THE WINGS OF THE DOVE

AN AUTHORITATIVE TEXT

THE AUTHOR AND THE NOVEL

CRITICISM

W. W. NORTON & COMPANY, INC.
also publishes

THE NORTON ANTHOLOGY OF AMERICAN LITERATURE
edited by Nina Baym et al.

THE NORTON ANTHOLOGY OF CONTEMPORARY FICTION
edited by R. V. Cassill

THE NORTON ANTHOLOGY OF ENGLISH LITERATURE
edited by M. H. Abrams et al.

THE NORTON ANTHOLOGY OF LITERATURE BY WOMEN
edited by Sandra M. Gilbert and Susan Gubar

THE NORTON ANTHOLOGY OF MODERN POETRY
edited by Richard Ellmann and Robert O'Clair

THE NORTON ANTHOLOGY OF POETRY
edited by Alexander W. Allison et al.

THE NORTON ANTHOLOGY OF SHORT FICTION
edited by R. V. Cassill

THE NORTON ANTHOLOGY OF WORLD MASTERPIECES
edited by Maynard Mack et al.

THE NORTON FACSIMILE OF
THE FIRST FOLIO OF SHAKESPEARE
prepared by Charlton Hinman

THE NORTON INTRODUCTION TO LITERATURE
edited by Carl E. Bain, Jerome Beaty, and J. Paul Hunter

THE NORTON INTRODUCTION TO THE SHORT NOVEL
edited by Jerome Beaty

THE NORTON READER
edited by Arthur M. Eastman et al.

THE NORTON SAMPLER
edited by Thomas Cooley

A NORTON CRITICAL EDITION

HENRY JAMES

THE WINGS OF THE DOVE

AN AUTHORITATIVE TEXT
THE AUTHOR AND THE NOVEL
CRITICISM

Edited by

J. DONALD CROWLEY
and
RICHARD A. HOCKS
UNIVERSITY OF MISSOURI

W · W · NORTON & COMPANY · INC · *New York*

R. P. Blackmur: Introduction to *The Golden Bowl.* Copyright © 1952 by Grove Press, Inc. Reprinted by permission of Grove Press, Inc.

Alvin Langdon Coburn: Photographs of "The Doctor's Door" and "The Venetian Palace" reprinted by permission of the Houghton Library, Harvard University.

Laurence Bedwell Holland: Excerpts from Laurence Bedwell Holland, *The Expense of Vision: Essays on the Craft of Henry James,* pp. 285–91, 298–301, and 306–10. Copyright © 1964 by Princeton University Press. Reprinted by permission of Princeton University Press.

Henry James: Letters to James B. Pinker quoted by permission of the Collection of American Literature, Beinecke Rare Book and Manuscript Library, Yale University, and Donald Gallup, Curator. Selections from *The Notebooks of Henry James,* edited by F. O. Matthiessen and Kenneth B. Murdock, copyright 1947 by Oxford University Press, Inc. Reprinted by permission. Correspondence with William James reprinted by permission of Alexander James.

Dorothea Krook: From *The Ordeal of Consciousness in Henry James,* pp. 203–15, 221–29. (Cambridge: Cambridge University Press, 1962). Copyright © 1962 by Cambridge University Press. Reprinted by permission of Cambridge University Press.

F. O. Matthiessen: From *Henry James: The Major Phase,* by F. O. Matthiessen. Copyright 1944 by Oxford University Press, Inc. Renewed by Mrs. Peter Putnam. Reprinted by permission of Oxford University Press, Inc.

Charles Thomas Samuels: From *The Ambiguity of Henry James,* pp. 61–65, 66–68, 69–72. Copyright © 1971 by The Board of Trustees of the University of Illinois. Reprinted by permission of the University of Illinois Press.

Ernest Sandeen: From "*The Wings of the Dove* and *The Portrait of a Lady:* A Study of Henry James's Later Phase," *PMLA* 69 (1954), pp. 1060–61, 1064–75. Reprinted by permission of the Modern Language Association of America.

Sallie Sears: From *The Negative Imagination: Form and Perspectives in the Novels of Henry James.* © 1963 Sallie Goldstein, © 1968 Cornell University. Used by permission of Cornell University Press.

J. A. Ward: "Social Disintegration in *The Wings of the Dove,*" Criticism, vol. 2, No. 2 (1960). Reprinted by permission of Wayne State University Press.

Christof Wegelin: From *The Image of Europe in Henry James,* by Christof Wegelin, © 1958 by Southern Methodist University Press. Reprinted by permission of the publisher and the author.

Library of Congress Cataloging in Publication Data

James, Henry, 1843–1916.

The wings of the dove.

(A Norton critical edition)

Bibliography: p.

1. James, Henry, 1843–1916. The wings of the dove.

I. Crowley, J. Donald. II. Hocks, Richard A., 1936– III. Title.

PZ3.J234Wi 1978 [PS2116.W5] 813'.4 77-19062

ISBN 0-393-04478-5

ISBN 0-393-09088-4 pbk.

Contents

Preface

The Wings of the Dove is but one of numerous pieces of American literature that have always commanded critical acclaim and controversy without ever enjoying the massive sales and the large popular audience their achievement deserves. Written after *The Ambassadors* but published before that novel, the book epitomizes the new conditions of Henry James's "major phase." It is the first of his later works to have been consciously conceived and designed without regard to the formal requirements—and, alas, without hope of the economic assurances—deriving from serial publication in magazines. The reader of this novel begins, then, knowing that James saw the book as a new departure and as representing new difficulties. He should know too, however, that while James considered *The Wings of the Dove* to be one of his more "advanced" works—an especially appetizing dessert, as he put it, to be partaken of only after the main course—he also invitingly insisted that the novel belongs as well to his "beef and potatoes."[1] That reader who is engaged with the drama of James's developing vision of the burdens of the American character as "heir of all the ages"—that reader who has tasted the urgent beginnings of that theme in Daisy Miller and its round amplification in Isabel Archer—will have savored only half the feast should he fail to take in its ultimate complication in Milly Theale.

This edition of *The Wings of the Dove* makes available for the first time a corrected and annotated reprint of the New York Edition text of 1909, together with the author's Preface for that edition. It is based on an analysis of thorough comparisons of that text with the two earlier editions of the novel—the first American and the first English—both published in 1902. The Textual Appendix discusses the nature, extent, and significance of James's typical revisions and suggests some of the ways in which those changes can be said to define his late manner; it also lists all of the most important variants and revisions found in these editions and cites those few instances in which the present text departs from New York Edition readings. The editors have made no silent alterations.

The second section, The Author and the Novel, comprises numerous materials excerpted from James's notebooks and letters, his

1. See p. 456 of this volume for James's comments in his letter to Mrs. G. W. Prothero.

travel literature, and his autobiographical writing. Included also are certain pertinent observations found in his New York Edition Preface to *The Ambassadors* and in his correspondence with his brother William. In addition, this section prints much of the novelist's all-but-unknown essay on immortality, a document which provides a rich analogue to the thinking and consciousness pervading the novel and its redemptive theme. An Editors' Commentary gives a fuller rationale and perspective for both this section and the following one.

The essays found in the Criticism section are meant primarily to reflect the lively critical interest which *The Wings of the Dove* has stimulated over the years. These analyses and assessments range from two early statements contemporary with the novel's publication, through the vigorous Jamesian criticism of the 1940s and 1950s, to the newer emphases which began in the 1960s. They present a variety of perspectives and discussions of specific problems of theme, character, and style. A Selected Bibliography contains additional items of criticism on the novel and other helpful writings for the reader of James's fiction.

For their diligent and painstaking help in the textual collations, we wish to express our deep gratitude to Albert von Frank and Nancy Zguta; and to Professor Norman Land, a colleague in the Department of Art History at the University of Missouri–Columbia, our gratitude for his aid in confirming the identity of paintings referred to in the novel. We are grateful also to the Research Council of the University of Missouri–Columbia for providing a small grant which helped defray various costs in the preparation of this edition. We wish, finally, to thank John W. N. Francis and Emily Garlin of W. W. Norton & Company, Inc., and Donald Jones, for their painstaking editing and most helpful suggestions.

J. Donald Crowley
Richard A. Hocks

The Text of
The Wings of the Dove

Preface to the New York Edition (1909)

"The Wings of the Dove," published in 1902, represents to my memory a very old—if I shouldn't perhaps rather say a very young—motive; I can scarce remember the time when the situation on which this long-drawn fiction mainly rests was not vividly present to me. The idea, reduced to its essence, is that of a young person conscious of a great capacity for life, but early stricken and doomed, condemned to die under short respite, while also enamoured of the world; aware moreover of the condemnation and passionately desiring to "put in" before extinction as many of the finer vibrations as possible, and so achieve, however briefly and brokenly, the sense of having lived. Long had I turned it over, standing off from it, yet coming back to it; convinced of what might be done with it, yet seeing the theme as formidable. The image so figured would be, at best, but half the matter; the rest would be all the picture of the struggle involved, the adventure brought about, the gain recorded or the loss incurred, the precious experience somehow compassed. These things, I had from the first felt, would require much working-out; that indeed was the case with most things worth working at all; yet there are subjects and subjects, and this one seemed particularly to bristle. It was formed, I judged, to make the wary adventurer walk round and round it—it had in fact a charm that invited and mystified alike that attention; not being somehow what one thought of as a "frank" subject, after the fashion of some, with its elements well in view and its whole character in its face. It stood there with secrets and compartments, with possible treacheries and traps; it might have a great deal to give, but would probably ask for equal services in return, and would collect this debt to the last shilling. It involved, to begin with, the placing in the strongest light a person infirm and ill—a case sure to prove difficult and to require much handling; though giving perhaps, with other matters, one of those chances for good taste, possibly even for the play of the very best in the world, that are not only always to be invoked and cultivated, but that are absolutely to be jumped at from the moment they make a sign.

Yes then, the case prescribed for its central figure a sick young woman, at the whole course of whose disintegration and the whole ordeal of whose consciousness one would have quite honestly to assist. The expression of her state and that of one's intimate relation to it might therefore well need to be discreet and ingenious; a reflexion that fortunately grew and grew, however, in proportion as I focussed my image—roundabout which, as it persisted, I repeat, the interesting possibilities and the attaching wonderments, not to say the insoluble mysteries, thickened apace. Why had one to look so straight in the face and so closely to cross-question that idea of making one's protagonist "sick"?—as if to be menaced with death or danger hadn't been from time immemorial, for heroine or hero, the very shortest of all cuts to the interesting state. Why should a figure be disqualified for a central position by the particular circumstance that might most quicken, that might crown with a fine intensity, its liability to many accidents, its consciousness of all relations? This circumstance, true enough, might disqualify it for many activities—even though we should have imputed to it the unsurpassable activity of passionate, of inspired resistance. This last fact was the real issue, for the way grew straight from the moment one recognised that the poet essentially *can't* be concerned with the act of dying. Let him deal with the sickest of the sick, it is still by the act of living that they appeal to him, and appeal the more as the conditions plot against them and prescribe the battle. The process of life gives way fighting, and often may so shine out on the lost ground as in no other connexion. One had had moreover, as a various chronicler, one's secondary physical weaklings and failures, one's accessory invalids—introduced with a complacency that made light of criticism. To Ralph Touchett in "The Portrait of a Lady," for instance, his deplorable state of health was not only no drawback; I had clearly been right in counting it, for any happy effect he should produce, a positive good mark, a direct aid to pleasantness and vividness. The reason of this moreover could never in the world have been his fact of sex; since men, among the mortally afflicted, suffer on the whole more overtly and more grossly than women, and resist with a ruder, an inferior strategy. I had thus to take *that* anomaly for what it was worth, and I give it here but as one of the ambiguities amid which my subject ended by making itself at home and seating itself quite in confidence.

With the clearness I have just noted, accordingly, the last thing in the world it proposed to itself was to be the record predominantly of a collapse. I don't mean to say that my offered victim was not present to my imagination, constantly, as dragged by a greater force than any she herself could exert; she had been given me from far back as contesting every inch of the road, as catching at every object the grasp of which might make for delay, as clutching these things to the last moment of her strength. Such an attitude and such movements, the passion they expressed and the success they in fact represented, what were they in truth but the soul of drama?—which is the portrayal, as we know, of a catastrophe determined in spite of oppositions. My young woman would *herself* be the opposition—to the catastrophe announced by the associated Fates,[1]

1. Daughters of the Night empowered to determine the mere mortal's length of life.

powers conspiring to a sinister end and, with their command of means, finally achieving it, yet in such straits really to *stifle* the sacred spark that, obviously, a creature so animated, an adversary so subtle, couldn't but be felt worthy, under whatever weaknesses, of the foreground and the limelight. She would meanwhile wish, moreover, all along, to live for particular things, she would found her struggle on particular human interests, which would inevitably determine, in respect to her, the attitude of other persons, persons affected in such a manner as to make them part of the action. If her impulse to wrest from her shrinking hour still as much of the fruit of life as possible, if this longing can take effect only by the aid of others, their participation (appealed to, entangled and coerced as they find themselves) becomes their drama too—that of their promoting her illusion, under her importunity, for reasons, for interests and advantages, from motives and points of view, of their own. Some of these promptings, evidently, would be of the highest order—others doubtless mightn't; but they would make up together, for her, contributively, her sum of experience, represent to her somehow, in good faith or in bad, what she should have *known*. Somehow, too, at such a rate, one would see the persons subject to them drawn in as by some pool of a Lorelei[2]—see them terrified and tempted and charmed; bribed away, it may even be, from more prescribed and natural orbits, inheriting from their connexion with her strange difficulties and still stranger opportunities, confronted with rare questions and called upon for new discriminations. Thus the scheme of her situation would, in a comprehensive way, see itself constituted; the rest of the interest would be in the number and nature of the particulars. Strong among these, naturally, the need that life should, apart from her infirmity, present itself to our young woman as quite dazzlingly liveable, and that if the great pang for her is in what she must give up we shall appreciate it the more from the sight of all she has.

One would see her then as possessed of all things, all but the single most precious assurance; freedom and money and a mobile mind and personal charm, the power to interest and attach; attributes, each one, enhancing the value of a future. From the moment his imagination began to deal with her at close quarters, in fact, nothing could more engage her designer than to work out the detail of her perfect rightness for her part; nothing above all more solicit him than to recognise fifty reasons for her national and social status. She should be the last fine flower—blooming alone, for the fullest attestation of her freedom—of an "old" New York stem; the happy congruities thus preserved for her being matters, however, that I may not now go into, and this even though the fine associa-

2. In German legend, an enchantress whose singing caused sailors to wreck their boats on her rock in the Rhine.

tion that shall yet elsewhere await me is of a sort, at the best, rather to defy than to encourage exact expression. There goes with it, for the heroine of "The Wings of the Dove," a strong and special implication of liberty, liberty of action, of choice, of appreciation, of contact—proceeding from sources that provide better for large independence, I think, than any other conditions in the world—and this would be in particular what we should feel ourselves deeply concerned with. I had from far back mentally projected a certain sort of young American as more the "heir of all the ages" than any other young person whatever (and precisely on those grounds I have just glanced at but to pass them by for the moment); so that here was a chance to confer on some such figure a supremely touching value. To be the heir of all the ages only to know yourself, as that consciousness should deepen, balked of your inheritance, would be to play the part, it struck me, or at least to arrive at the type, in the light on the whole the most becoming. Otherwise, truly, what a perilous part to play *out*—what a suspicion of "swagger" in positively attempting it! So at least I could reason—so I even think I *had* to—to keep my subject to a decent compactness. For already, from an early stage, it had begun richly to people itself: the difficulty was to see whom the situation I had primarily projected might, by this, that or the other turn, *not* draw in. My business was to watch its turns as the fond parent watches a child perched, for its first riding-lesson, in the saddle; yet its interest, I had all the while to recall, was just in its making, on such a scale, for developments.

What one had discerned, at all events, from an early stage, was that a young person so devoted and exposed, a creature with her security hanging so by a hair, couldn't but fall somehow into some abysmal trap—this being, dramatically speaking, what such a situation most naturally implied and imposed. Didn't the truth and a great part of the interest also reside in the appearance that she would constitute for others (given her passionate yearning to live while she might) a complication as great as any they might constitute for herself?—which is what I mean when I speak of such matters as "natural." They would be as natural, these tragic, pathetic, ironic, these indeed for the most part sinister, liabilities, to her living associates, as they could be to herself as prime subject. If her story was to consist, as it could so little help doing, of her being let in, as we say, for this, that and the other irreducible anxiety, how could she not have put a premium on the acquisition, by any close sharer of her life, of a consciousness similarly embarrassed? I have named the Rhine-maiden, but our young friend's existence would create rather, all round her, very much that whirlpool movement of the waters produced by the sinking of a big vessel or the failure of a great business; when we figure to ourselves the strong narrowing eddies, the immense force of suction, the general engulfment that, for any neighbouring object, makes immersion inevitable. I need scarce say, however, that in spite of these communities of doom I saw the main dramatic complication much more prepared *for* my vessel of sensibility than by her—the work of other hands (though with her own imbrued too, after all, in the measure of their never not being, in some direction, generous and extravagant, and thereby provoking).

The great point was, at all events, that if in a predicament she was to be, accordingly, it would be of the essence to create the predicament promptly and build it up solidly, so that it should have for us as much as possible its ominous air of awaiting her. That reflexion I found, betimes, not less inspiring than urgent; one begins so, in such a business, by looking about for one's compositional key, unable as one can only be to move till one has found it. To start without it is to pretend to enter the train and, still more, to remain in one's seat, without a ticket. Well—in the steady light and for the continued charm of these verifications—I had secured my ticket over the tolerably long line laid down for "The Wings of the Dove" from the moment I had noted that there could be no full presentation of Milly Theale as *engaged* with elements amid which she was to draw her breath in such pain, should not the elements have been, with all solicitude, duly prefigured. If one had seen that her stricken state was but half her case, the correlative half being the state of others as affected by her (they too should have a "case," bless them, quite as much as she!) then I was free to choose, as it were, the half with which I should begin. If, as I had fondly noted, the little world determined for her was to "bristle"—I delighted in the term!—with meanings, so, by the same token, could I but make my medal hang free, its obverse and its reverse, its face and its back, would beautifully become optional for the spectator. I somehow wanted them correspondingly embossed, wanted them inscribed and figured with an equal salience; yet it was none the less visibly my "key," as I have said, that though my regenerate young New Yorker, and what might depend on her, should form my centre, my circumference was every whit as treatable. Therefore I must trust myself to know when to proceed from the one and when from the other. Preparatively and, as it were, yearningly—given the whole ground—one began, in the event, with the outer ring, approaching the centre thus by narrowing circumvallations. There, full-blown, accordingly, from one hour to the other, rose one's process—for which there remained all the while so many amusing formulae.

The medal *did* hang free—I felt this perfectly, I remember, from the moment I had comfortably laid the ground provided in my first

Book, ground from which Milly is superficially so absent. I scarce remember perhaps a case—I like even with this public grossness to insist on it—in which the curiosity of "beginning far back," as far back as possible, and even of going, to the same tune, far "behind," that is behind the face of the subject, was to assert itself with less scruple. The free hand, in this connexion, was above all agreeable—the hand the freedom of which I owed to the fact that the work had ignominiously failed, in advance, of all power to see itself "serialised." This failure had repeatedly waited, for me, upon shorter fictions; but the considerable production we here discuss was (as "The Golden Bowl" was to be, two or three years later) born, not otherwise than a little bewilderedly, into a world of periodicals and editors, of roaring "successes" in fine, amid which it was well-nigh unnotedly to lose itself. There is fortunately something bracing, ever, in the alpine chill, that of some high icy *arête*,[3] shed by the cold editorial shoulder; sour grapes may at moments fairly intoxicate and the story-teller worth his salt rejoice to feel again how many accommodations he can practise. Those addressed to "conditions of publication" have in a degree their interesting, or at least their provoking, side; but their charm is qualified by the fact that the prescriptions here spring from a soil often wholly alien to the ground of the work itself. They are almost always the fruit of another air altogether and conceived in a light liable to represent *within* the circle of the work itself little else than darkness. Still, when not too blighting, they often operate as a tax on ingenuity—that ingenuity of the expert craftsman which likes to be taxed very much to the same tune to which a well-bred horse likes to be saddled. The best and finest ingenuities, nevertheless, with all respect to that truth, are apt to be, not one's compromises, but one's fullest conformities, and I well remember, in the case before us, the pleasure of feeling my divisions, my proportions and general rhythm, rest all on permanent rather than in any degree on momentary proprieties. It was enough for my alternations, thus, that they were good in themselves; it was in fact so much for them that I really think any further account of the constitution of the book reduces itself to a just notation of the law they followed.

There was the "fun," to begin with, of establishing one's successive centres—of fixing them so exactly that the portions of the subject commanded by them as by happy points of view, and accordingly treated from them, would constitute, so to speak, sufficiently solid *blocks* of wrought material, squared to the sharp edge, as to have weight and mass and carrying power; to make for construction, that is, to conduce to effect and to provide for beauty. Such a block, obviously, is the whole preliminary presentation of Kate Croy,

3. A sharp ascending ridge of a mountain.

which, from the first, I recall, absolutely declined to enact itself save in terms of amplitude. Terms of amplitude, terms of atmosphere, those terms, and those terms only, in which images assert their fulness and roundness, their power to revolve, so that they have sides and backs, parts in the shade as true as parts in the sun—these were plainly to be my conditions, right and left, and I was so far from overrating the amount of expression the whole thing, as I saw and felt it, would require, that to retrace the way at present is, alas, more than anything else, but to mark the gaps and the lapses, to miss, one by one, the intentions that, with the best will in the world, were not to fructify. I have just said that the process of the general attempt is described from the moment the "blocks" are numbered, and that would be a true enough picture of my plan. Yet one's plan, alas, is one thing and one's result another; so that I am perhaps nearer the point in saying that this last strikes me at present as most characterised by the happy features that *were*, under my first and most blest illusion, to have contributed to it. I meet them all, as I renew acquaintance, I mourn for them all as I remount the stream, the absent values, the palpable voids, the missing links, the mocking shadows, that reflect, taken together, the early bloom of one's good faith. Such cases are of course far from abnormal—so far from it that some acute mind ought surely to have worked out by this time the "law" of the degree in which the artist's energy fairly depends on his fallibility. How much and how often, and in what connexions and with what almost infinite variety, must he be a dupe, that of his prime object, to be at all measurably a master, that of his actual substitute for it—or in other words at all appreciably to exist? He places, after an earnest survey, the piers of his bridge—he has at least sounded deep enough, heaven knows, for their brave position; yet the bridge spans the stream, after the fact, in apparently complete independence of these properties, the principal grace of the original design. *They* were an illusion, for their necessary hour; but the span itself, whether of a single arch or of many, seems by the oddest chance in the world to be a reality; since, actually, the rueful builder, passing under it, sees figures and hears sounds above: he makes out, with his heart in his throat, that it bears and is positively being "used."

The building-up of Kate Croy's consciousness to the capacity for the load little by little to be laid on it was, by way of example, to have been a matter of as many hundred close-packed bricks as there are actually poor dozens. The image of her so compromised and compromising father was all effectively to have pervaded her life, was in a certain particular way to have tampered with her spring; by which I mean that the shame and the irritation and the depression, the general poisonous influence of him, were to have been *shown*, with a truth beyond the compass even of one's most emphasised "word of honour" for it, to do these things. But where do we find him, at this time of day, save in a beggarly scene or two which scarce arrives at the dignity of functional reference? He but "looks in," poor beautiful dazzling, damning apparition that he was to have been; he sees his place so taken, his company so little missed, that, cocking again that fine form of hat which has yielded him for so long his one effective cover, he turns away with a whistle of indifference that nobly misrepresents the deepest disappointment of his life. One's poor word of honour has *had* to pass muster for the show. Every one, in short, was to have enjoyed so much better a chance that, like stars of the theatre condescending to oblige, they have had to take small parts, to content themselves with minor identities, in order to come on at all. I haven't the heart now, I confess, to adduce the detail of so many lapsed importances; the explanation of most of which, after all, I take to have been in the crudity of a truth beating full upon me through these reconsiderations, the odd inveteracy with which picture, at almost any turn, is jealous of drama, and drama (though on the whole with a greater patience, I think) suspicious of picture. Between them, no doubt, they do much for the theme; yet each baffles insidiously the other's ideal and eats round the edges of its position; each is too ready to say "I can take the thing for 'done' only when done in *my* way." The residuum of comfort for the witness of these broils is of course meanwhile in the convenient reflexion, invented for him in the twilight of time and the infancy of art by the Angel, not to say by the Demon, of Compromise, that nothing is so easy to "do" as not to be thankful for almost any stray help in its getting done. It wasn't, after this fashion, by making good one's dream of Lionel Croy that my structure was to stand on its feet—any more than it was by letting him go that I was to be left irretrievably lamenting. The who and the what, the how and the why, the whence and the whither of Merton Densher, these, no less, were quantities and atrributes that should have danced about him with the antique grace of nymphs and fauns[4] circling round a bland Hermes[5] and crowning him with flowers. One's main anxiety, for each one's agents, is that the air of each shall be *given;* but what does the whole thing become, after all, as one goes, but a series of sad places at which the hand of generosity has been cautioned and stayed? The young man's situation, personal, professional, social, was to have been so decanted for us that we should get all the taste; we were to have been penetrated with Mrs. Lowder, by the same token, saturated with her presence,

4. Nymphs: female personifications of natural objects, long-lived but not immortal. Fauns: spirits of the countryside.

5. The god of luck and wealth, patron both of merchants and of thieves; trickster of Apollo. Among his numerous roles, Hermes was the conductor of the souls of the dead to Hades.

her "personality," and felt all her weight in the scale. We were to have revelled in Mrs. Stringham, my heroine's attendant friend, her fairly choral Bostonian, a subject for innumerable touches, and in an extended and above all an *animated* reflexion of Milly Theale's experience of English society; just as the strength and sense of the situation in Venice, for our gathered friends, was to have come to us in a deeper draught out of a larger cup, and just as the pattern of Densher's final position and fullest consciousness there was to have been marked in fine stitches, all silk and gold, all pink and silver, that have had to remain, alas, but entwined upon the reel.

It isn't, no doubt, however—to recover, after all, our critical balance—that the pattern didn't, for each compartment, get itself somehow wrought, and that we mightn't thus, piece by piece, opportunity offering, trace it over and study it. The thing has doubtless, as a whole, the advantage that each piece is true to its pattern, and that while it pretends to make no simple statement it yet never lets go its scheme of clearness. Applications of this scheme are continuous and exemplary enough, though I scarce leave myself room to glance at them. The clearness is obtained in Book First—or otherwise, as I have said, in the first "piece," each Book having its subordinate and contributive pattern—through the associated consciousness of my two prime young persons, for whom I early recognised that I should have to consent, under stress, to a practical *fusion* of consciousness. It is into the young woman's "ken" that Merton Densher is represented as swimming; but her mind is not here, rigorously, the one reflector. There are occasions when it plays this part, just as there are others when his plays it, and an intelligible plan consists naturally not a little in fixing such occasions and making them, on one side and the other, sufficient to themselves. Do I sometimes in fact forfeit the advantage of that distinctness? Do I ever abandon one centre for another after the former has been postulated? From the moment we proceed by "centres"—and I have never, I confess, embraced the logic of any superior process—they must *be*, each, as a basis, selected and fixed; after which it is that, in the high interest of economy of treatment, they determine and rule. There is no economy of treatment without an adopted, a related point of view, and though I understand, under certain degrees of pressure, a represented community of vision between several parties to the action when it makes for concentration, I understand no breaking-up of the register, no sacrifice of the recording consistency, that doesn't rather scatter and weaken. In this truth resides the secret of the discriminated occasion—that aspect of the subject which we have our noted choice of treating either as picture or scenically, but which is apt, I think, to show its fullest worth in the Scene. Beautiful exceedingly, for that matter, those occasions or parts of an occasion when the boundary line between picture and scene bears a little the weight of the double pressure.

Such would be the case, I can't but surmise, for the long passage that forms here before us the opening of Book Fourth, where all the offered life centres, to intensity, in the disclosure of Milly's single throbbing consciousness, but where, for a due rendering, everything has to be brought to a head. This passage, the view of her introduction to Mrs. Lowder's circle, has its mate, for illustration, later on in the book and at a crisis for which the occasion submits to another rule. My registers or "reflectors," as I so conveniently name them (burnished indeed as they generally are by the intelligence, the curiosity, the passion, the force of the moment, whatever it be, directing them), work, as we have seen, in arranged alternation; so that in the second connexion I here glance at it is Kate Croy who is, "for all she is worth," turned on. She is turned on largely at Venice, where the appearances, rich and obscure and portentous (another word I rejoice in) as they have by that time become and altogether exquisite as they remain, are treated almost wholly through her vision of them and Densher's (as to the lucid interplay of which conspiring and conflicting agents there would be a great deal to say). It is in Kate's consciousness that at the stage in question the drama is brought to a head, and the occasion on which, in the splendid saloon of poor Milly's hired palace, she takes the measure of her friend's festal evening, squares itself to the same synthetic firmness as the compact constructional block inserted by the scene at Lancaster Gate. Milly's situation ceases at a given moment to be "renderable" in terms closer than those supplied by Kate's intelligence, or, in a richer degree, by Densher's, or, for one fond hour, by poor Mrs. Stringham's (since to that sole brief futility is this last participant, crowned by my original plan with the quaintest functions, in fact reduced); just as Kate's relation with Densher and Densher's with Kate have ceased previously, and are then to cease again, to be projected for us, so far as Milly is concerned with them, on any more responsible plate than that of the latter's admirable anxiety. It is as if, for these aspects, the impersonal plate—in other words the poor author's comparatively cold affirmation or thin guarantee—had felt itself a figure of attestation at once too gross and too bloodless, likely to affect us as an abuse of privilege when not as an abuse of knowledge.

Heaven forbid, we say to ourselves during almost the whole Venetian climax, heaven forbid we should "know" anything more of our ravaged sister than what Densher darkly pieces together, or than what Kate Croy pays, heroically, it must be owned, at the hour of her visit alone to Densher's lodging, for her superior handling and her dire profanation of. For we have time, while this passage lasts, to turn round critically; we have time to recognise intentions and proprieties; we have time to catch glimpses of an economy of composition, as I put it, interesting in itself: all in spite of the author's scarce more than half-dissimulated despair at the inveterate displacement of his general centre. "The Wings of the Dove" happens to offer perhaps the most striking example I may cite (though with public penance for it already performed) of my regular failure to keep the appointed halves of my whole equal. Here the makeshift middle—for which the best I can say is that it's always rueful and never impudent—reigns with even more than its customary contrition, though passing itself off perhaps too with more than its usual craft. Nowhere, I seem to recall, had the need of dissimulation been felt so as anguish; nowhere had I condemned a luckless theme to complete its revolution, burdened with the accumulation of its difficulties, the difficulties that grow with a theme's development, in quarters so cramped. Of course, as every novelist knows, it is difficulty that inspires; only, for that perfection of charm, it must have been difficulty inherent and congenital, and not difficulty "caught" by the wrong frequentations. The latter half, that is the false and deformed half, of "The Wings" would verily, I think, form a signal object-lesson for a literary critic bent on improving his occasion to the profit of the budding artist. This whole corner of the picture bristles with "dodges"—such as he should feel himself all committed to recognise and denounce—for disguising the reduced scale of the exhibition, for foreshortening at any cost, for imparting to patches the value of presences, for dressing objects in an *air* as of the dimensions they can't possibly have. Thus he would have his free hand for pointing out what a tangled web we weave when—well, when, through our mislaying or otherwise trifling with our blest pair of compasses, we have to produce the illusion of mass without the illusion of extent. *There* is a job quite to the measure of most of our monitors—and with the interest for them well enhanced by the preliminary cunning quest for the spot where deformity has begun.

I recognise meanwhile, throughout the long earlier reach of the book, not only no deformities but, I think, a positively close and felicitous application of method, the preserved consistencies of which, often illusive, but never really lapsing, it would be of a certain diversion, and might be of some profit, to follow. The author's accepted task at the outset has been to suggest with force the nature of the tie formed between the two young persons first introduced—to give the full impression of its peculiar worried and baffled, yet clinging and confident, ardour. The picture constituted, so far as may be, is that of a pair of natures well-nigh consumed by a sense of their intimate affinity and congruity, the reciprocity of their desire, and thus passionately impatient of barriers and delays, yet with qualities of intelligence and character that they are meanwhile extraordinarily able to draw upon for the enrichment of their relation, the extension of their prospect and the support of their "game." They are far from a common couple, Merton Densher and Kate Croy, as befits the remarkable fashion in which fortune was to waylay and opportunity was to distinguish them—the whole strange truth of their response to which opening involves also, in its order, no vulgar art of exhibition; but what they have most to tell us is that, all unconsciously and with the best faith in the world, all by mere force of the terms of their superior passion combined with their superior diplomacy, they are laying a trap for the great innocence to come. If I like, as I have confessed, the "portentous" look, I was perhaps never to set so high a value on it as for all this prompt provision of forces unwittingly waiting to close round my eager heroine (to the eventual deep chill of her eagerness) as the result of her mere lifting of a latch. Infinitely interesting to have built up the relation of the others to the point at which its aching restlessness, its need to affirm itself otherwise than by an exasperated patience, meets as with instinctive relief and recognition the possibilities shining out of Milly Theale. Infinitely interesting to have prepared and organised, correspondingly, that young woman's precipitations and liabilities, to have constructed, for Drama essentially to take possession, the whole bright house of her exposure.

These references, however, reflect too little of the detail of the treatment imposed; such a detail as I for instance get hold of in the fact of Densher's interview with Mrs. Lowder before he goes to America. It forms, in this preliminary picture, the one patch not strictly seen over Kate Croy's shoulder; though it's notable that immediately after, at the first possible moment, we surrender again to our major convenience, as it happens to be at the time, that of our drawing breath through the young woman's lungs. Once more, in other words, before we know it, Densher's direct vision of the scene at Lancaster Gate is replaced by her apprehension, her contributive assimilation, of his experience: it melts back into that accumulation, which we have been, as it were, saving up. Does my apparent deviation here count accordingly as a muddle?—one of the muddles ever blooming so thick in any soil that fails to grow reasons and determinants. No, distinctly not; for I had definitely opened the door, as attention of perusal of the first two Books will show, to the subjective community of my young pair. (Attention of perusal, I thus confess by the way, is what I at every point, as well as here, absolutely invoke and take for granted; a truth I avail myself of this occasion to note once for all—in the interest of that variety of ideal reigning, I gather, in the connexion. The enjoyment of a work of art, the acceptance of an irresistible illusion, constituting, to my sense, our highest experience of "luxury," the luxury is not greatest, by my consequent measure, when the work asks for as little attention as possible. It is greatest, it is delightfully, divinely great, when we feel the surface, like the thick ice of the skater's pond, bear without cracking the strongest pressure we throw on it. The sound of the crack one may recognise, but never surely to call it a luxury.) That I had scarce availed myself of the privilege of seeing with Densher's eyes is another matter; the point is that I had intelligently marked my possible, my occasional need of it. So, at all events, the constructional "block" of the first two Books compactly forms itself. A new block, all of the squarest and not a little of the smoothest, begins with the Third—by which I mean of course a new mass of interest governed from a new centre. Here again I make prudent *provision*—to be sure to keep my centre strong. It dwells mainly, we at once see, in the depths of Milly Theale's "case," where, close beside it, however, we meet a supplementary reflector, that of the lucid even though so quivering spirit of her dedicated friend.

The more or less associated consciousness of the two women deals thus, unequally, with the next presented face of the subject—deals with it to the exclusion of the dealing of others; and if, for a highly particular moment, I allot to Mrs. Stringham the responsibility of the direct appeal to us, it is again, charming to relate, on behalf of that play of the portentous which I cherish so as a "value" and am accordingly for ever setting in motion. There is an hour of evening, on the alpine height, at which it becomes of the last importance that our young woman should testify eminently in this direction. But as I was to find it long since of a blest wisdom that no expense should be incurred or met, in any corner of picture of mine, without some concrete image of the account kept of it, that is of its being organically re-economised, so under that dispensation Mrs. Stringham has to register the transaction. Book Fifth is a new block mainly in its provision of a new set of occasions, which readopt, for their order, the previous centre, Milly's now almost full-blown consciousness. At my game, with renewed zest, of driving portents home, I have by this time all the choice of those that are to brush that surface with a dark wing. They are used, to our profit, on an elastic but a definite system; by which I mean that having to sound here and there a little deep, as a test, for my basis of method, I find it everywhere obstinately present. It draws the "occasion" into tune and keeps it so, to repeat my tiresome term; my nearest approach to muddlement is to have sometimes—but not too often—to break my occasions small. Some of them succeed in remaining ample and in really aspiring then to the higher, the sustained lucidity. The whole actual centre of the work, resting on a misplaced pivot and lodged in Book Fifth, pretends to a long reach, or at any rate to the larger foreshortening—though bringing home to me, on re-perusal, what I find striking, charming and curious, the author's instinct everywhere for the *indirect* presentation of his main image. I note how, again and again, I go but a little way with the direct—that is with the straight exhibition of Milly; it resorts for relief, this process, whenever it can, to some kinder, some merciful indirection: all as if to approach her circuitously, deal with her at second hand, as an unspotted princess is ever dealt with; the pressure all round her kept easy for her, the sounds, the movements regulated, the forms and ambiguities made charming. All of which proceeds, obviously, from her painter's tenderness of imagination about her, which reduces him to watching her, as it were, through the successive windows of other people's interest in her. So, if we talk of princesses, do the balconies opposite the palace gates, do the coigns of vantage and respect enjoyed for a fee, rake from afar the mystic figure in the gilded coach as it comes forth into the great *place*. But my use of windows and balconies is doubtless at best an extravagance by itself, and as to what there may be to note, of this and other supersubtleties, other arch-refinements, of tact and taste, of design and instinct, in "The Wings of the Dove," I become conscious of overstepping my space without having brought the full quantity to light. The failure leaves me with a burden of residuary comment of which I yet boldly hope elsewhere to discharge myself.

HENRY JAMES.

The Doctor's Door

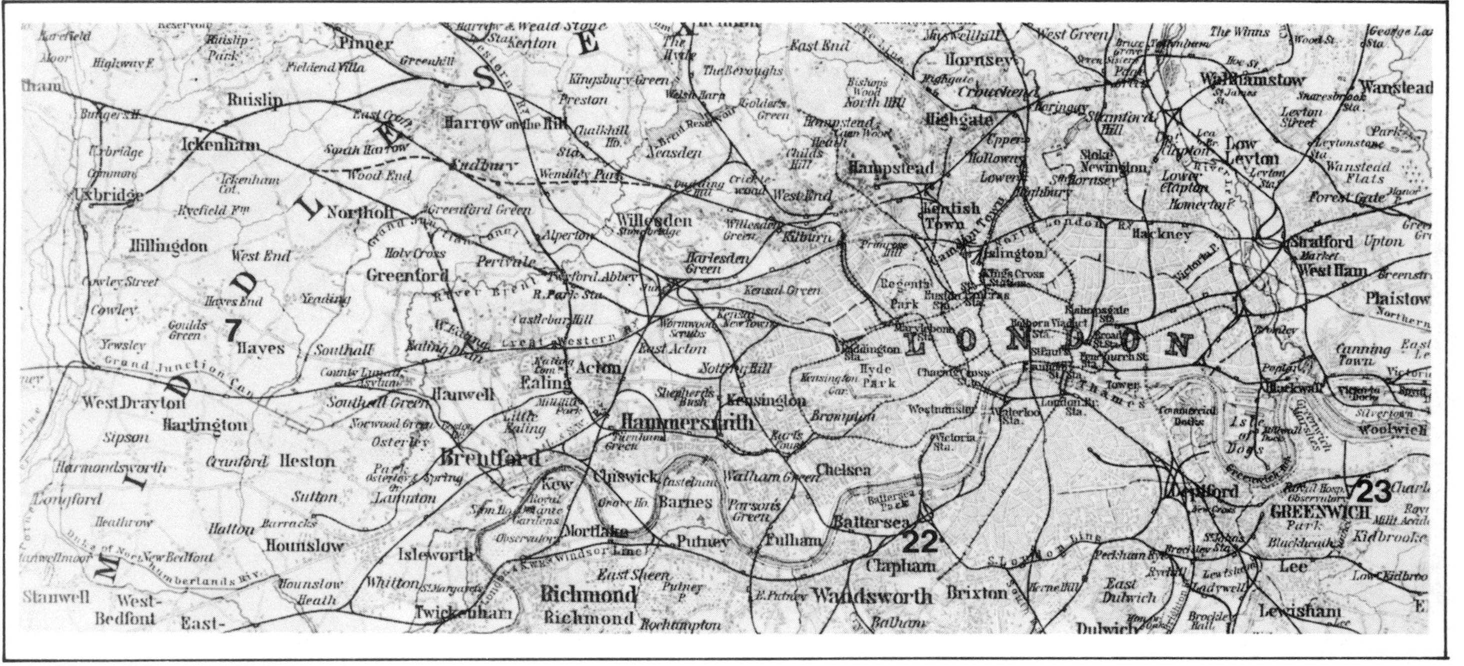

London in 1909

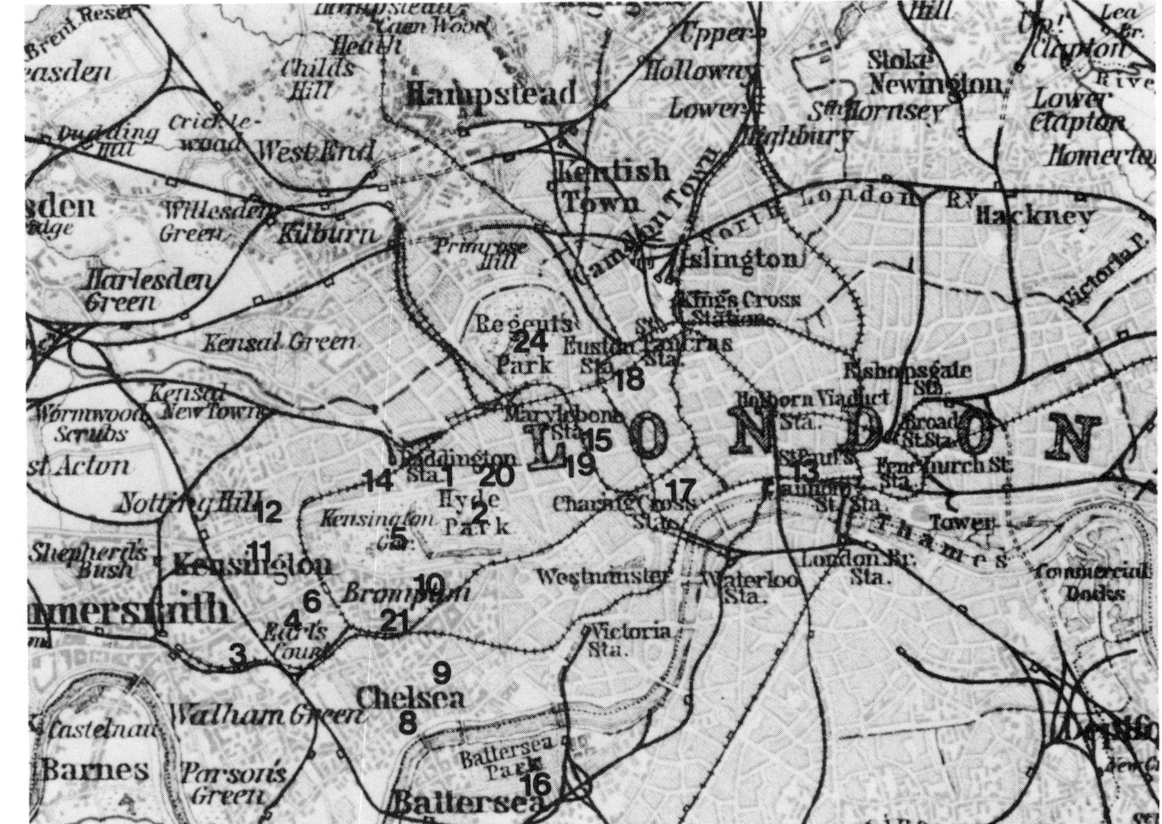

Legend

1. Lancaster Gate
2. Hyde Park
3. South Kensington
4. Cromwell Road
5. Kensington Gardens
6. Lexham Gardens
7. Middlesex
8. Chelsea
9. Sloane Square
10. Queen's Road
11. High Street Kensington
12. Notting Hill Gate
13. Fleet Street
14. Bayswater Road
15. Wigmore Street
16. Battersea Park
17. National Gallery
18. Euston Station
19. Brook Street
20. Marble Arch
21. Brompton Oratory
22. Clapham
23. Greenwich
24. Regent's Park

Volume One

Book First

I

She waited, Kate Croy, for her father to come in, but he kept her unconscionably, and there were moments at which she showed herself, in the glass over the mantel, a face positively pale with the irritation that had brought her to the point of going away without sight of him. It was at this point, however, that she remained; changing her place, moving from the shabby sofa to the armchair upholstered in a glazed cloth that gave at once—she had tried it—the sense of the slippery and of the sticky. She had looked at the sallow prints on the walls and at the lonely magazine, a year old, that combined, with a small lamp in coloured glass and a knitted white centre-piece wanting in freshness, to enhance the effect of the purplish cloth on the principal table; she had above all from time to time taken a brief stand on the small balcony to which the pair of long windows gave access. The vulgar little street, in this view, offered scant relief from the vulgar little room; its main office was to suggest to her that the narrow black house-fronts, adjusted to a standard that would have been low even for backs, constituted quite the publicity implied by such privacies. One felt them in the room exactly as one felt the room—the hundred like it or worse—in the street. Each time she turned in again, each time, in her impatience, she gave him up, it was to sound to a deeper depth, while she tasted the faint flat emanation of things, the failure of fortune and of honour. If she continued to wait it was really in a manner that she mightn't add the shame of fear, of individual, of personal collapse, to all the other shames. To feel the street, to feel the room, to feel the table-cloth and the centre-piece and the lamp, gave her a small salutary sense at least of neither shirking nor lying. This whole vision was the worst thing yet—as including in particular the interview to which she had braced herself; and for what had she come but for the worst? She tried to be sad so as not to be angry, but it made her angry that she couldn't be sad. And yet where was misery, misery too beaten for blame and chalk-marked by fate like a "lot" at a common auction, if not in these merciless signs of mere mean stale feelings?

Her father's life, her sister's, her own, that of her two lost brothers—the whole history of their house had the effect of some fine florid voluminous phrase, say even a musical, that dropped first into words and notes without sense and then, hanging unfinished, into no words nor any notes at all. Why should a set of people have been put in motion, on such a scale and with such an air of being equipped for a profitable journey, only to break down without an accident, to stretch themselves in the wayside dust without a reason? The answer to these questions was not in Chirk Street,[1] but the questions themselves bristled there, and the girl's repeated pause before the mirror and the chimney-place might have represented her nearest approach to an escape from them. Wasn't it in fact the partial escape from this "worst" in which she was steeped to be able to make herself out again as agreeable to see? She stared into the tarnished glass too hard indeed to be staring at her beauty alone. She readjusted the poise of her black closely-feathered hat; retouched, beneath it, the thick fall of her dusky hair; kept her eyes aslant no less on her beautiful averted than on her beautiful presented oval. She was dressed altogether in black, which gave an even tone, by contrast, to her clear face and made her hair more harmoniously dark. Outside, on the balcony, her eyes showed as blue; within, at the mirror, they showed almost as black. She was handsome, but the degree of it was not sustained by items and aids; a circumstance moreover playing its part at almost any time in the impression she produced. The impression was one that remained, but as regards the sources of it no sum in addition would have made up the total. She had stature without height, grace without motion, presence without mass. Slender and simple, frequently soundless, she was somehow always in the line of the eye—she counted singularly for its pleasure. More "dressed," often, with fewer accessories, than other women, or less dressed, should occasion require, with more, she probably couldn't have given the key to these felicities. They were mysteries of which her friends were conscious—those friends whose general explanation was to say that she was clever, whether or no it were taken by the world as the cause or as the effect of her charm. If she saw more things than her fine face in the dull glass of her father's lodgings she might have seen that after all she was not herself a fact in the collapse. She didn't hold herself cheap, she didn't make for misery. Personally, no, she wasn't chalk-marked for auction. She hadn't given up yet, and the broken sentence, if she was the last word, *would* end with a sort of meaning. There was a minute during which, though her eyes were fixed, she quite visibly lost herself in the thought of the way she might still pull things round had she only been a man. It was the name, above all, she would take in hand—the precious name she so liked and that, in spite of the harm her wretched father had done it, wasn't yet past praying for. She

1. We have not been able to identify this as an authentic London street. The *Oxford English Dictionary* lists "chirk" as an American colloquialism meaning "lively, cheerful, in good spirits." Given the tense irritation of the scene, the irony is apparent.

loved it in fact the more tenderly for that bleeding wound. But what could a penniless girl do with it but let it go?

When her father at last appeared she became, as usual, instantly aware of the futility of any effort to hold him to anything. He had written her he was ill, too ill to leave his room, and that he must see her without delay; and if this had been, as was probable, the sketch of a design he was indifferent even to the moderate finish required for deception. He had clearly wanted, for the perversities he called his reasons, to see her, just as she herself had sharpened for a talk; but she now again felt, in the inevitability of the freedom he used with her, all the old ache, her poor mother's very own, that he couldn't touch you ever so lightly without setting up. No relation with him could be so short or so superficial as not to be somehow to your hurt; and this, in the strangest way in the world, not because he desired it to be—feeling often, as he surely must, the profit for him of its not being—but because there was never a mistake for you that he could leave unmade, nor a conviction of his impossibility in you that he could approach you without strengthening. He might have awaited her on the sofa in his sitting-room, or might have stayed in bed and received her in that situation. She was glad to be spared the sight of such penetralia, but it would have reminded her a little less that there was no truth in him. This was the weariness of every fresh meeting; he dealt out lies as he might the cards from the greasy old pack for the game of diplomacy to which you were to sit down with him. The inconvenience—as always happens in such cases—was not that you minded what was false, but that you missed what was true. He might be ill and it might suit you to know it, but no contact with him, for this, could ever be straight enough. Just so he even might die, but Kate fairly wondered on what evidence of his own she would some day have to believe it.

He had not at present come down from his room, which she knew to be above the one they were in: he had already been out of the house, though he would either, should she challenge him, deny it or present it as a proof of his extremity. She had, however, by this time, quite ceased to challenge him; not only, face to face with him, vain irritation dropped, but he breathed upon the tragic consciousness in such a way that after a moment nothing of it was left. The difficulty was not less that he breathed in the same way upon the comic: she almost believed that with this latter she might still have found a foothold for clinging to him. He had ceased to be amusing—he was really too inhuman. His perfect look, which had floated him so long, was practically perfect still; but one had long since for every occasion taken it for granted. Nothing could have better shown than the actual how right one had been. He looked exactly as much as usual—all pink and silver as to skin and hair, all straightness and starch as to figure and dress; the man in the world least connected with anything unpleasant. He was so particularly the English gentleman and the fortunate settled normal person. Seen at a foreign table d'hôte he suggested but one thing: "In what perfection England produces them!" He had kind safe eyes, and a voice which, for all its clean fulness, told the quiet tale of its having never had once to raise itself. Life had met him so, halfway, and had turned round so to walk with him, placing a hand in his arm and fondly leaving him to choose the pace. Those who knew him a little said "How he does dress!"—those who knew him better said "How *does* he?" The one stray gleam of comedy just now in his daughter's eyes was the absurd feeling he momentarily made her have of being herself "looked up" by him in sordid lodgings. For a minute after he came in it was as if the place were her own and he the visitor with susceptibilities. He gave you absurd feelings, he had indescribable arts, that quite turned the tables: this had been always how he came to see her mother so long as her mother would see him. He came from places they had often not known about, but he patronised Lexham Gardens. Kate's only actual expression of impatience, however, was "I'm glad you're so much better!"

"I'm not so much better, my dear—I'm exceedingly unwell; the proof of which is precisely that I've been out to the chemist's—that beastly fellow at the corner." So Mr. Croy showed he could qualify the humble hand that assuaged him. "I'm taking something he has made up for me. It's just why I've sent for you—that you may see me as I really am."

"Oh papa, it's long since I've ceased to see you otherwise than as you really are! I think we've all arrived by this time at the right word for that: 'You're beautiful—*n'en parlons plus*.'[2] You're as beautiful as ever—you look lovely." He judged meanwhile her own appearance, as she knew she could always trust him to do; recognising, estimating, sometimes disapproving, what she wore, showing her the interest he continued to take in her. He might really take none at all, yet she virtually knew herself the creature in the world to whom he was least indifferent. She had often enough wondered what on earth, at the pass he had reached, could give him pleasure, and had come back on these occasions to that. It gave him pleasure that she was handsome, that she was in her way a tangible value. It was at least as marked, nevertheless, that he derived none from similar conditions, so far as they *were* similar, in his other child. Poor Marian might be handsome, but he certainly didn't care. The hitch here of course was that, with whatever beauty, her sister,

2. "Let's not talk about it anymore."

widowed and almost in want, with four bouncing children, had no such measure. She asked him the next thing how long he had been in his actual quarters, though aware of how little it mattered, how little any answer he might make would probably have in common with the truth. She failed in fact to notice his answer, truthful or not, already occupied as she was with what she had on her own side to say to him. This was really what had made her wait—what superseded the small remainder of her resentment at his constant practical impertinence; the result of all of which was that within a minute she had brought it out. "Yes—even now I'm willing to go with you. I don't know what you may have wished to say to me, and even if you hadn't written you would within a day or two have heard from me. Things have happened, and I've only waited, for seeing you, till I should be quite sure. I *am* quite sure. I'll go with you."

It produced an effect. "Go with me where?"

"Anywhere. I'll stay with you. Even here." She had taken off her gloves and, as if she had arrived with her plan, she sat down.

Lionel Croy hung about in his disengaged way—hovered there as if looking, in consequence of her words, for a pretext to back out easily: on which she immediately saw she had discounted, as it might be called, what he had himself been preparing. He wished her not to come to him, still less to settle with him, and had sent for her to give her up with some style and state; a part of the beauty of which, however, was to have been his sacrifice to her own detachment. There was no style, no state, unless she wished to forsake him. His idea had accordingly been to surrender her to her wish with all nobleness; it had by no means been to have positively to keep her off. She cared, however, not a straw for his embarrassment— feeling how little, on her own part, she was moved by charity. She had seen him, first and last, in so many attitudes that she could now deprive him quite without compunction of the luxury of a new one. Yet she felt the disconcerted gasp in his tone as he said: "Oh my child, I can never consent to that!"

"What then are you going to do?"

"I'm turning it over," said Lionel Croy. "You may imagine if I'm not thinking."

"Haven't you thought then," his daughter asked, "of what I speak of? I mean of my being ready."

Standing before her with his hands behind him and his legs a little apart, he swayed slightly to and fro, inclined toward her as if rising on his toes. It had an effect of conscientious deliberation. "No—I haven't. I couldn't. I wouldn't." It was so respectable a show that she felt afresh, and with the memory of their old despair, the despair at home, how little his appearance ever by any chance told about him. His plausibility had been the heaviest of her mother's crosses; inevitably so much more present to the world than whatever it was that was horrid—thank God they didn't really know!—that he had done. He had positively been, in his way, by the force of his particular type, a terrible husband not to live with; his type reflecting so invidiously on the woman who had found him distasteful. Had this thereby not kept directly present to Kate herself that it might, on some sides, prove no light thing for her to leave uncompanion'd a parent with such a face and such a manner? Yet if there was much she neither knew nor dreamed of it passed between them at this very moment that he was quite familiar with himself as the subject of such quandaries. If he recognised his younger daughter's happy aspect as a tangible value, he had from the first still more exactly appraised every point of his own. The great wonder was not that in spite of everything these points had helped him; the great wonder was that they hadn't helped him more. However, it was, to its eternal recurrent tune, helping him all the while; her drop into patience with him showed how it was helping him at this moment. She saw the next instant precisely the line he would take. "Do you really ask me to believe you've been making up your mind to that?"

She had to consider her own line. "I don't think I care, papa, what you believe. I never, for that matter, think of you as believing anything; hardly more," she permitted herself to add, "than I ever think of you as yourself believed. I don't know you, father, you see."

"And it's your idea that you may make that up?"

"Oh dear, no; not at all. That's no part of the question. If I haven't understood you by this time I never shall, and it doesn't matter. It has seemed to me you may be lived with, but not that you may be understood. Of course I've not the least idea how you get on."

"I don't get on," Mr. Croy almost gaily replied.

His daughter took the place in again, and it might well have seemed odd that with so little to meet the eye there should be so much to show. What showed was the ugliness—so positive and palpable that it was somehow sustaining. It was a medium, a setting, and to that extent, after all, a dreadful sign of life; so that it fairly gave point to her answer. "Oh I beg your pardon. You flourish."

"Do you throw it up at me again," he pleasantly put to her, "that I've not made away with myself?"

She treated the question as needing no reply; she sat there for real things. "You know how all our anxieties, under mamma's will, have come out. She had still less to leave than she feared. We don't know how we lived. It all makes up about two hundred a year for Marian, and two for me, but I give up a hundred to Marian."

"Oh you weak thing!" her father sighed as from depths of enlightened experience.

"For you and me together," she went on, "the other hundred would do something."

"And what would do the rest?"

"Can you yourself do nothing?"

He gave her a look; then, slipping his hands into his pockets and turning away, stood for a little at the window she had left open. She said nothing more—she had placed him there with that question, and the silence lasted a minute, broken by the call of an appealing costermonger,[3] which came in with the mild March air, with the shabby sunshine, fearfully unbecoming to the room, and with the small homely hum of Chirk Street. Presently he moved nearer, but as if her question had quite dropped. "I don't see what has so suddenly wound you up."

"I should have thought you might perhaps guess. Let me at any rate tell you. Aunt Maud has made me a proposal. But she has also made me a condition. She wants to keep me."

"And what in the world else *could* she possibly want?"

"Oh I don't know—many things. I'm not so precious a capture," the girl a little dryly explained. "No one has ever wanted to keep me before."

Looking always what was proper, her father looked now still more surprised than interested. "You've not had proposals?" He spoke as if that were incredible of Lionel Croy's daughter; as if indeed such an admission scarce consorted, even in filial intimacy, with her high spirit and general form.

"Not from rich relations. She's extremely kind to me, but it's time, she says, that we should understand each other."

Mr. Croy fully assented. "Of course it is—high time; and I can quite imagine what she means by it."

"Are you very sure?"

"Oh perfectly. She means that she'll 'do' for you handsomely if you'll break off all relations with me. You speak of her condition. Her condition's of course that."

"Well then," said Kate, "it's what has wound me up. Here I am."

He showed with a gesture how thoroughly he had taken it in; after which, within a few seconds, he had quite congruously turned the situation about. "Do you really suppose me in a position to justify your throwing yourself upon me?"

She waited a little, but when she spoke it was clear. "Yes."

3. A hawker of fresh fruit, vegetables, and other produce.

"Well then, you're of feebler intelligence than I should have ventured to suppose you."

"Why so? You live. You flourish. You bloom."

"Ah how you've all always hated me!" he murmured with a pensive gaze again at the window.

"No one could be less of a mere cherished memory," she declared as if she had not heard him. "You're an actual person, if there ever was one. We agreed just now that you're beautiful. You strike me, you know, as—in your own way—much more firm on your feet than I. Don't put it to me therefore as monstrous that the fact that we're after all parent and child should at present in some manner count for us. My idea has been that it should have some effect for each of us. I don't at all, as I told you just now," she pursued, "make out your life; but whatever it is I hereby offer to accept it. And, on my side, I'll do everything I can for you."

"I see," said Lionel Croy. Then with the sound of extreme relevance: "And what *can* you?" She only, at this, hesitated, and he took up her silence. "You can describe yourself—*to* yourself—as, in a fine flight, giving up your aunt for me; but what good, I should like to know, would your fine flight do me?" As she still said nothing he developed a little. "We're not possessed of so much, at this charming pass, please to remember, as that we can afford not to take hold of any perch held out to us. I like the way you talk, my dear, about 'giving up'! One doesn't give up the use of a spoon because one's reduced to living on broth. And your spoon, that is your aunt, please consider, is partly mine as well." She rose now, as if in sight of the term of her effort, in sight of the futility and the weariness of many things, and moved back to the poor little glass with which she had communed before. She retouched here again the poise of her hat, and this brought to her father's lips another remark—in which impatience, however, had already been replaced by a free flare of appreciation. "Oh you're all right! Don't muddle yourself up with *me!*"

His daughter turned round to him. "The condition Aunt Maud makes is that I shall have absolutely nothing to do with you; never see you, nor speak nor write to you, never go near you nor make you a sign, nor hold any sort of communication with you. What she requires is that you shall simply cease to exist for me."

He had always seemed—it was one of the marks of what they called the "unspeakable" in him—to walk a little more on his toes, as if for jauntiness, under the touch of offence. Nothing, however, was more wonderful than what he sometimes would take for offence, unless it might be what he sometimes wouldn't. He walked at any rate on his toes now. "A very proper requirement of your

Aunt Maud, my dear—I don't hesitate to say it!" Yet as this, much as she had seen, left her silent at first from what might have been a sense of sickness, he had time to go on: "That's her condition then. But what are her promises? Just what does she engage to do? You must work it, you know."

"You mean make her feel," Kate asked after a moment, "how much I'm attached to you?"

"Well, what a cruel invidious treaty it is for you to sign. I'm a poor ruin of an old dad to make a stand about giving up—I quite agree. But I'm not, after all, quite the old ruin not to get something *for* giving up."

"Oh I think her idea," said Kate almost gaily now, "is that I shall get a great deal."

He met her with his inimitable amenity. "But does she give you the items?"

The girl went through the show. "More or less, I think. But many of them are things I dare say I may take for granted—things women can do for each other and that you wouldn't understand."

"There's nothing I understand so well, always, as the things I needn't! But what I want to do, you see," he went on, "is to put it to your conscience that you've an admirable opportunity; and that it's moreover one for which, after all, damn you, you've really to thank *me*."

"I confess I don't see," Kate observed, "what my 'conscience' has to do with it."

"Then, my dear girl, you ought simply to be ashamed of yourself. Do you know what you're a proof of, all you hard hollow people together?" He put the question with a charming air of sudden spiritual heat. "Of the deplorably superficial morality of the age. The family sentiment, in our vulgarised brutalised life, has gone utterly to pot. There was a day when a man like me—by which I mean a parent like me—would have been for a daughter like you quite a distinct value; what's called in the business world, I believe, an 'asset.'" He continued sociably to make it out. "I'm not talking only of what you might, with the right feeling, do *for* me, but of what you might—it's what I call your opportunity—do *with* me. Unless indeed," he the next moment imperturbably threw off, "they come a good deal to the same thing. Your duty as well as your chance, if you're capable of seeing it, is to use me. Show family feeling by seeing what I'm good for. If you had it as *I* have it you'd see I'm still good—well, for a lot of things. There's in fact, my dear," Mr. Croy wound up, "a coach-and-four to be got out of me." His lapse, or rather his climax, failed a little of effect indeed through an undue precipitation of memory. Something his daughter had said came back to him. "You've settled to give away half your little inheritance?"

Her hesitation broke into laughter. "No—I haven't 'settled' anything."

"But you mean practically to let Marian collar it?" They stood there face to face, but she so denied herself to his challenge that he could only go on. "You've a view of three hundred a year for her in addition to what her husband left her with? Is *that*," the remote progenitor of such wantonness audibly wondered, "your morality?"

Kate found her answer without trouble. "Is it your idea that I should give you everything?"

The "everything" clearly struck him—to the point even of determining the tone of his reply. "Far from it. How can you ask that when I refuse what you tell me you came to offer? Make of my idea what you can; I think I've sufficiently expressed it, and it's at any rate to take or to leave. It's the only one, I may nevertheless add; it's the basket with all my eggs. It's my conception, in short, of your duty."

The girl's tired smile watched the word as if it had taken on a small grotesque visibility. "You're wonderful on such subjects! I think I should leave you in no doubt," she pursued, "that if I were to sign my aunt's agreement I should carry it out, in honour, to the letter."

"Rather, my own love! It's just your honour that I appeal to. The only way to play the game *is* to play it. There's no limit to what your aunt can do for you."

"Do you mean in the way of marrying me?"

"What else should I mean? Marry properly—"

"And then?" Kate asked as he hung fire.

"And then—well, I *will* talk with you. I'll resume relations."

She looked about her and picked up her parasol. "Because you're not so afraid of any one else in the world as you are of *her?* My husband, if I should marry, would be at the worst less of a terror? If that's what you mean there may be something in it. But doesn't it depend a little also on what you mean by my getting a proper one? However," Kate added as she picked out the frill of her little umbrella, "I don't suppose your idea of him is *quite* that he should persuade you to live with us."

"Dear no—not a bit." He spoke as not resenting either the fear or the hope she imputed; met both imputations in fact with a sort of intellectual relief. "I place the case for you wholly in your aunt's hands. I take her view with my eyes shut; I accept in all confidence any man she selects. If he's good enough for *her*—elephantine snob as she is—he's good enough for me; and quite in spite of the fact that she'll be sure to select one who can be trusted to be nasty to me. My only interest is in your doing what she wants. You shan't be so beastly poor, my darling," Mr. Croy declared, "if I can help it."

"Well then good-bye, papa," the girl said after a reflexion on this that had perceptibly ended for her in a renunciation of further debate. "Of course you understand that it may be for long."

Her companion had hereupon one of his finest inspirations. "Why not frankly for ever? You must do me the justice to see that I don't do things, that I've never done them, by halves—that if I offer you to efface myself it's for the final fatal sponge I ask, well saturated and well applied."

She turned her handsome quiet face upon him at such length that it might indeed have been for the last time. "I don't know what you're like."

"No more do I, my dear. I've spent my life in trying in vain to discover. Like nothing—more's the pity. If there had been many of us and we could have found each other out there's no knowing what we mightn't have done. But it doesn't matter now. Good-bye, love." He looked even not sure of what she would wish him to suppose on the subject of a kiss, yet also not embarrassed by his uncertainty.

She forbore in fact for a moment longer to clear it up. "I wish there were some one here who might serve—for any contingency—as a witness that I *have* put it to you that I'm ready to come."

"Would you like me," her father asked, "to call the landlady?"

"You may not believe me," she pursued, "but I came really hoping you might have found some way. I'm very sorry at all events to leave you unwell." He turned away from her on this and, as he had done before, took refuge, by the window, in a stare at the street. "Let me put it—unfortunately without a witness," she added after a moment, "that there's only one word you really need speak."

When he took these words up it was still with his back to her. "If I don't strike you as having already spoken it our time has been singularly wasted."

"I'll engage with you in respect to my aunt exactly to what she wants of me in respect to you. She wants me to choose. Very well, I *will* choose. I'll wash my hands of her for you to just that tune."

He at last brought himself round. "Do you know, dear, you make me sick? I've tried to be clear, and it isn't fair."

But she passed this over; she was too visibly sincere. "Father!"

"I don't quite see what's the matter with you," he said, "and if you can't pull yourself together I'll—upon my honour—take you in hand. Put you into a cab and deliver you again safe at Lancaster Gate."[4]

She was really absent, distant. "Father."

It was too much, and he met it sharply. "Well?"

"Strange as it may be to you to hear me say it, there's a good you can do me and a help you can render."

"Isn't it then exactly what I've been trying to make you feel?"

"Yes," she answered patiently, "but so in the wrong way. I'm perfectly honest in what I say, and I know what I'm talking about. It isn't that I'll pretend I could have believed a month ago in anything to call aid or support from you. The case is changed—that's what has happened; my difficulty is a new one. But even now it's not a question of anything I should ask you in a way to 'do.' It's simply a question of your not turning me away—taking yourself out of my life. It's simply a question of your saying: 'Yes then, since you will, we'll stand together. We won't worry in advance about how or where; we'll have a faith and find a way.' That's all—*that* would be the good you'd do me. I should *have* you, and it would be for my benefit. Do you see?"

If he didn't it wasn't for want of looking at her hard. "The matter with you is that you're in love, and that your aunt knows and—for reasons, I'm sure, perfect—hates and opposes it. Well she may! It's a matter in which I trust her with my eyes shut. Go, please." Though he spoke not in anger—rather in infinite sadness—he fairly turned her out. Before she took it up he had, as the fullest expression of what he felt, opened the door of the room. He had fairly, in his deep disapproval, a generous compassion to spare. "I'm sorry for her, deluded woman, if she builds on you."

Kate stood a moment in the draught. "She's not the person *I* pity most, for, deluded in many ways though she may be, she's not the person who's most so. I mean," she explained, "if it's a question of what you call building on me."

He took it as if what she meant might be other than her description of it. "You're deceiving *two* persons then, Mrs. Lowder and somebody else?"

She shook her head with detachment. "I've no intention of that sort with respect to any one now—to Mrs. Lowder least of all. If you fail me"—she seemed to make it out for herself—"that has the merit at least that it simplifies. I shall go my way—as I see my way."

4. That is, at Aunt Maud's—Mrs. Lowder's—home, located on the north side of Hyde Park and Kensington Gardens, in the highly fashionable, wealthy, and aristocratic Near West End of London. Before construction of Buckingham Palace, the Royal family made its residence in Kensington Palace. See the map of London, p. 000. For James's personal impressions of the area, see his essay "London" in *Essays in London and Elsewhere* (1893).

"Your way, you mean then, will be to marry some blackguard without a penny?"

"You demand a great deal of satisfaction," she observed, "for the little you give."

It brought him up again before her as with a sense that she was not to be hustled, and though he glared at her a little this had long been the practical limit to his general power of objection. "If you're base enough to incur your aunt's reprobation you're base enough for my argument. What, if you're not thinking of an utterly improper person, do your speeches to me signify? Who *is* the beggarly sneak?" he went on as her response failed.

Her response, when it came, was cold but distinct. "He has every disposition to make the best of you. He only wants in fact to be kind to you."

"Then he *must* be an ass! And how in the world can you consider it to improve him for me," her father pursued, "that he's also destitute and impossible? There are boobies and boobies even—the right and the wrong—and you appear to have carefully picked out one of the wrong. Your aunt knows *them*, by good fortune; I perfectly trust, as I tell you, her judgement for them; and you may take it from me once for all that I won't hear of any one of whom *she* won't." Which led up to his last word. "If you should really defy us both—!"

"Well, papa?"

"Well, my sweet child, I think that—reduced to insignificance as you may fondly believe me—I should still not be quite without some way of making you regret it."

She had a pause, a grave one, but not, as appeared, that she might measure this danger. "If I shouldn't do it, you know, it wouldn't be because I'm afraid of you."

"Oh if you don't do it," he retorted, "you may be as bold as you like!"

"Then you can do nothing at all for me?"

He showed her, this time unmistakeably—it was before her there on the landing, at the top of the tortuous stairs and in the midst of the strange smell that seemed to cling to them—how vain her appeal remained. "I've never pretended to do more than my duty; I've given you the best and the clearest advice." And then came up the spring that moved him. "If it only displeases you, you can go to Marian to be consoled." What he couldn't forgive was her dividing with Marian her scant share of the provision their mother had been able to leave them. She should have divided it with *him*.

II

She had gone to Mrs. Lowder on her mother's death—gone with an effort the strain and pain of which made her at present, as she recalled them, reflect on the long way she had travelled since then. There had been nothing else to do—not a penny in the other house, nothing but unpaid bills that had gathered thick while its mistress lay mortally ill, and the admonition that there was nothing she must attempt to raise money on, since everything belonged to the "estate." How the estate would turn out at best presented itself as a mystery altogether gruesome; it had proved in fact since then a residuum a trifle less scant than, with her sister, she had for some weeks feared; but the girl had had at the beginning rather a wounded sense of its being watched on behalf of Marian and her children. What on earth was it supposed that *she* wanted to do to it? She wanted in truth only to give up—to abandon her own interest, which she doubtless would already have done hadn't the point been subject to Aunt Maud's sharp intervention. Aunt Maud's intervention was all sharp now, and the other point, the great one, was that it was to be, in this light, either all put up with or all declined. Yet at the winter's end, nevertheless, she could scarce have said what stand she conceived she had taken. It wouldn't be the first time she had seen herself obliged to accept with smothered irony other people's interpretation of her conduct. She often ended by giving up to them—it seemed really the way to live—the version that met their convenience.

The tall rich heavy house at Lancaster Gate, on the other side of the Park and the long South Kensington stretches, had figured to her, through childhood, through girlhood, as the remotest limit of her vague young world. It was further off and more occasional than anything else in the comparatively compact circle in which she revolved, and seemed, by a rigour early marked, to be reached through long, straight, discouraging vistas, perfect telescopes of streets, and which kept lengthening and straightening, whereas almost everything else in life was either at the worst roundabout Cromwell Road or at the furthest in the nearer parts of Kensington Gardens. Mrs. Lowder was her only "real" aunt, not the wife of an uncle, and had been thereby, both in ancient days and when the greater trouble came, the person, of all persons, properly to make some sign; in accord with which our young woman's feeling was founded on the impression, quite cherished for years, that the signs made across the interval just mentioned had never been really in the note of the situation. The main office of this relative for the young Croys—apart from giving them their fixed measure of social greatness—had struck them as being to form them to a conception of what they were not to expect. When Kate came to think matters over with wider knowledge, she failed quite to see how Aunt Maud could have been different—she had rather perceived by this time how many other things might have been; yet she also made out that if they had all consciously lived under a liability to the chill breath of *ultima Thule*[1] they couldn't either, on the facts, very well have done less. What in the event appeared established was that if Mrs. Lowder had disliked them she yet hadn't disliked them so much as they supposed. It had at any rate been for the purpose of showing how she struggled with her aversion that she sometimes came to see them, that she at regular periods invited them to her house and in short, as it now looked, kept them along on the terms that would best give her sister the perennial luxury of a grievance. This sister, poor Mrs. Croy, the girl knew, had always judged her resentfully, and had brought them up, Marian, the boys and herself, to the idea of a particular attitude, for signs of the practice of which they watched each other with awe. The attitude was to make plain to Aunt Maud, with the same regularity as her invitations, that they sufficed—thanks awfully—to themselves. But the ground of it, Kate lived to discern, was that this was only because *she* didn't suffice to them. The little she offered was to be accepted under protest, yet not really because it was excessive. It wounded them—there was the rub!—because it fell short.

The number of new things our young lady looked out on from the high south window that hung over the Park—this number was so great (though some of the things were only old ones altered and, as the phrase was of other matters, done up) that life at present turned to her view from week to week more and more the face of a striking and distinguished stranger. She had reached a great age—for it quite seemed to her that at twenty-five it was late to reconsider, and her most general sense was a shade of regret that she hadn't known earlier. The world was different—whether for worse or for better—from her rudimentary readings, and it gave her the feeling of a wasted past. If she had only known sooner she might have arranged herself more to meet it. She made at all events discoveries every day, some of which were about herself and others about other persons. Two of these—one under each head—more particularly engaged, in alternation, her anxiety. She saw as she had never seen before how material things spoke to her. She saw, and she blushed to see, that if in contrast with some of its old aspects life now affected her as a dress successfully "done up," this was exactly by reason of the trimmings and lace, was a matter of ribbons and silk and velvet. She had a dire accessibility to pleasure

1. Literally, the farthest out; way out in the cold. James almost certainly had in mind the ancient geography of antiquity, in which Ultima Thule refers to the extreme limit of travel and discovery, hence the farthest northern limits of the habitable world—and the home of the gods; figuratively, the ultimate in anything. James may well have picked up the expression from Poe, who refers to "an ultimate dim Thule" in his poem "Dream-Land," and to the reference to the pit as the "Ultima Thule of all . . . punishments" in "The Pit and the Pendulum."

from such sources. She liked the charming quarters her aunt had assigned her—liked them literally more than she had in all her other days liked anything; and nothing could have been more uneasy than her suspicion of her relative's view of this truth. Her relative was prodigious—she had never done her relative justice. These larger conditions all tasted of her, from morning till night; but she was a person in respect to whom the growth of acquaintance could only—strange as it might seem—keep your heart in your mouth.

The girl's second great discovery was that, so far from having been for Mrs. Lowder a subject of superficial consideration, the blighted home in Lexham Gardens[2] had haunted her nights and her days. Kate had spent, all winter, hours of observation that were not less pointed for being spent alone; recent events, which her mourning explained, assured her a measure of isolation, and it was in the isolation above all that her neighbour's influence worked. Sitting far downstairs Aunt Maud was yet a presence from which a sensitive niece could feel herself extremely under pressure. She knew herself now, the sensitive niece, as having been marked from far back. She knew more than she could have told you, by the upstairs fire, in a whole dark December afternoon. She knew so much that her knowledge was what fairly kept her there, making her at times circulate more endlessly between the small silk-covered sofa that stood for her in the firelight and the great grey map of Middlesex[3] spread beneath her lookout. To go down, to forsake her refuge, was to meet some of her discoveries halfway, to have to face them or fly before them; whereas they were at such a height only like the rumble of a far-off siege heard in the provisioned citadel. She had almost liked, in these weeks, what had created her suspense and her stress: the loss of her mother, the submersion of her father, the discomfort of her sister, the confirmation of their shrunken prospects, the certainty, in especial, of her having to recognise that should she behave, as she called it, decently—that is still do something for others—she would be herself wholly without supplies. She held that she had a right to sadness and stillness; she nursed them for their postponing power. What they mainly postponed was the question of a surrender, though she couldn't yet have said exactly of what: a general surrender of everything—that was at moments the way it presented itself—to Aunt Maud's looming "personality." It was by her personality that Aunt Maud was prodigious, and the great mass of it loomed because, in the thick, the foglike air of her arranged existence, there were parts doubtless magnified and parts certainly

2. The home of the Croys before the death of Kate's mother.

3. The county that, bordered on the south by the Thames, incorporates the regions to the west and northwest of central London.

vague. They represented at all events alike, the dim and the distinct, a strong will and a high hand. It was perfectly present to Kate that she might be devoured, and she compared herself to a trembling kid, kept apart a day or two till her turn should come, but sure sooner or later to be introduced into the cage of the lioness.

The cage was Aunt Maud's own room, her office, her counting-house, her battlefield, her especial scene, in fine, of action, situated on the ground-floor, opening from the main hall and figuring rather to our young woman on exit and entrance as a guard-house or a toll-gate. The lioness waited—the kid had at least that consciousness; was aware of the neighbourhood of a morsel she had reason to suppose tender. She would have been meanwhile a wonderful lioness for a show, an extraordinary figure in a cage or anywhere; majestic, magnificent, high-coloured, all brilliant gloss, perpetual satin, twinkling bugles and flashing gems, with a lustre of agate eyes, a sheen of raven hair, a polish of complexion that was like that of well-kept china and that—as if the skin were too tight—told especially at curves and corners. Her niece had a quiet name for her—she kept it quiet: thinking of her, with a free fancy, as somehow typically insular, she talked to herself of Britannia of the Market Place[4]—Britannia unmistakeable but with a pen on her ear—and felt she should not be happy till she might on some occasion add to the rest of the panoply a helmet, a shield, a trident and a ledger. It wasn't in truth, however, that the forces with which, as Kate felt, she would have to deal were those most suggested by an image simple and broad; she was learning after all each day to know her companion, and what she had already most perceived was the mistake of trusting to easy analogies. There was a whole side of Britannia, the side of her florid philistinism,[5] her plumes and her train, her fantastic furniture and heaving bosom, the false gods of her taste and false notes of her talk, the sole contemplation of which would be dangerously misleading. She was a complex and subtle Britannia, as passionate as she was practical, with a reticule for her prejudices as deep as that other pocket, the pocket full of coins stamped in her image, that the world best knew her by. She carried on in short, behind her aggressive and defensive front, operations determined by her wisdom. It was in fact as a besieger, we have hinted, that our young lady, in the provisioned citadel, had for the present most to think of her, and what made her formidable in this character was that she was unscrupulous and immoral. So at all

4. A play on the feminine personification of Britain and the British Empire, often celebrated in the heavy bronze sculptures of the Victorian period. Cf. also the later references to the columns of Saint Theodore and the Winged Lion in Venice.

5. A term meaning lack of culture, prosaic commonplaceness, introduced into English in Thomas Carlyle's *Sartor Resartus* (1833) and made widely known in Matthew Arnold's *Essays in Criticism* (1865) and "Culture and Anarchy" (1869).

events in silent sessions and a youthful off-hand way Kate conveniently pictured her: what this sufficiently represented being that her weight was in the scale of certain dangers—those dangers that, by our showing, made the younger woman linger and lurk above, while the elder, below, both militant and diplomatic, covered as much of the ground as possible. Yet what were the dangers, after all, but just the dangers of life and of London? Mrs. Lowder *was* London, *was* life—the roar of the siege and the thick of the fray. There were some things, after all, of which Britannia was afraid; but Aunt Maud was afraid of nothing—not even, it would appear, of arduous thought.

These impressions, none the less, Kate kept so much to herself that she scarce shared them with poor Marian, the ostensible purpose of her frequent visits to whom yet continued to be to talk over everything. One of her reasons for holding off from the last concession to Aunt Maud was that she might be the more free to commit herself to this so much nearer and so much less fortunate relative, with whom Aunt Maud would have almost nothing direct to do. The sharpest pinch of her state, meanwhile, was exactly that all intercourse with her sister had the effect of casting down her courage and tying her hands, adding daily to her sense of the part, not always either uplifting or sweetening, that the bond of blood might play in one's life. She was face to face with it now, with the bond of blood; the consciousness of it was what she seemed most clearly to have "come into" by the death of her mother, much of that consciousness as her mother had absorbed and carried away. Her haunting harassing father, her menacing uncompromising aunt, her portionless little nephews and nieces, were figures that caused the chord of natural piety superabundantly to vibrate. Her manner of putting it to herself—but more especially in respect to Marian—was that she saw what you might be brought to by the cultivation of consanguinity. She had taken, in the old days, as she supposed, the measure of this liability; those being the days when, as the second-born, she had thought no one in the world so pretty as Marian, no one so charming, so clever, so assured in advance of happiness and success. The view was different now, but her attitude had been obliged, for many reasons, to show as the same. The subject of this estimate was no longer pretty, as the reason for thinking her clever was no longer plain; yet, bereaved, disappointed, demoralised, querulous, she was all the more sharply and insistently Kate's elder and Kate's own. Kate's most constant feeling about her was that she would make her, Kate, do things; and always, in comfortless Chelsea,[6] at the door of the small house the small rent of which

6. A decidedly less affluent residential area than Lexham Gardens; an area that had become notable as an artists' colony, particularly around Cheyne Row.

she couldn't help having on her mind, she fatalistically asked herself, before going in, which thing it would probably be this time. She noticed with profundity that disappointment made people selfish; she marvelled at the serenity—it was the poor woman's only one—of what Marian took for granted: her own state of abasement as the second-born, her life reduced to mere inexhaustible sisterhood. She existed in that view wholly for the small house in Chelsea; the moral of which moreover, of course, was that the more you gave yourself the less of you was left. There were always people to snatch at you, and it would never occur to *them* that they were eating you up. They did that without tasting.

There was no such misfortune, or at any rate no such discomfort, she further reasoned, as to be formed at once for being and for seeing. You always saw, in this case something else than what you were, and you got in consequence none of the peace of your condition. However, as she never really let Marian see what she was Marian might well not have been aware that she herself saw. Kate was accordingly to her own vision not a hypocrite of virtue, for she gave herself up; but she was a hypocrite of stupidity, for she kept to herself everything that was not herself. What she most kept was the particular sentiment with which she watched her sister instinctively neglect nothing that would make for her submission to their aunt; a state of the spirit that perhaps marked most sharply how poor you might become when you minded so much the absence of wealth. It was through Kate that Aunt Maud should be worked, and nothing mattered less than what might become of Kate in the process. Kate was to burn her ships in short, so that Marian should profit; and Marian's desire to profit was quite oblivious of a dignity that had after all its reasons—if it had only understood them—for keeping itself a little stiff. Kate, to be properly stiff for both of them, would therefore have had to be selfish, have had to prefer an ideal of behaviour—than which nothing ever was more selfish—to the possibility of stray crumbs for the four small creatures. The tale of Mrs. Lowder's disgust at her elder niece's marriage to Mr. Condrip had lost little of its point; the incredibly fatuous behaviour of Mr. Condrip, the parson of a dull suburban parish, with a saintly profile which was always in evidence, being so distinctly on record to keep criticism consistent. He had presented his profile on system, having, goodness knew, nothing else to present—nothing at all to full-face the world with, no imagination of the propriety of living and minding his business. Criticism had remained on Aunt Maud's part consistent enough; she was not a person to regard such proceedings as less of a mistake for having acquired more of the privilege of pathos. She hadn't been forgiving, and the only approach she made to overlooking them was by overlooking—with the surviving delinquent—the solid little phalanx that now represented them. Of the two sinister ceremonies that she lumped together, the marriage and the interment, she had been present at the former, just as she had sent Marian before it a liberal cheque; but this had not been for her more than the shadow of an admitted link with Mrs. Condrip's course. She disapproved of clamorous children for whom there was no prospect; she disapproved of weeping widows who couldn't make their errors good; and she had thus put within Marian's reach one of the few luxuries left when so much else had gone, an easy pretext for a constant grievance. Kate Croy remembered well what their mother, in a different quarter, had made of it; and it was Marian's marked failure to pluck the fruit of resentment that committed them as sisters to an almost equal fellowship in abjection. If the theory was that, yes, alas, one of the pair had ceased to be noticed, but that the other was noticed enough to make up for it, who would fail to see that Kate couldn't separate herself without a cruel pride? That lesson became sharp for our young lady the day after her interview with her father.

"I can't imagine," Marian on this occasion said to her, "how you can think of anything else in the world but the horrid way we're situated."

"And, pray, how do you know," Kate enquired in reply, "anything about my thoughts? It seems to me I give you sufficient proof of how much I think of *you*. I don't really, my dear, know what else you've to do with!"

Marian's retort on this was a stroke as to which she had supplied herself with several kinds of preparation, but there was none the less something of an unexpected note in its promptitude. She had foreseen her sister's general fear; but here, ominously, was the special one. "Well, your own business is of course your own business, and you may say there's no one less in a position than I to preach to you. But, all the same, if you wash your hands of me for ever in consequence, I won't, for this once, keep back that I don't consider you've a right, as we all stand, to throw yourself away."

It was after the children's dinner, which was also their mother's, but which their aunt mostly contrived to keep from ever becoming her own luncheon; and the two young women were still in the presence of the crumpled table-cloth, the dispersed pinafores, the scraped dishes, the lingering odour of boiled food. Kate had asked with ceremony if she might put up a window a little, and Mrs. Condrip had replied without it that she might do as she liked. She often received such enquiries as if they reflected in a manner on the pure essence of her little ones. The four had retired, with much movement and noise, under imperfect control of the small Irish governess whom their aunt had hunted up for them and whose brooding resolve not to prolong so uncrowned a martyrdom she already more than suspected. Their mother had become for Kate—who took it just for the effect of being their mother—quite a different thing from the mild Marian of the past: Mr. Condrip's widow expansively obscured that image. She was little more than a ragged relic, a plain prosaic result of him—as if she had somehow been pulled through him as through an obstinate funnel, only to be left crumpled and useless and with nothing in her but what he accounted for. She had grown red and almost fat, which were not happy signs of mourning; less and less like any Croy, particularly a Croy in trouble, and sensibly like her husband's two unmarried sisters, who came to see her, in Kate's view, much too often and stayed too long, with the consequence of inroads upon the tea and bread-and-butter—matters as to which Kate, not unconcerned with the tradesmen's books, had feelings. About them moreover Marian *was* touchy, and her nearer relative, who observed and weighed things, noted as an oddity that she would have taken any reflexion on them as a reflexion on herself. If that was what marriage necessarily did to you Kate Croy would have questioned marriage. It was at any rate a grave example of what a man—and such a man!—might make of a woman. She could see how the Condrip pair pressed their brother's widow on the subject of Aunt Maud—who wasn't, after all, *their* aunt; made her, over their interminable cups, chatter and even swagger about Lancaster Gate, made her more vulgar than it had seemed written that any Croy could possibly become on such a subject. They laid it down, they rubbed it in, that Lancaster Gate was to be kept in sight, and that she, Kate, was to keep it; so that, curiously, or at all events sadly, our young woman was sure of being in her own person more permitted to them as an object of comment than they would in turn ever be permitted to herself. The beauty of which too was that Marian didn't love them. But they were Condrips—they had grown near the rose; they were almost like Bertie and Maudie, like Kitty and Guy. They talked of the dead to her, which Kate never did; it being a relation in which Kate could but mutely listen. She couldn't indeed too often say to herself that if that was what marriage did to you—! It may easily be guessed therefore that the ironic light of such reserves fell straight across the field of Marian's warning. "I don't quite see," she answered, "where in particular it strikes you that my danger lies. I'm not conscious, I assure you, of the least disposition to 'throw' myself anywhere. I feel that for the present I've been quite sufficiently thrown."

"You don't feel"—Marian brought it all out—"that you'd like to marry Merton Densher?"

Kate took a moment to meet this enquiry. "Is it your idea that if I should feel so I would be bound to give you notice, so that you might step in and head me off? Is that your idea?" the girl asked. Then as her sister also had a pause, "I don't know what makes you talk of Mr. Densher," she observed.

"I talk of him just because you don't. That you never do, in spite of what I know—that's what makes me think of him. Or rather perhaps it's what makes me think of *you*. If you don't know by this time what I hope for you, what I dream of—my attachment being what it is—it's no use my attempting to tell you." But Marian had in fact warmed to her work, and Kate was sure she had discussed Mr. Densher with the Miss Condrips. "If I name that person I suppose it's because I'm so afraid of him. If you want really to know, he fills me with terror. If you want really to know, in fact, I dislike him as much as I dread him."

"And yet don't think it dangerous to abuse him to me?"

"Yes," Mrs. Condrip confessed, "I do think it dangerous; but how can I speak of him otherwise? I dare say, I admit, that I shouldn't speak of him at all. Only I do want you for once, as I said just now, to know."

"To know what, my dear?"

"That I should regard it," Marian promptly returned, "as far and away the worst thing that has happened to us yet."

"Do you mean because he hasn't money?"

"Yes, for one thing. And because I don't believe in him."

Kate was civil but mechanical. "What do you mean by not believing in him?"

"Well, being sure he'll never get it. And you *must* have it. You *shall* have it."

"To give it to you?"

Marian met her with a readiness that was practically pert. "To *have* it, first. Not at any rate to go on not having it. Then we should see."

"We should indeed!" said Kate Croy. It was talk of a kind she loathed, but if Marian chose to be vulgar what was one to do? It made her think of the Miss Condrips with renewed aversion. "I like the way you arrange things—I like what you take for granted. If it's so easy for us to marry men who want us to scatter gold, I wonder we any of us do anything else. I don't see so many of them about, nor what interest I might ever have for them. You live, my dear," she presently added, "in a world of vain thoughts."

"Not so much as you, Kate; for I see what I see and you can't turn it off that way." The elder sister paused long enough for the younger's face to show, in spite of superiority, an apprehension. "I'm not talking of any man but Aunt Maud's man, nor of any money even, if you like, but Aunt Maud's money. I'm not talking of anything but your doing what *she* wants. You're wrong if you speak of anything that I want of you; I want nothing but what she does. That's good enough for me!"—and Marian's tone struck her companion as of the lowest. "If I don't believe in Merton Densher I do at least in Mrs. Lowder."

"Your ideas are the more striking," Kate returned, "that they're the same as papa's. I had them from him, you'll be interested to know—and with all the brilliancy you may imagine—yesterday."

Marian clearly was interested to know. "He has been to see you?"

"No, I went to him."

"Really?" Marian wondered. "For what purpose?"

"To tell him I'm ready to go to him."

Marian stared. "To leave Aunt Maud—?"

"For my father, yes."

She had fairly flushed, poor Mrs. Condrip, with horror. "You're ready—?"

"So I told him. I couldn't tell him less."

"And pray could you tell him more?" Marian gasped in her distress. "What in the world is he *to* us? You bring out such a thing as that this way?"

They faced each other—the tears were in Marian's eyes. Kate watched them there a moment and then said: "I had thought it well over—over and over. But you needn't feel injured. I'm not going. He won't have me."

Her companion still panted—it took time to subside. "Well, *I* wouldn't have you—wouldn't receive you at all, I can assure you —if he had made you any other answer. I do feel injured—at your having been willing. If you were to go to papa, my dear, you'd have to stop coming to me." Marian put it thus, indefinably, as a picture of privation from which her companion might shrink. Such were the threats she could complacently make, could think herself masterful for making. "But if he won't take you," she continued, "he shows at least his sharpness."

Marian had always her views of sharpness; she was, as her sister privately commented, great on that resource. But Kate had her refuge from irritation. "He won't take me," she simply repeated. "But he believes, like you, in Aunt Maud. He threatens me with his curse if I leave her."

"So you *won't?*" As the girl at first said nothing her companion caught at it. "You won't, of course? I see you won't. But I don't see why, conveniently, I shouldn't insist to you once for all on the plain truth of the whole matter. The truth, my dear, of your duty. Do you ever think about *that?* It's the greatest duty of all."

"There you are again," Kate laughed. "Papa's also immense on my duty."

"Oh I don't pretend to be immense, but I pretend to know more than you do of life; more even perhaps than papa." Marian seemed to see that personage at this moment, nevertheless, in the light of a kinder irony. "Poor old papa!"

She sighed it with as many condonations as her sister's ear had more than once caught in her "Dear old Aunt Maud!" These were things that made Kate turn for the time sharply away, and she gathered herself now to go. They were the note again of the abject; it was hard to say which of the persons in question had most shown how little they liked her. The younger woman proposed at any rate to let discussion rest, and she believed that, for herself, she had done so during the ten minutes elapsing, thanks to her wish not to break off short, before she could gracefully withdraw. It then appeared, however, that Marian had been discussing still, and there was something that at the last Kate had to take up. "Whom do you mean by Aunt Maud's young man?"

"Whom should I mean but Lord Mark?"

"And where do you pick up such vulgar twaddle?" Kate demanded with her clear face. "How does such stuff, in this hole, get to you?"

She had no sooner spoken than she asked herself what had become of the grace to which she had sacrificed. Marian certainly did little to save it, and nothing indeed was so inconsequent as her ground of complaint. She desired her to "work" Lancaster Gate as she believed that scene of abundance could be worked; but she now didn't see why advantage should be taken of the bloated connexion to put an affront on her own poor home. She appeared in fact for the moment to take the position that Kate kept her in her "hole" and then heartlessly reflected on her being in it. Yet she didn't explain how she had picked up the report on which her sister had challenged her—so that it was thus left to her sister to see in it once more a sign of the creeping curiosity of the Miss Condrips. They lived in a deeper hole than Marian, but they kept their ear to the ground, they spent their days in prowling, whereas Marian, in garments and shoes that seemed steadily to grow looser and larger, never prowled. There were times when Kate wondered if the Miss Condrips were offered her by fate as a warning for her own future—to be taken as showing her what she herself might become at forty if she let things too recklessly go. What was expected of her by others—and by so many of them—could, all the same, on occasion, present itself as beyond a joke; and this was just now the aspect it particularly wore. She was not only to quarrel with Merton Densher for the pleasure of her five spectators—with the Miss Condrips there were five; she was to set forth in pursuit of Lord Mark on some preposterous theory of the premium attached to success. Mrs. Lowder's hand had hung out the premium, and it figured at the end of the course as a bell that would ring, break out into public clamour, as soon as touched. Kate reflected sharply enough on the weak points of this fond fiction, with the result at last of a certain chill for her sister's confidence; though Mrs. Condrip still took refuge in the plea—which was after all the great point—that their aunt would be munificent when their aunt should be content. The exact identity of her candidate was a detail; what was of the essence was her conception of the kind of match it was open to her niece to make with her aid. Marian always spoke of marriages as "matches," but that was again a detail. Mrs. Lowder's "aid" meanwhile awaited them—if not to light the way to Lord Mark, then to somebody better. Marian would put up, in fine, with somebody better; she only wouldn't put up with somebody so much worse. Kate had once more to go through all this before a graceful issue was reached. It was reached by her paying with the sacrifice of Mr. Densher for her reduction of Lord Mark to the absurd. So they separated softly enough. She was to be let off hearing about Lord Mark so long as she made it good that she wasn't underhand about any one else. She had denied everything and every one, she reflected as she went away—and that was a relief; but it also made rather a clean sweep of the future. The prospect put on a bareness that already gave her something in common with the Miss Condrips.

Book Second

I

Merton Densher, who passed the best hours of each night at the office of his newspaper, had at times, during the day, to make up for it, a sense, or at least an appearance, of leisure, in accordance with which he was not infrequently to be met in different parts of the town at moments when men of business are hidden from the public eye. More than once during the present winter's end he had deviated toward three o'clock, or toward four, into Kensington Gardens, where he might for a while, on each occasion, have been observed to demean himself as a person with nothing to do. He made his way indeed, for the most part, with a certain directness over to the north side; but once that ground was reached his behaviour was noticeably wanting in point. He moved, seemingly at random, from alley to alley; he stopped for no reason and remained idly agaze; he sat down in a chair and then changed to a bench; after which he walked about again, only again to repeat both the vagueness and the vivacity. Distinctly he was a man either with nothing at all to do or with ever so much to think about; and it was not to be denied that the impression he might often thus easily make had the effect of causing the burden of proof in certain directions to rest on him. It was a little the fault of his aspect, his personal marks, which made it almost impossible to name his profession.

He was a longish, leanish, fairish young Englishman, not unamenable, on certain sides, to classification—as for instance by being a gentleman, by being rather specifically one of the educated, one of the generally sound and generally civil; yet, though to that degree neither extraordinary nor abnormal, he would have failed to play straight into an observer's hands. He was young for the House of Commons, he was loose for the Army. He was refined, as might have been said, for the City and, quite apart from the cut of his cloth, sceptical, it might have been felt, for the Church. On the other hand he was credulous for diplomacy, or perhaps even for science, while he was perhaps at the same time too much in his mere senses for poetry and yet too little in them for art. You would have got fairly near him by making out in his eyes the potential recognition of ideas; but you would have quite fallen away again on the question of the ideas themselves. The difficulty with Densher was that he looked vague without looking weak—idle without looking empty. It was the accident, possibly, of his long legs, which were apt to stretch themselves; of his straight hair and his well-shaped head, never, the latter, neatly smooth, and apt into the bargain, at the time of quite other calls upon it, to throw itself suddenly back and, supported behind by his uplifted arms and interlocked hands, place him for unconscionable periods in communion with the ceiling, the tree-tops, the sky. He was in short visibly absent-minded, irregularly clever, liable to drop what was near and to take up what was far; he was more a prompt critic than a prompt follower of custom. He suggested above all, however, that wondrous state of youth in which the elements, the metals more or less precious, are so in fusion and fermentation that the question of the final stamp, the pressure that fixes the value, must wait for comparative coolness. And it was a mark of his interesting mixture that if he was irritable it was by a law of considerable subtlety—a law that in intercourse with him it might be of profit, though not easy, to master. One of the effects of it was that he had for you surprises of tolerance as well as of temper.

He loitered, on the best of the relenting days, the several occasions we speak of, along the part of the Gardens nearest to Lancaster Gate, and when, always, in due time, Kate Croy came out of her aunt's house, crossed the road and arrived by the nearest entrance, there was a general publicity in the proceeding which made it slightly anomalous. If their meeting was to be bold and free it might have taken place within-doors; if it was to be shy or secret it might have taken place almost anywhere better than under Mrs.

Lowder's windows. They failed indeed to remain attached to that spot; they wandered and strolled, taking in the course of more than one of these interviews a considerable walk, or else picked out a couple of chairs under one of the great trees and sat as much apart —apart from every one else—as possible. But Kate had each time, at first, the air of wishing to expose herself to pursuit and capture if those things were in question. She made the point that she wasn't underhand, any more than she was vulgar; that the Gardens were charming in themselves and this use of them a matter of taste; and that, if her aunt chose to glare at her from the drawing-room or to cause her to be tracked and overtaken, she could at least make it convenient that this should be easily done. The fact was that the relation between these young persons abounded in such oddities as were not inaptly symbolised by assignations that had a good deal more appearance than motive. Of the strength of the tie that held them we shall sufficiently take the measure; but it was meanwhile almost obvious that if the great possibility had come up for them it had done so, to an exceptional degree, under the protection of the famous law of contraries. Any deep harmony that might eventually govern them would not be the result of their having much in common—having anything in fact but their affection; and would really find its explanation in some sense, on the part of each, of being poor where the other was rich. It is nothing new indeed that generous young persons often admire most what nature hasn't given them—from which it would appear, after all, that our friends were both generous.

Merton Densher had repeatedly said to himself—and from far back—that he should be a fool not to marry a woman whose value would be in her differences; and Kate Croy, though without having quite so philosophised, had quickly recognised in the young man a precious unlikeness. He represented what her life had never given her and certainly, without some such aid as his, never would give her; all the high dim things she lumped together as of the mind. It was on the side of the mind that Densher was rich for her and mysterious and strong; and he had rendered her in especial the sovereign service of making that element real. She had had all her days to take it terribly on trust, no creature she had ever encountered having been able to testify for it directly. Vague rumours of its existence had made their precarious way to her; but nothing had, on the whole, struck her as more likely than that she should live and die without the chance to verify them. The chance had come—it was an extraordinary one—on the day she first met Densher; and it was to the girl's lasting honour that she knew on the spot what she was in presence of. That occasion indeed, for everything that straightway flowered in it, would be worthy of high commemoration; Densher's perception went out to meet the young woman's and quite kept pace with her own recognition. Having so often concluded on the fact of his weakness, as he called it, for life—his strength merely for thought—life, he logically opined, was what he must somehow arrange to annex and possess. This was so much a necessity that thought by itself only went on in the void; it was from the immediate air of life that it must draw its breath. So the young man, ingenious but large, critical but ardent too, made out both his case and Kate Croy's. They had originally met before her mother's death—an occasion marked for her as the last pleasure permitted by the approach of that event; after which the dark months had interposed a screen and, for all Kate knew, made the end one with the beginning.

The beginning—to which she often went back—had been a scene, for our young woman, of supreme brilliancy; a party given at a "gallery" hired by a hostess who fished with big nets. A Spanish dancer, understood to be at that moment the delight of the town, an American reciter, the joy of a kindred people, an Hungarian fiddler, the wonder of the world at large—in the name of these and other attractions the company in which Kate, by a rare privilege, found herself had been freely convoked. She lived under her mother's roof, as she considered, obscurely, and was acquainted with few persons who entertained on that scale; but she had had dealings with two or three connected, as appeared, with such—two or three through whom the stream of hospitality, filtered or diffused, could thus now and then spread to outlying receptacles. A good-natured lady in fine, a friend of her mother and a relative of the lady of the gallery, had offered to take her to the party in question and had there fortified her, further, with two or three of those introductions that, at large parties, lead to other things—that had at any rate on this occasion culminated for her in conversation with a tall fair, a slightly unbrushed and rather awkward, but on the whole a not dreary, young man. The young man had affected her as detached, as—it was indeed what he called himself—awfully at sea, as much more distinct from what surrounded them than any one else appeared to be, and even as probably quite disposed to be making his escape when pulled up to be placed in relation with her. He gave her his word for it indeed, this same evening, that only their meeting had prevented his flight, but that now he saw how sorry he should have been to miss it. This point they had reached by midnight, and though for the value of such remarks everything was in the tone, by midnight the tone was there too. She had had originally her full apprehension of his coerced, certainly of his vague, condition—full apprehensions often being with her immediate; then she had had her equal consciousness that within five minutes something between them had—well, she couldn't call it anything but *come.* It was nothing to look at or to handle, but was somehow everything to feel and to know; it was that something for each of them had happened.

They had found themselves regarding each other straight, and for a longer time on end than was usual even at parties in galleries; but that in itself after all would have been a small affair for two such handsome persons. It wasn't, in a word, simply that their eyes had met; other conscious organs, faculties, feelers had met as well, and when Kate afterwards imaged to herself the sharp deep fact she saw it, in the oddest way, as a particular performance. She had observed a ladder against a garden-wall and had trusted herself so to climb it as to be able to see over into the probable garden on the other side. On reaching the top she had found herself face to face with a gentleman engaged in a like calculation at the same moment, and the two enquirers had remained confronted on their ladders. The great point was that for the rest of that evening they had been perched—they had not climbed down; and indeed during the time that followed Kate at least had had the perched feeling—it was as if she were there aloft without a retreat. A simpler expression of all this is doubtless but that they had taken each other in with interest; and without a happy hazard six months later the incident would have closed in that account of it. The accident meanwhile had been as natural as anything in London ever is: Kate had one afternoon found herself opposite Mr. Densher on the Underground Railway.[1] She had entered the train at Sloane Square to go to Queen's Road, and the carriage in which she took her place was all but full. Densher was already in it—on the other bench and at the furthest angle; she was sure of him before they had again started. The day and the hour were darkness, there were six other persons and she had been busy seating herself; but her consciousness had gone to him as straight as if they had come together in some bright stretch of a desert. They had on neither part a second's hesitation; they looked across the choked compartment exactly as if she had known he would be there and he had expected her to come in; so that, though in the conditions they could only exchange the greeting of movements, smiles, abstentions, it would have been quite in the key of these passages that they should have alighted for ease at the very next station. Kate was in fact sure the very next station was the young man's true goal—which made it clear he was going on only from the wish to speak to her. He had to go on, for this purpose, to High Street Kensington, as it was not till then that the exit of a passenger gave him his chance.

His chance put him however in quick possession of the seat

1. London's subway system, known as the "Metro" or the "Tube."

facing her, the alertness of his capture of which seemed to show her his impatience. It helped them moreover, with strangers on either side, little to talk; though this very restriction perhaps made such a mark for them as nothing else could have done. If the fact that their opportunity had again come round for them could be so intensely expressed without a word, they might very well feel on the spot that it had not come round for nothing. The extraordinary part of the matter was that they were not in the least meeting where they had left off, but ever so much further on, and that these added links added still another between High Street and Notting Hill Gate, and then worked between the latter station and Queen's Road an extension really inordinate. At Notting Hill Gate Kate's right-hand neighbour descended, whereupon Densher popped straight into that seat; only there was not much gained when a lady the next instant popped into Densher's. He could say almost nothing—Kate scarce knew, at least, what he said; she was so occupied with a certainty that one of the persons opposite, a youngish man with a single eye-glass which he kept constantly in position, had made her out from the first as visibly, as strangely affected. If such a person made her out what then did Densher do?—a question in truth sufficiently answered when, on their reaching her station, he instantly followed her out of the train. That had been the real beginning—the beginning of everything else; the other time, the time at the party, had been but the beginning of *that*. Never in life before had she so let herself go; for always before—so far as small adventures could have been in question for her—there had been, by the vulgar measure, more to go upon. He had walked with her to Lancaster Gate, and then she had walked with him away from it—for all the world, she said to herself, like the housemaid giggling to the baker.

This appearance, she was afterwards to feel, had been all in order for a relation that might precisely best be described in the terms of the baker and the housemaid. She could say to herself that from that hour they had kept company: that had come to represent, technically speaking, alike the range and the limit of their tie. He had on the spot, naturally, asked leave to call upon her—which, as a young person who wasn't really young, who didn't pretend to be a sheltered flower, she as rationally gave. That—she was promptly clear about it—was now her only possible basis; she was just the contemporary London female, highly modern, inevitably battered, honourably free. She had of course taken her aunt straight into her confidence—had gone through the form of asking her leave; and she subsequently remembered that though on this occasion she had left the history of her new alliance as scant as the facts themselves, Mrs. Lowder had struck her at the time as surprisingly mild. The occasion had been in every way full of the reminder that her hostess was deep: it was definitely then that she had begun to ask herself what Aunt Maud was, in vulgar parlance, "up to." "You may receive, my dear, whom you like"—that was what Aunt Maud, who in general objected to people's doing as they liked, had replied; and it bore, this unexpectedness, a good deal of looking into. There were many explanations, and they were all amusing—amusing, that is, in the line of the sombre and brooding amusement cultivated by Kate in her actual high retreat. Merton Densher came the very next Sunday; but Mrs. Lowder was so consistently magnanimous as to make it possible to her niece to see him alone. She saw him, however, on the Sunday following, in order to invite him to dinner; and when, after dining, he came again—which he did three times, she found means to treat his visit as preponderantly to herself. Kate's conviction that she didn't like him made that remarkable; it added to the evidence, by this time voluminous, that she was remarkable all round. If she had been, in the way of energy, merely usual she would have kept her dislike direct; whereas it was now as if she were seeking to know him in order to see best where to "have" him. That was one of the reflexions made in our young woman's high retreat; she smiled from her lookout, in the silence that was only the fact of hearing irrelevant sounds, as she caught the truth that you could easily accept people when you wanted them so to be delivered to you. When Aunt Maud wished them dispatched it was not to be done by deputy; it was clearly always a matter reserved for her own hand.

But what made the girl wonder most was the implication of so much diplomacy in respect to her own value. What view might she take of her position in the light of this appearance that her companion feared so as yet to upset her? It was as if Densher were accepted partly under the dread that if he hadn't been she would act in resentment. Hadn't her aunt considered the danger that she would in that case have broken off, have seceded? The danger was exaggerated—she would have done nothing so gross; but that, it would seem, was the way Mrs. Lowder saw her and believed her to be reckoned with. What importance therefore did she really attach to her, what strange interest could she take in their keeping on terms? Her father and her sister had their answer to this—even without knowing how the question struck her: they saw the lady of Lancaster Gate as panting to make her fortune, and the explanation of that appetite was that, on the accident of a nearer view than she had before enjoyed, she had been charmed, been dazzled. They approved, they admired in her one of the belated fancies of rich capricious violent old women—the more marked moreover because the result of no plot; and they piled up the possible fruits for the person concerned. Kate knew what to think of her own power thus to carry by storm; she saw herself as handsome, no doubt, but as hard, and felt herself as clever but as cold; and as so much too imperfectly ambitious, futhermore, that it was a pity, for a quiet life, she couldn't decide to be either finely or stupidly indifferent. Her intelligence sometimes kept her still—too still—but her want of it was restless; so that she got the good, it seemed to her, of neither extreme. She saw herself at present, none the less, in a situation, and even her sad disillusioned mother, dying, but with Aunt Maud interviewing the nurse on the stairs, had not failed to remind her that it was of the essence of situations to be, under Providence, worked. The dear woman had died in the belief that she was actually working the one then recognised.

Kate took one of her walks with Densher just after her visit to Mr. Croy; but most of it went, as usual, to their sitting in talk. They had under the trees by the lake the air of old friends—particular phases of apparent earnestness in which they might have been settling every question in their vast young world; and periods of silence, side by side, perhaps even more, when "A long engagement!" would have been the final reading of the signs on the part of a passer struck with them, as it was so easy to be. They would have presented themselves thus as very old friends rather than as young persons who had met for the first time but a year before and had spent most of the interval without contact. It was indeed for each, already, as if they were older friends; and though the succession of their meetings might, between them, have been straightened out, they only had a confused sense of a good many, very much alike, and a confused intention of a good many more, as little different as possible. The desire to keep them just as they were had perhaps to do with the fact that in spite of the presumed diagnosis of the stranger there had been for them as yet no formal, no final understanding. Densher had at the very first pressed the question, but that, it had been easy to reply, was too soon; so that a singular thing had afterwards happened. They had accepted their acquaintance as too short for an engagement, but they had treated it as long enough for almost anything else, and marriage was somehow before them like a temple without an avenue. They belonged to the temple and they met in the grounds; they were in the stage at which grounds in general offered much scattered refreshment. But Kate had meanwhile had so few confidants that she wondered at the source of her father's suspicions. The diffusion of rumour was of course always remarkable in London, and for Marian not less—as Aunt Maud touched neither directly—the mystery had worked. No doubt she had been seen. Of course she had been seen. She had taken no trouble not to be seen, and it was a thing she was clearly incapable of taking. But she had been seen how?—and what *was* there to see? She was in love—she knew that: but it was wholly her own business, and she had the sense of having conducted herself, of still so doing, with almost violent conformity.

"I've an idea—in fact I feel sure—that Aunt Maud means to write to you; and I think you had better know it." So much as this she said to him as soon as they met, but immediately adding to it: "So as to make up your mind how to take her. I know pretty well what she'll say to you."

"Then will you kindly tell me?"

She thought a little. "I can't do that. I should spoil it. She'll do the best for her own idea."

"Her idea, you mean, that I'm a sort of a scoundrel; or, at the best, not good enough for you?"

They were side by side again in their penny chairs, and Kate had another pause. "Not good enough for *her*."

"Oh I see. And that's necessary."

He put it as a truth rather more than as a question; but there had been plenty of truths between them that each had contradicted. Kate, however, let this one sufficiently pass, only saying the next moment: "She has behaved extraordinarily."

"And so have we," Densher declared. "I think, you know, we've been awfully decent."

"For ourselves, for each other, for people in general, yes. But not for *her*. For her," said Kate, "we've been monstrous. She has been giving us rope. So if she does send for you," the girl repeated, "you must know where you are."

"That I always know. It's where *you* are that concerns me."

"Well," said Kate after an instant, "her idea of that is what you'll have from her." He gave her a long look, and whatever else people who wouldn't let her alone might have wished, for her advancement, his long looks were the thing in the world she could never have enough of. What she felt was that, whatever might happen, she must keep them, must make them most completely her possession; and it was already strange enough that she reasoned, or at all events began to act, as if she might work them in with other and alien things, privately cherish them and yet, as regards the rigour of it, pay no price. She looked it well in the face, she took it intensely home, that they were lovers; she rejoiced to herself and, frankly, to him, in their wearing of the name; but, distinguished creature that, in her way, she was, she took a view of this character that scarce squared with the conventional. The character itself she insisted on as their right, taking that so for granted that it didn't seem even bold; but Densher, though he agreed with her, found himself moved to wonder at her simplifications, her values. Life might prove difficult—was evidently going to; but meanwhile they had each other, and that was everything. This was her reasoning, but meanwhile, for *him*, each other was what they didn't have, and it was just the point. Repeatedly, however, it was a point that, in the face of strange and special things, he judged it rather awkwardly gross to urge. It was impossible to keep Mrs. Lowder out of their scheme. She stood there too close to it and too solidly; it had to open a gate, at a given point, do what they would, to take her in. And she came in, always, while they sat together rather helplessly watching her, as in a coach-and-four; she drove round their prospect as the principal lady at the circus drives round the ring, and she stopped the coach in the middle to alight with majesty. It was our young man's sense that she was magnificently vulgar, but yet quite that this wasn't all. It wasn't with her vulgarity that she felt his want of means, though that might have helped her richly to embroider it; nor was it with the same infirmity that she was strong original dangerous.

His want of means—of means sufficient for any one but himself—was really the great ugliness, and was moreover at no time more ugly for him than when it rose there, as it did seem to rise, all shameless, face to face with the elements in Kate's life colloquially and conveniently classed by both of them as funny. He sometimes indeed, for that matter, asked himself if these elements were as funny as the innermost fact, so often vivid to him, of his own consciousness—his private inability to believe he should ever be rich. His conviction on this head was in truth quite positive and a thing by itself; he failed, after analysis, to understand it, though he had naturally more lights on it than any one else. He knew how it subsisted in spite of an equal consciousness of his being neither mentally nor physically quite helpless, neither a dunce nor a cripple; he knew it to be absolute, though secret, and also, strange to say, about common undertakings, not discouraging, not prohibitive. Only now was he having to think if it were prohibitive in respect to marriage; only now, for the first time, had he to weigh his case in scales. The scales, as he sat with Kate, often dangled in the line of his vision; he saw them, large and black, while he talked or listened, take, in the bright air, singular positions. Sometimes the right was down and sometimes the left; never a happy equipoise—one or the other always kicking the beam. Thus was kept before him the question of whether it were more ignoble to ask a woman to take her chance with you, or to accept it from your conscience that her chance could be at the best but one of the degrees of privation; whether too, otherwise, marrying for money mightn't after all be a smaller cause of shame than the mere dread of marrying without. Through these variations of mood and view, nevertheless, the mark on his forehead stood clear; he saw himself remain without whether he married or not. It was a line on which his fancy could be admirably active; the innumerable ways of making money were beautifully present to him; he could have handled them for his newspaper as easily as he handled everything. He was quite aware how he handled everything; it was another mark on his forehead: the pair of smudges from the thumb of fortune, the brand on the passive fleece, dated from the primal hour and kept each other company. He wrote, as for print, with deplorable ease; since there had been nothing to stop him even at the age of ten, so there was as little at twenty; it was part of his fate in the first place and part of the wretched public's in the second. The innumerable ways of making money were, no doubt, at all events, what his imagination often was busy with after he had tilted his chair and thrown back his head with his hands clasped behind it. What would most have prolonged that attitude, moreover, was the reflexion that the ways were ways only for others. Within the minute now—however this might be—he was aware of a nearer view than he had yet quite had of those circumstances on his companion's part that made least for simplicity of relation. He saw above all how she saw them herself, for she spoke of them at present with the last frankness, telling him of her visit to her father and giving him, in an account of her subsequent scene with her sister, an instance of how she was perpetually reduced to patching-up, in one way or another, that unfortunate woman's hopes.

"The tune," she exclaimed, "to which we're a failure as a family!" With which he had it all again from her—and this time, as it seemed to him, more than all: the dishonour her father had brought them, his folly and cruelty and wickedness; the wounded state of her mother, abandoned despoiled and helpless, yet, for the management of such a home as remained to them, dreadfully unreasonable too; the extinction of her two young brothers—one, at nineteen, the eldest of the house, by typhoid fever contracted at a poisonous little place, as they had afterwards found out, that they had taken for a summer; the other, the flower of the flock, a middy on the *Britannia,* dreadfully drowned, and not even by an accident at sea, but by cramp, unrescued, while bathing, too late in the autumn, in a wretched little river during a holiday visit to the home of a shipmate. Then Marian's unnatural marriage, in itself a kind of spiritless turning of the other cheek to fortune: her actual wretchedness and plaintiveness, her greasy children, her impossible claims, her odious visitors—these things completed the proof of the heaviness, for them all, of the hand of fate. Kate confessedly described them with an excess of impatience; it was much of her charm for Densher that she gave in general that turn to her descriptions, partly as if to amuse him by free and humorous colour, partly—and that charm was the greatest—as if to work off, for her own relief, her constant perception of the incongruity of things. She had seen the general show too early and too sharply, and was so intelligent that she knew it and allowed for that misfortune; therefore when, in talk with him, she was violent and almost unfeminine, it was quite as if they had settled, for intercourse, on the short cut of the fantastic and the happy language of exaggeration. It had come to be definite between them at a primary stage that, if they could have no other straight way, the realm of thought at least was open to them. They could think whatever they liked about whatever they would—in other words they could say it. Saying it for each other, for each other alone, only of course added to the taste. The implication was thereby constant that what they said when not together had no taste for them at all, and nothing could have served more to launch them, at special hours, on their small floating island than such an assumption that they were only making believe everywhere else. Our young man, it must be added, was conscious enough that it was Kate who profited most by this particular play of the fact of intimacy. It always struck him she had more life than he to react from, and when she recounted the dark disasters of her house and glanced at the hard odd offset of her present exaltation—since as exaltation it was apparently to be considered—he felt his own grey domestic annals make little show. It was naturally, in all such reference, the question of her father's character that engaged him most, but her picture of her adventure in Chirk Street gave him a sense of how little as yet that character was clear to him. What was it, to speak plainly, that Mr. Croy had originally done?

"I don't know—and I don't want to. I only know that years and years ago—when I was about fifteen—something or other happened that made him impossible. I mean impossible for the world at large first, and then, little by little, for mother. We of course didn't know it at the time," Kate explained, "but we knew it later; and it was, oddly enough, my sister who first made out that he had done something. I can hear her now—the way, one cold black Sunday morning when, on account of an extraordinary fog, we hadn't gone to church, she broke it to me by the school-room fire. I was reading a history-book by the lamp—when we didn't go to church we had to read history-books—and I suddenly heard her say, out of the fog, which was in the room, and apropos of nothing: 'Papa has done something wicked.' And the curious thing was that I believed it on the spot and have believed it ever since, though she could tell me nothing more—neither what was the wickedness, nor how she knew, nor what would happen to him, nor anything else about it. We had our sense always that all sorts of things *had* happened, were all the while happening, to him; so that when Marian only said she was sure, tremendously sure, that she had made it out for herself, but that that was enough, I took her word for it—it seemed somehow so natural. We were not, however, to ask mother—which made it more natural still, and I said never a word. But mother, strangely enough, spoke of it to me, in time, of her own accord—this was very much later on. He hadn't been with us for ever so long, but we were used to that. She must have had some fear, some conviction that I had an idea, some idea of her own that it was the best thing to do. She came out as abruptly as Marian had done: 'If you hear anything against your father—anything I mean except that he's odious and vile—remember it's perfectly false.' That was the way I knew it was true, though I recall my saying to her then that I of course knew it wasn't. She might have told me it was true, and yet have trusted me to contradict fiercely enough any accusation of him that I should meet—to contradict it much more fiercely and effectively, I think, than she would have done herself. As it happens, however," the girl went on, "I've never had occasion, and I've been conscious of it with a sort of surprise. It has made the world seem at times more decent. No one has so much as breathed to me. That has been a part of the silence, the silence that surrounds him, the silence that, for the world, has washed him out. He doesn't exist for people. And yet I'm as sure as ever. In fact, though I know no more than I did then, I'm more sure. And that," she wound up,"is what I sit here and tell you about my own father. If you don't call it a proof of confidence I don't know what will satisfy you."

"It satisfies me beautifully," Densher returned, "but it doesn't, my dear child, very greatly enlighten me. You don't, you know, really tell me anything. It's so vague that what am I to think but that you may very well be mistaken? What has he done, if no one can name it?"

"He has done everything."

"Oh—everything! Everything's nothing."

"Well then," said Kate, "he has done some particular thing. It's known—only, thank God, not to us. But it has been the end of him. *You* could doubtless find out with a little trouble. You can ask about."

Densher for a moment said nothing; but the next moment he made it up. "I wouldn't find out for the world, and I'd rather lose my tongue than put a question."

"And yet it's a part of me," said Kate.

"A part of you?"

"My father's dishonour." Then she sounded for him, but more deeply than ever yet, her note of proud still pessimism. "How can such a thing as that not be the great thing in one's life?"

She had to take from him again, on this, one of his long looks, and she took it to its deepest, its headiest dregs. "I shall ask you, for the great thing in your life," he said, "to depend on *me* a little more." After which, just debating, "Doesn't he belong to some club?" he asked.

She had a grave headshake. "He used to—to many."

"But he has dropped them?"

"They've dropped *him.* Of that I'm sure. It ought to do for you. I offered him," the girl immediately continued—"and it was for that I went to him—to come and be with him, make a home for him so far as is possible. But he won't hear of it."

Densher took this in with marked but generous wonder. "You offered him—'impossible' as you describe him to me—to live with him and share his disadvantages?" The young man saw for the moment only the high beauty of it. "You *are* gallant!"

"Because it strikes you as being brave for him?" She wouldn't in the least have this. "It wasn't courage—it was the opposite. I did it to save myself—to escape."

He had his air, so constant at this stage, as of her giving him finer things than any one to think about. "Escape from what?"

"From everything."

"Do you by any chance mean from me?"

"No; I spoke to him of you, told him—or what amounted to it—that I would bring you, if he would allow it, with me."

"But he won't allow it," said Densher.

"Won't hear of it on any terms. He won't help me, won't save me, won't hold out a finger to me," Kate went on. "He simply wriggles away, in his inimitable manner, and throws me back."

"Back then, after all, thank goodness," Densher concurred, "on me."

But she spoke again as with the sole vision of the whole scene she had evoked. "It's a pity, because you'd like him. He's wonderful—he's charming." Her companion gave one of the laughs that showed again how inveterately he felt in her tone something that banished the talk of other women, so far as he knew other women, to the dull desert of the conventional, and she had already continued. "He would make himself delightful to you."

"Even while objecting to me?"

"Well, he likes to please," the girl explained—"personally. I've seen it make him wonderful. He would appreciate you and be clever with you. It's to *me* he objects—that is as to my liking you."

"Heaven be praised then," cried Densher, "that you like me enough for the objection!"

But she met it after an instant with some inconsequence. "I don't. I offered to give you up, if necessary, to go to him. But it made no difference, and that's what I mean," she pursued, "by his declining me on any terms. The point is, you see, that I don't escape."

Densher wondered. "But if you didn't wish to escape *me?*"

"I wished to escape Aunt Maud. But he insists that it's through her and through her only that I may help him; just as Marian insists that it's through her, and through her only, that I can help *her*. That's what I mean," she again explained, "by their turning me back."

The young man thought. "Your sister turns you back too?"

"Oh with a push!"

"But have you offered to live with your sister?"

"I would in a moment if she'd have me. That's all my virtue—a narrow little family feeling. I've a small stupid piety—I don't know what to call it." Kate bravely stuck to that; she made it out. "Sometimes, alone, I've to smother my shrieks when I think of my poor mother. She went through things—they pulled her down; I know what they were now—I didn't then, for I was a pig; and my position, compared with hers, is an insolence of success. That's what Marian keeps before me; that's what papa himself, as I say, so inimitably does. My position's a value, a great value, for them both"—she followed and followed. Lucid and ironic, she knew no merciful muddle. "It's *the* value—the only one they have."

Everything between our young couple moved today, in spite of their pauses, their margin, to a quicker measure—the quickness and anxiety playing lightning-like in the sultriness. Densher watched, decidedly, as he had never done before. "And the fact you speak of holds you!"

"Of course it holds me. It's a perpetual sound in my ears. It makes me ask myself if I've any right to personal happiness, any right to anything but to be as rich and overflowing, as smart and shining, as I can be made."

Densher had a pause. "Oh you might by good luck have the personal happiness too."

Her immediate answer to this was a silence like his own; after which she gave him straight in the face, but quite simply and quietly: "Darling!"

It took him another moment; then he was also quiet and simple. "Will you settle it by our being married to-morrow—as we can, with perfect ease, civilly?"

"Let us wait to arrange it," Kate presently replied, "till after you've seen her."

"Do you call that adoring me?" Densher demanded.

They were talking, for the time, with the strangest mixture of deliberation and directness, and nothing could have been more in the tone of it than the way she at last said: "You're afraid of her yourself."

He gave rather a glazed smile. "For young persons of a great distinction and a very high spirit we're a caution!"

"Yes," she took it straight up; "we're hideously intelligent. But there's fun in it too. We must get our fun where we can. I think," she added, and for that matter not without courage, "our relation's quite beautiful. It's not a bit vulgar. I cling to some saving romance in things."

It made him break into a laugh that had more freedom than his smile. "How you must be afraid you'll chuck me!"

"No, no, *that* would be vulgar. But of course," she admitted, "I do see my danger of doing something base."

"Then what can be so base as sacrificing me?"

"I *shan't* sacrifice you. Don't cry out till you're hurt. I shall sacrifice nobody and nothing, and that's just my situation, that I want and that I shall try for everything. That," she wound up, "is how I see myself (and how I see you quite as much) acting for them."

"For 'them'?"—and the young man extravagantly marked his coldness. "Thank you!"

"Don't you care for them?"

"Why should I? What are they to me but a serious nuisance?"

As soon as he had permitted himself this qualification of the unfortunate persons she so perversely cherished he repented of his roughness—and partly because he expected a flash from her. But it was one of her finest sides that she sometimes flashed with a mere mild glow. "I don't see why you don't make out a little more that if we avoid stupidity we may do *all*. We may keep her."

He stared. "Make her pension us?"

"Well, wait at least till we've seen."

He thought. "Seen what can be got out of her?"

Kate for a moment said nothing. "After all I never asked her; never, when our troubles were at the worst, appealed to her nor went near her. She fixed upon me herself, settled on me with her wonderful gilded claws."

"You speak," Densher observed, "as if she were a vulture."

"Call it an eagle—with a gilded beak as well, and with wings for great flights. If she's a thing of the air, in short—say at once a great seamed silk balloon—I never myself got into her car. I was her choice."

It had really, her sketch of the affair, a high colour and a great style; at all of which he gazed a minute as at a picture by a master. "What she must see in you!"

"Wonders!" And, speaking it loud, she stood straight up. "Everything. There it is."

Yes, there it was, and as she remained before him he continued to face it. "So that what you mean is that I'm to do my part in somehow squaring her?"

"See her, see her," Kate said with impatience.

"And grovel to her?"

"Ah do what you like!" And she walked in her impatience away.

II

His eyes had followed her at this time quite long enough, before he overtook her, to make out more than ever in the poise of her head, the pride of her step—he didn't know what best to call it—a part at least of Mrs. Lowder's reasons. He consciously winced while he figured his presenting himself as a reason opposed to these; though at the same moment, with the source of Aunt Maud's inspiration thus before him, he was prepared to conform, by almost any abject attitude or profitable compromise, to his companion's easy injunction. He would do as *she* liked—his own liking might come off as it would. He would help her to the utmost of his power; for, all the rest of this day and the next, her easy injunction, tossed off that way as she turned her beautiful back, was like the crack of a great whip in the blue air, the high element in which Mrs. Lowder hung. He wouldn't grovel perhaps—he wasn't quite ready for that; but he would be patient, ridiculous, reasonable, unreasonable, and above all deeply diplomatic. He would be clever with all his cleverness—which he now shook hard, as he sometimes shook his poor dear shabby old watch, to start it up again. It wasn't, thank goodness, as if there weren't plenty of that "factor" (to use one of his great newspaper-words), and with what they could muster between them it would be little to the credit of their star, however pale, that defeat and surrender—surrender so early, so immediate—should have to ensue. It was not indeed that he thought of that disaster as at the worst a direct sacrifice of their possibilities: he imaged it—which was enough—as some proved vanity, some exposed fatuity in the idea of bringing Mrs. Lowder round. When shortly afterwards, in this lady's vast drawing-room—the apartments at Lancaster Gate had struck him from the first as of prodigious extent—he awaited her, at her request, conveyed in a "reply-paid" telegram, his theory was that of their still clinging to their idea, though with a sense of the difficulty of it really enlarged to the scale of the place.

He had the place for a long time—it seemed to him a quarter of an hour—to himself; and while Aunt Maud kept him and kept him, while observation and reflexion crowded on him, he asked himself what was to be expected of a person who could treat one like that. The visit, the hour were of her own proposing, so that her delay, no doubt, was but part of a general plan of putting him to inconvenience. As he walked to and fro, however, taking in the message of her massive florid furniture, the immense expression of her signs and symbols, he had as little doubt of the inconvenience he was prepared to suffer. He found himself even facing the thought that he had nothing to fall back on, and that that was as great an humiliation in a good cause as a proud man could desire. It hadn't yet been so distinct to him that he made no show—literally not the smallest; so complete a show seemed made there all about him; so almost abnormally affirmative, so aggressively erect, were the huge heavy objects that syllabled his hostess's story. "When all's said and done, you know, she's colossally vulgar"—he had once all but noted that of her to her niece; only just keeping it back at the last, keeping it to himself with all its danger about it. It mattered because it bore so directly, and he at all events quite felt it a thing that Kate herself would some day bring out to him. It bore directly at present, and really all the more that somehow, strangely, it didn't in the least characterise the poor woman as dull or stale. She was vulgar with freshness, almost with beauty, since there was beauty, to a degree, in the play of so big and bold a temperament. She was in fine quite the largest possible quantity to deal with; and he was in the cage of the lioness without his whip—the whip, in a word, of a supply of proper retorts. He had no retort but that he loved the girl—which in such a house as that was painfully cheap. Kate had mentioned to him more than once that her aunt was Passionate, speaking of it as a kind of offset and uttering it as with a capital P, marking it as something that he might, that he in fact ought to, turn about in some way to their advantage. He wondered at this hour to what advantage he could turn it; but the case grew less simple the longer he waited. Decidedly there was something he hadn't enough of.

His slow march to and fro seemed to give him the very measure; as he paced and paced the distance it became the desert of his poverty; at the sight of which expanse moreover he could pretend to himself as little as before that the desert looked redeemable. Lancaster Gate looked rich—that was all the effect; which it was unthinkable that any state of his own should ever remotely resemble. He read more vividly, more critically, as has been hinted, the appearances about him; and they did nothing so much as make him wonder at his aesthetic reaction. He hadn't known—and in spite of Kate's repeated reference to her own rebellions of taste—that he should "mind" so much how an independent lady might decorate her house. It was the language of the house itself that spoke to him, writing out for him with surpassing breadth and freedom the associations and conceptions, the ideals and possibilities of the mistress.

Never, he felt sure, had he seen so many things so unanimously ugly—operatively, ominously so cruel. He was glad to have found this last name for the whole character; "cruel" somehow played into the subject for an article—an article that his impression put straight into his mind. He would write about the heavy horrors that could still flourish, that lifted their undiminished heads, in an age so proud of its short way with false gods; and it would be funny if what he should have got from Mrs. Lowder were to prove after all but a small amount of copy. Yet the great thing, really the dark thing, was that, even while he thought of the quick column he might add up, he felt it less easy to laugh at the heavy horrors than to quail before them. He couldn't describe and dismiss them collectively, call them either Mid-Victorian or Early—not being certain they were rangeable under one rubric. It was only manifest they were splendid and were furthermore conclusively British. They constituted an order and abounded in rare material—precious woods, metals, stuffs, stones. He had never dreamed of anything so fringed and scalloped, so buttoned and corded, drawn everywhere so tight and curled everywhere so thick. He had never dreamed of so much gilt and glass, so much satin and plush, so much rosewood and marble and malachite. But it was above all the solid forms, the wasted finish, the misguided cost, the general attestation of morality and money, a good conscience and a big balance. These things finally represented for him a portentous negation of his own world of thought—of which, for that matter, in presence of them, he became as for the first time hopelessly aware. They revealed it to him by their merciless difference.

His interview with Aunt Maud, none the less, took by no means the turn he had expected. Passionate though her nature, no doubt, Mrs. Lowder on this occasion neither threatened nor appealed. Her arms of aggression, her weapons of defence, were presumably close at hand, but she left them untouched and unmentioned, and was in fact so bland that he properly perceived only afterwards how adroit she had been. He properly perceived something else as well, which complicated his case; he shouldn't have known what to call it if he hadn't called it her really imprudent good nature. Her blandness, in other words, wasn't mere policy—he wasn't dangerous enough for policy: it was the result, he could see, of her fairly liking him a little. From the moment she did that she herself became more interesting, and who knew what might happen should he take to liking *her?* Well, it was a risk he naturally must face. She fought him at any rate but with one hand, with a few loose grains of stray powder. He recognised at the end of ten minutes, and even without her explaining it, that if she had made him wait it hadn't been to wound him; they had by that time almost directly met on the fact of her intention. She had wanted him to think for himself of what she proposed to say to him—not having otherwise announced it; wanted to let it come home to him on the spot, as she had shrewdly believed it would. Her first question, on appearing, had practically been as to whether he hadn't taken her hint, and this enquiry assumed so many things that it immediately made discussion frank and large. He knew, with the question put, that the hint was just what he *had* taken; knew that she had made him quickly forgive her the display of her power; knew that if he didn't take care he should understand her, and the strength of her purpose, to say nothing of that of her imagination, nothing of the length of her purse, only too well. Yet he pulled himself up with the thought too that he wasn't going to be afraid of understanding her; he was just going to understand and understand without detriment to the feeblest, even, of his passions. The play of one's mind gave one away, at the best, dreadfully, in action, in the need for action, where simplicity was all; but when one couldn't prevent it the thing was to make it complete. There would never be mistakes but for the original fun of mistakes. What he must *use* his fatal intelligence for was to resist. Mrs. Lowder meanwhile might use it for whatever she liked.

It was after she had begun her statement of her own idea about Kate that he began on his side to reflect that—with her manner of offering it as really sufficient if he would take the trouble to embrace it—she couldn't half hate him. That was all, positively, she seemed to show herself for the time as attempting; clearly, if she did her intention justice she would have nothing more disagreeable to do. "If I hadn't been ready to go very much further, you understand, I wouldn't have gone so far. I don't care what you repeat to her—the more you repeat to her perhaps the better; and at any rate there's nothing she doesn't already know. I don't say it for her; I say it for you—when I want to reach my niece I know how to do it straight." So Aunt Maud delivered herself—as with homely benevolence, in the simplest but the clearest terms; virtually conveying that, though a word to the wise was doubtless, in spite of the adage, *not* always enough, a word to the good could never fail to be. The sense our young man read into her words was that she liked him because he was good—was really by her measure good enough: good enough that is to give up her niece for her and go his way in peace. But *was* he good enough—by his own measure? He fairly wondered, while she more fully expressed herself, if it might be his doom to prove so. "She's the finest possible creature—of course you flatter yourself you know it. But I know it quite as well as you possibly can—by which I mean a good deal better yet; and the tune to which I'm ready to prove my faith compares favourably enough, I think, with anything you can do. I don't say it because she's my niece—that's nothing to me: I might have had fifty nieces, and I wouldn't have brought one of them to this place if I hadn't found her to my taste. I don't say I wouldn't have done something else, but I wouldn't have put up with her presence. Kate's presence, by good fortune, I marked early. Kate's presence—unluckily for *you*—is everything I could possibly wish. Kate's presence is, in short, as fine as you know, and I've been keeping it for the comfort of my declining years. I've watched it long; I've been saving it up and letting it, as you say of investments, appreciate; and you may judge whether, now it has begun to pay so, I'm likely to consent to treat for it with any but a high bidder. I can do the best with her, and I've my idea of the best."

"Oh I quite conceive," said Densher, "that your idea of the best isn't me."

It was an oddity of Mrs. Lowder's that her face in speech was like a lighted window at night, but that silence immediately drew the curtain. The occasion for reply allowed by her silence was never easy to take, yet she was still less easy to interrupt. The great glaze of her surface, at all events, gave her visitor no present help. "I didn't ask you to come to hear what it isn't—I asked you to come to hear what it *is*."

"Of course," Densher laughed, "that's very great indeed."

His hostess went on as if his contribution to the subject were barely relevant. "I want to see her high, high up—high up and in the light."

"Ah you naturally want to marry her to a duke and are eager to smooth away any hitch."

She gave him so, on this, the mere effect of the drawn blind that it quite forced him at first into the sense, possibly just, of his having shown for flippant, perhaps even for low. He had been looked at so, in blighted moments of presumptuous youth, by big cold public men, but never, so far as he could recall, by any private lady. More than anything yet it gave him the measure of his companion's subtlety, and thereby of Kate's possible career. "Don't be *too* impossible!"—he feared from his friend, for a moment, some such answer as that; and then felt, as she spoke otherwise, as if she were letting him off easily. "I want her to marry a great man." That was all; but, more and more, it was enough; and if it hadn't been her next words would have made it so. "And I think of her what I think. There you are."

They sat for a little face to face upon it, and he was conscious of something deeper still, of something she wished him to understand if he only would. To that extent she did appeal—appealed to the intelligence she desired to show she believed him to possess. He was meanwhile, at all events, not the man wholly to fail of comprehension. "Of course I'm aware how little I can answer to any fond proud dream. You've a view—a grand one; into which I perfectly enter. I thoroughly understand what I'm not, and I'm much obliged to you for not reminding me of it in any rougher way." She said nothing—she kept that up; it might even have been to let him go further, if he was capable of it, in the way of poorness of spirit. It was one of those cases in which a man couldn't show, if he showed at all, save for poor; unless indeed he preferred to show for asinine. It was the plain truth: he *was*—on Mrs. Lowder's basis, the only one in question—a very small quantity, and he did know, damnably, what made quantities large. He desired to be perfectly simple, yet in the midst of that effort a deeper apprehension throbbed. Aunt Maud clearly conveyed it, though he couldn't later on have said how. "You don't really matter, I believe, so much as you think, and I'm not going to make you a martyr by banishing you. Your performances with Kate in the Park are ridiculous so far as they're meant as consideration for me; and I had much rather see you myself—since you're, in your way, my dear young man, delightful—and arrange with you, count with you, as I easily, as I perfectly should. Do you suppose me so stupid as to quarrel with you if it's not really necessary? It won't—it would be too absurd! —*be* necessary. I can bite your head off any day, any day I really open my mouth; and I'm dealing with you now, see—and successfully judge—without opening it. I do things handsomely all round —I place you in the presence of the plan with which, from the moment it's a case of taking you seriously, you're incompatible. Come then as near it as you like, walk all round it—don't be afraid you'll hurt it!—and live on with it before you."

He afterwards felt that if she hadn't absolutely phrased all this it was because she so soon made him out as going with her far enough. He was so pleasantly affected by her asking no promise of him, her not proposing he should pay for her indulgence by his word of honour not to interfere, that he gave her a kind of general assurance of esteem. Immediately afterwards then he was to speak of these things to Kate, and what by that time came back to him first of all was the way he had said to her—he mentioned it to the girl—very much as one of a pair of lovers says in a rupture by mutual consent: "I hope immensely of course that you'll always regard me as a friend." This had perhaps been going far—he submitted it all to Kate; but really there had been so much in it that it was to be looked at, as they might say, wholly in its own light. Other things than those we have presented had come up before the close of his scene with Aunt Maud, but this matter of her not treating him as a peril of the first order easily predominated. There was moreover plenty to talk about on the occasion of his subsequent passage with our young woman, it having been put to him abruptly, the night before, that he might give himself a lift and do his newspaper a service—so flatteringly was the case expressed—by going for fifteen or twenty weeks to America. The idea of a series of letters from the United States from the strictly social point of view had for some time been nursed in the inner sanctuary at whose door he sat, and the moment was now deemed happy for letting it loose. The imprisoned thought had, in a word, on the opening of the door, flown straight out into Densher's face, or perched at least on his shoulder, making him look up in surprise from his mere inky office-table. His account of the matter to Kate was that he couldn't refuse—not being in a position as yet to refuse anything; but that his being chosen for such an errand confounded his sense of proportion. He was definite as to his scarce knowing how to measure the honour, which struck him as equivocal; he hadn't quite supposed himself the man for the class of job. This confused consciousness, he intimated, he had promptly enough betrayed to his manager; with the effect, however, of seeing the question surprisingly clear up. What it came to was that the sort of twaddle that wasn't in his chords was, unexpectedly, just what they happened this time not to want. They wanted his letters, for queer reasons, about as good as he could let them come; he was to play his own little tune and not be afraid: that was the whole point.

It would have been the whole, that is, had there not been a sharper one still in the circumstance that he was to start at once. His mission, as they called it at the office, would probably be over by the end of June, which was desirable; but to bring that about he must now not lose a week; his enquiries, he understood, were to cover the whole ground, and there were reasons of state—reasons operating at the seat of empire in Fleet Street[1]—why the nail should be struck on the head. Densher made no secret to Kate of his having asked for a day to decide; and his account of that matter was that he felt he owed it to her to speak to her first. She assured him on this that nothing so much as that scruple had yet shown her how they were bound together: she was clearly proud of his letting a thing of such importance depend on her, but she was clearer still as to his instant duty. She rejoiced in his prospect and urged him to his task; she should miss him too dreadfully—of course she should miss him; but she made so little of it that she spoke with jubilation of what he would see and would do. She made so much of this last quantity that he laughed at her innocence, though also with scarce the heart to give her the real size of his drop in the daily bucket. He was struck at the same time with her happy grasp of what had really occurred in Fleet Street—all the more that it was his own

1. Long the center of the newspaper and printing businesses.

final reading. He was to pull the subject up—that was just what they wanted; and it would take more than all the United States together, visit them each as he might, to let *him* down. It was just because he didn't nose about and babble, because he wasn't the usual gossip-monger, that they had picked him out. It was a branch of their correspondence with which they evidently wished a new tone associated, such a tone as, from now on, it would have always to take from his example.

"How you ought indeed, when you understand so well, to be a journalist's wife!" Densher exclaimed in admiration even while she struck him as fairly hurrying him off.

But she was almost impatient of the praise. "What do you expect one *not* to understand when one cares for you?"

"Ah then I'll put it otherwise and say 'How much you care for me!' "

"Yes," she assented; "it fairly redeems my stupidity. I *shall*, with a chance to show it," she added, "have some imagination for you."

She spoke of the future this time as so little contingent that he felt a queerness of conscience in making her the report that he presently arrived at on what had passed for him with the real arbiter of their destiny. The way for that had been blocked a little by his news from Fleet Street; but in the crucible of their happy discussion this element soon melted into the other, and in the mixture that ensued the parts were not to be distinguished. The young man moreover, before taking his leave, was to see why Kate had spoken with a wisdom indifferent to that, and was to come to the vision by a devious way that deepened the final cheer. Their faces were turned to the illumined quarter as soon as he had answered her question on the score of their being to appearance able to play patience, a prodigious game of patience, with success. It was for the possibility of the appearance that she had a few days before so earnestly pressed him to see her aunt; and if after his hour with that lady it had not struck Densher that he had seen her to the happiest purpose the poor facts flushed with a better meaning as Kate, one by one, took them up.

"If she consents to your coming why isn't that everything?"

"It *is* everything; everything *she* thinks it. It's the probability—I mean as Mrs. Lowder measures probability—that I may be prevented from becoming a complication for her by some arrangement, *any* arrangement, through which you shall see me often and easily. She's sure of my want of money, and that gives her time. She believes in my having a certain amount of delicacy, in my wishing to better my state before I put the pistol to your head in respect to sharing it. The time this will take figures for her as the time that will help her if she doesn't spoil her chance by treating me badly.

She doesn't at all wish moreover," Densher went on, "to treat me badly, for I believe, upon my honour, odd as it may sound to you, that she personally rather likes me and that if you weren't in question I might almost become her pet young man. She doesn't disparage intellect and culture—quite the contrary; she wants them to adorn her board and be associated with her name; and I'm sure it has sometimes cost her a real pang that I should be so desirable, at once, and so impossible." He paused a moment, and his companion then saw how strange a smile was in his face—a smile as strange even as the adjunct in her own of this informing vision. "I quite suspect her of believing that, if the truth were known, she likes me literally better than—deep down—you yourself do: wherefore she does me the honour to think I may be safely left to kill my own cause. There, as I say, comes in her margin. I'm not the sort of stuff of romance that wears, that washes, that survives use, that resists familiarity. Once in any degree admit that, and your pride and prejudice will take care of the rest!—the pride fed full, meanwhile, by the system she means to practise with you, and the prejudice excited by the comparisons she'll enable you to make, from which I shall come off badly. She likes me, but she'll never like me so much as when she has succeeded a little better in making me look wretched. For then *you'll* like me less."

Kate showed for this evocation a due interest, but no alarm; and it was a little as if to pay his tender cynicism back in kind that she after an instant replied: "I see, I see—what an immense affair she must think me! One was aware, but you deepen the impression."

"I think you'll make no mistake," said Densher, "in letting it go as deep as it will."

He had given her indeed, she made no scruple of showing, plenty to amuse herself with. "Her facing the music, her making you boldly as welcome as you say—that's an awfully big theory, you know, and worthy of all the other big things that in one's acquaintance with people give her a place so apart."

"Oh she's grand," the young man allowed; "she's on the scale altogether of the car of Juggernaut—which was a kind of image that came to me yesterday while I waited for her at Lancaster Gate. The things in your drawing-room there were like the forms of the strange idols, the mystic excrescences, with which one may suppose the front of the car to bristle."

"Yes, aren't they?" the girl returned; and they had, over all that aspect of their wonderful lady, one of those deep and free interchanges that made everything but confidence a false note for them. There were complications, there were questions; but they were so much more together than they were anything else. Kate uttered for a while no word of refutation of Aunt Maud's "big" diplomacy, and they left it there, as they would have left any other fine product, for a monument to her powers. But, Densher related further, he had had in other respects too the car of Juggernaut to face; he omitted nothing from his account of his visit, least of all the way Aunt Maud had frankly at last—though indeed only under artful pressure—fallen foul of his very type, his want of the right marks, his foreign accidents, his queer antecedents. She had told him he was but half a Briton, which, he granted Kate, would have been dreadful if he hadn't so let himself in for it.

"I was really curious, you see," he explained, "to find out from her what sort of queer creature, what sort of social anomaly, in the light of such conventions as hers, such an education as mine makes one pass for."

Kate said nothing for a little; but then, "Why should you care?" she asked.

"Oh," he laughed, "I like her so much; and then, for a man of my trade, her views, her spirit, are essentially a thing to get hold of: they belong to the great public mind that we meet at every turn and that we must keep setting up 'codes' with. Besides," he added, "I want to please her personally."

"Ah yes, we must please her personally!" his companion echoed; and the words may represent all their definite recognition, at the time, of Densher's politic gain. They had in fact between this and his start for New York many matters to handle, and the question he now touched upon came up for Kate above all. She looked at him as if he had really told her aunt more of his immediate personal story than he had ever told herself. This, if it had been so, was an accident, and it perched him there with her for half an hour, like a cicerone[2] and his victim on a tower-top, before as much of the bird's-eye view of his early years abroad, his migratory parents, his Swiss schools, his German university,[3] as she had easy attention for. A man, he intimated, a man of their world, would have spotted him straight as to many of these points; a man of their world, so far as they had a world, would have been through the English mill. But it was none the less charming to make his confession to a woman; women had in fact for such differences blessedly more imagination and blessedly more sympathy. Kate showed at present as much of both as his case could require; when she had had it from beginning to end she declared that she now made out more than ever yet what she loved him for. She had herself, as a child, lived with some continuity in the world across the Channel, coming home again still a child; and had participated after that, in

2. A tourist guide who explains antiquities to travelers.

3. Densher's education, cosmopolitan and eclectic like James's own, is central to his character.

her teens, in her mother's brief but repeated retreats to Dresden, to Florence, to Biarritz, weak and expensive attempts at economy from which there stuck to her—though in general coldly expressed, through the instinctive avoidance of cheap raptures—the religion of foreign things. When it was revealed to her how many more foreign things were in Merton Densher than he had hitherto taken the trouble to catalogue, she almost faced him as if he were a map of the continent or a handsome present of a delightful new "Murray."[4] He hadn't meant to swagger, he had rather meant to plead, though with Mrs. Lowder he had meant also a little to explain. His father had been, in strange countries, in twenty settlements of the English, British chaplain, resident or occasional, and had had for years the unusual luck of never wanting a billet. His career abroad had therefore been unbroken, and as his stipend had never been great he had educated his children, at the smallest cost, in the schools nearest; which was also a saving of railway-fares. Densher's mother, it further appeared, had practised on her side a distinguished industry, to the success of which—so far as success ever crowned it—this period of exile had much contributed: she copied, patient lady, famous pictures in great museums, having begun with a happy natural gift and taking in betimes the scale of her opportunity. Copyists abroad of course swarmed, but Mrs. Densher had had a sense and a hand of her own, had arrived at a perfection that persuaded, that even deceived, and that made the "placing" of her work blissfully usual. Her son, who had lost her, held her image sacred, and the effect of his telling Kate all about her, as well as about other matters until then mixed and dim, was to render his history rich, his sources full, his outline anything but common. He had come round, he had come back, he insisted abundantly, to being a Briton: his Cambridge years, his happy connexion, as it had proved, with his father's college, amply certified to that, to say nothing of his subsequent plunge into London, which filled up the measure. But brave enough though his descent to English earth, he had passed, by the way, through zones of air that had left their ruffle on his wings—he had been exposed to initiations indelible. Something had happened to him that could never be undone.

When Kate Croy said to him as much he besought her not to insist, declaring that this indeed was what was gravely the matter with him, that he had been but too probably spoiled for native, for insular use. On which, not unnaturally, she insisted the more, assuring him, without mitigation, that if he was various and complicated, complicated by wit and taste, she wouldn't for the world

4. One of a series of handbooks for tourists published by the London firm of John Murray.

have had him more helpless; so that he was driven in the end to accuse her of putting the dreadful truth to him in the hollow guise of flattery. She was making him out as all abnormal in order that she might eventually find him impossible, and since she could make it out but with his aid she had to bribe him by feigned delight to help her. If her last word for him in the connexion was that the way he saw himself was just a precious proof the more of his having tasted of the tree and being thereby prepared to assist her to eat, this gives the happy tone of their whole talk, the measure of the flight of time in the near presence of his settled departure. Kate showed, however, that she was to be more literally taken when she spoke of the relief Aunt Maud would draw from the prospect of his absence.

"Yet one can scarcely see why," he replied, "when she fears me so little."

His friend weighed his objection. "Your idea is that she likes you so much that she'll even go so far as to regret losing you?"

Well, he saw it in their constant comprehensive way. "Since what she builds on is the gradual process of your alienation, she may take the view that the process constantly requires me. Mustn't I be there to keep it going? It's in my exile that it may languish."

He went on with that fantasy, but at this point Kate ceased to attend. He saw after a little that she had been following some thought of her own, and he had been feeling the growth of something determinant even through the extravagance of much of the pleasantry, the warm transparent irony, into which their livelier intimacy kept plunging like a confident swimmer. Suddenly she said to him with extraordinary beauty: "I engage myself to you for ever."

The beauty was in everything, and he could have separated nothing—couldn't have thought of her face as distinct from the whole joy. Yet her face had a new light. "And I pledge you—I call God to witness!—every spark of my faith; I give you every drop of my life." That was all, for the moment, but it was enough, and it was almost as quiet as if it were nothing. They were in the open air, in an alley of the Gardens; the great space, which seemed to arch just then higher and spread wider for them, threw them back into deep concentration. They moved by a common instinct to a spot, within sight, that struck them as fairly sequestered, and there, before their time together was spent, they had extorted from concentration every advance it could make them. They had exchanged vows and tokens, sealed their rich compact, solemnised, so far as breathed words and murmured sounds and lighted eyes and clasped hands could do it, their agreement to belong only, and to belong tremendously, to each other. They were to leave the place accordingly an affianced couple, but before they left it other things still had passed. Densher had declared his horror of bringing to a premature end her happy relation with her aunt; and they had worked round together to a high level of discretion. Kate's free profession was that she wished not to deprive *him* of Mrs. Lowder's countenance, which in the long run she was convinced he would continue to enjoy; and as by a blest turn Aunt Maud had demanded of him no promise that would tie his hands they should be able to propitiate their star in their own way and yet remain loyal. One difficulty alone stood out, which Densher named.

"Of course it will never do—we must remember that—from the moment you allow her to found hopes of you for any one else in particular. So long as her view is content to remain as general as at present appears I don't see that we deceive her. At a given hour, you see, she must be undeceived: the only thing therefore is to be ready for the hour and to face it. Only, after all, in that case," the young man observed, "one doesn't quite make out what we shall have got from her."

"What she'll have got from *us?*" Kate put it with a smile. "What she'll have got from us," the girl went on, "is her own affair—it's for *her* to measure. I asked her for nothing," she added; "I never put myself upon her. She must take her risks, and she surely understands them. What we shall have got from her is what we've already spoken of," Kate further explained; "it's that we shall have gained time. And so, for that matter, will she."

Densher gazed a little at all this clearness; his gaze was not at the present hour into romantic obscurity. "Yes; no doubt, in our particular situation, time's everything. And then there's the joy of it."

She hesitated. "Of our secret?"

"Not so much perhaps of our secret in itself, but of what's represented and, as we must somehow feel, secured to us and made deeper and closer by it." And his fine face, relaxed into happiness, covered her with all his meaning. "Our being as we are."

It was as if for a moment she let the meaning sink into her. "So gone?"

"So gone. So extremely gone. However," he smiled, "we shall go a good deal further." Her answer to which was only the softness of her silence—a silence that looked out for them both at the far reach of their prospect. This was immense, and they thus took final possession of it. They were practically united and splendidly strong; but there were other things—things they were precisely strong enough to be able successfully to count with and safely to allow for; in consequence of which they would for the present, subject to some better reason, keep their understanding to themselves. It was not indeed however till after one more observation of Densher's that they felt the question completely straightened out. "The only thing of course is that she may any day absolutely put it to you."

Kate considered. "Ask me where, on my honour, we are? She

may, naturally; but I doubt if in fact she will. While you're away she'll make the most of that drop of the tension. She'll leave me alone."

"But there'll be my letters."

The girl faced his letters. "Very, very many?"

"Very, very, very many—more than ever; and you know what that is! And then," Densher added, "there'll be yours."

"Oh I shan't leave mine on the hall-table. I shall post them myself."

He looked at her a moment. "Do you think then I had best address you elsewhere?" After which, before she could quite answer, he added with some emphasis: "I'd rather not, you know. It's straighter."

She might again have just waited. "Of course it's straighter. Don't be afraid I shan't be straight. Address me," she continued, "where you like. I shall be proud enough of its being known you write to me."

He turned it over for the last clearness. "Even at the risk of its really bringing down the inquisition?"

Well, the last clearness now filled her. "I'm not afraid of the inquisition. If she asks if there's anything definite between us I know perfectly what I shall say."

"That I *am* of course 'gone' for you?"

"That I love you as I shall never in my life love any one else, and that she can make what she likes of that." She said it out so splendidly that it was like a new profession of faith, the fulness of a tide breaking through; and the effect of that in turn was to make her companion meet her with such eyes that she had time again before he could otherwise speak. "Besides, she's just as likely to ask *you.*"

"Not while I'm away."

"Then when you come back."

"Well then," said Densher, "we shall have had our particular joy. But what I feel is," he candidly added, "that, by an idea of her own, her superior policy, she *won't* ask me. She'll let me off. I shan't have to lie to her."

"It will be left all to me?" asked Kate.

"All to you!" he tenderly laughed.

But it was oddly, the very next moment, as if he had perhaps been a shade too candid. His discrimination seemed to mark a possible, a natural reality, a reality not wholly disallowed by the account the girl had just given of her own intention. There *was* a difference in the air—even if none other than the supposedly usual difference in truth between man and woman; and it was almost as if the sense of this provoked her. She seemed to cast about an instant, and then she went back a little resentfully to something she had suffered to pass a minute before. She appeared to take up rather more seriously than she need the joke about her freedom to deceive. Yet she did this too in a beautiful way. "Men are too stupid—even you. You didn't understand just now why, if I post my letters myself, it won't be for anything so vulgar as to hide them."

"Oh you named it—for the pleasure."

"Yes; but you didn't, you don't, understand what the pleasure may be. There are refinements—!" she more patiently dropped. "I mean of consciousness, of sensation, of appreciation," she went on. "No," she sadly insisted—"men *don't* know. They know in such matters almost nothing but what women show them."

This was one of the speeches, frequent in her, that, liberally, joyfully, intensely adopted and, in itself, as might be, embraced, drew him again as close to her, and held him as long, as their conditions permitted. "Then that's exactly why we've such an abysmal need of you!"

Book Third

I

The two ladies who, in advance of the Swiss season, had been warned that their design was unconsidered, that the passes wouldn't be clear, nor the air mild, nor the inns open—the two ladies who, characteristically, had braved a good deal of possibly interested remonstrance were finding themselves, as their adventure turned out, wonderfully sustained. It was the judgement of the head-waiters and other functionaries on the Italian lakes that approved itself now as interested; they themselves had been conscious of impatiences, of bolder dreams—at least the younger had; so that one of the things they made out together—making out as they did an endless variety—was that in those operatic palaces of the Villa d'Este, of Cadenabbia, of Pallanza and Stresa,[1] lone women, however reenforced by a travelling-library of instructive volumes, were apt to be beguiled and undone. Their flights of fancy moreover had been modest; they had for instance risked nothing vital in hoping to make their way by the Brünig. They were making it in fact happily enough as we meet them, and were only wishing that, for the wondrous beauty of the early high-climbing spring, it might have been longer and the places to pause and rest more numerous.

Such at least had been the intimated attitude of Mrs. Stringham, the elder of the companions, who had her own view of the impatiences of the younger, to which, however, she offered an opposition but of the most circuitous. She moved, the admirable Mrs.

1. Elegant Swiss hotels in towns on Lakes Como and Maggiore, near the Italian border.

Stringham, in a fine cloud of observation and suspicion; she was in the position, as she believed, of knowing much more about Milly Theale than Milly herself knew, and yet of having to darken her knowledge as well as make it active. The woman in the world least formed by nature, as she was quite aware, for duplicities and labyrinths, she found herself dedicated to personal subtlety by a new set of circumstances, above all by a new personal relation; had now in fact to recognise that an education in the occult—she could scarce say what to call it—had begun for her the day she left New York with Mildred. She had come on from Boston for that purpose; had seen little of the girl—or rather had seen her but briefly, for Mrs. Stringham, when she saw anything at all, saw much, saw everything—before accepting her proposal; and had accordingly placed herself, by her act, in a boat that she more and more estimated as, humanly speaking, of the biggest, though likewise, no doubt, in many ways, by reason of its size, of the safest. In Boston, the winter before, the young lady in whom we are interested had, on the spot, deeply, yet almost tacitly, appealed to her, dropped into her mind the shy conceit of some assistance, some devotion to render. Mrs. Stringham's little life had often been visited by shy conceits—secret dreams that had fluttered their hour between its narrow walls without, for any great part, so much as mustering courage to look out of its rather dim windows. But this imagination—the fancy of a possible link with the remarkable young thing from New York—*had* mustered courage: had perched, on the instant, at the clearest lookout it could find, and might be said to have remained there till, only a few months later, it had caught, in surprise and joy, the unmistakeable flash of a signal.

Milly Theale had Boston friends, such as they were, and of recent making; and it was understood that her visit to them—a visit that was not to be meagre—had been undertaken, after a series of bereavements, in the interest of the particular peace that New York couldn't give. It was recognised, liberally enough, that there were many things—perhaps even too many—New York *could* give; but this was felt to make no difference in the important truth that what you had most to do, under the discipline of life, or of death, was really to feel your situation as grave. Boston could help you to that as nothing else could, and it had extended to Milly, by every presumption, some such measure of assistance. Mrs. Stringham was never to forget—for the moment had not faded, nor the infinitely fine vibration it set up in any degree ceased—her own first sight of the striking apparition, then unheralded and unexplained: the slim, constantly pale, delicately haggard, anomalously, agreeably angular young person, of not more than two-and-twenty summers, in spite of her marks, whose hair was somehow exceptionally red even for the real thing, which it innocently confessed to being, and whose clothes were remarkably black even for robes of mourning, which was the meaning they expressed. It was New York mourning, it was New York hair, it was a New York history, confused as yet, but multitudinous, of the loss of parents, brothers, sisters, almost every human appendage, all on a scale and with a sweep that had required the greater stage; it was a New York legend of affecting, of romantic isolation, and, beyond everything, it was by most accounts, in respect to the mass of money so piled on the girl's back, a set of New York possibilities. She was alone, she was stricken, she was rich, and in particular was strange—a combination in itself of a nature to engage Mrs. Stringham's attention. But it was the strangeness that most determined our good lady's sympathy, convinced as she had to be that it was greater than any one else—any one but the sole Susan Stringham—supposed. Susan privately settled it that Boston was not in the least seeing her, was only occupied with her seeing Boston, and that any assumed affinity between the two characters was delusive and vain. *She* was seeing her, and she had quite the finest moment of her life in now obeying the instinct to conceal the vision. She couldn't explain it—no one would understand. They would say clever Boston things—Mrs. Stringham was from Burlington Vermont, which she boldly upheld as the real heart of New England, Boston being "too far south"—but they would only darken counsel.

There could be no better proof (than this quick intellectual split) of the impression made on our friend, who shone herself, she was well aware, with but the reflected light of the admirable city. She too had had her discipline, but it had not made her striking; it had been prosaically usual, though doubtless a decent dose; and had only made her usual to match it—usual, that is, as Boston went. She had lost first her husband and then her mother, with whom, on her husband's death, she had lived again; so that now, childless, she was but more sharply single than before. Yet she sat rather coldly light, having, as she called it, enough to live on—so far, that is, as she lived by bread alone: how little indeed she was regularly content with that diet appeared from the name she had made—Susan Shepherd Stringham—as a contributor to the best magazines. She wrote short stories, and she fondly believed she had her "note," the art of showing New England without showing it wholly in the kitchen. She had not herself been brought up in the kitchen; she knew others who had not; and to speak for them had thus become with her a literary mission. To *be* in truth literary had ever been her dearest thought, the thought that kept her bright little nippers perpetually in position. There were masters, models, celebrities, mainly foreign, whom she finally accounted so and in whose light she ingeniously laboured; there were others whom, however chattered about, she ranked with the inane, for she bristled with discriminations; but all categories failed her—they ceased at least to signify—as soon as she found herself in presence of the real thing, the romantic life itself. That was what she saw in Mildred—what positively made her hand a while tremble too much for the pen. She had had, it seemed to her, a revelation—such as even New England refined and grammatical couldn't give; and, all made up as she was of small neat memories and ingenuities, little industries and ambitions, mixed with something moral, personal, that was still more intensely responsive, she felt her new friend would have done her an ill turn if their friendship shouldn't develop, and yet that nothing would be left of anything else if it should. It was for the surrender of everything else that she was, however, quite prepared, and while she went about her usual Boston business with her usual Boston probity she was really all the while holding herself. She wore her "handsome" felt hat, so Tyrolese, yet somehow, though feathered from the eagle's wing, so truly domestic, with the same straightness and security; she attached her fur boa with the same honest precautions; she preserved her balance on the ice-slopes with the same practised skill; she opened, each evening, her *Transcript*[2] with the same interfusion of suspense and resignation; she attended her almost daily concert with the same expenditure of patience and the same economy of passion; she flitted in and out of the Public Library with the air of conscientiously returning or bravely carrying off in her pocket the key of knowledge itself; and finally—it was what she most did—she watched the thin trickle of a fictive "love-interest" through that somewhat serpentine channel, in the magazines, which she mainly managed to keep clear for it. But the real thing all the while was elsewhere; the real thing had gone back to New York, leaving behind it the two unsolved questions, quite distinct, of why it *was* real, and whether she should ever be so near it again.

For the figure to which these questions attached themselves she had found a convenient description—she thought of it for herself always as that of a girl with a background. The great reality was in the fact that, very soon, after but two or three meetings, the girl with the background, the girl with the crown of old gold and the mourning that was not as the mourning of Boston, but at once more rebellious in its gloom and more frivolous in its frills, had told her she had never seen any one like her. They had met thus as opposed curiosities, and that simple remark of Milly's—if simple it was—became the most important thing that had ever happened to her; it deprived the love-interest, for the time, of actuality and even

2. The *Boston Daily Evening Transcript* (1830–1941), a newspaper noted for its New England conservatism and its reporting of national cultural events.

of pertinence; it moved her first, in short, in a high degree, to gratitude, and then to no small compassion. Yet in respect to this relation at least it was what did prove the key of knowledge; it lighted up as nothing else could do the poor young woman's history. That the potential heiress of all the ages should never have seen any one like a mere typical subscriber, after all, to the *Transcript* was a truth that—in especial as announced with modesty, with humility, with regret—described a situation. It laid upon the elder woman, as to the void to be filled, a weight of responsibility; but in particular it led her to ask whom poor Mildred *had* then seen, and what range of contacts it had taken to produce such queer surprises. That was really the enquiry that had ended by clearing the air: the key of knowledge was felt to click in the lock from the moment it flashed upon Mrs. Stringham that her friend had been starved for culture. Culture was what she herself represented for her, and it was living up to that principle that would surely prove the great business. She knew, the clever lady, what the principle itself represented, and the limits of her own store; and a certain alarm would have grown upon her if something else hadn't grown faster. This was, fortunately for her—and we give it in her own words—the sense of a harrowing pathos. That, primarily, was what appealed to her, what seemed to open the door of romance for her still wider than any, than a still more reckless, connexion with the "picture-papers." For such was essentially the point: it was rich, romantic, abysmal, to have, as was evident, thousands and thousands a year, to have youth and intelligence and, if not beauty, at least in equal measure a high dim charming ambiguous oddity, which was even better, and then on top of all to enjoy boundless freedom, the freedom of the wind in the desert—it was unspeakably touching to be so equipped and yet to have been reduced by fortune to little humble-minded mistakes.

It brought our friend's imagination back again to New York, where aberrations were so possible in the intellectual sphere, and it in fact caused a visit she presently paid there to overflow with interest. As Milly had beautifully invited her, so she would hold out if she could against the strain of so much confidence in her mind; and the remarkable thing was that even at the end of three weeks she *had* held out. But by this time her mind had grown comparatively bold and free; it was dealing with new quantities, a different proportion altogether—and that had made for refreshment: she had accordingly gone home in convenient possession of her subject. New York was vast, New York was startling, with strange histories, with wild cosmopolite backward generations that accounted for anything; and to have got nearer the luxuriant tribe of which the rare creature was the final flower, the immense extravagant unregulated cluster, with free-living ancestors, handsome dead cousins, lurid uncles, beautiful vanished aunts, persons all busts and curls, preserved, though so exposed, in the marble of famous French chisels—all this, to say nothing of the effect of closer growths of the stem, was to have had one's small world-space both crowded and enlarged. Our couple had at all events effected an exchange; the elder friend had been as consciously intellectual as possible, and the younger, abounding in personal revelation, had been as unconsciously distinguished. This was poetry—it was also history—Mrs. Stringham thought, to a finer tune even than Maeterlinck and Pater, than Marbot and Gregorovius.[3] She appointed occasions for the reading of these authors with her hostess, rather perhaps than actually achieved great spans; but what they managed and what they missed speedily sank for her into the dim depths of the merely relative, so quickly, so strongly had she clutched her central clue. All her scruples and hesitations, all her anxious enthusiasms, had reduced themselves to a single alarm—the fear that she really might act on her companion clumsily and coarsely. She was positively afraid of what she might do to her, and to avoid that, to avoid it with piety and passion, to do, rather, nothing at all, to leave her untouched because no touch one could apply, however light, however just, however earnest and anxious, would be half good enough, would be anything but an ugly smutch upon perfection—this now imposed itself as a consistent, an inspiring thought.

Less than a month after the event that had so determined Mrs. Stringham's attitude—close upon the heels, that is, of her return from New York—she was reached by a proposal that brought up for her the kind of question her delicacy might have to contend with. Would she start for Europe with her young friend at the earliest possible date, and should she be willing to do so without making conditions? The enquiry was launched by wire; explanations, in sufficiency, were promised; extreme urgency was suggested and a general surrender invited. It was to the honour of her sincerity that she made the surrender on the spot, though it was not perhaps altogether to that of her logic. She had wanted, very consciously, from the first, to give something up for her new acquaintance, but she had now no doubt that she was practically giving up all. What settled this was the fulness of a particular impression, the impression

3. Maurice Maeterlinck (1862–1949), a Belgian dramatist and poet whose early works are sombre accounts of the ways in which love and death mysteriously govern human life; Walter Pater (1839–94), whose influential *Studies in the History of the Renaissance* (1873) made him the chief prophet of the Aesthetic Movement, popularized as the ideal of "art for art's sake"; Jean Baptiste Antoine Marcelin Marbot (1782–1854), a French baron who became a staunch republican, serving as a colonel under Napolean I, and whose *Memoirs* were highly successful, the first edition of 1891 going through six printings that year; Ferdinand Adolph Gregorovius (1821–91), a German historian whose works include volumes on Lucrezia Borgia and Hadrian, a history of Rome in the Middle Ages, and histories of Athens in the Middle Ages and in the Byzantine period.

that had throughout more and more supported her and which she would have uttered so far as she might by saying that the charm of the creature was positively in the creature's greatness. She would have been content so to leave it; unless indeed she had said, more familiarly, that Mildred was the biggest impression of her life. That was at all events the biggest account of her, and none but a big clearly would do. Her situation, as such things were called, was on the grand scale; but it still was not that. It was her nature, once for all—a nature that reminded Mrs. Stringham of the term always used in the newspapers about the great new steamers, the inordinate number of "feet of water" they drew; so that if, in your little boat, you had chosen to hover and approach, you had but yourself to thank, when once motion was started, for the way the draught pulled you. Milly drew the feet of water, and odd though it might seem that a lonely girl, who was not robust and who hated sound and show, should stir the stream like a leviathan, her companion floated off with the sense of rocking violently at her side. More than prepared, however, for that excitement, Mrs. Stringham mainly failed of ease in respect to her own consistency. To attach herself for an indefinite time seemed a roundabout way of holding her hands off. If she wished to be sure of neither touching nor smutching, the straighter plan would doubtless have been not to keep her friend within reach. This in fact she fully recognised, and with it the degree to which she desired that the girl should lead her life, a life certain to be so much finer than that of anybody else. The difficulty, however, by good fortune, cleared away as soon as she had further recognised, as she was speedily able to do, that she Susan Shepherd—the name with which Milly for the most part amused herself—was *not* anybody else. She had renounced that character; she had now no life to lead; and she honestly believed that she was thus supremely equipped for leading Milly's own. No other person whatever, she was sure, had to an equal degree this qualification, and it was really to assert it that she fondly embarked.

Many things, though not in many weeks, had come and gone since then, and one of the best of them doubtless had been the voyage itself, by the happy southern course, to the succession of Mediterranean ports, with the dazzled wind-up at Naples. Two or three others had preceded this; incidents, indeed rather lively marks, of their last fortnight at home, and one of which had determined on Mrs. Stringham's part a rush to New York, forty-eight breathless hours there, previous to her final rally. But the great sustained sea-light had drunk up the rest of the picture, so that for many days other questions and other possibilities sounded with as little effect as a trio of penny whistles might sound in a Wagner overture. It was the Wagner overture that practically prevailed, up through

Italy, where Milly had already been, still further up and across the Alps, which were also partly known to Mrs. Stringham; only perhaps "taken" to a time not wholly congruous, hurried in fact on account of the girl's high restlessness. She had been expected, she had frankly promised, to be restless—that was partly why she was "great"—or was a consequence, at any rate, if not a cause; yet she had not perhaps altogether announced herself as straining so hard at the cord. It was familiar, it was beautiful to Mrs. Stringham that she had arrears to make up, the chances that had lapsed for her through the wanton ways of forefathers fond of Paris, but not of its higher sides, and fond almost of nothing else; but the vagueness, the openness, the eagerness without point and the interest without pause—all a part of the charm of her oddity as at first presented—had become more striking in proportion as they triumphed over movement and change. She had arts and idiosyncrasies of which no great account could have been given, but which were a daily grace if you lived with them; such as the art of being almost tragically impatient and yet making it as light as air; of being inexplicably sad and yet making it as clear as noon; of being unmistakeably gay and yet making it as soft as dusk. Mrs. Stringham by this time understood everything, was more than ever confirmed in wonder and admiration, in her view that it was life enough simply to feel her companion's feelings; but there were special keys she had not yet added to her bunch, impressions that of a sudden were apt to affect her as new.

This particular day on the great Swiss road had been, for some reason, full of them, and they referred themselves, provisionally, to some deeper depth than she had touched—though into two or three such depths, it must be added, she had peeped long enough to find herself suddenly draw back. It was not Milly's unpacified state, in short, that now troubled her—though certainly, as Europe was the great American sedative, the failure was to some extent to be noted: it was the suspected presence of something behind the state —which, however, could scarcely have taken its place there since their departure. What a fresh motive of unrest could suddenly have sprung from was in short not to be divined. It was but half an explanation to say that excitement, for each of them, had naturally dropped, and that what they had left behind, or tried to—the great serious facts of life, as Mrs. Stringham liked to call them—was once more coming into sight as objects loom through smoke when smoke begins to clear; for these were general appearances from which the girl's own aspect, her really larger vagueness, seemed rather to disconnect itself. The nearest approach to a personal anxiety indulged in as yet by the elder lady was on her taking occasion to wonder if what she had more than anything else got hold of mightn't be one of the finer, one of the finest, one of the rarest—as she called it so that she might call it nothing worse—cases of American intensity. She had just had a moment of alarm—asked herself if her young friend were merely going to treat her to some complicated drama of nerves. At the end of a week, however, with their further progress, her young friend had effectively answered the question and given her the impression, indistinct indeed as yet, of something that had a reality compared with which the nervous explanation would have been coarse. Mrs. Stringham found herself from that hour, in other words, in presence of an explanation that remained a muffled and intangible form, but that assuredly, should it take on sharpness, would explain everything and more than everything, would become instantly the light in which Milly was to be read.

Such a matter as this may at all events speak of the style in which our young woman could affect those who were near her, may testify to the sort of interest she could inspire. She worked—and seemingly quite without design—upon the sympathy, the curiosity, the fancy of her associates, and we shall really ourselves scarce otherwise come closer to her than by feeling their impression and sharing, if need be, their confusion. She reduced them, Mrs. Stringham would have said, to a consenting bewilderment; which was precisely, for that good lady, on a last analysis, what was most in harmony with her greatness. She exceeded, escaped measure, was surprising only because *they* were so far from great. Thus it was that on this wondrous day by the Brünig the spell of watching her had grown more than ever irresistible; a proof of what—or of a part of what—Mrs. Stringham had, with all the rest, been reduced to. She had almost the sense of tracking her young friend as if at a given moment to pounce. She knew she shouldn't pounce, she hadn't come out to pounce; yet she felt her attention secretive, all the same, and her observation scientific. She struck herself as hovering like a spy, applying tests, laying traps, concealing signs. This would last, however, only till she should fairly know what was the matter; and to watch was after all, meanwhile, a way of clinging to the girl, not less than an occupation, a satisfaction in itself. The pleasure of watching moreover, if a reason were needed, came from a sense of her beauty. Her beauty hadn't at all originally seemed a part of the situation, and Mrs. Stringham had even in the first flush of friendship not named it grossly to any one; having seen early that for stupid people—and who, she sometimes secretly asked herself, wasn't stupid?—it would take a great deal of explaining. She had learned not to mention it till it was mentioned first—which occasionally happened, but not too often; and then she was there in force. Then she both warmed to the perception that met her own perception, and disputed it, suspiciously, as to special items; while, in general, she had learned to refine even to the point of herself employing the word that most people employed. She employed it to pretend she was also stupid and so have done with the matter; spoke of her friend as plain, as ugly even, in a case of especially dense insistence; but as, in appearance, so "awfully full of things." This was her own way of describing a face that, thanks doubtless to rather too much forehead, too much nose and too much mouth, together with too little mere conventional colour and conventional line, was expressive, irregular, exquisite, both for speech and for silence. When Milly smiled it was a public event—when she didn't it was a chapter of history. They had stopped on the Brünig for luncheon, and there had come up for them under the charm of the place the question of a longer stay.

Mrs. Stringham was now on the ground of thrilled recognitions, small sharp echoes of a past which she kept in a well-thumbed case, but which, on pressure of a spring and exposure to the air, still showed itself ticking as hard as an honest old watch. The embalmed "Europe" of her younger time had partly stood for three years of Switzerland, a term of continuous school at Vevey,[4] with rewards of merit in the form of silver medals tied by blue ribbons and mild mountain-passes attacked with alpenstocks. It was the good girls who, in the holidays, were taken highest, and our friend could now judge, from what she supposed her familiarity with the minor peaks, that she had been one of the best. These reminiscences, sacred today because prepared in the hushed chambers of the past, had been part of the general train laid for the pair of sisters, daughters early fatherless, by their brave Vermont mother, who struck her at present as having apparently, almost like Columbus, worked out, all unassisted, a conception of the other side of the globe. She had focussed Vevey, by the light of nature and with extraordinary completeness, at Burlington; after which she had embarked, sailed, landed, explored and, above all, made good her presence. She had given her daughters the five years in Switzerland and Germany that were to leave them ever afterwards a standard of comparison for all cycles of Cathay,[5] and to stamp the younger in especial—Susan was the younger—with a character, that, as Mrs. Stringham had often had occasion, through life, to say to herself, made all the difference. It made all the difference for Mrs. Stringham, over and over again and in the most remote connexions, that, thanks to her parent's lonely thrifty hardy faith, she was a woman of the world. There were plenty of women who were all sorts of things that she wasn't,

4. Located in western Switzerland, on the north bank of Lake Geneva, Vevey became a favorite stopping place for Americans abroad.

5. An allusion to Tennyson's judgment in "Locksley Hall" (1842)—"Better fifty years of Europe than a cycle of Cathay"—and one of many references describing a provincial-cosmopolitan motif in the novel.

but who, on the other hand, were not that, and who didn't know *she* was (which she liked—it relegated them still further) and didn't know either how it enabled her to judge them. She had never seen herself so much in this light as during the actual phase of her associated, if slightly undirected, pilgrimage; and the consciousness gave perhaps to her plea for a pause more intensity than she knew. The irrecoverable days had come back to her from far off; they were part of the sense of the cool upper air and of everything else that hung like an indestructible scent to the torn garment of youth—the taste of honey and the luxury of milk, the sound of cattle-bells and the rush of streams, the fragrance of trodden balms and the dizziness of deep gorges.

Milly clearly felt these things too, but they affected her companion at moments—that was quite the way Mrs. Stringham would have expressed it—as the princess in a conventional tragedy might have affected the confidant if a personal emotion had ever been permitted to the latter. That a princess could only be a princess was a truth with which, essentially, a confidant, however responsive, had to live. Mrs. Stringham was a woman of the world, but Milly Theale was a princess, the only one she had yet had to deal with, and this, in its way too, made all the difference. It was a perfectly definite doom for the wearer—it was for every one else an office nobly filled. It might have represented possibly, with its involved loneliness and other mysteries, the weight under which she fancied her companion's admirable head occasionally, and ever so submissively, bowed. Milly had quite assented at luncheon to their staying over, and had left her to look at rooms, settle questions, arrange about their keeping on their carriage and horses; cares that had now moreover fallen to Mrs. Stringham as a matter of course and that yet for some reason, on this occasion particularly, brought home to her—all agreeably, richly, almost grandly—what it was to live with the great. Her young friend had in a sublime degree a sense closed to the general question of difficulty, which she got rid of furthermore not in the least as one had seen many charming persons do, by merely passing it on to others. She kept it completely at a distance: it never entered the circle; the most plaintive confidant couldn't have dragged it in; and to tread the path of a confidant was accordingly to live exempt. Service was in other words so easy to render that the whole thing was like court life without the hardships. It came back of course to the question of money, and our observant lady had by this time repeatedly reflected that if one were talking of the "difference," it was just this, this incomparably and nothing else, that when all was said and done most made it. A less vulgarly, a less obviously purchasing or parading person she couldn't have imagined; but it prevailed even as the truth of truths that the girl couldn't get away from her wealth. She might leave her conscientious companion as freely alone with it as possible and never ask a question, scarce even tolerate a reference; but it was in the fine folds of the helplessly expensive little black frock that she drew over the grass as she now strolled vaguely off; it was in the curious and splendid coils of hair, "done" with no eye whatever to the *mode du jour*,[6] that peeped from under the corresponding indifference of her hat, the merely personal tradition that suggested a sort of noble inelegance; it lurked between the leaves of the uncut but antiquated Tauchnitz volume[7] of which, before going out, she had mechanically possessed herself. She couldn't dress it away, nor walk it away, nor read it away, nor think it away; she could neither smile it away in any dreamy absence nor blow it away in any softened sigh. She couldn't have lost it if she had tried—that was what it was to be really rich. It had to be *the* thing you were. When at the end of an hour she hadn't returned to the house Mrs. Stringham, though the bright afternoon was yet young, took, with precautions, the same direction, went to join her in case of her caring for a walk. But the purpose of joining her was in truth less distinct than that of a due regard for a possibly preferred detachment: so that, once more, the good lady proceeded with a quietness that made her slightly "underhand" even in her own eyes. She couldn't help that, however, and she didn't care, sure as she was that what she really wanted wasn't to overstep but to stop in time. It was to be able to stop in time that she went softly, but she had on this occasion further to go than ever yet, for she followed in vain, and at last with some anxiety, the footpath she believed Milly to have taken. It wound up a hillside and into the higher Alpine meadows in which, all these last days, they had so often wanted, as they passed above or below, to stray; and then it obscured itself in a wood, but always going up, up, and with a small cluster of brown old high-perched châlets evidently for its goal. Mrs. Stringham reached in due course the châlets, and there received from a bewildered old woman, a very fearful person to behold, an indication that sufficiently guided her. The young lady had been seen not long before passing further on, over a crest and to a place where the way would drop again, as our unappeased enquirer found it in fact, a quarter of an hour later, markedly and almost alarmingly to do. It led somewhere, yet apparently quite into space, for the great side of the mountain appeared, from where she pulled up, to fall away altogether, though probably but to some issue below and out of sight. Her uncertainty moreover was brief, for she next became aware of

6. Fashion of the day.

7. The German publishing house of Tauchnitz, taking advantage of the lack of an international copyright law, began reprinting in 1841 a large number of works by British and American writers. Milly's volume, being uncut, cannot have been read.

the presence on a fragment of rock, twenty yards off, of the Tauchnitz volume the girl had brought out and that therefore pointed to her shortly previous passage. She had rid herself of the book, which was an encumbrance, and meant of course to pick it up on her return; but as she hadn't yet picked it up what on earth had become of her? Mrs. Stringham, I hasten to add, was within a few moments to see; but it was quite an accident that she hadn't, before they were over, betrayed by her deeper agitation the fact of her own nearness.

The whole place, with the descent of the path and as a sequel to a sharp turn that was masked by rocks and shrubs, appeared to fall precipitously and to become a "view" pure and simple, a view of great extent and beauty, but thrown forward and vertiginous. Milly, with the promise of it from just above, had gone straight down to it, not stopping till it was all before her; and here, on what struck her friend as the dizzy edge of it, she was seated at her ease. The path somehow took care of itself and its final business, but the girl's seat was a slab of rock at the end of a short promontory or excrescence that merely pointed off to the right at gulfs of air and that was so placed by good fortune, if not by the worst, as to be at last completely visible. For Mrs. Stringham stifled a cry on taking in what she believed to be the danger of such a perch for a mere maiden; her liability to slip, to slide, to leap, to be precipitated by a single false movement, by a turn of the head—how could one tell?—into whatever was beneath. A thousand thoughts, for the minute, roared in the poor lady's ears, but without reaching, as happened, Milly's. It was a commotion that left our observer intensely still and holding her breath. What had first been offered her was the possibility of a latent intention—however wild the idea—in such a posture; of some betrayed accordance of Milly's caprice with a horrible hidden obsession. But since Mrs. Stringham stood as motionless as if a sound, a syllable, must have produced the start that would be fatal, so even the lapse of a few seconds had partly a reassuring effect. It gave her time to receive the impression which, when she some minutes later softly retraced her steps, was to be the sharpest she carried away. This was the impression that if the girl was deeply and recklessly meditating there she wasn't meditating a jump; she was on the contrary, as she sat, much more in a state of uplifted and unlimited possession that had nothing to gain from violence. She was looking down on the kingdoms of the earth, and though indeed that of itself might well go to the brain, it wouldn't be with a view of renouncing them. Was she choosing among them or did she want them all? This question, before Mrs. Stringham had decided what to do, made others vain; in accordance with which she saw, or believed she did, that if it might be dangerous to call out, to sound in any way a surprise, it would probably be safe enough to withdraw as she had come. She watched a while longer, she held her breath, and she never knew afterwards what time had elapsed.

Not many minutes probably, yet they hadn't seemed few, and they had given her so much to think of, not only while creeping home, but while waiting afterwards at the inn, that she was still busy with them when, late in the afternoon, Milly reappeared. She had stopped at the point of the path where the Tauchnitz lay, had taken it up and, with the pencil attached to her watch-guard, had scrawled a word—*à bientôt!*[8]—across the cover; after which, even under the girl's continued delay, she had measured time without a return of alarm. For she now saw that the great thing she had brought away was precisely a conviction that the future wasn't to exist for her princess in the form of any sharp or simple release from the human predicament. It wouldn't be for her a question of a flying leap and thereby of a quick escape. It would be a question of taking full in the face the whole assault of life, to the general muster of which indeed her face might have been directly presented as she sat there on her rock. Mrs. Stringham was thus able to say to herself during still another wait of some length that if her young friend still continued absent it wouldn't be because—whatever the opportunity—she had cut short the thread. She wouldn't have committed suicide; she knew herself unmistakeably reserved for some more complicated passage; this was the very vision in which she had, with no little awe, been discovered. The image that thus remained with the elder lady kept the character of a revelation. During the breathless minutes of her watch she had seen her companion afresh; the latter's type, aspect, marks, her history, her state, her beauty, her mystery, all unconsciously betrayed themselves to the Alpine air, and all had been gathered in again to feed Mrs. Stringham's flame. They are things that will more distinctly appear for us, and they are meanwhile briefly represented by the enthusiasm that was stronger on our friend's part than any doubt. It was a consciousness she was scarce yet used to carrying, but she had as beneath her feet a mine of something precious. She seemed to herself to stand near the mouth, not yet quite cleared. The mine but needed working and would certainly yield a treasure. She wasn't thinking, either, of Milly's gold.

II

The girl said nothing, when they met, about the words scrawled on the Tauchnitz, and Mrs. Stringham then noticed that she hadn't the book with her. She had left it lying and probably would never remember it at all. Her comrade's decision was therefore quickly made not to speak of having followed her; and within five

8. "See you soon."

minutes of her return, wonderfully enough, the preoccupation denoted by her forgetfulness further declared itself. "Should you think me quite abominable if I were to say that after all—?"

Mrs. Stringham had already thought, with the first sound of the question, everything she was capable of thinking, and had immediately made such a sign that Milly's words gave place to visible relief at her assent. "You don't care for our stop here—you'd rather go straight on? We'll start then with the peep of tomorrow's dawn—or as early as you like; it's only rather late now to take the road again." And she smiled to show how she meant it for a joke that an instant onward rush was what the girl would have wished. "I bullied you into stopping," she added; "so it serves me right."

Milly made in general the most of her good friend's jokes; but she humoured this one a little absently. "Oh yes, you do bully me." And it was thus arranged between them, with no discussion at all, that they would resume their journey in the morning. The younger tourist's interest in the detail of the matter—in spite of a declaration from the elder that she would consent to be dragged anywhere—appeared almost immediately afterwards quite to lose itself; she promised, however, to think till supper of where, with the world all before them, they might go—supper having been ordered for such time as permitted of lighted candles. It had been agreed between them that lighted candles at wayside inns, in strange countries, amid mountain scenery, gave the evening meal a peculiar poetry—such being the mild adventures, the refinements of impression, that they, as they would have said, went in for. It was now as if, before this repast, Milly had designed to "lie down"; but at the end of three minutes more she wasn't lying down, she was saying instead, abruptly, with a transition that was like a jump of four thousand miles: "What was it that, in New York, on the ninth, when you saw him alone, Doctor Finch said to you?"

It was not till later that Mrs. Stringham fully knew why the question had startled her still more than its suddenness explained; though the effect of it even at the moment was almost to frighten her into a false answer. She had to think, to remember the occasion, the "ninth," in New York, the time she had seen Doctor Finch alone, and to recall the words he had then uttered; and when everything had come back it was quite, at first, for a moment, as if he had said something that immensely mattered. He hadn't, however, in fact; it was only as if he might perhaps after all have been going to. It was on the sixth—within ten days of their sailing—that she had hurried from Boston under the alarm, a small but a sufficient shock, of hearing that Mildred had suddenly been taken ill, had had, from some obscure cause, such an upset as threatened to stay their journey. The bearing of the accident had happily soon presented itself as slight, and there had been in the event but a few hours of anxiety; the journey had been pronounced again not only possible, but, as representing "change," highly advisable; and if the zealous guest had had five minutes by herself with the Doctor this was clearly no more at his instance than at her own. Almost nothing had passed between them but an easy exchange of enthusiasms in respect to the remedial properties of "Europe"; and due assurance, as the facts came back to her, she was now able to give. "Nothing whatever, on my word of honour, that you mayn't know or mightn't then have known. I've no secret with him about you. What makes you suspect it? I don't quite make out how you know I did see him alone."

"No—you never told me," said Milly. "And I don't mean," she went on, "during the twenty-four hours while I was bad, when your putting your heads together was natural enough. I mean after I was better—the last thing before you went home."

Mrs. Stringham continued to wonder. "Who told you I saw him then?"

"*He* didn't himself—nor did you write me it afterwards. We speak of it now for the first time. That's exactly why!" Milly declared—with something in her face and voice that, the next moment, betrayed for her companion that she had really known nothing, had only conjectured and, chancing her charge, made a hit. Yet why had her mind been busy with the question? "But if you're not, as you now assure me, in his confidence," she smiled, "it's no matter."

"I'm not in his confidence—he had nothing to confide. But are you feeling unwell?"

The elder woman was earnest for the truth, though the possibility she named was not at all the one that seemed to fit—witness the long climb Milly had just indulged in. The girl showed her constant white face, but this her friends had all learned to discount, and it was often brightest when superficially not bravest. She continued for a little mysteriously to smile. "I don't know—haven't really the least idea. But it might be well to find out."

Mrs. Stringham at this flared into sympathy. "Are you in trouble—in pain?"

"Not the least little bit. But I sometimes wonder—!"

"Yes"—she pressed: "wonder what?"

"Well, if I shall have much of it."

Mrs. Stringham stared. "Much of what? Not of pain?"

"Of everything. Of everything I have."

Anxiously again, tenderly, our friend cast about. "You 'have' everything; so that when you say 'much' of it—"

"I only mean," the girl broke in, "shall I have it for long? That is if I *have* got it."

She had at present the effect, a little, of confounding, or at least of perplexing her comrade, who was touched, who was always touched, by something helpless in her grace and abrupt in her turns, and yet actually half made out in her a sort of mocking light. "If you've got an ailment?"

"If I've got everything," Milly laughed.

"Ah *that*—like almost nobody else."

"Then for how long?"

Mrs. Stringham's eyes entreated her; she had gone close to her, half-enclosed her with urgent arms. "Do you want to see some one?" And then as the girl only met it with a slow headshake, though looking perhaps a shade more conscious: "We'll go straight to the best near doctor." This too, however, produced but a gaze of qualified assent and a silence, sweet and vague, that left everything open. Our friend decidedly lost herself. "Tell me, for God's sake, if you're in distress."

"I don't think I've really *everything*," Milly said as if to explain —and as if also to put it pleasantly.

"But what on earth can I do for you?"

The girl debated, then seemed on the point of being able to say; but suddenly changed and expressed herself otherwise. "Dear, dear thing—I'm only too happy!"

It brought them closer, but it rather confirmed Mrs. Stringham's doubt. "Then what's the matter?"

"That's the matter—that I can scarcely bear it."

"But what is it you think you haven't got?"

Milly waited another moment; then she found it, and found for it a dim show of joy. "The power to resist the bliss of what I *have!*"

Mrs. Stringham took it in—her sense of being "put off" with it, the possible, probable irony of it—and her tenderness renewed itself in the positive grimness of a long murmur. "Whom will you see?" —for it was as if they looked down from their height at a continent of doctors. "Where will you first go?"

Milly had for the third time her air of consideration; but she came back with it to her plea of some minutes before. "I'll tell you at supper—good-bye till then." And she left the room with a lightness that testified for her companion to something that again particularly pleased her in the renewed promise of motion. The odd passage just concluded, Mrs. Stringham mused as she once more sat alone with a hooked needle and a ball of silk, the "fine" work with which she was always provided—this mystifying mood had simply been precipitated, no doubt, by their prolonged halt, with which the girl hadn't really been in sympathy. One had only to admit that her complaint was in fact but the excess of the joy of life, and everything *did* then fit. She couldn't stop for the joy, but she could go on for it, and with the pulse of her going on she floated again, was restored to her great spaces. There was no evasion of any truth—so at least Susan Shepherd hoped—in one's sitting there while the twilight deepened and feeling still more finely that the position of this young lady was magnificent. The evening at that height had naturally turned to cold, and the travellers had bespoken a fire with their meal; the great Alpine road asserted its brave presence through the small panes of the low clean windows, with incidents at the inn-door, the yellow diligence,[2] the great waggons, the hurrying hooded private conveyances, reminders, for our fanciful friend, of old stories, old pictures, historic flights, escapes, pursuits, things that had happened, things indeed that by a sort of strange congruity helped her to read the meanings of the greatest interest into the relation in which she was now so deeply involved. It was natural that this record of the magnificence of her companion's position should strike her as after all the best meaning she could extract; for she herself was seated in the magnificence as in a court-carriage—she came back to that, and such a method of progression, such a view from crimson cushions, would evidently have a great deal more to give. By the time the candles were lighted for supper and the short white curtains drawn Milly had reappeared, and the little scenic room had then all its romance. That charm moreover was far from broken by the words in which she, without further loss of time, satisfied her patient mate. "I want to go straight to London."

It was unexpected, corresponding with no view positively taken at their departure; when England had appeared, on the contrary, rather relegated and postponed—seen for the moment, as who should say, at the end of an avenue of preparations and introductions. London, in short, might have been supposed to be the crown, and to be achieved, like a siege, by gradual approaches. Milly's actual fine stride was therefore the more exciting, as any simplification almost always was to Mrs. Stringham; who, besides, was afterwards to recall as a piece of that very "exposition" dear to the dramatist the terms in which, between their smoky candles, the girl had put her preference and in which still other things had come up, come while the clank of waggon-chains in the sharp air reached their ears, with the stamp of hoofs, the rattle of buckets and the foreign questions, foreign answers, that were all alike a part of the cheery converse of the road. The girl brought it out in truth as she might have brought a huge confession, something she admitted her-

2. Public stagecoach.

self shy about and that would seem to show her as frivolous; it had rolled over her that what she wanted of Europe was "people," so far as they were to be had, and that, if her friend really wished to know, the vision of this same equivocal quantity was what had haunted her during their previous days, in museums and churches, and what was again spoiling for her the pure taste of scenery. She was all for scenery—yes; but she wanted it human and personal, and all she could say was that there would be in London—wouldn't there?—more of that kind than anywhere else. She came back to her idea that if it wasn't for long—if nothing should happen to be so for *her*—why the particular thing she spoke of would probably have most to give her in the time, would probably be less than anything else a waste of her remainder. She produced this last consideration indeed with such gaiety that Mrs. Stringham was not again disconcerted by it, was in fact quite ready—if talk of early dying was in order—to match it from her own future. Good, then; they would eat and drink because of what might happen to-morrow; and they would direct their course from that moment with a view to such eating and drinking. They ate and drank that night, in truth, as in the spirit of this decision; whereby the air, before they separated, felt itself the clearer.

It had cleared perhaps to a view only too extensive—extensive, that is, in proportion to the signs of life presented. The idea of "people" was not so entertained on Milly's part as to connect itself with particular persons, and the fact remained for each of the ladies that they would, completely unknown, disembark at Dover amid the completely unknowing. They had no relation already formed; this plea Mrs. Stringham put forward to see what it would produce. It produced nothing at first but the observation on the girl's side that what she had in mind was no thought of society nor of scraping acquaintance; nothing was further from her than to desire the opportunities represented for the compatriot in general by a trunkful of "letters." It wasn't a question, in short, of the people the compatriot was after; it was the human, the English picture itself, as they might see it in their own way—the concrete world inferred so fondly from what one had read and dreamed. Mrs. Stringham did every justice to this concrete world, but when later on an occasion chanced to present itself she made a point of not omitting to remark that it might be a comfort to know in advance one or two of the human particles of its concretion. This still, however, failed, in vulgar parlance, to "fetch" Milly, so that she had presently to go all the way. "Haven't I understood from you, for that matter, that you gave Mr. Densher something of a promise?"

There was a moment, on this, when Milly's look had to be taken as representing one of two things—either that she was completely vague about the promise or that Mr. Densher's name itself started no train. But she really couldn't be so vague about the promise, the partner of these hours quickly saw, without attaching it to something; it had to be a promise to somebody in particular to be so repudiated. In the event, accordingly, she acknowledged Mr. Merton Densher, the so unusually "bright" young Englishman who had made his appearance in New York on some special literary business—wasn't it?—shortly before their departure, and who had been three or four times in her house during the brief period between her visit to Boston and her companion's subsequent stay with her; but she required much reminding before it came back to her that she had mentioned to this companion just afterwards the confidence expressed by the personage in question in her never doing so dire a thing as to come to London without, as the phrase was, looking a fellow up. She had left him the enjoyment of his confidence, the form of which might have appeared a trifle free—this she now reasserted; she had done nothing either to impair or to enhance it; but she had also left Mrs. Stringham, in the connexion and at the time, rather sorry to have missed Mr. Densher. She had thought of him again after that, the elder woman; she had likewise gone so far as to notice that Milly appeared not to have done so—which the girl might easily have betrayed; and, interested as she was in everything that concerned her, she had made out for herself, for herself only and rather idly, that, but for interruptions, the young Englishman might have become a better acquaintance. His being an acquaintance at all was one of the signs that in the first days had helped to place Milly, as a young person with the world before her, for sympathy and wonder. Isolated, unmothered, unguarded, but with her other strong marks, her big house, her big fortune, her big freedom, she had lately begun to "receive," for all her few years, as an older woman might have done—as was done, precisely, by princesses who had public considerations to observe and who came of age very early. If it was thus distinct to Mrs. Stringham then that Mr. Densher had gone off somewhere else in connexion with his errand before her visit to New York, it had been also not undiscoverable that he had come back for a day or two later on, that is after her own second excursion—that he had in fine reappeared on a single occasion on his way to the West: his way from Washington as she believed, though he was out of sight at the time of her joining her friend for their departure. It hadn't occurred to her before to exaggerate—it had not occurred to her that she could; but she seemed to become aware to-night that there had been just enough in this relation to meet, to provoke, the free conception of a little more.

She presently put it that, at any rate, promise or no promise,

Milly would at a pinch be able, in London, to act on his permission to make him a sign; to which Milly replied with readiness that her ability, though evident, would be none the less quite wasted, inasmuch as the gentleman would to a certainty be still in America. He had a great deal to do there—which he would scarce have begun; and in fact she might very well not have thought of London at all if she hadn't been sure he wasn't yet near coming back. It was perceptible to her companion that the moment our young woman had so far committed herself she had a sense of having overstepped; which was not quite patched up by her saying the next minute, possibly with a certain failure of presence of mind, that the last thing she desired was the air of running after him. Mrs. Stringham wondered privately what question there could be of any such appearance—the danger of which thus suddenly came up; but she said for the time nothing of it—she only said other things: one of which was, for instance, that if Mr. Densher was away he was away, and this the end of it: also that of course they must be discreet at any price. But what was the measure of discretion, and how was one to be sure? So it was that, as they sat there, she produced her own case: *she* had a possible tie with London, which she desired as little to disown as she might wish to risk presuming on it. She treated her companion, in short, for their evening's end, to the story of Maud Manningham, the odd but interesting English girl who had formed her special affinity in the old days at the Vevey school; whom she had written to, after their separation, with a regularity that had at first faltered and then altogether failed, yet that had been for the time quite a fine case of crude constancy; so that it had in fact flickered up again of itself on the occasion of the marriage of each. They had then once more fondly, scrupulously written—Mrs. Lowder first; and even another letter or two had afterwards passed. This, however, had been the end—though with no rupture, only a gentle drop: Maud Manningham had made, she believed, a great marriage, while she herself had made a small; on top of which, moreover, distance, difference, diminished community and impossible reunion had done the rest of the work. It was but after all these years that reunion had begun to show as possible—if the other party to it, that is, should be still in existence. That was exactly what it now appeared to our friend interesting to ascertain, as, with one aid and another, she believed she might. It was an experiment she would at all events now make if Milly didn't object.

Milly in general objected to nothing, and though she asked a question or two she raised no present plea. Her questions—or at least her own answers to them—kindled on Mrs. Stringham's part a backward train: she hadn't known till to-night how much she remembered, or how fine it might be to see what had become of large high-coloured Maud, florid, alien, exotic—which had been just the spell—even to the perceptions of youth. There was the danger —she frankly touched it—that such a temperament mightn't have matured, with the years, all in the sense of fineness: it was the sort of danger that, in renewing relations after long breaks, one had always to look in the face. To gather in strayed threads was to take a risk—for which, however, she was prepared if Milly was. The possible "fun," she confessed, was by itself rather tempting; and she fairly sounded, with this—wound up a little as she was—the note of fun as the harmless final right of fifty years of mere New England virtue. Among the things she was afterwards to recall was the indescribable look dropped on her, at that, by her companion; she was still seated there between the candles and before the finished supper, while Milly moved about, and the look was long to figure for her as an inscrutable comment on *her* notion of freedom. Challenged, at any rate, as for the last wise word, Milly showed perhaps, musingly, charmingly, that, though her attention had been mainly soundless, her friend's story—produced as a resource unsuspected, a card from up the sleeve—half-surprised, half-beguiled her. Since the matter, such as it was, depended on that, she brought out before she went to bed an easy, a light "Risk everything!"

This quality in it seemed possibly a little to deny weight to Maud Lowder's evoked presence—as Susan Stringham, still sitting up, became, in excited reflexion, a trifle more conscious. Something determinant, when the girl had left her, took place in her—nameless but, as soon as she had given way, coercive. It was as if she knew again, in this fulness of time, that she had been, after Maud's marriage, just sensibly outlived or, as people nowadays said, shunted. Mrs. Lowder had left her behind, and on the occasion, subsequently, of the corresponding date in her own life—not the second, the sad one, with its dignity of sadness, but the first, with the meagreness of its supposed felicity—she had been, in the same spirit, almost patronisingly pitied. If that suspicion, even when it had ceased to matter, had never quite died out for her, there was doubtless some oddity in its now offering itself as a link, rather than as another break, in the chain; and indeed there might well have been for her a mood in which the notion of the development of patronage in her quondam schoolmate would have settled her question in another sense. It was actually settled—if the case be worth our analysis—by the happy consummation, the poetic justice, the generous revenge, of her having at last something to show. Maud, on their parting company, had appeared to have so much, and would now—for wasn't it also in general quite the rich law of English life?—have, with accretions, promotions, expansions, ever so much more. Very good; such things might be; she rose to the sense of being ready for them. Whatever Mrs. Lowder might have to

their simplicity. She thrilled, she consciously flushed, and all to turn pale again, with the certitude—it had never been so present—that she should find herself completely involved: the very air of the place, the pitch of the occasion, had for her both so sharp a ring and so deep an undertone. The smallest things, the faces, the hands, the jewels of the women, the sound of words, especially of names, across the table, the shape of the forks, the arrangement of the flowers, the attitude of the servants, the walls of the room, were all touches in a picture and denotements in a play; and they marked for her moreover her alertness of vision. She had never, she might well believe, been in such a state of vibration; her sensibility was almost too sharp for her comfort: there were for example more indications than she could reduce to order in the manner of the friendly niece, who struck her as distinguished and interesting, as in fact surprisingly genial. This young woman's type had, visibly, other possibilities; yet here, of its own free movement, it had already sketched a relation. Were they, Miss Croy and she, to take up the tale where their two elders had left it off so many years before?—were they to find they liked each other and to try for themselves whether a scheme of constancy on more modern lines could be worked? She had doubted, as they came to England, of Maud Manningham, had believed her a broken reed and a vague resource, had seen their dependence on her as a state of mind that would have been shamefully silly—so far as it *was* dependence—had they wished to do anything so inane as "get into society." To have made their pilgrimage all for the sake of such society as Mrs. Lowder might have in reserve for them—that didn't bear thinking of at all, and she herself had quite chosen her course for curiosity about other matters. She would have described this curiosity as a desire to see the places she had read about, and *that* description of her motive she was prepared to give her neighbour—even though, as a consequence of it, he should find how little she had read. It was almost at present as if her poor prevision had been rebuked by the majesty—she could scarcely call it less—of the event, or at all events by the commanding character of the two figures (she could scarcely call *that* less either) mainly presented. Mrs. Lowder and her niece, however dissimilar, had at least in common that each was a great reality. That was true, primarily, of the aunt—so true that Milly wondered how her own companion had arrived in other years at so odd an alliance; yet she none the less felt Mrs. Lowder as a person of whom the mind might in two or three days roughly make the circuit. She would sit there massive at least while one attempted it; whereas Miss Croy, the handsome girl, would indulge in incalculable movements that might interfere with one's tour. She was the amusing resisting ominous fact, none the less, and each other person and thing was just such a fact; and it served them right, no doubt, the pair of them, for having rushed into their adventure.

Lord Mark's intelligence meanwhile, however, had met her own quite sufficiently to enable him to tell her how little he could clear up her situation. He explained, for that matter—or at least he hinted—that there was no such thing to-day in London as saying where any one was. Every one was everywhere—nobody was anywhere. He should be put to it—yes, frankly—to give a name of any sort or kind to their hostess's "set." *Was* it a set at all, or wasn't it, and were there not really no such things as sets in the place any more? —was there anything but the groping and pawing, that of the vague billows of some great greasy sea in mid-Channel, of masses of bewildered people trying to "get" they didn't know what or where? He threw out the question, which seemed large; Milly felt that at the end of five minutes he had thrown out a great many, though he followed none more than a step or two; perhaps he would prove suggestive, but he helped her as yet to no discriminations: he spoke as if he had given them up from too much knowledge. He was thus at the opposite extreme from herself, but, as a consequence of it, also wandering and lost; and he was furthermore, for all his temporary incoherence, to which she guessed there would be some key, as packed a concretion as either Mrs. Lowder or Kate. The only light in which he placed the former of these ladies was that of an extraordinary woman—a most extraordinary woman, and "the more extraordinary the more one knows her," while of the latter he said nothing for the moment but that she was tremendously, yes, quite tremendously, good-looking. It was some time, she thought, before his talk showed his cleverness, and yet each minute she believed in that mystery more, quite apart from what her hostess had told her on first naming him. Perhaps he was one of the cases she had heard of at home—those characteristic cases of people in England who concealed their play of mind so much more than they advertised it. Even Mr. Densher a little did that. And what made Lord Mark, at any rate, so real either, when this was a trick he had apparently so mastered? His type somehow, as by a life, a need, an intention of its own, took all care for vividness off his hands; that was enough. It was difficult to guess his age—whether he were a young man who looked old or an old man who looked young; it seemed to prove nothing, as against other things, that he was bald and, as might have been said, slightly stale, or, more delicately perhaps, dry: there was such a fine little fidget of preoccupied life in him, and his eyes, at moments—though it was an appearance they could suddenly lose —were as candid and clear as those of a pleasant boy. Very neat, very light, and so fair that there was little other indication of his moustache than his constantly feeling it—which was again boyish

—he would have affected her as the most intellectual person present if he had not affected her as the most frivolous. The latter quality was rather in his look than in anything else, though he constantly wore his double eye-glass, which was, much more, Bostonian and thoughtful.

The idea of his frivolity had, no doubt, to do with his personal designation, which represented—as yet, for our young woman, a little confusedly—a connexion with an historic patriciate, a class that in turn, also confusedly, represented an affinity with a social element she had never heard otherwise described than as "fashion." The supreme social element in New York had never known itself but as reduced to that category, and though Milly was aware that, as applied to a territorial and political aristocracy, the label was probably too simple, she had for the time none other at hand. She presently, it is true, enriched her idea with the perception that her interlocutor was indifferent; yet this, indifferent as aristocracies notoriously were, saw her but little further, inasmuch as she felt that, in the first place, he would much rather get on with her than not, and in the second was only thinking of too many matters of his own. If he kept her in view on the one hand and kept so much else on the other—the way he crumbed up his bread was a proof—why did he hover before her as a potentially insolent noble? She couldn't have answered the question, and it was precisely one of those that swarmed. They were complicated, she might fairly have said, by his visibly knowing, having known from afar off, that she was a stranger and an American, and by his none the less making no more of it than if she and her like were the chief of his diet. He took her, kindly enough, but, imperturbably, irreclaimably, for granted, and it wouldn't in the least help that she herself knew him, as quickly, for having been in her country and threshed it out. There would be nothing for her to explain or attenuate or brag about; she could neither escape nor prevail by her strangeness; he would have, for that matter, on such a subject, more to tell her than to learn from her. She might learn from *him* why she was so different from the handsome girl—which she didn't know, being merely able to feel it; or at any rate might learn from him why the handsome girl was so different from her.

On these lines, however, they would move later; the lines immediately laid down were, in spite of his vagueness for his own convenience, definite enough. She was already, he observed to her, thinking what she should say on her other side—which was what Americans were always doing. She needn't in conscience say anything at all; but Americans never knew that, nor ever, poor creatures, yes (*she* had interposed the "poor creatures!") what not to do. The burdens they took on—the things, positively, they made an affair of! This easy and after all friendly jibe at her race was really for her, on her new friend's part, the note of personal recognition so far as she required it; and she gave him a prompt and conscious example of morbid anxiety by insisting that her desire to be, herself, "lovely" all round was justly founded on the lovely way Mrs. Lowder had met her. He was directly interested in that, and it was not till afterwards she fully knew how much more information about their friend he had taken than given. Here again for instance was a characteristic note: she had, on the spot, with her first plunge into the obscure depths of a society constituted from far back, encountered the interesting phenomenon of complicated, of possibly sinister motive. However, Maud Manningham (her name, even in her presence, somehow still fed the fancy) *had*, all the same, been lovely, and one was going to meet her now quite as far on as one had one's self been met. She had been with them at their hotel—they were a pair—before even they had supposed she could have got their letter. Of course indeed they had written in advance, but they had followed that up very fast. She had thus engaged them to dine but two days later, and on the morrow again, without waiting for a return visit, without waiting for anything, she had called with her niece. It was as if she really cared for them, and it was magnificent fidelity—fidelity to Mrs. Stringham, her own companion and Mrs. Lowder's former schoolmate, the lady with the charming face and the rather high dress down there at the end.

Lord Mark took in through his nippers these balanced attributes of Susie. "But isn't Mrs. Stringham's fidelity then equally magnificent?"

"Well, it's a beautiful sentiment; but it isn't as if she had anything to *give*."

"Hasn't she got you?" Lord Mark asked without excessive delay.

"Me—to give Mrs. Lowder?" Milly had clearly not yet seen herself in the light of such an offering. "Oh I'm rather a poor present; and I don't feel as if, even at that, I had as yet quite been given."

"You've been shown, and if our friend has jumped at you it comes to the same thing." He made his jokes, Lord Mark, without amusement for himself; yet it wasn't that he was grim. "To be seen, you must recognise, *is*, for you, to be jumped at; and, if it's a question of being shown, here you are again. Only it has now been taken out of your friend's hands; it's Mrs. Lowder already who's getting the benefit. Look round the table, and you'll make out, I think, that you're being, from top to bottom, jumped at."

"Well then," said Milly, "I seem also to feel that I like it better than being made fun of."

It was one of the things she afterwards saw—Milly was for ever seeing things afterwards—that her companion had here had some way of his own, quite unlike any one's else, of assuring her of his consideration. She wondered how he had done it, for he had neither apologised nor protested. She said to herself at any rate that he had led her on; and what was most odd was the question by which he had done so. "Does she know much about you?"

"No, she just likes us."

Even for this his travelled lordship, seasoned and saturated, had no laugh. "I mean *you* particularly. Has that lady with the charming face, which *is* charming, told her?"

Milly cast about. "Told her what?"

"Everything."

This, with the way he dropped it, again considerably moved her—made her feel for a moment that as a matter of course she was a subject for disclosures. But she quickly found her answer. "Oh as for that you must ask *her*."

"Your clever companion?"

"Mrs. Lowder."

He replied to this that their hostess was a person with whom there were certain liberties one never took, but that he was none the less fairly upheld, inasmuch as she was for the most part kind to him and as, should he be very good for a while, she would probably herself tell him. "And I shall have at any rate in the meantime the interest of seeing what she does with you. That will teach me more or less, you see, how much she knows."

Milly followed this—it was lucid, but it suggested something apart. "How much does she know about *you?*"

"Nothing," said Lord Mark serenely. "But that doesn't matter—for what she does with me." And then as to anticipate Milly's question about the nature of such doing: "This for instance—turning me straight on for *you*."

The girl thought. "And you mean she wouldn't if she did know—?"

He met it as if it were really a point. "No. I believe, to do her justice, she still would. So you can be easy."

Milly had the next instant then acted on the permission. "Because you're even at the worst the best thing she has?"

With this he was at last amused. "I was till you came. You're the best now."

It was strange his words should have given her the sense of his knowing, but it was positive that they did so, and to the extent of making her believe them, though still with wonder. That really from this first of their meetings was what was most to abide with her: she accepted almost helplessly—she surrendered so to the inevitable in it—being the sort of thing, as he might have said, that he at least thoroughly believed he had, in going about, seen enough of for all practical purposes. Her submission was naturally moreover not to be impaired by her learning later on that he had paid at short intervals, though at a time apparently just previous to her own emergence from the obscurity of extreme youth, three separate visits to New York, where his nameable friends and his contrasted contacts had been numerous. His impression, his recollection of the whole mixed quantity, was still visibly rich. It had helped him to place her, and she was more and more sharply conscious of having—as with the door sharply slammed upon her and the guard's hand raised in signal to the train—been popped into the compartment in which she was to travel for him. It was a use of her that many a girl would have been doubtless quick to resent; and the kind of mind that thus, in our young lady, made all for mere seeing and taking is precisely one of the charms of our subject. Milly had practically just learned from him, had made out, as it were, from her rumbling compartment, that he gave her the highest place among their friend's actual properties. She was a success, that was what it came to, he presently assured her, and this was what it was to be a success; it always happened before one could know it. One's ignorance was in fact often the greatest part of it. "You haven't had time yet," he said; "this is nothing. But you'll see. You'll see everything. You *can*, you know—everything you dream of."

He made her more and more wonder; she almost felt as if he were showing her visions while he spoke; and strangely enough, though it was visions that had drawn her on, she hadn't had them in connexion—that is in such preliminary and necessary connexion—with such a face as Lord Mark's, such eyes and such a voice, such a tone and such a manner. He had for an instant the effect of making her ask herself if she were after all going to be afraid; so distinct was it for fifty seconds that a fear passed over her. There they were again—yes, certainly: Susie's overture to Mrs. Lowder had been their joke, but they had pressed in that gaiety an electric bell that continued to sound. Positively while she sat there she had the loud rattle in her ears, and she wondered during these moments why the others didn't hear it. They didn't stare, they didn't smile, and the fear in her that I speak of was but her own desire to stop it. That dropped, however, as if the alarm itself had ceased; she seemed to have seen in a quick though tempered glare that there were two courses for her, one to leave London again the first thing in the morning, the other to do nothing at all. Well, she would do nothing at all; she was already doing it; more than that, she had already done it, and her chance was gone. She gave herself up—she had the strangest sense, on the spot, of so deciding; for she had turned a corner before she went on again with Lord Mark. Inexpressive but intensely significant, he met as no one else could have done the very question she had suddenly put to Mrs. Stringham on the Brünig. Should she have it, whatever she did have, that question had been, for long? "Ah so possibly not," her neighbour appeared to reply; "therefore, don't you see? *I 'm* the way." It was vivid that he might be, in spite of his absence of flourish; the way being doubtless just *in* that absence. The handsome girl, whom she didn't lose sight of and who, she felt, kept her also in view—Mrs. Lowder's striking niece would perhaps be the way as well, for in her too was the absence of flourish, though she had little else, so far as one could tell, in common with Lord Mark. Yet how indeed *could* one tell, what did one understand, and of what was one, for that matter, provisionally conscious but of their being somehow together in what they represented? Kate Croy, fine but friendly, looked over at her as really with a guess at Lord Mark's effect on her. If she could guess this effect what then did she know about it and in what degree had she felt it herself? Did that represent, as between them, anything particular, and should she have to count with them as duplicating, as intensifying by a mutual intelligence, the relation into which she was sinking? Nothing was so odd as that she should have to recognise so quickly in each of these glimpses of an instant the various signs of a relation; and this anomaly itself, had she had more time to give to it, might well, might almost terribly have suggested to her that her doom was to live fast. It was queerly a question of the short run and the consciousness proportionately crowded.

These were immense excursions for the spirit of a young person at Mrs. Lowder's mere dinner-party; but what was so significant and so admonitory as the fact of their being possible? What could they have been but just a part, already, of the crowded consciousness? And it was just a part likewise that while plates were changed and dishes presented and periods in the banquet marked; while appearances insisted and phenomena multiplied and words reached her from here and there like plashes of a slow thick tide; while Mrs. Lowder grew somehow more stout and more instituted and Susie, at her distance and in comparison, more thinly improvised and more different—different, that is, from every one and every thing: it was just a part that while this process went forward our young lady alighted, came back, taking up her destiny again as if she had been able by a wave or two of her wings to place herself briefly in sight of an alternative to it. Whatever it was it had showed in this brief interval as better than the alternative; and it now presented itself altogether in the image and in the place in which she had left it. The image was that of her being, as Lord Mark had declared, a success. This depended more or less of course on his idea of the thing —into which at present, however, she wouldn't go. But, renewing soon, she had asked him what he meant then that Mrs. Lowder would do with her, and he had replied that this might safely be left. "She'll get back," he pleasantly said, "her money." He could say it too—which was singular—without affecting her either as vulgar or as "nasty"; and he had soon explained himself by adding: "Nobody here, you know, does anything for nothing."

"Ah if you mean that we shall reward her as hard as ever we can, nothing is more certain. But she's an idealist," Milly continued, "and idealists, in the long run, I think, *don't* feel that they lose."

Lord Mark seemed, within the limits of his enthusiasm, to find this charming. "Ah she strikes you as an idealist?"

"She idealises *us*, my friend and me, absolutely. She sees us in a light," said Milly. "That's all I've got to hold on by. So don't deprive me of it."

"I wouldn't think of such a thing for the world. But do you suppose," he continued as if it were suddenly important for him—"do you suppose she sees *me* in a light?"

She neglected his question for a little, partly because her attention attached itself more and more to the handsome girl, partly because, placed so near their hostess, she wished not to show as discussing her too freely. Mrs. Lowder, it was true, steering in the other quarter a course in which she called at subjects as if they were islets in an archipelago, continued to allow them their ease, and Kate Croy at the same time steadily revealed herself as interesting. Milly in fact found of a sudden her ease—found it all as she bethought herself that what Mrs. Lowder was really arranging for was a report on her quality and, as perhaps might be said her value, from Lord Mark. She wished him, the wonderful lady, to have no pretext for not knowing what he thought of Miss Theale. Why his judgement so mattered remained to be seen; but it was this divination that in any case now determined Milly's rejoinder. "No. She knows you. She has probably reason to. And you all here know each other—I see that—so far as you know anything. You know what you're used to, and it's your being used to it—that, and that only—that makes you. But there are things you don't know."

He took it in as if it might fairly, to do him justice, be a point. "Things that *I* don't—with all the pains I take and the way I've run about the world to leave nothing unlearned?"

Milly thought, and it was perhaps the very truth of his claim—its not being negligible—that sharpened her impatience and thereby her wit. "You're *blasé*, but you're not enlightened. You're familiar with everything, but conscious really of nothing. What I mean is that you've no imagination."

Lord Mark at this threw back his head, ranging with his eyes the opposite side of the room and showing himself at last so much more flagrantly diverted that it fairly attracted their hostess's notice. Mrs. Lowder, however, only smiled on Milly for a sign that something racy was what she had expected, and resumed, with a splash of her screw, her cruise among the islands. "Oh I've heard that," the young man replied, "before!"

"There it is then. You've heard everything before. You've heard *me* of course before, in my country, often enough."

"Oh never too often," he protested. "I'm sure I hope I shall still hear you again and again."

"But what good then has it done you?" the girl went on as if now frankly to amuse him.

"Oh you'll see when you know me."

"But most assuredly I shall never know you."

"Then that will be exactly," he laughed, "the good!"

If it established thus that they couldn't or wouldn't mix, why did Milly none the less feel through it a perverse quickening of the relation to which she had been in spite of herself appointed? What queerer consequence of their not mixing than their talking—for it was what they had arrived at—almost intimately? She wished to get away from him, or indeed, much rather, away from herself so far as she was present to him. She saw already—wonderful creature, after all, herself too—that there would be a good deal more of him to come for her, and that the special sign of their intercourse would be to keep herself out of the question. Everything else might come in—only never that; and with such an arrangement they would perhaps even go far. This in fact might quite have begun, on the spot, with her returning again to the topic of the handsome girl. If she was to keep herself out she could naturally best do so by putting in somebody else. She accordingly put in Kate Croy, being ready to that extent—as she was not at all afraid for her—to sacrifice her if necessary. Lord Mark himself, for that matter, had made it easy by saying a little while before that no one among them did anything for nothing. "What then"—she was aware of being abrupt— "does Miss Croy, if she's so interested, do it for? What has she to gain by *her* lovely welcome? Look at her *now!*" Milly broke out with characteristic freedom of praise, though pulling herself up also with a compunctious "Oh!" as the direction thus given to their eyes happened to coincide with a turn of Kate's face to them. All she had meant to do was to insist that this face was fine; but what she had in fact done was to renew again her effect of showing herself to its possessor as conjoined with Lord Mark for some interested view of it. He had, however, promptly met her question.

"To gain? Why your acquaintance."

"Well, what's my acquaintance to *her?* She can care for me—she must feel that—only by being sorry for me; and that's why she's lovely: to be already willing to take the trouble to be. It's the height of the disinterested."

There were more things in this than one that Lord Mark might have taken up; but in a minute he had made his choice. "Ah then I'm nowhere, for I'm afraid *I'm* not sorry for you in the least. What do you make then," he asked, "of your success?"

"Why just the great reason of all. It's just because our friend there sees it that she pities me. She understands," Milly said; "she's better than any of you. She's beautiful."

He appeared struck with this at last—with the point the girl made of it; to which she came back even after a diversion created by a dish presented between them. "Beautiful in character, I see. *Is* she so? You must tell me about her."

Milly wondered. "But haven't you known her longer than I? Haven't you seen her for yourself?"

"No—I've failed with her. It's no use. I don't make her out. And I assure you I really should like to." His assurance had in fact for his companion a positive suggestion of sincerity; he affected her as now saying something he did feel; and she was the more struck with it as she was still conscious of the failure even of curiosity he had just shown in respect to herself. She had meant something—though indeed for herself almost only—in speaking of their friend's natural pity; it had doubtless been a note of questionable taste, but it had quavered out in spite of her and he hadn't so much as cared to enquire "Why 'natural'?" Not that it wasn't really much better for her that he shouldn't: explanations would in truth have taken her much too far. Only she now perceived that, in comparison, her word about this other person really "drew" him; and there were things in that probably, many things, as to which she would learn more and which glimmered there already as part and parcel of that larger "real" with which, in her new situation, she was to be beguiled. It was in fact at the very moment, this element, not absent from what Lord Mark was further saying. "So you're wrong, you see, as to our knowing all about each other. There are cases where we break down. I at any rate give *her* up—up, that is, to you. You must do her for me—tell me, I mean, when you know more. You'll notice," he pleasantly wound up, "that I've confidence in you."

"Why shouldn't you have?" Milly asked, observing in this, as she thought, a fine, though for such a man a surprisingly artless, fatuity. It was as if there might have been a question of her falsifying for the sake of her own show—that is of the failure of her honesty to be proof against her desire to keep well with him herself. She didn't, none the less, otherwise protest against his remark; there was something else she was occupied in seeing. It was the handsome girl alone, one of his own species and his own society, who had made him feel uncertain; of his certainties about a mere little American, a cheap exotic, imported almost wholesale and whose habitat, with its conditions of climate, growth and cultivation, its immense profusion but its few varieties and thin development, he was perfectly satisfied. The marvel was too that Milly understood his satisfaction—feeling she expressed the truth in presently saying: "Of course; I make out that she must be difficult; just as I see that I myself must be easy." And that was what, for all the rest of this occasion, remained with her—as the most interesting thing that *could* remain. She was more and more content herself to be easy; she would have been resigned, even had it been brought straighter home to her, to passing for a cheap exotic. Provisionally, at any rate, that protected her wish to keep herself, with Lord Mark, in abeyance. They *had* all affected her as inevitably knowing each other, and if the handsome girl's place among them was something even their initiation couldn't deal with—why then she would indeed be a quantity.

II

That sense of quantities, separate or mixed, was really, no doubt, what most prevailed at first for our slightly gasping American pair; it found utterance for them in their frequent remark to each other that they had no one but themselves to thank. It dropped from Milly more than once that if she had ever known it was so easy—! though her exclamation mostly ended without completing her idea. This, however, was a trifle to Mrs. Stringham, who cared little whether she meant that in this case she would have come sooner. She couldn't have come sooner, and she perhaps on the contrary meant—for it would have been like her—that she wouldn't have come at all; why it was so easy being at any rate a matter as to which her companion had begun quickly to pick up views. Susie kept some of these lights for the present to herself, since, freely communicated, they might have been a little disturbing; with which, moreover, the quantities that we speak of as surrounding the two ladies were in many cases quantities of things—and of other things—to talk about. Their immediate lesson accordingly was that they just had been caught up by the incalculable strength of a wave that was actually holding them aloft and that would naturally dash them wherever it liked. They meanwhile, we hasten to add, made the best of their precarious position, and if Milly had had no other help for it she would have found not a little in the sight of Susan Shepherd's state. The girl had had nothing to say to her, for three days, about the "success" announced by Lord Mark—which they saw, besides, otherwise established; she was too taken up, too touched, by Susie's own exaltation. Susie glowed in the light of her justified faith; everything had happened that she had been acute enough to think least probable; she had appealed to a possible delicacy in Maud Manningham—a delicacy, mind you, but *barely* possible—and her appeal had been met in a way that was an honour to human nature. This proved sensibility of the lady of Lancaster Gate performed verily for both our friends during these first days the office of a fine floating gold-dust, something that threw over the prospect a harmonising blur. The forms, the colours behind it were strong and deep—we have seen how they already stood out for Milly; but nothing, comparatively, had had so much of the dignity of truth as the fact of Maud's fidelity to a sentiment. That was what Susie was proud of, much more than of her great place in the world, which she was moreover conscious of not as yet wholly measuring. That was what was more vivid even than her being—in senses more worldly and in fact almost in the degree of a revelation—English and distinct and positive, with almost no inward but with the finest outward resonance.

Susan Shepherd's word for her, again and again, was that she was "large"; yet it was not exactly a case, as to the soul, of echoing chambers: she might have been likened rather to a capacious receptacle, originally perhaps loose, but now drawn as tightly as possible over its accumulated contents—a packed mass, for her American admirer, of curious detail. When the latter good lady, at home, had handsomely figured her friends as not small—which was the way she mostly figured them—there was a certain implication that they were spacious because they were empty. Mrs. Lowder, by a different law, was spacious because she was full, because she had something in common, even in repose, with a projectile, of great size, loaded and ready for use. That indeed, to Susie's romantic mind, announced itself as half the charm of their renewal—a charm as of sitting in springtime, during a long peace, on the daisied grassy bank of some great slumbering fortress. True to her psychological instincts, certainly, Mrs. Stringham had noted that the "sentiment" she rejoiced in on her old schoolmate's part was all a matter of action and movement, was not, save for the interweaving of a more frequent plump "dearest" than she would herself perhaps have used, a matter of much other embroidery. She brooded with interest on this further mark of race, feeling in her own spirit a different economy. The joy, for her, was to know *why* she acted—the reason was half the business; whereas with Mrs. Lowder there might have been no reason: "why" was the trivial seasoning-substance, the vanilla or the nutmeg, omittable from the nutritive pudding without spoiling it. Mrs. Lowder's desire was clearly sharp that their young companions should also prosper together; and Mrs. Stringham's account of it all to Milly, during the first days, was that when, at Lancaster Gate, she was not occupied in telling, as it were, about her, she was occupied in hearing much of the history of her hostess's brilliant niece.

They had plenty, on these lines, the two elder women, to give and to take, and it was even not quite clear to the pilgrim from Boston that what she should mainly have arranged for in London was not a series of thrills for herself. She had a bad conscience, indeed almost a sense of immorality, in having to recognise that she was, as she said, carried away. She laughed to Milly when she also said that she didn't know where it would end; and the principle of her uneasiness was that Mrs. Lowder's life bristled for her with elements that she was really having to look at for the first time. They represented, she believed, the world, the world that, as a consequence of the cold shoulder turned to it by the Pilgrim Fathers, had never yet boldly crossed to Boston—it would surely have sunk the stoutest Cunarder—and she couldn't pretend that she faced the prospect simply because Milly had had a caprice. She was in the act herself of having one, directed precisely to their present spectacle. She could but seek strength in the thought that she had never had one—or had never yielded to one, which came to the same thing—before. The sustaining sense of it all moreover as literary material—that quite dropped from her. She must wait, at any rate, she should see: it struck her, so far as she had got, as vast, obscure, lurid. She reflected in the watches of the night that she was probably just going to love it for itself—that is for itself and Milly. The odd thing was that she could think of Milly's loving it without dread—or with dread at least not on the score of conscience, only on the score of peace. It was a mercy at all events, for the hour, that their two spirits jumped together.

While, for this first week that followed their dinner, she drank deep at Lancaster Gate, her companion was no less happily, appeared to be indeed on the whole quite as romantically, provided for. The handsome English girl from the heavy English house had been as a figure in a picture stepping by magic out of its frame: it was a case in truth for which Mrs. Stringham presently found the perfect image. She had lost none of her grasp, but quite the contrary, of that other conceit in virtue of which Milly was the wandering princess: so what could be more in harmony now than to see the princess waited upon at the city gate by the worthiest maiden, the chosen daughter of the burgesses? It was the real again, evidently, the amusement of the meeting for the princess too; princesses living for the most part, in such an appeased way, on the plane of mere elegant representation. That was why they pounced, at city gates, on deputed flower-strewing damsels; that was why, after effigies, processions and other stately games, frank human company was pleasant to them. Kate Croy really presented herself to Milly—the latter abounded for Mrs. Stringham in accounts of it—as the wondrous London girl in person (by what she had conceived, from far back, of the London girl; conceived from the tales of travellers and the anecdotes of New York, from old porings over *Punch*[1] and a liberal acquaintance with the fiction of the day). The only thing was that she was nicer, since the creature in question had rather been, to our young woman, an image of dread. She had thought of her, at her best, as handsome just as Kate was, with turns of head and tones of voice, felicities of stature and attitude, things "put on" and, for that matter, put off, all the marks of the product of a packed society who should be at the same time the heroine of a strong story. She placed this striking young person from the first in a story, saw her, by a necessity of the imagination, for a heroine, felt it the only character in which she wouldn't be wasted; and this in spite of the heroine's pleasant abruptness, her forbearance from gush, her umbrellas and jackets and shoes—as these things sketched themselves to Milly—and something rather of a breezy boy in the carriage of her arms and the occasional freedom of her slang.

When Milly had settled that the extent of her good will itself made her shy, she had found for the moment quite a sufficient key, and they were by that time thoroughly afloat together. This might well have been the happiest hour they were to know, attacking in friendly independence their great London—the London of shops and streets and suburbs oddly interesting to Milly, as well as of museums, monuments, "sights" oddly unfamiliar to Kate, while their elders pursued a separate course; these two rejoicing not less in their intimacy and each thinking the other's young woman a great acquisition for her own. Milly expressed to Susan Shepherd more than once that Kate had some secret, some smothered trouble, besides all the rest of her history; and that if she had so good-naturedly helped Mrs. Lowder to meet them this was exactly to create a diversion, to give herself something else to think about. But on the case thus postulated our young American had as yet had no light: she only felt that when the light should come it would greatly deepen the colour; and she liked to think she was prepared for anything. What she already knew moreover was full, to her vision, of English, of eccentric, of Thackerayan character—Kate Croy having gradually become not a little explicit on the subject of her situation, her past, her present, her general predicament, her small success, up to the present hour, in contenting at the same time her father, her sister, her aunt and herself. It was Milly's subtle guess, imparted to her Susie, that the girl had somebody else as well, as yet unnamed,

1. The famous illustrated weekly, founded in London in 1841 as a radical, satiric commentary on English life. Emerson found its wit and humor refreshingly democratic in spirit, and Thackeray took occasion to praise it because it was fit even for young girls to read. Among the various objects of satire were the Aesthetes, for their self-conscious affectation.

to content—it being manifest that such a creature couldn't help having; a creature not perhaps, if one would, exactly formed to inspire passions, since that always implied a certain silliness, but essentially seen, by the admiring eye of friendship, under the clear shadow of some probably eminent male interest. The clear shadow, from whatever source projected, hung at any rate over Milly's companion the whole week, and Kate Croy's handsome face smiled out of it, under bland skylights, in the presence alike of old masters passive in their glory and of thoroughly new ones, the newest, who bristled restlessly with pins and brandished snipping shears.

It was meanwhile a pretty part of the intercourse of these young ladies that each thought the other more remarkable than herself—that each thought herself, or assured the other she did, a comparatively dusty object and the other a favourite of nature and of fortune and covered thereby with the freshness of the morning. Kate was amused, amazed, at the way her friend insisted on "taking" her, and Milly wondered if Kate were sincere in finding her the most extraordinary—quite apart from her being the most charming—person she had come across. They had talked, in long drives, and quantities of history had not been wanting—in the light of which Mrs. Lowder's niece might superficially seem to have had the best of the argument. Her visitor's American references, with their bewildering immensities, their confounding moneyed New York, their excitements of high pressure, their opportunities of wild freedom, their record of used-up relatives, parents, clever eager fair slim brothers—these the most loved—all engaged, as well as successive superseded guardians, in a high extravagance of speculation and dissipation that had left this exquisite being her black dress, her white face and her vivid hair as the mere last broken link: such a picture quite threw into the shade the brief biography, however sketchily amplified, of a mere middle-class nobody in Bayswater. And though that indeed might be but a Bayswater way of putting it, in addition to which Milly was in the stage of interest in Bayswater ways, this critic so far prevailed that, like Mrs. Stringham herself, she fairly got her companion to accept from her that she was quite the nearest approach to a practical princess Bayswater could hope ever to know. It was a fact—it became one at the end of three days—that Milly actually began to borrow from the handsome girl a sort of view of her state; the handsome girl's impression of it was clearly so sincere. This impression was a tribute, a tribute positively to power, power the source of which was the last thing Kate treated as a mystery. There were passages, under all their skylights, the succession of their shops being large, in which the latter's easy yet the least bit dry manner sufficiently gave out that if *she* had had so deep a pocket—!

It was not moreover by any means with not having the imagination of expenditure that she appeared to charge her friend, but with not having the imagination of terror, of thrift, the imagination or in any degree the habit of a conscious dependence on others. Such moments, when all Wigmore Street,[2] for instance, seemed to rustle about and the pale girl herself to be facing the different rustlers, usually so undiscriminated, as individual Britons too, Britons personal, parties to a relation and perhaps even intrinsically remarkable —such moments in especial determined for Kate a perception of the high happiness of her companion's liberty. Milly's range was thus immense; she had to ask nobody for anything, to refer nothing to any one; her freedom, her fortune and her fancy were her law; an obsequious world surrounded her, she could sniff up at every step its fumes. And Kate, these days, was altogether in the phase of forgiving her so much bliss; in the phase moreover of believing that, should they continue to go on together, she would abide in that generosity. She had at such a point as this no suspicion of a rift within the lute—by which we mean not only none of anything's coming between them, but none of any definite flaw in so much clearness of quality. Yet, all the same, if Milly, at Mrs. Lowder's banquet, had described herself to Lord Mark as kindly used by the young woman on the other side because of some faintly-felt special propriety in it, so there really did match with this, privately, on the young woman's part, a feeling not analysed but divided, a latent impression that Mildred Theale was not, after all, a person to change places, to change even chances with. Kate, verily, would perhaps not quite have known what she meant by this discrimination, and she came near naming it only when she said to herself that, rich as Milly was, one probably wouldn't—which was singular—ever hate her for it. The handsome girl had, with herself, these felicities and crudities: it wasn't obscure to her that, without some very particular reason to help, it might have proved a test of one's philosophy not to be irritated by a mistress of millions, or whatever they were, who, as a girl, so easily might have been, like herself, only vague and cruelly female. She was by no means sure of liking Aunt Maud as much as *she* deserved, and Aunt Maud's command of funds was obviously inferior to Milly's. There was thus clearly, as pleading for the latter, some influence that would later on become distinct; and meanwhile, decidedly, it was enough that she was as charming as she was queer and as queer as she was charming—all of which was a rare amusement; as well, for that matter, as further sufficient that there were objects of value she had already pressed on Kate's acceptance. A week of her society in these conditions—con-

2. Wigmore Street is in the center of an area offering aristocratic homes, elegant shops, and fine art collections.

ditions that Milly chose to sum up as ministering immensely, for a blind vague pilgrim, to aid and comfort—announced itself from an early hour as likely to become a week of presents, acknowledgements, mementoes, pledges of gratitude and admiration, that were all on one side. Kate as promptly embraced the propriety of making it clear that she must forswear shops till she should receive some guarantee that the contents of each one she entered as a humble companion shouldn't be placed at her feet; yet that was in truth not before she had found herself in possession, under whatever protests, of several precious ornaments and other minor conveniences.

Great was the absurdity too that there should have come a day, by the end of the week, when it appeared that all Milly would have asked in definite "return," as might be said, was to be told a little about Lord Mark and to be promised the privilege of a visit to Mrs. Condrip. Far other amusements had been offered her, but her eagerness was shamelessly human, and she seemed really to count more on the revelation of the anxious lady at Chelsea than on the best nights of the opera. Kate admired, and showed it, such an absence of fear: to the fear of being bored in such a connexion she would have been so obviously entitled. Milly's answer to this was the plea of her curiosities—which left her friend wondering as to their odd direction. Some among them, no doubt, were rather more intelligible, and Kate had heard without wonder that she was blank about Lord Mark. This young lady's account of him, at the same time, professed itself frankly imperfect; for what they best knew him by at Lancaster Gate was a thing difficult to explain. One knew people in general by something they had to show, something that, either for them or against, could be touched or named or proved; and she could think of no other case of a value taken as so great and yet flourishing untested. His value was his future, which had somehow got itself as accepted by Aunt Maud as if it had been his good cook or his steamlaunch. She, Kate, didn't mean she thought him a humbug; he might do great things—but they were as yet, so to speak, all he had done. On the other hand it was of course something of an achievement, and not open to every one, to have got one's self taken so seriously by Aunt Maud. The best thing about him doubtless, on the whole, was that Aunt Maud believed in him. She was often fantastic, but she knew a humbug, and—no, Lord Mark wasn't that. He had been a short time in the House, on the Tory side, but had lost his seat on the first opportunity, and this was all he had to point to. However, he pointed to nothing; which was very possibly just a sign of his real cleverness, one of those that the really clever had in common with the really void. Even Aunt Maud frequently admitted that there was a good deal, for her view of him, to bring up the rear. And he wasn't meanwhile himself indifferent—indifferent to himself—for he was working Lancaster Gate for all it was worth: just as it was, no doubt, working *him*, and just as the working and the worked were in London, as one might explain, the parties to every relation.

Kate did explain, for her listening friend; every one who had anything to give—it was true they were the fewest—made the sharpest possible bargain for it, got at least its value in return. The strangest thing furthermore was that this might be in cases a happy understanding. The worker in one connexion was the worked in another; it was as broad as it was long—with the wheels of the system, as might be seen, wonderfully oiled. People could quite like each other in the midst of it, as Aunt Maud, by every appearance, quite liked Lord Mark, and as Lord Mark, it was to be hoped, liked Mrs. Lowder, since if he didn't he was a greater brute than one could believe. She, Kate, hadn't yet, it was true, made out what he was doing for her—besides which the dear woman needed him, even at the most he could do, much less than she imagined; so far as all of which went, moreover, there were plenty of things on every side she hadn't yet made out. She believed, on the whole, in any one Aunt Maud took up; and she gave it to Milly as worth thinking of that, whatever wonderful people this young lady might meet in the land, she would meet no more extraordinary woman. There were greater celebrities by the million, and of course greater swells, but a bigger *person*, by Kate's view, and a larger natural handful every way, would really be far to seek. When Milly enquired with interest if Kate's belief in *her* was primarily on the lines of what Mrs. Lowder "took up," her interlocutress could handsomely say yes, since by the same principle she believed in herself. Whom but Aunt Maud's niece, pre-eminently, had Aunt Maud taken up, and who was thus more in the current, with her, of working and of being worked? "You may ask," Kate said, "what in the world *I* have to give; and that indeed is just what I'm trying to learn. There must be something, for her to think she can get it out of me. She *will* get it—trust her; and then I shall see what it is; which I beg you to believe I should never have found out for myself." She declined to treat any question of Milly's own "paying" power as discussable; that Milly would pay a hundred per cent—and even to the end, doubtless, through the nose—was just the beautiful basis on which they found themselves.

These were fine facilities, pleasantries, ironies, all these luxuries of gossip and philosophies of London and of life, and they became quickly, between the pair, the common form of talk, Milly professing herself delighted to know that something was to be done with her. If the most remarkable woman in England was to do it, so much the better, and if the most remarkable woman in England had them both in hand together why what could be jollier for each? When she reflected indeed a little on the oddity of her wanting two at once Kate had the natural reply that it was exactly what showed her sincerity. She invariably gave way to feeling, and feeling had distinctly popped up in her on the advent of her girlhood's friend. The way the cat would jump was always, in presence of anything that moved her, interesting to see; visibly enough, moreover, it hadn't for a long time jumped anything like so far. This in fact, as we already know, remained the marvel for Milly Theale, who, on sight of Mrs. Lowder, had found fifty links in respect to Susie absent from the chain of association. She knew so herself what she thought of Susie that she would have expected the lady of Lancaster Gate to think something quite different; the failure of which endlessly mystified her. But her mystification was the cause for her of another fine impression, inasmuch as when she went so far as to observe to Kate that Susan Shepherd—and especially Susan Shepherd emerging so uninvited from an irrelevant past—ought by all the proprieties simply to have bored Aunt Maud, her confidant agreed to this without a protest and abounded in the sense of her wonder. Susan Shepherd at least bored the niece—that was plain; this young woman saw nothing in her—nothing to account for anything, not even for Milly's own indulgence: which little fact became in turn to the latter's mind a fact of significance. It was a light on the handsome girl—representing more than merely showed—that poor Susie was simply as nought to her. This was in a manner too a general admonition to poor Susie's companion, who seemed to see marked by it the direction in which she had best most look out. It just faintly rankled in her that a person who was good enough and to spare for Milly Theale shouldn't be good enough for another girl; though, oddly enough, she could easily have forgiven Mrs. Lowder herself the impatience. Mrs. Lowder didn't feel it, and Kate Croy felt it with ease; yet in the end, be it added, she grasped the reason, and the reason enriched her mind. Wasn't it sufficiently the reason that the handsome girl was, with twenty other splendid qualities, the least bit brutal too, and didn't she suggest, as no one yet had ever done for her new friend, that there might be a wild beauty in that, and even a strange grace? Kate wasn't brutally brutal—which Milly had hitherto benightedly supposed the only way; she wasn't even aggressively so, but rather indifferently, defensively and, as might be said, by the habit of anticipation. She simplified in advance, was beforehand with her doubts, and knew with singular quickness what she wasn't, as they said in New York, going to like. In that way at least people were clearly quicker in England than at home; and Milly could quite see after a little how such instincts might become usual in a world in which dangers abounded. There were clearly more dangers roundabout Lancaster Gate than one suspected in New York or could dream of in Boston. At all events, with more sense of them, there were more precautions, and it was a remarkable world altogether in which there could be precautions, on whatever ground, against Susie.

III

She certainly made up with Susie directly, however, for any allowance she might have had privately to extend to tepid appreciation; since the late and long talks of these two embraced not only everything offered and suggested by the hours they spent apart, but a good deal more besides. She might be as detached as the occasion required at four o'clock in the afternoon, but she used no such freedom to any one about anything as she habitually used about everything to Susan Shepherd at midnight. All the same, it should with much less delay than this have been mentioned, she hadn't yet—hadn't, that is, at the end of six days—produced any news for her comrade to compare with an announcement made her by the latter as a result of a drive with Mrs. Lowder, for a change, in the remarkable Battersea Park.[1] The elder friends had sociably revolved there while the younger ones followed bolder fancies in the admirable equipage appointed to Milly at the hotel—a heavier, more emblazoned, more amusing chariot than she had ever, with "stables" notoriously mismanaged, known at home; whereby, in the course of the circuit, more than once repeated, it had "come out," as Mrs. Stringham said, that the couple at Lancaster Gate were, of all people, acquainted with Mildred's other English friend, the gentleman, the one connected with the English newspaper (Susie hung fire a little over his name) who had been with her in New York so shortly previous to present adventures. He had been named of course in Battersea Park—else he couldn't have been identified; and Susie had naturally, before she could produce her own share in the matter as a kind of confession, to make it plain that her allusion was to Mr. Merton Densher. This was because Milly had at first a little air of not knowing whom she meant; and the girl really kept, as well, a certain control of herself while she remarked that the case was surprising, the chance one in a thousand. They knew him, both Maud and Miss Croy knew him, she gathered too, rather well, though indeed it wasn't on any show of intimacy that he had happened to be mentioned. It hadn't been—Susie made the point—she herself who brought him in: he had in fact not been brought in at all, but only referred to as a young journalist known to Mrs. Lowder and who had lately gone to their wonderful country—Mrs.

1. Originally marshland, this large area was reclaimed in the 1850s as a municipal park enjoyed for its artificial rock formations, alpine and sub-tropical gardens, and pathways.

Lowder always said "your wonderful country"—on behalf of his journal. But Mrs. Stringham had taken it up—with the tips of her fingers indeed; and that was the confession: she had, without meaning any harm, recognised Mr. Densher as an acquaintance of Milly's, though she had also pulled herself up before getting in too far. Mrs. Lowder had been struck, clearly—it wasn't too much to say; then she also, it had rather seemed, had pulled herself up; and there had been a little moment during which each might have been keeping something from the other. "Only," said Milly's informant, "I luckily remembered in time that I had nothing whatever to keep—which was much simpler and nicer. I don't know what Maud has, but there it is. She was interested, distinctly, in your knowing him—in his having met you over there with so little loss of time. But I ventured to tell her it hadn't been so long as to make you as yet great friends. I don't know if I was right."

Whatever time this explanation might have taken, there had been moments enough in the matter now—before the elder woman's conscience had done itself justice—to enable Milly to reply that although the fact in question doubtless had its importance she imagined they wouldn't find the importance overwhelming. It *was* odd that their one Englishman should so instantly fit; it wasn't, however, miraculous—they surely all had often seen how extraordinarily "small," as every one said, was the world. Undoubtedly also Susie had done just the plain thing in not letting his name pass. Why in the world should there be a mystery?—and what an immense one they would appear to have made if he should come back and find they had concealed their knowledge of him! "I don't know, Susie dear," the girl observed, "what you think I have to conceal."

"It doesn't matter, at a given moment," Mrs. Stringham returned, "what you know or don't know as to what I think; for you always find out the very next minute, and when you do find out, dearest, you never *really* care. Only," she presently asked, "have you heard of him from Miss Croy?"

"Heard of Mr. Densher? Never a word. We haven't mentioned him. Why should we?"

"That *you* haven't I understand; but that your friend hasn't," Susie opined, "may mean something."

"May mean what?"

"Well," Mrs. Stringham presently brought out, "I tell you all when I tell you that Maud asks me to suggest to you that it may perhaps be better for the present not to speak of him: not to speak of him to her niece, that is, unless she herself speaks to you first. But Maud thinks she won't."

Milly was ready to engage for anything; but in respect to the facts—as they so far possessed them—it all sounded a little complicated. "Is it because there's anything between them?"

"No—I gather not; but Maud's state of mind is precautionary. She's afraid of something. Or perhaps it would be more correct to say she's afraid of everything."

"'She's afraid, you mean," Milly asked, "of their—a—liking each other?"

Susie had an intense thought and then an effusion. "My dear child, we move in a labyrinth."

"Of course we do. That's just the fun of it!" said Milly with a strange gaiety. Then she added: "Don't tell me that—in this for instance—there are not abysses. I want abysses."

Her friend looked at her—it was not unfrequently the case—a little harder than the surface of the occasion seemed to require; and another person present at such times might have wondered to what inner thought of her own the good lady was trying to fit the speech. It was too much her disposition, no doubt, to treat her young companion's words as symptoms of an imputed malady. It was none the less, however, her highest law to be light when the girl was light. She knew how to be quaint with the new quaintness—the great Boston gift; it had been happily her note in the magazines; and Maud Lowder, to whom it was new indeed and who had never heard anything remotely like it, quite cherished her, as a social resource, by reason of it. It shouldn't therefore fail her now; with it in fact one might face most things. "Ah then let us hope we shall sound the depths—I'm prepared for the worst—of sorrow and sin! But she would like her niece—we're not ignorant of that, are we?—to marry Lord Mark. Hasn't she told you so?"

"Hasn't Mrs. Lowder told me?"

"No; hasn't Kate? It isn't, you know, that she doesn't know it."

Milly had, under her comrade's eyes, a minute of mute detachment. She had lived with Kate Croy for several days in a state of intimacy as deep as it had been sudden, and they had clearly, in talk, in many directions, proceeded to various extremities. Yet it now came over her as in a clear cold wave that there was a possible account of their relations in which the quantity her new friend had told her might have figured as small, as smallest, beside the quantity she hadn't. She couldn't say at any rate whether or no Kate had made the point that her aunt designed her for Lord Mark: it had only sufficiently come out—which had been, moreover, eminently guessable—that she was involved in her aunt's designs. Somehow, for Milly, brush it over nervously as she might and with whatever simplifying hand, this abrupt extrusion of Mr. Densher altered all proportions, had an effect on all values. It was fantastic of her to let it make a difference that she couldn't in the least have defined—

and she was at least, even during these instants, rather proud of being able to hide, on the spot, the difference it did make. Yet all the same the effect for her was, almost violently, of that gentleman's having been there—having been where she had stood till now in her simplicity—before her. It would have taken but another free moment to make her see abysses—since abysses were what she wanted—in the mere circumstance of his own silence, in New York, about his English friends. There had really been in New York little time for anything; but, had she liked, Milly could have made it out for herself that he had avoided the subject of Miss Croy and that Miss Croy was yet a subject it could never be natural to avoid. It was to be added at the same time that even if his silence had been a labyrinth—which was absurd in view of all the other things too he couldn't possibly have spoken of—this was exactly what must suit her, since it fell under the head of the plea she had just uttered to Susie. These things, however, came and went, and it set itself up between the companions, for the occasion, in the oddest way, both that their happening all to know Mr. Densher—except indeed that Susie didn't, but probably would—was a fact attached, in a world of rushing about, to one of the common orders of chance; and yet further that it was amusing—oh awfully amusing!—to be able fondly to hope that there was "something *in*" its having been left to crop up with such suddenness. There seemed somehow a possibility that the ground or, as it were, the air might in a manner have undergone some pleasing preparation; though the question of this possibility would probably, after all, have taken some threshing out. The truth, moreover—and there they were, already, our pair, talking about it, the "truth"!—hadn't in fact quite cropped out. This, obviously, in view of Mrs. Lowder's request to her old friend.

It was accordingly on Mrs. Lowder's recommendation that nothing should be said to Kate—it was on all this might cover in Aunt Maud that the idea of an interesting complication could best hope to perch; and when in fact, after the colloquy we have reported, Milly saw Kate again without mentioning any name, her silence succeeded in passing muster with her as the beginning of a new sort of fun. The sort was all the newer by its containing measurably a small element of anxiety: when she had gone in for fun before it had been with her hands a little more free. Yet it *was*, none the less, rather exciting to be conscious of a still sharper reason for interest in the handsome girl, as Kate continued even now pre-eminently to remain for her; and a reason—this was the great point—of which the young woman herself could have no suspicion. Twice over thus, for two or three hours together, Milly found herself seeing Kate, quite fixing her, in the light of the knowledge that it was a face on which Mr. Densher's eyes had more or less familiarly rested and which, by the same token, had looked, rather *more* beautifully than less, into his own. She pulled herself up indeed with the thought that it had inevitably looked, as beautifully as one would, into thousands of faces in which one might one's self never trace it; but just the odd result of the thought was to intensify for the girl that side of her friend which she had doubtless already been more prepared than she quite knew to think of as the "other," the not wholly calculable. It was fantastic, and Milly was aware of this; but the other side was what had, of a sudden, been turned straight toward her by the show of Mr. Densher's propinquity. She hadn't the excuse of knowing it for Kate's own, since nothing whatever as yet proved it particularly to be such. Never mind; it was with this other side now fully presented that Kate came and went, kissed her for greeting and for parting, talked, as usual, of everything but—as it had so abruptly become for Milly—*the* thing. Our young woman, it is true, would doubtless not have tasted so sharply a difference in this pair of occasions hadn't she been tasting so peculiarly her own possible betrayals. What happened was that afterwards, on separation, she wondered if the matter hadn't mainly been that she herself was so "other," so taken up with the unspoken; the strangest thing of all being, still subsequently, that when she asked herself how Kate could have failed to feel it she became conscious of being here on the edge of a great darkness. She should never know how Kate truly felt about anything such a one as Milly Theale should give her to feel. Kate would never—and not from ill will nor from duplicity, but from a sort of failure of common terms—reduce it to such a one's comprehension or put it within her convenience.

It was as such a one, therefore, that, for three or four days more, Milly watched Kate as just such another; and it was presently as such a one that she threw herself into their promised visit, at last achieved, to Chelsea, the quarter of the famous Carlyle,[1] the field of exercise of his ghost, his votaries, and the residence of "poor Marian," so often referred to and actually a somewhat incongruous spirit there. With our young woman's first view of poor Marian everything gave way but the sense of how in England, apparently, the social situation of sisters could be opposed, how common ground for a place in the world could quite fail them: a state of things sagely perceived to be involved in an hierarchical, an aristocratic order. Just whereabouts in the order Mrs. Lowder had established her niece was a question not wholly void as yet, no doubt, of ambiguity—though Milly was withal sure Lord Mark could exactly

1. Carlyle (1795–1881), as a social critic and philosopher of history, was preeminent among Victorian sages. Rebelling against the earlier mechanistic views of John Locke, Carlyle drew heavily upon German and French thought—Kant, Fichte, Goethe, Herder, Saint-Simon—to create an eclectic view of history and culture as organically evolutionary in its cyclical changes. His influence extended to Emerson and later nineteenth-century American thought.

have fixed the point if he would, fixing it at the same time for Aunt Maud herself; but it was clear Mrs. Condrip was, as might have been said, in quite another geography. She wouldn't have been to be found on the same social map, and it was as if her visitors had turned over page after page together before the final relief of their benevolent "Here!" The interval was bridged of course, but the bridge verily was needed, and the impression left Milly to wonder if, in the general connexion, it were of bridges or of intervals that the spirit not locally disciplined would find itself most conscious. It was as if at home, by contrast, there were neither—neither the difference itself, from position to position, nor, on either side, and particularly on one, the awfully good manner, the conscious sinking of a consciousness, that made up for it. The conscious sinking, at all events, and the awfully good manner, the difference, the bridge, the interval, the skipped leaves of the social atlas—these, it was to be confessed, had a little, for our young lady, in default of stouter stuff, to work themselves into the light literary legend—a mixed wandering echo of Trollope, of Thackeray, perhaps mostly of Dickens—under favour of which her pilgrimage had so much appealed. She could relate to Susie later on, late the same evening, that the legend, before she had done with it, had run clear, that the adored author of "The Newcomes," in fine, had been on the whole the note: the picture lacking thus more than she had hoped, or rather perhaps showing less than she had feared, a certain possibility of Pickwickian outline. She explained how she meant by this that Mrs. Condrip hadn't altogether proved another Mrs. Nickleby, nor even —for she might have proved almost anything, from the way poor worried Kate had spoken—a widowed and aggravated Mrs. Micawber.[2]

Mrs. Stringham, in the midnight conference, intimated rather yearningly that, however the event might have turned, the side of English life such experiences opened to Milly were just those she herself seemed "booked"—as they were all, roundabout her now, always saying—to miss: she had begun to have a little, for her fellow observer, these moments of fanciful reaction (reaction in which she was once more all Susan Shepherd) against the high sphere of colder conventions into which her overwhelming connexion with Maud Manningham had rapt her. Milly never lost sight for long of the Susan Shepherd side of her, and was always there to meet it when it came up and vaguely, tenderly, impatiently to pat it, abounding in the assurance that they would still provide for it. They had, however, to-night another matter in hand; which proved

2. Thackeray's *The Newcomers*, like Dickens's *Pickwick Papers, Nicholas Nickleby*, and *David Copperfield*, turns on the complications of love and money: love is unfulfilled and financial circumstances reduced until, according to the conventions of much Victorian fiction, the happy, comic resolution finds lovers secure romantically and parents economically comfortable.

to be presently, on the girl's part, in respect to her hour of Chelsea, the revelation that Mrs. Condrip, taking a few minutes when Kate was away with one of the children, in bed upstairs for some small complaint, had suddenly (without its being in the least "led up to") broken ground on the subject of Mr. Densher, mentioned him with impatience as a person in love with her sister. "She wished me, if I cared for Kate, to know," Milly said—"for it would be quite too dreadful, and one might do something."

Susie wondered. "Prevent anything coming of it? That's easily said. Do what?"

Milly had a dim smile. "I think that what she would like is that I should come a good deal to see *her* about it."

"And doesn't she suppose you've anything else to do?"

The girl had by this time clearly made it out. "Nothing but to admire and make much of her sister—whom she doesn't, however, herself in the least understand—and give up one's time, and everything else, to it." It struck the elder friend that she spoke with an almost unprecedented approach to sharpness; as if Mrs. Condrip had been rather indescribably disconcerting. Never yet so much as just of late had Mrs. Stringham seen her companion exalted, and by the very play of something within, into a vague golden air that left irritation below. That was the great thing with Milly—it was her characteristic poetry, or at least it was Susan Shepherd's. "But she made a point," the former continued, "of my keeping what she says from Kate. I'm not to mention that she has spoken."

"And why," Mrs. Stringham presently asked, "is Mr. Densher so dreadful?"

Milly had, she thought, a delay to answer—something that suggested a fuller talk with Mrs. Condrip than she inclined perhaps to report. "It isn't so much he himself." Then the girl spoke a little as for the romance of it; one could never tell, with her, where romance would come in. "It's the state of his fortunes."

"And is that very bad?"

"He has no 'private means,' and no prospect of any. He has no income, and no ability, according to Mrs. Condrip, to make one. He's as poor, she calls it, as 'poverty,' and she says she knows what that is."

Again Mrs. Stringham considered, and it presently produced something. "But isn't he brilliantly clever?"

Milly had also then an instant that was not quite fruitless. "I haven't the least idea."

To which, for the time, Susie only replied "Oh!"—though by the end of a minute she had followed it with a slightly musing "I see"; and that in turn with: "It's quite what Maud Lowder thinks."

"That he 'll never do anything?"

"No—quite the contrary: that he's exceptionally able."

"Oh yes; I know"—Milly had again, in reference to what her friend had already told her of this, her little tone of a moment before. "But Mrs. Condrip's own great point is that Aunt Maud herself won't hear of any such person. Mr. Densher, she holds—that's the way, at any rate, it was explained to me—won't ever be either a public man or a rich man. If he were public she'd be willing, as I understand, to help him; if he were rich—without being anything else—she'd do her best to swallow him. As it is she taboos him."

"In short," said Mrs. Stringham as with a private purpose, "she told you, the sister, all about it. But Mrs. Lowder likes him," she added.

"Mrs. Condrip didn't tell me that."

"Well, she does, all the same, my dear, extremely."

"Then there it is!" On which, with a drop and one of those sudden slightly sighing surrenders to a vague reflux and a general fatigue that had recently more than once marked themselves for her companion, Milly turned away. Yet the matter wasn't left so, that night, between them, albeit neither perhaps could afterwards have said which had first come back to it. Milly's own nearest approach at least, for a little, to doing so, was to remark that they appeared all—every one they saw—to think tremendously of money. This prompted in Susie a laugh, not untender, the innocent meaning of which was that it came, as a subject for indifference, money did, easier to some people than to others: she made the point in fairness, however, that you couldn't have told, by any too crude transparency of air, what place it held for Maud Manningham. She did her worldliness with grand proper silences—if it mightn't better be put perhaps that she did her detachment with grand occasional pushes. However Susie put it, in truth, she was really, in justice to herself, thinking of the difference, as favourites of fortune, between her old friend and her new. Aunt Maud sat somehow in the midst of her money, founded on it and surrounded by it, even if with a masterful high manner about it, her manner of looking, hard and bright, as if it weren't there. Milly, about hers, had no manner at all—which was possibly, from a point of view, a fault: she was at any rate far away on the edge of it, and you hadn't, as might be said, in order to get at her nature, to traverse, by whatever avenue, any piece of her property. It was clear, on the other hand, that Mrs. Lowder was keeping her wealth as for purposes, imaginations, ambitions, that would figure as large, as honourably unselfish, on the day they should take effect. She would impose her will, but her will would be only that a person or two shouldn't lose a benefit by not submitting if they could be made to submit. To Milly, as so much younger, such far views couldn't be imputed: there was nobody she was supposable as interested for. It was too soon, since she wasn't interested for herself. Even the richest woman, at her age, lacked motive, and Milly's motive doubtless had plenty of time to arrive. She was meanwhile beautiful, simple, sublime without it—whether missing it and vaguely reaching out for it or not; and with it, for that matter, in the event, would really be these things just as much. Only then she might very well have, like Aunt Maud, a manner. Such were the connexions, at all events, in which the colloquy of our two ladies freshly flickered up—in which it came round that the elder asked the younger if she had herself, in the afternoon, named Mr. Densher as an acquaintance.

"Oh no—I said nothing of having seen him. I remembered," the girl explained, "Mrs. Lowder's wish."

"But that," her friend observed after a moment, "was for silence to Kate."

"Yes—but Mrs. Condrip would immediately have told Kate."

"Why so?—since she must dislike to talk about him."

"Mrs. Condrip must?" Milly thought. "What she would like most is that her sister should be brought to think ill of him; and if anything she can tell her will help that—" But the girl dropped suddenly here, as if her companion would see.

Her companion's interest, however, was all for what she herself saw. "You mean she'll immediately speak?" Mrs. Stringham gathered that this was what Milly meant, but it left still a question. "How will it be against him that you know him?"

"Oh how can I say? It won't be so much one's knowing him as one's having kept it out of sight."

"Ah," said Mrs. Stringham as for comfort, "*you* haven't kept it out of sight. Isn't it much rather Miss Croy herself who has?"

"It isn't my acquaintance with him," Milly smiled, "that she has dissimulated."

"She has dissimulated only her own? Well then the responsibility's hers."

"Ah but," said the girl, not perhaps with marked consequence, "she has a right to do as she likes."

"Then so, my dear, have you!" smiled Susan Shepherd.

Milly looked at her as if she were almost venerably simple, but also as if this were what one loved her for. "We're not quarrelling about it, Kate and I, *yet*."

"I only meant," Mrs. Stringham explained, "that I don't see what Mrs. Condrip would gain."

"By her being able to tell Kate?" Milly thought. "I only meant that I don't see what I myself should gain."

"But it will have to come out—that he knows you both—some time."

Milly scarce assented. "Do you mean when he comes back?"

"He'll find you both here, and he can hardly be looked to, I take it, to 'cut' either of you for the sake of the other."

This placed the question at last on a basis more distinctly cheerful. "I might get at him somehow beforehand," the girl suggested; "I might give him what they call here the 'tip'—that he's not to know me when we meet. Or, better still, I mightn't be here at all."

"Do you want to run away from him?"

It was, oddly enough, an idea Milly seemed half to accept. "I don't know *what* I want to run away from!"

It dispelled, on the spot—something, to the elder woman's ear, in the sad, sweet sound of it—any ghost of any need of explaining. The sense was constant for her that their relation might have been afloat, like some island of the south, in a great warm sea that represented, for every conceivable chance, a margin, an outer sphere, of general emotion; and the effect of the occurrence of anything in particular was to make the sea submerge the island, the margin flood the text. The great wave now for a moment swept over. "I'll go anywhere else in the world you like."

But Milly came up through it. "Dear old Susie—how I do work you!"

"Oh this is nothing yet."

"No indeed—to what it will be."

"You're not—and it's vain to pretend," said dear old Susie, who had been taking her in, "as sound and strong as I insist on having you."

"Insist, insist—the more the better. But the day I *look* as sound and strong as that, you know," Milly went on—"on that day I shall be just sound and strong enough to take leave of you sweetly for ever. That's where one is," she continued thus agreeably to embroider, "when even one's *most* 'beaux moments'[3] aren't such as to qualify, so far as appearance goes, for anything gayer than a handsome cemetery. Since I've lived all these years as if I were dead, I shall die, no doubt, as if I were alive—which will happen to be as you want me. So, you see," she wound up, "you'll never really know where I am. Except indeed when I'm gone; and then you'll only know where I'm not."

"I'd die *for* you," said Susan Shepherd after a moment.

" 'Thanks awfully'! Then stay here for me."

"But we can't be in London for August, nor for many of all these next weeks."

"Then we'll go back."

Susie blenched. "Back to America?"

"No, abroad—to Switzerland, Italy, anywhere. I mean by your staying 'here' for me," Milly pursued, "your staying with me wher-

3. Beautiful moments.

ever I may be, even though we may neither of us know at the time where it is. No," she insisted, "I *don't* know where I am, and you never will, and it doesn't matter—and I dare say it's quite true," she broke off, "that everything will have to come out." Her friend would have felt of her that she joked about it now, hadn't her scale from grave to gay been a thing of such unnameable shades that her contrasts were never sharp. She made up for failures of gravity by failures of mirth; if she hadn't, that is, been at times as earnest as might have been liked, so she was certain not to be at other times as easy as she would like herself. "I must face the music. It isn't at any rate its 'coming out,'" she added; "it's that Mrs. Condrip would put the fact before her to his injury."

Her companion wondered. "But how to *his?*"

"Why if he pretends to love her—!"

"And does he only 'pretend'?"

"I mean if, trusted by her in strange countries, he forgets her so far as to make up to other people."

The amendment, however, brought Susie in, as with gaiety, for a comfortable end. "Did he make up, the false creature, to *you?*"

"No—but the question isn't of that. It's of what Kate might be made to believe."

"That, given the fact of his having evidently more or less followed up his acquaintance with you, to say nothing of your obvious weird charm, he must have been all ready if you had a little bit led him on?"

Milly neither accepted nor qualified this; she only said after a moment and as with a conscious excess of the pensive: "No, I don't think she'd quite wish to suggest that I made up to *him*; for that I should have had to do so would only bring out his constancy. All I mean is," she added—and now at last, as with a supreme impatience —"that her being able to make him out a little a person who could give cause for jealousy would evidently help her, since she's afraid of him, to do him in her sister's mind a useful ill turn."

Susan Shepherd perceived in this explanation such signs of an appetite for motive as would have sat gracefully even on one of her own New England heroines. It was seeing round several corners; but that was what New England heroines did, and it was moreover interesting for the moment to make out how many her young friend had actually undertaken to see round. Finally, too, weren't they braving the deeps? They got their amusement where they could. "Isn't it only," she asked, "rather probable she'd see that Kate's knowing him as (what's the pretty old word?) *volage*[4]—?"

"Well?" She hadn't filled out her idea, but neither, it seemed, could Milly.

4. Inconstant, fickle.

"Well, might but do what that often does—by all *our* blessed little laws and arrangements at least: excite Kate's own sentiment instead of depressing it."

The idea was bright, yet the girl but beautifully stared. "Kate's own sentiment? Oh she didn't speak of that. I don't think," she added as if she had been unconsciously giving a wrong impression, "I don't think Mrs. Condrip imagines *she's* in love."

It made Mrs. Stringham stare in turn. "Then what's her fear?"

"Well, only the fact of Mr. Densher's possibly himself keeping it up—the fear of some final result from *that*."

"Oh," said Susie, intellectually a little disconcerted—"she looks far ahead!"

At this, however, Milly threw off another of her sudden vague "sports." "No—it's only we who do."

"Well, don't let us be more interested for them than they are for themselves!"

"Certainly not"—the girl promptly assented. A certain interest nevertheless remained; she appeared to wish to be clear. "It wasn't of anything on Kate's own part she spoke."

"You mean she thinks her sister distinctly doesn't care for him?"

It was still as if, for an instant, Milly had to be sure of what she meant; but there it presently was. "If she did care Mrs. Condrip would have told me."

What Susan Shepherd seemed hereupon for a little to wonder was why then they had been talking so. "But did you ask her?"

"Ah no!"

"Oh!" said Susan Shepherd.

Milly, however, easily explained that she wouldn't have asked her for the world.

Book Fifth

I

Lord Mark looked at her to-day in particular as if to wring from her a confession that she had originally done him injustice; and he was entitled to whatever there might be in it of advantage or merit that his intention really in a manner took effect: he cared about something, after all, sufficiently to make her feel absurdly as if she *were* confessing—all the while it was quite the case that neither justice nor injustice was what had been in question between them. He had presented himself at the hotel, had found her and had found Susan Shepherd at home, had been "civil" to Susan—it was just that shade, and Susan's fancy had fondly caught it; and then had come again and missed them, and then had come and found them once more: besides letting them easily see that if it hadn't by this time been the end of everything—which they could feel in the exhausted air, that of the season at its last gasp—the places they might have liked to go to were such as they would have had only to mention. Their feeling was—or at any rate their modest general plea—that there was no place they would have liked to go to; there was only the sense of finding they liked, wherever they were, the place to which they had been brought. Such was highly the case as to their current consciousness—which could be indeed, in an equally eminent degree, but a matter of course; impressions this afternoon having by a happy turn of their wheel been gathered for them into a splendid cluster, an offering like an armful of the rarest flowers. They were in presence of the offering—they had been led up to it; and if it had been still their habit to look at each other across distances for increase of unanimity his hand would have been silently named between them as the hand applied to the wheel. He had administered the touch that, under light analysis, made the difference—the difference of their not having lost, as Susie on the spot and at the hour phrased it again and again, both for herself and for such others as the question might concern, so beautiful and interesting an experience; the difference also, in fact, of Mrs. Lowder's not having lost it either, though it was superficially with Mrs. Lowder they had come, and though it was further with that lady that our young woman was directly engaged during the half-hour or so of her most agreeably inward response to the scene.

The great historic house had, for Milly, beyond terrace and garden, as the centre of an almost extravagantly grand Watteau-composition,[1] a tone as of old gold kept "down" by the quality of the air, summer full-flushed but attuned to the general perfect taste. Much, by her measure, for the previous hour, appeared, in connexion with this revelation of it, to have happened to her—a quantity expressed in introductions of charming new people, in walks through halls of armour, of pictures, of cabinets, of tapestry, of tea-tables, in an assault of reminders that this largeness of style was the sign of *appointed* felicity. The largeness of style was the great containing vessel, while everything else, the pleasant personal affluence, the easy murmurous welcome, the honoured age of illustrious host and hostess, all at once so distinguished and so plain, so public and so shy, became but this or that element of the infusion. The elements melted together and seasoned the draught, the essence of which might have struck the girl as distilled into the small cup of iced coffee she had vaguely accepted from somebody, while a fuller flood somehow kept bearing her up—all the freshness of response of

1. Jean-Antoine Watteau (1684–1721), a French painter influenced by Titian and Veronese, whose special genre was *fêtes galantes*—festivals attended by exquisitely dressed young ladies and gentlemen in parks and gardens. His figures are characteristically small in relation to the canvas's space.

her young life, the freshness of the first and only prime. What had perhaps brought on just now a kind of climax was the fact of her appearing to make out, through Aunt Maud, what was really the matter. It couldn't be less than a climax for a poor shaky maiden to find it put to her of a sudden that she herself was the matter—for that was positively what, on Mrs. Lowder's part, it came to. Everything was great, of course, in great pictures, and it was doubtless precisely a part of the brilliant life—since the brilliant life, as one had faintly figured it, just *was* humanly led—that all impressions within its area partook of its brilliancy; still, letting that pass, it fairly stamped an hour as with the official seal for one to be able to take in so comfortably one's companion's broad blandness. "You must stay among us—you must stay; anything else is impossible and ridiculous; you don't know yet, no doubt—you can't; but you will soon enough: you can stay in *any* position." It had been as the murmurous consecration to follow the murmurous welcome; and even if it were but part of Aunt Maud's own spiritual ebriety—for the dear woman, one could see, was spiritually "keeping" the day—it served to Milly, then and afterwards, as a high-water mark of the imagination.

It was to be the end of the short parenthesis which had begun but the other day at Lancaster Gate with Lord Mark's informing her that she was a "success"—the key thus again struck; and though no distinct, no numbered revelations had crowded in, there had, as we have seen, been plenty of incident for the space and the time. There had been thrice as much, and all gratuitous and genial—if, in portions, not exactly hitherto *the* revelation—as three unprepared weeks could have been expected to produce. Mrs. Lowder had improvised a "rush" for them, but out of elements, as Milly was now a little more freely aware, somewhat roughly combined. Therefore if at this very instant she had her reasons for thinking of the parenthesis as about to close—reasons completely personal—she had on behalf of her companion a divination almost as deep. The parenthesis would close with this admirable picture, but the admirable picture still would show Aunt Maud as not absolutely sure either if she herself were destined to remain in it. What she was doing, Milly might even not have escaped seeming to see, was to talk herself into a sublimer serenity while she ostensibly talked Milly. It was fine, the girl fully felt, the way she did talk *her*, little as, at bottom, our young woman needed it or found other persuasions at fault. It was in particular during the minutes of her grateful absorption of iced coffee—qualified by a sharp doubt of her wisdom—that she most had in view Lord Mark's relation to her being there, or at least to the question of her being amused at it. It wouldn't have taken much by the end of five minutes quite to make her feel that this relation was charming. It might, once more, simply have been that everything, anything, was charming when one was so justly and completely charmed; but, frankly, she hadn't supposed anything so serenely sociable could settle itself between them as the friendly understanding that was at present somehow in the air. They were, many of them together, near the marquee that had been erected on a stretch of sward as a temple of refreshment and that happened to have the property—which was all to the good—of making Milly think of a "durbar";[2] her iced coffee had been a consequence of this connexion, through which, further, the bright company scattered about fell thoroughly into place. Certain of its members might have represented the contingent of "native princes"—familiar, but scarce the less grandly gregarious term!—and Lord Mark would have done for one of these even though for choice he but presented himself as a supervisory friend of the family. The Lancaster Gate family, he clearly intended, in which he included its American recruits, and included above all Kate Croy—a young person blessedly easy to take care of. She knew people, and people knew her, and she was the handsomest thing there—this last a declaration made by Milly, in a sort of soft midsummer madness, a straight skylark-flight of charity, to Aunt Maud.

Kate had for her new friend's eyes the extraordinary and attaching property of appearing at a given moment to show as a beautiful stranger, to cut her connexions and lose her identity, letting the imagination for the time make what it would of them—make her merely a person striking from afar, more and more pleasing as one watched, but who was above all a subject for curiosity. Nothing could have given her, as a party to a relation, a greater freshness than this sense, which sprang up at its own hours, of one's being as curious about her as if one hadn't known her. It had sprung up, we have gathered, as soon as Milly had seen her after hearing from Mrs. Stringham of her knowledge of Merton Densher; she had *looked* then other and, as Milly knew the real critical mind would call it, more objective; and our young woman had foreseen it of her on the spot that she would often look so again. It was exactly what she was doing this afternoon; and Milly, who had amusements of thought that were like the secrecies of a little girl playing with dolls when conventionally "too big," could almost settle to the game of what one would suppose her, how one would place her, if one didn't know her. She became thus, intermittently, a figure conditioned only by the great facts of aspect, a figure to be waited for, named and fitted. This was doubtless but a way of feeling that it was of her essence to be peculiarly what the occasion, whatever it might be, demanded when its demand was highest. There were probably

2. In India, the court of a native ruler; more generally, an official reception.

ways enough, on these lines, for such a consciousness; another of them would be for instance to say that she was made for great social uses. Milly wasn't wholly sure she herself knew what great social uses might be—unless, as a good example, to exert just that sort of glamour in just that sort of frame were one of them: she would have fallen back on knowing sufficiently that they existed at all events for her friend. It imputed a primness, all round, to be reduced but to saying, by way of a translation of one's amusement, that she was always so *right*—since that, too often, was what the *insupportables*[3] themselves were; yet it was, in overflow to Aunt Maud, what she had to content herself withal—save for the lame enhancement of saying she was lovely. It served, despite everything, the purpose, strengthened the bond that for the time held the two ladies together, distilled in short its drop of rose-colour for Mrs. Lowder's own view. That was really the view Milly had, for most of the rest of the occasion, to give herself to immediately taking in; but it didn't prevent the continued play of those swift cross-lights, odd beguilements of the mind, at which we have already glanced.

Mrs. Lowder herself found it enough simply to reply, in respect to Kate, that she was indeed a luxury to take about the world: she expressed no more surprise than that at her "rightness" to-day. Didn't it by this time sufficiently shine out that it was precisely *as* the very luxury she was proving that she had, from far back, been appraised and waited for? Crude elation, however, might be kept at bay, and the circumstance none the less made clear that they were all swimming together in the blue. It came back to Lord Mark again, as he seemed slowly to pass and repass and conveniently to linger before them; he was personally the note of the blue—like a suspended skein of silk within reach of the broiderer's hand. Aunt Maud's free-moving shuttle took a length of him at rhythmic intervals; and one of the accessory truths that flickered across to Milly was that he ever so consentingly knew he was being worked in. This was almost like an understanding with her at Mrs. Lowder's expense, which she would have none of; she wouldn't for the world have had him make any such point as that he wouldn't have launched them at Matcham—or whatever it was he *had* done—only for Aunt Maud's *beaux yeux*.[4] What he had done, it would have been guessable, was something he had for some time been desired in vain to do; and what they were all now profiting by was a change comparatively sudden, the cessation of hope delayed. What had caused the cessation easily showed itself as none of Milly's business; and she was luckily, for that matter, in no real danger of hearing from him directly that her individual weight had been felt in the scale. Why then indeed was it an effect of his diffused but subdued

3. Disagreeable, unbearable people.

4. Lovely eyes.

participation that he might absolutely have been saying to her "Yes, let the dear woman take her own tone"? "Since she's here she may stay," he might have been adding—"for whatever she can make of it. But you and I are different." Milly knew *she* was different in truth—his own difference was his own affair; but also she knew that after all, even at their distinctest, Lord Mark's "tips" in this line would be tacit. He practically placed her—it came round again to that—under no obligation whatever. It was a matter of equal ease, moreover, her letting Mrs. Lowder take a tone. She might have taken twenty—they would have spoiled nothing.

"You must stay on with us; you *can*, you know, in any position you like; any, any, *any*, my dear child"—and her emphasis went deep. "You must make your home with us; and it's really open to you to make the most beautiful one in the world. You mustn't be under a mistake—under any of any sort; and you must let us all think for you a little, take care of you and watch over you. Above all you must help me with Kate, and you must stay a little *for* her; nothing for a long time has happened to me so good as that you and she should have become friends. It's beautiful; it's great; it's everything. What makes it perfect is that it should have come about through our dear delightful Susie, restored to me, after so many years, by such a miracle. No—that's more charming to me than even your hitting it off with Kate. God has been good to one—positively; for I couldn't, at my age, have made a new friend—undertaken, I mean, out of whole cloth, the real thing. It's like changing one's bankers—after fifty: one doesn't do that. That's why Susie has been kept for me, as you seem to keep people in your wonderful country, in lavender and pink paper—coming back at last as straight as out of a fairy-tale and with you as an attendant fairy." Milly hereupon replied appreciatively that such a description of herself made her feel as if pink paper were her dress and lavender its trimming; but Aunt Maud wasn't to be deterred by a weak joke from keeping it up. The young person under her protection could feel besides that she kept it up in perfect sincerity. She was somehow at this hour a very happy woman, and a part of her happiness might precisely have been that her affections and her views were moving as never before in concert. Unquestionably she loved Susie; but she also loved Kate and loved Lord Mark, loved their funny old host and hostess, loved every one within range, down to the very servant who came to receive Milly's empty ice-plate—down, for that matter, to Milly herself, who was, while she talked, really conscious of the enveloping flap of a protective mantle, a shelter with the weight of an Eastern carpet. An Eastern carpet, for wishing-purposes of one's own, was a thing to be on rather than under; still, however, if the girl should fail of breath it wouldn't be, she could feel, by Mrs. Lowder's fault. One of the last things she was afterwards to recall of this was Aunt Maud's going on to say that she and Kate must stand together because together they could do anything. It was for Kate of course she was essentially planning; but the plan, enlarged and uplifted now, somehow required Milly's prosperity too for its full operation, just as Milly's prosperity at the same time involved Kate's. It was nebulous yet, it was slightly confused, but it was comprehensive and genial, and it made our young woman understand things Kate had said of her aunt's possibilities, as well as characterisations that had fallen from Susan Shepherd. One of the most frequent on the lips of the latter had been that dear Maud was a grand natural force.

II

A prime reason, we must add, why sundry impressions were not to be fully present to the girl till later on was that they yielded at this stage, with an effect of sharp supersession, to a detached quarter of an hour—her only one—with Lord Mark. "Have you seen the picture in the house, the beautiful one that's so like you?"—he was asking that as he stood before her; having come up at last with his smooth intimation that any wire he had pulled and yet wanted not to remind her of wasn't quite a reason for his having no joy at all.

"I've been through rooms and I've seen pictures. But if I'm 'like' anything so beautiful as most of them seemed to me—!" It needed in short for Milly some evidence which he only wanted to supply. She was the image of the wonderful Bronzino,[1] which she must have a look at on every ground. He had thus called her off and led her away; the more easily that the house within was above all what had already drawn round her its mystic circle. Their progress meanwhile was not of the straightest; it was an advance, without haste, through innumerable natural pauses and soft concussions, determined for the most part by the appearance before them of ladies and gentlemen, singly, in couples, in clusters, who brought them to a stand with an inveterate "I say, Mark." What they said she never quite made out; it was their all so domestically knowing him, and his knowing them, that mainly struck her, while her impression, for the rest, was but of fellow strollers more vaguely afloat than themselves, supernumeraries mostly a little battered, whether as jaunty males or as ostensibly elegant women. They might have been moving a good deal by a momentum that had begun far back, but they were still

1. Angelo Bronzino (1503–72), a foremost Venetian portraitist whose paintings are said to record the social atmosphere and ceremony of the Medicean court of the mid-sixteenth century. The portrait is not imaginary (as is Lord Mark's estate, Matcham) but a painting of Lucrezia Panciatichi (ca. 1540) in the Uffizi, Florence. The typical aloofness of the figure is in striking contrast to the unusual background, a darkened sculpture niche looming above her. (A reproduction of the portrait appears on the cover of this book.)

brave and personable, still warranted for continuance as long again, and they gave her, in especial collectively, a sense of pleasant voices, pleasanter than those of actors, of friendly empty words and kind lingering eyes that took somehow pardonable liberties. The lingering eyes looked her over, the lingering eyes were what went, in almost confessed simplicity, with the pointless "I say, Mark"; and what was really most flagrant of all was that, as a pleasant matter of course, if she didn't mind, he seemed to suggest their letting people, poor dear things, have the benefit of her.

The odd part was that he made her herself believe, for amusement, in the benefit, measured by him in mere manner—for wonderful, of a truth, was, as a means of expression, his slightness of emphasis—that her present good nature conferred. It was, as she could easily see, a mild common carnival of good nature—a mass of London people together, of sorts and sorts, but who mainly knew each other and who, in their way, did, no doubt, confess to curiosity. It had gone round that she was there; questions about her would be passing; the easiest thing was to run the gauntlet with *him*—just as the easiest thing was in fact to trust him generally. Couldn't she know for herself, passively, how little harm they meant her?—to that extent that it made no difference whether or not he introduced them. The strangest thing of all for Milly was perhaps the uplifted assurance and indifference with which she could simply give back the particular bland stare that appeared in such cases to mark civilisation at its highest. It was so little her fault, this oddity of what had "gone round" about her, that to accept it without question might be as good a way as another of feeling life. It was inevitable to supply the probable description—that of the awfully rich young American who was so queer to behold, but nice, by all accounts, to know; and she had really but one instant of speculation as to fables or fantasies perchance originally launched. She asked herself once only if Susie could, inconceivably, have been blatant about her; for the question, on the spot, was really blown away for ever. She knew in fact on the spot and with sharpness just why she had "elected" Susan Shepherd: she had had from the first hour the conviction of her being precisely the person in the world least possibly a trumpeter. So it wasn't their fault, it wasn't their fault, and anything might happen that would, and everything now again melted together, and kind eyes were always kind eyes—if it were never to be worse than that! She got with her companion into the house; they brushed, beneficently, past all their accidents. The Bronzino was, it appeared, deep within, and the long afternoon light lingered for them on patches of old colour and waylaid them, as they went, in nooks and opening vistas.

It was all the while for Milly as if Lord Mark had really had something other than this spoken pretext in view; as if there were something he wanted to say to her and were only—consciously yet not awkwardly, just delicately—hanging fire. At the same time it was as if the thing had practically been said by the moment they came in sight of the picture; since what it appeared to amount to was "Do let a fellow who isn't a fool take care of you a little." The thing somehow, with the aid of the Bronzino, was done; it hadn't seemed to matter to her before if he were a fool or no; but now, just where they were, she liked his not being; and it was all more-over none the worse for coming back to something of the same sound as Mrs. Lowder's so recent reminder. She too wished to take care of her—and wasn't it, *à peu près,*[2] what all the people with the kind eyes were wishing? Once more things melted together—the beauty and the history and the facility and the splendid mid-summer glow: it was a sort of magnificent maximum, the pink dawn of an apotheosis coming so curiously soon. What in fact befell was that, as she afterwards made out, it was Lord Mark who said nothing in particular—it was she herself who said all. She couldn't help that—it came; and the reason it came was that she found herself, for the first moment, looking at the mysterious portrait through tears. Perhaps it was her tears that made it just then so strange and fair—as wonderful as he had said: the face of a young woman, all splendidly drawn, down to the hands, and splendidly dressed; a face almost livid in hue, yet handsome in sadness and crowned with a mass of hair, rolled back and high, that must, before fading with time, have had a family resemblance to her own. The lady in question, at all events, with her slightly Michael-angelesque squareness, her eyes of other days, her full lips, her long neck, her recorded jewels, her brocaded and wasted reds, was a very great personage—only unaccompanied by a joy. And she was dead, dead, dead. Milly recognised her exactly in words that had nothing to do with her. "I shall never be better than this."

He smiled for her at the portrait. "Than she? You'd scarce need to be better, for surely that's well enough. But you *are*, one feels, as it happens, better; because, splendid as she is, one doubts if she was good."

He hadn't understood. She was before the picture, but she had turned to him, and she didn't care if for the minute he noticed her tears. It was probably as good a moment as she should ever have with him. It was perhaps as good a moment as she should have with any one, or have in any connexion whatever. "I mean that everything this afternoon has been too beautiful, and that perhaps everything together will never be so right again. I'm very glad therefore you've been a part of it."

2. More or less, just about.

Though he still didn't understand her he was as nice as if he had; he didn't ask for insistence, and that was just a part of his looking after her. He simply protected her now from herself, and there was a world of practice in it. "Oh we must talk about these things!"

Ah they had already done that, she knew, as much as she ever would; and she was shaking her head at her pale sister the next moment with a world, on her side, of slowness. "I wish I could see the resemblance. Of course her complexion's green," she laughed; "but mine's several shades greener."

"It's down to the very hands," said Lord Mark.

"Her hands are large," Milly went on, "but mine are larger. Mine are huge."

"Oh you go her, all round, 'one better'—which is just what I said. But you're a pair. You must surely catch it," he added as if it were important to his character as a serious man not to appear to have invented his plea.

"I don't know—one never knows one's self. It's a funny fancy, and I don't imagine it would have occurred—"

"I see it *has* occurred"—he had already taken her up. She had her back, as she faced the picture, to one of the doors of the room, which was open, and on her turning as he spoke she saw that they were in the presence of three other persons, also, as appeared, interested enquirers. Kate Croy was one of these; Lord Mark had just become aware of her, and she, all arrested, had immediately seen, and made the best of it, that she was far from being first in the field. She had brought a lady and a gentleman to whom she wished to show what Lord Mark was showing Milly, and he took her straightway as a re-enforcement. Kate herself had spoken, however, before he had had time to tell her so.

"*You* had noticed too?"—she smiled at him without looking at Milly. "Then I'm not original—which one always hopes one has been. But the likeness is so great." And now she looked at Milly—for whom again it was, all round indeed, kind, kind eyes. "Yes, there you are, my dear, if you want to know. And you're superb." She took now but a glance at the picture, though it was enough to make her question to her friends not too straight. "Isn't she superb?"

"I brought Miss Theale," Lord Mark explained to the latter, "quite off my own bat."

"I wanted Lady Aldershaw," Kate continued to Milly, "to see for herself."

"Les grands esprits se rencontrent!"[3] laughed her attendant gen-

3. "Great spirits seek one another out!"

tleman, a high but slightly stooping, shambling and wavering person who represented urbanity by the liberal aid of certain prominent front teeth and whom Milly vaguely took for some sort of great man.

Lady Aldershaw meanwhile looked at Milly quite as if Milly had been the Bronzino and the Bronzino only Milly. "Superb, superb. Of course I had noticed you. It *is* wonderful," she went on with her back to the picture, but with some other eagerness which Milly felt gathering, felt directing her motions now. It was enough—they were introduced, and she was saying "I wonder if you could give us the pleasure of coming—" She wasn't fresh, for she wasn't young, even though she denied at every pore that she was old; but she was vivid and much bejewelled for the midsummer daylight; and she was all in the palest pinks and blues. She didn't think, at this pass, that she could "come" anywhere—Milly didn't; and she already knew that somehow Lord Mark was saving her from the question. He had interposed, taking the words out of the lady's mouth and not caring at all if the lady minded. That was clearly the right way to treat her—at least for him; as she had only dropped, smiling, and then turned away with him. She had been dealt with—it would have done an enemy good. The gentleman still stood, a little helpless, addressing himself to the intention of urbanity as if it were a large loud whistle; he had been sighing sympathy, in his way, while the lady made her overture; and Milly had in this light soon arrived at their identity. They were Lord and Lady Aldershaw, and the wife was the clever one. A minute or two later the situation had changed, and she knew it afterwards to have been by the subtle operation of Kate. She was herself saying that she was afraid she must go now if Susie could be found; but she was sitting down on the nearest seat to say it. The prospect, through opened doors, stretched before her into other rooms, down the vista of which Lord Mark was strolling with Lady Aldershaw, who, close to him and much intent, seemed to show from behind as peculiarly expert. Lord Aldershaw, for his part, had been left in the middle of the room, while Kate, with her back to him, was standing before her with much sweetness of manner. The sweetness was all for *her*; she had the sense of the poor gentleman's having somehow been handled as Lord Mark had handled his wife. He dangled there, he shambled a little; then he bethought himself of the Bronzino, before which, with his eye-glass, he hovered. It drew from him an odd vague sound, not wholly distinct from a grunt, and a "Humph—most remarkable!" which lighted Kate's face with amusement. The next moment he had creaked away over polished floors after the others and Milly was feeling as if *she* had been rude. But Lord

Aldershaw was in every way a detail and Kate was saying to her that she hoped she wasn't ill.

Thus it was that, aloft there in the great gilded historic chamber and the presence of the pale personage on the wall, whose eyes all the while seemed engaged with her own, she found herself suddenly sunk in something quite intimate and humble and to which these grandeurs were strange enough witnesses. It had come up, in the form in which she had had to accept it, all suddenly, and nothing about it, at the same time, was more marked than that she had in a manner plunged into it to escape from something else. Something else, from her first vision of her friend's appearance three minutes before, had been present to her even through the call made by the others on her attention; something that was perversely *there*, she was more and more uncomfortably finding, at least for the first moments and by some spring of its own, with every renewal of their meeting. "Is it the way she looks to *him?*" she asked herself—the perversity being how she kept in remembrance that Kate was known to him. It wasn't a fault in Kate—nor in him assuredly; and she had a horror, being generous and tender, of treating either of them as if it had been. To Densher himself she couldn't make it up—he was too far away; but her secondary impulse was to make it up to Kate. She did so now with a strange soft energy—the impulse immediately acting. "Will you render me to-morrow a great service?"

"Any service, dear child, in the world."

"But it's a secret one—nobody must know. I must be wicked and false about it."

"Then I'm your woman," Kate smiled, "for that's the kind of thing I love. *Do* let us do something bad. You're impossibly without sin, you know."

Milly's eyes, on this, remained a little with their companion's. "Ah I shan't perhaps come up to your idea. It's only to deceive Susan Shepherd."

"Oh!" said Kate as if this were indeed mild.

"But thoroughly—as thoroughly as I can."

"And for cheating," Kate asked, "my powers will contribute? Well, I'll do my best for you." In accordance with which it was presently settled between them that Milly should have the aid and comfort of her presence for a visit to Sir Luke Strett. Kate had needed a minute for enlightenment, and it was quite grand for her comrade that this name should have said nothing to her. To Milly herself it had for some days been secretly saying much. The personage in question was, as she explained, the greatest of medical lights—if she had got hold, as she believed (and she had used to this end the wisdom of the serpent) of the right, the special man. She had written to him three days before, and he had named her an hour, eleven-twenty; only it had come to her on the eve that she couldn't go alone. Her maid on the other hand wasn't good enough, and Susie was too good. Kate had listened above all with high indulgence. "And I'm betwixt and between, happy thought! Too good for what?"

Milly thought. "Why to be worried if it's nothing. And to be still more worried—I mean before she need be—if it isn't."

Kate fixed her with deep eyes. "What in the world is the matter with you?" It had inevitably a sound of impatience, as if it had been a challenge really to produce something; so that Milly felt her for the moment only as a much older person, standing above her a little, doubting the imagined ailments, suspecting the easy complaints, of ignorant youth. It somewhat checked her, further, that the matter with her was what exactly as yet she wanted knowledge about; and she immediately declared, for conciliation, that if she were merely fanciful Kate would see her put to shame. Kate vividly uttered, in return, the hope that, since she could come out and be so charming, could so universally dazzle and interest, she wasn't all the while in distress or in anxiety—didn't believe herself to be in any degree seriously menaced. "Well, I want to make out—to make out!" was all that this consistently produced. To which Kate made clear answer: "Ah then let us by all means!"

"I thought," Milly said, "you'd like to help me. But I must ask you, please, for the promise of absolute silence."

"And how, if you *are* ill, can your friends remain in ignorance?"

"Well, if I am it must of course finally come out. But I can go for a long time." Milly spoke with her eyes again on her painted sister's—almost as if under their suggestion. She still sat there before Kate, yet not without a light in her face. "That will be one of my advantages. I think I could die without its being noticed."

"You're an extraordinary young woman," her friend, visibly held by her, declared at last. "What a remarkable time to talk of such things!"

"Well, we won't talk, precisely"—Milly got herself together again. "I only wanted to make sure of you."

"Here in the midst of—!" But Kate could only sigh for wonder —almost visibly too for pity.

It made a moment during which her companion waited on her word; partly as if from a yearning, shy but deep, to have her case put to her just as Kate was struck by it; partly as if the hint of pity were already giving a sense to her whimsical "shot," with Lord Mark, at Mrs. Lowder's first dinner. Exactly this—the handsome girl's compassionate manner, her friendly descent from her own strength—was what she had then foretold. She took Kate up as if positively for the deeper taste of it. "Here in the midst of what?"

"Of everything. There's nothing you can't have. There's nothing you can't do."

"So Mrs. Lowder tells me."

It just kept Kate's eyes fixed as possibly for more of that; then, however, without waiting, she went on. "We all adore you."

"You're wonderful—you dear things!" Milly laughed.

"No, it's *you.*" And Kate seemed struck with the real interest of it. "In three weeks!"

Milly kept it up. "Never were people on such terms! All the more reason," she added, "that I shouldn't needlessly torment you."

"But me? what becomes of *me?*" said Kate.

"Well, you"—Milly thought—"if there's anything to bear you'll bear it."

"But I *won't* bear it!" said Kate Croy.

"Oh yes you will: all the same! You'll pity me awfully, but you'll help me very much. And I absolutely trust you. So there we are." There they were then, since Kate had so to take it; but there, Milly felt, she herself in particular was; for it was just the point at which she had wished to arrive. She had wanted to prove to herself that she didn't horribly blame her friend for any reserve; and what better proof could there be than this quite special confidence? If she desired to show Kate that she really believed Kate liked her, how could she show it more than by asking her help?

III

What it really came to, on the morrow, this first time—the time Kate went with her—was that the great man had, a little, to excuse himself; had, by a rare accident—for he kept his consulting-hours in general rigorously free—but ten minutes to give her; ten mere minutes which he yet placed at her service in a manner that she admired still more than she could meet it: so crystal-clean the great empty cup of attention that he set between them on the table. He was presently to jump into his carriage, but he promptly made the point that he must see her again, see her within a day or two; and he named for her at once another hour—easing her off beautifully too even then in respect to her possibly failing of justice to her errand. The minutes affected her in fact as ebbing more swiftly than her little army of items could muster, and they would probably have gone without her doing much more than secure another hearing, hadn't it been for her sense, at the last, that she had gained above all an impression. The impression—all the sharp growth of the final few moments—was neither more nor less than that she might make, of a sudden, in quite another world, another straight friend, and a friend who would moreover be, wonderfully, the most appointed, the most thoroughly adjusted of the whole collection, inasmuch as he would somehow wear the character scientifically, ponderably, proveably—not just loosely and sociably. Literally, furthermore, it wouldn't really depend on herself, Sir Luke Strett's friendship, in the least: perhaps what made her most stammer and pant was its thus queerly coming over her that she might find she had interested him even beyond her intention, find she was in fact launched in some current that would lose itself in the sea of science. At the same time that she struggled, however, she also surrendered; there was a moment at which she almost dropped the form of stating, of explaining, and threw herself, without violence, only with a supreme pointless quaver that had turned the next instant to an intensity of interrogative stillness, upon his general good will. His large settled face, though firm, was not, as she had thought at first, hard; he looked, in the oddest manner, to her fancy, half like a general and half like a bishop, and she was soon sure that, within some such handsome range, what it would show her would be what was good, what was best for her. She had established, in other words, in this time-saving way, a relation with it; and the relation was the special trophy that, for the hour, she bore off. It was like an absolute possession, a new resource altogether, something done up in the softest silk and tucked away under the arm of memory. She hadn't had it when she went in, and she had it when she came out; she had it there under her cloak, but dissimulated, invisibly carried, when smiling, smiling, she again faced Kate Croy. That young lady had of course awaited her in another room, where, as the great man was to absent himself, no one else was in attendance; and she rose for her with such a face of sympathy as might have graced the vestibule of a dentist. "Is it out?" she seemed to ask as if it had been a question of a tooth; and Milly indeed kept her in no suspense at all.

"He's a dear. I'm to come again."

"But what does he say?"

Milly was almost gay. "That I'm not to worry about anything in the world, and that if I'll be a good girl and do exactly what he tells me he'll take care of me for ever and ever."

Kate wondered as if things scarce fitted. "But does he allow then that you're ill?"

"I don't know what he allows, and I don't care. I *shall* know, and whatever it is it will be enough. He knows all about me, and I like it. I don't hate it a bit."

Still, however, Kate stared. "But could he, in so few minutes, ask you enough—?"

"He asked me scarcely anything—he doesn't need to do anything so stupid," Milly said. "He can tell. He knows," she repeated;

"and when I go back—for he'll have thought me over a little—it will be all right."

Kate after a moment made the best of this. "Then when are we to come?"

It just pulled her friend up, for even while they talked—at least it was one of the reasons—she stood there suddenly, irrelevantly, in the light of her *other* identity, the identity she would have for Mr. Densher. This was always, from one instant to another, an incalculable light, which, though it might go off faster than it came on, necessarily disturbed. It sprang, with a perversity all its own, from the fact that, with the lapse of hours and days, the chances themselves that made for his being named continued so oddly to fail. There were twenty, there were fifty, but none of them turned up. This in particular was of course not a juncture at which the least of them would naturally be present; but it would make, none the less, Milly saw, another day practically all stamped with avoidance. She saw in a quick glimmer, and with it all Kate's unconsciousness; and then she shook off the obsession. But it had lasted long enough to qualify her response. No, she had shown Kate how she trusted her; and that, for loyalty, would somehow do. "Oh, dear thing, now that the ice is broken I shan't trouble *you* again."

"You'll come alone?"

"Without a scruple. Only I shall ask you, please, for your absolute discretion still."

Outside, at a distance from the door, on the wide pavement of the great contiguous square, they had to wait again while their carriage, which Milly had kept, completed a further turn of exercise, engaged in by the coachman for reasons of his own. The footman was there and had indicated that he was making the circuit; so Kate went on while they stood. "But don't you ask a good deal, darling, in proportion to what you give?"

This pulled Milly up still shorter—so short in fact that she yielded as soon as she had taken it in. But she continued to smile. "I see. Then you *can* tell."

"I don't want to 'tell,' " said Kate. "I'll be as silent as the tomb if I can only have the truth from you. All I want is that you shouldn't keep from me how you find out that you really are."

"Well then I won't ever. But you see for yourself," Milly went on, "how I really am. I'm satisfied. I'm happy."

Kate looked at her long. "I believe you like it. The way things turn out for you—!"

Milly met her look now without a thought of anything but the spoken. She had ceased to be Mr. Densher's image; she stood for nothing but herself, and she was none the less fine. Still, still, what had passed was a fair bargain and it would do. "Of course I like it. I feel—I can't otherwise describe it—as if I had been on my knees to the priest. I've confessed and I've been absolved. It has been lifted off."

Kate's eyes never quitted her. "He must have liked *you.*"

"Oh—doctors!" Milly said. "But I hope," she added, "he didn't like me too much." Then as if to escape a little from her friend's deeper sounding, or as impatient for the carriage, not yet in sight, her eyes, turning away, took in the great stale square. As its staleness, however, was but that of London fairly fatigued, the late hot London with its dance all danced and its story all told, the air seemed a thing of blurred pictures and mixed echoes, and an impression met the sense—an impression that broke the next moment through the girl's tightened lips. "Oh it's a beautiful big world, and every one, yes, every one—!" It presently brought her back to Kate, and she hoped she didn't actually look as much as if she were crying as she must have looked to Lord Mark among the portraits at Matcham.

Kate at all events understood. "Every one wants to be so nice?"

"So nice," said the grateful Milly.

"Oh," Kate laughed, "we'll pull you through! And won't you now bring Mrs. Stringham?"

But Milly after an instant was again clear about that. "Not till I've seen him once more."

She was to have found this preference, two days later, abundantly justified; and yet when, in prompt accordance with what had passed between them, she reappeared before her distinguished friend—that character having for him in the interval built itself up still higher—the first thing he asked her was whether she had been accompanied. She told him, on this, straightway, everything; completely free at present from her first embarrassment, disposed even—as she felt she might become—to undue volubility, and conscious moreover of no alarm from his thus perhaps wishing she had not come alone. It was exactly as if, in the forty-eight hours that had passed, her acquaintance with him had somehow increased and his own knowledge in particular received mysterious additions. They had been together, before, scarce ten minutes; but the relation, the one the ten minutes had so beautifully created, was there to take straight up: and this not, on his own part, from mere professional heartiness, mere bedside manner, which she would have disliked—much rather from a quiet pleasant air in him of having positively asked about her, asked here and asked there and found out. Of course he couldn't in the least have asked, or have wanted to; there was no source of information to his hand, and he had really needed none: he had found out simply by his genius—and found out, she meant, literally everything. Now she knew not only that she didn't dislike this—the state of being found out about; but that on the contrary it was truly what she had come for, and that for the time at least it would give her something firm to stand on. She struck herself as aware, aware as she had never been, of really not having had from the beginning anything firm. It would be strange for the firmness to come, after all, from her learning in these agreeable conditions that she was in some way doomed; but above all it would prove how little she had hitherto had to hold her up. If she was now to be held up by the mere process—since that was perhaps on the cards—of being let down, this would only testify in turn to her queer little history. *That* sense of loosely rattling had been no process at all; and it was ridiculously true that her thus sitting there to see her life put into the scales represented her first approach to the taste of orderly living. Such was Milly's romantic version—that her life, especially by the fact of this second interview, *was* put into the scales; and just the best part of the relation established might have been, for that matter, that the great grave charming man knew, had known at once, that it was romantic, and in that measure allowed for it. Her only doubt, her only fear, was whether he perhaps wouldn't even take advantage of her being a little romantic to treat her as romantic altogether. This doubtless was her danger with him; but she should see, and dangers in general meanwhile dropped and dropped.

The very place, at the end of a few minutes, the commodious "handsome" room, far back in the fine old house, soundless from position, somewhat sallow with years of celebrity, somewhat sombre even at midsummer—the very place put on for her a look of custom and use, squared itself solidly round her as with promises and certainties. She had come forth to see the world, and this then was to be the world's light, the rich dusk of a London "back," these the world's walls, those the world's curtains and carpet. She should be intimate with the great bronze clock and mantel-ornaments, conspicuously presented in gratitude and long ago; she should be as one of the circle of eminent contemporaries, photographed, engraved, signatured, and in particular framed and glazed, who made up the rest of the decoration, and made up as well so much of the human comfort; and while she thought of all the clean truths, unfringed, unfingered, that the listening stillness, strained into pauses and waits, would again and again, for years, have kept distinct, she also wondered what *she* would eventually decide upon to present in gratitude. She would give something better at least than the brawny Victorian bronzes. This was precisely an instance of what she felt he knew of her before he had done with her: that she was secretly romancing at that rate, in the midst of so much else that was more urgent, all over the place. So much for her secrets with him, none of which really required to be phrased. It would have been thoroughly a secret for her from any one else that without a dear lady she had picked up just before coming over she wouldn't have a decently near connexion of any sort, for such an appeal as she was making, to put forward: no one in the least, as it were, to produce for respectability. But *his* seeing it she didn't mind a scrap, and not a scrap either his knowing how she had left the dear lady in the dark. She had come alone, putting her friend off with a fraud: giving a pretext of shops, of a whim, of she didn't know what—the amusement of being for once in the streets by herself. The streets by herself were new to her—she had always had in them a companion or a maid; and he was never to believe moreover that she couldn't take full in the face anything he might have to say. He was softly amused at her account of her courage; though he yet showed it somehow without soothing her too grossly. Still, he did want to know whom she had. Hadn't there been a lady with her on Wednesday?

"Yes—a different one. Not the one who's travelling with me. I've told *her*."

Distinctly he was amused, and it added to his air—the greatest charm of all—of giving her lots of time. "You've told her what?"

"Well," said Milly, "that I visit you in secret."

"And how many persons will she tell?"

"Oh she's devoted. Not one."

"Well, if she's devoted doesn't that make another friend for you?"

It didn't take much computation, but she nevertheless had to think a moment, conscious as she was that he distinctly *would* want to fill out his notion of her—even a little, as it were, to warm the air for her. That however—and better early than late—he must accept as of no use; and she herself felt for an instant quite a competent certainty on the subject of any such warming. The air, for Milly Theale, was, from the very nature of the case, destined never to rid itself of a considerable chill. This she could tell him with authority, if she could tell him nothing else; and she seemed to see now, in short, that it would importantly simplify. "Yes, it makes another; but they all together wouldn't make—well, I don't know what to call it but the difference. I mean when one *is*—really alone. I've never seen anything like the kindness." She pulled up a minute while he waited—waited again as if with his reasons for letting her, for almost making her, talk. What she herself wanted was not, for the third time, to cry, as it were, in public. She *had* never seen anything like the kindness, and she wished to do it justice; but she knew what she was about, and justice was not wronged by her being able presently to stick to her point. "Only one's situation is what it is. It's *me* it concerns. The rest is delightful and useless. Nobody can really help. That's why I'm by myself to-day. I *want* to be—in spite of Miss Croy, who came with me last. If you can help, so much the better—and also of course if one can a little one's self. Except for that—you and me doing our best—I like you to see me just as I am. Yes, I like it—and I don't exaggerate. Shouldn't one, at the start, show the worst—so that anything after that may be better? It wouldn't make any real difference—it *won't* make any, anything that may happen won't—to any one. Therefore I feel myself, this way, with you, just as I am; and—if you do in the least care to know—it quite positively bears me up."

She put it as to his caring to know, because his manner seemed to give her all her chance, and the impression was there for her to take. It was strange and deep for her, this impression, and she did accordingly take it straight home. It showed him—showed him in spite of himself—as allowing, somewhere far within, things comparatively remote, things in fact quite, as she would have said, outside, delicately to weigh with him; showed him as interested on her behalf in other questions beside the question of what was the matter with her. She accepted such an interest as regular in the highest type of scientific mind—his own *being* the highest, magnificently—because otherwise obviously it wouldn't be there; but she could at the same time take it as a direct source of light upon herself, even though that might present her a little as pretending to equal him. Wanting to know more about a patient than how a patient was constructed or deranged couldn't be, even on the part of the greatest of doctors, anything but some form or other of the desire to let the patient down easily. When that was the case the reason, in turn, could only be, too manifestly, pity; and when pity held up its telltale face like a head on a pike, in a French revolution, bobbing before a window, what was the inference but that the patient was bad? He might say what he would now—she would always have seen the head at the window; and in fact from this moment she only wanted him to say what he would. He might say it too with the greater ease to himself as there wasn't one of her divinations that—*as* her own—he would in any way put himself out for. Finally, if he was making her talk she *was* talking, and what it could at any rate come to for him was that she wasn't afraid. If he wanted to do the dearest thing in the world for her he would show her he believed she wasn't; which undertaking of hers—not to have misled him—was what she counted at the moment as her presumptuous little hint to him that she was as good as himself. It put forward the bold idea that he could really *be* misled; and there actually passed between them for some seconds a sign, a sign of the eyes only, that they knew together where they were. This made, in their brown old temple of truth, its momentary flicker; then what followed it was that he had her, all the same, in his pocket; and the whole thing wound up for that consummation with his kind dim smile. Such kindness was wonderful with such dimness; but brightness—that even of sharp steel—was of course for the other side of the business, and it would all come in for her to one tune or another. "Do you mean," he asked, "that you've no relations at all?—not a parent, not a sister, not even a cousin nor an aunt?"

She shook her head as with the easy habit of an interviewed heroine or a freak of nature at a show. "Nobody whatever"—but the last thing she had come for was to be dreary about it. "I'm a survivor—a survivor of a general wreck. You see," she added, "how that's to be taken into account—that every one else *has* gone. When I was ten years old there were, with my father and my mother, six of us. I'm all that's left. But they died," she went on, to be fair all round, "of different things. Still, there it is. And, as I told you before, I'm American. Not that I mean that makes me worse. However, you'll probably know what it makes me."

"Yes"—he even showed amusement for it. "I know perfectly what it makes you. It makes you, to begin with, a capital case."

She sighed, though gratefully, as if again before the social scene. "Ah there you are!"

"Oh no; there 'we' aren't at all! There I am only—but as much as you like. I've no end of American friends: there *they* are, if you please, and it's a fact that you couldn't very well be in a better place than in their company. It puts you with plenty of others—and that isn't pure solitude." Then he pursued: "I'm sure you've an excellent spirit; but don't try to bear more things than you need." Which after an instant he further explained. "Hard things have come to you in youth, but you mustn't think life will be for you all hard things. You've the right to be happy. You must make up your mind to it. You must accept any form in which happiness may come."

"Oh I'll accept any whatever!" she almost gaily returned. "And it seems to me, for that matter, that I'm accepting a new one every day. Now *this!*" she smiled.

"This is very well so far as it goes. You can depend on me," the great man said, "for unlimited interest. But I'm only, after all, one element in fifty. We must gather in plenty of others. Don't mind who knows. Knows, I mean, that you and I are friends."

"Ah you do want to see some one!" she broke out. "You want to get at some one who cares for me." With which, however, as he simply met this spontaneity in a manner to show that he had often had it from young persons of her race, and that he was familiar even with the possibilities of *their* familiarity, she felt her freedom rendered vain by his silence, and she immediately tried to think of the most reasonable thing she could say. This would be, precisely, on the subject of that freedom, which she now quickly spoke of as complete. "That's of course by itself a great boon; so please don't think I don't know it. I can do exactly what I like—anything in all the wide world. I haven't a creature to ask—there's not a finger to stop me. I can shake about till I'm black and blue. That perhaps isn't *all* joy; but lots of people, I know, would like to try it." He had appeared about to put a question, but then had let her go on, which she promptly did, for she understood him the next moment as having thus taken it from her that her means were as great as might be. She had simply given it to him so, and this was all that would ever pass between them on the odious head. Yet she couldn't help also knowing that an important effect, for his judgement, or at least for his amusement—which was his feeling, since, marvellously, he did have feeling—was produced by it. All her little pieces had now then fallen together for him like the morsels of coloured glass that used to make combinations, under the hand, in the depths of one of the polygonal peepshows of childhood. "So that if it's a question of my doing anything under the sun that will help—!"

"You'll *do* anything under the sun? Good." He took that beautifully, ever so pleasantly, for what it was worth; but time was needed—the minutes or so were needed on the spot—to deal even provisionally with the substantive question. It was convenient, in its degree, that there was nothing she wouldn't do; but it seemed also highly and agreeably vague that she should have to do anything. They thus appeared to be taking her, together, for the moment, and almost for sociability, as prepared to proceed to gratuitous extremities; the upshot of which was in turn that after much interrogation, auscultation, exploration, much noting of his own sequences and neglecting of hers, had duly kept up the vagueness, they might have struck themselves, or may at least strike us, as coming back from an undeterred but useless voyage to the North Pole.[1] Milly was ready, under orders, for the North Pole; which fact was doubtless what made a blinding anticlimax of her friend's actual abstention from orders. "No," she heard him again distinctly repeat it, "I don't want you for the present to do anything at all; anything, that is, but obey a small prescription or two that will be made clear to you, and let me within a few days come to see you at home."

1. Much in the news were the Arctic explorations of Robert Edwin Peary (1856–1930), whose *Northward over the "Great Ice"* (1898) described his searches. Only on a later expedition, in 1909, did he claim to have reached the North Pole.

It was at first heavenly. "Then you'll see Mrs. Stringham." But she didn't mind a bit now.

"Well, I shan't be afraid of Mrs. Stringham." And he said it once more as she asked once more: "Absolutely not; I 'send' you nowhere. England's all right—anywhere that's pleasant, convenient, decent, will be all right. You say you can do exactly as you like. Oblige me therefore by being so good as to do it. There's only one thing: you ought of course, now, as soon as I've seen you again, to get out of London."

Milly thought. "May I then go back to the Continent?"

"By all means back to the Continent. Do go back to the Continent."

"Then how will you keep seeing me? But perhaps," she quickly added, "you won't want to keep seeing me."

He had it all ready; he had really everything all ready. "I shall follow you up; though if you mean that I don't want you to keep seeing *me*—"

"Well?" she asked.

It was only just here that he struck her the least bit as stumbling. "Well, see all you can. That's what it comes to. Worry about nothing. You *have* at least no worries. It's a great rare chance."

She had got up, for she had had from him both that he would send her something and would advise her promptly of the date of his coming to her, by which she was virtually dismissed. Yet for herself one or two things kept her. "May I come back to England too?"

"Rather! Whenever you like. But always, when you do come, immediately let me know."

"Ah," said Milly, "it won't be a great going to and fro."

"Then if you'll stay with us so much the better."

It touched her, the way he controlled his impatience of her; and the fact itself affected her as so precious that she yielded to the wish to get more from it. "So you don't think I'm out of my mind?"

"Perhaps that *is*," he smiled, "all that's the matter."

She looked at him longer. "No, that's too good. Shall I at any rate suffer?"

"Not a bit."

"And yet then live?"

"My dear young lady," said her distinguished friend, "isn't to 'live' exactly what I'm trying to persuade you to take the trouble to do?"

IV

She had gone out with these last words so in her ears that when once she was well away—back this time in the great square alone

—it was as if some instant application of them had opened out there before her. It was positively, that effect, an excitement that carried her on; she went forward into space under the sense of an impulse received—an impulse simple and direct, easy above all to act upon. She was borne up for the hour, and now she knew why she had wanted to come by herself. No one in the world could have sufficiently entered into her state; no tie would have been close enough to enable a companion to walk beside her without some disparity. She literally felt, in this first flush, that her only company must be the human race at large, present all round her, but inspiringly impersonal, and that her only field must be, then and there, the grey immensity of London. Grey immensity had somehow of a sudden become her element; grey immensity was what her distinguished friend had, for the moment, furnished her world with and what the question of "living," as he put it to her, living by option, by volition, inevitably took on for its immediate face. She went straight before her, without weakness, altogether with strength; and still as she went she was more glad to be alone, for nobody—not Kate Croy, not Susan Shepherd either—would have wished to rush with her as she rushed. She had asked him at the last whether, being on foot, she might go home so, or elsewhere, and he had replied as if almost amused again at her extravagance: "You're active, luckily, by nature—it's beautiful: therefore rejoice in it. *Be* active, without folly—for you're not foolish: be as active as you can and as you like." That had been in fact the final push, as well as the touch that most made a mixture of her consciousness—a strange mixture that tasted at one and the same time of what she had lost and what had been given her. It was wonderful to her, while she took her random course, that these quantities felt so equal: she had been treated—hadn't she?—as if it were in her power to live; and yet one wasn't treated so—was one?—unless it had come up, quite as much, that one might die. The beauty of the bloom had gone from the small old sense of safety—that was distinct: she had left it behind her there for ever. But the beauty of the idea of a great adventure, a big dim experiment or struggle in which she might more responsibly than ever before take a hand, had been offered her instead. It was as if she had had to pluck off her breast, to throw away, some friendly ornament, a familiar flower, a little old jewel, that was part of her daily dress; and to take up and shoulder as a substitute some queer defensive weapon, a musket, a spear, a battle-axe—conducive possibly in a higher degree to a striking appearance, but demanding all the effort of the military posture.

She felt this instrument, for that matter, already on her back, so that she proceeded now in very truth after the fashion of a soldier on a march—proceeded as if, for her initiation, the first charge had been sounded. She passed along unknown streets, over dusty littery ways, between long rows of fronts not enhanced by the August light; she felt good for miles and only wanted to get lost; there were moments at corners, where she stopped and chose her direction, in which she quite lived up to his injunction to rejoice that she was active. It was like a new pleasure to have so new a reason; she would affirm without delay her option, her volition; taking this personal possession of what surrounded her was a fair affirmation to start with; and she really didn't care if she made it at the cost of alarms for Susie. Susie would wonder in due course "whatever," as they said at the hotel, had become of her; yet this would be nothing either, probably, to wonderments still in store. Wonderments in truth, Milly felt, even now attended her steps: it was quite as if she saw in people's eyes the reflexion of her appearance and pace. She found herself moving at times in regions visibly not haunted by odd-looking girls from New York, duskily draped, sable-plumed, all but incongruously shod and gazing about them with extravagance; she might, from the curiosity she clearly excited in by-ways, in side-streets peopled with grimy children and costermongers' carts, which she hoped were slums, literally have had her musket on her shoulder, have announced herself as freshly on the war-path. But for the fear of overdoing the character she would here and there have begun conversation, have asked her way; in spite of the fact that, as this would help the requirements of adventure, her way was exactly what she wanted not to know. The difficulty was that she at last accidentally found it; she had come out, she presently saw, at the Regent's Park,[1] round which on two or three occasions with Kate Croy her public chariot had solemnly rolled. But she went into it further now; this was the real thing; the real thing was to be quite away from the pompous roads, well within the centre and on the stretches of shabby grass. Here were benches and smutty sheep; here were idle lads at games of ball, with their cries mild in the thick air; here were wanderers anxious and tired like herself; here doubtless were hundreds of others just in the same box. Their box, their great common anxiety, what was it, in this grim breathing-space, but the practical question of life? They could live if they would; that is, like herself, they had been told so: she saw them all about her, on seats, digesting the information, recognising it again as something in a slightly different shape familiar enough, the blessed old truth that they would live if they could. All she thus shared with them made her wish to sit in their company; which she so far did that she

1. Named for the Prince Regent, afterwards George IV, the park is known for its zoological and botanical gardens.

looked for a bench that was empty, eschewing a still emptier chair that she saw hard by and for which she would have paid, with superiority, a fee.

The last scrap of superiority had soon enough left her, if only because she before long knew herself for more tired than she had proposed. This and the charm, after a fashion, of the situation in itself made her linger and rest; there was an accepted spell in the sense that nobody in the world knew where she was. It was the first time in her life that this had happened; somebody, everybody appeared to have known before, at every instant of it, where she was; so that she was now suddenly able to put it to herself that that hadn't been a life. This present kind of thing therefore might be —which was where precisely her distinguished friend seemed to be wishing her to come out. He wished her also, it was true, not to make, as she was perhaps doing now, too much of her isolation; at the same time, however, as he clearly desired to deny her no decent source of interest. He was interested—she arrived at that—in her appealing to as many sources as possible; and it fairly filtered into her, as she sat and sat, that he was essentially propping her up. Had she been doing it herself she would have called it bolstering—the bolstering that was simply for the weak; and she thought and thought as she put together the proofs that it was as one of the weak he was treating her. It was of course as one of the weak that she had gone to him—but oh with how sneaking a hope that he might pronounce her, as to all indispensables, a veritable young lioness! What indeed she was really confronted with was the consciousness that he hadn't after all pronounced her anything: she nursed herself into the sense that he had beautifully got out of it. Did he think, however, she wondered, that he could keep out of it to the end?—though as she weighed the question she yet felt it a little unjust. Milly weighed, in this extraordinary hour, questions numerous and strange; but she had happily, before she moved, worked round to a simplification. Stranger than anything for instance was the effect of its rolling over her that, when one considered it, he might perhaps have "got out" by one door but to come in with a beautiful beneficent dishonesty by another. It kept her more intensely motionless there that what he might fundamentally be "up to" was some disguised intention of standing by her as a friend. Wasn't that what women always said they wanted to do when they deprecated the addresses of gentlemen they couldn't more intimately go on with? It was what they, no doubt, sincerely fancied they could make of men of whom they couldn't make husbands. And she didn't even reason that it was by a similar law the expedient of doctors in general for the invalids of whom they couldn't make patients: she was somehow so sufficiently aware that *her* doctor was—however fatuous it might sound—exceptionally moved. This was the damning little fact—if she could talk of damnation: that she could believe herself to have caught him in the act of irrelevantly liking her. She hadn't gone to him to be liked, she had gone to him to be judged; and he was quite a great enough man to be in the habit, as a rule, of observing the difference. She could like *him*, as she distinctly did—that was another matter; all the more that her doing so was now, so obviously for herself, compatible with judgement. Yet it would have been all portentously mixed had not, as we say, a final and merciful wave, chilling rather, but washing clear, come to her assistance.

It came of a sudden when all other thought was spent. She had been asking herself why, if her case was grave—and she knew what she meant by that—he should have talked to her at all about what she might with futility "do"; or why on the other hand, if it were light, he should attach an importance to the office of friendship. She had him, with her little lonely acuteness—as acuteness went during the dog-days in the Regent's Park—in a cleft stick: she either mattered, and then she was ill; or she didn't matter, and then she was well enough. Now he was "acting," as they said at home, as if she did matter—until he should prove the contrary. It was too evident that a person at his high pressure must keep his inconsistencies, which were probably his highest amusements, only for the very greatest occasions. Her prevision, in fine, of just where she should catch him furnished the light of that judgement in which we describe her as daring to indulge. And the judgement it was that made her sensation simple. He *had* distinguished her—that was the chill. He hadn't known—how could he?—that she was devilishly subtle, subtle exactly in the manner of the suspected, the suspicious, the condemned. He in fact confessed to it, in his way, as to an interest in her combinations, her funny race, her funny losses, her funny gains, her funny freedom, and, no doubt, above all, her funny manners—funny, like those of Americans at their best, without being vulgar, legitimating amiability and helping to pass it off. In his appreciation of these redundancies he dressed out for her the compassion he so signally permitted himself to waste; but its operation for herself was as directly divesting, denuding, exposing. It reduced her to her ultimate state, which was that of a poor girl—with her rent to pay for example—staring before her in a great city. Milly had her rent to pay, her rent for her future; everything else but how to meet it fell away fom her in pieces, in tatters. This was the sensation the great man had doubtless not purposed. Well, she must go home, like the poor girl, and see. There might after all be ways; the poor girl too would be thinking. It came back for that matter perhaps to views already presented. She looked about her again, on her feet, at her scattered melancholy comrades—some of them so melancholy as to be down on their stomachs in the grass, turned away, ignoring, burrowing; she saw once more, with them, those two faces of the question between which there was so little to choose for inspiration. It was perhaps superficially more striking that one could live if one would; but it was more appealing, insinuating, irresistible in short, that one would live if one could.

She found after this, for the day or two, more amusement than she had ventured to count on in the fact, if it were not a mere fancy, of deceiving Susie; and she presently felt that what made the difference was the mere fancy—as this *was* one—of a countermove to her great man. His taking on himself—should he do so—to get at her companion made her suddenly, she held, irresponsible, made any notion of her own all right for her; though indeed at the very moment she invited herself to enjoy this impunity she became aware of new matter for surprise, or at least for speculation. Her idea would rather have been that Mrs. Stringham would have looked at her hard—her sketch of the grounds of her independent long excursion showing, she could feel, as almost cynically superficial. Yet the dear woman so failed, in the event, to avail herself of any right of criticism that it was sensibly tempting to wonder for an hour if Kate Croy had been playing perfectly fair. Hadn't she possibly, from motives of the highest benevolence, promptings of the finest anxiety, just given poor Susie what she would have called the straight tip? It must immediately be mentioned, however, that, quite apart from a remembrance of the distinctness of Kate's promise, Milly, the next thing, found her explanation in a truth that had the merit of being general. If Susie at this crisis suspiciously spared her, it was really that Susie was always suspiciously sparing her—yet occasionally too with portentous and exceptional mercies. The girl was conscious of how she dropped at times into inscrutable impenetrable deferences—attitudes that, though without at all intending it, made a difference for familiarity, for the ease of intimacy. It was as if she recalled herself to manners, to the law of court-etiquette—which last note above all helped our young woman to a just appreciation. It was definite for her, even if not quite solid, that to treat her as a princess was a positive need of her companion's mind; wherefore she couldn't help it if this lady had her transcendent view of the way the class in question were treated. Susan had read history, had read Gibbon and Froude and Saint-Simon;[2] she had

2. Edward Gibbon (1737–94), whose *Decline and Fall of the Roman Empire* (1776–88) was one of the first historiographic studies to focus on the disintegration of high civilization; J. A. Froude (1818–94), author of a *History of England from the Fall of Wolsey to the Defeat of the Spanish Armada* (1856–70) and chief disciple of Carlyle; Claude Henri de Saint-Simon (1760–1825), socialist reformer and founder of positivist philosophy, which substituted for the truths of metaphysics and revelation an ethics of sociology and humanism.

high lights as to the special allowances made for the class, and, since she saw them, when young, as effete and overtutored, inevitably ironic and infinitely refined, one must take it for amusing if she inclined to an indulgence verily Byzantine.[3] If one *could* only be Byzantine!—wasn't *that* what she insidiously led one on to sigh? Milly tried to oblige her—for it really placed Susan herself so handsomely to be Byzantine now. The great ladies of that race—it would be somewhere in Gibbon—were apparently not questioned about their mysteries. But oh poor Milly and hers! Susan at all events proved scarce more inquisitive than if she had been a mosaic at Ravenna.[4] Susan was a porcelain monument to the odd moral that consideration might, like cynicism, have abysses. Besides, the Puritan finally disencumbered—! What starved generations wasn't Mrs. Stringham, in fancy, going to make up for?

Kate Croy came straight to the hotel—came that evening shortly before dinner; specifically and publicly moreover, in a hansom that, driven apparently very fast, pulled up beneath their windows almost with the clatter of an accident, a "smash." Milly, alone, as happened, in the great garnished void of their sitting-room, where, a little, really, like a caged Byzantine, she had been pacing through the queer long-drawn almost sinister delay of night, an effect she yet liked—Milly, at the sound, one of the French windows standing open, passed out to the balcony that overhung, with pretensions, the general entrance, and so was in time for the look that Kate, alighting, paying her cabman, happened to send up to the front. The visitor moreover had a shilling[5] back to wait for, during which Milly, from the balcony, looked down at her, and a mute exchange, but with smiles and nods, took place between them on what had occurred in the morning. It was what Kate had called for, and the tone was thus almost by accident determined for Milly before her friend came up. What was also, however, determined for her was, again, yet irrepressibly again, that the image presented to her, the splendid young woman who looked so particularly handsome in impatience, with the fine freedom of her signal, was the peculiar property of somebody else's vision, that this fine freedom in short was the fine freedom she showed Mr. Densher. Just so was how she looked to him, and just so was how Milly was held by her—held as by the strange sense of seeing through that distant person's eyes. It lasted, as usual, the strange sense, but fifty seconds; yet in so lasting it produced an effect. It produced in fact more than one, and we

3. The term designating the art and architecture of the eastern Roman Empire roughly in the thousand years ending with the Turks' capture of Constantinople, formerly Byzantium, in 1453. Saint Mark's in Venice epitomizes most of its features.

4. Such mosaics are another high Byzantine form.

5. A shilling at this time was worth about twenty-five or thirty cents.

take them in their order. The first was that it struck our young woman as absurd to say that a girl's looking so to a man could possibly be without connexions; and the second was that by the time Kate had got into the room Milly was in mental possession of the main connexion it must have for herself.

She produced this commodity on the spot—produced it in straight response to Kate's frank "Well, what?" The enquiry bore of course, with Kate's eagerness, on the issue of the morning's scene, the great man's latest wisdom, and it doubtless affected Milly a little as the cheerful demand for news is apt to affect troubled spirits when news is not, in one of the neater forms, prepared for delivery. She couldn't have said what it was exactly that on the instant determined her; the nearest description of it would perhaps have been as the more vivid impression of all her friend took for granted. The contrast between this free quantity and the maze of possibilities through which, for hours, she had herself been picking her way, put on, in short, for the moment, a grossness that even friendly forms scarce lightened: it helped forward in fact the revelation to herself that she absolutely had nothing to tell. Besides which, certainly, there was something else—an influence at the particular juncture still more obscure. Kate had lost, on the way upstairs, the look—*the* look—that made her young hostess so subtly think and one of the signs of which was that she never kept it for many moments at once; yet she stood there, none the less, so in her bloom and in her strength, so completely again the "handsome girl" beyond all others, the "handsome girl" for whom Milly had at first gratefully taken her, that to meet her now with the note of the plaintive would amount somehow to a surrender, to a confession. *She* would never in her life be ill; the greatest doctor would keep her, at the worst, the fewest minutes; and it was as if she had asked just *with* all this practical impeccability for all that was most mortal in her friend. These things, for Milly, inwardly danced their dance; but the vibration produced and the dust kicked up had lasted less than our account of them. Almost before she knew it she was answering, and answering beautifully, with no consciousness of fraud, only as with a sudden flare of the famous "will-power" she had heard about, read about, and which was what her medical adviser had mainly thrown her back on. "Oh it's all right. He's lovely."

Kate was splendid, and it would have been clear for Milly now, had the further presumption been needed, that she had said no word to Mrs. Stringham. "You mean you've been absurd?"

"Absurd." It was a simple word to say, but the consequence of it, for our young woman, was that she felt it, as soon as spoken, to have done something for her safety.

And Kate really hung on her lips. "There's nothing at all the matter?"

"Nothing to worry about. I shall need a little watching, but I shan't have to do anything dreadful, or even in the least inconvenient. I can do in fact as I like." It was wonderful for Milly how just to put it so made all its pieces fall at present quite properly into their places.

Yet even before the full effect came Kate had seized, kissed, blessed her. "My love, you're too sweet! It's too dear! But it's as I was sure." Then she grasped the full beauty. "You can do as you like?"

"Quite. Isn't it charming?"

"Ah but catch you," Kate triumphed with gaiety, "*not* doing—! And what *shall* you do?"

"For the moment simply enjoy it. Enjoy"—Milly was completely luminous—"having got out of my scrape."

"Learning, you mean, so easily, that you *are* well?"

It was as if Kate had but too conveniently put the words into her mouth. "Learning, I mean, so easily, that I *am* well."

"Only no one's of course well enough to stay in London now. He can't," Kate went on, "want this of you."

"Mercy no—I'm to knock about. I'm to go to places."

"But not beastly 'climates'—Engadines,[6] Rivieras, boredoms?"

"No; just, as I say, where I prefer. I'm to go in for pleasure."

"Oh the duck!"—Kate, with her own shades of familiarity, abounded. "But what kind of pleasure?"

"The highest," Milly smiled.

Her friend met it as nobly. "Which *is* the highest?"

"Well, it's just our chance to find out. You must help me."

"What have I wanted to do but help you," Kate asked, "from the moment I first laid eyes on you?" Yet with this too Kate had her wonder. "I like your talking, though, about that. What help, with your luck all round, do you need?"

V

Milly indeed at last couldn't say; so that she had really for the time brought it along to the point so oddly marked for her by her visitor's arrival, the truth that she was enviably strong. She carried this out, from that evening, for each hour still left her, and the more easily perhaps that the hours were now narrowly numbered. All she actually waited for was Sir Luke Strett's promised visit; as to her proceeding on which, however, her mind was quite made up. Since he wanted to get at Susie he should have the freest access, and then perhaps he would see how he liked it. What was between

6. The Upper Engadine, a large valley near St. Moritz, was one of the best-known health spas in the world.

them they might settle as between them, and any pressure it should lift from her own spirit they were at liberty to convert to their use. If the dear man wished to fire Susan Shepherd with a still higher ideal, he would only after all, at the worst, have Susan on his hands. If devotion, in a word, was what it would come up for the interested pair to organise, she was herself ready to consume it as the dressed and served dish. He had talked to her of her "appetite," her account of which, she felt, must have been vague. But for devotion, she could now see, this appetite would be of the best. Gross, greedy, ravenous—these were doubtless the proper names for her: she was at all events resigned in advance to the machinations of sympathy. The day that followed her lonely excursion was to be the last but two or three of their stay in London; and the evening of that day practically ranked for them as, in the matter of outside relations, the last of all. People were by this time quite scattered, and many of those who had so liberally manifested in calls, in cards, in evident sincerity about visits, later on, over the land, had positively passed in music out of sight; whether as members, these latter, more especially, of Mrs. Lowder's immediate circle or as members of Lord Mark's—our friends being by this time able to make the distinction. The general pitch had thus decidedly dropped, and the occasions still to be dealt with were special and few. One of these, for Milly, announced itself as the doctor's call already mentioned, as to which she had now had a note from him: the single other, of importance, was their appointed leave-taking—for the shortest separation—in respect to Mrs. Lowder and Kate. The aunt and the niece were to dine with them alone, intimately and easily—as easily as should be consistent with the question of their afterwards going on together to some absurdly belated party, at which they had had it from Aunt Maud that they would do well to show. Sir Luke was to make his appearance on the morrow of this, and in respect to that complication Milly had already her plan.

The night was at all events hot and stale, and it was late enough by the time the four ladies had been gathered in, for their small session, at the hotel, where the windows were still open to the high balconies and the flames of the candles, behind the pink shades—disposed as for the vigil of watchers—were motionless in the air in which the season lay dead. What was presently settled among them was that Milly, who betrayed on this occasion a preference more marked than usual, shouldn't hold herself obliged to climb that evening the social stair, however it might stretch to meet her, and that, Mrs. Lowder and Mrs. Stringham facing the ordeal together, Kate Croy should remain with her and await their return. It was a pleasure to Milly, ever, to send Susan Shepherd forth; she saw her go with complacency, liked, as it were, to put people off with her, and noted with satisfaction, when she so moved to the carriage, the further denudation—a markedly ebbing tide—of her little benevolent back. If it wasn't quite Aunt Maud's ideal, moreover, to take out the new American girl's funny friend instead of the new American girl herself, nothing could better indicate the range of that lady's merit than the spirit in which—as at the present hour for instance—she made the best of the minor advantage. And she did this with a broad cheerful absence of illusion; she did it—confessing even as much to poor Susie—because, frankly, she *was* good-natured. When Mrs. Stringham observed that her own light was too abjectly borrowed and that it was as a link alone, fortunately not missing, that she was valued, Aunt Maud concurred to the extent of the remark: "Well, my dear, you're better than nothing." To-night furthermore it came up for Milly that Aunt Maud had something particular in mind. Mrs. Stringham, before adjourning with her, had gone off for some shawl or other accessory, and Kate, as if a little impatient for their withdrawal, had wandered out to the balcony, where she hovered for the time unseen, though with scarce more to look at than the dim London stars and the cruder glow, up the street, on a corner, of a small public-house in front of which a fagged cab-horse was thrown into relief. Mrs. Lowder made use of the moment: Milly felt as soon as she had spoken that what she was doing was somehow for use.

"Dear Susan tells me that you saw in America Mr. Densher—whom I've never till now, as you may have noticed, asked you about. But do you mind at last, in connexion with him, doing something for me?" She had lowered her fine voice to a depth, though speaking with all her rich glibness; and Milly, after a small sharpness of surprise, was already guessing the sense of her appeal. "Will you name him, in any way you like, to *her*"—and Aunt Maud gave a nod at the window; "so that you may perhaps find out whether he's back?"

Ever so many things, for Milly, fell into line at this; it was a wonder, she afterwards thought, that she could be conscious of so many at once. She smiled hard, however, for them all. "But I don't know that it's important to me to 'find out.' " The array of things was further swollen, however, even as she said this, by its striking her as too much to say. She therefore tried as quickly to say less. "Except you mean of course that it's important to *you*." She fancied Aunt Maud was looking at her almost as hard as she was herself smiling, and that gave her another impulse. "You know I never *have* yet named him to her; so that if I should break out now—"

"Well?"—Mrs. Lowder waited.

"Why she may wonder what I've been making a mystery of. She hasn't mentioned him, you know," Milly went on, "herself."

"No"—her friend a little heavily weighed it—"she wouldn't. So it's she, you see then, who has made the mystery."

Yes, Milly but wanted to see; only there was so much. "There has been of course no particular reason." Yet that indeed was neither here nor there. "Do you think," she asked, "he *is* back?"

"It will be about his time, I gather, and rather a comfort to me definitely to know."

"Then can't you ask her yourself?"

"Ah we never speak of him!"

It helped Milly for the moment to the convenience of a puzzled pause. "Do you mean he's an acquaintance of whom you disapprove for her?"

Aunt Maud, as well, just hung fire. "I disapprove of *her* for the poor young man. She doesn't care for him."

"And *he* cares so much—?"

"Too much, too much. And my fear is," said Mrs. Lowder, "that he privately besets her. She keeps it to herself, but I don't want her worried. Neither, in truth," she both generously and confidentially concluded, "do I want *him*."

Milly showed all her own effort to meet the case. "But what can *I* do?"

"You can find out where they are. If I myself try," Mrs. Lowder explained, "I shall appear to treat them as if I supposed them deceiving me."

"And you don't. You don't," Milly mused for her, "suppose them deceiving you."

"Well," said Aunt Maud, whose fine onyx eyes failed to blink even though Milly's questions might have been taken as drawing her rather further than she had originally meant to go—"well, Kate's thoroughly aware of my views for her, and that I take her being with me at present, in the way she *is* with me, if you know what I mean, for a loyal assent to them. Therefore as my views don't happen to provide a place at all for Mr. Densher, much, in a manner, as I like him"—therefore in short she had been prompted to this step, though she completed her sense, but sketchily, with the rattle of her large fan.

It assisted them for the moment perhaps, however, that Milly was able to pick out of her sense what might serve as the clearest part of it. "You do like him then?"

"Oh dear yes. Don't you?"

Milly waited, for the question was somehow as the sudden point of something sharp on a nerve that winced. She just caught her breath, but she had ground for joy afterwards, she felt, in not really having failed to choose with quickness sufficient, out of fifteen possible answers, the one that would best serve her. She was then almost proud, as well, that she had cheerfully smiled. "I did—three times—in New York." So came and went, in these simple words, the speech that was to figure for her, later on, that night, as the one she had ever uttered that cost her most. She was to lie awake for the gladness of not having taken any line so really inferior as the denial of a happy impression.

For Mrs. Lowder also moreover her simple words were the right ones; they were at any rate, that lady's laugh showed, in the natural note of the racy. "You dear American thing! But people may be very good and yet not good for what one wants."

"Yes," the girl assented, "even I suppose when what one wants is something very good."

"Oh my child, it would take too long just now to tell you all *I* want! I want everything at once and together—and ever so much for you too, you know. But you've seen us," Aunt Maud continued; "you'll have made out."

"Ah," said Milly, "I *don't* make out;" for again—it came that way in rushes—she felt an obscurity in things. "Why, if our friend here doesn't like him—"

"Should I conceive her interested in keeping things from me?" Mrs. Lowder did justice to the question. "My dear, how can you ask? Put yourself in her place. She meets me, but on *her* terms. Proud young women are proud young women. And proud old ones are—well, what *I* am. Fond of you as we both are, you can help us."

Milly tried to be inspired. "Does it come back then to my asking her straight?"

At this, however, finally, Aunt Maud threw her up. "Oh if you've so many reasons not—!"

"I've not so many," Milly smiled—"but I've one. If I break out so suddenly on my knowing him, what will she make of my not having spoken before?"

Mrs. Lowder looked blank at it. "Why should you care what she makes? You may have only been decently discreet."

"Ah I *have* been," the girl made haste to say.

"Besides," her friend went on, "I suggested to you, through Susan, your line."

"Yes, that reason's a reason for *me*."

"And for *me*," Mrs. Lowder insisted. "She's not therefore so stupid as not to do justice to grounds so marked. You can tell her perfectly that I had asked you to say nothing."

"And may I tell her that you've asked me now to speak?"

Mrs. Lowder might well have thought, yet, oddly, this pulled her up. "You can't do it without—?"

Milly was almost ashamed to be raising so many difficulties. "I'll do what I can if you'll kindly tell me one thing more." She faltered a little—it was so prying; but she brought it out. "Will he have been writing to her?"

"It's exactly, my dear, what I should like to know!" Mrs. Lowder was at last impatient. "Push in for yourself and I dare say she'll tell you."

Even now, all the same, Milly had not quite fallen back. "It will be pushing in," she continued to smile, "for *you*." She allowed her companion, however, no time to take this up. "The point will be that if he *has* been writing she may have answered."

"But what point, you subtle thing, is that?"

"It isn't subtle, it seems to me, but quite simple," Milly said, "that if she has answered she has very possibly spoken of me."

"Very certainly indeed. But what difference will it make?"

The girl had a moment, at this, of thinking it natural Mrs. Lowder herself should so fail of subtlety. "It will make the difference that he'll have written her in reply that he knows me. And that, in turn," our young woman explained, "will give an oddity to my own silence."

"How so, if she's perfectly aware of having given you no opening? The only oddity," Aunt Maud lucidly professed, "is for yourself. It's in *her* not having spoken."

"Ah there we are!" said Milly.

And she had uttered it, evidently, in a tone that struck her friend. "Then it *has* troubled you?"

But the enquiry had only to be made to bring the rare colour with fine inconsequence to her face. "Not really the least little bit!" And, quickly feeling the need to abound in this sense, she was on the point, to cut short, of declaring that she cared, after all, no scrap how much she obliged. Only she felt at this instant too the intervention of still other things. Mrs. Lowder was in the first place already beforehand, already affected as by the sudden vision of her having herself pushed too far. Milly could never judge from her face of her uppermost motive—it was so little, in its hard smooth sheen, that kind of human countenance. She looked hard when she spoke fair; the only thing was that when she spoke hard she didn't likewise look soft. Something, none the less, had arisen in her now—a full appreciable tide, entering by the rupture of some bar. She announced that if what she had asked was to prove in the least a bore her young friend was not to dream of it; making her young friend at the same time, by the change in her tone, dream on the spot more profusely. She spoke, with a belated light, Milly could apprehend—she could always apprehend—from pity; and the result of that perception, for the girl, was singular: it proved to her as quickly that Kate, keeping her secret, had been straight with her.

From Kate distinctly then, as to why she was to be pitied, Aunt Maud knew nothing, and was thereby simply putting in evidence the fine side of her own character. This fine side was that she could almost at any hour, by a kindled preference or a diverted energy, glow for another interest than her own. She exclaimed as well, at this moment, that Milly must have been thinking round the case much more than she had supposed; and this remark could affect the girl as quickly and as sharply as any other form of the charge of weakness. It was what every one, if she didn't look out, would soon be saying—"There's something the matter with you!" What one was therefore one's self concerned immediately to establish was that there was nothing at all. "I shall like to help you; I shall like, so far as that goes, to help Kate herself," she made such haste as she could to declare; her eyes wandering meanwhile across the width of the room to that dusk of the balcony in which their companion perhaps a little unaccountably lingered. She suggested hereby her impatience to begin; she almost overtly wondered at the length of the opportunity this friend was giving them—referring it, however, so far as words went, to the other friend and breaking off with an amused: "How tremendously Susie must be beautifying!"

It only marked Aunt Maud, none the less, as too preoccupied for her allusion. The onyx eyes were fixed upon her with a polished pressure that must signify some enriched benevolence. "Let it go, my dear. We shall after all soon enough see."

"If he *has* come back we shall certainly see," Milly after a moment replied; "for he'll probably feel that he can't quite civilly not come to see me. Then *there*," she remarked, "we shall be. It wouldn't then, you see, come through Kate at all—it would come through him. Except," she wound up with a smile, "that he won't find me."

She had the most extraordinary sense of interesting her guest, in spite of herself, more than she wanted; it was as if her doom so floated her on that she couldn't stop—by very much the same trick it had played her with her doctor. "Shall you run away from him?"

She neglected the question, wanting only now to get off. "Then," she went on, "you'll deal with Kate directly."

"Shall you run away from *her*?" Mrs. Lowder profoundly enquired, while they became aware of Susie's return through the room, opening out behind them, in which they had dined.

This affected Milly as giving her but an instant; and suddenly, with it, everything she felt in the connexion rose to her lips for a question that, even as she put it, she knew she was failing to keep colourless. "Is it your own belief that he *is* with her?"

Aunt Maud took it in—took in, that is, everything of the tone that she just wanted her not to; and the result for some seconds was but to make their eyes meet in silence. Mrs. Stringham had rejoined them and was asking if Kate had gone—an enquiry at once answered by this young lady's reappearance. They saw her again in the open window, where, looking at them, she had paused—producing thus on Aunt Maud's part almost too impressive a "Hush!" Mrs. Lowder indeed without loss of time smothered any danger in a sweeping retreat with Susie; but Milly's words to her, just uttered, about dealing with her niece directly, struck our young woman as already recoiling on herself. Directness, however evaded, would be, fully, for *her*; nothing in fact would ever have been for her so direct as the evasion. Kate had remained in the window, very handsome and upright, the outer dark framing in a highly favourable way her summery simplicities and lightnesses of dress. Milly had, given the relation of space, no real fear she had heard their talk; only she hovered there as with conscious eyes and some added advantage. Then indeed, with small delay, her friend sufficiently saw. The conscious eyes, the added advantage were but those she had now always at command—those proper to the person Milly knew as known to Merton Densher. It was for several seconds again as if the *total* of her identity had been that of the person known to him—a determination having for result another sharpness of its own. Kate had positively but to be there just as she was to tell her he had come back. It seemed to pass between them in fine without a word that he was in London, that he was perhaps only round the corner; and surely therefore no dealing of Milly's with her would yet have been so direct.

VI

It was doubtless because this queer form of directness had in itself, for the hour, seemed so sufficient that Milly was afterwards aware of having really, all the while—during the strange indescribable session before the return of their companions—done nothing to intensify it. If she was most aware only afterwards, under the long and discurtained ordeal of the morrow's dawn, that was because she had really, till their evening's end came, ceased after a little to miss anything from their ostensible comfort. What was behind showed but in gleams and glimpses; what was in front never at all confessed to not holding the stage. Three minutes hadn't passed before Milly quite knew she should have done nothing Aunt Maud had just asked her. She knew it moreover by much the same light that had acted for her with that lady and with Sir Luke Strett. It pressed upon her then and there that she was still in a current determined, through her indifference, timidity, bravery, generosity—she scarce could say which—by others; that not she but the current acted, and that somebody else always was the keeper of the lock or the dam. Kate for example had but to open the flood-gate: the current moved in its mass—the current, as it had been, of her doing as Kate wanted. What, somehow, in the most extraordinary way in the world, *had* Kate wanted but to be, of a sudden, more interesting than she had ever been? Milly, for their evening then, quite held her breath with the appreciation of it. If she hadn't been sure her companion would have had nothing, from her moments with Mrs. Lowder, to go by, she would almost have seen the admirable creature "cutting in" to anticipate a danger. This fantasy indeed, while they sat together, dropped after a little; even if only because other fantasies multiplied and clustered, making fairly, for our young woman, the buoyant medium in which her friend talked and moved. They sat together, I say, but Kate moved as much as she talked; she figured there, restless and charming, just perhaps a shade perfunctory, repeatedly quitting her place, taking slowly, to and fro, in the trailing folds of her light dress, the length of the room—almost avowedly performing for the pleasure of her hostess.

Mrs. Lowder had said to Milly at Matcham that she and her niece, as allies, could practically conquer the world; but though it was a speech about which there had even then been a vague grand glamour the girl read into it at present more of an approach to a meaning. Kate, for that matter, by herself, could conquer anything, and *she*, Milly Theale, was probably concerned with the "world" only as the small scrap of it that most impinged on her and that was therefore first to be dealt with. On this basis of being dealt with she would doubtless herself do her share of the conquering: she would have something to supply, Kate something to take—each of them thus, to that tune, something for squaring with Aunt Maud's ideal. This in short was what it came to now—that the occasion, in the quiet late lamplight, had the quality of a rough rehearsal of the possible big drama. Milly knew herself dealt with —handsomely, completely: she surrendered to the knowledge, for so it was, she felt, that she supplied her helpful force. And what Kate had to take Kate took as freely and to all appearance as gratefully; accepting afresh, with each of her long, slow walks, the relation between them so established and consecrating her companion's surrender simply by the interest she gave it. The interest to Milly herself we naturally mean; the interest to Kate Milly felt as probably inferior. It easily and largely came for their present talk, for the quick flight of the hour before the breach of the spell—it all came, when considered, from the circumstance, not in the least abnormal, that the handsome girl was in extraordinary "form." Milly remembered her having said that she was at her best late at night; remembered it by its having, with its fine assurance, made her wonder when *she* was at her best and how happy people must be who had such a fixed time. She had no time at all; she was never at her best

—unless indeed it were exactly, as now, in listening, watching, admiring, collapsing. If Kate moreover, quite mercilessly, had never been so good, the beauty and the marvel of it was that she had never really been so frank: being a person of such a calibre, as Milly would have said, that, even while "dealing" with you and thereby, as it were, picking her steps, she could let herself go, could, in irony, in confidence, in extravagance, tell you things she had never told before. That was the impression—that she was telling things, and quite conceivably for her own relief as well; almost as if the errors of vision, the mistakes of proportion, the residuary innocence of spirit still to be remedied on the part of her auditor, had their moments of proving too much for her nerves. She went at them just now, these sources of irritation, with an amused energy that it would have been open to Milly to regard as cynical and that was nevertheless called for—as to this the other was distinct—by the way that in certain connexions the American mind broke down. It seemed at least—the American mind as sitting there thrilled and dazzled in Milly—not to understand English society without a separate confrontation with *all* the cases. It couldn't proceed by—there was some technical term she lacked until Milly suggested both analogy and induction, and then, differently, instinct, none of which were right: it had to be led up and introduced to each aspect of the monster, enabled to walk all round it, whether for the consequent exaggerated ecstasy or for the still more (as appeared to this critic) disproportionate shock. It might, the monster, Kate conceded, loom large for those born amid forms less developed and therefore no doubt less amusing; it might on some sides be a strange and dreadful monster, calculated to devour the unwary, to abase the proud, to scandalise the good; but if one had to live with it one must, not to be for ever sitting up, learn how: which was virtually in short to-night what the handsome girl showed herself as teaching.

She gave away publicly, in this process, Lancaster Gate and everything it contained; she gave away, hand over hand, Milly's thrill continued to note, Aunt Maud and Aunt Maud's glories and Aunt Maud's complacencies; she gave herself away most of all, and it was naturally what most contributed to her candour. She didn't speak to her friend once more, in Aunt Maud's strain, of how they could scale the skies; she spoke, by her bright perverse preference on this occasion, of the need, in the first place, of being neither stupid nor vulgar. It might have been a lesson, for our young American, in the art of seeing things as they were—a lesson so various and so sustained that the pupil had, as we have shown, but receptively to gape. The odd thing furthermore was that it could serve its purpose while explicitly disavowing every personal bias. It wasn't that she disliked Aunt Maud, who was everything she had on other occasions declared; but the dear woman, ineffaceably stamped by inscrutable nature and a dreadful art, wasn't—how *could* she be?—what she wasn't. She wasn't any one. She wasn't anything. She wasn't anywhere. Milly mustn't think it—one couldn't, as a good friend, let her. Those hours at Matcham were *inespérées*,[1] were pure manna from heaven; or if not wholly that perhaps, with humbugging old Lord Mark as a backer, were vain as a ground for hopes and calculations. Lord Mark was very well, but he wasn't *the* cleverest creature in England, and even if he had been he still wouldn't have been the most obliging. He weighed it out in ounces, and indeed each of the pair was really waiting for what the other would put down.

"She has put down *you*," said Milly, attached to the subject still; "and I think what you mean is that, on the counter, she still keeps hold of you."

"Lest"—Kate took it up—"he should suddenly grab me and run? Oh as he isn't ready to run he's much less ready, naturally, to grab. I *am*—you're so far right as that—on the counter, when I'm not in the shop-window; in and out of which I'm thus conveniently, commercially whisked: the essence, all of it, of my position, and the price, as properly, of my aunt's protection." Lord Mark was substantially what she had begun with as soon as they were alone; the impression was even yet with Milly of her having sounded his name, having imposed it, as a topic, in direct opposition to the other name that Mrs. Lowder had left in the air and that all her own look, as we have seen, kept there at first for her companion. The immediate strange effect had been that of her consciously needing, as it were, an *alibi*—which, successfully, she so found. She had worked it to the end, ridden it to and fro across the course marked for Milly by Aunt Maud, and now she had quite, so to speak, broken it in. "The bore is that if she wants him so much—wants him, heaven forgive her! for *me*—he has put us all out, since your arrival, by wanting somebody else. I don't mean somebody else than you."

Milly threw off the charm sufficiently to shake her head. "Then I haven't made out who it is. If I'm any part of his alternative he had better stop where he is."

"Truly, truly?—always, always?"

Milly tried to insist with an equal gaiety. "Would you like me to swear?"

Kate appeared for a moment—though that was doubtless but gaiety too—to think. "Haven't we been swearing enough?"

"You have perhaps, but I haven't, and I ought to give you the

1. Unhoped for.

equivalent. At any rate there it is. 'Truly, truly' as you say—'always, always.' So I'm not in the way."

"Thanks," said Kate—"but that doesn't help me."

"Oh it's as simplifying for *him* that I speak of it."

"The difficulty really is that he's a person with so many ideas that it's particularly hard to simplify for him. That's exactly of course what Aunt Maud has been trying. He won't," Kate firmly continued, "make up his mind about me."

"Well," Milly smiled, "give him time."

Her friend met it in perfection. "One's *doing* that—one *is*. But one remains all the same but one of his ideas."

"There's no harm in that," Milly returned, "if you come out in the end as the best of them. What's a man," she pursued, "especially an ambitious one, without a variety of ideas?"

"No doubt. The more the merrier." And Kate looked at her grandly. "One can but hope to come out, and do nothing to prevent it."

All of which made for the impression, fantastic or not, of the *alibi*. The splendour, the grandeur were for Milly the bold ironic spirit behind it, so interesting too in itself. What, further, was not less interesting was the fact, as our young woman noted it, that Kate confined her point to the difficulties, so far as *she* was concerned, raised only by Lord Mark. She referred now to none that her own taste might present; which circumstance again played its little part. She was doing what she liked in respect to another person, but she was in no way committed to the other person, and her moreover talking of Lord Mark as not young and not true were only the signs of her clear self-consciousness, were all in the line of her slightly hard but scarce the less graceful extravagance. She didn't wish to show too much her consent to be arranged for, but that was a different thing from not wishing sufficiently to give it. There was something on it all, as well, that Milly still found occasion to say. "If your aunt has been, as you tell me, put out by me, I feel she has remained remarkably kind."

"Oh but she has—whatever might have happened in that respect—plenty of use for you! You put her in, my dear, more than you put her out. You don't half see it, but she has clutched your petticoat. You can do anything—you can do, I mean, lots that *we* can't. You're an outsider, independent and standing by yourself; you're not hideously relative to tiers and tiers of others." And Kate, facing in that direction, went further and further; wound up, while Milly gaped, with extraordinary words. "We're of no use to you—it's decent to tell you. You'd be of use to us, but that's a different matter. My honest advice to you would be—" she went indeed all lengths—"to drop us while you can. It would be funny if you didn't soon see how awfully better you can do. We've not really done for you the least thing worth speaking of—nothing you mightn't easily have had in some other way. Therefore you're under no obligation. You won't want us next year; we shall only continue to want *you*. But that's no reason for you, and you mustn't pay too dreadfully for poor Mrs. Stringham's having let you in. She has the best conscience in the world; she's enchanted with what she had done; but you shouldn't take your people from *her*. It has been quite awful to see you do it."

Milly tried to be amused, so as not—it was too absurd—to be fairly frightened. Strange enough indeed—if not natural enough—that, late at night thus, in a mere mercenary house, with Susie away, a want of confidence should possess her. She recalled, with all the rest of it, the next day, piecing things together in the dawn, that she had felt herself alone with a creature who paced like a panther. That was a violent image, but it made her a little less ashamed of having been scared. For all her scare, none the less, she had now the sense to find words. "And yet without Susie I shouldn't have had *you*."

It had been at this point, however, that Kate flickered highest. "Oh you may very well loathe me yet!"

Really at last, thus, it had been too much; as, with her own least feeble flare, after a wondering watch, Milly had shown. She hadn't cared; she had too much wanted to know; and, though a small solemnity of remonstrance, a sombre strain, had broken into her tone, it was to figure as her nearest approach to serving Mrs. Lowder. "Why do you say such things to me?"

This unexpectedly had acted, by a sudden turn of Kate's attitude, as a happy speech. She had risen as she spoke, and Kate had stopped before her, shining at her instantly with a softer brightness. Poor Milly hereby enjoyed one of her views of how people, wincing oddly, were often touched by her. "Because you're a dove." With which she felt herself ever so delicately, so considerately, embraced; not with familiarity or as a liberty taken, but almost ceremonially and in the manner of an *accolade*; partly as if, though a dove who could perch on a finger, one were also a princess with whom forms were to be observed. It even came to her, through the touch of her companion's lips, that this form, this cool pressure, fairly sealed the sense of what Kate had just said. It was moreover, for the girl, like an inspiration: she found herself accepting as the right one, while she caught her breath with relief, the name so given her. She met it on the instant as she would have met revealed truth; it lighted up the strange dusk in which she lately had walked. *That* was what was the matter with her. She was a dove. Oh *wasn't* she?—it echoed within her as she became aware of the sound, outside, of the return of their friends. There was, the next thing, little enough doubt about it after Aunt Maud had been two minutes in the room. She had come up, Mrs. Lowder, with Susan—which she needn't have done, at that hour, instead of letting Kate come down to her; so that Milly could be quite sure it was to catch hold, in some way, of the loose end they had left. Well, the way she did catch was simply to make the point that it didn't now in the least matter. She had mounted the stairs for this, and she had her moment again with her younger hostess while Kate, on the spot, as the latter at the time noted, gave Susan Shepherd unwonted opportunities. Kate was in other words, as Aunt Maud engaged her friend, listening with the handsomest response to Mrs. Stringham's impression of the scene they had just quitted. It was in the tone of the fondest indulgence—almost, really, that of dove cooing to dove—that Mrs. Lowder expressed to Milly the hope that it had all gone beautifully. Her "all" had an ample benevolence; it soothed and simplified; she spoke as if it were the two young women, not she and her comrade, who had been facing the town together. But Milly's answer had prepared itself while Aunt Maud was on the stair; she had felt in a rush all the reasons that would make it the most dovelike; and she gave it, while she was about it, as earnest, as candid. "I don't *think*, dear lady, he's here."

It gave her straightway the measure of the success she could have as a dove: that was recorded in the long look of deep criticism, a look without a word, that Mrs. Lowder poured forth. And the word, presently, bettered it still. "Oh you exquisite thing!" The luscious innuendo of it, almost startling, lingered in the room, after the visitors had gone, like an oversweet fragrance. But left alone with Mrs. Stringham Milly continued to breathe it: she studied again the dovelike and so set her companion to mere rich reporting that she averted all enquiry into her own case.

That, with the new day, was once more her law—though she saw before her, of course, as something of a complication, her need, each time, to decide. She should have to be clear as to how a dove *would* act. She settled it, she thought, well enough this morning by quite readopting her plan in respect to Sir Luke Strett. That, she was pleased to reflect, had originally been pitched in the key of a merely iridescent drab; and although Mrs. Stringham, after breakfast, began by staring at it as if it had been a priceless Persian carpet suddenly unrolled at her feet, she had no scruple, at the end of five minutes, in leaving her to make the best of it. "Sir Luke Strett comes, by appointment, to see me at eleven, but I'm going out on purpose. He's to be told, please, deceptively, that I'm at home, and you, as my representative, when he comes up, are to see him instead. He'll like that, this time, better. So do be nice to him." It had taken, naturally, more explanation, and the mention, above all, of the fact that the visitor was the greatest of doctors; yet when once the key had been offered Susie slipped it on her bunch, and her young friend could again feel her lovely imagination operate. It operated in truth very much as Mrs. Lowder's, at the last, had done the night before: it made the air heavy once more with the extravagance of assent. It might, afresh, almost have frightened our young woman to see how people rushed to meet her: *had* she then so little time to live that the road must always be spared her? It was as if they were helping her to take it out on the spot. Susie —she couldn't deny, and didn't pretend to—might, of a truth, on *her* side, have treated such news as a flash merely lurid; as to which, to do Susie justice, the pain of it was all there. But, none the less, the margin always allowed her young friend was all there as well; and the proposal now made her—what was it in short but Byzantine? The vision of Milly's perception of the propriety of the matter had, at any rate, quickly engulfed, so far as her attitude was concerned, any surprise and any shock; so that she only desired, the next thing, perfectly to possess the facts. Milly could easily speak, on this, as if there were only one: she made nothing of such another as that she had felt herself menaced. The great fact, in fine, was that she *knew* him to desire just now, more than anything else, to meet, quite apart, some one interested in her. Who therefore so interested as her faithful Susan? The only other circumstance that, by the time she had quitted her friend, she had treated as worth mentioning was the circumstance of her having at first intended to keep quiet. She had originally best seen herself as sweetly secretive. As to that she had changed, and her present request was the result. She didn't say why she had changed, but she trusted her faithful Susan. Their visitor would trust her not less, and she herself would adore their visitor. Moreover he wouldn't—the girl felt sure—tell her anything dreadful. The worst would be that he was in love and that he needed a confidant to work it. And now she was going to the National Gallery.[2]

VII

The idea of the National Gallery had been with her from the moment of her hearing from Sir Luke Strett about his hour of coming. It had been in her mind as a place so meagrely visited, as one of the places that had seemed at home one of the attractions of Europe and one of its highest aids to culture, but that—the old story—the typical frivolous always ended by sacrificing to vulgar pleasures. She had had perfectly, at those whimsical moments on the

2. On the north side of Trafalgar Square, the National Gallery at the turn of the century housed especially fine collections of Dutch, Italian, and British masterpieces.

Brünig, the half-shamed sense of turning her back on such opportunities for real improvement as had figured to her, from of old, in connexion with the continental tour, under the general head of "pictures and things"; and at last she knew for what she had done so. The plea had been explicit—she had done so for life as opposed to learning; the upshot of which had been that life was now beautifully provided for. In spite of those few dips and dashes into the many-coloured stream of history for which of late Kate Croy had helped her to find time, there were possible great chances she had neglected, possible great moments she should, save for to-day, have all but missed. She might still, she had felt, overtake one or two of them among the Titians and the Turners;[1] she had been honestly nursing the hour, and, once she was in the benignant halls, her faith knew itself justified. It was the air she wanted and the world she would now exclusively choose; the quiet chambers, nobly overwhelming, rich but slightly veiled, opened out round her and made her presently say "If I could lose myself *here!*" There were people, people in plenty, but, admirably, no personal question. It was immense, outside, the personal question; but she had blissfully left it outside, and the nearest it came, for a quarter of an hour, to glimmering again into view was when she watched for a little one of the more earnest of the lady-copyists. Two or three in particular, spectacled, aproned, absorbed, engaged her sympathy to an absurd extent, seemed to show her for the time the right way to live. She should have been a lady-copyist—it met so the case. The case was the case of escape, of living under water, of being at once impersonal and firm. There it was before one—one had only to stick and stick.

Milly yielded to this charm till she was almost ashamed; she watched the lady-copyists till she found herself wondering what would be thought by others of a young woman, of adequate aspect, who should appear to regard them as the pride of the place. She would have liked to talk to them, to get, as it figured to her, into their lives, and was deterred but by the fact that she didn't quite see herself as purchasing imitations and yet feared she might excite the expectation of purchase. She really knew before long that what held her was the mere refuge, that something within her was after all too weak for the Turners and Titians. They joined hands about her in a circle too vast, though a circle that a year before she would

1. Titian (1477–1576), the great Venetian painter, and J.M.W. Turner (1775-1851), celebrated most for his watercolor paintings, provide vivid contrasts. Titian's subjects are typically sacred or mythological; his figures often dominate the landscape completely; religious passion elevates the worldly to the idealistic. Turner's early landscapes tend to be topographical renderings, his human figures rarely individualistic. Yet the art of both tends toward greater expressionism: Titian's, in the full integration of figure and background, conveying a metaphysical significance rather than physical appearance, and Turner's, encompassing wider scenes, directing the eye, not to a central focus, but to a diversionary one.

only have desired to trace. They were truly for the larger, not for the smaller life, the life of which the actual pitch, for example, was an interest, the interest of compassion, in misguided efforts. She marked absurdly her little stations, blinking, in her shrinkage of curiosity, at the glorious walls, yet keeping an eye on vistas and approaches, so that she shouldn't be flagrantly caught. The vistas and approaches drew her in this way from room to room, and she had been through many parts of the show, as she supposed, when she sat down to rest. There were chairs in scant clusters, places from which one could gaze. Milly indeed at present fixed her eyes more than elsewhere on the appearance, first, that she couldn't quite, after all, have accounted to an examiner for the order of her "schools," and then on that of her being more tired than she had meant, in spite of her having been so much less intelligent. They found, her eyes, it should be added, other occupation as well, which she let them freely follow: they rested largely, in her vagueness, on the vagueness of other visitors; they attached themselves in especial, with mixed results, to the surprising stream of her compatriots. She was struck with the circumstance that the great museum, early in August, was haunted with these pilgrims, as also with that of her knowing them from afar, marking them easily, each and all, and recognising not less promptly that they had ever new lights for her—new lights on their own darkness. She gave herself up at last, and it was a consummation like another: what she should have come to the National Gallery for to-day would be to watch the copyists and reckon the Baedekers.[2] That perhaps was the moral of a menaced state of health—that one would sit in public places and count the Americans. It passed the time in a manner; but it seemed already the second line of defence, and this notwithstanding the pattern, so unmistakeable, of her country-folk. They were cut out as by scissors, coloured, labelled, mounted; but their relation to her failed to act—they somehow did nothing for her. Partly, no doubt, they didn't so much as notice or know her, didn't even recognise their community of collapse with her, the sign on her, as she sat there, that for her too Europe was "tough." It came to her idly thus—for her humour could still play—that she didn't seem then the same success with them as with the inhabitants of London, who had taken her up on scarce more of an acquaintance. She could wonder if they would be different should she go back with this glamour attached; and she could also wonder, if it came to that, whether she should ever go back. Her friends straggled past, at any rate, in all the vividness of their absent criticism, and she had even at last the sense of taking a mean advantage.

2. Edited and published by Karl Baedeker in Leipzig, "Baedekers" became one of the most popular and useful guides for European travel.

There was a finer instant, however, at which three ladies, clearly a mother and daughters, had paused before her under compulsion of a comment apparently just uttered by one of them and referring to some object on the other side of the room. Milly had her back to the object, but her face very much to her young compatriot, the one who had spoken and in whose look she perceived a certain gloom of recognition. Recognition, for that matter, sat confessedly in her own eyes: she *knew* the three, generically, as easily as a school-boy with a crib in his lap would know the answer in class; she felt, like the school-boy, guilty enough—questioned, as honour went, as to her right so to possess, to dispossess, people who hadn't consciously provoked her. She would have been able to say where they lived, and also how, had the place and the way been but amenable to the positive; she bent tenderly, in imagination, over marital, paternal Mr. Whatever-he-was, at home, eternally named, with all the honours and placidities, but eternally unseen and existing only as some one who could be financially heard from. The mother, the puffed and composed whiteness of whose hair had no relation to her apparent age, showed a countenance almost chemically clean and dry; her companions wore an air of vague resentment humanised by fatigue; and the three were equally adorned with short cloaks of coloured cloth surmounted by little tartan hoods. The tartans were doubtless conceivable as different, but the cloaks, curiously, only thinkable as one. "Handsome? Well, if you choose to say so." It was the mother who had spoken, who herself added, after a pause during which Milly took the reference as to a picture: "In the English style." The three pair of eyes had converged, and their possessors had for an instant rested, with the effect of a drop of the subject, on this last characterisation—with that, too, of a gloom not less mute in one of the daughters than murmured in the other. Milly's heart went out to them while they turned their backs; she said to herself that they ought to have known her, that there was something between them they might have beautifully put together. But she had lost *them* also—they were cold; they left her in her weak wonder as to what they had been looking at. The "handsome" disposed her to turn—all the more that the "English style" would be the English school, which she liked; only she saw, before moving, by the array on the side facing her, that she was in fact among small Dutch pictures.[3] The action of this was again appreciable—the dim surmise that it wouldn't then be by a picture that the spring in the three ladies had been pressed. It was at all events time she should go, and she turned as she got on her feet. She had had behind her one of the entrances and various visitors who had come in while she sat, visi-

3. In all probability, interior domestic scenes, whose scale, subject, and style contrast markedly with the Turners and the Titians.

tors single and in pairs—by one of the former of whom she felt her eyes suddenly held.

This was a gentleman in the middle of the place, a gentleman who had removed his hat and was for a moment, while he glanced, absently, as she could see, at the top tier of the collection, tapping his forehead with his pocket-handkerchief. The occupation held him long enough to give Milly time to take for granted—and a few seconds sufficed—that his face was the object just observed by her friends. This could only have been because she concurred in their tribute, even qualified; and indeed "the English style" of the gentleman—perhaps by instant contrast to the American—was what had had the arresting power. This arresting power, at the same time—and that was the marvel—had already sharpened almost to pain, for in the very act of judging the bared head with detachment she felt herself shaken by a knowledge of it. It was Merton Densher's own, and he was standing there, standing long enough unconscious for her to fix him and then hesitate. These successions were swift, so that she could still ask herself in freedom if she had best let him see her. She could still reply to this that she shouldn't like him to catch her in the effort to prevent it; and she might further have decided that he was too preoccupied to see anything had not a perception intervened that surpassed the first in violence. She was unable to think afterwards how long she had looked at him before knowing herself as otherwise looked at; all she was coherently to put together was that she had had a second recognition without his having noticed her. The source of this latter shock was nobody less than Kate Croy—Kate Croy who was suddenly also in the line of vision and whose eyes met her eyes at their next movement. Kate was but two yards off——Mr. Densher wasn't alone. Kate's face specifically said so, for after a stare as blank at first as Milly's it broke into a far smile. That was what, wonderfully—in addition to the marvel of their meeting—passed from her for Milly; the instant reduction to easy terms of the fact of their being there, the two young women, together. It was perhaps only afterwards that the girl fully felt the connexion between this touch and her already established conviction that Kate was a prodigious person; yet on the spot she none the less, in a degree, knew herself handled and again, as she had been the night before, dealt with—absolutely even dealt with for her greater pleasure. A minute in fine hadn't elapsed before Kate had somehow made her provisionally take everything as natural. The provisional was just the charm—acquiring that character from one moment to the other; it represented happily so much that Kate would explain on the very first chance. This left moreover —and that was the greatest wonder—all due margin for amusement at the way things happened, the monstrous oddity of their turning up in such a place on the very heels of their having separated without allusion to it. The handsome girl was thus literally in control of the scene by the time Merton Densher was ready to exclaim with a high flush or a vivid blush—one didn't distinguish the embarrassment from the joy—"Why Miss Theale: fancy!" and "Why Miss Theale: what luck!"

Miss Theale had meanwhile the sense that for him too, on Kate's part, something wonderful and unspoken was determinant; and this although, distinctly, his companion had no more looked at him with a hint than he had looked at her with a question. He had looked and was looking only at Milly herself, ever so pleasantly and considerately—she scarce knew what to call it; but without prejudice to her consciousness, all the same, that women got out of predicaments better than men. The predicament of course wasn't definite nor phraseable—and the way they let all phrasing pass was presently to recur to our young woman as a characteristic triumph of the civilised state; but she took it for granted, insistently, with a small private flare of passion, because the one thing she could think of to do for him was to show him how she eased him off. She would really, tired and nervous, have been much disconcerted if the opportunity in question hadn't saved her. It was what had saved her most, what had made her, after the first few seconds, almost as brave for Kate as Kate was for her, had made her only ask herself what their friend would like of her. That he was at the end of three minutes, without the least complicated reference, so smoothly "their" friend was just the effect of their all being sublimely civilised. The flash in which he saw this was, for Milly, fairly inspiring—to that degree in fact that she was even now, on such a plane, yearning to be supreme. It took, no doubt, a big dose of inspiration to treat as not funny—or at least as not unpleasant—the anomaly, for Kate, that *she* knew their gentleman, and for herself, that Kate was spending the morning with him; but everything continued to make for this after Milly had tasted of her draught. She was to wonder in subsequent reflexion what in the world they had actually said, since they had made such a success of what they didn't say; the sweetness of the draught for the time, at any rate, was to feel success assured. What depended on this for Mr. Densher was all obscurity to her, and she perhaps but invented the image of his need as a short cut to accommodation. Whatever the facts, their perfect manners, all round, saw them through. The finest part of Milly's own inspiration, it may further be mentioned, was the quick perception that what would be of most service was, so to speak, her own native wood-note. She had long been conscious with shame for her thin blood, or at least for her poor economy, of her unused margin as an American girl—closely indeed as in English air the text might appear to cover the page. She still had reserves of spontaneity, if not of comicality; so that all this cash in hand could now find employment. She became as spontaneous as possible and as American as it might conveniently appeal to Mr. Densher, after his travels, to find her. She said things in the air, and yet flattered herself that she struck him as saying them not in the tone of agitation but in the tone of New York. In the tone of New York agitation was beautifully discounted, and she had now a sufficient view of how much it might accordingly help her.

The help was fairly rendered before they left the place; when her friends presently accepted her invitation to adjourn with her to luncheon at her hotel it was in Fifth Avenue[4] that the meal might have waited. Kate had never been there so straight, but Milly was at present taking her; and if Mr. Densher had been he had at least never had to come so fast. She proposed it as the natural thing—proposed it as the American girl; and she saw herself quickly justified by the pace at which she was followed. The beauty of the case was that to do it all she had only to appear to take Kate's hint. This had said in its fine first smile "Oh yes, our look's queer—but give me time"; and the American girl could give time as nobody else could. What Milly thus gave she therefore made them take—even if, as they might surmise, it was rather more than they wanted. In the porch of the museum she expressed her preference for a four-wheeler; they would take their course in that guise precisely to multiply the minutes. She was more than ever justified by the positive charm that her spirit imparted even to their use of this conveyance; and she touched her highest point—that is certainly for herself—as she ushered her companions into the presence of Susie. Susie was there with luncheon as well as with her return in prospect; and nothing could now have filled her own consciousness more to the brim than to see this good friend take in how little she was abjectly anxious. The cup itself actually offered to this good friend might in truth well be startling, for it was composed beyond question of ingredients oddly mixed. She caught Susie fairly looking at her as if to know whether she had brought in guests to hear Sir Luke Strett's report. Well, it was better her companion should have too much than too little to wonder about; she had come out "anyway," as they said at home, for the interest of the thing; and interest truly sat in her eyes. Milly was none the less, at the sharpest crisis, a little sorry for her; she could of necessity extract from the odd scene so comparatively little of a soothing secret. She saw Mr. Densher suddenly popping up, but she saw nothing else that had happened. She saw in the same way her young friend indifferent to her young friend's doom, and she lacked what would explain it. The only

4. That is, in New York.

thing to keep her in patience was the way, after luncheon, Kate almost, as might be said, made up to her. This was actually perhaps as well what most kept Milly herself in patience. It had in fact for our young woman a positive beauty—was so marked as a deviation from the handsome girl's previous courses. Susie had been a bore to the handsome girl, and the change was now suggestive. The two sat together, after they had risen from table, in the apartment in which they had lunched, making it thus easy for the other guest and his entertainer to sit in the room adjacent. This, for the latter personage, was the beauty; it was almost, on Kate's part, like a prayer to be relieved. If she honestly liked better to be "thrown with" Susan Shepherd than with their other friend, why that said practically everything. It didn't perhaps altogether say why she had gone out with him for the morning, but it said, as one thought, about as much as she could say to his face.

Little by little indeed, under the vividness of Kate's behaviour, the probabilities fell back into their order. Merton Densher was in love and Kate couldn't help it—could only be sorry and kind: wouldn't that, without wild flurries, cover everything? Milly at all events tried it as a cover, tried it hard, for the time; pulled it over her, in the front, the larger room, drew it up to her chin with energy. If it didn't, so treated, do everything for her, it did so much that she could herself supply the rest. She made that up by the interest of her great question, the question of whether, seeing him once more, with all that, as she called it to herself, had come and gone, her impression of him would be different from the impression received in New York. That had held her from the moment of their leaving the museum; it kept her company through their drive and during luncheon; and now that she was a quarter of an hour alone with him it became acute. She was to feel at this crisis that no clear, no common answer, no direct satisfaction on this point, was to reach her; she was to see her question itself simply go to pieces. She couldn't tell if he were different or not, and she didn't know nor care if *she* were: these things had ceased to matter in the light of the only thing she did know. This was that she liked him, as she put it to herself, as much as ever; and if that were to amount to liking a new person the amusement would be but the greater. She had thought him at first very quiet, in spite of his recovery from his original confusion; though even the shade of bewilderment, she yet perceived, had not been due to such vagueness on the subject of her reintensified identity as the probable sight, over there, of many thousands of her kind would sufficiently have justified. No, he was quiet, inevitably, for the first half of the time, because Milly's own lively line—the line of spontaneity—made everything else relative; and because too, so far as

Kate was spontaneous, it was ever so finely in the air among them that the normal pitch must be kept. Afterwards, when they had got a little more used, as it were, to each other's separate felicity, he had begun to talk more, clearly bethinking himself at a given moment of what *his* natural lively line would be. It would be to take for granted she must wish to hear of the States, and to give her in its order everything he had seen and done there. He abounded, of a sudden—he almost insisted; he returned, after breaks, to the charge; and the effect was perhaps the more odd as he gave no clue whatever to what he had admired, as he went, or to what he hadn't. He simply drenched her with his sociable story—especially during the time they were away from the others. She had stopped then being American—all to let him be English; a permission of which he took, she could feel, both immense and unconscious advantage. She had really never cared less for the States than at this moment; but that had nothing to do with the matter. It would have been the occasion of her life to learn about them, for nothing could put him off, and he ventured on no reference to what had happened for herself. It might have been almost as if he had known that the greatest of all these adventures was her doing just what she did then.

It was at this point that she saw the smash of her great question complete, saw that all she had to do with was the sense of being there with him. And there was no chill for this in what she also presently saw—that, however he had begun, he was now acting from a particular desire, determined either by new facts or new fancies, to be like every one else, simplifyingly "kind" to her. He had caught on already as to manner—fallen into line with every one else; and if his spirits verily *had* gone up it might well be that he had thus felt himself lighting on the remedy for all awkwardness. Whatever he did or he didn't Milly knew she should still like him—there was no alternative to that; but her heart could none the less sink a little on feeling how much his view of her was destined to have in common with—as she now sighed over it—*the* view. She could have dreamed of his not having *the* view, of his having something or other, if need be quite viewless, of his own; but he might have what he could with least trouble, and *the* view wouldn't be after all a positive bar to her seeing him. The defect of it in general—if she might so ungraciously criticise—was that, by its sweet universality, it made relations rather prosaically a matter of course. It anticipated and superseded the—likewise sweet—operation of real affinities. It was this that was doubtless marked in her power to keep him now—this and her glassy lustre of attention to his pleasantness about the scenery in the Rockies. She was in truth a little measuring her success in detaining him by Kate's success in "standing" Susan. It wouldn't be, if she could help it, Mr. Densher who should first break down. Such at least was one of the forms of the girl's inward tension; but beneath even this deep reason was a motive still finer. What she had left at home on going out to give it a chance was meanwhile still, was more sharply and actively, there. What had been at the top of her mind about it and then been violently pushed down—this quantity was again working up. As soon as their friends should go Susie would break out, and what she would break out upon wouldn't be—interested in that gentleman as she had more than once shown herself—the personal fact of Mr. Densher. Milly had found in her face at luncheon a feverish glitter, and it told what she was full of. She didn't care now for Mr. Densher's personal fact. Mr. Densher had risen before her only to find his proper place in her imagination already of a sudden occupied. His personal fact failed, so far as she was concerned, to *be* personal, and her companion noticed the failure. This could only mean that she was full to the brim of Sir Luke Strett and of what she had had from him. What *had* she had from him? It was indeed now working upward again that Milly would do well to know, though knowledge looked stiff in the light of Susie's glitter. It was therefore on the whole because Densher's young hostess was divided from it by so thin a partition that she continued to cling to the Rockies.

END OF VOLUME I

The Venetian Palace

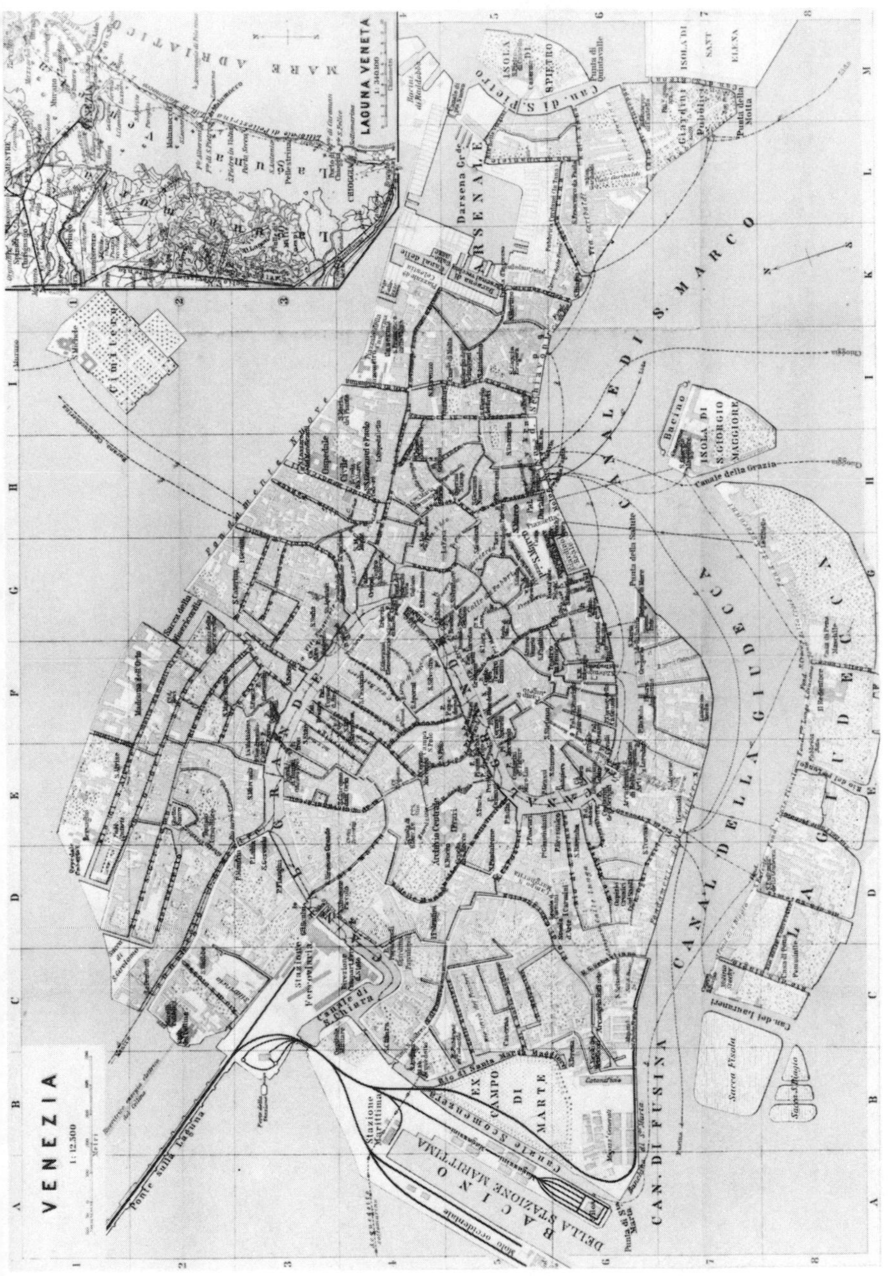

Venice in 1909

Legend

1. Palazzo Leporelli
2. The Rialto
3. The Bridge of Sighs
4. Palace of the Doges
5. The Grand Canal
6. Saint Mark's Square
7. Church of Saint Mark
8. The Molo
9. Columns of Saint Theodore and the Winged Lion of Saint Mark
10. Florian's

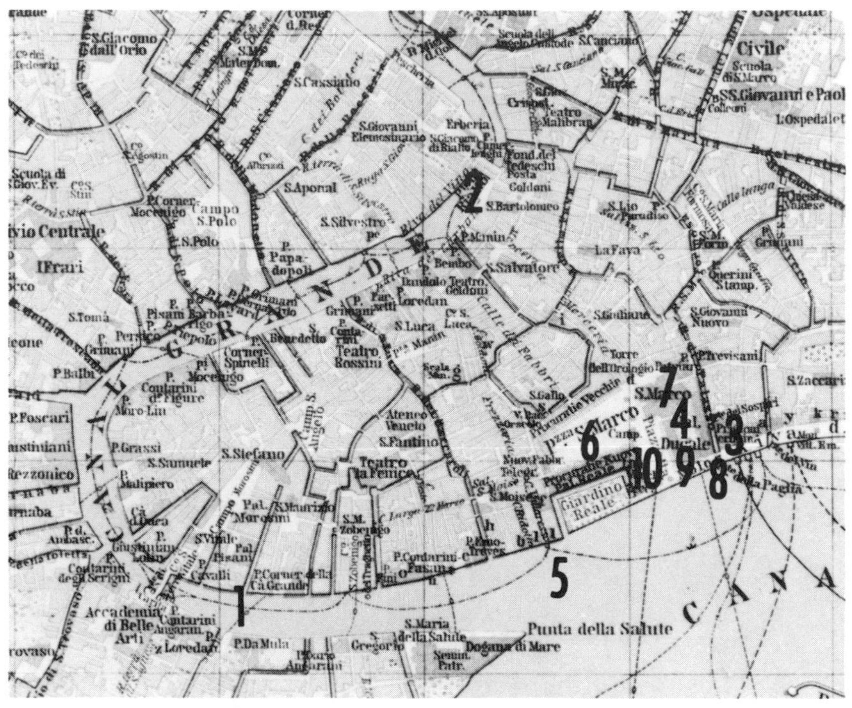

Volume Two

Book Sixth

I

"I say, you know, Kate—you *did* stay!" had been Merton Densher's punctual remark on their adventure after they had, as it were, got out of it; an observation which she not less promptly, on her side, let him see that she forgave in him only because he was a man. She had to recognise, with whatever disappointment, that it was doubtless the most helpful he could make in this character. The fact of the adventure was flagrant between them; they had looked at each other, on gaining the street, as people look who have just rounded together a dangerous corner, and there was therefore already enough unanimity sketched out to have lighted, for her companion, anything equivocal in her action. But the amount of light men *did* need!—Kate could have been eloquent at this moment about that. What, however, on his seeing more, struck him as most distinct in her was her sense that, reunited after his absence and having been now half the morning together, it behooved them to face without delay the question of handling their immediate future. That it would require some handling, that they should still have to deal, deal in a crafty manner, with difficulties and delays, was the great matter he had come back to, greater than any but the refreshed consciousness of their personal need of each other. This need had had twenty minutes, the afternoon before, to find out where it stood, and the time was fully accounted for by the charm of the demonstration. He had arrived at Euston[1] at five, having wired her from Liverpool the moment he landed, and she had quickly decided to meet him at the station, whatever publicity might attend such an act. When he had praised her for it on alighting from his train she had answered frankly enough that such things should be taken at a jump. She didn't care to-day who saw her, and she profited by it for her joy. To-morrow, inevitably, she should have time to think and then, as inevitably, would become a baser creature, a creature of alarms and precautions. It was none the less for to-morrow at an early hour that she had appointed their next meeting, keeping in mind for the present a particular obligation to show at Lancaster Gate by six o'clock. She had given, with imprecations, her reason—people to tea, eternally, and a promise to Aunt Maud; but she had been liberal enough on the spot and had suggested the National Gallery for the morning quite as with an idea that had ripened in expectancy. They might be seen there too, but

1. London terminus of the London and North Western Railway.

nobody would know them; just as, for that matter, now, in the refreshment-room to which they had adjourned, they would incur the notice but, at the worst, of the unacquainted. They would "have something" there for the facility it would give. Thus had it already come up for them again that they had no place of convenience.

He found himself on English soil with all sorts of feelings, but he hadn't quite faced having to reckon with a certain ruefulness in regard to that subject as one of the strongest. He was aware later on that there were questions his impatience had shirked; whereby it actually rather smote him, for want of preparation and assurance, that he had nowhere to "take" his love. He had taken it thus, at Euston—and on Kate's own suggestion—into the place where people had beer and buns, and had ordered tea at a small table in the corner; which, no doubt, as they were lost in the crowd, did well enough for a stop-gap. It perhaps did as well as her simply driving with him to the door of his lodging, which had had to figure as the sole device of his own wit. That wit, the truth was, had broken down a little at the sharp prevision that once at his door they would have to hang back. She would have to stop there, wouldn't come in with him, couldn't possibly; and he shouldn't be able to ask her, would feel he couldn't without betraying a deficiency of what would be called, even at their advanced stage, respect for her: that again was all that was clear except the further fact that it was maddening. Compressed and concentrated, confined to a single sharp pang or two, but none the less in wait for him there on the Euston platform and lifting its head as that of a snake in the garden, was the disconcerting sense that "respect," in their game, seemed somehow—he scarce knew what to call it—a fifth wheel to the coach. It was properly an inside thing, not an outside, a thing to make love greater, not to make happiness less. They had met again for happiness, and he distinctly felt, during his most lucid moment or two, how he must keep watch on anything that really menaced that boon. If Kate had consented to drive away with him and alight at his house there would probably enough have occurred for them, at the foot of his steps, one of those strange instants between man and woman that blow upon the red spark, the spark of conflict, ever latent in the depths of passion. She would have shaken her head—oh sadly, divinely—on the question of coming in; and he, though doing all justice to her refusal, would have yet felt his eyes reach further into her own than a possible word at such a time could reach. This would have meant the suspicion, the dread of the shadow, of an adverse will. Lucky therefore in the actual case that the scant minutes took another turn and that by the half-hour she did in spite of everything contrive to spend with him Kate showed so well how she could deal with things that maddened. She seemed to ask him, to beseech him, and all for his better comfort, to leave her, now and henceforth, to treat them in her own way.

She had still met it in naming so promptly, for their early convenience, one of the great museums; and indeed with such happy art that his fully seeing where she had placed him hadn't been till after he left her. His absence from her for so many weeks had had such an effect upon him that his demands, his desires had grown; and only the night before, as his ship steamed, beneath summer stars, in sight of the Irish coast, he had felt all the force of his particular necessity. He hadn't in other words at any point doubted he was on his way to say to her that really their mistake must end. Their mistake was to have believed that they *could* hold out—hold out, that is, not against Aunt Maud, but against an impatience that, prolonged and exasperated, made a man ill. He had known more than ever, on their separating in the court of the station, how ill a man, and even a woman, could feel from such a cause; but he struck himself as also knowing that he had already suffered Kate to begin finely to apply antidotes and remedies and subtle sedatives. It had a vulgar sound—as throughout, in love, the names of things, the verbal terms of intercourse, were, compared with love itself, horribly vulgar; but it was as if, after all, he might have come back to find himself "put off," though it would take him of course a day or two to see. His letters from the States had pleased whom it concerned, though not so much as he had meant they should; and he should be paid according to agreement and would now take up his money. It wasn't in truth very much to take up, so that he hadn't in the least come back flourishing a chequebook; that new motive for bringing his mistress to terms he couldn't therefore pretend to produce. The ideal certainty would have been to be able to present a change of prospect as a warrant for the change of philosophy, and without it he should have to make shift but with the pretext of the lapse of time. The lapse of time—not so many weeks after all, she might always of course say—couldn't at any rate have failed to do something for him; and that consideration it was that had just now tided him over, all the more that he had his vision of what it had done personally for Kate. This had come out for him with a splendour that almost scared him even in their small corner of the room at Euston—almost scared him because it just seemed to blaze at him that waiting was the game of dupes. Not yet had she been so the creature he had originally seen; not yet had he felt so soundly safely sure. It was all there for him, playing on his pride of possession as a hidden master in a great dim church might play on the grandest organ. His final sense was that a woman couldn't be like that and then ask of one the impossible.

She had been like that afresh on the morrow; and so for the hour they had been able to float in the mere joy of contact—such contact as their situation in pictured public halls permitted. This poor makeshift for closeness confessed itself in truth, by twenty small signs of unrest even on Kate's part, inadequate; so little could a decent interest in the interesting place presume to remind them of its claims. They had met there in order not to meet in the streets and not again, with an equal want of invention and of style, at a railway-station; not again, either, in Kensington Gardens, which, they could easily and tacitly agree, would have had too much of the taste of their old frustrations. The present taste, the taste that morning in the pictured halls, had been a variation; yet Densher had at the end of a quarter of an hour fully known what to conclude from it. This fairly consoled him for their awkwardness, as if he had been watching it affect her. She might be as nobly charming as she liked, and he had seen nothing to touch her in the States; she couldn't pretend that in such conditions as those she herself *believed* it enough to appease him. She couldn't pretend she believed he would believe it enough to render her a like service. It wasn't enough for that purpose—she as good as showed him it wasn't. That was what he could be glad, by demonstration, to have brought her to. He would have said to her had he put it crudely and on the spot: "*Now* am I to understand you that you consider this sort of thing can go on?" It would have been open to her, no doubt, to reply that to have him with her again, to have him all kept and treasured, so still, under her grasping hand, as she had held him in their yearning interval, was a sort of thing that he must allow her to have no quarrel about; but that would be a mere gesture of her grace, a mere sport of her subtlety. She knew as well as he what they wanted; in spite of which indeed he scarce could have said how beautifully he mightn't once more have named it and urged it if she hadn't, at a given moment, blurred, as it were, the accord. They had soon seated themselves for better talk, and so they had remained a while, intimate and superficial. The immediate things to say had been many, for they hadn't exhausted them at Euston. They drew upon them freely now, and Kate appeared quite to forget—which was prodigiously becoming to her—to look about for surprises. He was to try afterwards, and try in vain, to remember what speech or what silence of his own, what natural sign of the eyes or accidental touch of the hand, had precipitated for her, in the midst of this, a sudden different impulse. She had got up, with inconsequence, as if to break the charm, though he wasn't aware of what he had done at the moment to make the charm a danger. She had patched it up agreeably enough the next minute by some odd remark about some picture, to which he hadn't so much as replied;

it being quite independently of this that he had himself exclaimed on the dreadful closeness of the rooms. He had observed that they must go out again to breathe; and it was as if their common consciousness, while they passed into another part, was that of persons who, infinitely engaged together, had been startled and were trying to look natural. It was probably while they were so occupied—as the young man subsequently reconceived—that they had stumbled upon his little New York friend. He thought of her for some reason as little, though she was of about Kate's height, to which, any more than to any other felicity in his mistress, he had never applied the diminutive.

What was to be in the retrospect more distinct to him was the process by which he had become aware that Kate's acquaintance with her was greater than he had gathered. She had written of it in due course as a new and amusing one, and he had written back that he had met over there, and that he much liked, the young person; whereupon she had answered that he must find out about her at home. Kate, in the event, however, had not returned to that, and he had of course, with so many things to find out about, been otherwise taken up. Little Miss Theale's individual history was not stuff for his newspaper; besides which, moreover, he was seeing but too many little Miss Theales. They even went so far as to impose themselves as one of the groups of social phenomena that fell into the scheme of his public letters. For this group in especial perhaps—the irrepressible, the supereminent young persons—his best pen was ready. Thus it was that there could come back to him in London, an hour or two after their luncheon with the American pair, the sense of a situation for which Kate hadn't wholly prepared him. Possibly indeed as marked as this was his recovered perception that preparations, of more than one kind, had been exactly what, both yesterday and to-day, he felt her as having in hand. That appearance in fact, if he dwelt on it, so ministered to apprehension as to require some brushing away. He shook off the suspicion to some extent, on their separating first from their hostesses and then from each other, by the aid of a long and rather aimless walk. He was to go to the office later, but he had the next two or three hours, and he gave himself as a pretext that he had eaten much too much. After Kate had asked him to put her into a cab—which, as an announced, a resumed policy on her part, he found himself deprecating—he stood a while by a corner and looked vaguely forth at his London. There was always doubtless a moment for the absentee recaptured—*the* moment, that of the reflux of the first emotion—at which it was beyond disproof that one was back. His full parenthesis was closed, and he was once more but a sentence, of a sort, in the general text, the text that, from his momentary street-corner, showed as a great grey page of print that somehow managed to be crowded without being "fine." The grey, however, was more or less the blur of a point of view not yet quite seized again; and there would be colour enough to come out. He was back, flatly enough, but back to possibilities and prospects, and the ground he now somewhat sightlessly covered was the act of renewed possession.

He walked northward without a plan, without suspicion, quite in the direction his little New York friend, in her restless ramble, had taken a day or two before. He reached, like Milly, the Regent's Park; and though he moved further and faster he finally sat down, like Milly, from the force of thought. For him too in this position, be it added—and he might positively have occupied the same bench—various troubled fancies folded their wings. He had no more yet said what he really wanted than Kate herself had found time. She should hear enough of that in a couple of days. He had practically not pressed her as to what most concerned them; it had seemed so to concern them during these first hours but to hold each other, spiritually speaking, close. This at any rate was palpable, that there were at present more things rather than fewer between them. The explanation about the two ladies would be part of the lot, yet could wait with all the rest. They were not meanwhile certainly what most made him roam—the missing explanations weren't. That was what she had so often said before, and always with the effect of suddenly breaking off: "Now please call me a good cab." Their previous encounters, the times when they had reached in their stroll the south side of the park, had had a way of winding up with this special irrelevance. It was effectively what most divided them, for he would generally, but for her reasons, have been able to jump in with her. What did she think he wished to do to her?—it was a question he had had occasion to put. A small matter, however, doubtless—since, when it came to that, they didn't depend on cabs good or bad for the sense of union: its importance was less from the particular loss than as a kind of irritating mark of her expertness. This expertness, under providence, had been great from the first, so far as joining him was concerned; and he was critical only because it had been still greater, even from the first too, in respect to leaving him. He had put the question to her again that afternoon, on the repetition of her appeal—had asked her once more what she supposed he wished to do. He recalled, on his bench in the Regent's Park, the freedom of fancy, funny and pretty, with which she had answered; recalled the moment itself, while the usual hansom charged them, during which he felt himself, disappointed as he was, grimacing back at the superiority of her very "humour," in its added grace of gaiety, to the celebrated solemn American. Their fresh appointment had been at all events by that time made, and he should see what her choice in respect to it—a surprise as well as a relief—would do toward really simplifying. It meant either new help or new hindrance, though it took them at least out of the streets. And her naming this privilege had naturally made him ask if Mrs. Lowder knew of his return.

"Not from me," Kate had replied. "But I shall speak to her now." And she had argued, as with rather a quick fresh view, that it would now be quite easy. "We've behaved for months so properly that I've margin surely for my mention of you. You'll come to see *her*, and she'll leave you with me; she'll show her good nature, and her lack of betrayed fear, in that. With her, you know, you've never broken, quite the contrary, and she likes you as much as ever. We're leaving town; it will be the end; just now therefore it's nothing to ask. I'll ask to-night," Kate had wound up, "and if you'll leaving it to me—my cleverness, I assure you, has grown infernal—I'll make it all right."

He had of course thus left it to her and he was wondering more about it now than he had wondered there in Brook Street.[2] He repeated to himself that if it wasn't in the line of triumph it was in the line of muddle. This indeed, no doubt, was as a part of his wonder for still other questions. Kate had really got off without meeting his little challenge about the terms of their intercourse with her dear Milly. Her dear Milly, it was sensible, *was* somehow in the picture. Her dear Milly, popping up in his absence, occupied—he couldn't have said quite why he felt it—more of the foreground than one would have expected her in advance to find clear. She took up room, and it was almost as if room had been made for her. Kate had appeared to take for granted he would know why it had been made; but that was just the point. It was a foreground in which he himself, in which his connexion with Kate, scarce enjoyed a space to turn round. But Miss Theale was perhaps at the present juncture a possibility of the same sort as the softened, if not the squared, Aunt Maud. It might be true of her also that if she weren't a bore she'd be a convenience. It rolled over him of a sudden, after he had resumed his walk, that this might easily be what Kate had meant. The charming girl adored her—Densher had for himself made out that—and would protect, would lend a hand, to their interviews. These might take place, in other words, on her premises, which would remove them still better from the streets. *That* was an explanation which did hang together. It was impaired a little, of a truth, by this fact that their next encounter was rather markedly not to depend upon her. Yet this fact in turn would be

2. The location of Milly's hotel, perhaps Claridge's.

accounted for by the need of more preliminaries. One of the things he conceivably should gain on Thursday at Lancaster Gate would be a further view of that propriety.

II

It was extraordinary enough that he should actually be finding himself, when Thursday arrived, none so wide of the mark. Kate hadn't come all the way to this for him, but she had come to a good deal by the end of a quarter of an hour. What she had begun with was her surprise at her appearing to have left him on Tuesday anything more to understand. The parts, as he now saw, under her hand, did fall more or less together, and it wasn't even as if she had spent the interval in twisting and fitting them. She was bright and handsome, not fagged and worn, with the general clearness; for it certainly stuck out enough that if the American ladies themselves weren't to be squared, which was absurd, they fairly imposed the necessity of trying Aunt Maud again. One couldn't say to them, kind as she had been to them: "We'll meet, please, whenever you'll let us, at your house; but we count on you to help us to keep it secret." They must in other terms inevitably speak to Aunt Maud—it would be of the last awkwardness to ask them not to: Kate had embraced all this in her choice of speaking first. What Kate embraced altogether was indeed wonderful to-day for Densher, though he perhaps struck himself rather as getting it out of her piece by piece than as receiving it in a steady light. He had always felt, however, that the more he asked of her the more he found her prepared, as he imaged it, to hand out. He had said to her more than once even before his absence: "You keep the key of the cupboard, and I foresee that when we're married you'll dole me out my sugar by lumps." She had replied that she rejoiced in his assumption that sugar would be his diet, and the domestic arrangement so prefigured might have seemed already to prevail. The supply from the cupboard at this hour was doubtless, of a truth, not altogether cloyingly sweet; but it met in a manner his immediate requirements. If her explanations at any rate prompted questions the questions no more exhausted them than they exhausted her patience. And they were naturally, of the series, the simpler; as for instance in his taking it from her that Miss Theale then could do nothing for them. He frankly brought out what he had ventured to think possible. "If we can't meet here and we've really exhausted the charms of the open air and the crowd, some such little raft in the wreck, some occasional opportunity like that of Tuesday, has been present to me these two days as better than nothing. But if our friends are so accountable to this house of course there's no more to be said. And it's one more nail, thank God, in the coffin of our odious delay." He was but too glad without more ado to point the moral. "Now I hope you see we can't work it anyhow."

If she laughed for this—and her spirits seemed really high—it was because of the opportunity that, at the hotel, he had most shown himself as enjoying. "Your idea's beautiful when one remembers that you hadn't a word except for Milly." But she was as beautifully good-humoured. "You might of course get used to her—you *will*. You're quite right—so long as they're with us or near us." And she put it, lucidly, that the dear things couldn't *help*, simply as charming friends, giving them a lift. "They'll speak to Aunt Maud. but they won't shut their doors to us: that would be another matter. A friend always helps—and she's a friend." She had left Mrs. Stringham by this time out of the question; she had reduced it to Milly. "Besides, she particularly likes us. She particularly likes *you*. I say, old boy, make something of that." He felt her dodging the ultimatum he had just made sharp, his definite reminder of how little, at the best, they could work it; but there were certain of his remarks—those mostly of the sharper penetration—that it had been quite her practice from the first not formally, not reverently to notice. She showed the effect of them in ways less trite. This was what happened now: he didn't think in truth that she wasn't really minding. She took him up, none the less, on a minor question. "You say we can't meet here, but you see it's just what we do. What could be more lovely than this?"

It wasn't to torment him—that again he didn't believe; but he had to come to the house in some discomfort, so that he frowned a little at her calling it thus a luxury. Wasn't there an element in it of coming back into bondage? The bondage might be veiled and varnished, but he knew in his bones how little the very highest privileges of Lancaster Gate could ever be a sign of their freedom. They were upstairs, in one of the smaller apartments of state, a room arranged as a boudoir, but visibly unused—it defied familiarity—and furnished in the ugliest of blues. He had immediately looked with interest at the closed doors, and Kate had met his interest with the assurance that it was all right, that Aunt Maud did them justice —so far, that was, as this particular time was concerned; that they should be alone and have nothing to fear. But the fresh allusion to this that he had drawn from her acted on him now more directly, brought him closer still to the question. They *were* alone—it *was* all right: he took in anew the shut doors and the permitted privacy, the solid stillness of the great house. They connected themselves on the spot with something made doubly vivid in him by the whole present play of her charming strong will. What it amounted to was that he couldn't have her—hanged if he could!—evasive. He couldn't and he wouldn't—wouldn't have her inconvenient and elusive. He didn't want her deeper than himself, fine as it might be as wit or as character; he wanted to keep her where their communications would be straight and easy and their intercourse independent. The effect of this was to make him say in a moment: "Will you take me just as I am?"

She turned a little pale for the tone of truth in it—which qualified to his sense delightfully the strength of her will; and the pleasure he found in this was not the less for her breaking out after an instant into a strain that stirred him more than any she had ever used with him. "Ah do let me try myself! I assure you I see my way—so don't spoil it: wait for me and give me time. Dear man," Kate said, "only believe in me, and it will be beautiful."

He hadn't come back to hear her talk of his believing in her as if he didn't; but he had come back—and it all was upon him now—to seize her with a sudden intensity that her manner of pleading with him had made, as happily appeared, irresistible. He laid strong hands upon her to say, almost in anger, "Do you love me, love me, love me?" and she closed her eyes as with the sense that he might strike her but that she could gratefully take it. Her surrender was her response, her response her surrender; and, though scarce hearing what she said, he so profited by these things that it could for the time be ever so intimately appreciable to him that he was keeping her. The long embrace in which they held each other was the rout of evasion, and he took from it the certitude that what she had from him was real to her. It was stronger than an uttered vow, and the name he was to give it in afterthought was that she had been sublimely sincere. *That* was all he asked—sincerity making a basis that would bear almost anything. This settled so much, and settled it so thoroughly, that there was nothing left to ask her to swear to. Oaths and vows apart, now they could talk. It seemed in fact only now that their questions were put on the table. He had taken up more expressly at the end of five minutes her plea for her own plan, and it was marked that the difference made by the passage just enacted was a difference in favour of her choice of means. Means had somehow suddenly become a detail—her province and her care; it had grown more consistently vivid that her intelligence was one with her passion. "I certainly don't want," he said—and he could say it with a smile of indulgence—"to be all the while bringing it up that I don't trust you."

"I should hope not! What do you think I want to do?"

He had really at this to make out a little what he thought, and the first thing that put itself in evidence was of course the oddity, after all, of their game, to which he could but frankly allude. "We're doing, at the best, in trying to temporise in so special a way, a thing most people would call us fools for." But his visit passed, all the same, without his again attempting to make "just as he was" serve. He had no more money just as he was than he had had just as he had been, or than he should have, probably, when it came to that, just as he always would be; whereas she, on her side, in comparison with her state of some months before, had measureably more to relinquish. He easily saw how their meeting at Lancaster Gate gave more of an accent to that quantity than their meeting at stations or in parks; and yet on the other hand he couldn't urge this against it. If Mrs. Lowder was indifferent her indifference added in a manner to what Kate's taking him as he was would call on her to sacrifice. Such in fine was her art with him that she seemed to put the question of their still waiting into quite other terms than the terms of ugly blue, of florid Sèvres,[1] of complicated brass, in which their boudoir expressed it. She said almost all in fact by saying, on this article of Aunt Maud, after he had once more pressed her, that when he should see her, as must inevitably soon happen, he would understand. "Do you mean," he asked at this, "that there's any *definite* sign of her coming round? I'm not talking," he explained, "of mere hypocrisies in her, or mere brave duplicities. Remember, after all, that supremely clever as we are, and as strong a team, I admit, as there is going—remember that she can play with us quite as much as we play with her."

"She doesn't want to play with *me*, my dear," Kate lucidly replied; "she doesn't want to make me suffer a bit more than she need. She cares for me too much, and everything she does or doesn't do has a value. *This* has a value—her being as she has been about us to-day. I believe she's in her room, where she's keeping strictly to herself while you're here with me. But that isn't 'playing'—not a bit."

"What is it then," the young man returned—"from the moment it isn't her blessing and a cheque?"

Kate was complete. "It's simply her absence of smallness. There *is* somthing in her above trifles. She *generally* trusts us; she doesn't propose to hunt us into corners: and if we frankly ask for a thing—why," said Kate, "she shrugs, but she lets it go. She has really but one fault—she's indifferent, on such ground as she has taken about us, to details. However," the girl cheerfully went on, "it isn't in detail we fight her."

"It seems to me," Densher brought out after a moment's thought of this, "that it's in detail we deceive her"—a speech that, as soon as he had uttered it, applied itself for him, as also visibly for his companion, to the afterglow of their recent embrace.

1. A fine porcelain made in Sèvres, France.

Any confusion attaching to this adventure, however, dropped from Kate, whom, as he could see with sacred joy, it must take more than that to make compunctious. "I don't say we can do it again. I mean," she explained, "meet here."

Densher indeed had been wondering where they could do it again. If Lancaster Gate was so limited that issue reappeared. "I mayn't come back at all?"

"Certainly—to see her. It's she, really," his companion smiled, "who's in love with you."

But it made him—a trifle more grave—look at her a moment. "Don't make out, you know, that every one's in love with me."

She hesitated. "I don't say every one."

"You said just now Miss Theale."

"I said she liked you—yes."

"Well, it comes to the same thing." With which, however, he pursued: "Of course I ought to thank Mrs. Lowder in person. I mean for *this*—as from myself."

"Ah but, you know, not too much!" She had an ironic gaiety for the implications of his "this," besides wishing to insist on a general prudence. "She'll wonder what you're thanking her for!"

Densher did justice to both considerations. "Yes, I can't very well tell her all."

It was perhaps because he said it so gravely that Kate was again in a manner amused. Yet she gave out light. "You can't very well 'tell' her anything, and that doesn't matter. Only be nice to her. Please her; make her see how clever you are—only without letting her see that you're trying. If you're charming to her you've nothing else to do."

But she oversimplified too. "I can be 'charming' to her, so far as I see, only by letting her suppose I give you up—which I'll be hanged if I do! It *is*," he said with feeling, "a game."

"Of course it's a game. But she'll never suppose you give me up —or I give *you*—if you keep reminding her how you enjoy our interviews."

"Then if she has to see us as obstinate and constant," Densher asked, "what good does it do?"

Kate was for a moment checked. "What good does what—?"

"Does my pleasing her—does anything. I *can't*," he impatiently declared, "please her."

Kate looked at him hard again, disappointed at his want of consistency; but it appeared to determine in her something better than a mere complaint. "Then *I* can! Leave it to me." With which she came to him under the compulsion, again, that had united them shortly before, and took hold of him in her urgency to the same tender purpose. It was her form of entreaty renewed and repeated, which made after all, as he met it, their great fact clear. And it somehow clarified *all* things so to possess each other. The effect of it was that, once more, on these terms, he could only be generous. He had so on the spot then left everything to her that she reverted in the course of a few moments to one of her previous—and as positively seemed—her most precious ideas. "You accused me just now of saying that Milly's in love with you. Well, if you come to that, I do say it. So there you are. That's the good she'll do us. It makes a basis for her seeing you—so that she'll help us to go on."

Densher stared—she was wondrous all round. "And what sort of a basis does it make for my seeing *her?*"

"Oh I don't mind!" Kate smiled.

"Don't mind my leading her on?"

She put it differently. "Don't mind her leading *you.*"

"Well, she won't—so it's nothing not to mind. But how can that 'help,' " he pursued, "with what she knows?"

"What she knows?" That needn't prevent."

He wondered. "Prevent her loving us?"

"Prevent her helping you. She's *like* that," Kate Croy explained.

It took indeed some understanding. "Making nothing of the fact that I love another?"

"Making everything," said Kate. "To console you."

"But for what?"

"For not getting your other."

He continued to stare. "But how does she know—?"

"That you *won't* get her? She doesn't; but on the other hand she doesn't know you will. Meanwhile she sees you baffled, for she knows of Aunt Maud's stand. *That*"—Kate was lucid—"gives her the chance to be nice to you."

"And what does it give *me,*" the young man none the less rationally asked, "the chance to be? A brute of a humbug to her?"

Kate so possessed her facts, as it were, that she smiled at his violence. "You'll extraordinarily like her. She's exquisite. And there are reasons. I mean others."

"What others?"

"Well, I'll tell you another time. Those I give you," the girl added, "are enough to go on with."

"To go on to what?"

"Why, to seeing her again—say as soon as you can: which, moreover, on all grounds, is no more than decent of you."

He of course took in her reference, and he had fully in mind what had passed between them in New York. It had been no great quantity, but it had made distinctly at the time for his pleasure; so that anything in the nature of an appeal in the name of it could have a slight kindling consequence. "Oh I shall naturally call again without delay. Yes," said Densher, "her being in love with me is nonsense; but I must, quite independently of that, make every acknowledgement of favours received."

It appeared practically all Kate asked. "Then you see. I shall meet you there."

"I don't quite see," he presently returned, "why she should wish to receive *you* for it."

"She receives me for myself—that is for *her* self. She thinks no end of me. That I should have to drum it into you!"

Yet still he didn't take it. "Then I confess she's beyond me."

Well, Kate could but leave it as she saw it. "She regards me as already—in these few weeks—her dearest friend. It's quite separate. We're in, she and I, ever so deep." And it was to confirm this that, as if it had flashed upon her that he was somewhere at sea, she threw out at last her own real light. "She doesn't of course know I care for *you*. She thinks I care so little that it's not worth speaking of." That he *had* been somewhere at sea these remarks made quickly clear, and Kate hailed the effect with surprise. "Have you been supposing that she does know—?"

"About our situation? Certainly, if you're such friends as you show me—and if you haven't otherwise represented it to her." She uttered at this such a sound of impatience that he stood artlessly vague. "You *have* denied it to her?"

She threw up her arms at his being so backward. " 'Denied it'? My dear man, we've never spoken of you."

"Never, never?"

"Strange as it may appear to your glory—never."

He couldn't piece it together. "But won't Mrs. Lowder have spoken?"

"Very probably. But of *you*. Not of me."

This struck him as obscure. "How does she know me but as part and parcel of you?"

"How?" Kate triumphantly asked. "Why exactly to make nothing of it, to have nothing to do with it, to stick consistently to her line about it. Aunt Maud's line is to keep all reality out of our relation—that is out of my being in danger from you—by not having so much as suspected or heard of it. She'll get rid of it, as she believes, by ignoring it and sinking it—if she only does so hard enough. Therefore *she*, in her manner, 'denies' it if you will. That's how she knows you otherwise than as part and parcel of me. She won't for a moment have allowed either to Mrs. Stringham or to Milly that I've in any way, as they say, distinguished you."

"And you don't suppose," said Densher, "that they must have made it out for themselves?"

"No, my dear, I don't; not even," Kate declared, "after Milly's so funnily bumping against us on Tuesday."

"She doesn't see from *that*—?"

"That you're, so to speak, mad about me. Yes, she sees, no doubt, that you regard me with a complacent eye—for you show it, I think, always too much and too crudely. But nothing beyond that. *I* don't show it too much; I don't perhaps—to please you completely where others are concerned—show it enough."

"Can you show it or not as you like?" Densher demanded.

It pulled her up a little, but she came out resplendent. "Not where *you* are concerned. Beyond seeing that you're rather gone," she went on, "Milly only sees that I'm decently good to you."

"Very good indeed she must think it!"

"Very good indeed then. She easily sees me," Kate smiled, "as very good indeed."

The young man brooded. "But in a sense to take some explaining."

"Then I explain." She was really fine; it came back to her essential plea for her freedom of action and his beauty of trust. "I mean," she added, "I *will* explain."

"And what will *I* do?"

"Recognise the difference it must make if she thinks." But here in truth Kate faltered. It was his silence alone that, for the moment, took up her apparent meaning; and before he again spoke she had returned to remembrance and prudence. They were now not to forget that, Aunt Maud's liberality having put them on their honour, they mustn't spoil their case by abusing it. He must leave her in time; they should probably find it would help them. But she came back to Milly too. "Mind you go to see her."

Densher still, however, took up nothing of this. "Then I may come again?"

"For Aunt Maud—as much as you like. But we can't again," said Kate, "play her *this* trick. I can't see you here alone."

"Then where?"

"Go to see Milly," she for all satisfaction repeated.

"And what good will that do me?"

"Try it and you'll see."

"You mean you'll manage to be there?" Densher asked. "Say you are, how will that give us privacy?"

"Try it—you'll see," the girl once more returned. "We must manage as we can."

"That's precisely what *I* feel. It strikes me we might manage better." His idea of this was a thing that made him an instant hesitate; yet he brought it out with conviction. "Why won't you come to *me?*"

It was a question her troubled eyes seemed to tell him he was scarce generous in expecting her definitely to answer, and by looking to him to wait at least she appealed to something that she presently made him feel as his pity. It was on that special shade of tenderness that he thus found himself thrown back; and while he asked of his spirit and of his flesh just what concession they could arrange she pressed him yet again on the subject of her singular remedy for their embarrassment. It might have been irritating had she ever struck him as having in her mind a stupid corner. "You'll see," she said, "the difference it will make."

Well, since she wasn't stupid she was intelligent; it was he who was stupid—the proof of which was that he would do what she liked. But he made a last effort to understand, her allusion to the "difference" bringing him round to it. He indeed caught at something subtle but strong even as he spoke. "Is what you meant a moment ago that the difference will be in her being made to believe you hate me?"

Kate, however, had simply, for this gross way of putting it, one of her more marked shows of impatience; with which in fact she sharply closed their discussion. He opened the door on a sign from her, and she accompanied him to the top of the stairs with an air of having so put their possibilities before him that questions were idle and doubts perverse. "I verily believe I *shall* hate you if you spoil for me the beauty of what I see!"

III

He was really, notwithstanding, to hear more from her of what she saw; and the very next occasion had for him still other surprises than that. He received from Mrs. Lowder on the morning after his visit to Kate the telegraphic expression of a hope that he might be free to dine with them that evening; and his freedom affected him as fortunate even though in some degree qualified by her missive. "Expecting American friends whom I'm so glad to find you know!" His knowledge of American friends was clearly an accident of which he was to taste the fruit to the last bitterness. This apprehension, however, we hasten to add, enjoyed for him, in the immediate event, a certain merciful shrinkage; the immediate event being that, at Lancaster Gate, five minutes after his due arrival, prescribed him for eight-thirty, Mrs. Stringham came in alone. The long daylight, the postponed lamps, the habit of the hour, made dinners late and guests still later; so that, punctual as he was, he had found Mrs. Lowder alone, with Kate herself not yet in the field. He had thus had with her several bewildering moments—bewildering by reason, fairly, of their tacit invitation to him to be supernaturally simple. This was exactly, goodness knew, what he wanted to be; but he had never had it so largely and freely—*so* supernaturally simply, for that matter—imputed to him as of easy achievement. It was a particular in which Aunt Maud appeared to offer herself as an example, appeared to say quite agreeably: "What I want of you, don't you see? is to be just exactly as *I* am." The quantity of the article required was what might especially have caused him to stagger—he liked so, in general, the quantities in which Mrs. Lowder dealt. He would have liked as well to ask her how feasible she supposed it for a poor young man to resemble her at any point; but he had after all soon enough perceived that he was doing as she wished by letting his wonder show just a little as silly. He was conscious moreover of a small strange dread of the results of discussion with her—strange, truly, because it was her good nature, not her asperity, that he feared. Asperity might have made him angry—in which there was always a comfort; good nature, in his conditions, had a tendency to make him ashamed—which Aunt Maud indeed, wonderfully, liking him for himself, quite struck him as having guessed. To spare him therefore she also avoided discussion; she kept him down by refusing to quarrel with him. This was what she now proposed to him to enjoy, and his secret discomfort was his sense that on the whole it was what would best suit him. Being kept down was a bore, but his great dread, verily, was of being ashamed, which was a thing distinct; and it mattered but little that he was ashamed of that too.

It was of the essence of his position that in such a house as this the tables could always be turned on him. "What do you offer, what do you offer?"—the place, however muffled in convenience and decorum, constantly hummed for him with that thick irony. The irony was a renewed reference to obvious bribes, and he had already seen how little aid came to him from denouncing the bribes as ugly in form. That was what the precious metals—they alone—could afford to be; it was vain enough for him accordingly to try to impart a gloss to his own comparative brummagem. The humiliation of this impotence was precisely what Aunt Maud sought to mitigate for him by keeping him down; and as her effort to that end had doubtless never yet been so visible he had probably never felt so definitely placed in the world as while he waited with her for her half-dozen other guests. She welcomed him genially back from the States, as to his view of which her few questions, though not coherent, were comprehensive, and he had the amusement of seeing in her, as through a clear glass, the outbreak of a plan and the sudden consciousness of a curiosity. She became aware of America, under his eyes, as a possible scene for social operations; the idea of a visit to the wonderful country had clearly but just occurred to her, yet she was talking of it, at the end of a minute, as her favourite dream. He didn't believe in it, but he pretended to; this helped her as well as anything else to treat him as harmless and blameless. She was so engaged, with the further aid of a complete absence of allusions, when the highest effect was given her method by the beautiful entrance of Kate. The method therefore received support all round, for no young man could have been less formidable than the person to the relief of whose shyness her niece ostensibly came. The ostensible, in Kate, struck him altogether, on this occasion, as prodigious; while scarcely less prodigious, for that matter, was his own reading, on the spot, of the relation between his companions—a relation lighted for him by the straight look, not exactly loving nor lingering, yet searching and soft, that, on the part of their hostess, the girl had to reckon with as she advanced. It took her in from head to foot, and in doing so it told a story that made poor Densher again the least bit sick: it marked so something with which Kate habitually and consummately reckoned.

That was the story—that she was always, for her beneficent dragon, under arms; living up, every hour, but especially at festal hours, to the "value" Mrs. Lowder had attached to her. High and fixed, this estimate ruled on each occasion at Lancaster Gate the social scene; so that he now recognised in it something like the artistic idea, the plastic substance, imposed by tradition, by genius, by criticism, in respect to a given character, on a distinguished actress. As such a person was to dress the part, to walk, to look, to speak, in every way to express, the part, so all this was what Kate was to do for the character she had undertaken, under her aunt's roof, to represent. It was made up, the character, of definite elements and touches—things all perfectly ponderable to criticism; and the way for her to meet criticism was evidently at the start to be sure her make-up had had the last touch and that she looked at least no worse than usual. Aunt Maud's appreciation of that tonight was indeed managerial, and the performer's own contribution fairly that of the faultless soldier on parade. Densher saw himself for the moment as in his purchased stall at the play; the watchful manager was in the depths of a box and the poor actress in the glare of the footlights. But she *passed*, the poor performer—he could see how she always passed; her wig, her paint, her jewels, every mark of her expression impeccable, and her entrance accordingly greeted with the proper round of applause. Such impressions as we thus note for Densher come and go, it must be granted, in very much less time than notation demands; but we may none the less make the point that there was, still further, time among them for him to feel almost too scared to take part in the ovation. He struck himself as having lost, for the minute, his presence of mind

—so that in any case he only stared in silence at the older woman's technical challenge and at the younger one's disciplined face. It was as if the drama—it thus came to him, for the fact of a drama there was no blinking—was between *them*, them quite preponderantly; with Merton Densher relegated to mere spectatorship, a paying place in front, and one of the most expensive. This was why his appreciation had turned for the instant to fear—had just turned, as we have said, to sickness; and in spite of the fact that the disciplined face did offer him over the footlights, as he believed, the small gleam, fine faint but exquisite, of a special intelligence. So might a practised performer, even when raked by double-barrelled glasses, seem to be all in her part and yet convey a sign to the person in the house she loved best.

The drama, at all events, as Densher saw it, meanwhile went on —amplified soon enough by the advent of two other guests, stray gentlemen both, stragglers in the rout of the season, who visibly presented themselves to Kate during the next moments as subjects for a like impersonal treatment and sharers in a like usual mercy. At opposite ends of the social course, they displayed, in respect to the "figure" that each, in his way, made, one the expansive, the other the contractile effect of the perfect white waistcoat. A scratch company of two innocuous youths and a pacified veteran was therefore what now offered itself to Mrs. Stringham, who rustled in a little breathless and full of the compunction of having had to come alone. Her companion, at the last moment, had been indisposed—positively not well enough, and so had packed her off, insistently, with excuses, with wild regrets. This circumstance of their charming friend's illness was the first thing Kate took up with Densher on their being able after dinner, without bravado, to have ten minutes "naturally," as she called it—which wasn't what *he* did—together; but it was already as if the young man had, by an odd impression, throughout the meal, not been wholly deprived of Miss Theale's participation. Mrs. Lowder had made dear Milly the topic, and it proved, on the spot, a topic as familiar to the enthusiastic younger as to the sagacious older man. Any knowledge they might lack Mrs. Lowder's niece was moreover alert to supply, while Densher himself was freely appealed to as the most privileged, after all, of the group. Wasn't it he who had in a manner invented the wonderful creature —through having seen her first, caught her in her native jungle? Hadn't he more or less paved the way for her by his prompt recognition of her rarity, by preceding her, in a friendly spirit—as he had the "ear" of society—with a sharp flashlight or two?

He met, poor Densher, these enquiries as he could, listening with interest, yet with discomfort; wincing in particular, dry journalist as he was, to find it seemingly supposed of him that he had put his pen—oh his "pen!"—at the service of private distinction. The ear of society?—they were talking, or almost, as if he had publicly paragraphed a modest young lady. They dreamt dreams, in truth, he appeared to perceive, that fairly waked *him* up, and he settled himself in his place both to resist his embarrassment and to catch the full revelation. His embarrassment came naturally from the fact that if he could claim no credit for Miss Theale's success, so neither could he gracefully insist on his not having been concerned with her. What touched him most nearly was that the occasion took on somehow the air of a commemorative banquet, a feast to celebrate a brilliant if brief career. There was of course more said about the heroine than if she hadn't been absent, and he found himself rather stupefied at the range of Milly's triumph. Mrs. Lowder had wonders to tell of it; the two wearers of the waistcoat, either with sincerity or with hypocrisy, professed in the matter an equal expertness; and Densher at last seemed to know himself in presence of a social "case." It was Mrs. Stringham, obviously, whose testimony would have been most invoked hadn't she been, as her friend's representative, rather confined to the function of inhaling the incense; so that Kate, who treated her beautifully, smiling at her, cheering and consoling her across the table, appeared benevolently both to speak and to interpret for her. Kate spoke as if she wouldn't perhaps understand *their* way of appreciating Milly, but would let them none the less, in justice to their good will, express it in their coarser fashion. Densher himself wasn't unconscious in respect to this of a certain broad brotherhood with Mrs. Stringham; wondering indeed, while he followed the talk, how it might move American nerves. He had only heard of them before, but in his recent tour he had caught them in the remarkable fact, and there was now a moment or two when it came to him that he had perhaps—and not in the way of an escape—taken a lesson from them.

They quivered, clearly, they hummed and drummed, they leaped and bounded in Mrs. Stringham's typical organism—this lady striking him as before all things excited, as, in the native phrase, keyed-up, to a perception of more elements in the occasion than he was himself able to count. She was accessible to sides of it, he imagined, that were as yet obscure to him; for, though she unmistakeably rejoiced and soared, he none the less saw her at moments as even more agitated than pleasure required. It was a state of emotion in her that could scarce represent simply an impatience to report at home. Her little dry New England brightness—he had "sampled" all the shades of the American complexity, if complexity it were—had its actual reasons for finding relief most in silence; so that before the subject was changed he perceived (with surprise at the others) that they had given her enough of it. He had quite had enough of it himself by the time he was asked if it were true that their friend had really not made in her own country the mark she had chalked so large in London. It was Mrs. Lowder herself who addressed him that enquiry; while he scarce knew if he were the more impressed with her launching it under Mrs. Stringham's nose or with her hope that he would allow to London the honour of discovery. The less expansive of the white waistcoats propounded the theory that they saw in London—for all that was said—much further than in the States: it wouldn't be the first time, he urged, that they had taught the Americans to appreciate (especially when it was funny) some native product. He didn't mean that Miss Theale was funny—though she was weird, and this was precisely her magic; but it might very well be that New York, in having her to show, hadn't been aware of its luck. There *were* plenty of people who were nothing over there and yet were awfully taken up in England; just as—to make the balance right, thank goodness—they sometimes sent out beauties and celebrities who left the Briton cold. The Briton's temperature in truth wasn't to be calculated—a formulation of the matter that was not reached, however, without producing in Mrs. Stringham a final feverish sally. She announced that if the point of view for a proper admiration of her young friend *had* seemed to fail a little in New York, there was no manner of doubt of her having carried Boston by storm. It pointed the moral that Boston, for the finer taste, left New York nowhere; and the good lady, as the exponent of this doctrine—which she set forth at a certain length—made, obviously, to Densher's mind, her nearest approach to supplying the weirdness in which Milly's absence had left them deficient. She made it indeed effective for him by suddenly addressing him. "You know nothing, sir—but not the least little bit—about my friend."

He hadn't pretended he did, but there was a purity of reproach in Mrs. Stringham's face and tone, a purity charged apparently with solemn meanings; so that for a little, small as had been his claim, he couldn't but feel that she exaggerated. He wondered what she did mean, but while doing so he defended himself. "I certainly don't know enormously much—beyond her having been most kind to me, in New York, as a poor bewildered and newly landed alien, and my having tremendously appreciated it." To which he added, he scarce knew why, what had an immediate success. "Remember, Mrs. Stringham, that you weren't then present."

"Ah there you are!" said Kate with much gay expression, though what it expressed he failed at the time to make out.

"You weren't present *then*, dearest," Mrs. Lowder richly concurred. "You don't know," she continued with mellow gaiety, "how far things may have gone."

It made the little woman, he could see, really lose her head. She had more things in that head than any of them in any other; unless perhaps it were Kate, whom he felt as indirectly watching him during this foolish passage, though it pleased him—and because of the foolishness—not to meet her eyes. He met Mrs. Stringham's, which affected him: with her he could on occasion clear it up—a sense produced by the mute communion between them and really the beginning, as the event was to show, of something extraordinary. It was even already a little the effect of this communion that Mrs. Stringham perceptibly faltered in her retort to Mrs. Lowder's joke. "Oh it's precisely my point that Mr. Densher *can't* have had vast opportunities." And then she smiled at him. "I wasn't away, you know, long."

It made everything, in the oddest way in the world, immediately right for him. "And I wasn't *there* long, either." He positively saw with it that nothing for him, so far as she was concerned, would again be wrong. "She's beautiful, but I don't say she's easy to know."

"Ah she's a thousand and one things!" replied the good lady, as if now to keep well with him.

He asked nothing better. "She was off with you to these parts before I knew it. I myself was off too—away off to wonderful parts, where I had endlessly more to see."

"But you didn't forget her!" Aunt Maud interposed with almost menacing archness.

"No, of course I didn't forget her. One doesn't forget such charming impressions. But I never," he lucidly maintained, "chattered to others about her."

"She'll thank you for that, sir," said Mrs. Stringham with a flushed firmness.

"Yet doesn't silence in such a case," Aunt Maud blandly enquired, "very often quite prove the depth of the impression?"

He would have been amused, hadn't he been slightly displeased. at all they seemed desirous to fasten on him. "Well, the impression was as deep as you like. But I really want Miss Theale to know," he pursued for Mrs. Stringham, "that I don't figure by any consent of my own as an authority about her."

Kate came to his assistance—if assistance it was—before their friend had had time to meet this charge. "You're right about her not being easy to know. One *sees* her with intensity—sees her more than one sees almost any one; but then one discovers that that isn't knowing her and that one may know better a person whom one doesn't 'see,' as I say, half so much."

The discrimination was interesting, but it brought them back to the fact of her success; and it was at that comparatively gross circumstance, now so fully placed before them, that Milly's anxious companion sat and looked—looked very much as some spectator in an old-time circus might have watched the oddity of a Christian maiden, in the arena, mildly, caressingly, martyred. It was the nosing and fumbling not of lions and tigers but of domestic animals let loose as for the joke. Even the joke made Mrs. Stringham uneasy, and her mute communion with Densher, to which we have alluded, was more and more determined by it. He wondered afterwards if Kate had made this out; though it was not indeed till much later on that he found himself, in thought, dividing the things she might have been conscious of from the things she must have missed. If she actually missed, at any rate, Mrs. Stringham's discomfort, that but showed how her own idea held her. Her own idea was, by insisting on the fact of the girl's prominence as a feature of the season's end, to keep Densher in relation, for the rest of them, both to present and to past. "It's everything that has happened *since* that makes you naturally a little shy about her. You don't know what has happened since, but we do; we've seen it and followed it; we've a little been *of* it." The great thing for him, at this, as Kate gave it, *was* in fact quite irresistibly that the case was a real one—the kind of thing that, when one's patience was shorter than one's curiosity, one had vaguely taken for possible in London, but in which one had never been even to this small extent concerned. The little American's sudden social adventure, her happy and, no doubt, harmless flourish, had probably been favoured by several accidents, but it had been favoured above all by the simple spring-board of the scene, by one of those common caprices of the numberless foolish flock, gregarious movements as inscrutable as ocean-currents. The huddled herd had drifted to her blindly—it might as blindly have drifted away. There had been of course a signal, but the great reason was probably the absence at the moment of a larger lion. The bigger beast would come and the smaller would then incontinently vanish. It was at all events characteristic, and what was of the essence of it was grist to his scribbling mill, matter for his journalising hand. That hand already, in intention, played over it, the "motive," as a sign of the season, a feature of the time, of the purely expeditious and rough-and-tumble nature of the social boom. The boom as in *itself* required—that would be the note; the subject of the process a comparatively minor question. Anything was boomable enough when nothing else was more so: the author of the "rotten" book, the beauty who was no beauty, the heiress who was only that, the stranger who was for the most part saved from being inconveniently strange but by being inconveniently familiar, the American whose Americanism had been long desperately discounted, the creature in fine as to whom spangles or spots of any sufficiently marked and exhibited sort could be loudly enough predicated.

So he judged at least, within his limits, and the idea that what he had thus caught in the fact was the trick of fashion and the tone of society went so far as to make him take up again his sense of independence. He had supposed himself civilised; but if this was civilisation—! One could smoke one's pipe outside when twaddle was within. He had rather avoided, as we have remarked, Kate's eyes, but there came a moment when he would fairly have liked to put it, across the table, to her: "I say, light of my life, is *this* the great world?" There came another, it must be added—and doubtless as a result of something that, over the cloth, did hang between them—when she struck him as having quite answered: "Dear no—for what do you take me? Not the least little bit: only a poor silly, though quite harmless, imitation." What she might have passed for saying, however, was practically merged in what she did say, for she came overtly to his aid, very much as if guessing some of his thoughts. She enunciated, to relieve his bewilderment, the obvious truth that you couldn't leave London for three months at that time of the year and come back to find your friends just where they were. As they had *of course* been jigging away they might well be so red in the face that you wouldn't know them. She reconciled in fine his disclaimer about Milly with that honour of having discovered her which it was vain for him modestly to shirk. He *had* unearthed her, but it was they, all of them together, who had developed her. She was always a charmer, one of the greatest ever seen, but she wasn't the person he had "backed."

Densher was to feel sure afterwards that Kate had had in these pleasantries no conscious, above all no insolent purpose of making light of poor Susan Shepherd's property in their young friend—which property, by such remarks, was very much pushed to the wall; but he was also to know that Mrs. Stringham had secretly resented them, Mrs. Stringham holding the opinion, of which he was ultimately to have a glimpse, that all the Kate Croys in Christendom were but dust for the feet of her Milly. That, it was true, would be what she must reveal only when driven to her last entrenchments and well cornered in her passion—the rare passion of friendship, the sole passion of her little life save the one other, more imperturbably cerebral, that she entertained for the art of Guy de Maupassant.[1] She slipped in the observation that her Milly was

1. Maupassant (1850–93), a naturalistic novelist and master of the short story, was often viewed by British and American readers as at once too morbid and too concerned with sexuality. James, for years an admirer of Maupassant's concision and compactness, wrote a lengthy essay on his work (1888) praising it but finding it deficient in that it ignored what he called the reflective consciousness which informs character and behavior.

incapable of change, was just exactly, on the contrary, the same Milly; but this made little difference in the drift of Kate's contention. She was perfectly kind to Susie: it was as if she positively knew her as handicapped for any disagreement by feeling that she, Kate, had "type," and by being committed to admiration of type. Kate had occasion subsequently—she found it somehow—to mention to our young man Milly's having spoken to her of this view on the good lady's part. She would like—Milly had had it from her—to put Kate Croy in a book and see what she could so do with her. "Chop me up fine or serve me whole"—it was a way of being got at that Kate professed she dreaded. It would be Mrs. Stringham's, however, she understood, because Mrs. Stringham, oddly, felt that with such stuff as the strange English girl was made of, stuff that (in spite of Maud Manningham, who was full of sentiment) she had never known, there was none other to be employed. These things were of later evidence, yet Densher might even then have felt them in the air. They were practically in it already when Kate, waiving the question of her friend's chemical change, wound up with the comparatively unobjectionable proposition that he must now, having missed so much, take them all up, on trust, further on. He met it peacefully, a little perhaps as an example to Mrs. Stringham—"Oh as far on as you like!" This even had its effect: Mrs. Stringham appropriated as much of it as might be meant for herself. The nice thing about her was that she could measure how much; so that by the time dinner was over they had really covered ground.

IV

The younger of the other men, it afterwards appeared, was most in his element at the piano; so that they had coffee and comic songs upstairs—the gentlemen, temporarily relinquished, submitting easily in this interest to Mrs. Lowder's parting injunction not to sit too tight. Our especial young man sat tighter when restored to the drawing-room; he made it out perfectly with Kate that they might, off and on, foregather without offence. He had perhaps stronger needs in this general respect than she; but she had better names for the scant risks to which she consented. It was the blessing of a big house that intervals were large and, of an August night, that windows were open; whereby, at a given moment, on the wide balcony, with the songs sufficiently sung, Aunt Maud could hold her little court more freshly. Densher and Kate, during these moments, occupied side by side a small sofa—a luxury formulated by the latter as the proof, under criticism, of their remarkably good conscience. "To seem not to know each other—once you're here—would be," the girl said, "to overdo it"; and she arranged it charmingly that they *must* have some passage to put Aunt Maud off the scent. She would be wondering otherwise what in the world they found their account in. For Densher, none the less, the profit of snatched moments, snatched contacts, was partial and poor; there were in particular at present more things in his mind than he could bring out while watching the windows. It was true, on the other hand, that she suddenly met most of them—and more than he could see on the spot —by coming out for him with a reference to Milly that was not in the key of those made at dinner. "She's not a bit right, you know. I mean in health. Just see her tonight. I mean it looks grave. For you she would have come, you know, if it had been at all possible."

He took this in such patience as he could muster. "What in the world's the matter with her?"

But Kate continued without saying. "Unless indeed your being here has been just a reason for her funking it."

"What in the world's the matter with her?" Densher asked again.

"Why just what I've told you—that she likes you so much."

"Then why should she deny herself the joy of meeting me?"

Kate cast about—it would take so long to explain. "And perhaps it's true that she *is* bad. She easily may be."

"Quite easily, I should say, judging by Mrs. Stringham, who's visibly preoccupied and worried."

"Visibly enough. Yet it mayn't," said Kate, "be only for that."

"For what then?"

But this question too, on thinking, she neglected. "Why, if it's anything real, doesn't that poor lady go home? She'd be anxious, and she has done all she need to be civil."

"I think," Densher remarked, "she has been quite beautifully civil."

It made Kate, he fancied, look at him the least bit harder; but she was already, in a manner, explaining. "Her preoccupation is probably on two different heads. One of them would make her hurry back, but the other makes her stay. She's commissioned to tell Milly all about you."

"Well then," said the young man between a laugh and a sigh, "I'm glad I felt, downstairs, a kind of 'drawing' to her. Wasn't I rather decent to her?"

"Awfully nice. You've instincts, you fiend. It's all," Kate declared, "as it should be."

"Except perhaps," he after a moment cynically suggested, "that she isn't getting much good of me now. Will she report to Milly on *this*?" And then as Kate seemed to wonder what "this" might be: "On our present disregard for appearances."

"Ah leave appearances to me!" She spoke in her high way. "I'll make them all right. Aunt Maud, moreover," she added, "has her so engaged that she won't notice." Densher felt, with this, that his companion had indeed perceptive flights he couldn't hope to match—had for instance another when she still subjoined: "And Mrs. Stringham's appearing to respond just in order to make that impression."

"Well," Densher dropped with some humour, "life's very interesting! I hope it's really as much so for you as you make it for others; I mean judging by what you make it for me. You seem to me to represent it as thrilling for *ces dames*,[1] and in a different way for each: Aunt Maud, Susan Shepherd, Milly. But what *is*," he wound up, "the matter? Do you mean she's as ill as she looks?"

Kate's face struck him as replying at first that his derisive speech deserved no satisfaction; then she appeared to yield to a need of her own—the need to make the point that "as ill as she looked" was what Milly scarce could be. If she had been as ill as she looked she could scarce be a question with them, for her end would in that case be near. She believed herself nevertheless—and Kate couldn't help believing her too—seriously menaced. There was always the fact that they had been on the point of leaving town, the two ladies, and had suddenly been pulled up. "We bade them good-bye—or all but—Aunt Maud and I, the night before Milly, popping so very oddly into the National Gallery for a farewell look, found you and me together. They were then to get off a day or two later. But they've not got off—they're not getting off. When I see them—and I saw them this morning—they have showy reasons. They do mean to go, but they've postponed it." With which the girl brought out: "They've postponed it for *you*." He protested so far as a man might without fatuity, since a protest was itself credulous; but Kate, as ever, understood herself. "You've made Milly change her mind. She wants not to miss you—though she wants also not to show she wants you; which is why, as I hinted a moment ago, she may consciously have hung back to-night. She doesn't know when she may see you again—she doesn't know she ever may. She doesn't see the future. It has opened out before her in these last weeks as a dark confused thing."

Densher wondered. "After the tremendous time you've all been telling me she has had?"

"That's it. There's a shadow across it."

"The shadow, you consider, of some physical break-up?"

"Some physical break-down. Nothing less. She's scared. She has so much to lose. And she wants more."

"Ah well," said Densher with a sudden strange sense of discomfort, "couldn't one say to her that she can't have everything?"

"No—for one wouldn't want to. She really," Kate went on, "has

1. "Those ladies."

been somebody here. Ask Aunt Maud—you may think me prejudiced," the girl oddly smiled. "Aunt Maud will tell you—the world's before her. It has all come since you saw her, and it's a pity you've missed it, for it certainly would have amused you. She has really been a perfect success—I mean of course so far as possible in the scrap of time—and she has taken it like a perfect angel. If you can imagine an angel with a thumping bank-account you'll have the simplest expression of the kind of thing. Her fortune's absolutely huge; Aunt Maud has had all the facts, or enough of them, in the last confidence, from 'Susie,' and Susie speaks by book. Take them then, in the last confidence, from *me*. There she is." Kate expressed above all what it most came to. "It's open to her to make, you see, the very greatest marriage. I assure you we're not vulgar about her. Her possibilities are quite plain."

Densher showed he neither disbelieved nor grudged them. "But what good then on earth can I do her?"

Well, she had it ready. "You can console her."

"And for what?"

"For all that, if she's stricken, she must see swept away. I shouldn't care for her if she hadn't so much," Kate very simply said. And then as it made him laugh not quite happily: "I shouldn't trouble about her if there were one thing she did have." The girl spoke indeed with a noble compassion. "She has nothing."

"Not all the young dukes?"

"Well we must see—see if anything can come of them. She at any rate does love life. To have met a person like you," Kate further explained, "is to have felt you become, with all the other fine things, a part of life. Oh she has you arranged!"

"*You* have, it strikes me, my dear"—and he looked both detached and rueful. "Pray what am I to do with the dukes?"

"Oh the dukes will be disappointed!"

"Then why shan't I be?"

"You'll have expected less," Kate wonderfully smiled. "Besides, you *will* be. You'll have expected enough for that."

"Yet it's what you want to let me in for?"

"I want," said the girl, "to make things pleasant for her. I use, for the purpose, what I have. You're what I have of most precious, and you're therefore what I use most."

He looked at her long. "I wish I could use *you* a little more." After which, as she continued to smile at him, "Is it a bad case of lungs?" he asked.

Kate showed for a little as if she wished it might be. "Not lungs, I think. Isn't consumption, taken in time, now curable?"

"People are, no doubt, patched up." But he wondered. "Do you mean she has something that's past patching?" And before she could answer: "It's really as if her appearance put her outside of such things—being, in spite of her youth, that of a person who has been through all it's conceivable she should be exposed to. She affects one, I should say, as a creature saved from a shipwreck. Such a creature may surely, in these days, on the doctrine of chances, go to sea again with confidence. She has *had* her wreck—she has met her adventure."

"Oh I grant you her wreck!"—Kate was all response so far. "But do let her have still her adventure. There are wrecks that are not adventures."

"Well—if there be also adventures that are not wrecks!" Densher in short was willing, but he came back to his point. "What I mean is that she has none of the effect—on one's nerves or whatever—of an invalid."

Kate on her side did this justice. "No—that's the beauty of her."

"The beauty—?"

"Yes, she's so wonderful. She won't show for that, any more than your watch, when it's about to stop for want of being wound up, gives you convenient notice or shows as different from usual. She won't die, she won't live, by inches. She won't smell, as it were, of drugs. She won't taste, as it were, of medicine. No one will know."

"Then what," he demanded, frankly mystified now, "are we talking about? In what extraordinary state *is* she?"

Kate went on as if, at this, making it out in a fashion for herself. "I believe that if she's ill at all she's very ill. I believe that if she's bad she's not a *little* bad. I can't tell you why, but that's how I see her. She'll really live or she'll really not. She'll have it all or she'll miss it all. Now I don't think she'll have it all."

Densher had followed this with his eyes upon her, her own having thoughtfully wandered, and as if it were more impressive than lucid. "You 'think' and you 'don't think,' and yet you remain all the while without an inkling of her complaint?"

"No, not without an inkling; but it's a matter in which I don't want knowledge. She moreover herself doesn't want one to want it: she has, as to what may be preying upon her, a kind of ferocity of modesty, a kind of—I don't know what to call it—intensity of pride. And then and then—" But with this she faltered.

"And then what?"

"I'm a brute about illness. I hate it. It's well for you, my dear," Kate continued, "that you're as sound as a bell."

"Thank you!" Densher laughed. "It's rather good then for yourself too that you're as strong as the sea."

She looked at him now a moment as for the selfish gladness of their young immunities. It was all they had together, but they had it at least without a flaw—each had the beauty, the physical felicity, the personal virtue, love and desire of the other. Yet it was as if that very consciousness threw them back the next moment into pity for the poor girl who had everything else in the world, the great genial good they, alas, didn't have, but failed on the other hand of this. "How we're talking about her!" Kate compunctiously sighed. But there were the facts. "From illness I keep away."

"But you don't—since here you are, in spite of all you say, in the midst of it."

"Ah I'm only watching—!"

"And putting me forward in your place? Thank you!"

"Oh," said Kate, "I'm breaking you in. Let it give you the measure of what I shall expect of you. One can't begin too soon."

She drew away, as from the impression of a stir on the balcony, the hand of which he had a minute before possessed himself; and the warning brought him back to attention. "You haven't even an idea if it's a case for surgery?"

"I dare say it may be; that is that if it comes to anything it may come to that. Of course she's in the highest hands."

"The doctors are after her then?"

"She's after *them*—it's the same thing. I think I'm free to say it now—she sees Sir Luke Strett."

It made him quickly wince. "Ah fifty thousand knives!" Then after an instant: "One seems to guess."

Yes, but she waved it away. "Don't guess. Only do as I tell you."

For a moment now, in silence, he took it all in, might have had it before him. "What you want of me then is to make up to a sick girl."

"Ah but you admit yourself that she doesn't affect you as sick. You understand moreover just how much—and just how little."

"It's amazing," he presently answered, "what you think I understand."

"Well, if you've brought me to it, my dear," she returned, "that has been your way of breaking *me* in. Besides which, so far as making up to her goes, plenty of others will."

Densher for a little, under this suggestion, might have been seeing their young friend on a pile of cushions and in a perpetual tea-gown, amid flowers and with drawn blinds, surrounded by the higher nobility. "Others can follow their tastes. Besides, others are free."

"But so are you, my dear!"

She had spoken with impatience, and her suddenly quitting him had sharpened it; in spite of which he kept his place, only looking up at her. "You're prodigious!"

"Of course I'm prodigious!"—and, as immediately happened, she gave a further sign of it that he fairly sat watching. The door from the lobby had, as she spoke, been thrown open for a gentleman who, immediately finding her within his view, advanced to greet her before the announcement of his name could reach her companion. Densher none the less felt himself brought quickly into relation; Kate's welcome to the visitor became almost precipitately an appeal to her friend, who slowly rose to meet it. "I don't know whether you know Lord Mark." And then for the other party: "Mr. Merton Densher—who has just come back from America."

"Oh!" said the other party while Densher said nothing—occupied as he mainly was on the spot with weighing the sound in question. He recognised it in a moment as less imponderable than it might have appeared, as having indeed positive claims. It wasn't, that is, he knew, the "Oh!" of the idiot, however great the superficial resemblance: it was that of the clever, the accomplished man; it was the very specialty of the speaker, and a deal of expensive training and experience had gone to producing it. Densher felt somehow that, as a thing of value accidentally picked up, it would retain an interest of curiosity. The three stood for a little together in an awkwardness to which he was conscious of contributing his share; Kate failing to ask Lord Mark to be seated, but letting him know that he would find Mrs. Lowder, with some others, on the balcony.

"Oh and Miss Theale I suppose?—as I seemed to hear outside, from below, Mrs. Stringham's unmistakeable voice."

"Yes, but Mrs. Stringham's alone. Milly's unwell," the girl explained, "and was compelled to disappoint us."

"Ah 'disappoint'—rather!" And, lingering a little, he kept his eyes on Densher. "She isn't really bad, I trust?"

Densher, after all he had heard, easily supposed him interested in Milly; but he could imagine him also interested in the young man with whom he had found Kate engaged and whom he yet considered without visible intelligence. That young man concluded in a moment that he was doing what he wanted, satisfying himself as to each. To this he was aided by Kate, who produced a prompt: "Oh dear no; I think not. I've just been reassuring Mr. Densher," she added—"who's as concerned as the rest of us. I've been calming his fears."

"Oh!" said Lord Mark again—and again it was just as good. That was for Densher, the latter could see, or think he saw. And then for the others: "*My* fears would want calming. We must take great care of her. This way?"

She went with him a few steps, and while Densher, hanging about, gave them frank attention, presently paused again for some further colloquy. What passed between them their observer lost, but she was presently with him again, Lord Mark joining the rest.

Densher was by this time quite ready for her. "It's *he* who's your aunt's man?"

"Oh immensely."

"I mean for *you*."

"That's what I mean too," Kate smiled. "There he is. Now you can judge."

"Judge of what?"

"Judge of him."

"Why should I judge of him?" Densher asked. "I've nothing to do with him."

"Then why do you ask about him?"

"To judge of you—which is different."

Kate seemed for a little to look at the difference. "To take the measure, do you mean, of my danger?"

He hesitated; then he said: "I'm thinking, I dare say, of Miss Theale's. How does your aunt reconcile his interest in her—?"

"With his interest in me?"

"With her own interest in you," Densher said while she reflected. "If that interest—Mrs. Lowder's—takes the form of Lord Mark, hasn't he rather to look out for the forms *he* takes?"

Kate seemed interested in the question, but "Oh he takes them easily," she answered. "The beauty is that she doesn't trust him."

"That Milly doesn't?"

"Yes—Milly either. But I mean Aunt Maud. Not really."

Densher gave it his wonder. "Takes him to her heart and yet thinks he cheats?"

"Yes," said Kate—"that's the way people are. What they think of their enemies, goodness knows, is bad enough; but I'm still more struck with what they think of their friends. Milly's own state of mind, however," she went on, "is lucky. That's Aunt Maud's security, though she doesn't yet fully recognise it—besides being Milly's own."

"You conceive it a real escape then not to care for him?"

She shook her head in beautiful grave deprecation. "You oughtn't to make me say too much. But I'm glad I don't."

"Don't say too much?"

"Don't care for Lord Mark."

"Oh!" Densher answered with a sound like his lordship's own. To which he added: "You absolutely hold that that poor girl doesn't?"

"Ah you know what I hold about that poor girl!" It had made her again impatient.

Yet he stuck a minute to the subject. "You scarcely call him, I suppose, one of the dukes."

"Mercy, no—far from it. He's not, compared with other possibilities, 'in' it. Milly, it's true," she said, to be exact, "has no natural sense of social values, doesn't in the least understand our differences or know who's who or what's what."

"I see. That," Densher laughed, "is her reason for liking *me*."

"Precisely. She doesn't resemble me," said Kate, "who at least know what I lose."

Well, it had all risen for Densher to a considerable interest. "And Aunt Maud—why shouldn't *she* know? I mean that your friend there isn't really anything. Does she suppose him of ducal value?"

"Scarcely; save in the sense of being uncle to a duke. That's undeniably something. He's the best moreover we can get."

"Oh, oh!" said Densher; and his doubt was not all derisive.

"It isn't Lord Mark's grandeur," she went on without heeding this; "because perhaps in the line of that alone—as he has no money—more could be done. But she's not a bit sordid; she only counts with the sordidness of others. Besides, he's grand enough, with a duke in his family and at the other end of the string. *The* thing's his genius."

"And do you believe in that?"

"In Lord Mark's genius?" Kate, as if for a more final opinion than had yet been asked of her, took a moment to think. She balanced indeed so that one would scarce have known what to expect; but she came out in time with a very sufficient "Yes!"

"Political?"

"Universal. I don't know at least," she said, "what else to call it when a man's able to make himself without effort, without violence, without machinery of any sort, so intensely felt. He has somehow an effect without his being in any traceable way a cause."

"Ah but if the effect," said Densher with conscious superficiality, "isn't agreeable—?"

"Oh but it is!"

"Not surely for every one."

"If you mean not for you," Kate returned, "you may have reasons—and men don't count. Women don't know if it's agreeable or not."

"Then there you are!"

"Yes, precisely—that takes, on his part, genius."

Densher stood before her as if he wondered what everything she thus promptly, easily and above all amusingly met him with, would have been found, should it have come to an analysis, to "take." Something suddenly, as if under a last determinant touch, welled up in him and overflowed—the sense of his good fortune and her variety, of the future she promised, the interest she supplied. "All women but you are stupid. How can I look at another? You're different and different—and then you're different again. No marvel Aunt Maud builds on you—except that you're so much too good for what she builds *for*. Even 'society' won't know how good for it you are; it's too stupid, and you're beyond it. You'd have to pull it uphill—it's you yourself who are at the top. The women one meets—what are they but books one has already read? You're a whole library of the unknown, the uncut." He almost moaned, he ached, from the depth of his content. "Upon my word I've a subscription!"

She took it from him with her face again giving out all it had in answer, and they remained once more confronted and united in their essential wealth of life. "It's you who draw me out. I exist in you. Not in others."

It had been, however, as if the thrill of their association itself pressed in him, as great felicities do, the sharp spring of fear. "See here, you know: don't, *don't*—!"

"Don't what?"

"Don't fail me. It would kill me."

She looked at him a minute with no response but her eyes. "So you think you'll kill *me* in time to prevent it?" She smiled, but he saw her the next instant as smiling through tears; and the instant after this she had got, in respect to the particular point, quite off. She had come back to another, which was one of her own; her own were so closely connected that Densher's were at best but parenthetic. Still she had a distance to go. "You do then see your way?" She put it to him before they joined—as was high time—the others. And she made him understand she meant his way with Milly.

He had dropped a little in presence of the explanation; then she had brought him up to a sort of recognition. He could make out by this light something of what he saw, but a dimness also there was, undispelled since his return. "There's something you must definitely tell me. If our friend knows that all the while—?"

She came straight to his aid, formulating for him his anxiety, though quite to smooth it down. "All the while she and I here were growing intimate, you and I were in unmentioned relation? If she knows that, yes, she knows our relation must have involved your writing to me."

"Then how could she suppose you weren't answering?"

"She doesn't suppose it."

"How then can she imagine you never named her?"

"She doesn't. She knows now I did name her. I've told her everything. She's in possession of reasons that will perfectly do."

Still he just brooded. "She takes things from you exactly as I take them?"

"Exactly as you take them."

"She's just such another victim?"

"Just such another. You're a pair."

"Then if anything happens," said Densher, "we can console each other?"

"Ah something *may* indeed happen," she returned, "if you'll only go straight!"

He watched the others an instant through the window. "What do you mean by going straight?"

"Not worrying. Doing as you like. Try, as I've told you before, and you'll see. You'll have me perfectly, always, to refer to."

"Oh rather, I hope! But if she's going away?"

It pulled Kate up but a moment. "I'll bring her back. There you are. You won't be able to say I haven't made it smooth for you."

He faced it all, and certainly it was queer. But it wasn't the queerness that after another minute was uppermost. He was in a wondrous silken web, and it *was* amusing. "You spoil me!"

He wasn't sure if Mrs. Lowder, who at this juncture reappeared, had caught his word as it dropped from him; probably not, he thought, her attention being given to Mrs. Stringham, with whom she came through and who was now, none too soon, taking leave of her. They were followed by Lord Mark and by the other men, but two or three things happened before any dispersal of the company began. One of these was that Kate found time to say to him with furtive emphasis: "You must go now!" Another was that she next addressed herself in all frankness to Lork Mark, drew near to him with an almost reproachful "Come and talk to *me!*"—a challenge resulting after a minute for Densher in a consciousness of their installation together in an out-of-the-way corner, though not the same he himself had just occupied with her. Still another was that Mrs. Stringham, in the random intensity of her farewells, affected him as looking at him with a small grave intimation, something into which he afterwards read the meaning that if he had happened to desire a few words with her after dinner he would have found her ready. This impression was naturally light, but it just left him with the sense of something by his own act overlooked, unappreciated. It gathered perhaps a slightly sharper shade from the mild formality of her "Good-night, sir!" as she passed him; a matter as to which there was now nothing more to be done, thanks to the alertness of the young man he by this time had appraised as even more harmless than himself. This personage had forestalled him in opening the door for her and was evidently—with a view, Densher might have judged, to ulterior designs on Milly—proposing to attend her to her carriage. What further occurred was that Aunt Maud, having released her, immediately had a word for himself. It was an imperative "Wait a minute," by which she both detained and dismissed him; she was particular about her minute, but he hadn't yet given her, as happened, a sign of withdrawal.

"Return to our little friend. You'll find her really interesting."

"If you mean Miss Theale," he said, "I shall certainly not forget her. But you must remember that, so far as her 'interest' is concerned, I myself discovered, I—as was said at dinner—invented her."

"Well, one seemed rather to gather that you hadn't taken out the patent. Don't, I only mean, in the press of other things, too much neglect her."

Affected, surprised by the coincidence of her appeal with Kate's, he asked himself quickly if it mightn't help him with her. He at any rate could but try. "You're all looking after my manners. That's exactly, you know, what Miss Croy has been saying to me. *She* keeps me up—she has had so much to say about them."

He found pleasure in being able to give his hostess an account of his passage with Kate that, while quite veracious, might be reassuring to herself. But Aunt Maud, wonderfully and facing him straight, took it as if her confidence were supplied with other props. If she saw his intention in it she yet blinked neither with doubt nor with acceptance; she only said imperturbably: "Yes, she'll herself do anything for her friend; so that she but preaches what she practises."

Densher really quite wondered if Aunt Maud knew how far Kate's devotion went. He was moreover a little puzzled by this special harmony; in face of which he quickly asked himself if Mrs. Lowder had bethought herself of the American girl as a distraction for him, and if Kate's mastery of the subject were therefore but an appearance addressed to her aunt. What might really *become* in all this of the American girl was therefore a question that, on the latter contingency, would lose none of its sharpness. However, questions could wait, and it was easy, so far as he understood, to meet Mrs. Lowder. "It isn't a bit, all the same, you know, that I resist. I find Miss Theale charming."

Well, it was all she wanted. "Then don't miss a chance."

"The only thing is," he went on, "that she's—naturally now—leaving town and, as I take it, going abroad."

Aunt Maud looked indeed an instant as if she herself had been dealing with this difficulty. "She won't go," she smiled in spite of it, "till she has seen you. Moreover, when she does go—" She paused, leaving him uncertain. But the next minute he was still more at sea. "We shall go too."

He gave a smile that he himself took for slightly strange. "And what good will that do *me*?"

"We shall be near them somewhere, and you'll come out to us."

"Oh!" he said a little awkwardly.

"I'll see that you do. I mean I'll write to you."

"Ah thank you, thank you!" Merton Densher laughed. She was indeed putting him on his honour, and his honour winced a little at the use he rather helplessly saw himself suffering her to believe she could make of it. "There are all sorts of things," he vaguely remarked, "to consider."

"No doubt. But there's above all the great thing."

"And pray what's that?"

"Why the importance of your not losing the occasion of your life. I'm treating you handsomely, I'm looking after it for you. I *can*—I can smooth your path. She's charming, she's clever and she's good. And her fortune's a real fortune."

Ah there she was, Aunt Maud! The pieces fell together for him as he felt her thus buying him off, and buying him—it would have been funny if it hadn't been so grave—with Miss Theale's money. He ventured, derisive, fairly to treat it as extravagant. "I'm much obliged to you for the handsome offer—"

"Of what doesn't belong to me?" She wasn't abashed. "I don't say it does—but there's no reason it shouldn't to *you*. Mind you moreover"—she kept it up—"I'm not one who talks in the air. And you owe me something—if you want to know why."

Distinct he felt her pressure; he felt, given her basis, her consistency; he even felt, to a degree that was immediately to receive an odd confirmation, her truth. Her truth, for that matter, was that she believed him bribeable: a belief that for his own mind as well, while they stood there, lighted up the impossible. What then in this light did Kate believe him? But that wasn't what he asked aloud. "Of course I know I owe you thanks for a deal of kind treatment. Your inviting me for instance to-night—!"

"Yes, my inviting you to-night's a part of it. But you don't know," she added, "how far I've gone for you."

He felt himself red and as if his honour were colouring up; but he laughed again as he could. "I see how far you're going."

"I'm the most honest woman in the world, but I've nevertheless done for you what was necessary." And then as her now quite sombre gravity only made him stare: "To start you it *was* necessary. From *me* it has the weight." He but continued to stare, and she met his blankness with surprise. "Don't you understand me?

I've told the proper lie for you." Still he only showed her his flushed strained smile; in spite of which, speaking with force and as if he must with a minute's reflexion see what she meant, she turned away from him. "I depend upon you now to make me right!"

The minute's reflexion he was of course more free to take after he had left the house. He walked up the Bayswater Road, but he stopped short, under the murky stars, before the modern church, in the middle of the square that, going eastward, opened out on his left. He had had his brief stupidity, but now he understood. She had guaranteed to Milly Theale through Mrs. Stringham that Kate didn't care for him. She had affirmed through the same source that the attachment was only his. He made it out, he made it out, and he could see what she meant by its starting him. She had described Kate as merely compassionate, so that Milly might be compassionate too. "Proper" indeed it was, her lie—the very properest possible and the most deeply, richly diplomatic. So Milly was successfully deceived.

V

To see her alone, the poor girl, he none the less promptly felt, was to see her after all very much on the old basis, the basis of his three visits in New York; the new element, when once he was again face to face with her, not really amounting to much more than a recognition, with a little surprise, of the positive extent of the old basis. Everything but that, everything embarrassing fell away after he had been present five minutes: it was in fact wonderful that their excellent, their pleasant, their permitted and proper and harmless American relation—the legitimacy of which he could thus scarce express in names enough—should seem so unperturbed by other matters. They had both since then had great adventures—such an adventure for him was his mental annexation of her country; and it was now, for the moment, as if the greatest of them all were this acquired consciousness of reasons other than those that had already served. Densher had asked for her, at her hotel, the day after Aunt Maud's dinner, with a rich, that is with a highly troubled, preconception of the part likely to be played for him at present, in any contact with her, by Kate's and Mrs. Lowder's so oddly conjoined and so really superfluous attempts to make her interesting. She had been interesting enough without them—that appeared to-day to come back to him; and, admirable and beautiful as was the charitable zeal of the two ladies, it might easily have nipped in the bud the germs of a friendship inevitably limited but still perfectly open to him. What had happily averted the need of his breaking off, what would as happily continue to avert it, was his own good sense and good humour, a certain spring of mind in him which ministered, imagination aiding, to understandings and allowances and which he had positively never felt such ground as just now to rejoice in the possession of. Many men—he practically made the reflexion—wouldn't have taken the matter that way, would have lost patience, finding the appeal in question irrational, exorbitant; and, thereby making short work with it, would have let it render any further acquaintance with Miss Theale impossible. He had talked with Kate of this young woman's being "sacrificed," and that would have been one way, so far as he was concerned, to sacrifice her. Such, however, had not been the tune to which his at first bewildered view had, since the night before, cleared itself up. It wasn't so much that he failed of being the kind of man who "chucked," for he knew himself as the kind of man wise enough to mark the case in which chucking might be the minor evil and the least cruelty. It was that he liked too much every one concerned willingly to show himself merely impracticable. He liked Kate, goodness knew, and he also clearly enough liked Mrs. Lowder. He liked in particular Milly herself; and hadn't it come up for him the evening before that he quite liked even Susan Shepherd? He had never known himself so generally merciful. It was a footing, at all events, whatever accounted for it, on which he should surely be rather a muff not to manage by one turn or another to escape disobliging. Should he find he couldn't work it there would still be time enough. The idea of working it crystallised before him in such guise as not only to promise much interest—fairly, in case of success, much enthusiasm; but positively to impart to failure an appearance of barbarity.

Arriving thus in Brook Street both with the best intentions and with a margin consciously left for some primary awkwardness, he found his burden, to his great relief, unexpectedly light. The awkwardness involved in the responsibility so newly and so ingeniously traced for him turned round on the spot to present him another face. This was simply the face of his old impression, which he now fully recovered—the impression that American girls, when, rare case, they had the attraction of Milly, were clearly the easiest people in the world. Had what had happened been that this specimen of the class was from the first so committed to ease that nothing subsequent *could* ever make her difficult? That affected him now as still more probable than on the occasion of the hour or two lately passed with her in Kate's society. Milly Theale had recognised no complication, to Densher's view, while bringing him, with his companion, from the National Gallery and entertaining them at luncheon; it was therefore scarce supposable that complications had become so soon too much for her. His pretext for presenting himself was fortunately of the best and simplest; the least he could decently do, given their happy acquaintance, was to call with an enquiry after learning that she had been prevented by illness from meeting him at dinner. And then there was the beautiful accident of her other demonstration; he must at any rate have given a sign as a sequel to the hospitality he had shared with Kate. Well, he was giving one now—such as it was; he was finding her, to begin with, accessible, and very naturally and prettily glad to see him. He had come, after luncheon, early, though not so early but that she might already be out if she were well enough; and she was well enough and yet was still at home. He had an inner glimpse, with this, of the comment Kate would have made on it; it wasn't absent from his thought that Milly would have been at home by *her* account because expecting, after a talk with Mrs. Stringham, that a certain person might turn up. He even—so pleasantly did things go—enjoyed freedom of mind to welcome, on that supposition, a fresh sign of the beautiful hypocrisy of women. He went so far as to enjoy believing the girl *might* have stayed in for him; it helped him to enjoy her behaving as if she hadn't. She expressed, that is, exactly the right degree of surprise; she didn't a bit overdo it: the lesson of which was, perceptibly, that, so far as his late lights had opened the door to any want of the natural in their meetings, he might trust her to take care of it for him as well as for herself.

She had begun this, admirably, on his entrance, with her turning away from the table at which she had apparently been engaged in letter-writing; it was the very possibility of his betraying a concern for her as one of the afflicted that she had within the first minute conjured away. She was never, never—did he understand?—to be one of the afflicted for him; and the manner in which he understood it, something of the answering pleasure that he couldn't help knowing he showed, constituted, he was very soon after to acknowledge, something like a start for intimacy. When things like that could pass people had in truth to be equally conscious of a relation. It soon made one, at all events, when it didn't find one made. She had let him ask—there had been time for that, his allusion to her friend's explanatory arrival at Lancaster Gate without her being inevitable; but she had blown away, and quite as much with the look in her eyes as with the smile on her lips, every ground for anxiety and every chance for insistence. How was she?—why she was as he thus saw her and as she had reasons of her own, nobody else's business, for desiring to appear. Kate's account of her as too proud for pity, as fiercely shy about so personal a secret, came back to him; so that he rejoiced he could take a hint, especially when he wanted to. The question the girl had quickly disposed of—"Oh it was nothing: I'm all right, thank you!"—was one he was glad enough to be able to banish. It wasn't at all, in spite of the appeal Kate had made to him on it, his affair; for his interest had been invoked in the name of compassion, and the name of compassion was exactly what he felt himself at the end of two minutes forbidden so much as to whisper. He had been sent to see her in order to be sorry for her, and how sorry he might be, quite privately, he was yet to make out. Didn't that signify, however, almost not at all?—inasmuch as, whatever his upshot, he was never to give her a glimpse of it. Thus the ground was unexpectedly cleared; though it was not till a slightly longer time had passed that he read clear, at first with amusement and then with a strange shade of respect, what had most operated. Extraordinarily, quite amazingly, he began to see that if his pity hadn't had to yield to still other things it would have had to yield quite definitely to her own. That was the way the case had turned round: he had made his visit to be sorry for her, but he would repeat it—if he did repeat it—in order that she might be sorry for him. His situation made him, she judged—when once one liked him—a subject for that degree of tenderness: he felt this judgement in her, and felt it as something he should really, in decency, in dignity, in common honesty, have very soon to reckon with.

Odd enough was it certainly that the question originally before him, the question placed there by Kate, should so of a sudden find itself quite dislodged by another. This other, it was easy to see, came straight up with the fact of her beautiful delusion and her wasted charity; the whole thing preparing for him as pretty a case of conscience as he could have desired, and one at the prospect of which he was already wincing. If he was interesting it was because he was unhappy; and if he was unhappy it was because his passion for Kate had spent itself in vain; and if Kate was indifferent, inexorable, it was because she had left Milly in no doubt of it. That above all was what came up for him—how clear an impression of this attitude, how definite an account of his own failure, Kate must have given her friend. His immediate quarter of an hour there with the girl lighted up for him almost luridly such an inference; it was almost as if the other party to their remarkable understanding had been with them as they talked, had been hovering about, had dropped in to look after her work. The value of the work affected him as different from the moment he saw it so expressed in poor Milly. Since it was false that he wasn't loved, so his right was quite quenched to figure on that ground as important; and if he didn't look out he should find himself appreciating in a way quite at odds with straightness the good faith of Milly's benevolence. *There* was the place for scruples; there the need absolutely to mind what he was about. If it wasn't proper for him to enjoy consideration on a perfectly false footing, where was the guarantee that, if he kept on, he mightn't soon himself pretend to the grievance in order not to miss the sweet? Consideration—from a charming girl —was soothing on whatever theory; and it didn't take him far to remember that he had himself as yet done nothing deceptive. It was Kate's description of him, his defeated state, it was none of his own; his responsibility would begin, as he might say, only with acting it out. The sharp point was, however, in the difference between acting and not acting: this difference in fact it was that made the case of conscience. He saw it with a certain alarm rise before him that everything was acting that was not speaking the particular word. "If you like me because you think *she* doesn't, it isn't a bit true: she *does* like me awfully!"—that would have been the particular word; which there were at the same time but too palpably such difficulties about his uttering. Wouldn't it be virtually as indelicate to challenge her as to leave her deluded?—and this quite apart from the exposure, so to speak, of Kate, as to whom it would constitute a kind of betrayal. Kate's design was something so extraordinarily special to Kate that he felt himself shrink from the complications involved in judging it. Not to give away the woman one loved, but to back her up in her mistakes—once they had gone a certain length—that was perhaps chief among the inevitabilities of the abjection of love. Loyalty was of course supremely prescribed in presence of any design on her part, however roundabout, to do one nothing but good.

Densher had quite to steady himself not to be awestruck at the immensity of the good his own friend must on all this evidence have wanted to do him. Of one thing indeed meanwhile he was sure: Milly Theale wouldn't herself precipitate his necessity of intervention. She would absolutely never say to him: "*Is* it so impossible she shall ever care for you seriously?"—without which nothing could well be less delicate than for him aggressively to set her right. Kate would be free to do that if Kate, in some prudence, some contrition, for some better reason in fine, should revise her plan; but he asked himself what, failing this, *he* could do that wouldn't be after all more gross than doing nothing. This brought him round again to the acceptance of the fact that the poor girl liked him. She put it, for reasons of her own, on a simple, a beautiful ground, a ground that already supplied her with the pretext she required. The ground was there, that is, in the impression she had received, retained, cherished; the pretext, over and above it, was the pretext for acting on it. That she now believed as she did made her sure at last that she might act; so that what Densher therefore would have struck at would be the root, in her soul, of a pure pleasure. It positively lifted its head and flowered, this pure pleasure, while the young man now sat with her, and there were things she seemed to say that took the words out of his mouth. These were not all the things she did say; they were rather what such things meant in the light of what he knew. Her warning him for instance off the question of how she was, the quick brave little art with which she did that, represented to his fancy a truth she didn't utter. "I'm well for *you*—that's all you have to do with or need trouble about: I shall never be anything so horrid as ill for you. So there you are; worry about me, spare me, please, as little as you can. Don't be afraid, in short, to ignore my 'interesting' side. It isn't, you see, even now while you sit here, that there aren't lots of others. Only do *them* justice and we shall get on beautifully." This was what was folded finely up in her talk—all quite ostensibly about her impressions and her intentions. She tried to put Densher again on his American doings, but he wouldn't have that to-day. As he thought of the way in which, the other afternoon, before Kate, he had sat complacently "jawing," he accused himself of excess, of having overdone it, having made—at least apparently—more of a "set" at their entertainer than he was at all events then intending. He turned the tables, drawing her out about London, about her vision of life there, and only too glad to treat her as a person with whom he could easily have other topics than her aches and pains. He spoke to her above all of the evidence offered him at Lancaster Gate that she had come but to conquer; and when she had met this with full and gay assent—"How could I help being the feature of the season, the what-do-you-call-it, the theme of every tongue?"—they fraternised freely over all that had come and gone for each since their interrupted encounter in New York.

At the same time, while many things in quick succession came up for them, came up in particular for Densher, nothing perhaps was just so sharp as the odd influence of their present conditions on their view of their past ones. It was as if they hadn't known how "thick" they had originally become, as if, in a manner, they had really fallen to remembrance of more passages of intimacy than there had in fact at the time quite been room for. They were in a relation now so complicated, whether by what they said or by what they didn't say, that it might have been seeking to justify its speedy growth by reaching back to one of those fabulous periods in which prosperous states place their beginnings. He recalled what had been said at Mrs. Lowder's about the steps and stages, in people's careers, that absence caused one to miss, and about the resulting frequent sense of meeting them further on; which, with some other matters also recalled, he took occasion to communicate to Milly. The matters he couldn't mention mingled themselves with those he did; so that it would doubtless have been hard to say which of the two groups now played most of a part. He was kept face to face with this young lady by a force absolutely resident in their situation and operating, for his nerves, with the swiftness of the forces commonly regarded by sensitive persons as beyond their control. The current thus determined had positively become for him, by the time he had been ten minutes in the room, something that, but for the absurdity of comparing the very small with the very great, he would freely have likened to the rapids of Niagara. An uncriticised acquaintance between a clever young man and a responsive young woman could do nothing more, at the most, than go, and his actual experiment went and went and went. Nothing probably so conduced to make it go as the marked circumstance that they had spoken all the while not a word about Kate; and this in spite of the fact that, if it were a question for them of what had occurred in the past weeks, nothing had occurred comparable to Kate's predominance. Densher had but the night before appealed to her for instruction as to what he must do about her, but he fairly winced to find how little this came to. She had foretold him of course how little; but it was a truth that looked different when shown him by Milly. It proved to him that the latter had in fact been dealt with, but it produced in him the thought that Kate might perhaps again conveniently be questioned. He would have liked to speak to her before going further—to make sure she really meant him to succeed quite so much. With all the difference that, as we say, came up for him, it came up afresh, naturally, that he might make his visit brief and never renew it; yet the strangest thing of all was that the argument against that issue would have sprung precisely from the beautiful little eloquence involved in Milly's avoidances.

Precipitate these well might be, since they emphasised the fact that she was proceeding in the sense of the assurances she had taken. Over the latter she had visibly not hesitated, for hadn't they had the merit of giving her a chance? Densher quite saw her, felt her take it; the chance, neither more nor less, of help rendered him according to her freedom. It was what Kate had left her with: "Listen to him, *I?* Never! So do as you like." What Milly "liked" was to do, it thus appeared, as she was doing: our young man's glimpse of which was just what would have been for him not less a glimpse of the peculiar brutality of shaking her off. The choice exhaled its shy fragrance of heroism, for it was not aided by any question of parting with Kate. She would be charming to Kate as well as to Kate's adorer; she would incur whatever pain could dwell for her in the sight—should she continue to be exposed to the sight—of the adorer thrown with the adored. It wouldn't really have taken much more to make him wonder if he hadn't before him one of those rare cases of exaltation—food for fiction, food for poetry—

in which a man's fortune with the woman who doesn't care for him is positively promoted by the woman who does. It was as if Milly had said to herself: "Well, he can at least meet her in my society, if that's anything to him; so that my line can only be to make my society attractive." She certainly couldn't have made a different impression if she *had* so reasoned. All of which, none the less, didn't prevent his soon enough saying to her, quite as if she were to be whirled into space: "And now, then, what becomes of you? Do you begin to rush about on visits to country-houses?"

She disowned the idea with a headshake that, put on what face she would, couldn't help betraying to him something of her suppressed view of the possibility—ever, ever perhaps—of any such proceedings. They weren't at any rate for her now. "Dear no. We go abroad for a few weeks somewhere of high air. That has been before us for many days; we've only been kept on by last necessities here. However, everything's done and the wind's in our sails."

"May you scud then happily before it! But when," he asked, "do you come back?"

She looked ever so vague; then as if to correct it: "Oh when the wind turns. And what do you do with your summer?"

"Ah I spend it in sordid toil. I drench it with mercenary ink. My work in your country counts for play as well. You see what's thought of the pleasure your country can give. My holiday's over."

"I'm sorry you had to take it," said Milly, "at such a different time from ours. If you could but have worked while we've been working—"

"I might be playing while you play? Oh the distinction isn't great with me. There's a little of each for me, of work and of play, in either. But you and Mrs. Stringham, with Miss Croy and Mrs. Lowder—you all," he went on, "have been given up, like navvies or niggers, to real physical toil. Your rest is something you've earned and you need. My labour's comparatively light."

"Very true," she smiled; "but all the same I like mine."

"It doesn't leave you 'done'?"

"Not a bit. I don't get tired when I'm interested. Oh I could go far."

He bethought himself. "Then why don't you?—since you've got here, as I learn, the whole place in your pocket."

"Well, it's a kind of economy—I'm saving things up. I've enjoyed so what you speak of—though your account of it's fantastic—that I'm watching over its future, that I can't help being anxious and careful. I want—in the interest itself of what I've had and may still have—not to make stupid mistakes. The way not to make them is to get off again to a distance and see the situation from there. I shall keep it fresh," she wound up as if herself rather pleased with the ingenuity of her statement—"I shall keep it fresh, by that prudence, for my return."

"Ah then you *will* return? Can you promise one that?"

Her face fairly lighted at his asking for a promise; but she made as if bargaining a little. "Isn't London rather awful in winter?"

He had been going to ask her if she meant for the invalid; but he checked the infelicity of this and took the enquiry as referring to social life. "No—I like it, with one thing and another; it's less of a mob than later on; and it would have for *us* the merit—should you come here then—that we should probably see more of you. So do reappear for us—if it isn't a question of climate."

She looked at that a little graver. "If what isn't a question—?"

"Why the determination of your movements. You spoke just now of going somewhere for that."

"For better air?"—she remembered. "Oh yes, one certainly wants to get out of London in August."

"Rather, of course!"—he fully understood. "Though I'm glad you've hung on long enough for me to catch you. Try us at any rate," he continued, "once more."

"Whom do you mean by 'us'?" she presently asked.

It pulled him up an instant—representing, as he saw it might have seemed, an allusion to himself as conjoined with Kate, whom he was proposing not to mention any more than his hostess did. But the issue was easy. "I mean all of us together, every one you'll find ready to surround you with sympathy."

It made her, none the less, in her odd charming way, challenge him afresh. "Why do you say sympathy?"

"Well, it's doubtless a pale word. What we *shall* feel for you will be much nearer worship."

"As near then as you like!" With which at last Kate's name was sounded. "The people I'd most come back for are the people you know. I'd do it for Mrs. Lowder, who has been beautifully kind to me."

"So she has to *me*," said Densher. "I feel," he added as she at first answered nothing, "that, quite contrary to anything I originally expected, I've made a good friend of her."

"*I* didn't expect it either—its turning out as it has. But I did," said Milly, "with Kate. I shall come back for her too. I'd do anything"—she kept it up—"for Kate."

Looking at him as with conscious clearness while she spoke, she might for the moment have effectively laid a trap for whatever remains of the ideal straightness in him were still able to pull themselves together and operate. He was afterwards to say to himself that something had at that moment hung for him by a hair. "Oh I know what one would do for Kate!"—it had hung for him by a hair to break out with that, which he felt he had really been kept from by an element in his consciousness stronger still. The proof of the truth in question was precisely in his silence; resisting the impulse to break out was what he *was* doing for Kate. This at the time moreover came and went quickly enough; he was trying the next minute but to make Milly's allusion easy for herself. "Of course I know what friends you are—and of course I understand," he permitted himself to add, "any amount of devotion to a person so charming. That's the good turn then she'll do us all—I mean her working for your return."

"Oh you don't know," said Milly, "how much I'm really on her hands."

He could but accept the appearance of wondering how much he might show he knew. "Ah she's very masterful."

"She's great. Yet I don't say she bullies me."

"No—that's not the way. At any rate it isn't hers," he smiled. He remembered, however, then that an undue acquaintance with Kate's ways was just what he mustn't show; and he pursued the subject no further than to remark with a good intention that had the further merit of representing a truth: "I don't feel as if I knew her—really to call know."

"Well, if you come to that, I don't either!" she laughed. The words gave him, as soon as they were uttered, a sense of responsibility for his own; though during a silence that ensued for a minute he had time to recognise that his own contained after all no element of falsity. Strange enough therefore was it that he could go too far—if it *was* too far—without being false. His observation was one he would perfectly have made to Kate herself. And before he again spoke, and before Milly did, he took time for more still—for feeling how just here it was that he must break short off if his mind was really made up not to go further. It was as if he had been at a corner—and fairly put there by his last speech; so that it depended on him whether or no to turn it. The silence, if prolonged but an instant, might even have given him a sense of her waiting to see what he would do. It was filled for them the next thing by the sound, rather voluminous for the August afternoon, of the approach, in the street below them, of heavy carriage-wheels and of horses trained to "step." A rumble, a great shake, a considerable effective clatter, had been apparently succeeded by a pause at the door of the hotel, which was in turn accompanied by a due display of diminished prancing and stamping. "You've a visitor," Densher laughed, "and it must be at least an ambassador."

"It's only my own carriage; it does that—isn't it wonderful?—every day. But we find it, Mrs. Stringham and I, in the innocence of our hearts, very amusing." She had got up, as she spoke, to assure herself of what she said; and at the end of a few steps they were together on the balcony and looking down at her waiting chariot, which made indeed a brave show. "Is it very awful?"

It was to Densher's eyes—save for its absurd heaviness—only pleasantly pompous. "It seems to me delightfully rococo.[1] But how do I know? You're mistress of these things, in contact with the highest wisdom. You occupy a position, moreover, thanks to which your carriage—well, by this time, in the eye of London, also occupies one." But she was going out, and he mustn't stand in her way. What had happened the next minute was first that she had denied she was going out, so that he might prolong his stay; and second that she had said she would go out with pleasure if he would like to drive—that in fact there were always things to do, that there had been a question for her to-day of several in particular, and that this in short was why the carriage had been ordered so early. They perceived, as she said these things, that an enquirer had presented himself, and, coming back, they found Milly's servant announcing the carriage and prepared to accompany her. This appeared to have for her the effect of settling the matter—on the basis, that is, of Densher's happy response. Densher's happy response, however, had as yet hung fire, the process we have described in him operating by this time with extreme intensity. The system of not pulling up, not breaking off, had already brought him headlong, he seemed to feel, to where they actually stood; and just now it was, with a vengeance, that he must do either one thing or the other. He had been waiting for some moments, which probably seemed to him longer than they were; this was because he was anxiously watching himself wait. He couldn't keep that up for ever; and since one thing or the other was what he must do, it was for the other that he presently became conscious of having decided. If he had been drifting it settled itself in the manner of a bump, of considerable violence, against a firm object in the stream. "Oh yes; I'll go with you with pleasure. It's a charming idea."

She gave no look to thank him—she rather looked away; she only said at once to her servant, "In ten minutes"; and then to her visitor, as the man went out, "We'll go somewhere—I shall like that. But I must ask of you time—as little as possible—to get ready." She looked over the room to provide for him, keep him there. "There are books and things—plenty; and I dress very quickly." He caught her eyes only as she went, on which he thought them pretty and touching.

1. An artistic style of the mid-eighteenth century, begun in France and developed fully in Germany; it is deliberately excessive in its ornateness.

Why especially touching at that instant he could certainly scarce have said; it was involved, it was lost in the sense of her wishing to oblige him. Clearly what had occurred was her having wished it so that she had made him simply wish, in civil acknowledgement, to oblige *her*; which he had now fully done by turning his corner. He was quite round it, his corner, by the time the door had closed upon her and he stood there alone. Alone he remained for three minutes more—remained with several very living little matters to think about. One of these was the phenomenon—typical, highly American, he would have said—of Milly's extreme spontaneity. It was perhaps rather as if he had sought refuge—refuge from another question—in the almost exclusive contemplation of this. Yet this, in its way, led him nowhere; not even to a sound generalisation about American girls. It was spontaneous for his young friend to have asked him to drive with her alone—since she hadn't mentioned her companion; but she struck him after all as no more advanced in doing it than Kate, for instance, who wasn't an American girl, might have struck him in not doing it. Besides, Kate *would* have done it, though Kate wasn't at all, in the same sense as Milly, spontaneous. And then in addition Kate *had* done it—or things very like it. Furthermore he was engaged to Kate—even if his ostensibly not being put her public freedom on other grounds. On all grounds, at any rate, the relation between Kate and freedom, between freedom and Kate, was a different one from any he could associate or cultivate, as to anything, with the girl who had just left him to prepare to give herself up to him. It had never struck him before, and he moved about the room while he thought of it, touching none of the books placed at his disposal. Milly was forward, as might be said, but not advanced; whereas Kate was backward—backward still, comparatively, as an English girl—and yet advanced in a high degree. However—though this didn't straighten it out—Kate was of course two or three years older; which at their time of life considerably counted.

Thus ingeniously discriminating, Densher continued slowly to wander; yet without keeping at bay for long the sense of having rounded his corner. He had so rounded it that he felt himself lose even the option of taking advantage of Milly's absence to retrace his steps. If he might have turned tail, vulgarly speaking, five minutes before, he couldn't turn tail now; he must simply wait there with his consciousness charged to the brim. Quickly enough moreover that issue was closed from without; in the course of three minutes more Miss Theale's servant had returned. He preceded a visitor whom he had met, obviously, at the foot of the stairs and whom, throwing open the door, he loudly announced as Miss Croy. Kate, on following him in, stopped short at sight of Densher—only, after an instant, as the young man saw with free amusement, not from surprise and still less from discomfiture. Densher immediately gave his explanation—Miss Theale had gone to prepare to drive—on receipt of which the servant effaced himself.

"And you're going with her?" Kate asked.

"Yes—with your approval; which I've taken, as you see, for granted."

"Oh, she laughed, "my approval's complete!" She was thoroughly consistent and handsome about it.

"What I mean is of course," he went on—for he was sensibly affected by her gaiety—"at your so lively instigation."

She had looked about the room—she might have been vaguely looking for signs of the duration, of the character of his visit, a momentary aid in taking a decision. "Well, instigation then, as much as you like." She treated it as pleasant, the success of her plea with him; she made a fresh joke of this direct impression of it. "So much so as that? Do you know I think I won't wait?"

"Not to see her—after coming?"

"Well, with you in the field—! I came for news of her, but she must be all right. If she *is*—"

But he took her straight up. "Ah how do I know?" He was moved to say more. "It's not *I* who am responsible for her, my dear. It seems to me it's you." She struck him as making light of a matter that had been costing him sundry qualms; so that they couldn't both be quite just. Either she was too easy or he had been too anxious. He didn't want at all events to feel a fool for that. "I'm doing nothing—and shall not, I assure you, do anything but what I'm told."

Their eyes met with some intensity over the emphasis he had given his words; and he had taken it from her the next moment that he really needn't get into a state. What in the world was the matter? She asked it, with interest, for all answer. "Isn't she better—if she's able to see you?"

"She assures me she's in perfect health."

Kate's interest grew. "I knew she would." On which she added: "It won't have been really for illness that she stayed away last night."

"For what then?"

"Well—for nervousness."

"Nervousness about what?"

"Oh you know!" She spoke with a hint of impatience, smiling however the next moment. "I've told you that."

He looked at her to recover in her face what she had told him;

then it was as if what he saw there prompted him to say: "What have you told *her?*"

She gave him her controlled smile, and it was all as if they remembered where they were, liable to surprise, talking with softened voices, even stretching their opportunity, by such talk, beyond a quite right feeling. Milly's room would be close at hand, and yet they were saying things—! For a moment, none the less, they kept it up. "Ask *her*, if you like; you're free—she'll tell you. Act as you think best; don't trouble about what you think I may or mayn't have told. I'm all right with her," said Kate. "So there you are."

"If you mean *here* I am," he answered, "it's unmistakeable. If you also mean that her believing in you is all I have to do with you're so far right as that she certainly does believe in you."

"Well then take example by her."

"She's really doing it for you," Densher continued. "She's driving me out for you."

"In that case," said Kate with her soft tranquillity, "you can do it a little for *her*. I'm not afraid," she smiled.

He stood before her a moment, taking in again the face she put on it and affected again, as he had already so often been, by more things in this face and in her whole person and presence than he was, to his relief, obliged to find words for. It wasn't, under such impressions, a question of words. "I do nothing for any one in the world but you. But for you I'll do anything."

"Good, good," said Kate. "That's how I like you."

He waited again an instant. "Then you swear to it?"

"To 'it'? To what?"

"Why that you do 'like' me. Since it's all for that, you know, that I'm letting you do—well, God knows what with me."

She gave at this, with a stare, a disheartened gesture—the sense of which she immediately further expressed. "If you don't believe in me then, after all, hadn't you better break off before you've gone further?"

"Break off with you?"

"Break off with Milly. You might go now," she said, "and I'll stay and explain to her why it is."

He wondered—as if it struck him. "What would you say?"

"Why that you find you can't stand her, and that there's nothing for me but to bear with you as I best may."

He considered of this. "How much do you abuse me to her?"

"Exactly enough. As much as you see by her attitude."

Again he thought. "It doesn't seem to me I ought to mind her attitude."

"Well then, just as you like. I'll stay and do my best for you."

He saw she was sincere, was really giving him a chance; and that of itself made things clearer. The feeling of how far he had gone came back to him not in repentance, but in this very vision of an escape; and it was not of what he had done, but of what Kate offered, that he now weighed the consequence. "Won't it make her —her not finding me here—be rather more sure there's something between us?"

Kate thought. "Oh I don't know. It will of course greatly upset her. But you needn't trouble about that. She won't die of it."

"Do you mean she *will?*" Densher presently asked.

"Don't put me questions when you don't believe what I say. You make too many conditions."

She spoke now with a shade of rational weariness that made the want of pliancy, the failure to oblige her, look poor and ugly; so that what it suddenly came back to for him was his deficiency in the things a man of any taste, so engaged, so enlisted, would have liked to make sure of being able to show—imagination, tact, positively even humour. The circumstance is doubtless odd, but the truth is none the less that the speculation uppermost with him at this juncture was: "What if I should begin to bore this creature?" And that, within a few seconds, had translated itself. "If you'll swear again you love me—!"

She looked about, at door and window, as if he were asking for more than he said. "Here? There's nothing between us here," Kate smiled.

"Oh *isn't* there?" Her smile itself, with this, had so settled something for him that he had come to her pleadingly and holding out his hands, which she immediately seized with her own as if both to check him and to keep him. It was by keeping him thus for a minute that she did check him; she held him long enough, while, with their eyes deeply meeting, they waited in silence for him to recover himself and renew his discretion. He coloured as with a return of the sense of where they were, and that gave her precisely one of her usual victories, which immediately took further form. By the time he had dropped her hands he had again taken hold, as it were, of Milly's. It was not at any rate with Milly he had broken. "I'll do all you wish," he declared as if to acknowledge the acceptance of his condition that he had practically, after all, drawn from her—a declaration on which she then, recurring to her first idea, promptly acted.

"If you *are* as good as that I go. You'll tell her that, finding you with her, I wouldn't wait. Say that, you know, from yourself. She'll understand."

She had reached the door with it—she was full of decision; but he had before she left him one more doubt. "I don't see how she can understand enough, you know, without understanding too much."

"You don't need to see."

He required then a last injunction. "I must simply go it blind?"

"You must simply be kind to her."

"And leave the rest to you?"

"Leave the rest to *her*," said Kate disappearing.

It came back then afresh to that, as it had come before. Milly, three minutes after Kate had gone, returned in her array—her big black hat, so little superstitiously in the fashion, her fine black garments throughout, the swathing of her throat, which Densher vaguely took for an infinite number of yards of priceless lace, and which, its folded fabric kept in place by heavy rows of pearls, hung down to her feet like the stole of a priestess. He spoke to her at once of their friend's visit and flight. "She hadn't known she'd find me," he said—and said at present without difficulty. He had so rounded his corner that it wasn't a question of a word more or less.

She took this account of the matter as quite sufficient; she glossed over whatever might be awkward. "I'm sorry—but I of course often see *her*." He felt the discrimination in his favour and how it justified Kate. This was Milly's tone when the matter was left to her. Well, it should now be wholly left.

Book Seventh

I

When Kate and Densher abandoned her to Mrs. Stringham on the day of her meeting them together and bringing them to luncheon, Milly, face to face with that companion, had had one of those moments in which the warned, the anxious fighter of the battle of life, as if once again feeling for the sword at his side, carries his hand straight to the quarter of his courage. She laid hers firmly on her heart, and the two women stood there showing each other a strange front. Susan Shepherd had received their great doctor's visit, which had been clearly no small affair for her; but Milly had since then, with insistence, kept in place, against communication and betrayal, as she now practically confessed, the barrier of their invited guests. "You've been too dear. With what I see you're full of you treated them beautifully. *Isn't* Kate charming when she wants to be?"

Poor Susie's expression, contending at first, as in a high fine spasm, with different dangers, had now quite let itself go. She had to make an effort to reach a point in space already so remote. "Miss

Croy? Oh she was pleasant and clever. She knew," Mrs. Stringham added. "She knew."

Milly braced herself—but conscious above all, at the moment, of a high compassion for her mate. She made her out as struggling—struggling in all her nature against the betrayal of pity, which in itself, given her nature, could only be a torment. Milly gathered from the struggle how much there was of the pity, and how therefore it was both in her tenderness and in her conscience that Mrs. Stringham suffered. Wonderful and beautiful it was that this impression instantly steadied the girl. Ruefully asking herself on what basis of ease, with the drop of their barrier, they were to find themselves together, she felt the question met with a relief that was almost joy. The basis, the inevitable basis, was that she was going to be sorry for Susie, who, to all appearance, had been condemned in so much more uncomfortable a manner to be sorry for *her*. Mrs. Stringham's sorrow would hurt Mrs. Stringham, but how could her own ever hurt? She had, the poor girl, at all events, on the spot, five minutes of exaltation in which she turned the tables on her friend with a pass of the hand, a gesture of an energy that made a wind in the air. "Kate knew," she asked, "that you were full of Sir Luke Strett?"

"She spoke of nothing, but she was gentle and nice; she seemed to want to help me through." Which the good lady had no sooner said, however, than she almost tragically gasped at herself. She glared at Milly with a pretended pluck. "What I mean is that she saw one had been taken up with something. When I say she knows I should say she's a person who guesses." And her grimace was also, on its side, heroic. "But *she* doesn't matter, Milly."

The girl felt she by this time could face anything. "Nobody matters, Susie. Nobody." Which her next words, however, rather contradicted. "Did he take it ill that I wasn't here to see him? Wasn't it really just what he wanted—to have it out, so much more simply, with *you*?"

"We didn't have anything 'out,' Milly," Mrs. Stringham delicately quavered.

"Didn't he awfully like you," Milly went on, "and didn't he think you the most charming person I could possibly have referred him to for an account of me? Didn't you hit it off tremendously together and in fact fall quite in love, so that it will really be a great advantage for you to have me as a common ground? You're going to make, I can see, no end of a good thing of me."

"My own child, my own child!" Mrs. Stringham pleadingly murmured; yet showing as she did so that she feared the effect even of deprecation.

"Isn't he beautiful and good too himself?—altogether, whatever he may say, a lovely acquaintance to have made? You're just the right people for me—I see it now; and do you know what, between you, you must do?" Then as Susie still but stared, wonderstruck and holding herself: "You must simply see me through. Any way you choose. Make it out together. I, on my side, will be beautiful too, and we'll be—the three of us, with whatever others, oh as many as the case requires, any one you like!—a sight for the gods. I'll be as easy for you as carrying a feather." Susie took it for a moment in such silence that her young friend almost saw her—and scarcely withheld the observation—as taking it for "a part of the disease." This accordingly helped Milly to be, as she judged, definite and wise. "He's at any rate awfully interesting, isn't he?—which is so much to the good. We haven't at least—as we might have, with the way we tumbled into it—got hold of one of the dreary."

"Interesting, dearest?"—Mrs. Stringham felt her feet firmer. "I don't know if he's interesting or not; but I do know, my own," she continued to quaver, "that he's just as much interested as you could possibly desire."

"Certainly—that's it. Like all the world."

"No, my precious, not like all the world. Very much more deeply and intelligently."

"'Ah there you are!" Milly laughed. "That's the way, Susie, I want you. So 'buck' up, my dear. We'll have beautiful times with him. Don't worry."

"I'm not worrying, Milly." And poor Susie's face registered the sublimity of her lie.

It was at this that, too sharply penetrated, her companion went to her, met by her with an embrace in which things were said that exceeded speech. Each held and clasped the other as if to console her for this unnamed woe, the woe for Mrs. Stringham of learning the torment of helplessness, the woe for Milly of having *her*, at such a time, to think of. Milly's assumption was immense, and the difficulty for her friend was that of not being able to gainsay it without bringing it more to the proof than tenderness and vagueness could permit. Nothing in fact came to the proof between them but that they could thus cling together—except indeed that, as we have indicated, the pledge of protection and support was all the younger woman's own. "I don't ask you," she presently said, "what he told you for yourself, nor what he told you to tell me, nor how he took it, really, that I had left him to you, nor what passed between you about me in any way. It wasn't to get that out of you that I took my means to make sure of your meeting freely—for there are things I don't want to know. I shall see him again and again and shall know more than enough. All I do want is that you shall see me through on *his* basis, whatever it is; which it's enough

—for the purpose—that you yourself should know: that is with him to show you how. I'll make it charming for you—that's what I mean; I'll keep you up to it in such a way that half the time you won't know you're doing it. And for that you're to rest upon me. There. It's understood. We keep each other going, and you may absolutely feel of me that I shan't break down. So, with the way you haven't so much as a dig of the elbow to fear, how could you be safer?"

"He told me I *can* help you—of course he told me that," Susie, on her side, eagerly contended. "Why shouldn't he, and for what else have I come out with you? But he told me nothing dreadful—nothing, nothing, nothing," the poor lady passionately protested. "Only that you must do as you like and as he tells you—which *is* just simply to do as you like."

"I must keep in sight of him. I must from time to time go to him. But that's of course doing as I like. It's lucky," Milly smiled, "that I like going to him."

Mrs. Stringham was here in agreement; she gave a clutch at the account of their situation that most showed it as workable. "That's what *will* be charming for me, and what I'm sure he really wants of me—to help you to do as you like."

"And also a little, won't it be," Milly laughed, "to save me from the consequences? Of course," she added, "there must first *be* things I like."

"Oh I think you'll find some," Mrs. Stringham more bravely said. "I think there *are* some—as for instance just this one. I mean," she explained, "really having us so."

Milly thought. "Just as if I wanted you comfortable about *him*, and him the same about you? Yes—I shall get the good of it."

Susan Shepherd appeared to wander from this into a slight confusion. "Which of them are you talking of?"

Milly wondered an instant—then had a light. "I'm not talking of Mr. Densher." With which moreover she showed amusement. "Though if you can be comfortable about Mr. Densher too so much the better."

"Oh you meant Sir Luke Strett? Certainly he's a fine type. Do you know," Susie continued, "whom he reminds me of? Of *our* great man—Dr. Buttrick of Boston."

Milly recognised Dr. Buttrick of Boston, but she dropped him after a tributary pause. "What do you think, now that you've seen him, of Mr. Densher?"

It was not till after consideration, with her eyes fixed on her friend's, that Susie produced her answer. "I think he's very handsome."

Milly remained smiling at her, though putting on a little the manner of a teacher with a pupil. "Well, that will do for the first time. I *have* done," she went on, "what I wanted."

"Then that's all *we* want. You see there are plenty of things."

Milly shook her head for the "plenty." "The best is not to know—that includes them all. I don't—I don't know. Nothing about anything—except that you're *with* me. Remember that, please. There won't be anything that, on my side, for you, I shall forget. So it's all right."

The effect of it by this time was fairly, as intended, to sustain Susie, who dropped in spite of herself into the reassuring. "Most certainly it's all right. I think you ought to understand that he sees no reason—"

"Why I shouldn't have a grand long life?" Milly had taken it straight up, as to understand it and for a moment consider it. But she disposed of it otherwise. "Oh of course I know *that*." She spoke as if her friend's point were small.

Mrs. Stringham tried to enlarge it. "Well, what I mean is that he didn't say to me anything that he hasn't said to yourself."

"Really?—I would in his place!" She might have been disappointed, but she had her good humour. "He tells me to *live*"—and she oddly limited the word.

It left Susie a little at sea. "Then what do you want more?"

"My dear," the girl presently said, "I don't 'want,' as I assure you, anything. Still," she added, "I *am* living. Oh yes, I'm living."

It put them again face to face, but it had wound Mrs. Stringham up. "So am I then, you'll see!"—she spoke with the note of her recovery. Yet it was her wisdom now—meaning by it as much as she did—not to say more than that. She had risen by Milly's aid to a certain command of what was before them; the ten minutes of their talk had in fact made her more distinctly aware of the presence in her mind of a new idea. It was really perhaps an old idea with a new value; it had at all events begun during the last hour, though at first but feebly, to shine with a special light. That was because in the morning darkness had so suddenly descended—a sufficient shade of night to bring out the power of a star. The dusk might be thick yet, but the sky had comparatively cleared; and Susan Shepherd's star from this time on continued to twinkle for her. It was for the moment, after her passage with Milly, the one spark left in the heavens. She recognised, as she continued to watch it, that it had really been set there by Sir Luke Strett's visit and that the impressions immediately following had done no more than fix it. Milly's reappearance with Mr. Densher at her heels—or, so oddly perhaps, at Miss Croy's heels, Miss Croy being at Milly's—had contributed to this effect, though it was only with the lapse of the greater obscurity that Susie made that out. The obscurity had reigned during the hour of their friends' visit, faintly clearing indeed while, in one of the rooms, Kate Croy's remarkable advance to her intensified the fact that Milly and the young man were conjoined in the other. If it hadn't acquired on the spot all the intensity of which it was capable, this was because the poor lady still sat in her primary gloom, the gloom the great benignant doctor had practically left behind him.

The intensity the circumstance in question *might* wear to the informed imagination would have been sufficiently revealed for us, no doubt—and with other things to our purpose—in two or three of those confidential passages with Mrs. Lowder that she now permitted herself. She hadn't yet been so glad that she believed in her old friend: for if she hadn't had, at such a pass, somebody or other to believe in she should certainly have stumbled by the way. Discretion had ceased to consist of silence; silence was gross and thick, whereas wisdom should taper, however tremulously, to a point. She betook herself to Lancaster Gate the morning after the colloquy just noted; and there, in Maud Manningham's own sanctum, she gradually found relief in giving an account of herself. An account of herself was one of the things that she had long been in the habit of expecting herself regularly to give—the regularity depending of course much on such tests of merit as might, by laws beyond her control, rise in her path. She never spared herself in short a proper sharpness of conception of how she had behaved, and it was a statement that she for the most part found herself able to make. What had happened at present was that nothing, as she felt, was left of her to report to; she was all too sunk in the inevitable and the abysmal. To give an account of herself she must give it to somebody else, and her first instalment of it to her hostess was that she must please let her cry. She couldn't cry, with Milly in observation, at the hotel, which she had accordingly left for that purpose; and the power happily came to her with the good opportunity. She cried and cried at first—she confined herself to that; it was for the time the best statement of her business. Mrs. Lowder moreover intelligently took it as such, though knocking off a note or two more, as she said, while Susie sat near her table. She could resist the contagion of tears, but her patience did justice to her visitor's most vivid plea for it. "I shall never be able, you know, to cry again—at least not ever with *her*; so I must take it out when I can. Even if she does herself it won't be for me to give away; for what would that be but a confession of despair? I'm not with her for that—I'm with her to be regularly sublime. Besides, Milly won't cry herself."

"I'm sure I hope," said Mrs. Lowder, "that she won't have occasion to."

"She won't even if she does have occasion. She won't shed a tear. There's something that will prevent her."

"Oh!" said Mrs. Lowder.

"Yes, her pride," Mrs. Stringham explained in spite of her friend's doubt, and it was with this that her communication took consistent form. It had never been pride, Maud Manningham had hinted, that kept *her* from crying when other things made for it; it had only been that these same things, at such times, made still more for business, arrangements, correspondence, the ringing of bells, the marshalling of servants, the taking of decisions. "I might be crying now," she said, "if I weren't writing letters"—and this quite without harshness for her anxious companion, to whom she allowed just the administrative margin for difference. She had interrupted her no more than she would have interrupted the piano-tuner. It gave poor Susie time; and when Mrs. Lowder, to save appearances and catch the post, had, with her addressed and stamped notes, met at the door of the room the footman summoned by the pressure of a knob, the facts of the case were sufficiently ready for her. It took but two or three, however, given their importance, to lay the ground for the great one—Mrs. Stringham's interview of the day before with Sir Luke, who had wished to see her about Milly.

"He had wished it himself?"

"I think he was glad of it. Clearly indeed he was. He stayed a quarter of an hour. I could see that for *him* it was long. He's interested," said Mrs. Stringham.

"Do you mean in her case?"

"He says it *isn't* a case."

"What then is it?"

"It isn't, at least," Mrs. Stringham explained, "the case she believed it to be—thought it at any rate *might* be—when, without my knowledge, she went to see him. She went because there was something she was afraid of, and he examined her thoroughly—he has made sure. She's wrong—she hasn't what she thought."

"And what did she think?" Mrs. Lowder demanded.

"He didn't tell me."

"And you didn't ask?"

"I asked nothing," said poor Susie—"I only took what he gave me. He gave me no more than he had to—he was beautiful," she went on. "He *is*, thank God, interested."

"He must have been interested in *you*, dear," Maud Manningham observed with kindness.

Her visitor met it with candour. "Yes, love, I think he *is*. I mean that he sees what he can do with me."

Mrs. Lowder took it rightly. "For *her*."

"For her. Anything in the world he will or he must. He can use me to the last bone, and he likes at least that. He says the great thing for her is to be happy."

"It's surely the great thing for every one. Why, therefore," Mrs. Lowder handsomely asked, "should we cry so hard about it?"

"Only," poor Susie wailed, "that it's so strange, so beyond us. I mean if she can't be."

"She must be." Mrs. Lawder knew no impossibles. "She *shall* be."

"Well—if you'll help. He thinks, you know, we *can* help."

Mrs. Lowder faced a moment, in her massive way, what Sir Luke Strett thought. She sat back there, her knees apart, not unlike a picturesque ear-ringed matron at a market-stall; while her friend, before her, dropped their items, tossed the separate truths of the matter one by one, into her capacious apron. "But is that all he came to you for—to tell you she must be happy?"

"That she must be *made* so—that's the point. It seemed enough, as he told me," Mrs. Stringham went on; "he makes it somehow such a grand possible affair."

"Ah well, if he makes it possible!"

"I mean especially he makes it grand. He gave it to me, that is, as *my* part. The rest's his own."

"And what's the rest?" Mrs. Lowder asked.

"I don't know. *His* business. He means to keep hold of her."

"Then why do you say it isn't a 'case'? It must be very much of one."

Everything in Mrs. Stringham confessed to the extent of it. "It's only that it isn't *the* case she herself supposed."

"It's another?"

"It's another."

"Examining her for what she supposed he finds something else?"

"Something else."

"And what does he find?"

"Ah," Mrs. Stringham cried, "God keep me from knowing!"

"He didn't tell you that?"

But poor Susie had recovered herself. "What I mean is that if it's there I shall know in time. He's considering, but I can trust him for it—because he does, I feel, trust me. He's considering," she repeated.

"He's in other words not sure?"

"Well, he's watching. I think that's what he means. She's to get away now, but to come back to him in three months."

"Then I think," said Maud Lowder, "that he oughtn't meanwhile to scare us."

It roused Susie a little, Susie being already enrolled in the great doctor's cause. This came out at least in her glimmer of reproach. "Does it scare us to enlist us for her happiness?"

Mrs. Lowder was rather stiff for it. "Yes; it scares *me*. I'm always scared—I may call it so—till I understand. What happiness is he talking about?"

Mrs. Stringham at this came straight. "Oh you know!"

She had really said it so that her friend had to take it; which the latter in fact after a moment showed herself as having done. A strange light humour in the matter even perhaps suddenly aiding, she met it with a certain accommodation. "Well, say one seems to see. The point is—!" But, fairly too full now of her question, she dropped.

"The point is will it *cure?*"

"Precisely. Is it absolutely a remedy—*the* specific?"

"Well, I should think we might know!" Mrs. Stringham delicately declared.

"Ah but we haven't the complaint."

"Have you never, dearest, been in love?" Susan Shepherd enquired.

"Yes, my child; but not by the doctor's direction."

Maud Manningham had spoken perforce with a break into momentary mirth, which operated—and happily too—as a challenge to her visitor's spirit. "Oh of course we don't ask his leave to fall. But it's something to know he thinks it good for us."

"My dear woman," Mrs. Lowder cried, "it strikes me we know it without hiim. So that when *that's* all he has to tell us—!"

"Ah," Mrs. Stringham interposed, "it isn't 'all.' I feel Sir Luke will have more; he won't have put me off with anything inadequate. I'm to see him again; he as good as told me that he'll wish it. So it won't be for nothing."

"Then what will it be for? Do you mean he has somebody of his own to propose? Do you mean you told him nothing?"

Mrs. Stringham dealt with these questions. "I showed him I understood him. That was all I could do. I didn't feel at liberty to be explicit; but I felt, even though his visit so upset me, the comfort of what I had from you night before last."

"What I spoke to you of in the carriage when we had left her with Kate?"

"You had *seen*, apparently, in three minutes. And now that he's here, now that I've met him and had my impression of him, I feel," said Mrs. Stringham, "that you've been magnificent."

"Of course I've been magnificent. When," asked Maud Manningham, "was I anything else? But Milly won't be, you know, if she marries Merton Densher."

"Oh it's always magnificent to marry the man one loves. But we're going fast!" Mrs. Stringham woefully smiled.

"The thing *is* to go fast if I see the case right. What had I after all but my instinct of that on coming back with you, night before last, to pick up Kate? I felt what I felt—I knew in my bones the man had returned."

That's just where, as I say, you're magnificent. But wait," said Mrs. Stringram, "till you've seen him."

"I shall see him immediately"—Mrs. Lowder took it up with decision. "What *is* then," she asked, "your impression?"

Mrs. Stringham's impression seemed lost in her doubts. "How can he ever care for her?"

Her companion, in her companion's heavy manner, sat on it. "By being put in the way of it."

"For God's sake then," Mrs. Stringham wailed, "*put* him in the way! You have him, one feels, in your hand."

Maud Lowder's eyes at this rested on her friend's. "Is that your impression of him?"

"It's my impression, dearest, of you. You handle every one."

Mrs. Lowder's eyes still rested, and Susan Shepherd now felt, for a wonder, not less sincere by seeing that she pleased her. But there was a great limitation. "I don't handle Kate."

It suggested something that her visitor hadn't yet had from her—something the sense of which made Mrs. Stringham gasp. "Do you mean Kate cares for *him?*"

That fact the lady of Lancaster Gate had up to this moment, as we know, enshrouded, and her friend's quick question had produced a change in her face. She blinked—then looked at the question hard; after which, whether she had inadvertently betrayed herself or had only reached a decision and then been affected by the quality of Mrs. Stringham's surprise, she accepted all results. What took place in her for Susan Shepherd was not simply that she made the best of them, but that she suddenly saw more in them to her purpose than she could have imagined. A certain impatience in fact marked in her this transition: she had been keeping back, very hard, an important truth and wouldn't have liked to hear that she hadn't concealed it cleverly. Susie nevertheless felt herself pass as not a little of a fool with her for not having thought of it. What Susie indeed, however, most thought of at present, in the quick, new light of it, was the wonder of Kate's dissimulation. She had time for that view while she waited for an answer to her cry. "Kate thinks she cares. But she's mistaken. And no one knows it." These things, distinct and responsible, were Mrs. Lowder's retort. Yet they weren't all of it. "*You* don't know it—that must be your line. Or rather your line must be that you deny it utterly."

"Deny that she cares for him?"

"Deny that she so much as thinks that she does. Positively and absolutely. Deny that you've so much as heard of it."

Susie faced this new duty. "To Milly, you mean—if she asks?"

"To Milly, naturally. No one else *will* ask."

"Well," said Mrs. Stringham after a moment, "Milly won't."

Mrs. Lowder wondered. "Are you sure?"

"Yes, the more I think of it. And luckily for *me*. I lie badly."

"*I* lie well, thank God," Mrs. Lowder almost snorted, "when, as sometimes will happen, there's nothing else so good. One must always do the best. But without lies then," she went on, "perhaps we can work it out." Her interest had risen; her friend saw her, as within some minutes, more enrolled and inflamed—presently felt in her what had made the difference. Mrs. Stringham, it was true, descried this at the time but dimly; she only made out at first that Maud had found a reason for helping her. The reason was that, strangely, she might help Maud too, for which she now desired to profess herself ready even to lying. What really perhaps most came out for her was that her hostess was a little disappointed at her doubt of the social solidity of this appliance; and that in turn was to become a steadier light. The truth about Kate's delusion, as her aunt presented it, the delusion about the state of her affections, which might be removed—this was apparently the ground on which they now might more intimately meet. Mrs. Stringham saw herself recruited for the removal of Kate's delusion—by arts, however, in truth, that she as yet quite failed to compass. Or was it perhaps to be only for the removal of Mr. Densher's?—success in which indeed might entail other successes. Before that job, unfortunately, her heart had already failed. She felt that she believed in her bones what Milly believed, and what would now make working for Milly such a dreadful upward tug. All this within her was confusedly present—a cloud of questions out of which Maud Manningham's large seated self loomed, however, as a mass more and more definite, taking in fact for the consultative relation something of the form of an oracle. From the oracle the sound did come—or at any rate the sense did, a sense all accordant with the insufflation she had just seen working. "Yes," the sense was, "I'll help you for Milly, because if that comes off I shall be helped, by its doing so, for Kate"—a view into which Mrs. Stringham could now sufficiently enter. She found herself of a sudden, strange to say, quite willing to operate to Kate's harm, or at least to Kate's good as Mrs. Lowder with a noble anxiety measured it. She found herself in short not caring what became of Kate—only convinced at bottom of the predominance of Kate's star. Kate wasn't in danger. Kate wasn't pathetic; Kate Croy, whatever happened, would take care of Kate Croy. She saw moreover by this time that her friend was travelling even beyond her own speed. Mrs. Lowder had already, in mind, drafted a rough plan of action, a plan vividly enough thrown off as she said: "You must stay on a few days, and you must immediately, both of you, meet him at dinner." In addition to which Maud claimed the merit of having by an instinct of pity, of prescient wisdom, done much, two nights before, to prepare that ground. "The poor child, when I was with her there while you were getting your shawl, quite gave herself away to me."

"Oh I remember how you afterwards put it to me. Though it was nothing more," Susie did herself the justice to observe, "than what I too had quite felt."

But Mrs. Lowder fronted her so on this that she wondered what she had said. "I suppose I ought to be edified at what you can so beautifully give up."

"Give up?" Mrs. Stringham echoed. "Why, I give up nothing—I cling."

Her hostess showed impatience, turning again with some stiffness to her great brass-bound cylinder-desk and giving a push to an object or two disposed there. "*I* give up then. You know how little such a person as Mr. Densher was to be my idea for her. You know what I've been thinking perfectly possible."

"Oh you've been great"—Susie was perfectly fair. "A duke, a duchess, a princess, a palace: you've made me believe in them too. But where we break down is that *she* doesn't believe in them. Luckily for her—as it seems to be turning out—she doesn't want them. So what's one to do? I assure you I've had many dreams. But I've only one dream now."

Mrs. Stringham's tone in these last words gave so fully her meaning that Mrs. Lowder could but show herself as taking it in. They sat a moment longer confronted on it. "Her having what she does want?"

"If it *will* do anything for her."

Mrs. Lowder seemed to think what it might do; but she spoke for the instant of something else. "It does provoke me a bit, you know—for of course I'm a brute. And I had thought of all sorts of things. Yet it doesn't prevent the fact that we must be decent."

"We must take her"—Mrs. Stringham carried that out—"as she is."

"And we must take Mr. Densher as *he* is." With which Mrs. Lowder gave a sombre laugh. "It's a pity he isn't better!"

"Well, if he were better," her friend rejoined, "you'd have liked him for your niece; and in that case Milly would interfere. I mean," Susie added, "interfere with *you*."

"She interferes with me as it is—not that it matters now. But I saw Kate and her—really as soon as you came to me—set up side by side. I saw your girl—I don't mind telling you—helping my girl;

and when I say that," Mrs. Lowder continued, "you'll probably put in for yourself that it was part of the reason of my welcome to you. So you see what I give up. I do give it up. But when I take that line," she further set forth, "I take it handsomely. So good-bye to it all. Good-day to Mrs. Densher! Heavens!" she growled.

Susie held herself a minute. "Even as Mrs. Densher my girl will be somebody."

"Yes, she won't be nobody. Besides," said Mrs. Lowder, "we're talking in the air."

Her companion sadly assented. "We're leaving everything out."

"It's nevertheless interesting." And Mrs. Lowder had another thought. "*He's* not quite nobody either." It brought her back to the question she had already put and which her friend hadn't at the time dealt with. "What in fact do you make of him?"

Susan Shepherd, at this, for reasons not clear even to herself, was moved a little to caution. So she remained general. "He's charming."

She had met Mrs. Lowder's eyes with that extreme pointedness in her own to which people resort when they are not quite candid—a circumstance that had its effect. "Yes; he's charming."

The effect of the words, however, was equally marked; they almost determined in Mrs. Stringham a return of amusement. "I thought you didn't like him!"

"I don't like him for Kate."

"But you don't like him for Milly either."

Mrs. Stringham rose as she spoke, and her friend also got up. "I like him, my dear, for myself."

"Then that's the best way of all."

"Well, it's one way. He's not good enough for my niece, and he's not good enough for you. One's an aunt, one's a wretch and one's a fool."

"Oh *I'm* not—not either," Susie declared.

But her companion kept on. "One lives for others. *You* do that. If I were living for myself I shouldn't at all mind him."

But Mrs. Stringham was sturdier. "Ah if I find him charming it's however I'm living."

Well, it broke Mrs. Lowder down. She hung fire but an instant, giving herself away with a laugh. "Of course he's all right in himself."

"That's all I contend," Susie said with more reserve; and the note in question—what Merton Densher was "in himself"—closed practically, with some inconsequence, this first of their councils.

II

It had at least made the difference for them, they could feel, of an informed state in respect to the great doctor, whom they were now to take as watching, waiting, studying, or at any rate as proposing to himself some such process before he should make up his mind. Mrs. Stringham understood him as considering the matter meanwhile in a spirit that, on this same occasion, at Lancaster Gate, she had come back to a rough notation of before retiring. She followed the course of his reckoning. If what they had talked of *could* happen—if Milly, that is, could have her thoughts taken off herself—it wouldn't do any harm and might conceivably do much good. If it couldn't happen—if, anxiously, though tactfully working, they themselves, conjoined, could do nothing to contribute to it—they would be in no worse a box than before. Only in this latter case the girl would have had her free range for the summer, for the autumn; she would have done her best in the sense enjoined on her, and, coming back at the end to her eminent man, would—besides having more to show him—find him more ready to go on with her. It was visible further to Susan Shepherd—as well as being ground for a second report to her old friend—that Milly did her part for a working view of the general case, inasmuch as she mentioned frankly and promptly that she meant to go and say good-bye to Sir Luke Strett and thank him. She even specified what she was to thank him for, his having been so easy about her behaviour.

"You see I didn't know that—for the liberty I took—I shouldn't afterwards get a stiff note from him."

So much Milly had said to her, and it had made her a trifle rash. "Oh you'll never get a stiff note from him in your life."

She felt her rashness, the next moment, at her young friend's question. "Why not, as well as any one else who has played him a trick?"

"Well, because he doesn't regard it as a trick. He could understand your action. It's all right, you see."

"Yes—I do see. It *is* all right. He's easier with me than with any one else, because that's the way to let me down. He's only making believe, and I'm not worth hauling up."

Rueful at having provoked again this ominous flare, poor Susie grasped at her only advantage. "Do you really accuse a man like Sir Luke Strett of trifling with you?"

She couldn't blind herself to the look her companion gave her—a strange half-amused perception of what she made of it. "Well, so far as it's trifling with me to pity me so much."

"He doesn't pity you," Susie earnestly reasoned. "He just—the same as any one else—likes you."

"He has no business then to like me. He's not the same as any one else."

"Why not, if he wants to work for you?"

Milly gave her another look, but this time a wonderful smile. "Ah there you are!" Mrs. Stringham coloured, for there indeed she was again. But Milly let her off. "Work for me, all the same—work for me! It's of course what I want." Then as usual she embraced her friend. "I'm not going to be as nasty as this to *him*."

"I'm sure I hope not!"—and Mrs. Stringham laughed for the kiss. "I've no doubt, however, he'd take it from you! It's *you*, my dear, who are not the same as any one else."

Milly's assent to which, after an instant, gave her the last word. "No, so that people can take anything from me." And what Mrs. Stringham did indeed resignedly take after this was the absence on her part of any account of the visit then paid. It was the beginning in fact between them of an odd independence—an independence positively of action and custom—on the subject of Milly's future. They went their separate ways with the girl's intense assent; this being really nothing but what she had so wonderfully put in her plea for after Mrs. Stringham's first encounter with Sir Luke. She fairly favoured the idea that Susie had or was to have other encounters—private pointed personal; she favoured every idea, but most of all the idea that she herself was to go on as if nothing were the matter. Since she was to be worked for that would be her way; and though her companion learned from herself nothing of it this was in the event her way with her medical adviser. She put her visit to him on the simplest ground; she had come just to tell him how touched she had been by his good nature. That required little explaining, for, as Mrs. Stringham had said, he quite understood he could but reply that it was all right.

"I had a charming quarter of an hour with that clever lady. You've got good friends."

"So each one of them thinks of all the others. But so I also think," Milly went on, "of all of them together. You're excellent for each other. And it's in that way, I dare say, that you're best for me."

There came to her on this occasion one of the strangest of her impressions, which was at the same time one of the finest of her alarms—the glimmer of a vision that if she should go, as it were, too far, she might perhaps deprive their relation of facility if not of value. Going too far was failing to try at least to remain simple. He would be quite ready to hate her if she did, by heading him off at every point, embarrass his exercise of a kindness that, no doubt, rather constituted for him a high method. Susie wouldn't hate her, since Susie positively wanted to suffer for her; Susie had a noble idea that she might somehow so do her good. Such, however, was not the way in which the greatest of London doctors was to be expected to wish to do it. He wouldn't have time even should he wish; whereby, in a word, Milly felt herself intimately warned. Face to face there with her smooth strong director, she enjoyed at a given moment quite such another lift of feeling as she had known in her crucial talk with Susie. It came round to the same thing; him too she would help to help her if that could possibly be; but if it couldn't possibly be she would assist also to make this right. It wouldn't have taken many minutes more, on the basis in question, almost to reverse for her their characters of patient and physician. What *was* he in fact but patient, what was she but physician, from the moment she embraced once for all the necessity, adopted once for all the policy, of saving him alarms about her subtlety? She would leave the subtlety to him, he would enjoy his use of it, and she herself, no doubt, would in time enjoy his enjoyment. She went so far as to imagine that the inward success of these reflexions flushed her for the minute, to his eyes, with a certain bloom, a comparative appearance of health; and what verily next occurred was that he gave colour to the presumption. "Every little helps, no doubt!"—he noticed good-humouredly her harmless sally. "But, help or no help, you're looking, you know, remarkably well."

"Oh I thought I was," she answered; and it was as if already she saw his line. Only she wondered what he would have guessed. If he had guessed anything at all it would be rather remarkable of him. As for what there *was* to guess, he couldn't—if this was present to him—have arrived at it save by his own acuteness. That acuteness was therefore immense; and if it supplied the subtlety she thought of leaving him to, his portion would be none so bad. Neither, for that matter, would hers be—which she was even actually enjoying. She wondered if really then there mightn't be something for her. She hadn't been sure in coming to him that she was "better," and he hadn't used, he would be awfully careful not to use, that compromising term about her; in spite of all of which she would have been ready to say, for the amiable sympathy of it, "Yes, I *must* be," for he had this unaided sense of something that had happened to her. It was a sense unaided, because who could have told him of anything? Susie, she was certain, hadn't yet seen him again, and there were things it was impossible she could have told him the first time. Since such was his penetration, therefore, why shouldn't she gracefully, in recognition of it, accept the new circumstance, the one he was clearly wanting to congratulate her on, as a sufficient cause? If one nursed a cause tenderly enough it might produce an effect; and this, to begin with, would be a way of nursing. "You gave me the other day," she went on, "plenty to think over, and I've been doing that—thinking it over—quite as you'll have probably wished me. I think I must be pretty easy to treat," she smiled, "since you've already done me so much good."

The only obstacle to reciprocity with him was that he looked in advance so closely related to all one's possibilities that one missed the pleasure of really improving it. "Oh no, you're extremely difficult to treat. I've need with you, I assure you, of all my wit."

"Well, I mean I do come up." She hadn't meanwhile a bit believed in his answer, convinced as she was that if she *had* been difficult it would be the last thing he would have told her. "I'm doing," she said, "as I like."

"Then it's as *I* like. But you must really, though we're having such a decent month, get straight away." In pursuance of which, when she had replied with promptitude that her departure—for the Tyrol[1] and then for Venice—was quite fixed for the fourteenth, he took her up with alacrity. "For Venice? That's perfect, for we shall meet there. I've a dream of it for October, when I'm hoping for three weeks off; three weeks during which, if I can get them clear, my niece, a young person who has quite the whip hand of me, is to take me where she prefers. I heard from her only yesterday that she expects to prefer Venice."

"That's lovely then. I shall expect you there. And anything that, in advance or in any way, I can do for you—!"

"Oh thank you. My niece, I seem to feel, does for me. But it will be capital to find you there."

"I think it ought to make you feel," she said after a moment, "that I *am* easy to treat."

But he shook his head again; he wouldn't have it. "You've not come to that *yet*."

"One has to be so bad for it?"

"Well, I don't think I've ever come to it—to 'ease' of treatment. I doubt if it's possible. I've not, if it is, found any one bad enough. The ease, you see, is for *you*."

"I see—I see."

They had an odd friendly, but perhaps the least bit awkward pause on it; after which Sir Luke asked: "And that clever lady—she goes with you?"

"Mrs. Stringham? Oh dear, yes. She'll stay with me, I hope, to the end."

He had a cheerful blankness. "To the end of what?"

"Well—of everything."

"Ah then," he laughed, "you're in luck. The end of everything is far off. This, you know, I'm hoping," said Sir Luke, "is only the beginning." And the next question he risked might have been a part of his hope. "Just you and she together?"

"No, two other friends; two ladies of whom we've seen more here than of any one and who are just the right people for us."

He thought a moment. "You'll be four women together then?"

"Ah," said Milly, "we're widows and orphans. But I think," she added as if to say what she saw would reassure him, "that we shall

1. An alpine region in northern Italy and western Austria.

not be unattractive, as we move, to gentlemen. When you talk of 'life' I suppose you mean mainly gentlemen."

"When I talk of 'life,' " he made answer after a moment during which he might have been appreciating her raciness—"when I talk of life I think I mean more than anything else the beautiful show of it, in its freshness, made by young persons of your age. So go on as you are. I see more and more *how* you are. You can't," he went so far as to say for pleasantness, "better it."

She took it from him with a great show of peace. "One of our companions will be Miss Croy, who came with me here first. It's in *her* that life is splendid; and a part of that is even that she's devoted to me. But she's above all magnificent in herself. So that if you'd like," she freely threw out, "to see *her*—"

"Oh I shall like to see any one who's devoted to you, for clearly it will be jolly to be 'in' it. So that if she's to be at Venice I *shall* see her?"

"We must arrange it—I shan't fail. She moreover has a friend who may also be there"—Milly found herself going on to this. "He's likely to come, I believe, for he always follows her."

Sir Luke wondered. "You mean they're lovers?"

"*He* is," Milly smiled; "but not she. She doesn't care for him."

Sir Luke took an interest. "What's the matter with him?"

"Nothing but that she doesn't like him."

Sir Luke kept it up. "Is he all right?"

"Oh he's very nice. Indeed he's remarkably so."

"And he's to be in Venice?"

"So she tells me she fears. For if he is there he'll be constantly about with her."

"And she'll be constantly about with you?"

"As we're great friends—yes."

"Well then," said Sir Luke, "you won't be four women alone."

"Oh no; I quite recognise the chance of gentlemen. But he won't," Milly pursued in the same wondrous way, "have come, you see, for *me*."

"No—I see. But can't you help him?"

"Can't *you*?" Milly after a moment quaintly asked. Then for the joke of it she explained. "I'm putting you, you see, in relation with my entourage."

It might have been for the joke of it too, by this time, that her eminent friend fell in. "But if this gentleman *isn't* of your 'entourage'? I mean if he's of—what do you call her?—Miss Croy's. Unless indeed you also take an interest in him."

"Oh certainly I take an interest in him!"

"You think there may be then some chance for him?"

"I like him," said Milly, "enough to hope so."

"Then that's all right. But what, pray," Sir Luke next asked, "have I to do with him?"

"Nothing," said Milly, "except that if you're to be there, so may he be. And also that we shan't in that case be simply four dreary women."

He considered her as if at this point she a little tried his patience. "*You're* the least 'dreary' woman I've ever, ever seen. Ever, do you know? There's no reason why you shouldn't have a really splendid life."

"So every one tells me," she promptly returned.

"The conviction—strong already when I had seen you once—is strengthened in me by having seen your friend. There's no doubt about it. The world's before you."

"What did my friend tell you?" Milly asked.

"Nothing that wouldn't have given you pleasure. We talked about you—and freely. I don't deny that. But it shows me I don't require of you the impossible."

She was now on her feet. "I think I know what you require of me."

"Nothing, for you," he went on, "*is* impossible. So go on." He repeated it again—wanting her so to feel that to-day he saw it. "You're all right."

"Well," she smiled—"keep me so."

"Oh you'll get away from me."

"Keep me, keep me," she simply continued with her gentle eyes on him.

She had given him her hand for good-bye, and he thus for a moment did keep her. Something then, while he seemed to think if there were anything more, came back to him; though something of which there wasn't too much to be made. "Of course if there's anything I *can* do for your friend: I mean the gentleman you speak of—?" He gave out in short that he was ready.

"Oh Mr. Densher?" It was as if she had forgotten.

"Mr. Densher—is that his name?"

"Yes—but his case isn't so dreadful." She had within a minute got away from that.

"No doubt—if *you* take an interest." She had got away, but it was as if he made out in her eyes—though they also had rather got away—a reason for calling her back. "Still, if there's anything one can do—?"

She looked at him while she thought, while she smiled. "I'm afraid there's really nothing one can do."

III

Not yet so much as this morning had she felt herself sink into possession; gratefully glad that the warmth of the Southern summer was still in the high florid rooms, palatial chambers where hard cool pavements took reflexions in their lifelong polish, and where the sun on the stirred sea-water, flickering up through open windows, played over the painted "subjects" in the splendid ceilings—medallions of purple and brown, of brave old melancholy colour, medals as of old reddened gold, embossed and beribboned, all toned with time and all flourished and scolloped and gilded about, set in their great moulded and figured concavity (a nest of white cherubs, friendly creatures of the air) and appreciated by the aid of that second tier of smaller lights, straight openings to the front, which did everything, even with the Baedekers and photographs of Milly's party dreadfully meeting the eye, to make of the place an apartment of state. This at last only, though she had enjoyed the palace for three weeks, seemed to count as effective occupation; perhaps because it was the first time she had been alone—really to call alone—since she had left London, it ministered to her first full and unembarrassed sense of what the great Eugenio had done for her. The great Eugenio, recommended by grand-dukes and Americans, had entered her service during the last hours of all—had crossed from Paris, after multiplied *pourparlers*[1] with Mrs. Stringham, to whom she had allowed more than ever a free hand, on purpose to escort her to the Continent and encompass her there, and had dedicated to her, from the moment of their meeting, all the treasures of his experience. She had judged him in advance—polyglot and universal, very dear and very deep—as probably but a swindler finished to the finger-tips; for he was for ever carrying one well-kept Italian hand to his heart and plunging the other straight into her pocket, which, as she had instantly observed him to recognise, fitted it like a glove. The remarkable thing was that these elements of their common consciousness had rapidly gathered into an indestructible link, formed the ground of a happy relation; being by this time, strangely, grotesquely, delightfully, what most kept up confidence between them and what most expressed it.

She had seen quickly enough what was happening—the usual thing again, yet once again. Eugenio had, in an interview of five minutes, understood her, had got hold, like all the world, of the idea not so much of the care with which she must be taken up as of the care with which she must be let down. All the world understood her, all the world had got hold; but for nobody yet, she felt, would the idea have been so close a tie or won from herself so patient a surrender. Gracefully, respectfully, consummately enough—always with hands in position and the look, in his thick neat white hair, smooth fat face and black professional, almost theatrical eyes, as of some famous tenor grown too old to make love, but with an art still

1. Negotiations.

to make money—did he on occasion convey to her that she was, of all the clients of his glorious career, the one in whom his interest was most personal and paternal. The others had come in the way of business, but for her his sentiment was special. Confidence rested thus on her completely believing that: there was nothing of which she felt more sure. It passed between them every time they conversed; he was abysmal, but this intimacy lived on the surface. He had taken his place already for her among those who were to see her through, and meditation ranked him, in the constant perspective, for the final function, side by side with poor Susie—whom she was now pitying more than ever for having to be herself so sorry and to say so little about it. Eugenio had the general tact of a residuary legatee—which was a character that could be definitely worn; whereas she could see Susie, in the event of her death, in no character at all, Susie being insistently, exclusively concerned in her mere makeshift duration. This principle, for that matter, Milly at present, with a renewed flare of fancy, felt she should herself have liked to believe in. Eugenio had really done for her more than he probably knew—he didn't after all know everything—in having, for the wind-up of the autumn, on a weak word from her, so admirably, so perfectly established her. Her weak word, as a general hint, had been: "At Venice, please, if possible, no dreadful, no vulgar hotel; but, if it can be at all managed—you know what I mean—some fine old rooms, wholly independent, for a series of months. Plenty of them too, and the more interesting the better: part of a palace, historic and picturesque, but strictly inodorous, where we shall be to ourselves, with a cook, don't you know?—with servants, frescoes, tapestries, antiquities, the thorough make-believe of a settlement."

The proof of how he better and better understood her was in all the place; as to his masterly acquisition of which she had from the first asked no questions. She had shown him enough what she thought of it, and her forbearance pleased him; with the part of the transaction that mainly concerned her she would soon enough become acquainted, and his connexion with such values as she would then find noted could scarce help growing, as it were, still more residuary. Charming people, conscious Venice-lovers, evidently, had given up their house to her, and had fled to a distance, to other countries, to hide their blushes alike over what they had, however briefly, alienated, and over what they had, however durably, gained. They had preserved and consecrated, and she now—her part of it was shameless—appropriated and enjoyed. Palazzo Leporelli[2] held its history still in its great lap, even like a painted

2. The Palazzo (reproduced in the photograph of "The Venetian Palace") is the Palazzo Barbaro, built in the fifteenth century; in 1887 James, staying there with his friends the Daniel Curtises, the owners, wrote *A London Life*.

idol, a solemn puppet hung about with decorations. Hung about with pictures and relics, the rich Venetian past, the ineffaceable character, was here the presence revered and served: which brings us back to our truth of a moment ago—the fact that, more than ever, this October morning, awkward novice though she might be, Milly moved slowly to and fro as the priestess of the worship. Certainly it came from the sweet taste of solitude, caught again and cherished for the hour; always a need of her nature, moreover, when things spoke to her with penetration. It was mostly in stillness they spoke to her best; amid voices she lost the sense. Voices had surrounded her for weeks, and she had tried to listen, had cultivated them and had answered back; these had been weeks in which there were other things they might well prevent her from hearing. More than the prospect had at first promised or threatened she had felt herself going on in a crowd and with a multiplied escort; the four ladies pictured by her to Sir Luke Strett as a phalanx comparatively closed and detached had in fact proved a rolling snowball, condemned from day to day to cover more ground. Susan Shepherd had compared this portion of the girl's excursion to the Empress Catherine's famous progress across the steppes of Russia;[3] improvised settlements appeared at each turn of the road, villagers waiting with addresses drawn up in the language of London. Old friends in fine were in ambush, Mrs. Lowder's, Kate Croy's, her own; when the addresses weren't in the language of London they were in the more insistent idioms of American centres. The current was swollen even by Susie's social connexions; so that there were days, at hotels, at Dolomite[4] picnics, on lake steamers, when she could almost repay to Aunt Maud and Kate with interest the debt contracted by the London "success" to which they had opened the door.

Mrs. Lowder's success and Kate's, amid the shock of Milly's and Mrs. Stringham's compatriots, failed but little, really, of the concert-pitch; it had gone almost as fast as the boom, over the sea, of the last great native novel. Those ladies were "so different"—different, observably enough, from the ladies so appraising them; it being throughout a case mainly of ladies, of a dozen at once sometimes, in Milly's apartment, pointing, also at once, that moral and many others. Milly's companions were acclaimed not only as perfectly fascinating in themselves, the nicest people yet known to the acclaimers, but as obvious helping hands, socially speaking, for the eccentric young woman, evident initiators and smoothers of her

3. Catherine the Great (1729–96), in order to impress herself and various European visitors with the enlightenment of her rule, created "Potemkin Villages" —mock facades of buildings with gaily dressed peasants in front of them—to be passed in review. The "villages" take their name from one of her paramours, who was charged with making the elaborate preparations.

4. The Dolomites are an alpine mountain range in northern Italy.

path, possible subduers of her eccentricity. Short intervals, to her own sense, stood now for great differences, and this renewed inhalation of her native air had somehow left her to feel that she already, that she mainly, struck the compatriot as queer and dissociated. She moved such a critic, it would appear, as to rather an odd suspicion, a benevolence induced by a want of complete trust: all of which showed her in the light of a person too plain and too ill-clothed for a thorough good time, and yet too rich and too befriended—an intuitive cunning within her managing this last—for a thorough bad one. The compatriots, in short, by what she made out, approved her friends for their expert wisdom with her; in spite of which judicial sagacity it was the compatriots who recorded themselves as the innocent parties. She saw things in these days that she had never seen before, and she couldn't have said why save on a principle too terrible to name; whereby she saw that neither Lancaster Gate was what New York took it for, nor New York what Lancaster Gate fondly fancied it in coquetting with the plan of a series of American visits. The plan might have been, humorously, on Mrs. Lowder's part, for the improvement of her social position—and it had verily in that direction lights that were perhaps but half a century too prompt; at all of which Kate Croy assisted with the cool controlled facility that went so well, as the others said, with her particular kind of good looks, the kind that led you to expect the person enjoying them *would* dispose of disputations, speculations, aspirations, in a few very neatly and brightly uttered words, so simplified in sense, however, that they sounded, even when guiltless, like rather aggravated slang. It wasn't that Kate hadn't pretended too that *she* should like to go to America; it was only that with this young woman Milly had constantly proceeded, and more than ever of late, on the theory of intimate confessions, private frank ironies that made up for their public grimaces and amid which, face to face, they wearily put off the mask.

These puttings-off of the mask had finally quite become the form taken by their moments together, moments indeed not increasingly frequent and not prolonged, thanks to the consciousness of fatigue on Milly's side whenever, as she herself expressed it, she got out of harness. They flourished their masks, the independent pair, as they might have flourished Spanish fans; they smiled and sighed on removing them; but the gesture, the smiles, the sighs, strangely enough, might have been suspected the greatest reality in the business. Strangely enough, we say, for the volume of effusion in general would have been found by either on measurement to be scarce proportional to the paraphernalia of relief. It was when they called each other's attention to their ceasing to pretend, it was then that what they were keeping back was most in the air. There was a difference, no doubt, and mainly to Kate's advantage: Milly didn't quite see what her friend could keep back, was possessed of, in fine, that would be so subject to retention; whereas it was comparatively plain sailing for Kate that poor Milly had a treasure to hide. This was not the treasure of a shy, an abject affection—concealment, on that head, belonging to quite another phase of such states; it was much rather a principle of pride relatively bold and hard, a principle that played up like a fine steel spring at the lightest pressure of too near a footfall. Thus insuperably guarded was the truth about the girl's own conception of her validity; thus was a wondering pitying sister condemned wistfully to look at her from the far side of the moat she had dug round her tower. Certain aspects of the connexion of these young women show for us, such is the twilight that gathers about them, in the likeness of some dim scene in a Maeterlinck play; we have positively the image, in the delicate dusk, of the figures so associated and yet so opposed, so mutually watchful: that of the angular pale princess, ostrich-plumed, black-robed, hung about with amulets, reminders, relics, mainly seated, mainly still, and that of the upright restless slow-circling lady of her court who exchanges with her, across the black water streaked with evening gleams, fitful questions and answers. The upright lady, with thick dark braids down her back, drawing over the grass a more embroidered train, makes the whole circuit, and makes it again, and the broken talk, brief and sparingly allusive, seems more to cover than to free their sense. This is because, when it fairly comes to not having others to consider, they meet in an air that appears rather anxiously to wait for their words. Such an impression as that was in fact grave, and might be tragic; so that, plainly enough, systematically at last, they settled to a care of what they said.

There could be no gross phrasing to Milly, in particular, of the probability that if she wasn't so proud she might be pitied with more comfort—more to the person pitying; there could be no spoken proof, no sharper demonstration than the consistently considerate attitude, that this marvellous mixture of her weakness and of her strength, her peril, if such it were, and her option, made her, kept her, irresistibly interesting. Kate's predicament in the matter was, after all, very much Mrs. Stringham's own, and Susan Shepherd herself indeed, in our Maeterlinck picture, might well have hovered in the gloaming by the moat. It may be declared for Kate, at all events, that her sincerity about her friend, through this time, was deep, her compassionate imagination strong; and that these things gave her a virtue, a good conscience, a credibility for herself, so to speak, that were later to be precious to her. She grasped with her keen intelligence the logic of their common duplicity, went unassisted through the same ordeal as Milly's other hushed follower, easily saw that for the girl to be explicit was to betray divinations, gratitudes, glimpses of the felt contrast between her fortune and her fear—all of which would have contradicted her systematic bravado. That was it, Kate wonderingly saw: to recognise was to bring down the avalanche—the avalanche Milly lived so in watch for and that might be started by the lightest of breaths; though less possibly the breath of her own stifled plaint than that of the vain sympathy, the mere helpless gaping inference of others. With so many suppressions as these, therefore, between them, their withdrawal together to unmask had to fall back, as we have hinted, on a nominal motive—which was decently represented by a joy at the drop of chatter. Chatter had in truth all along attended their steps, but they took the despairing view of it on purpose to have ready, when face to face, some view or other of something. The relief of getting out of harness—that was the moral of their meetings; but the moral of this, in turn, was that they couldn't so much as ask each other why harness need be worn. Milly wore it as a general armour.

She was out of it at present, for some reason, as she hadn't been for weeks; she was always out of it, that is, when alone, and her companions had never yet so much as just now affected her as dispersed and suppressed. It was as if still again, still more tacitly and wonderfully, Eugenio had understood her, taking it from her without a word and just bravely and brilliantly in the name, for instance, of the beautiful day: "Yes, get me an hour alone; take them off—I don't care where; absorb, amuse, detain them; drown them, kill them if you will: so that I may just a little, all by myself, see where I am." She was conscious of the dire impatience of it, for she gave up Susie as well as the others to him—Susie who would have drowned her very self for her; gave her up to a mercenary monster through whom she thus purchased respites. Strange were the turns of life and the moods of weakness; strange the flickers of fancy and the cheats of hope; yet lawful, all the same—weren't they?—those experiments tried with the truth that consisted, at the worst, but in practising on one's self. She was now playing with the thought that Eugenio might *inclusively* assist her: he had brought home to her, and always by remarks that were really quite soundless, the conception, hitherto ungrasped, of some complete use of her wealth itself, some use of it as a counter-move to fate. It had passed between them as preposterous that with so much money she should just stupidly and awkwardly *want*—any more want a life, a career, a consciousness, than want a house, a carriage or a cook. It was as if she had had from him a kind of expert professional measure of what he was in a position, at a stretch, to undertake for her; the thoroughness of which, for that matter, she could closely compare with a looseness on Sir Luke Strett's part that—at least in Palazzo Leporelli when mornings were fine—showed as almost amateurish. Sir Luke hadn't said to her "Pay enough money and leave the rest to *me*"—which was distinctly what Eugenio did say. Sir Luke had appeared indeed to speak of purchase and payment, but in reference to a different sort of cash. Those were amounts not to be named nor reckoned, and such moreover as she wasn't sure of having at her command. Eugenio—this was the difference—could name, could reckon, and prices of *his* kind were things she had never suffered to scare her. She had been willing, goodness knew, to pay enough for anything, for everything, and here was simply a new view of the sufficient quantity. She amused herself—for it came to that, since Eugenio was there to sign the receipt—with possibilities of meeting the bill. She was more prepared than ever to pay enough, and quite as much as ever to pay too much. What else—if such were points at which your most trusted servant failed—was the use of being, as the dear Susies of earth called you, a princess in a palace?

She made now, alone, the full circuit of the place, noble and peaceful while the summer sea, stirring here and there a curtain or an outer blind, breathed into its veiled spaces. She had a vision of clinging to it; that perhaps Eugenio could manage. She was *in* it, as in the ark of her deluge, and filled with such a tenderness for it that why shouldn't this, in common mercy, be warrant enough? She would never, never leave it—she would engage to that; would ask nothing more than to sit tight in it and float on and on. The beauty and intensity, the real momentary relief of this conceit, reached their climax in the positive purpose to put the question to Eugenio on his return as she had not yet put it; though the design, it must be added, dropped a little when, coming back to the great saloon from which she had started on her pensive progress, she found Lord Mark, of whose arrival in Venice she had been unaware, and who had now—while a servant was following her through empty rooms—been asked, in her absence, to wait. He had waited then, Lord Mark, he was waiting—oh unmistakeably; never before had he so much struck her as the man to do that on occasion with patience, to do it indeed almost as with gratitude for the chance, though at the same time with a sort of notifying firmness. The odd thing, as she was afterwards to recall, was that her wonder for what had brought him was not immediate, but had come at the end of five minutes; and also, quite incoherently, that she felt almost as glad to see him, and almost as forgiving of his interruption of her solitude, as if he had already been in her thought or acting at her suggestion. He was somehow, at the best, the end of a respite; one might like him very much and yet feel that his presence tempered precious solitude more than any other known to one: in spite of all of which, as he was neither dear Susie, nor dear Kate, nor dear Aunt Maud, nor even, for the least, dear Eugenio in person, the sight of him did no damage to her sense of the dispersal of her friends. She hadn't been so thoroughly alone with him since those moments of his showing her the great portrait at Matcham, the moments that had exactly made the high-water-mark of her security, the moments during which her tears themselves, those she had been ashamed of, were the sign of her consciously rounding her protective promontory, quitting the blue gulf of comparative ignorance and reaching her view of the troubled sea. His presence now referred itself to his presence then, reminding her how kind he had been, altogether, at Matcham, and telling her, unexpectedly, at a time when she could particularly feel it, that, for such kindness and for the beauty of what they remembered together, she hadn't lost him—quite the contrary. To receive him handsomely, to receive him there, to see him interested and charmed, as well, clearly, as delighted to have found her without some other person to spoil it—these things were so pleasant for the first minutes that they might have represented on her part some happy foreknowledge.

She gave an account of her companions while he on his side failed to press her about them, even though describing his appearance, so unheralded, as the result of an impulse obeyed on the spot. He had been shivering at Carlsbad, belated there and blue, when taken by it; so that, knowing where they all were, he had simply caught the first train. He explained how he had known where they were; he had heard—what more natural?—from their friends, Milly's and his. He mentioned this betimes, but it was with his mention, singularly, that the girl became conscious of her inner question about his reason. She noticed his plural, which added to Mrs. Lowder or added to Kate; but she presently noticed also that it didn't affect her as explaining. Aunt Maud had written to him, Kate apparently—and this was interesting—had written to him; but their design presumably hadn't been that he should come and sit there as if rather relieved, so far as *they* were concerned, at postponements. He only said "Oh!" and again "Oh!" when she sketched their probable morning for him, under Eugenio's care and Mrs. Stringham's—sounding it quite as if any suggestion that he should overtake them at the Rialto or the Bridge of Sighs[5] would leave him temporarily cold. This precisely it was that, after a little, operated for Milly as an obscure but still fairly direct check to confidence. He had known where they all were from the others, but it was not for the others that, in his actual dispositions, he had come. That, strange to say, was a pity; for, stranger still to say, she could

5. The Rialto is the largest bridge over the Grand Canal and is a bustling center of commerce; the Bridge of Sighs is a passageway connecting the upper arcade of the Palace of the Doges to the prison which housed those condemned to death by the Republic.

have shown him more confidence if he himself had had less intention. His intention so chilled her, from the moment she found herself divining it, that, just for the pleasure of going on with him fairly, just for the pleasure of their remembrance together of Matcham and the Bronzino, the climax of her fortune, she could have fallen to pleading with him and to reasoning, to undeceiving him in time. There had been, for ten minutes, with the directness of her welcome to him and the way this clearly pleased him, something of the grace of amends made, even though he couldn't know it—amends for her not having been originally sure, for instance at that first dinner of Aunt Maud's, that he was adequately human. That first dinner of Aunt Maud's added itself to the hour at Matcham, added itself to other things, to consolidate, for her present benevolence, the ease of their relation, making it suddenly delightful that he had thus turned up. He exclaimed, as he looked about, on the charm of the place: "What a temple to taste and an expression of the pride of life, yet, with all that, what a jolly *home!*"—so that, for his entertainment, she could offer to walk him about though she mentioned that she had just been, for her own purposes, in a general prowl, taking everything in more susceptibly than before. He embraced her offer without a scruple and seemed to rejoice that he was to find her susceptible.

IV

She couldn't have said what it was, in the conditions, that renewed the whole solemnity, but by the end of twenty minutes a kind of wistful hush had fallen upon them, as before something poignant in which her visitor also participated. That was nothing verily but the perfection of the charm—or nothing rather but their excluded disinherited state in the presence of it. The charm turned on them a face that was cold in its beauty, that was full of a poetry never to be theirs, that spoke with an ironic smile of a possible but forbidden life. It all rolled afresh over Milly: "Oh the impossible romance—!" The romance for her, yet once more, would be to sit there for ever, through all her time, as in a fortress; and the idea became an image of never going down, of remaining aloft in the divine dustless air, where she would hear but the plash of the water against stone. The great floor on which they moved was at an altitude, and this prompted the rueful fancy. "Ah not to go down—never, never to go down!" she strangely sighed to her friend.

"But why shouldn't you," he asked, "with that tremendous old staircase in your court? There ought of course always to be people at top and bottom, in Veronese costumes,[1] to watch you do it."

She shook her head both lightly and mournfully enough at his not understanding. "Not even for people in Veronese costumes. I

1. Paolo Veronese (1528–88), the Venetian master, typically painted figures in richly colored and sumptuous dress.

mean that the positive beauty is that one needn't go down. I don't move in fact," she added—"now. I've not been out, you know. I stay up. That's how you happily found me."

Lord Mark wondered—he was, oh yes, adequately human. "You don't go about?"

She looked over the place, the storey above the apartments in which she had received him, the sala[2] corresponding to the sala below and fronting the great canal with its gothic arches. The casements between the arches were open, the ledge of the balcony broad, the sweep of the canal, so overhung, admirable, and the flutter toward them of the loose white curtain an invitation to she scarce could have said what. But there was no mystery after a moment; she had never felt so invited to anything as to make that, and that only, just where she was, her adventure. It would be—to this it kept coming back—the adventure of not stirring. "I go about just here."

"Do you mean," Lord Mark presently asked, "that you're really not well?"

They were at the window, pausing, lingering, with the fine old faded palaces opposite and the slow Adriatic tide beneath; but after a minute, and before she answered, she had closed her eyes to what she saw and unresistingly dropped her face into her arms, which rested on the coping. She had fallen to her knees on the cushion of the window-place, and she leaned there, in a long silence, with her forehead down. She knew that her silence was itself too straight an answer, but it was beyond her now to say that she saw her way. She would have made the question itself impossible to others—impossible for example to such a man as Merton Densher; and she could wonder even on the spot what it was a sign of in her feeling for Lord Mark that from his lips it almost tempted her to break down. This was doubtless really because she cared for him so little; to let herself go with him thus, suffer his touch to make her cup overflow, would be the relief—since it was actually, for her nerves, a question of relief—that would cost her least. If he had come to her moreover with the intention she believed, or even if this intention had but been determined in him by the spell of their situation, he mustn't be mistaken about her value—for what value did she now have? It throbbed within her as she knelt there that she had none at all; though, holding herself, not yet speaking, she tried, even in the act, to recover what might be possible of it. With that there came to her a light: wouldn't her value, for the man who should marry her, be precisely in the ravage of her disease? *She* mightn't last, but her money would. For a man in whom the vision of her money should be intense, in whom it should be most of the ground for "making up" to her, any prospective failure on her part to be long for this

2. A hall or large apartment.

world might easily count as a positive attraction. Such a man, proposing to please, persuade, secure her, appropriate her for such a time, shorter or longer, as nature and the doctors should allow, would make the best of her, ill, damaged, disagreeable though she might be, for the sake of eventual benefits: she being clearly a person of the sort esteemed likely to do the handsome thing by a stricken and sorrowing husband.

She had said to herself betimes, in a general way, that whatever habits her youth might form, that of seeing an interested suitor in every bush should certainly never grow to be one of them—an attitude she had early judged as ignoble, as poisonous. She had had accordingly in fact as little to do with it as possible and she scarce knew why at the present moment she should have had to catch herself in the act of imputing an ugly motive. It didn't sit, the ugly motive, in Lord Mark's cool English eyes; the darker side of it at any rate showed, to her imagination, but briefly. Suspicion moreover, with this, simplified itself: there was a beautiful reason—indeed there were two—why her companion's motive shouldn't matter. One was that even should he desire her without a penny she wouldn't marry him for the world; the other was that she felt him, after all, perceptively, kindly, very pleasantly and humanly, concerned for her. They were also two things, his wishing to be well, to be very well, with her, and his beginning to feel her as threatened, haunted, blighted; but they were melting together for him, making him, by their combination, only the more sure that, as he probably called it to himself, he liked her. That was presently what remained with her—his really doing it; and with the natural and proper incident of being conciliated by her weakness. Would she really have had him—she could ask herself that—disconcerted or disgusted by it? If he could only be touched enough to do what she preferred, not to raise, not to press any question, he might render her a much better service than by merely enabling her to refuse him. Again, again it was strange, but he figured to her for the moment as the one safe sympathiser. It would have made her worse to talk to others, but she wasn't afraid with him of how he might wince and look pale. She would keep him, that is, her one easy relation—in the sense of easy for himself. Their actual outlook had meanwhile such charm, what surrounded them within and without did so much toward making appreciative stillness as natural as at the opera, that she could consider she hadn't made him hang on her lips when at last, instead of saying if she were well or ill, she repeated: "I go about here. I don't get tired of it. I never should—it suits me so. I adore the place," she went on, "and I don't want in the least to give it up."

"Neither should I if I had your luck. Still, with that luck, for one's *all*—! Should you positively like to live here?"

"I think I should like," said poor Milly after an instant, "to die here."

Which made him, precisely, laugh. That was what she wanted—when a person did care: it was the pleasant human way, without depths of darkness. "Oh it's not good enough for *that!* That requires picking. But can't you keep it? It is, you know, the sort of place to see you in; you carry out the note, fill it, people it, quite by yourself, and you might do much worse—I mean for your friends—than show yourself here a while, three or four months, every year. But it's not my notion for the rest of the time. One has quite other uses for you."

"What sort of a use for me is it," she smilingly enquired, "to kill me?"

"Do you mean we should kill you in England?"

"Well, I've seen you and I'm afraid. You're too much for me—too many. England bristles with questions. This is more, as you say there, my form."

"Oho, oho!"—he laughed again as if to humour her. "Can't you then buy it—for a price? Depend upon it they'll treat for money. That is for money enough."

"I've exactly," she said, "been wondering if they won't. I think I shall try. But if I get it I shall cling to it." They were talking sincerely. "It will be my life—paid for as that. It will become my great gilded shell; so that those who wish to find me must come and hunt me up."

"Ah then you *will* be alive," said Lord Mark.

"Well, not quite extinct perhaps, but shrunken, wasted, wizened; rattling about here like the dried kernel of a nut."

"Oh," Lord Mark returned, "we, much as you mistrust us, can do better for you than that."

"In the sense that you'll feel it better for me really to have it over?"

He let her see now that she worried him, and after a look at her, of some duration, without his glasses—which always altered the expression of his eyes—he re-settled the nippers on his nose and went back to the view. But the view, in turn, soon enough released him. "Do you remember something I said to you that day at Matcham—or at least fully meant to?"

"Oh yes, I remember everything at Matcham. It's another life."

"Certainly it will be—I mean the kind of thing: what I then wanted it to represent for you. Matcham, you know," he continued, "is symbolic. I think I tried to rub that into you a little."

She met him with the full memory of what he had tried—not an inch, not an ounce of which was lost to her. "What I meant is that it seems a hundred years ago."

"Oh for me it comes in better. Perhaps a part of what makes me remember it," he pursued, "is that I was quite aware of what might have been said about what I was doing. I wanted you to take it from me that I should perhaps be able to look after you—well, rather better. Rather better, of course, than certain other persons in particular."

"Precisely—than Mrs. Lowder, than Miss Croy, even than Mrs. Stringham."

"Oh Mrs. Stringham's all right!" Lord Mark promptly amended.

It amused her even with what she had else to think of; and she could show him at all events how little, in spite of the hundred years, she had lost what he alluded to. The way he was with her at this moment made in fact the other moment so vivid as almost to start again the tears it had started at the time. "You could do so much for me, yes. I perfectly understood you."

"I wanted, you see," he despite this explained, "to *fix* your confidence. I mean, you know, in the right place."

"Well, Lord Mark, you did—it's just exactly now, my confidence, where you put it then. The only difference," said Milly, "is that I seem now to have no use for it. Besides," she then went on, "I do seem to feel you disposed to act in a way that would undermine it a little."

He took no more notice of these last words than if she hadn't said them, only watching her at present as with a gradual new light. "Are you *really* in any trouble?"

To this, on her side, she gave no heed. Making out his light was a little a light for herself. "Don't say, don't try to say, anything that's impossible. There are much better things you can do."

He looked straight at it and then straight over it. "It's too monstrous that one can't ask you as a friend what one wants so to know."

"What is it you want to know?" She spoke, as by a sudden turn, with a slight hardness. "Do you want to know if I'm badly ill?"

The sound of it in truth, though from no raising of her voice, invested the idea with a kind of terror, but a terror all for others. Lord Mark winced and flushed—clearly couldn't help it; but he kept his attitude together and spoke even with unwonted vivacity. "Do you imagine I can see you suffer and not say a word?"

"You won't see me suffer—don't be afraid. I shan't be a public nuisance. That's why I should have liked *this*: it's so beautiful in itself and yet it's out of the gangway. You won't know anything about anything," she added; and then as if to make with decision an end: "And you *don't!* No, not even you." He faced her through it with the remains of his expression, and she saw him as clearly—for *him*—bewildered; which made her wish to be sure not to have been unkind. She would be kind once for all; that would be the end. "I'm very badly ill."

"And you don't do anything?"

"I do everything. Everything's *this*," she smiled. "I'm doing it now. One can't do more than live."

"Ah than live in the right way, no. But is *that* what you do? Why haven't you advice?"

He had looked about at the rococo elegance as if there were fifty things it didn't give her, so that he suggested with urgency the most absent. But she met his remedy with a smile. "I've the best advice in the world. I'm acting under it now. I act upon it in receiving you, in talking with you thus. One can't, as I tell you, do more than live."

"Oh live!" Lord Mark ejaculated.

"Well, it's immense for *me*." She finally spoke as if for amusement; now that she had uttered her truth, that he had learnt it from herself as no one had yet done, her emotion had, by the fact, dried up. There she was; but it was as if she would never speak again. "I shan't," she added, "have missed everything."

"Why should you have missed *anything?*" She felt, as he sounded this, to what, within the minute, he had made up his mind. "You're the person in the world for whom that's least necessary; for whom one would call it in fact most impossible; for whom 'missing' at all will surely require an extraordinary amount of misplaced good will. Since you believe in advice, for God's sake take *mine*. I know what you want."

Oh she knew he would know it. But she had brought it on herself—or almost. Yet she spoke with kindness. "I think I want not to be too much worried."

"You want to be adored." It came at last straight. "Nothing would worry you less. I mean as I shall do it. It *is* so"—he firmly kept it up. "You're not loved enough."

"Enough for what, Lord Mark?"

"Why to get the full good of it."

Well, she didn't after all mock at him. "I see what you mean. That full good of it which consists in finding one's self forced to love in return." She had grasped it, but she hesitated. "Your idea is that I might find myself forced to love *you?*"

"Oh 'forced'—!" He was so fine and so expert, so awake to anything the least ridiculous, and of a type with which the preaching of passion somehow so ill consorted—he was so much all these things that he had absolutely to take account of them himself. And he did so, in a single intonation, beautifully. Milly liked him again, liked him for such shades as that, liked him so that it was woeful to see him spoiling it, and still more woeful to have to rank him among those minor charms of existence that she gasped at moments to remember she must give up. "Is it inconceivable to you that you might try?"

"To be so favourably affected by you—?"

"To believe in me. To believe in me," Lord Mark repeated.

Again she hesitated. "To 'try' in return for your trying?"

"Oh I shouldn't have to!" he quickly declared. The prompt neat accent, however, his manner of disposing of her question, failed of real expression, as he himself the next moment intelligently, helplessly, almost comically saw—a failure pointed moreover by the laugh into which Milly was immediately startled. As a suggestion to her of a healing and uplifting passion it *was* in truth deficient; it wouldn't do as the communication of a force that should sweep them both away. And the beauty of him was that he too, even in the act of persuasion, of self-persuasion, could understand that, and could thereby show but the better as fitting into the pleasant commerce of prosperity. The way she let him see that she looked at him was a thing to shut him out, of itself, from services of danger, a thing that made a discrimination against him never yet made—made at least to any consciousness of his own. Born to float in a sustaining air, this would be his first encounter with a judgement formed in the sinister light of tragedy. The gathering dusk of *her* personal world presented itself to him, in her eyes, as an element in which it was vain for him to pretend he could find himself at home, since it was charged with depressions and with dooms, with the chill of the losing game. Almost without her needing to speak, and simply by the fact that there could be, in such a case, no decent substitute for a felt intensity, he had to take it from her that practically he was afraid—whether afraid to protest falsely enough, or only afraid of what might be eventually disagreeable in a compromised alliance, being a minor question. She believed she made out besides, wonderful girl, that he had never quite expected to have to protest about anything beyond his natural convenience—more, in fine, than his disposition and habits, his education as well, his personal *moyens*,[3] in short, permitted. His predicament was therefore one he couldn't like, and also one she willingly would have spared him hadn't he brought it on himself. No man, she was quite aware, could enjoy thus having it from her that he wasn't good for what she would have called her reality. It wouldn't have taken much more to enable her positively to make out in him that he was virtually capable of hinting—had his innermost feeling spoken—at the propriety rather, in his interest, of some cutting down, some dressing up, of the offensive real. He would meet that halfway, but the real must also meet *him*. Milly's sense of it for herself, which was so conspicuously, so financially supported, couldn't, or wouldn't, so accommodate him, and the perception of that fairly showed in his face after a moment like the smart of a blow. It had marked the one minute during which he could again be touching to her. By the

3. Financial means.

time he had tried once more, after all, to insist, he had quite ceased to be so.

By this time she had turned from their window to make a diversion, had walked him through other rooms, appealing again to the inner charm of the place, going even so far for that purpose as to point afresh her independent moral, to repeat that if one only had such a house for one's own and loved it and cherished it enough, it would pay one back in kind, would close one in from harm. He quite grasped for the quarter of an hour the perch she held out to him—grasped it with one hand, that is, while she felt him attached to his own clue with the other; he was by no means either so sore or so stupid, to do him all justice, as not to be able to behave more or less as if nothing had happened. It was one of his merits, to which she did justice too, that both his native and his acquired notion of behaviour rested on the general assumption that nothing—nothing to make a deadly difference for him—ever *could* happen. It was, socially, a working view like another, and it saw them easily enough through the greater part of the rest of their adventure. Downstairs again, however, with the limit of his stay in sight, the sign of his smarting, when all was said, reappeared for her—breaking out moreover, with an effect of strangeness, in another quite possibly sincere allusion to her state of health. He might for that matter have been seeing what he could do in the way of making it a grievance that she should snub him for a charity, on his own part, exquisitely roused. "It's true, you know, all the same, and I don't care a straw for your trying to freeze one up." He seemed to show her, poor man, bravely, how little he cared. "Everybody knows affection often makes things out when indifference doesn't notice. And that's why I know that *I* notice."

Are you sure you've got it right?" the girl smiled. "I thought rather that affection was supposed to be blind."

"Blind to faults, not to beauties," Lord Mark promptly returned.

"And are my extremely private worries, my entirely domestic complications, which I'm ashamed to have given you a glimpse of —are they beauties?"

"Yes, for those who care for you—as every one does. Everything about you is a beauty. Besides which I don't believe," he declared, "in the seriousness of what you tell me. It's too absurd you should have *any* trouble about which something can't be done. If you can't get the right thing, who *can*, in all the world, I should like to know? You're the first young woman of your time. I mean what I say." He looked, to do him justice, quite as if he did; not ardent, but clear—simply so competent, in such a position, to compare, that his quiet assertion had the force not so much perhaps of a tribute as of a warrant. "We're all in love with you. I'll put it that way, dropping any claim of my own, if you can bear it better. I speak as one of the lot. You weren't born simply to torment us—you were born to make us happy. Therefore you must listen to us."

She shook her head with her slowness, but this time with all her mildness. "No, I mustn't listen to you—that's just what I mustn't do. The reason is, please, that it simply kills me. I must be as attached to you as you will, since you give that lovely account of yourselves. I give you in return the fullest possible belief of what it would be—" And she pulled up a little. "I give and give and give—there you are; stick to me as close as you like and see if I don't. Only I can't listen or receive or accept—I can't *agree*. I can't make a bargain. I can't really. You must believe that from me. It's all I've wanted to say to you, and why should it spoil anything?"

He let her question fall—though clearly, it might have seemed, because, for reasons or for none, there was so much that *was* spoiled. "You want somebody of your own." He came back, whether in good faith or in bad, to that; and it made her repeat her headshake. He kept it up as if his faith were of the best. "You want somebody, you want somebody."

She was to wonder afterwards if she hadn't been at this juncture on the point of saying something emphatic and vulgar—"Well, I don't at all events want *you!*" What somehow happened, nevertheless, the pity of it being greater than the irritation—the sadness, to her vivid sense, of his being so painfully astray, wandering in a desert in which there was nothing to nourish him—was that his error amounted to positive wrongdoing. She was moreover so acquainted with quite another sphere of usefulness for him that her having suffered him to insist almost convicted her of indelicacy. Why hadn't she stopped him off with her first impression of his purpose? She could do so now only by the allusion she had been wishing not to make. "Do you know I don't think you're doing very right?—and as a thing quite apart, I mean, from my listening to you. That's not right either—except that I'm *not* listening. You oughtn't to have come to Venice to see *me*—and in fact you've not come, and you mustn't behave as if you had. You've much older friends than I, and ever so much better. Really, if you've come at all, you can only have come—properly, and if I may say so honourably—for the best friend, as I believe her to be, that you have in the world."

When once she had said it he took it, oddly enough, as if he had been more or less expecting it. Still, he looked at her very hard, and they had a moment of this during which neither pronounced a name, each apparently determined that the other should. It was Milly's fine coercion, in the event, that was the stronger. "Miss Croy?" Lord Mark asked.

It might have been difficult to make out that she smiled. "Mrs. Lowder." He did make out something, and then fairly coloured for its attestation of his comparative simplicity. "I call *her* on the whole the best. I can't imagine a man's having a better."

Still with his eyes on her he turned it over. "Do you want me to marry Mrs. Lowder?"

At which it seemed to her that it was he who was almost vulgar! But she wouldn't in any way have that. "You know, Lord Mark, what I mean. One isn't in the least turning you out into the cold world. There's no cold world for you at all, I think," she went on; "nothing but a very warm and watchful and expectant world that's waiting for you at any moment you choose to take it up."

He never budged, but they were standing on the polished concrete and he had within a few minutes possessed himself again of his hat. "Do you want me to marry Kate Croy?"

"Mrs. Lowder wants it—I do no wrong, I think, in saying that; and she understands moreover that you know she does."

Well, he showed how beautifully he could take it; and it wasn't obscure to her, on her side, that it was a comfort to deal with a gentleman. "It's ever so kind of you to see such opportunities for me. But what's the use of my tackling Miss Croy?"

Milly rejoiced on the spot to be so able to point out. "Because she's the handsomest and cleverest and most charming creature I ever saw, and because if I were a man I should simply adore her. In fact I do as it is." It was a luxury of response.

"Oh, my dear lady, plenty of people adore her. But that can't further the case of *all*."

"Ah," she went on, "I know about 'people.' If the case of one's bad, the case of another's good. I don't see what you have to fear from any one else," she said, "save through your being foolish, this way, about *me*."

So she said, but she was aware the next moment of what he was making of what she didn't see. "Is it your idea—since we're talking of these things in these ways—that the young lady you describe in such superlative terms is to be had for the asking?"

"Well, Lord Mark, try. She *is* a great person. But don't be humble." She was almost gay.

It was this apparently, at last, that was too much for him. "But don't you really *know?*"

As a challenge, practically, to the commonest intelligence she could pretend to, it made her of course wish to be fair. "I 'know,' yes, that a particular person's very much in love with her."

"Then you must know by the same token that she's very much in love with a particular person."

"Ah I beg your pardon!"—and Milly quite flushed at having so crude a blunder imputed to her. "You're wholly mistaken."

"It's not true?"

"It's not true."

His stare became a smile. "Are you very, very sure?"

"As sure as one can be"—and Milly's manner could match it—"when one has every assurance. I speak on the best authority."

He hesitated. "Mrs. Lowder's?"

"No. I don't call Mrs. Lowder's the best."

"Oh I thought you were just now saying," he laughed, "that everything about her's so good."

"Good for you"—she was perfectly clear. "For you," she went on, "let her authority be the best. She doesn't believe what you mention, and you must know yourself how little she makes of it. So you can take it from her. *I* take it—" But Milly, with the positive tremor of her emphasis, pulled up.

"You take it from Kate?"

"From Kate herself."

"That she's thinking of no one at all?"

"Of no one at all." Then, with her intensity, she went on. "She has given me her word for it."

"Oh!" said Lord Mark. To which he next added: "And what do you call her word?"

It made Milly, on her side, stare—though perhaps partly but with the instinct of gaining time for the consciousness that she was already a little further "in" than she had designed. "Why, Lord Mark, what should *you* call her word?"

"Ah I'm not obliged to say. I've not asked her. You apparently have."

Well, it threw her on her defence—a defence that she felt, however, especially as of Kate. "We're very intimate," she said in a moment; "so that, without prying into each other's affairs, she naturally tells me things."

Lord Mark smiled as at a lame conclusion. "You mean then she made you of her own movement the declaration you quote?"

Milly thought again, though with hindrance rather than help in her sense of the way their eyes now met—met as for their each seeing in the other more than either said. What she most felt that she herself saw was the strange disposition on her companion's part to disparage Kate's veracity. She could be only concerned to "stand up" for that.

"I mean what I say: that when she spoke of her having no private interest—"

"She took her oath to you?" Lord Mark interrupted.

Milly didn't quite see why he should so catechise her; but she met it again for Kate. "She left me in no doubt whatever of her being free."

At this Lord Mark did look at her, though he continued to smile. "And thereby in no doubt of *your* being too?" It was as if as soon as he had said it, however, he felt it as something of a mistake, and she couldn't herself have told by what queer glare at him she had instantly signified that. He at any rate gave her glare no time to act further; he fell back on the spot, and with a light enough movement, within his rights. "That's all very well, but why in the world, dear lady, should she be swearing to you?"

She had to take this "dear lady" as applying to herself; which disconcerted her when he might now so gracefully have used it for the aspersed Kate. Once more it came to her that she must claim her own part of the aspersion. "Because, as I've told you, we're such tremendous friends."

"Oh," said Lord Mark, who for the moment looked as if that might have stood rather for an absence of such rigours. He was going, however, as if he had in a manner, at the last, got more or less what he wanted. Milly felt, while he addressed his next few words to leave-taking, that she had given rather more than she intended or than she should be able, when once more getting herself into hand, theoretically to defend. Strange enough in fact that he had had from her, about herself—and, under the searching spell of the place, infinitely straight—what no one else had had: neither Kate, nor Aunt Maud, nor Merton Densher, nor Susan Shepherd. He had made her within a minute, in particular, she was aware, lose her presence of mind, and she now wished he would take himself off, so that she might either recover it or bear the loss better in solitude. If he paused, however, she almost at the same time saw, it was because of his watching the approach, from the end of the sala, of one of the gondoliers, who, whatever excursions were appointed for the party with the attendance of the others, always, as the most decorative, most sashed and starched, remained at the palace on the theory that she might whimsically want him—which she never, in her caged freedom, had yet done. Brown Pasquale, slipping in white shoes over the marble and suggesting to her perpetually charmed vision she could scarce say what, either a mild Hindoo, too noiseless almost for her nerves, or simply a barefooted seaman on the deck of a ship—Pasquale offered to sight a small salver, which he obsequiously held out to her with its burden of a visiting-card. Lord Mark—and as if also for admiration of him—delayed his departure to let her receive it; on which she read it with the instant effect of another blow to her presence of mind. This precarious quantity was indeed now so gone that even for dealing with Pasquale she had to do her best to conceal its disappearance. The effort was made, none the less, by the time she had asked if the gentleman were below and had taken in the fact that he had come up. He had followed the gondolier and was waiting at the top of the staircase.

"I'll see him with pleasure." To which she added for her companion, while Pasquale went off: "Mr. Merton Densher."

"Oh!" said Lord Mark—in a manner that, making it resound through the great cool hall, might have carried it even to Densher's ear as a judgement of his identity heard and noted once before.

Book Eighth

I

Densher became aware, afresh, that he disliked his hotel—and all the more promptly that he had had occasion of old to make the same discrimination. The establishment, choked at that season with the polyglot herd, cockneys of all climes, mainly German, mainly American, mainly English, it appeared as the corresponding sensitive nerve was touched, sounded loud and not sweet, sounded anything and everything but Italian, but Venetian. The Venetian was all a dialect, he knew; yet it was pure Attic[1] beside some of the dialects at the bustling inn. It made, "abroad," both for his pleasure and his pain that he had to feel at almost any point how he had been through everything before. He had been three or four times, in Venice, during other visits, through this pleasant irritation of paddling away—away from the concert of false notes in the vulgarised hall, away from the amiable American families and overfed German porters. He had in each case made terms for a lodging more private and not more costly, and he recalled with tenderness these shabby but friendly asylums, the windows of which he should easily know again in passing on canal or through campo. The shabbiest now failed of an appeal to him, but he found himself at the end of forty-eight hours forming views in respect to a small independent *quartiere*,[2] far down the Grand Canal, which he had once occupied for a month with a sense of pomp and circumstance and yet also with a growth of initiation into the homelier Venetian mysteries. The humour of those days came back to him for an hour, and what further befell in this interval, to be brief, was that, emerging on a traghetto[3] in sight of the recognised house, he made out on the green shutters of his old, of his young windows the strips of white pasted paper that figure in Venice as an invitation to tenants. This was in the course of his very first walk apart, a walk replete with impressions to which he responded with force. He had been almost

1. A dialect of ancient Athens defining the pure, simple, polished style of the best writers.

2. Lodgings.

3. A ferry or public launch for crossing the Grand Canal.

without cessation, since his arrival, at Palazzo Leporelli, where, as happened, a turn of bad weather on the second day had kept the whole party continuously at home. The episode had passed for him like a series of hours in a museum, though without the fatigue of that; and it had also resembled something that he was still, with a stirred imagination, to find a name for. He might have been looking for the name while he gave himself up, subsequently, to the ramble—he saw that even after years he couldn't lose his way—crowned with his stare across the water at the little white papers.

He was to dine at the palace in an hour or two, and he had lunched there, at an early luncheon, that morning. He had then been out with the three ladies, the three being Mrs. Lowder, Mrs. Stringham and Kate, and had kept afloat with them, under a sufficient Venetian spell, until Aunt Maud had directed him to leave them and return to Miss Theale. Of two circumstances connected with this disposition of his person he was even now not unmindful; the first being that the lady of Lancaster Gate had addressed him with high publicity and as if expressing equally the sense of her companions, who had not spoken, but who might have been taken—yes, Susan Shepherd quite equally with Kate—for inscrutable parties to her plan. What he could as little contrive to forget was that he had, before the two others, as it struck him—that was to say especially before Kate—done exactly as he was bidden; gathered himself up without a protest and retraced his way to the palace. Present with him still was the question of whether he looked a fool for it, of whether the awkwardness he felt as the gondola rocked with the business of his leaving it—they could but make, in submission, for a landing-place that was none of the best—had furnished his friends with such entertainment as was to cause them, behind his back, to exchange intelligent smiles. He had found Milly Theale twenty minutes later alone, and he had sat with her till the others returned to tea. The strange part of this was that it had been very easy, extraordinarily easy. He knew it for strange only when he was away from her, because when he was away from her he was in contact with particular things that made it so. At the time, in her presence, it was as simple as sitting with his sister might have been, and not, if the point were urged, very much more thrilling. He continued to see her as he had first seen her—that remained ineffaceably behind. Mrs. Lowder, Susan Shepherd, his own Kate, might, each in proportion, see her as a princess, as an angel, as a star, but for himself, luckily, she hadn't as yet complications to any point of discomfort: the princess, the angel, the star, were muffled over, ever so lightly and brightly, with the little American girl who had been kind to him in New York and to whom certainly—though without making too much of it for either of them

—he was perfectly willing to be kind in return. She appreciated his coming in on purpose, but there was nothing in that—from the moment she was always at home—that they couldn't easily keep up. The only note the least bit high that had even yet sounded between them was this admission on her part that she found it best to remain within. She wouldn't let him call it keeping quiet, for she insisted that her palace—with all its romance and art and history—had set up round her a whirlwind of suggestion that never dropped for an hour. It wasn't therefore, within such walls, confinement, it was the freedom of all the centuries: in respect to which Densher granted good-humouredly that they were then blown together, she and he, as much as she liked, through space.

Kate had found on the present occasion a moment to say to him that he suggested a clever cousin calling on a cousin afflicted, and bored for his pains; and though he denied on the spot the "bored" he could so far see it as an impression he might make that he wondered if the same image wouldn't have occurred to Milly. As soon as Kate appeared again the difference came up—the oddity, as he then instantly felt it, of his having sunk so deep. It was sinking because it was all doing what Kate had conceived for him; it wasn't in the least doing—and that had been his notion of his life—anything he himself had conceived. The difference, accordingly, renewed, sharp, sore, was the irritant under which he had quitted the palace and under which he was to make the best of the business of again dining there. He said to himself that he must make the best of everything; that was in his mind, at the traghetto, even while, with his preoccupation about changing quarters, he studied, across the canal, the look of his former abode. It had done for the past, would it do for the present? would it play in any manner into the general necessity of which he was conscious? That necessity of making the best was the instinct—as he indeed himself knew—of a man somehow aware that if he let go at one place he should let go everywhere. If he took off his hand, the hand that at least helped to hold it together, the whole queer fabric that built him in would fall away in a minute and admit the light. It was really a matter of nerves; it was exactly because he was nervous that he *could* go straight; yet if that condition should increase he must surely go wild. He was walking in short on a high ridge, steep down on either side, where the proprieties—once he could face at all remaining there—reduced themselves to his keeping his head. It was Kate who had so perched him, and there came up for him at moments, as he found himself planting one foot exactly before another, a sensible sharpness of irony as to her management of him. It wasn't that she had put him in danger—to be in real danger with her would have had another quality. There glowed for him in fact a kind of rage at what he wasn't having; an exasperation, a resentment, begotten truly by the very impatience of desire, in respect to his postponed and relegated, his so extremely manipulated state. It was beautifully done of her, but what was the real meaning of it unless that he was perpetually bent to her will? His idea from the first, from the very first of his knowing her, had been to be, as the French called it, *bon prince*[4] with her, mindful of the good humour and generosity, the contempt, in the matter of confidence, for small outlays and small savings, that belonged to the man who wasn't generally afraid. There were things enough, goodness knew—for it was the moral of his plight—that he couldn't afford; but what had had a charm for him if not the notion of living handsomely, to make up for it, in another way? of not at all events reading the romance of his existence in a cheap edition. All he had originally felt in her came back to him, was indeed actually as present as ever—how he had admired and envied what he called to himself her pure talent for life, as distinguished from his own, a poor weak thing of the occasion, amateurishly patched up; only it irritated him the more that this was exactly what was now, ever so characteristically, standing out in her.

It was thanks to her pure talent for life, verily, that he was just where he was and that he was above all just *how* he was. The proof of a decent reaction in him against so much passivity was, with no great richness, that he at least knew—knew, that is, how he was, and how little he liked it as a thing accepted in mere helplessness. He was, for the moment, wistful—that above all described it; that was so large a part of the force that, as the autumn afternoon closed in, kept him, on his traghetto, positively throbbing with his question. His question connected itself, even while he stood, with his special smothered soreness, his sense almost of shame; and the soreness and the shame were less as he let himself, with the help of the conditions about him, regard it as serious. It was born, for that matter, partly of the conditions, those conditions that Kate had so almost insolently braved, had been willing, without a pang, to see him ridiculously—ridiculously so far as just complacently—exposed to. How little it *could* be complacently he was to feel with the last thoroughness before he had moved from his point of vantage. His question, as we have called it, was the interesting question of whether he had really no will left. How could he know—that was the point—without putting the matter to the test? It had been right to be *bon prince*, and the joy, something of the pride, of having lived, in spirit, handsomely, was even now compatible with the impulse to look into their account; but he held his breath a little as it came home to him with supreme sharpness that, whereas he

4. Open-handed, decent fellow.

had done absolutely everything that Kate had wanted, she had done nothing whatever that he had. So it was in fine that his idea of the test by which he must try that possibility kept referring itself, in the warm early dusk, the approach of the Southern night—"conditions" these, such as we just spoke of—to the glimmer, more and more ghostly as the light failed, of the little white papers on his old green shutters. By the time he looked at his watch he had been for a quarter of an hour at this post of observation and reflexion; but by the time he walked away again he had found his answer to the idea that had grown so importunate. Since a proof of his will was wanted it was indeed very exactly in wait for him—it lurked there on the other side of the Canal. A ferryman at the little pier had from time to time accosted him; but it was a part of the play of his nervousness to turn his back on that facility. He would go over, but he walked, very quickly, round and round, crossing finally by the Rialto. The rooms, in the event, were unoccupied; the ancient padrona[5] was there with her smile all a radiance but her recognition all a fable; the ancient rickety objects too, refined in their shabbiness, amiable in their decay, as to which, on his side, demonstrations were tenderly veracious; so that before he took his way again he had arranged to come in on the morrow.

He was amusing about it that evening at dinner—in spite of an odd first impulse, which at the palace quite melted away, to treat it merely as matter for his own satisfaction. This need, this propriety, he had taken for granted even up to the moment of suddenly perceiving, in the course of talk, that the incident would minister to innocent gaiety. Such was quite its effect, with the aid of his picture —an evocation of the quaint, of the humblest rococo, of a Venetian interior in the true old note. He made the point for his hostess that her own high chambers, though they were a thousand grand things, weren't really this; made it in fact with such success that she presently declared it his plain duty to invite her on some near day to tea. She had expressed as yet—he could feel it as felt among them all—no such clear wish to go anywhere, not even to make an effort for a parish feast, or an autumn sunset, nor to descend her staircase for Titian or Gianbellini.[6] It was constantly Densher's view that, as between himself and Kate, things were understood without saying, so that he could catch in her, as she but too freely could in him, innumerable signs of it, the whole soft breath of consciousness meeting and promoting consciousness. This view was so far justified to-night as that Milly's offer to him of her company was to his sense taken up by Kate in spite of her doing nothing to show it. It fell in

5. Proprietress.

6. Giovanni Bellini (c. 1430–1516), Venice's foremost painter until his death, and one of Titian's teachers; many of his paintings treat the Christian mysteries and subjects from the New Testament.

so perfectly with what she had desired and foretold that she was—and this was what most struck him—sufficiently gratified and blinded by it not to know, from the false quality of his response, from his tone and his very look, which for an instant instinctively sought her own, that he had answered inevitably, almost shamelessly, in a mere time-gaining sense. It gave him on the spot, her failure of perception, almost a beginning of the advantage he had been planning for—that is at least if she too were not darkly dishonest. She might, he was not unaware, have made out, from some deep part of her, the bearing, in respect to herself, of the little fact he had announced; for she was after all capable of that, capable of guessing and yet of simultaneously hiding her guess. It wound him up a turn or two further, none the less, to impute to her now a weakness of vision by which he could himself feel the stronger. Whatever apprehension of his motive in shifting his abode might have brushed her with its wings, she at all events certainly didn't guess that he was giving their friend a hollow promise. That was what she had herself imposed on him; there had been in the prospect from the first a definite particular point at which hollowness, to call it by its least compromising name, would have to begin. Therefore its hour had now charmingly sounded.

Whatever in life he had recovered his old rooms for, he had not recovered them to receive Milly Theale: which made no more difference in his expression of happy readiness than if he had been—just what he was trying not to be—fully hardened and fully base. So rapid in fact was the rhythm of his inward drama that the quick vision of impossibility produced in him by his hostess's direct and unexpected appeal had the effect, slightly sinister, of positively scaring him. It gave him a measure of the intensity, the reality of his now mature motive. It prompted in him certainly no quarrel with these things, but it made them as vivid as if they already flushed with success. It was before the flush of success that his heart beat almost to dread. The dread was but the dread of the happiness to be compassed; only that was in itself a symptom. That a visit from Milly should, in this projection of necessities, strike him as of the last incongruity, quite as a hateful idea, and above all as spoiling, should one put it grossly, his game—the adoption of such a view might of course have an identity with one of those numerous ways of being a fool that seemed so to abound for him. It would remain none the less the way to which he should be in advance most reconciled. His mature motive, as to which he allowed himself no grain of illusion, had thus in an hour taken imaginative possession of the place: that precisely was how he saw it seated there, already unpacked and settled, for Milly's innocence, for Milly's beauty, no matter how short a time, to be housed with. There were things she would never recognise, never feel, never catch in the air; but this made no difference in the fact that her brushing against them would do nobody any good. The discrimination and the scruple were for *him*. So he felt all the parts of the case together, while Kate showed admirably as feeling none of them. Of course, however —when hadn't it to be his last word?—Kate was always sublime.

That came up in all connexions during the rest of these first days; came up in especial under pressure of the fact that each time our plighted pair snatched, in its passage, at the good fortune of half an hour together, they were doomed—though Densher felt it as all by *his* act—to spend a part of the rare occasion in wonder at their luck and in study of its queer character. This was the case after he might be supposed to have got, in a manner, used to it; it was the case after the girl—ready always, as we say, with the last word—had given him the benefit of her righting of every wrong appearance, a support familiar to him now in reference to other phases. It was still the case after he possibly might, with a little imagination, as she freely insisted, have made out, by the visible working of the crisis, what idea on Mrs. Lowder's part had determined it. Such as the idea was—and that it suited Kate's own book she openly professed —he had only to see how things were turning out to feel it strikingly justified. Densher's reply to all this vividness was that of course Aunt Maud's intervention hadn't been occult, even for *his* vividness, from the moment she had written him, with characteristic concentration, that if he should see his way to come to Venice for a fortnight she should engage he would find it no blunder. It took Aunt Maud really to do such things in such ways; just as it took him, he was ready to confess, to do such others as he must now strike them all—didn't he?—as committed to Mrs. Lowder's admonition had been of course a direct reference to what she had said to him at Lancaster Gate before his departure the night Milly had failed them through illness; only it had at least matched that remarkable outbreak in respect to the quantity of good nature it attributed to him. The young man's discussions of his situation—which were confined to Kate; he had none with Aunt Maud herself —suffered a little, it may be divined, by the sense that he couldn't put everything off, as he privately expressed it, on other people. His ears, in solitude, were apt to burn with the reflexion that Mrs. Lowder had simply tested him, seen him as he was and made out what could be done with him. She had had but to whistle for him and he had come. If she had taken for granted his good nature she was as justified as Kate declared. This awkwardness of his conscience, both in respect to his general plasticity, the fruit of his feeling plasticity, within limits, to be a mode of life like another—certainly better than some, and particularly in respect to such confusion as might reign about what he had really come for—this inward ache was not wholly dispelled by the style, charming as that was, of Kate's poetic versions. Even the high wonder and delight of Kate couldn't set him right with himself when there was something quite distinct from these things that kept him wrong.

In default of being right with himself he had meanwhile, for one thing, the interest of seeing—and quite for the first time in his life—whether, on a given occasion, that might be quite so necessary to happiness as was commonly assumed and as he had up to this moment never doubted. He was engaged distinctly in an adventure—he who had never thought himself cut out for them, and it fairly helped him that he was able at moments to say to himself that he mustn't fall below it. At his hotel, alone, by night, or in the course of the few late strolls he was finding time to take through dusky labyrinthine alleys and empty *campi,*[7] overhung with mouldering palaces, where he paused in disgust at his want of ease and where the sound of a rare footstep on the enclosed pavement was like that of a retarded dancer in a banquet-hall deserted—during these interludes he entertained cold views, even to the point, at moments, on the principle that the shortest follies are the best, of thinking of immediate departure as not only possible but as indicated. He had however only to cross again the threshold of Palazzo Leporelli to see all the elements of the business compose, as painters called it, differently. It began to strike him then that departure wouldn't curtail, but would signally coarsen his folly, and that above all, as he hadn't really "begun" anything, had only submitted, consented, but too generously indulged and condoned the beginnings of others, he had no call to treat himself with superstitious rigour. The single thing that was clear in complications was that, whatever happened, one was to behave as a gentleman—to which was added indeed the perhaps slightly less shining truth that complications might sometimes have their tedium beguiled by a study of the question of how a gentleman would behave. This question, I hasten to add, was not in the last resort Densher's greatest worry. Three women were looking to him at once, and, though such a predicament could never be, from the point of view of facility, quite the ideal, it yet had, thank goodness, its immediate workable law. The law was not to be a brute—in return for amiabilities. He hadn't come all the way out from England to be a brute. He hadn't thought of what it might give him to have a fortnight, however handicapped, with Kate in Venice, to be a brute. He hadn't treated Mrs. Lowder as if in responding to her suggestion he had understood her—he hadn't done that either to be a brute. And what he had prepared least of all for such an anti-climax was the prompt and inevitable, the

7. Squares or open spaces.

achieved surrender—*as* a gentleman, oh that indubitably!—to the unexpected impression made by poor pale exquisite Milly as the mistress of a grand old palace and the dispenser of an hospitality more irresistible, thanks to all the conditions, than any ever known to him.

This spectacle had for him an eloquence, an authority, a felicity—he scarce knew by what strange name to call it—for which he said to himself that he had not consciously bargained. Her welcome, her frankness, sweetness, sadness, brightness, her disconcerting poetry, as he made shift at moments to call it, helped as it was by the beauty of her whole setting and by the perception at the same time, on the observer's part, that this element gained from her, in a manner, for effect and harmony, as much as it gave—her whole attitude had, to his imagination, meanings that hung about it, waiting upon her, hovering, dropping and quavering forth again, like vague faint snatches, mere ghosts of sound, of old-fashioned melancholy music. It was positively well for him, he had his times of reflecting, that he couldn't put it off on Kate and Mrs. Lowder, as a gentleman so conspicuously wouldn't, that—well, that he had been rather taken in by not having known in advance! There had been now five days of it all without his risking even to Kate alone any hint of what he ought to have known and of what in particular therefore had taken him in. The truth was doubtless that really, when it came to any free handling and naming of things, they were living together, the five of them, in an air in which an ugly effect of "blurting out" might easily be produced. He came back with his friend on each occasion to the blest miracle of renewed propinquity, which had a double virtue in that favouring air. He breathed on it as if he could scarcely believe it, yet the time had passed, in spite of this privilege, without his quite committing himself, for her ear, to any such comment on Milly's high style and state as would have corresponded with the amount of recognition it had produced in him. Behind everything for him was his renewed remembrance, which had fairly become a habit, that he had been the first to know her. This was what they had all insisted on, in her absence, that day at Mrs. Lowder's; and this was in especial what had made him feel its influence on his immediately paying her a second visit. Its influence had been all there, been in the high-hung, rumbling carriage with them, from the moment she took him to drive, covering them in together as if it had been a rug of softest silk. It had worked as a clear connexion with something lodged in the past, something already their own. He had more than once recalled how he had said to himself even at that moment, at some point in the drive, that he was not *there*, not just as he was in so doing it, through Kate and Kate's idea, but through Milly and Milly's own, and through himself and *his* own, unmistakeably—as well as through the little facts, whatever they had amounted to, of his time in New York.

II

There was at last, with everything that made for it, an occasion when he got from Kate, on what she now spoke of as his eternal refrain, an answer of which he was to measure afterwards the precipitating effect. His eternal refrain was the way he came back to the riddle of Mrs. Lowder's view of her profit—a view so hard to reconcile with the chances she gave them to meet. Impatiently, at this, the girl denied the chances, wanting to know from him, with a fine irony that smote him rather straight, whether he felt their opportunities as anything so grand. He looked at her deep in the eyes when she had sounded this note; it was the least he could let her off with for having made him visibly flush. For some reason then, with it, the sharpness dropped out of her tone, which became sweet and sincere. " 'Meet,' my dear man," she expressively echoed; "does it strike you that we get, after all, so very much out of our meetings?"

"On the contrary—they're starvation diet. All I mean is—and it's all I've meant from the day I came—that we at least get more than Aunt Maud."

"Ah but you see," Kate replied, "you don't understand what Aunt Maud gets."

"Exactly so—and it's what I don't understand that keeps me so fascinated with the question. *She* gives me no light; she's prodigious. She takes everything as of a natural—!"

"She takes it as 'of a natural' that at this rate I shall be making my reflexions about you. There's every appearance for her," Kate went on, "that what she had made her mind up to as possible *is* possible; that what she had thought more likely than not to happen *is* happening. The very essence of her, as you surely by this time have made out for yourself, is that when she adopts a view she—well, to her own sense, really brings the thing about, fairly terrorises with her view any other, any opposite view, and those, not less, who represent that. I've often thought success comes to her"—Kate continued to study the phenomenon—"by the spirit in her that dares and defies her idea not to prove the right one. One has seen it so again and again, in the face of everything, *become* the right one."

Densher had for this, as he listened, a smile of the largest response. "Ah my dear child, if you can explain I of course needn't not 'understand.' I'm condemned to that," he on his side presently explained, "only when understanding fails." He took a moment; then he pursued: "Does she think she terrorises *us*?" To which he added while, without immediate speech, Kate but looked over the place: "Does she believe anything so stiff as that you've really changed about me?" He knew now that he was probing the girl deep—something told him so; but that was a reason the more. "Has she got it into her head that you dislike me?"

To this, of a sudden, Kate's answer was strong. "You could yourself easily put it there!"

He wondered. "By telling her so?"

"No," said Kate as with amusement at his simplicity; "I don't ask that of you."

"Oh my dear," Densher laughed, "when you ask, you know, so little—!"

There was a full irony in this, on his own part, that he saw her resist the impulse to take up. "I'm perfectly justified in what I've asked," she quietly returned. "It's doing beautifully for you." Their eyes again intimately met, and the effect was to make her proceed. "You're not a bit unhappy."

"Oh ain't I?" he brought out very roundly.

"It doesn't practically show—which is enough for Aunt Maud. You're wonderful, you're beautiful," Kate said; "and if you really want to know whether I believe you're doing it you may take from me perfectly that I see it coming." With which, by a quick transition, as if she had settled the case, she asked him the hour.

"Oh only twelve-ten"—he had looked at his watch. "We've taken but thirteen minutes; we've time yet."

"Then we must walk. We must go toward them."

Densher, from where they had been standing, measured the long reach of the Square.[1] "They're still in their shop. They're safe for half an hour."

"That shows then, that shows!" said Kate.

This colloquy had taken place in the middle of Piazza San Marco, always, as a great social saloon, a smooth-floored, blue-roofed chamber of amenity, favourable to talk; or rather, to be exact, not in the middle, but at the point where our pair had paused by a common impulse after leaving the great mosque-like church. It rose now, domed and pinnacled, but a little way behind them, and they had in front the vast empty space, enclosed by its arcades, to which at that hour movement and traffic were mostly confined. Venice was at breakfast, the Venice of the visitor and the possible acquaintance, and, except for the parties of importunate pigeons picking up the crumbs of perpetual feasts, their prospect was clear and they could see their companions hadn't yet been, and

1. Piazza San Marco—Saint Mark's Square—the center of Venetian commerce, art, and culture.

weren't for a while longer likely to be, disgorged by the lace-shop, in one of the *loggie*,[2] where, shortly before, they had left them for a look-in—the expression was artfully Densher's—at Saint Mark's.[3] Their morning had happened to take such a turn as brought this chance to the surface; yet his allusion, just made to Kate, hadn't been an overstatement of their general opportunity. The worst that could be said of their general opportunity was that it was essentially in presence—in presence of every one; every one consisting at this juncture, in a peopled world, of Susan Shepherd, Aunt Maud and Milly. But the proof how, even in presence, the opportunity could become special was furnished precisely by this view of the compatibility of their comfort with a certain amount of lingering. The others had assented to their not waiting in the shop; it was of course the least the others could do. What had really helped them this morning was the fact that, on his turning up, as he always called it, at the palace, Milly had not, as before, been able to present herself. Custom and use had hitherto seemed fairly established; on his coming round, day after day—eight days had been now so conveniently marked—their friends, Milly's and his, conveniently dispersed and left him to sit with her till luncheon. Such was the perfect operation of the scheme on which he had been, as he phrased it to himself, had out; so that certainly there was that amount of justification for Kate's vision of success. He *had*, for Mrs. Lowder—he couldn't help it while sitting there—the air, which was the thing to be desired, of no absorption in Kate sufficiently deep to be alarming. He had failed their young hostess each morning as little as she had failed him; it was only to-day that she hadn't been well enough to see him.

That had made a mark, all round; the mark was in the way in which, gathered in the room of state, with the place, from the right time, all bright and cool and beflowered, as always, to receive her descent, they—the rest of them—simply looked at each other. It was lurid—lurid, in all probability, for each of them privately—that they had uttered no common regrets. It was strange for our young man above all that, if the poor girl was indisposed to *that* degree, the hush of gravity, of apprehension, of significance of some sort, should be the most the case—that of the guests—could permit itself. The hush, for that matter, continued after the party of four had gone down to the gondola and taken their places in it. Milly had sent them word that she hoped they would go out and enjoy themselves, and this indeed had produced a second remarkable look, a look as of their knowing, one quite as well as the other, what such

2. Galleries or arcades open to the air on at least one side.

3. The Church of Saint Mark, the patron saint of Venice since the year 828.

a message meant as provision for the alternative beguilement of Densher. She wished not to have spoiled his morning, and he had therefore, in civility, to take it as pleasantly patched up. Mrs. Stringham had helped the affair out, Mrs. Stringham who, when it came to that, knew their friend better than any of them. She knew her so well that she knew herself as acting in exquisite compliance with conditions comparatively obscure, approximately awful to them, by not thinking it necessary to stay at home. She had corrected that element of the perfunctory which was the slight fault, for all of them, of the occasion; she had invented a preference for Mrs. Lowder and herself; she had remembered the fond dreams of the visitation of lace that had hitherto always been brushed away by accidents, and it had come up as well for her that Kate had, the day before, spoken of the part played by fatality in her own failure of real acquaintance with the inside of Saint Mark's. Densher's sense of Susan Shepherd's conscious intervention had by this time a corner of his mind all to itself; something that had begun for them at Lancaster Gate was now a sentiment clothed in a shape; her action, ineffably discreet, had at all events a way of affecting him as for the most part subtly, even when not superficially, in his own interest. They were not, as a pair, as a "team," really united; there were too many persons, at least three, and too many things, between them; but meanwhile something was preparing that would draw them closer. He scarce knew what: probably nothing but his finding, at some hour when it would be a service to do so, that she had all the while understood him. He even had a presentiment of a juncture at which the understanding of every one else would fail and this deep little person's alone survive.

Such was to-day, in its freshnesss, the moral air, as we may say, that hung about our young friends; these had been the small accidents and quiet forces to which they owed the advantage we have seen them in some sort enjoying. It seemed in fact fairly to deepen for them as they stayed their course again; the splendid Square, which had so notoriously, in all the years, witnessed more of the joy of life than any equal area in Europe, furnished them, in their remoteness from earshot, with solitude and security. It was as if, being in possession, they could say what they liked; and it was also as if, in consequence of that, each had an apprehension of what the other wanted to say. It was most of all for them, moreover, as if this very quantity, seated on their lips in the bright historic air, where the only sign for their ears was the flutter of the doves, begot in the heart of each a fear. There might have been a betrayal of that in the way Densher broke the silence resting on her last words. "What did you mean just now that I can do to make Mrs. Lowder believe?

For myself, stupidly, if you will, I don't see, from the moment I can't lie to her, what else there *is* but lying."

Well, she could tell him. "You can say something both handsome and sincere to her about Milly—whom you honestly like so much. That wouldn't be lying; and, coming from you, it would have an effect. You don't, you know, say much about her." And Kate put before him the fruit of observation. "You don't, you know, speak of her at all."

"And has Aunt Maud," Densher asked, "told you so?" Then as the girl, for answer, only seemed to bethink herself, "You must have extraordinary conversations!" he exclaimed.

Yes, she had bethought herself. "We have extraordinary conversations."

His look, while their eyes met, marked him as disposed to hear more about them; but there was something in her own, apparently, that defeated the opportunity. He questioned her in a moment on a different matter, which had been in his mind a week, yet in respect to which he had had no chance so good as this. "Do you happen to know then, as such wonderful things pass between you, what she makes of the incident, the other day, of Lord Mark's so very superficial visit?—his having spent here, as I gather, but the two or three hours necessary for seeing our friend and yet taken no time at all, since he went off by the same night's train, for seeing any one else. What can she make of his not having waited to see *you*, or to see herself—with all he owes her?"

"Oh of course," said Kate, "she understands. He came to make Milly his offer of marriage—he came for nothing but that. As Milly wholly declined it his business was for the time at an end. He couldn't quite on the spot turn round to make up to *us*."

Kate had looked surprised that, as a matter of taste on such an adventurer's part, Densher shouldn't see it. But Densher was lost in another thought. "Do you mean that when, turning up myself, I found him leaving her, that was what had been taking place between them?"

"Didn't you make it out, my dear?" Kate enquired.

"What sort of a blundering weathercock then *is* he?" the young man went on in his wonder.

"Oh don't make too little of him!" Kate smiled. "Do you pretend that Milly didn't tell you?"

"How great an ass he had made of himself?"

Kate continued to smile. "You *are* in love with her, you know."

He gave her another long look. "Why, since she has refused him, should my opinion of Lord Mark show it? I'm not obliged, however, to think well of him for such treatment of the other persons

I've mentioned, and I feel I don't understand from you why Mrs. Lowder should."

"She doesn't—but she doesn't care," Kate explained. "You know perfectly the terms on which lots of London people live together even when they're supposed to live very well. He's not committed to us—he was having his try. Mayn't an unsatisfied man," she asked, "always have his try?"

"And come back afterwards, with confidence in a welcome, to the victim of his inconstancy?"

Kate consented, as for argument, to be thought of as a victim. "Oh but he has *had* his try at *me*. So it's all right."

"Through your also having, you mean, refused him?"

She balanced an instant during which Densher might have just wondered if pure historic truth were to suffer a slight strain. But she dropped on the right side. "I haven't let it come to that. I've been too discouraging. Aunt Maud," she went on—now as lucid as ever—"considers, no doubt, that she has a pledge from him in respect to me; a pledge that would have been broken if Milly had accepted him. As the case stands that makes no difference."

Densher laughed out. "It isn't *his* merit that he has failed."

"It's still his merit, my dear, that he's Lord Mark. He's just what he was, and what he knew he was. It's not for me either to reflect on him after I've so treated him."

"Oh," said Densher impatiently, "you've treated him beautifully."

"I'm glad," she smiled, "that you can still be jealous." But before he could take it up she had more to say. "I don't see why it need puzzle you that Milly's so marked line gratifies Aunt Maud more than anything else can displease her. What does she see but that Milly herself recognises her situation with you as too precious to be spoiled? Such a recognition as that can't but seem to her to involve in some degree your own recognition. Out of which she therefore gets it that the more you have for Milly the less you have for me."

There were moments again—we know that from the first they had been numerous—when he felt with a strange mixed passion the mastery of her mere way of putting things. There was something in it that bent him at once to conviction and to reaction. And this effect, however it be named, now broke into his tone. "Oh if she began to know what I have for you—!"

It wasn't ambiguous, but Kate stood up to it. "Luckily for us we may really consider she doesn't. So successful have we been."

"Well," he presently said, "I take from you what you give me, and I suppose that, to be consistent—to stand on my feet where I do stand at all—I ought to thank you. Only, you know, what you give me seems to me, more than anything else, the larger and larger size of my job. It seems to me more than anything else what you expect of me. It never seems to me somehow what I may expect of *you*. There's so much you *don't* give me."

She appeared to wonder. "And pray what is it I don't—?"

"I give you proof," said Densher. "You give me none."

"What then do you call proof?" she after a moment ventured to ask.

"Your doing something for me."

She considered with surprise. "Am I not doing *this* for you? Do you call this nothing?"

"Nothing at all."

"Ah I risk, my dear, everything for it."

They had strolled slowly further, but he was brought up short. "I thought you exactly contend that, with your aunt so bamboozled, you risk nothing!"

It was the first time since the launching of her wonderful idea that he had seen her at a loss. He judged the next instant moreover that she didn't like it—either the being so or the being seen, for she soon spoke with an impatience that showed her as wounded; an appearance that produced in himself, he no less quickly felt, a sharp pang of indulgence. "What then do you wish me to risk?"

The appeal from danger touched him, but all to make him, as he would have said, worse. "What I wish is to be loved. How can I feel at this rate that I *am?*" Oh she understood him, for all she might so bravely disguise it, and that made him feel straighter than if she hadn't. Deep, always, was his sense of life with her—deep as it had been from the moment of those signs of life that in the dusky London of two winters ago they had originally exchanged. He had never taken her for unguarded, ignorant, weak; and if he put to her a claim for some intenser faith between them this was because he believed it could reach her and she could meet it. "I can go on perhaps," he said, "with help. But I can't go on without."

She looked away from him now, and it showed him how she understood. "We ought to be there—I mean when they come out."

"They *won't* come out—not yet. And I don't care if they do." To which he straightway added, as if to deal with the charge of selfishness that his words, sounding for himself, struck him as enabling her to make: "Why not have done with it all and face the music as we are?" It broke from him in perfect sincerity. "Good God, if you'd only *take* me!"

It brought her eyes round to him again, and he could see how, after all, somewhere deep within, she felt his rebellion more sweet than bitter. Its effect on her spirit and her sense was visibly to hold her an instant. "We've gone too far," she none the less pulled herself together to reply. "Do you want to kill her?"

He had an hesitation that wasn't all candid. "Kill, you mean, Aunt Maud?"

"You know whom I mean. We've told too many lies."

Oh at this his head went up. "I, my dear, have told none!"

He had brought it out with a sharpness that did him good, but he had naturally, none the less, to take the look it made her give him. "Thank you very much."

Her expression, however, failed to check the words that had already risen to his lips. "Rather than lay myself open to the least appearance of it I'll go this very night."

"Then go," said Kate Croy.

He knew after a little, while they walked on again together, that what was in the air for him, and disconcertingly, was not the violence, but much rather the cold quietness, of the way this had come from her. They walked on together, and it was for a minute as if their difference had become of a sudden, in all truth, a split—as if the basis of his departure had been settled. Then, incoherently and still more suddenly, recklessly moreover, since they now might easily, from under the arcades, be observed, he passed his hand into her arm with a force that produced for them another pause. "I'll tell any lie you want, any your idea requires, if you'll only come to me."

"Come to you?"

"Come to me."

"How? Where?"

She spoke low, but there was somehow, for his uncertainty, a wonder in her being so equal to him. "To my rooms, which are perfectly possible, and in taking which, the other day, I had you, as you must have felt, in view. We can arrange it—with two grains of courage. People in our case always arrange it." She listened as for the good information, and there was support for him—since it was a question of his going step by step—in the way she took no refuge in showing herself shocked. He had in truth not expected of her that particular vulgarity, but the absence of it only added the thrill of a deeper reason to his sense of possibilities. For the knowledge of what she was he had absolutely to *see* her now, incapable of refuge, stand there for him in all the light of the day and of his admirable merciless meaning. Her mere listening in fact made him even understand himself as he hadn't yet done. Idea for idea, his own was thus already, and in the germ, beautiful. "There's nothing for me possible but to feel that I'm not a fool. It's all I have to say, but you must know what it means. *With* you I can do it—I'll go as far as you demand or as you will yourself. Without you—I'll be hanged! And I must be sure."

She listened so well that she was really listening after he had ceased to speak. He had kept his grasp of her, drawing her close, and though they had again, for the time, stopped walking, his talk —for others at a distance—might have been, in the matchless place, that of any impressed tourist to any slightly more detached companion. On possessing himself of her arm he had made her turn, so that they faced afresh to Saint Mark's, over the great presence of which his eyes moved while she twiddled her parasol. She now, however, made a motion that confronted them finally with the opposite end. Then only she spoke—"Please take your hand out of my arm." He understood at once: she had made out in the shade of the gallery the issue of the others from their place of purchase. So they went to them side by side, and it was all right. The others had seen them as well and waited for them, complacent enough, under one of the arches. They themselves too—he argued that Kate would argue—looked perfectly ready, decently patient, properly accommodating. They themselves suggested nothing worse—always by Kate's system—than a pair of the children of a supercivilised age making the best of an awkwardness. They didn't nevertheless hurry —that would overdo it; so he had time to feel, as it were, what he felt. He felt, ever so distinctly—it was with this he faced Mrs. Lowder—that he was already in a sense possessed of what he wanted. There was more to come—everything; he had by no means, with his companion, had it all out. Yet what he was possessed of was real—the fact that she hadn't thrown over his lucidity the horrid shadow of cheap reprobation. Of this he had had so sore a fear that its being dispelled was in itself of the nature of bliss. The danger had dropped—it was behind him there in the great sunny space. So far she was good for what he wanted.

III

She was good enough, as it proved, for him to put to her that evening, and with further ground for it, the next sharpest question that had been on his lips in the morning—which his other preoccupation had then, to his consciousness, crowded out. His opportunity was again made, as befell, by his learning from Mrs. Stringham, on arriving, as usual, with the close of day, at the palace, that Milly must fail them again at dinner, but would to all appearance be able to come down later. He had found Susan Shepherd alone in the great saloon, where even more candles than their friend's large common allowance—she grew daily more splendid; they were all struck with it and chaffed her about it—lighted up the pervasive mystery of Style. He had thus five minutes with the good lady before Mrs. Lowder and Kate appeared—minutes illumined indeed to a longer reach than by the number of Milly's candles.

"*May* she come down—ought she if she isn't really up to it?"

He had asked that in the wonderment always stirred in him by glimpses—rare as were these—of the inner truth about the girl. There was of course a question of health—it was in the air, it was in the ground he trod, in the food he tasted, in the sounds he heard, it was everywhere. But it was everywhere with the effect of a request to him—to his very delicacy, to the common discretion of others as well as his own—that no allusion to it should be made. There had practically been none, that morning, on her explained non-appearance—the absence of it, as we know, quite monstrous and awkward; and this passage with Mrs. Stringham offered him his first licence to open his eyes. He had gladly enough held them closed; all the more that his doing so performed for his own spirit a useful function. If he positively wanted not to be brought up with his nose against Milly's facts, what better proof could he have that his conduct was marked by straightness? It was perhaps pathetic for her, and for himself was perhaps even ridiculous; but he hadn't even the amount of curiosity that he would have had about an ordinary friend. He might have shaken himself at moments to try, for a sort of dry decency, to have it; but that too, it appeared, wouldn't come. In what therefore was the duplicity? He was at least sure about his feelings—it being so established that he had none at all. They were all for Kate, without a feather's weight to spare. He was acting for Kate—not, by the deviation of an inch, for her friend. He was accordingly not interested, for had he been interested he would have cared, and had he cared he would have wanted to know. Had he wanted to know he wouldn't have been purely passive, and it was his pure passivity that had to represent his dignity and his honour. His dignity and his honour, at the same time, let us add, fortunately fell short to-night of spoiling his little talk with Susan Shepherd. One glimpse—it was as if she had wished to give him that; and it was as if, for himself, on current terms, he could oblige her by accepting it. She not only permitted, she fairly invited him to open his eyes. "I'm so glad you're here." It was no answer to his question, but it had for the moment to serve. And the rest was fully to come.

He smiled at her and presently found himself, as a kind of consequence of communion with her, talking her own language. "It's a very wonderful experience."

"Well"—and her raised face shone up at him—"that's all I want you to feel about it. If I weren't afraid," she added, "there are things I should like to say to you."

"And what are you afraid of, please?" he encouragingly asked.

"Of other things that I may possibly spoil. Besides, I don't, you know, seem to have the chance. You're always, you know, *with* her."

He was strangely supported, it struck him, in his fixed smile;

which was the more fixed as he felt in these last words an exact description of his course. It was an odd thing to have come to, but he *was* always with her. "Ah," he none the less smiled, "I'm not with her now."

"No—and I'm so glad, since I get this from it. She's ever so much better."

"Better? Then she *has* been worse?"

Mrs. Stringham waited. "She has been marvelous—that's what she has been. She *is* marvellous. But she's really better."

"Oh then if she's really better—!" But he checked himself, wanting only to be easy about it and above all not to appear engaged to the point of mystification. "We shall miss her the more at dinner."

Susan Shephard, however, was all there for him. "She's keeping herself. You'll see. You'll not really need to miss anything. There's to be a little party."

"Ah I do see—by this aggravated grandeur."

"Well, it *is* lovely, isn't it? I want the whole thing. She's lodged for the first time as she ought, from her type, to be; and doing it—I mean bringing out all the glory of the place—makes her really happy. It's a Veronese picture, as near as can be—with me as the inevitable dwarf, the small blackamoor, put into a corner of the foreground for effect. If I only had a hawk or a hound or something of that sort I should do the scene more honour. The old housekeeper, the woman in charge here, has a big red cockatoo that I might borrow and perch on my thumb for the evening." These explanations and sundry others Mrs. Stringham gave, though not all with the result of making him feel that the picture closed him in. What part was there for *him*, with his attitude that lacked the highest style, in a composition in which everything else would have it? "They won't, however, be at dinner, the few people she expects—they come round afterwards from their respective hotels; and Sir Luke Strett and his niece, the principal ones, will have arrived from London but an hour or two ago. It's for *him* she has wanted to do something—to let it begin at once. We shall see more of him, because she likes him; and I'm so glad—she'll be glad too—that *you're* to see him." The good lady, in connexion with it, was urgent, was almost unnaturally bright. "So I greatly hope—!" But her hope fairly lost itself in the wide light of her cheer.

He considered a little this appearance, while she let him, he thought, into still more knowledge than she uttered. "What is it you hope?"

"Well, that you'll stay on."

"Do you mean after dinner?" She meant, he seemed to feel, so much that he could scarce tell where it ended or began.

"Oh that, of course. Why we're to have music—beautiful instruments and songs; and not Tasso[1] declaimed as in the guide-books either. She has arranged it—or at least I have. That is Eugenio has. Besides, you're in the picture."

"Oh—I!" said Densher almost with the gravity of a real protest.

"You'll be the grand young man who surpasses the others and holds up his head and the wine-cup. What we hope," Mrs. Stringham pursued, "is that you'll be faithful to us—that you've not come for a mere foolish few days."

Densher's more private and particular shabby realities turned, without comfort, he was conscious, at this touch, in the artificial repose he had in his anxiety about them but half-managed to induce. The way smooth ladies, travelling for their pleasure and housed in Veronese pictures, talked to plain embarrassed working-men, engaged in an unprecedented sacrifice of time and of the opportunity for modest acquisition! The things they took for granted and the general misery of explaining! He couldn't tell them how he had tried to work, how it was partly what he had moved into rooms for, only to find himself, almost for the first time in his life, stricken and sterile; because that would give them a false view of the source of his restlessness, if not of the degree of it. It would operate, indirectly perhaps, but infallibly, to add to that weight as of expected performance which these very moments with Mrs. Stringham caused more and more to settle on his heart. He had incurred it, the expectation of performance; the thing was done, and there was no use talking; again, again the cold breath of it was in the air. So there he was. And at best he floundered. "I'm afraid you won't understand when I say I've very tiresome things to consider. Botherations, necessities at home. The pinch, the pressure in London."

But she understood in perfection; she rose to the pinch and the pressure and showed how they had been her own very element. "Oh the daily task and the daily wage, the golden guerdon or reward? No one knows better than I how they haunt one in the flight of the precious deceiving days. Aren't they just what I myself have given up? I've given up all to follow *her*. I wish you could feel as I do. And can't you," she asked, "write about Venice?"

He very nearly wished, for the minute, that he could feel as she did; and he smiled for her kindly. "Do *you* write about Venice?"

"No; but I would—oh wouldn't I?—if I hadn't so completely given up. She's, you know, my princess, and to one's princess—"

"One makes the whole sacrifice?"

"Precisely. There you are!"

1. Tasso (1544–95) is the author of *Jerusalem Delivered;* he was also for years the subject of a legend of unrequited passion for Leonora d'Este, whose father first imprisoned and then exiled him from Ferrara.

It pressed on him with this that never had a man been in so many places at once. "I quite understand that she's yours. Only you see she's not mine." He felt he could somehow, for honesty, risk that, as he had the moral certainty she wouldn't repeat it and least of all to Mrs. Lowder, who would find in it a disturbing implication. This was part of what he liked in the good lady, that she didn't repeat, and also that she gave him a delicate sense of her shyly wishing him to know it. That was in itself a hint of possibilities between them, of a relation, beneficent and elastic for him, which wouldn't engage him further than he could see. Yet even as he afresh made this out he felt how strange it all was. She wanted, Susan Shepherd then, as appeared, the same thing Kate wanted, only wanted it, as still further appeared, in so different a way and from a motive so different, even though scarce less deep. Then Mrs. Lowder wanted, by so odd an evolution of her exuberance, exactly what each of the others did; and he was between them all, he was in the midst. Such perceptions made occasions—well, occasions for fairly wondering if it mightn't be best just to consent, luxuriously, to *be* the ass the whole thing involved. Trying not to be and yet keeping in it was of the two things the more asinine. He was glad there was no male witness; it was a circle of petticoats; he shouldn't have liked a man to see him. He only had for a moment a sharp thought of Sir Luke Strett, the great master of the knife whom Kate in London had spoken of Milly as in commerce with, and whose renewed intervention at such a distance, just announced to him, required some accounting for. He had a vision of great London surgeons—if this one was a surgeon—as incisive all round; so that he should perhaps after all not wholly escape the ironic attention of his own sex. The most he might be able to do was not to care; while he was trying not to he could take that in. It was a train, however, that brought up the vision of Lord Mark as well. Lord Mark had caught him twice in the fact—the fact of his absurd posture; and that made a second male. But it was comparatively easy not to mind Lord Mark.

His companion had before this taken him up, and in a tone to confirm her discretion, on the matter of Milly's not being his princess. "Of course she's not. You must do something first."

Densher gave it his thought. "Wouldn't it be rather *she* who must?"

It had more than he intended the effect of bringing her to a stand. "I see. No doubt, if one takes it so." Her cheer was for the time in eclipse, and she looked over the place, avoiding his eyes, as in the wonder of what Milly could do. "And yet she has wanted to be kind."

It made him on the spot feel a brute. "Of course she has. No one could be more charming. She has treated me as if *I* were somebody. Call her my hostess as I've never had nor imagined a hostess, and I'm with you altogether. Of course," he added in the right spirit for her, "I do see that it's quite court life."

She promptly showed how this was almost all she wanted of him. "That's all I mean, if you understand it of such a court as never was: one of the courts of heaven, the court of a reigning seraph, a sort of a vice-queen of an angel. That will do perfectly."

"Oh well then I grant it. Only court life as a general thing, you know," he observed, "isn't supposed to pay."

"Yes, one has read; but this is beyond any book. That's just the beauty here; it's why she's the great and only princess. With her, at her court," said Mrs. Stringham, "it does pay." Then as if she had quite settled it for him: "You'll see for yourself."

He waited a moment, but said nothing to discourage her. "I think you were right just now. One must do something first."

"Well, you've done something."

"No—I don't see that. I can do more."

Oh well, she seemed to say, if he would have it so! "You can do everything, you know."

"Everything" was rather too much for him to take up gravely, and he modestly let it alone, speaking the next moment, to avert fatuity, of a different but a related matter. "Why has she sent for Sir Luke Strett if, as you tell me, she's so much better?"

"She hasn't sent. He has come of himself," Mrs. Stringham explained. "He has wanted to come."

"Isn't that rather worse then—if it means he mayn't be easy?"

"He was coming, from the first, for his holiday. She has known that these several weeks." After which Mrs. Stringham added: "You can *make* him easy."

"*I* can?" he candidly wondered. It was truly the circle of petticoats. "What have I to do with it for a man like that?"

"How do you know," said his friend, "what he's like? He's not like any one you've ever seen. He's a great beneficent being."

"Ah then he can do without me. I've no call, as an outsider, to meddle."

"Tell him, all the same," Mrs. Stringham urged, "what you think."

"What I think of Miss Theale?" Densher stared. It was, as they said, a large order. But he found the right note. "It's none of his business."

It did seem a moment for Mrs. Stringham too the right note. She fixed him at least with an expression still bright, but searching, that showed almost to excess what she saw in it; though what this might be he was not to make out till afterwards. "Say *that* to him then. Anything will do for him as a means of getting at you."

"And why should he get at me?"

"Give him a chance to. Let him talk to you. Then you'll see."

All of which, on Mrs. Stringham's part, sharpened his sense of immersion in an element rather more strangely than agreeably warm—a sense that was moreover, during the next two or three hours, to be fed to satiety by several other impressions. Milly came down after dinner, half a dozen friends—objects of interest mainly, it appeared, to the ladies of Lancaster Gate—having by that time arrived; and with this call on her attention, the further call of her musicians ushered by Eugenio, but personally and separately welcomed, and the supreme opportunity offered in the arrival of the great doctor, who came last of all, he felt her diffuse in wide warm waves the spell of a general, a beatific mildness. There was a deeper depth of it, doubtless, for some than for others; what he in particular knew of it was that he seemed to stand in it up to his neck. He moved about in it and it made no plash; he floated, he noiselessly swam in it, and they were all together, for that matter, like fishes in a crystal pool. The effect of the place, the beauty of the scene, had probably much to do with it; the golden grace of the high rooms, chambers of art in themselves, took care, as an influence, of the general manner, and made people bland without making them solemn. They were only people, as Mrs. Stringham had said, staying for the week or two at the inns, people who during the day had fingered their Baedekers, gaped at their frescoes and differed, over fractions of francs, with their gondoliers. But Milly, let loose among them in a wonderful white dress, brought them somehow into relation with something that made them more finely genial; so that if the Veronese picture[2] of which he had talked with Mrs. Stringham was not quite constituted, the comparative prose of the previous hours, the traces of insensibility qualified by "beating down," were at last almost nobly disowned. There was perhaps something for him in the accident of his seeing her for the first time in white, but she hadn't yet had occasion—circulating with a clearness intensified—to strike him as so happily pervasive. She was different, younger, fairer, with the colour of her braided hair more than ever a not altogether lucky challenge to attention; yet he was loth wholly to explain it by her having quitted this once, for some obscure yet doubtless charming reason, her almost monastic, her hitherto invet-

2. The painting is almost certainly Veronese's *Marriage at Cana*, in which Veronese, by including several contemporaries in the banquet scene, transforms the sacramental event into a sumptuous, worldly feast. The figures comprising the analogue of James's scene are positioned in the left foreground of the painting. Cf. Veronese's later work, *Feast in the House of Levi*; originally entitled *The Last Supper*, it manifests a similar stress between the sacred and the profane.

erate black. Much as the change did for the value of her presence, she had never yet, when all was said, made it for *him;* and he was not to fail of the further amusement of judging her determined in the matter by Sir Luke Strett's visit. If he could in this connexion have felt jealous of Sir Luke Strett, whose strong face and type, less assimilated by the scene perhaps than any others, he was anon to study from the other side of the saloon, that would doubtless have been most amusing of all. But he couldn't be invidious, even to profit by so high a tide; he felt himself too much "in" it, as he might have said: a moment's reflexion put him more in than any one. The way Milly neglected him for other cares while Kate and Mrs. Lowder, without so much as the attenuation of a joke, introduced him to English ladies—that was itself a proof; for nothing really of so close a communion had up to this time passed between them as the single bright look and the three gay words (all ostensibly of the last lightness) with which her confessed consciousness brushed by him.

She was acquitting herself to-night as hostess, he could see, under some supreme idea, an inspiration which was half her nerves and half an inevitable harmony; but what he especially recognised was the character that had already several times broken out in her and that she so oddly appeared able, by choice or by instinctive affinity, to keep down or to display. She was the American girl as he had originally found her—found her at certain moments, it was true, in New York, more than at certain others; she was the American girl as, still more than then, he had seen her on the day of her meeting him in London and in Kate's company. It affected him as a large though queer social resource in her—such as a man, for instance, to his diminution, would never in the world be able to command; and he wouldn't have known whether to see it in an extension or a contraction of "personality," taking it as he did most directly for a confounding extension of surface. Clearly too it was the right thing this evening all round: that came out for him in a word from Kate as she approached him to wreak on him a second introduction. He had under cover of the music melted away from the lady toward whom she had first pushed him; and there was something in her to affect him as telling evasively a tale of their talk in the Piazza. To what did she want to coerce him as a form of penalty for what he had done to her there? It was thus in contact uppermost for him that he had done something; not only caused her perfect intelligence to act in his interest, but left her unable to get away, by any mere private effort, from his inattackable logic. With him thus in presence, and near him—and it had been as unmistakeable through dinner—there was no getting away for her at all, there was less of it than ever: so she could only either deal with the question straight, either frankly yield or ineffectually struggle or insincerely argue, or else merely express herself by following up the advantage she did possess. It was part of that advantage for the hour—a brief fallacious makeweight to his pressure—that there were plenty of things left in which he must feel her will. They only told him, these indications, how much she was, in such close quarters, feeling his; and it was enough for him again that her very aspect, as great a variation in its way as Milly's own, gave him back the sense of his action. It had never yet in life been granted him to know, almost materially to taste, as he could do in these minutes, the state of what was vulgarly called conquest. He had lived long enough to have been on occasion "liked," but it had never begun to be allowed him to be liked to any such tune in any such quarter. It was a liking greater than Milly's—or it would be: he felt it in him to answer for that. So at all events he read the case while he noted that Kate was somehow—for Kate—wanting in lustre. As a striking young presence she was practically superseded; of the mildness that Milly diffused she had assimilated all her share; she might fairly have been dressed to-night in the little black frock, superficially indistinguishable, that Milly had laid aside. This represented, he perceived, the opposite pole from such an effect as that of her wonderful entrance, under her aunt's eyes—he had never forgotten it—the day of their younger friend's failure at Lancaster Gate. She was, in her accepted effacement—it was actually her acceptance that made the beauty and repaired the damage—under her aunt's eyes now; but whose eyes were not effectually preoccupied? It struck him none the less certainly that almost the first thing she said to him showed an exquisite attempt to appear if not unconvinced at least self-possessed.

"Don't you think her good enough *now?*"

Almost heedless of the danger of overt freedoms, she eyed Milly from where they stood, noted her in renewed talk, over her further wishes, with the members of her little orchestra, who had approached her with demonstrations of deference enlivened by native humours—things quite in the line of old Venetian comedy.[3] The girl's idea of music had been happy—a real solvent of shyness, yet not drastic; thanks to the intermissions, discretions, a general habit of mercy to gathered barbarians, that reflected the good manners of its interpreters, representatives though these might be but of the order in which taste was natural and melody rank. It was easy at all events to answer Kate. "Ah my dear, you know how good I think her!"

3. The oldest Venetian comedy, predating the *Commedia dell' Arte* and Learned Comedy of the sixteenth century, is typically farcical and bawdy and centered on love intrigues and deceptions.

"But she's *too* nice," Kate returned with appreciation. "Everything suits her so—especially her pearls. They go so with her old lace. I'll trouble you really to look at them." Densher, though aware he had seen them before, had perhaps not "really" looked at them, and had thus not done justice to the embodied poetry—his mind, for Milly's aspects, kept coming back to that—which owed them part of its style. Kate's face, as she considered them, struck him: the long, priceless chain, wound twice round the neck, hung, heavy and pure, down the front of the wearer's breast—so far down that Milly's trick, evidently unconscious, of holding and vaguely fingering and entwining a part of it, conduced presumably to convenience. "She's a dove," Kate went on, "and one somehow doesn't think of doves as bejewelled. Yet they suit her down to the ground."

"Yes—down to the ground is the word." Densher saw now how they suited her, but was perhaps still more aware of something intense in his companion's feeling about them. Milly was indeed a dove; this was the figure, though it most applied to her spirit. Yet he knew in a moment that Kate was just now, for reasons hidden from him, exceptionally under the impression of that element of wealth in her which was a power, which was a great power, and which was dove-like only so far as one remembered that doves have wings and wondrous flights, have them as well as tender tints and soft sounds. It even came to him dimly that such wings could in a given case—*had*, truly, in the case with which he was concerned—spread themselves for protection. Hadn't they, for that matter, lately taken an inordinate reach, and weren't Kate and Mrs. Lowder, weren't Susan Shepherd and he, wasn't *he* in particular, nestling under them to a great increase of immediate ease? All this was a brighter blur in the general light, out of which he heard Kate presently going on.

"Pearls have such a magic that they suit every one."

"They would uncommonly suit you," he frankly returned.

"Oh yes, I see myself!"

As she saw herself, suddenly, he saw her—she would have been splendid; and with it he felt more what she was thinking of. Milly's royal ornament had—under pressure now not wholly occult—taken on the character of a symbol of differences, differences of which the vision was actually in Kate's face. It might have been in her face too that, well as she certainly would look in pearls, pearls were exactly what Merton Densher would never be able to give her. Wasn't *that* the great difference that Milly to-night symbolised? She unconsciously represented to Kate, and Kate took it in at every pore, that there was nobody with whom she had less in common than a remarkably handsome girl married to a man unable to make her on any such lines as that the least little present. Of these absurdities, however, it was not till afterwards that Densher thought. He could think now, to any purpose, only of what Mrs. Stringham had said to him before dinner. He could but come back to his friend's question of a minute ago. "She's certainly good enough, as you call it, in the sense that I'm assured she's better. Mrs. Stringham, an hour or two since, was in great feather to me about it. She evidently believes her better."

"Well, if they choose to call it so—!"

"And what do *you* call it—as against them?"

"I don't call it anything to any one but you. I'm not 'against' them!" Kate added as with just a fresh breath of impatience for all he had to be taught.

"That's what I'm talking about," he said. "What do you call it to me?"

It made her wait a little. "She isn't better. She's worse. But that has nothing to do with it."

"Nothing to do?" He wondered.

But she was clear. "Nothing to do with *us*. Except of course that we're doing our best for her. We're making her want to live." And Kate again watched her. "To-night she does want to live." She spoke with a kindness that had the strange property of striking him as inconsequent—so much, and doubtless so unjustly, had all her clearness been an implication of the hard. "It's wonderful. It's beautiful."

"It's beautiful indeed."

He hated somehow the helplessness of his own note; but she had given it no heed. "She's doing it for *him*"—and she nodded in the direction of Milly's medical visitor. "She wants to be for him at her best. But she can't deceive him."

Densher had been looking too; which made him say in a moment: "And do you think *you* can? I mean, if he's to be with us here, about your sentiments. If Aunt Maud's so thick with him—!"

Aunt Maud now occupied in fact a place at his side and was visibly doing her best to entertain him, though this failed to prevent such a direction of his own eyes—determined, in the way such things happen, precisely by the attention of the others—as Densher became aware of and as Kate promptly marked. "He's looking at *you*. He wants to speak to you."

"So Mrs. Stringham," the young man laughed, "advised me he would."

"Then let him. Be right with him. I don't need," Kate went on in answer to the previous question, "to deceive him. Aunt Maud, if it's necessary, will do that. I mean that, knowing nothing about me, he can see me only as she sees me. She sees me now so well. He has nothing to do with me."

"Except to reprobate you," Densher suggested.

"For not caring for *you?* Perfectly. As a brilliant young man driven by it into your relation with Milly—as all *that* I leave you to him."

"Well," said Densher sincerely enough, "I think I can thank you for leaving me to some one easier perhaps with me than yourself."

She had been looking about again meanwhile, the lady having changed her place, for the friend of Mrs. Lowder's to whom she had spoken of introducing him. "All the more reason why I should commit you then to Lady Wells."

"Oh but wait." It was not only that he distinguished Lady Wells from afar, that she inspired him with no eagerness, and that, somewhere at the back of his head, he was fairly aware of the question, in germ, of whether this was the kind of person he should be involved with when they were married. It was furthermore that the consciousness of something he had not got from Kate in the morning, and that logically much concerned him, had been made more keen by these very moments—to say nothing of the consciousness that, with their general smallness of opportunity, he must squeeze each stray instant hard. If Aunt Maud, over there with Sir Luke, noted him as a little "attentive," that might pass for a futile demonstration on the part of a gentleman who had to confess to having, not very gracefully, changed his mind. Besides, just now, he didn't care for Aunt Maud except in so far as he was immediately to show. "How can Mrs. Lowder think me disposed of with any finality, if I'm disposed of only to a girl who's dying? If you're right about that, about the state of the case, you're wrong about Mrs. Lowder's being squared. If Milly, as you say," he lucidly pursued, "can't deceive a great surgeon, or whatever, the great surgeon won't deceive other people—not those, that is, who are closely concerned. He won't at any rate deceive Mrs. Stringham, who's Milly's greatest friend; and it will be very odd if Mrs. Stringham deceives Aunt Maud, who's her own."

Kate showed him at this the cold glow of an idea that really was worth his having kept her for. "Why will it be odd? I marvel at your seeing your way so little."

Mere curiosity even, about his companion, had now for him its quick, its slightly quaking intensities. He had compared her once, we know, to a "new book," an uncut volume of the highest, the rarest quality; and his emotion (to justify that) was again and again like the thrill of turning the page. "Well, you know how deeply I marvel at the way *you* see it!"

"It doesn't in the least follow," Kate went on, "that anything in the nature of what you call deception on Mrs. Stringham's part will be what you call odd. Why shouldn't she hide the truth?"

"From Mrs. Lowder?" Densher stared. "Why should she?"

"To please you."

"And how in the world can it please me?"

Kate turned her head away as if really at last almost tired of his density. But she looked at him again as she spoke. "Well then to please Milly." And before he could question: "Don't you feel by this time that there's nothing Susan Shephard won't do for you?"

He had verily after an instant to take it in, so sharply it corresponded with the good lady's recent reception of him. It was queerer than anything again, the way they all came together round him. But that was an old story, and Kate's multiplied lights led him on and on. It was with a reserve, however, that he confessed this. "She's ever so kind. Only her view of the right thing may not be the same as yours."

"How can it be anything different if it's the view of serving you?"

Densher for an instant, but only for an instant, hung fire. "Oh the difficulty is that I don't, upon my honour, even yet quite make out how yours does serve me."

"It helps you—put it then," said Kate very simply—"to serve *me*. It gains you time."

"Time for what?"

"For everything!" She spoke at first, once more, with impatience; then as usual she qualified. "For anything that may happen."

Densher had a smile, but he felt it himself as strained. "You're cryptic, love!"

It made her keep her eyes on him, and he could thus see that, by one of those incalculable motions in her without which she wouldn't have been a quarter so interesting, they half-filled with tears from some source he had too roughly touched. "I'm taking a trouble for you I never dreamed I should take for any human creature."

Oh it went home, making him flush for it; yet he soon enough felt his reply on his lips. "Well, isn't my whole insistence to you now that I can conjure trouble away?" And he let it, his insistence, come out again; it had so constantly had, all the week, but its step or two to make. "There *need* be none whatever between us. There need be nothing but our sense of each other."

It had only the effect at first that her eyes grew dry while she took up again one of the so numerous links in her close chain. "You can tell her anything you like, anything whatever."

"Mrs. Stringham? I *have* nothing to tell her."

"You can tell her about *us*. I mean," she wonderfully pursued, "that you do still like me."

It was indeed so wonderful that it amused him. "Only not that you still like me."

She let his amusement pass. "I'm absolutely certain she wouldn't repeat it."

"I see. To Aunt Maud."

"You don't quite see. Neither to Aunt Maud nor to any one else." Kate then, he saw, was always seeing Milly much more, after all, than he was; and she showed it again as she went on. "*There*, accordingly, is your time."

She did at last make him think, and it was fairly as if light broke, though not quite all at once. "You must let me say I *do* see. Time for something in particular that I understand you regard as possible. Time too that, I further understand, is time for you as well."

"Time indeed for me as well." And encouraged visibly by his glow of concentration, she looked at him as through the air she had painfully made clear. Yet she was still on her guard. "Don't think, however, I'll do *all* the work for you. If you want things named you must name them."

He had quite, within the minute, been turning names over; and there was only one, which at last stared at him there dreadful, that properly fitted. "Since she's to die I'm to marry her?"

It struck him even at the moment as fine in her that she met it with no wincing nor mincing. She might for the grace of silence, for favour to their conditions, have only answered him with her eyes. But her lips bravely moved. "To marry her."

"So that when her death has taken place I shall in the natural course have money?"

It was before him enough now, and he had nothing more to ask; he had only to turn, on the spot, considerably cold with the thought that all along—to his stupidity, his timidity—it had been, it had been only, what she meant. Now that he was in possession moreover she couldn't forbear, strangely enough, to pronounce the words she hadn't pronounced: they broke through her controlled and colourless voice as if she should be ashamed, to the very end, to have flinched. "You'll in the natural course have money. We shall in the natural course be free."

"Oh, oh, oh!" Densher softly murmured.

"Yes, yes, yes." But she broke off. "Come to Lady Wells."

He never budged—there was too much else. "I'm to propose it then—marriage—on the spot?"

There was no ironic sound he needed to give it; the more simply he spoke the more he seemed ironic. But she remained consummately proof. "Oh I can't go into that with you, and from the moment you don't wash your hands of me I don't think you ought to ask me. You must act as you like and as you can."

He thought again. "I'm far—as I sufficiently showed you this morning—from washing my hands of you."

"Then," said Kate, "it's all right."

"All right?" His eagerness flamed. "You'll come?"

But he had had to see in a moment that it wasn't what she meant. "You'll have a free hand, a clear field, a chance—well, quite ideal."

"Your descriptions"—her "ideal" was such a touch!—"are prodigious. And what I don't make out is how, caring for me, you can like it."

"I don't like it, but I'm a person, thank goodness, who can do what I don't like."

It wasn't till afterwards that, going back to it, he was to read into this speech a kind of heroic ring, a note of character that belittled his own incapacity for action. Yet he saw indeed even at the time the greatness of knowing so well what one wanted. At the time too, moreover, he next reflected that he after all knew what *he* did. But something else on his lips was uppermost. "What I don't make out then is how you can even bear it."

"Well, when you know me better you'll find out how much I can bear." And she went on before he could take up, as it were, her too many implications. That it was left to him to know her, spiritually, "better" after his long sacrifice to knowledge—this for instance was a truth he hadn't been ready to receive so full in the face. She had mystified him enough, heaven knew, but that was rather by his own generosity than by hers. And what, with it, did she seem to suggest she might incur at his hands? In spite of these questions she was carrying him on. "All you'll have to do will be to stay."

"And proceed to my business under your eyes?"

"Oh dear no—we shall go."

" 'Go?' " he wondered. "Go when, go where?"

"In a day or two—straight home. Aunt Maud wishes it now."

It gave him all he could take in to think of. "Then what becomes of Miss Theale?"

"What I tell you. She stays on, and you stay with her."

He stared. "All alone?"

She had a smile that was apparently for his tone. "You're old enough—with plenty of Mrs. Stringham."

Nothing might have been so odd for him now, could he have measured it, as his being able to feel, quite while he drew from her these successive cues, that he was essentially "seing what she would say"—an instinct compatible for him therefore with that absence of a need to know her better to which she had a moment before done injustice. If it hadn't been appearing to him in gleams that she would somewhere break down, he probably couldn't have gone on. Still, as she wasn't breaking down there was nothing for him but to continue. "Is your going Mrs. Lowder's idea?"

"Very much indeed. Of course again you see what it does for us. And I don't," she added, "refer only to our going, but to Aunt Maud's view of the general propriety of it."

"I see again, as you say," Densher said after a moment. "It makes everything fit."

"Everything."

The word, for a little, held the air, and he might have seemed the while to be looking, by no means dimly now, at all it stood for. But he had in fact been looking at something else. "You leave her here then to die?"

"Ah she believes she won't die. Not if you stay. I mean," Kate explained, "Aunt Maud believes."

"And that's all that's necessary?"

Still indeed she didn't break down. "Didn't we long ago agree that what she believes is the principal thing for us?"

He recalled it, under her eyes, but it came as from long ago. "Oh yes. I can't deny it." Then he added: "So that if I stay—"

"It won't"—she was prompt—"be our fault."

"If Mrs. Lowder still, you mean, suspects us?"

"If she still suspects us. But she won't."

Kate gave it an emphasis that might have appeared to leave him nothing more; and he might in fact well have found nothing if he hadn't presently found: "But what if she doesn't accept me?"

It produced in her a look of weariness that made the patience of her tone the next moment touch him. "You can but try."

"Naturally I can but try. Only, you see, one has to try a little hard to propose to a dying girl."

"She isn't for you as if she's dying." It had determined in Kate the flash of *justesse*[4] he could perhaps most, on consideration, have admired, since her retort touched the truth. There before him was the fact of how Milly to-night impressed him, and his companion, with her eyes in his own and pursuing his impression to the depths of them, literally now perched on the fact in triumph. She turned her head to where their friend was again in range, and it made him turn his, so that they watched a minute in concert. Milly, from the other side, happened at the moment to notice them, and she sent across toward them in response all the candour of her smile, the lustre of her pearls, the value of her life, the essence of her wealth. It brought them together again with faces made fairly grave by the

4. Soundness, accuracy.

reality she put into their plan. Kate herself grew a little pale for it, and they had for a time only a silence. The music, however, gay and vociferous, had broken out afresh and protected more than interrupted them. When Densher at last spoke it was under cover.

"I might stay, you know, without trying."

"Oh to stay *is* to try."

"To have for herself, you mean, the appearance of it?"

"I don't see how you can have the appearance more."

Densher waited. "You think it then possible she may *offer* marriage?"

"I can't think—if you really want to know—what she may *not* offer!"

"In the manner of princesses, who do such things?"

"In any manner you like. So be prepared."

Well, he looked as if he almost were. "It will be for me then to accept. But that's the way it must come."

Kate's silence, so far, let it pass; but presently said: "You'll, on your honour, stay then?"

His answer made her wait, but when it came it was distinct. "Without you, you mean?"

"Without us."

"And you yourselves go at latest—?"

"Not later than Thursday."

It made three days. "Well," he said, "I'll stay, on my honour, if you'll come to me. On *your* honour."

Again, as before, this made her momentarily rigid, with a rigour out of which, at a loss, she vaguely cast about her. Her rigour was more to him, nevertheless, than all her readiness; for her readiness was the woman herself, and this other thing a mask, a stop-gap and a "dodge." She cast about, however, as happened, and not for the instant in vain. Her eyes, turned over the room, caught at a pretext. "Lady Wells is tired of waiting: she's coming—see—to *us*."

Densher saw in fact, but there was a distance for their visitor to cross, and he still had time. "If you decline to understand me I wholly decline to understand you. I'll do nothing."

"Nothing?" It was as if she tried for the minute to plead.

"I'll do nothing. I'll go off before you. I'll go to-morrow."

He was to have afterwards the sense of her having then, as the phrase was—and for vulgar triumphs too—seen he meant it. She looked again at Lady Wells, who was nearer, but she quickly came back. "And if I do understand?"

"I'll do everything."

She found anew a pretext in her approaching friend: he was fairly playing with her pride. He had never, he then knew, tasted, in all his relation with her, of anything so sharp—too sharp for mere sweetness—as the vividness with which he saw himself master in the conflict. "Well, I understand."

"On your honour?"

"On my honour."

"You'll come?"

"I'll come."

Book Ninth

I

It was after they had gone that he truly felt the difference, which was most to be felt moreover in his faded old rooms. He had recovered from the first a part of his attachment to this scene of contemplation, within sight, as it was, of the Rialto bridge, on the hither side of that arch of associations and the left going up the Canal; he had seen it in a particular light, to which, more and more, his mind and his hands adjusted it; but the interest the place now wore for him had risen at a bound, becoming a force that, on the spot, completely engaged and absorbed him, and relief from which—if relief was the name—he could find only by getting away and out of reach. What had come to pass within his walls lingered there as an obsession importunate to all his senses; it lived again, as a cluster of pleasant memories, at every hour and in every object; it made everything but itself irrelevant and tasteless. It remained, in a word, a conscious watchful presence, active on its own side, for ever to be reckoned with, in face of which the effort at detachment was scarcely less futile than frivolous. Kate had come to him; it was only once—and this not from any failure of their need, but from such impossibilities, for bravery alike and for subtlety, as there was at the last no blinking; yet she had come, that once, to stay, as people called it; and what survived of her, what reminded and insisted, was something he couldn't have banished if he had wished. Luckily he didn't wish, even though there might be for a man almost a shade of the awful in so unqualified a consequence of his act. It had simply *worked*, his idea, the idea he had made her accept; and all erect before him, really covering the ground as far as he could see, was the fact of the gained success that this represented. It was, otherwise, but the fact of the idea as directly applied, as converted from a luminous conception into an historic truth. He had known it before but as desired and urged, as convincingly insisted on for the help it would render; so that at present, *with* the help rendered, it seemed to acknowledge its office and to set up, for memory and faith, an insistence of its own. He had in fine judged his friend's pledge in advance as an inestimable value, and what he must now know his case for was that of a possession of the value to the full. Wasn't it perhaps even rather the value that possessed *him*, kept him thinking of it and waiting on it, turning round and round it and making sure of it again from this side and that?

It played for him—certainly in this prime afterglow—the part of a treasure kept at home in safety and sanctity, something he was sure of finding in its place when, with each return, he worked his heavy old key in the lock. The door had but to open for him to be with it again and for it to be all there; so intensely there that, as we say, no other act was possible to him than the renewed act, almost the hallucination, of intimacy. Wherever he looked or sat or stood, to whatever aspect he gave for the instant the advantage, it was in view as nothing of the moment, nothing begotten of time or of chance could be, or ever would; it was in view as, when the curtain has risen, the play on the stage is in view, night after night, for the fiddlers. He remained thus, in his own theatre, in his single person, perpetual orchestra to the ordered drama, the confirmed "run"; playing low and slow, moreover, in the regular way, for the situations of most importance. No other visitor was to come to him; he met, he bumped occasionally, in the Piazza or in his walks, against claimants to acquaintance, remembered or forgotten, at present mostly effusive, sometimes even inquisitive; but he gave no address and encouraged no approach; he couldn't for his life, he felt, have opened his door to a third person. Such a person would have interrupted him, would have profaned his secret or perhaps have guessed it; would at any rate have broken the spell of what he conceived himself—in the absence of anything "to show"—to be inwardly doing. He was giving himself up—that was quite enough—to the general feeling of his renewed engagement to fidelity. The force of the engagement, the quantity of the article to be supplied, the special solidity of the contract, the way, above all, as a service for which the price named by him had been magnificently paid, his equivalent office was to take effect—such items might well fill his consciousness when there was nothing from outside to interfere. Never was a consciousness more rounded and fastened down over what filled it; which is precisely what we have spoken of as, in its degree, the oppression of success, the somewhat chilled state—tending to the solitary—of supreme recognition. If it was slightly awful to feel so justified, this was by the loss of the warmth of the element of mystery. The lucid reigned instead of it, and it was into the lucid that he sat and stared. He shook himself out of it a dozen times a day, tried to break by his own act his constant still communion. It wasn't still communion she had meant to bequeath him; it was the very different business of that kind of fidelity of which the other name was careful action.

Nothing, he perfectly knew, was less like careful action than the immersion he enjoyed at home. The actual grand queerness was that to be faithful to Kate he had positively to take his eyes, his arms, his lips straight off her—he had to let her alone. He had to remember it was time to go to the palace—which in truth was a mercy, since the check was not less effectual than imperative. What it came to, fortunately, as yet, was that when he closed the door behind him for an absence he always shut her in. Shut her out—it came to that rather, when once he had got a little away; and before he reached the palace, much more after hearing at his heels the bang of the greater *portone*,[1] he felt free enough not to know his position as oppressively false. As Kate was *all* in his poor rooms, and not a ghost of her left for the grander, it was only on reflexion that the falseness came out; so long as he left it to the mercy of beneficent chance it offered him no face and made of him no claim that he couldn't meet without aggravation of his inward sense. This aggravation had been his original horror; yet what—in Milly's presence, each day—was horror doing with him but virtually letting him off? He shouldn't perhaps get off to the end; there was time enough still for the possibility of shame to pounce. Still, however, he did constantly a little more what he liked best, and that kept him for the time more safe. What he liked best was, in any case, to know *why* things were as he felt them; and he knew it pretty well, in this case, ten days after the retreat of his other friends. He then fairly perceived that—even putting their purity of motive at its highest—it was neither Kate nor he who made his strange relation to Milly, who made her own, so far as it might be, innocent; it was neither of them who practically purged it—if practically purged it was. Milly herself did everything—so far at least as he was concerned—Milly herself, and Milly's house, and Milly's hospitality, and Milly's manner, and Milly's character, and, perhaps still more than anything else, Milly's imagination, Mrs. Stringham and Sir Luke indeed a little aiding: whereby he knew the blessing of a fair pretext to ask himself what more he had to do. Something incalculable wrought for them—for him and Kate; something outside, beyond, above themselves, and doubtless ever so much better than they: which wasn't a reason, however—its being so much better—for them not to profit by it. Not to profit by it, so far as profit could be reckoned, would have been to go directly against it; and the spirit of generosity at present engendered in Densher could have felt no greater pang than by his having to go directly against Milly.

1. Entrance.

To go *with* her was the thing, so far as she could herself go; which, from the moment her tenure of her loved palace stretched on, was possible but by his remaining near her. This remaining was of course on the face of it the most "marked" of demonstrations—which was exactly why Kate had required it; it was so marked that on the very evening of the day it had taken effect Milly herself hadn't been able not to reach out to him, with an exquisite awkwardness, for some account of it. It was as if she had wanted from him some name that, now they were to be almost alone together, they could, for their further ease, know it and call it by—it being, after all, almost rudimentary that his presence, of which the absence of the others made quite a different thing, couldn't but have for himself some definite basis. She only wondered about the basis it would have for himself, and how he would describe it; that would quite do for her—it even would have done for her, he could see, had he produced some reason merely trivial, had he said he was waiting for money or clothes, for letters or for orders from Fleet Street, without which, as she might have heard, newspaper men never took a step. He hadn't in the event quite sunk to that; but he had none the less had there with her, that night, on Mrs. Stringham's leaving them alone—Mrs. Stringham proved really prodigious—his acquaintance with a shade of awkwardness darker than any Milly could know. He had supposed himself beforehand, on the question of what he was doing or pretending, in possession of some tone that would serve; but there were three minutes of his feeling incapable of promptness quite in the same degree in which a gentleman whose pocket has been picked feels incapable of purchase. It even didn't help him, oddly, that he was sure Kate would in some way have spoken for him—or rather not so much in some way as in one very particular way. He hadn't asked her, at the last, what she might, in the connexion, have said; nothing would have induced him to put such a question after she had been to see him: his lips were so sealed by that passage, his spirit in fact so hushed, in respect to any charge upon her freedom. There was something he could only therefore read back into the probabilities, and when he left the palace an hour afterwards it was with a sense of having breathed there, in the very air, the truth he had been guessing.

Just this perception it was, however, that had made him for the time ugly to himself in his awkwardness. It was horrible, with this creature, to *be* awkward; it was odious to be seeking excuses for the relation that involved it. Any relation that involved it was by the very fact as much discredited as a dish would be at dinner if one had to take medicine as a sauce. What Kate would have said in one of the young women's last talks was that—if Milly absolutely must have the truth about it—Mr. Densher was staying because she had really seen no way but to require it of him. If he stayed he didn't follow her—or didn't appear to her aunt to be doing so; and when she kept him from following her Mrs. Lowder couldn't pretend, in scenes, the renewal of which at this time of day was painful, that she after all didn't snub him as she might. She did nothing in fact *but* snub him—wouldn't that have been part of the story?—only Aunt Maud's suspicions were of the sort that had repeatedly to be dealt with. He had been, by the same token, reasonable enough—as he now, for that matter, well might; he had consented to oblige them, aunt and niece, by giving the plainest sign possible that he could exist away from London. To exist away from London was to exist away from Kate Croy—which was a gain, much appreciated, to the latter's comfort. There was a minute, at this hour, out of Densher's three, during which he knew the terror of Milly's uttering some such allusion to their friend's explanation as he must meet with words that wouldn't destroy it. To destroy it was to destroy everything, to destroy probably Kate herself, to destroy in particular by a breach of faith still uglier than anything else the beauty of their own last passage. He had given her his word of honour that if she would come to him he would act absolutely in her sense, and he had done so with a full enough vision of what her sense implied. What it implied for one thing was that to-night in the great saloon, noble in its half-lighted beauty, and straight in the white face of his young hostess, divine in her trust, or at any rate inscrutable in her mercy—what it implied was that he should lie with his lips. The single thing, of all things, that could save him from it would be Milly's letting him off after having thus scared him. What made her mercy inscrutable was that if she had already more than once saved him it was yet apparently without knowing how nearly he was lost.

These were transcendent motions, not the less blest for being obscure; whereby yet once more he was to feel the pressure lighten. He was kept on his feet in short by the felicity of her not presenting him with Kate's version as a version to adopt. He couldn't stand up to lie—he felt as if he should have to go down on his knees. As it was he just sat there shaking a little for nervousness the leg he had crossed over the other. She was sorry for his suffered snub, but he had nothing more to subscribe to, to perjure himself about, than the three or four inanities he had, on his own side, feebly prepared for the crisis. He scrambled a little higher than the reference to money and clothes, letters and directions from his manager; but he brought out the beauty of the chance for him—there before him like a temptress painted by Titian[2]—to do a little quiet writing. He was vivid for a moment on the difficulty of writing qui-

2. An allusion, perhaps, to Titian's *Venus and Adonis.*

etly in London; and he was precipitate, almost explosive, on his idea, long cherished, of a book.

The explosion lighted her face. "You'll do your book here?"

"I hope to begin it."

"It's something you haven't begun?"

"Well, only just."

"And since you came?"

She was so full of interest that he shouldn't perhaps after all be too easily let off. "I tried to think a few days ago that I had broken ground."

Scarcely anything, it was indeed clear, could have let him in deeper. "I'm afraid we've made an awful mess of your time."

"Of course you have. But what I'm hanging on for now is precisely to repair that ravage."

"Then you mustn't mind me, you know."

"You'll see," he tried to say with ease, "how little I shall mind anything."

"You'll want"—Milly had thrown herself into it—"the best part of your days."

He thought a moment: he did what he could to wreathe it in smiles. "Oh I shall make shift with the worst part. The best will be for *you*." And he wished Kate could hear him. It didn't help him moreover that he visibly, even pathetically, imaged to her by such touches his quest for comfort against discipline. He was to bury Kate's so signal snub, and also the hard law she had now laid on him, under a high intellectual effort. This at least was his crucifixion—that Milly was so interested. She was so interested that she presently asked him if he found his rooms propitious, while he felt that in just decently answering her he put on a brazen mask. He should need it quite particularly were she to express again her imagination of coming to tea with him—an extremity that he saw he was not to be spared. "We depend on you, Susie and I, you know, not to forget we're coming"—the extremity was but to face that remainder, yet it demanded all his tact. Facing their visit itself—to that, no matter what he might have to do, he would never consent, as we know, to be pushed; and this even though it might be exactly such a demonstration as would figure for him at the top of Kate's list of his proprieties. He could wonder freely enough, deep within, if Kate's view of that especial propriety had not been modified by a subsequent occurrence; but his deciding that it was quite likely not to have been had no effect on his own preference for tact. It pleased him to think of "tact" as his present prop in doubt; that glossed his predicament over, for it was of application among the sensitive and the kind. He wasn't inhuman, in fine, so long as it would serve. It had to serve now, accordingly, to help him not to sweeten Milly's hopes. He didn't want to be rude to them, but he still less wanted them to flower again in the particular connexion; so that, casting about him in his anxiety for a middle way to meet her, he put his foot, with unhappy effect, just in the wrong place. "Will it be safe for you to break into your custom of not leaving the house?"

" 'Safe'—?" She had for twenty seconds an exquisite pale glare. Oh but he didn't need it, by that time, to wince; he had winced for himself as soon as he had made his mistake. He had done what, so unforgettably, she had asked him in London not to do; he had touched, all alone with her here, the supersensitive nerve of which she had warned him. He had not, since the occasion in London, touched it again till now; but he saw himself freshly warned that it was able to bear still less. So for the moment he knew as little what to do as he had ever known it in his life. He couldn't emphasise that he thought of her as dying, yet he couldn't pretend he thought of her as indifferent to precautions. Meanwhile too she had narrowed his choice. "You suppose me so awfully bad?"

He turned, in his pain, within himself; but by the time the colour had mounted to the roots of his hair he had found what he wanted. "I'll believe whatever you tell me."

"Well then, I'm splendid."

"Oh I don't need you to tell me that."

"I mean I'm capable of life."

"I've never doubted it."

"I mean," she went on, "that I want so to live—!"

"Well?" he asked while she paused with the intensity of it.

"Well, that I know I *can*."

"Whatever you do?" He shrank from solemnity about it.

"Whatever I do. If I want to."

"If you want to do it?"

"If I want to live. I *can*," Milly repeated.

He had clumsily brought it on himself, but he hesitated with all the pity of it. "Ah then *that* I believe."

"I will, I will," she declared; yet with the weight of it somehow turned for him to mere light and sound.

He felt himself smiling through a mist. "You simply must!"

It brought her straight again to the fact. "Well then, if you say it, why mayn't we pay you our visit?"

"Will it help you to live?"

"Every little helps," she laughed; "and it's very little for me, in general, to stay at home. Only I shan't want to miss it—!"

"Yes?"—she had dropped again.

"Well, on the day you give us a chance."

It was amazing what so brief an exchange had at this point done with him. His great scruple suddenly broke, giving way to something inordinately strange, something of a nature to become clear to him only when he had left her. "You can come," he said, "when you like."

What had taken place for him, however—the drop, almost with violence, of everything but a sense of her own reality—apparently showed in his face or his manner, and even so vividly that she could take it for something else. "I see how you feel—that I'm an awful bore about it and that, sooner than have any such upset, you'll go. So it's no matter."

"No matter? Oh!"—he quite protested now.

"If it drives you away to escape us. We want you not to go."

It was beautiful how she spoke for Mrs. Stringham. Whatever it was, at any rate, he shook his head. "I won't go."

"Then *I* won't go!" she brightly declared.

"You mean you won't come to me?"

"No—never now. It's over. But it's all right. I mean, apart from that," she went on, "that I won't do anything I oughtn't or that I'm not forced to."

"Oh who can ever force you?" he asked with his hand-to-mouth way, at all times, of speaking for her encouragement. "You're the least coercible of creatures."

"Because, you think, I'm so free?"

"The freest person probably now in the world. You've got everything."

"Well," she smiled, "call it so. I don't complain."

On which again, in spite of himself, it let him in. "No I know you don't complain."

As soon as he had said it he had himself heard the pity in it. His telling her she had "everything" was extravagant kind humour, whereas his knowing so tenderly that she didn't complain was terrible kind gravity. Milly felt, he could see, the difference; he might as well have praised her outright for looking death in the face. This was the way she just looked *him* again, and it was of no attenuation that she took him up more gently than ever. "It isn't a merit—when one sees one's way."

"To peace and plenty? Well, I dare say not."

"I mean to keeping what one has."

"Oh that's success. If what one has is good," Densher said at random, "it's enough to try for."

"Well, it's my limit. I'm not trying for more." To which then she added with a change: "And now about your book."

"My book—?" He had got in a moment so far from it.

"The one you're now to understand that nothing will induce either Susie or me to run the risk of spoiling."

He cast about, but he made up his mind. "I'm not doing a book."

"Not what you said?" she asked in a wonder. "You're not writing?"

He already felt relieved. "I don't know, upon my honour, what I'm doing."

It made her visibly grave; so that, disconcerted in another way, he was afraid of what she would see in it. She saw in fact exactly what he feared, but again his honour, as he called it, was saved even while she didn't know she had threatened it. Taking his words for a betrayal of the sense that he, on his side, *might* complain, what she clearly wanted was to urge on him some such patience as he should be perhaps able to arrive at with her indirect help. Still more clearly, however, she wanted to be sure of how far she might venture; and he could see her make out in a moment that she had a sort of test.

"Then if it's not for your book—?"

"What *am* I staying for?"

"I mean with your London work—with all you have to do. Isn't it rather empty for you?"

"Empty for me?" He remembered how Kate had held that she might propose marriage, and he wondered if this were the way she would naturally begin it. It would leave him, such an incident, he already felt, at a loss, and the note of his finest anxiety might have been in the vagueness of his reply. "Oh well—!"

"I ask too many questions?" She settled it for herself before he could protest. "You stay because you've got to."

He grasped at it. "I stay because I've got to." And he couldn't have said when he had uttered it if it were loyal to Kate or disloyal. It gave her, in a manner, away; it showed the tip of the ear of her plan. Yet Milly took it, he perceived, but as a plain statement of his truth. He was waiting for what Kate would have told her of—the permission from Lancaster Gate to come any nearer. To remain friends with either niece or aunt he mustn't stir without it. All this Densher read in the girl's sense of the spirit of his reply; so that it made him feel he was lying, and he had to think of something to correct that. What he thought of was, in an instant, "Isn't it enough, whatever may be one's other complications, to stay after all for *you?*"

"Oh you must judge."

He was by this time on his feet to take leave, and was also at last too restless. The speech in question at least wasn't disloyal to Kate; that was the very tone of their bargain. So was it, by being loyal, another kind of lie, the lie of the uncandid profession of a motive. He was staying so little "for" Milly that he was staying positively against her. He didn't, none the less, know, and at last, thank goodness, didn't care. The only thing he could say might make it either better or worse. "Well then, so long as I don't go, you must think of me all *as* judging!"

II

He didn't go home, on leaving her—he didn't want to; he walked instead, through his narrow ways and his *campi* with gothic arches, to a small and comparatively sequestered café where he had already more than once found refreshment and comparative repose, together with solutions that consisted mainly and pleasantly of further indecisions. It was a literal fact that those awaiting him there to-night, while he leaned back on his velvet bench with his head against a florid mirror and his eyes not looking further than the fumes of his tobacco, might have been regarded by him as a little less limp than usual. This wasn't because, before getting to his feet again, there was a step he had seen his way to; it was simply because the acceptance of his position took sharper effect from his sense of what he had just had to deal with. When half an hour before, at the palace, he had turned about to Milly on the question of the impossibility so inwardly felt, turned about on the spot and under her eyes, he had acted, by the sudden force of his seeing much further, seeing how little, how not at all, impossibilities mattered. It wasn't a case for pedantry; when people were at *her* pass everything was allowed. And her pass was now, as by the sharp click of a spring, just completely his own—to the extent, as he felt, of her deep dependence on him. Anything he should do or shouldn't would have close reference to her life, which was thus absolutely in his hands—and ought never to have reference to anything else. It was on the cards for him that he might kill her—that was the way he read the cards as he sat in his customary corner. The fear in this thought made him let everything go, kept him there actually, all motionless, for three hours on end. He renewed his consumption and smoked more cigarettes than he had ever done in the time. What had come out for him had come out, with this first intensity, as a terror; so that action itself, of any sort, the right as well as the wrong—if the difference even survived—had heard in it a vivid "Hush!" the injunction to keep from that moment intensely still. He thought in fact while his vigil lasted of several different ways for his doing so, and the hour might have served him as a lesson in going on tiptoe.

What he finally took home, when he ventured to leave the place, was the perceived truth that he might on any other system go straight to destruction. Destruction was represented for him by the idea of his really bringing to a point, on Milly's side, anything whatever. Nothing so "brought," he easily argued, but *must* be in one way or another a catastrophe. He was mixed up in her fate, or her fate, if that should be better, was mixed up in *him*, so that a single false motion might either way snap the coil. They helped him, it was true, these considerations, to a degree of eventual peace, for what they luminously amounted to was that he was to do nothing, and that fell in after all with the burden laid on him by Kate. He was only not to budge without the girl's leave—not, oddly enough at the last, to move without it, whether further or nearer, any more than without Kate's. It was to this his wisdom reduced itself—to the need again simply to be kind. That was the same as being still—as studying to create the minimum of vibration. He felt himself as he smoked shut up to a room on the wall of which something precious was too precariously hung. A false step would bring it down, and it must hang as long as possible. He was aware when he walked away again that even Fleet Street wouldn't at this juncture successfully touch him. His manager might wire that he was wanted, but he could easily be deaf to his manager. His money for the idle life might be none too much; happily, however, Venice was cheap, and it was moreover the queer fact that Milly in a manner supported him. The greatest of his expenses really was to walk to the palace to dinner. He didn't want, in short, to give that up, and he should probably be able, he felt, to stay his breath and his hand. He should be able to be still enough through everything.

He tried that for three weeks, with the sense after a little of not having failed. There had to be a delicate art in it, for he wasn't trying—quite the contrary—to be either distant or dull. That would not have been being "nice," which in its own form was the real law. That too might just have produced the vibration he desired to avert; so that he best kept everything in place by not hesitating or fearing, as it were, to let himself go—go in the direction, that is to say, of staying. It depended on where he went; which was what he meant by taking care. When one went on tiptoe one could turn off for retreat without betraying the manœuvre. Perfect tact—the necessity for which he had from the first, as we know, happily recognised—was to keep all intercourse in the key of the absolutely settled. It was settled thus for instance that they were indissoluble good friends, and settled as well that her being the American girl was, just in time and for the relation they found themselves concerned in, a boon inappreciable. If, at least, as the days went on, she was to fall short of her prerogative of the great national, the great maidenly ease, if she didn't diviningly and responsively desire and labour to record herself as possessed of it, this wouldn't have been for want of Densher's keeping her, with his idea, well up to it—wouldn't have been in fine for want of his encouragement and reminder. He didn't perhaps in so many words speak to her of the quantity itself as of the thing she was least to intermit; but he talked of it, freely, in what he flattered himself was an impersonal way, and this held it there before her—since he was careful also to talk pleasantly. It was at once their idea, when all was said, and the most marked of their conveniences. The type was so elastic that it could be stretched to almost anything; and yet, not stretched, it kept down, remained normal, remained properly within bounds. And he *had* meanwhile, thank goodness, without being too much disconcerted, the sense, for the girl's part of the business, of the queerest conscious compliance, of her doing very much what he wanted, even though without her quite seeing why. She fairly touched this once in saying: "Oh yes, you like us to be as we are because it's a kind of facilitation to you that we don't quite measure: I think one would have to be English to measure it!"—and that too, strangely enough, without prejudice to her good nature. She might have been conceived as doing—that is of being—what he liked in order perhaps only to judge where it would take them. They really as it went on *saw* each other at the game; she knowing he tried to keep her in tune with his conception, and he knowing she thus knew it. Add that he again knew she knew, and yet that nothing was spoiled by it, and we get a fair impression of the line they found most completely workable. The strangest fact of all for us must be that the success he himself thus promoted was precisely what figured to his gratitude as the something above and beyond him, above and beyond Kate, that made for daily decency. There would scarce have been felicity—certainly too little of the right lubricant—had not the national character so invoked been, not less inscrutably than entirely, in Milly's chords. It made up her unity and was the one thing he could unlimitedly take for granted.

He did so then, daily, for twenty days, without deepened fear of the undue vibration that was keeping him watchful. He knew in his nervousness that he was living at best from day to day and from hand to mouth; yet he had succeeded, he believed, in avoiding a mistake. All women had alternatives, and Milly's would doubtless be shaky too; but the national character was firm in her, whether as all of her, practically, by this time, or but as a part; the national character that, in a woman still so young, made of the air breathed a virtual non-conductor. It wasn't till a certain occasion when the twenty days had passed that, going to the palace at tea-time, he was met by the information that the signorina padrona was not "receiving." The announcement met him, in the court, on the lips of one of the gondoliers, met him, he thought, with such a conscious eye as the knowledge of his freedoms of access, hitherto conspicuously shown, could scarce fail to beget. Densher had not been at Palazzo Leporelli among the mere receivable, but had taken his place once for all among the involved and included, so that on being so flagrantly braved he recognised after a moment the propriety of a further appeal. Neither of the two ladies, it appeared, received, and yet Pasquale was not prepared to say that either was *poco bene*.[1] He was yet not prepared to say that either was anything, and he would have been blank, Densher mentally noted, if the term could ever apply to members of a race in whom vacancy was but a nest of darknesses—not a vain surface, but a place of withdrawal in which something obscure, something always ominous, indistinguishably lived. He felt afresh indeed at this hour the force of the veto laid within the palace on any mention, any cognition, of the liabilities of its mistress. The state of her health was never confessed to there as a reason. How much it might deeply be taken for one was another matter; of which he grew fully aware on carrying his question further. This appeal was to his friend Eugenio, whom he immediately sent for, with whom, for three rich minutes, protected from the weather, he was confronted in the gallery that led from the water-steps to the court, and whom he always called, in meditation, his friend; seeing it was so elegantly presumable he would have put an end to him if he could. That produced a relation which required a name of its own, an intimacy of consciousness in truth for each—an intimacy of eye, of ear, of general sensibility, of everything but tongue. It had been, in other words, for the five weeks, far from occult to our young man that Eugenio took a view of him not less finely formal than essentially vulgar, but which at the same time he couldn't himself raise an eyebrow to prevent. It was all in the air now again; it was as much between them as ever while Eugenio waited on him in the court.

The weather, from early morning, had turned to storm, the first sea-storm of the autumn, and Densher had almost invidiously brought him down the outer staircase—the massive ascent, the great feature of the court, to Milly's *piano nobile*.[2] This was to pay him—it was the one chance—for all imputations; the imputation in particular that, clever, *tanto bello*[3] and not rich, the young man from London was—by the obvious way—pressing Miss Theale's fortune hard. It was to pay him for the further ineffable intimation that a gentleman must take the young lady's most devoted servant (interested scarcely less in the high attraction) for a strangely casual appendage if he counted in such a connexion on impunity and prosperity. These interpretations were odious to Densher for the simple reason that they might have been so true of the attitude of an inferior man, and three things alone, accordingly, had kept him from righting himself. One of these was that his critic sought

1. Not too well.
2. The main floor, containing the principal reception rooms.
3. So handsome.

expression only in an impersonality, a positive inhumanity, of politeness; the second was that refinements of expression in a friend's servant were not a thing a visitor could take action on; and the third was the fact that the particular attribution of motive did him after all no wrong. It was his own fault if the vulgar view, the view that might have been taken of an inferior man, happened so incorrigibly to fit him. He apparently wasn't so different from inferior men as that came to. If therefore, in fine, Eugenio figured to him as "my friend" because he was conscious of his seeing so much of him, what he made him see on the same lines in the course of their present interview was ever so much more. Densher felt that he marked himself, no doubt, as insisting, by dissatisfaction with the gondolier's answer, on the pursuit taken for granted in him; and yet felt it only in the augmented, the exalted distance that was by this time established between them. Eugenio had of course reflected that a word to Miss Theale from such a pair of lips would cost him his place; but he could also bethink himself that, so long as the word never came—and it was, on the basis he had arranged, impossible—he enjoyed the imagination of mounting guard. He had never so mounted guard, Densher could see, as during these minutes in the damp *loggia* where the storm-gusts were strong; and there came in fact for our young man, as a result of his presence, a sudden sharp sense that everything had turned to the dismal. Something had happened—he didn't know what; and it wasn't Eugenio who would tell him. What Eugenio told him was that he thought the ladies—as if their liability had been equal—were a "leetle" fatigued, just a "leetle leetle," and without any cause named for it. It was one of the signs of what Densher felt in him that, by a profundity, a true deviltry of resource, he always met the latter's Italian with English and his English with Italian. He now, as usual, slightly smiled at him in the process—but ever so slightly this time, his manner also being attuned, our young man made out, to the thing, whatever it was, that constituted the rupture of peace.

This manner, while they stood a long minute facing each other over all they didn't say, played a part as well in the sudden jar to Densher's protected state. It was a Venice all of evil that had broken out for them alike, so that they were together in their anxiety, if they really could have met on it; a Venice of cold lashing rain from a low black sky, of wicked wind raging through narrow passes, of general arrest and interruption, with the people engaged in all the water-life huddled, stranded and wageless, bored and cynical, under archways and bridges. Our young man's mute exchange with his friend contained meanwhile such a depth of reference that, had the pressure been but slightly prolonged, they might have reached a point at which they were equally weak. Each had verily something in mind that would have made a hash of mutual suspicion and in presence of which, as a possibility, they were more united than disjoined. But it was to have been a moment for Densher that nothing could ease off—not even the formal propriety with which his interlocutor finally attended him to the *portone* and bowed upon his retreat. Nothing had passed about his coming back, and the air had made itself felt as a non-conductor of messages. Densher knew of course, as he took his way again, that Eugenio's invitation to return was not what he missed; yet he knew at the same time that what had happened to him was part of his punishment. Out in the square beyond the *fondamenta*[4] that gave access to the land-gate of the palace, out where the wind was higher, he fairly, with the thought of it, pulled his umbrella closer down. It couldn't be, his consciousness, unseen enough by others—the base predicament of having, by a concatenation, just to *take* such things: such things as the fact that one very acute person in the world, whom he couldn't dispose of as an interested scoundrel, enjoyed an opinion of him that there was no attacking, no disproving, no (what was worst of all) even noticing. One had come to a queer pass when a servant's opinion so mattered. Eugenio's would have mattered even if, as founded on a low vision of appearances, it had been quite wrong. It was the more disagreeable accordingly that the vision of appearances was quite right, and yet was scarcely less low.

Such as it was, at any rate, Densher shook it off with the more impatience that he was independently restless. He had to walk in spite of weather, and he took his course, through crooked ways, to the Piazza, where he should have the shelter of the galleries. Here, in the high arcade, half Venice was crowded close, while, on the Molo,[5] at the limit of the expanse, the old columns of the Saint Theodore and of the Lion[6] were the frame of a door wide open to the storm. It was odd for him, as he moved, that it should have made such a difference—if the difference wasn't only that the palace had for the first time failed of a welcome. There was more, but it came from that; that gave the harsh note and broke the spell. The wet and the cold were now to reckon with, and it was to Densher precisely as if he had seen the obliteration, at a stroke, of the margin on a faith in which they were all living. The margin had been his name for it—for the thing that, though it had held out, could bear

4. A street flanked by a canal.

5. The gondola docking area at Saint Mark's Square.

6. Saint Theodore was the patron saint of the Byzantine years prior to the year 828; the Lion is the Winged Lion of Saint Mark. Sister Stephanie Vincec (see Bibliography) has pointed out that in *The Stones of Venice* (1851–53)—a work James knew well—John Ruskin had suggested that the area between these pillars was associated with fortune and death. According to Ruskin, the engineer who erected the columns in 1171 stipulated that "he might keep tables for forbidden games of chance between the shafts. Whereupon the Senate ordered that executions should also take place between them."

no shock. The shock, in some form, had come, and he wondered about it while, threading his way among loungers as vague as himself, he dropped his eyes sightlessly on the rubbish in shops. There were stretches of the gallery paved with squares of red marble, greasy now with the salt spray; and the whole place, in its huge elegance, the grace of its conception and the beauty of its detail, was more than ever like a great drawing-room, the drawing-room of Europe, profaned and bewildered by some reverse of fortune. He brushed shoulders with brown men whose hats askew, and the loose sleeves of whose pendent jackets, made them resemble melancholy maskers. The tables and chairs that overflowed from the cafés were gathered, still with a pretence of service, into the arcade, and here and there a spectacled German, with his coat-collar up, partook publicly of food and philosophy. These were impressions for Densher too, but he had made the whole circuit thrice before he stopped short, in front of Florian's,[7] with the force of his sharpest. His eye had caught a face within the café—he had spotted an acquaintance behind the glass. The person he had thus paused long enough to look at twice was seated, well within range, at a small table on which a tumbler, half-emptied and evidently neglected, still remained; and though he had on his knee, as he leaned back, a copy of a French newspaper—the heading of the *Figaro*[8] was visible—he stared straight before him at the little opposite rococo wall. Densher had him for a minute in profile, had him for a time during which his identity produced, however quickly, all the effect of establishing connexions—connexions startling and direct; and then, as if it were the one thing more needed, seized the look, determined by a turn of the head, that might have been a prompt result of the sense of being noticed. This wider view showed him *all* Lord Mark—Lord Mark as encountered, several weeks before, the day of the first visit of each to Palazzo Leporelli. For it had been all Lord Mark that was going out, on that occasion, as he came in—he had felt it, in the hall, at the time; and he was accordingly the less at a loss to recognise in a few seconds, as renewed meeting brought it to the surface, the same potential quantity.

It was a matter, the whole passage—it could only be—but of a few seconds; for as he might neither stand there to stare nor on the other hand make any advance from it, he had presently resumed his walk, this time to another pace. It had been for all the world, during his pause, as if he had caught his answer to the riddle of the day. Lord Mark had simply faced him—as he had faced *him*, not

7. A large open cafe in Saint Mark's Square.

8. The famous Parisian newspaper, founded in the 1810s as a weekly; begun again in 1856 in the reign of Napoleon III and given over to belletristic and cultural interests, regarding itself as the guardian of good taste. In the early struggles of the Third Republic, during the 1870s, it was overtly monarchist but shifted later to a moderate republican stance.

placed by him, not at first—as one of the damp shuffling crowd. Recognition, though hanging fire, had then clearly come; yet no light of salutation had been struck from these certainties. Acquaintance between them was scant enough for neither to take it up. That neither had done so was not, however, what now mattered, but that the gentleman at Florian's should be in the place at all. He couldn't have been in it long; Densher, as inevitably a haunter of the great meeting-ground, would in that case have seen him before. He paid short visits; he was on the wing; the question for him even as he sat there was of his train or of his boat. He had come back for something—as a sequel to his earlier visit; and whatever he had come back for it had had time to be done. He might have arrived but last night or that morning; he had already made the difference. It was a great thing for Densher to get this answer. He held it close, he hugged it, quite leaned on it as he continued to circulate. It kept him going and going—it made him no less restless. But it explained—and that was much, for with explanations he might somehow deal. The vice in the air, otherwise, was too much like the breath of fate. The weather had changed, the rain was ugly, the wind wicked, the sea impossible, *because* of Lord Mark. It was because of him, a *fortiori*,[9] that the palace was closed. Densher went round again twice; he found the visitor each time as he had found him first. Once, that is, he was staring before him; the next time he was looking over his *Figaro*, which he had opened out. Densher didn't again stop, but left him apparently unconscious of his passage—on another repetition of which Lord Mark had disappeared. He had spent but the day; he would be off that night; he had now gone to his hotel for arrangements. These things were as plain to Densher as if he had had them in words. The obscure had cleared for him—if cleared it was; there was something he didn't see, the great thing; but he saw so round it and so close to it that this was almost as good. He had been looking at a man who had done what he had come for, and for whom, as done, it temporarily sufficed. The man had come again to see Milly, and Milly had received him. His visit would have taken place just before or just after luncheon, and it was the reason why he himself had found her door shut.

He said to himself that evening, he still said even on the morrow, that he only wanted a reason, and that with this perception of one he could now mind, as he called it, his business. His business, he had settled, as we know, was to keep thoroughly still; and he asked himself why it should prevent this that he could feel, in connexion with the crisis, so remarkably blameless. He gave the appearances before him all the benefit of being critical, so that if blame were to

9. All the more.

accrue he shouldn't feel he had dodged it. But it wasn't a bit he who, that day, had touched her, and if she was upset it wasn't a bit his act. The ability so to think about it amounted for Densher during several hours to a kind of exhilaration. The exhilaration was heightened fairly, besides, by the visible conditions—sharp, striking, ugly to him—of Lord Mark's return. His constant view of it, for all the next hours, of which there were many, was as a demonstration on the face of it sinister even to his own actual ignorance. He didn't need, for seeing it as evil, seeing it as, to a certainty, in a high degree "nasty," to know more about it than he had so easily and so wonderfully picked up. You couldn't drop on the poor girl that way without, by the fact, being brutal. Such a visit was a descent, an invasion, an aggression, constituting precisely one or other of the stupid shocks he himself had so decently sought to spare her. Densher had indeed drifted by the next morning to the reflexion—which he positively, with occasion, might have brought straight out—that the only delicate and honourable way of treating a person in such a state was to treat her as *he*, Merton Densher, did. With time, actually—for the impression but deepened—this sense of the contrast, to the advantage of Merton Densher, became a sense of relief, and that in turn a sense of escape. It was for all the world—and he drew a long breath on it—as if a special danger for him had passed. Lord Mark had, without in the least intending such a service, got it straight out of the way. It was *he*, the brute, who had stumbled into just the wrong inspiration and who had therefore produced, for the very person he had wished to hurt, an impunity that was comparative innocence, that was almost like purification. The person he had wished to hurt could only be the person so unaccountably hanging about. To keep still meanwhile was, for this person, more comprehensively, to keep it all up; and to keep it all up was, if that seemed on consideration best, not, for the day or two, to go back to the palace.

The day or two passed—stretched to three days; and with the effect, extraordinarily, that Densher felt himself in the course of them washed but the more clean. Some sign would come if his return should have the better effect; and he was at all events, in absence, without the particular scruple. It wouldn't have been meant for him by either of the women that he was to come back but to face Eugenio. That was impossible—the being again denied; for it made him practically answerable, and answerable was what he wasn't. There was no neglect either in absence, inasmuch as, from the moment he didn't get in, the one message he could send up would be some hope on the score of health. Since accordingly that sort of expression was definitely forbidden him he had only to wait—which he was actually helped to do by his feeling with the lapse of each day more and more wound up to it. The days in themselves were anything but sweet; the wind and the weather lasted, the fireless cold hinted at worse; the broken charm of the world about was broken into smaller pieces. He walked up and down his rooms and listened to the wind—listened also to tinkles of bells and watched for some servant of the palace. He might get a note, but the note never came; there were hours when he stayed at home not to miss it. When he wasn't at home he was in circulation again as he had been at the hour of his seeing Lord Mark. He strolled about the Square with the herd of refugees; he raked the approaches and the cafés on the chance the brute, as he now regularly imaged him, *might* be still there. He could only be there, he knew, to be received afresh; and that—one had but to think of it—would be indeed stiff. He had gone, however—it was proved; though Densher's care for the question either way only added to what was most acrid in the taste of his present ordeal. It all came round to what he was doing for Milly—spending days that neither relief nor escape could purge of a smack of the abject. What was it but abject for a man of his parts to be reduced to such pastimes? What was it but sordid for him, shuffling about in the rain, to have to peep into shops and to consider possible meetings? What was it but odious to find himself wondering what, as between him and another man, a possible meeting would produce? There recurred moments when in spite of everything he felt no straighter than another man. And yet even on the third day, when still nothing had come, he more than ever knew that he wouldn't have budged for the world.

He thought of the two women, in their silence, at last—he at all events thought of Milly—as probably, for her reasons, now intensely wishing him to go. The cold breath of her reasons was, with everything else, in the air; but he didn't care for them any more than for her wish itself, and he would stay in spite of her, stay in spite of odium, stay in spite perhaps of some final experience that would be, for the pain of it, all but unbearable. That would be his one way, purified though he was, to mark his virtue beyond any mistake. It would be accepting the disagreeable, and the disagreeable would be a proof; a proof of his not having stayed for the thing—the agreeable, as it were—that Kate had named. The thing Kate had named was not to have been the odium of staying in spite of hints. It was part of the odium as actual too that Kate was, for her comfort, just now well aloof. These were the first hours since her flight in which his sense of what she had done for him on the eve of that event was to incur a qualification. It was strange, it was perhaps base, to be thinking such things so soon; but one of the intimations of his solitude was that she had provided for herself. She was out of it all, by her act, as much as he was in it; and this difference grew, positively, as his own intensity increased. She had said in their last sharp snatch of talk—sharp though thickly muffled, and with every word in it final and deep, unlike even the deepest words they had ever yet spoken: "Letters? Never—*now*. Think of it. Impossible." So that as he had sufficiently caught her sense—into which he read, all the same, a strange inconsequence—they had practically wrapped their understanding in the breach of their correspondence. He had moreover, on losing her, done justice to her law of silence; for there was doubtless a finer delicacy in his not writing to her than in his writing as he must have written had he spoken of themselves. That would have been a turbid strain, and her idea had been to be noble; which, in a degree, was a manner. Only it left her, for the pinch, comparatively at ease. And it left *him*, in the conditions, peculiarly alone. He was alone, that is, till, on the afternoon of his third day, in gathering dusk and renewed rain, with his shabby rooms looking doubtless, in their confirmed dreariness, for the mere eyes of others, at their worst, the grinning padrona threw open the door and introduced Mrs. Stringham. That made at a bound a difference, especially when he saw that his visitor was weighted. It appeared part of her weight that she was in a wet waterproof, that she allowed her umbrella to be taken from her by the good woman without consciousness or care, and that her face, under her veil, richly rosy with the driving wind, was—and the veil too—as splashed as if the rain were her tears.

III

They came to it almost immediately; he was to wonder afterwards at the fewness of their steps. "She has turned her face to the wall."

"You mean she's worse?"

The poor lady stood there as she had stopped; Densher had, in the instant flare of his eagerness, his curiosity, all responsive at sight of her, waved away, on the spot, the padrona, who had offered to relieve her of her mackintosh. She looked vaguely about through her wet veil, intensely alive now to the step she had taken and wishing it not to have been in the dark, but clearly, as yet, seeing nothing. "I don't know *how* she is—and it's why I've come to you."

"I'm glad enough you've come," he said, "and it's quite—you make me feel—as if I had been wretchedly waiting for you."

She showed him again her blurred eyes—she had caught at his word. "Have you been wretched?"

Now, however, on his lips, the word expired. It would have sounded for him like a complaint, and before something he already made out in his visitor he knew his own trouble as small. Hers, under her damp draperies, which shamed his lack of a fire, was great, and he felt she had brought it all with her. He answered that he had been patient and above all that he had been still. "As still as a mouse—you'll have seen it for yourself. Stiller, for three days together, than I've ever been in my life. It has seemed to me the only thing."

This qualification of it as a policy or a remedy was straightway for his friend, he saw, a light that her own light could answer. "It has been best. I've wondered for you. But it has been best," she said again.

"Yet it has done no good?"

"I don't know. I've been afraid you were gone." Then as he gave a headshake which, though slow, was deeply mature: "You *won't* go?"

"Is to 'go,' " he asked, "to be still?"

"Oh I mean if you'll stay for me."

"I'll do anything for you. Isn't it for you alone now I can?"

She thought of it, and he could see even more of the relief she was taking from him. His presence, his face, his voice, the old rooms themselves, so meagre yet so charged, where Kate had admirably been to him—these things counted for her, now she had them, as the help she had been wanting: so that she still only stood there taking them all in. With it however popped up characteristically a throb of her conscience. What she thus tasted was almost a personal joy. It told Densher of the three days she on her side had spent. "Well, anything you do for me—*is* for her too. Only, only—!"

"Only nothing now matters?"

She looked at him a minute as if he were the fact itself that he expressed. "Then you know?"

"Is she dying?" he asked for all answer.

Mrs. Stringham waited—her face seemed to sound him. Then her own reply was strange. "She hasn't so much as named you. We haven't spoken."

"Not for three days?"

"No more," she simply went on, "than if it were all over. Not even by the faintest allusion."

"Oh," said Densher with more light, "you mean you haven't spoken about *me?*"

"About what else? No more than if you were dead."

"Well," he answered after a moment, "I *am* dead."

"Then *I* am," said Susan Shepherd with a drop of her arms on her waterproof.

It was a tone that, for the minute, imposed itself in its dry despair; it represented, in the bleak place, which had no life of its own, none but the life Kate had left—the sense of which, for that matter, by mystic channels, might fairly be reaching the visitor—the very impotence of their extinction. And Densher had nothing to oppose it withal, nothing but again: "Is she dying?"

It made her, however, as if these were crudities, almost material pangs, only say as before: "Then you know?"

"Yes," he at last returned, "I know. But the marvel to me is that *you* do. I've no right in fact to imagine or to assume that you do."

"You may," said Susan Shepherd, "all the same. I know."

"Everything?"

Her eyes, through her veil, kept pressing him. "No—not everything. That's why I've come."

"That I shall really tell you?" With which, as she hesitated and it affected him, he brought out in a groan a doubting "Oh, oh!" It turned him from her to the place itself, which was a part of what was in him, was the abode, the worn shrine more than ever, of the fact in possession, the fact, now a thick association, for which he had hired it. *That* was not for telling, but Susan Shepherd was, none the less, so decidedly wonderful that the sense of it might really have begun, by an effect already operating, to be a part of her knowledge. He saw, and it stirred him, that she hadn't come to judge him; had come rather, so far as she might dare, to pity. This showed him her own abasement—that, at any rate, of grief; and made him feel with a rush of friendliness that he liked to be with her. The rush had quickened when she met his groan with an attenuation.

"We shall at all events—if that's anything—be together."

It was his own good impulse in herself. "It's what I've ventured to feel. It's much." She replied in effect, silently, that it was whatever he liked; on which, so far as he had been afraid for anything, he knew his fear had dropped. The comfort was huge, for it gave back to him something precious, over which, in the effort of recovery, his own hand had too imperfectly closed. Kate, he remembered, had said to him, with her sole and single boldness—and also on grounds he hadn't then measured—that Mrs. Stringham was a person who *wouldn't*, at a pinch, in a stretch of confidence, wince. It was but another of the cases in which Kate was always showing. "You don't think then very horridly of me?"

And her answer was the more valuable that it came without nervous effusion—quite as if she understood what he might conceivably have believed. She turned over in fact what she thought, and that was what helped him. "Oh you've been extraordinary!"

It made him aware the next moment of how they had been planted there. She took off her cloak with his aid, though when she had also, accepting a seat, removed her veil, he recognised in her personal ravage that the words she had just uttered to him were the one flower she had to throw. They were all her consolation for him, and the consolation even still depended on the event. She sat with him at any rate in the grey clearance, as sad as a winter dawn, made by their meeting. The image she again evoked for him loomed in it but the larger. "She has turned her face to the wall."

He saw with the last vividness, and it was as if, in their silences, they were simply so leaving what he saw. "She doesn't speak at all? I don't mean not of me."

"Of nothing—of no one." And she went on, Susan Shepherd, giving it out as she had had to take it. "She doesn't *want* to die. Think of her age. Think of her goodness. Think of her beauty. Think of all she is. Think of all she *has*. She lies there stiffening herself and clinging to it all. So I thank God—!" the poor lady wound up with a wan inconsequence.

He wondered. "You thank God—?"

"That she's so quiet."

He continued to wonder. "*Is* she so quiet?"

"She's more than quiet. She's grim. It's what she has never been. So you see—all these days. I can't tell you—but it's better so. It would kill me if she *were* to tell me."

"To tell you?" He was still at a loss.

"How she feels. How she clings. How she doesn't want it."

"How she doesn't want to die? Of course she doesn't want it." He had a long pause, and they might have been thinking together of what they could even now do to prevent it. This, however, was not what he brought out. Milly's "grimness" and the great hushed palace were present to him; present with the little woman before him as she must have been waiting there and listening. "Only, what harm have *you* done her?"

Mrs. Stringham looked about in her darkness. "I don't know. I come and talk of her here with you."

It made him again hesitate. "Does she utterly hate me?"

"I don't know. How *can* I? No one ever will."

"She'll never tell?"

"She'll never tell."

Once more he thought. "She must be magnificent."

"She *is* magnificent."

His friend, after all, helped him, and he turned it, so far as he could, all over. "Would she see me again?"

It made his companion stare. "Should you like to see her?"

"You mean as you describe her?" He felt her surprise, and it took him some time. "No."

"Ah then!" Mrs. Stringham sighed.

"But if she could bear it I'd do anything."

She had for the moment her vision of this, but it collapsed. "I don't see what you can do."

"I don't either. But *she* might."

Mrs. Stringham continued to think. "It's too late."

"Too late for her to see—?"

"Too late."

The very decision of her despair—it was after all so lucid—kindled in him a heat. "But the doctor, all the while—?"

"Tacchini? Oh he's kind. He comes. He's proud of having been approved and coached by a great London man. He hardly in fact goes away; so that I scarce know what becomes of his other patients. He thinks her, justly enough, a great personage; he treats her like royalty; he's waiting on events. But she has barely consented to see him, and, though she has told him, generously—for she *thinks* of me, dear creature—that he may come, that he may stay, for my sake, he spends most of his time only hovering at her door, prowling through the rooms, trying to entertain me, in that ghastly saloon, with the gossip of Venice, and meeting me, in doorways, in the sala, on the staircase, with an agreeable intolerable smile. We don't," said Susan Shepherd, "talk of her."

"By her request?"

"Absolutely. I don't do what she doesn't wish. We talk of the price of provisions."

"By her request too?"

"Absolutely. She named it to me as a subject when she said, the first time, that if it would be any comfort to me he might stay as much as we liked."

Densher took it all in. "But he isn't any comfort to you!"

"None whatever. That, however," she added, "isn't his fault. Nothing's any comfort."

"Certainly," Densher observed, "as I but too horribly feel, *I'm* not."

"No. But I didn't come for that."

"You came for *me*."

"Well then call it that." But she looked at him a moment with eyes filled full, and something came up in her the next instant from deeper still. "I came at bottom of course—"

"You came at bottom of course for our friend herself. But if it's, as you say, too late for me to do anything?"

She continued to look at him, and with an irritation, which he saw grow in her, from the truth itself. "So I did say. But, with you here"—and she turned her vision again strangely about her—"with you here, and with everything, I feel we mustn't abandon her."

"God forbid we should abandon her."

"Then you *won't?*" His tone had made her flush again.

"How do you mean I 'won't,' if she abandons *me?* What can I do if she won't see me?"

"But you said just now you wouldn't like it."

"I said I shouldn't like it in the light of what you tell me. I shouldn't like it only to see her as you make me. I should like it if I could help her. But even then," Densher pursued without faith, "she would have to want it first herself. And there," he continued to make out, "is the devil of it. She *won't* want it herself. She *can't!*"

He had got up in his impatience of it, and she watched him while he helplessly moved. "There's one thing you can do. There's only that, and even for that there are difficulties. But there *is* that." He stood before her with his hands in his pockets, and he had soon enough, from her eyes, seen what was coming. She paused as if waiting for his leave to utter it, and as he only let her wait they heard in the silence, on the Canal, the renewed downpour of rain. She had at last to speak, but, as if still with her fear, she only half-spoke. "I think you really know yourself what it is."

He did know what it was, and with it even, as she said—rather! —there were difficulties. He turned away on them, on everything, for a moment; he moved to the other window and looked at the sheeted channel, wider, like a river, where the houses opposite, blurred and belittled, stood at twice their distance. Mrs. Stringham said nothing, was as mute in fact, for the minute, as if she had "had" him, and he was the first again to speak. When he did so, however, it was not in straight answer to her last remark—he only started from that. He said, as he came back to her, "Let me, you know, *see*—one must understand," almost as if he had for the time accepted it. And what he wished to understand was where, on the essence of the question, was the voice of Sir Luke Strett. If they talked of not giving her up shouldn't *he* be the one least of all to do it? "Aren't we, at the worst, in the dark without him?"

"Oh," said Mrs. Stringham, "it's he who has kept me going. I wired the first night, and he answered like an angel. He'll come like one. Only he can't arrive, at the nearest, till Thursday afternoon."

"Well then that's something."

She considered. "Something—yes. She likes him."

"Rather! I can see it still, the face with which, when he was here in October—that night when she was in white, when she had people there and those musicians—she committed him to my care. It was beautiful for both of us—she put us in relation. She asked me, for the time, to take him about; I did so, and we quite hit it off. That proved," Densher said with a quick sad smile, "that she liked him."

"He liked *you*," Susan Shepherd presently risked.

"Ah I know nothing about that."

"You ought to then. He went with you to galleries and churches; you saved his time for him, showed him the choicest things, and you perhaps will remember telling me myself that if he hadn't been a great surgeon he might really have been a great judge. I mean of the beautiful."

"Well," the young man admitted, "that's what he is—in having judged *her*. He hasn't," he went on, "judged her for nothing. His interest in her—which we must make the most of—can only be supremely beneficent."

He still roamed, while he spoke, with his hands in his pockets, and she saw him, on this, as her eyes sufficiently betrayed, trying to keep his distance from the recognition he had a few moments before partly confessed to. "I'm glad," she dropped, "you like him!"

There was something for him in the sound of it. "Well, I do no more, dear lady, than you do yourself. Surely *you* like him. Surely, when he was here, we all liked him."

"Yes, but I seem to feel I know what he thinks. And I should think, with all the time you spent with him, you'd know it," she said, "yourself."

Densher stopped short, though at first without a word. "We never spoke of her. Neither of us mentioned her, even to sound her name, and nothing whatever in connexion with her passed between us."

Mrs. Stringham stared up at him, surprised at this picture. But she had plainly an idea that after an instant resisted it. "That was his professional propriety."

"Precisely. But it was also my sense of that virtue in him, and it was something more besides." And he spoke with sudden intensity. "I couldn't *talk* to him about her!"

"Oh!" said Susan Shepherd.

"I can't talk to any one about her."

"Except to *me*," his friend continued.

"Except to you." The ghost of her smile, a gleam of significance, had waited on her words, and it kept him, for honesty, looking at her. For honesty too—that is for his own words—he had quickly coloured: he was sinking so, at a stroke, the burden of his discourse with Kate. His visitor, for the minute, while their eyes met, might have been watching him hold it down. And he *had* to hold it down—the effort of which, precisely, made him red. He couldn't let it come up; at least not yet. She might make what she would of it. He attempted to repeat his statement, but he really modified it. "Sir Luke, at all events, had nothing to tell me, and I had nothing to tell him. Make-believe talk was impossible for us, and—"

"And *real*"—she had taken him right up with a huge emphasis—"was more impossible still." No doubt—he didn't deny it; and she had straightway drawn her conclusion. "Then that proves what I say—that there were immensities between you. Otherwise you'd have chattered."

"I dare say," Densher granted, "we were both thinking of her."

"You were neither of you thinking of any one else. That's why you kept together."

Well, that too, if she desired, he took from her; but he came straight back to what he had originally said. "I haven't a notion, all the same, of what he thinks." She faced him, visibly, with the question into which he had already observed that her special shade of earnestness was perpetually flowering, right and left—"Are you *very* sure?"—and he could only note her apparent difference from himself. "You, I judge, believe that he thinks she's gone."

She took it, but she bore up. "It doesn't matter what I believe."

"Well, we shall see"—and he felt almost basely superficial. More and more, for the last five minutes, had he known she had brought something with her, and never in respect to anything had he had such a wish to postpone. He would have liked to put everything off till Thursday; he was sorry it was now Tuesday; he wondered if he were afraid. Yet it wasn't of Sir Luke, who was coming; nor of Milly, who was dying; nor of Mrs. Stringham, who was sitting there. It wasn't, strange to say, of Kate either, for Kate's presence affected him suddenly as having swooned or trembled away. Susan Shepherd's, thus prolonged, had cast on it some influence under which it had ceased to act. She was as absent to his sensibility as she had constantly been, since her departure, absent, as an echo or a reference, from the palace; and it was the first time, among the objects now surrounding him, that his sensibility so noted her. He knew soon enough that it was of himself he was afraid, and that even, if he didn't take care, he should infallibly be more so. "Meanwhile," he added for his companion, "it has been everything for me to see you."

She slowly rose at the words, which might almost have conveyed to her the hint of his taking care. She stood there as if she had in fact seen him abruptly moved to dismiss her. But the abruptness would have been in this case so marked as fairly to offer ground for insistence to her imagination of his state. It would take her moreover, she clearly showed him she was thinking, but a minute or two to insist. Besides, she had already said it. "Will you do it if *he* asks you? I mean if Sir Luke himself puts it to you. And will you give him"—oh she was earnest now!—"the opportunity to put it to you?"

"The opportunity to put what?"

"That if you deny it to her, that may still do something."

Densher felt himself—as had already once befallen him in the quarter of an hour—turn red to the top of his forehead. Turning red had, however, for him, as a sign of shame, been, so to speak, discounted: his consciousness of it at the present moment was rather as a sign of his fear. It showed him sharply enough of what he was afraid. "If I deny what to her?"

Hesitation, on the demand, revived in her, for hadn't he all along been letting her see that he knew? "Why, what Lord Mark told her."

"And what did Lord Mark tell her?"

Mrs. Stringham had a look of bewilderment—of seeing him as suddenly perverse. "I've been judging that you yourself know." And it was she who now blushed deep.

It quickened his pity for her, but he was beset too by other things. "Then *you* know—"

"Of his dreadful visit?" She stared. "Why it's what has done it."

"Yes—I understand that. But you also know—"

He had faltered again, but all she knew she now wanted to say. "I'm speaking," she said soothingly, "of what he told her. It's *that* that I've taken you as knowing."

"Oh!" he sounded in spite of himself.

It appeared to have for her, he saw the next moment, the quality of relief, as if he had supposed her thinking of something else. Thereupon, straightway, that lightened it. "Oh you thought I've known it for *true!*"

Her light had heightened her flush, and he saw that he had betrayed himself. Not, however, that it mattered, as he immediately saw still better. There it was now, all of it at last, and this at least there was no postponing. They were left with her idea—the one she was wishing to make him recognise. He had expressed ten minutes before his need to understand, and she was acting after all but on that. Only what he was to understand was no small matter; it might be larger even than as yet appeared.

He took again one of his turns, not meeting what she had last said; he mooned a minute, as he would have called it, at a window; and of course she could see that she had driven him to the wall. She did clearly, without delay, see it; on which her sense of having "caught" him became as promptly a scruple, which she spoke as if not to press. "What I mean is that he told her you've been all the while engaged to Miss Croy."

He gave a jerk round; it was almost—to hear it—the touch of a lash; and he said—idiotically, as he afterwards knew—the first thing that came into his head. "All *what* while?"

"Oh it's not I who say it." She spoke in gentleness. "I only repeat to you what he told her."

Densher, from whom an impatience had escaped, had already caught himself up. "Pardon my brutality. Of course I know what you're talking about. I saw him, toward the evening," he further explained, "in the Piazza; only just saw him—through the glass at Florian's—without any words. In fact I scarcely know him—there wouldn't have been occasion. It was but once, moreover—he must have gone that night. But I knew he wouldn't have come for nothing, and I turned it over—what he would have come for."

Oh so had Mrs. Stringham. "He came for exasperation."

Densher approved. "He came to let her know that he knows

better than she for whom it was she had a couple of months before, in her fool's paradise, refused him."

"How you *do* know!"—and Mrs. Stringham almost smiled.

"I know that—but I don't know the good it does him."

"The good, he thinks, if he has patience—not too much—may be to come. He doesn't know what he has done to her. Only *we*, you see, do that."

He saw, but he wondered. "She kept from him—what she felt?"

"She was able—I'm sure of it—not to show anything. He dealt her his blow, and she took it without a sign." Mrs. Stringham, it was plain, spoke by book, and it brought into play again her appreciation of what she related. "She's magnificent."

Densher again gravely assented. "Magnificent!"

"And *he*," she went on, "is an idiot of idiots."

"An idiot of idiots." For a moment, on it all, on the stupid doom in it, they looked at each other. "Yet he's thought so awfully clever."

"So awfully—it's Maud Lowder's own view. And he was nice, in London," said Mrs. Stringham, "to *me*. One could almost pity him—he has had such a good conscience."

"That's exactly the inevitable ass."

"Yes, but it wasn't—I could see from the only few things she first told me—that he meant *her* the least harm. He intended none whatever."

"That's always the ass at his worst," Densher returned. "He only of course meant harm to me."

"And good to himself—he thought that would come. He had been unable to swallow," Mrs. Stringham pursued, "what had happened on his other visit. He had been then too sharply humiliated."

"Oh I saw that."

"Yes, and he also saw you. He saw you received, as it were, while he was turned away."

"Perfectly," Densher said—"I've filled it out. And also that he has known meanwhile for *what* I was then received. For a stay of all these weeks. He had had it to think of."

"Precisely—it was more than he could bear. But he has it," said Mrs. Stringham, "to think of still."

"Only, after all," asked Densher, who himself somehow, at this point, was having more to think of even than he had yet had—"only, after all, how has he happened to know? That is, to know enough."

"What do you call enough?" Mrs. Stringham enquired.

"He can only have acted—it would have been his sole safety—from full knowledge."

He had gone on without heeding her question; but, face to face as they were, something had none the less passed between them. It was this that, after an instant, made her again interrogative. "What do you mean by full knowledge?"

Densher met it indirectly. "Where has he been since October?"

"I think he has been back to England. He came in fact, I've reason to believe, straight from there."

"Straight to do this job? All the way for his half-hour?"

"Well, to try again—with the help perhaps of a new fact. To make himself possibly right with her—a different attempt from the other. He had at any rate something to tell her, and he didn't know his opportunity would reduce itself to half an hour. Or perhaps indeed half an hour would be just what was most effective. It *has* been!" said Susan Shepherd.

Her companion took it in, understanding but too well; yet as she lighted the matter for him more, really, than his own courage had quite dared—putting the absent dots on several i's—he saw new questions swarm. They had been till now in a bunch, entangled and confused; and they fell apart, each showing for itself. The first he put to her was at any rate abrupt. "Have you heard of late from Mrs. Lowder."

"Oh yes, two or three times. She depends naturally upon news of Milly."

He hesitated. "And does she depend, naturally, upon news of *me?*"

His friend matched for an instant his deliberation.

"I've given her none that hasn't been decently good. This will have been the first."

" 'This'?" Densher was thinking.

"Lord Mark's having been here, and her being as she is."

He thought a moment longer. "What has Mrs. Lowder written about him? Has she written that he has been with them?"

"She has mentioned him but once—it was in her letter before the last. Then she said something."

"And what did she say?"

Mrs. Stringham produced it with an effort. "Well it was in reference to Miss Croy. That she thought Kate was thinking of him. Or perhaps I should say rather that he was thinking of *her*—only it seemed this time to have struck Maud that he was seeing the way more open to him."

Densher listened with his eyes on the ground, but he presently raised them to speak, and there was that in his face which proved him aware of a queerness in his question. "Does she mean he has been encouraged to *propose* to her niece?"

"I don't know what she means."

"Of course not"—he recovered himself; "and I oughtn't to seem to trouble you to piece together what I can't piece myself. Only I 'guess,' " he added, "I *can* piece it."

She spoke a little timidly, but she risked it. "I dare say I can piece it too."

It was one of the things in her—and his conscious face took it from her as such—that from the moment of her coming in had seemed to mark for him, as to what concerned him, the long jump of her perception. They had parted four days earlier with many things, between them, deep down. But these things were now on their troubled surface, and it wasn't he who had brought them so quickly up. Women were wonderful—at least this one was. But so, not less, was Milly, was Aunt Maud; so, most of all, was his very Kate. Well, he already knew what he had been feeling about the circle of petticoats. They were all *such* petticoats! It was just the fineness of his tangle. The sense of that, in its turn, for us too, might have been not unconnected with his putting to his visitor a question that quite passed over her remark. "Has Miss Croy meanwhile written to our friend?"

"Oh," Mrs. Stringham amended, "*her* friend also. But not a single word that I know of."

He had taken it for certain she hadn't—the thing being after all but a shade more strange than his having himself, with Milly, never for six weeks mentioned the young lady in question. It was for that matter but a shade more strange than Milly's not having mentioned her. In spite of which, and however inconsequently, he blushed anew for Kate's silence. He got away from it in fact as quickly as possible, and the furthest he could get was by reverting for a minute to the man they had been judging. "How did he manage to get *at* her? She had only—with what had passed between them before—to say she couldn't see him."

"Oh she was disposed to kindness. She was easier," the good lady explained with a slight embarrassment, "than at the other time."

"Easier?"

"She was off her guard. There was a difference."

"Yes. But exactly not *the* difference."

"Exactly not the difference of her having to be harsh. Perfectly. She could afford to be the opposite." With which, as he said nothing, she just impatiently completed her sense. "She had had *you* here for six weeks."

"Oh!" Densher softly groaned.

"Besides, I think he must have written her first—written I mean in a tone to smooth his way. That it would be a kindness to himself. Then on the spot—"

"On the spot," Densher broke in, "he unmasked? The horrid little beast!"

It made Susan Shepherd turn slightly pale, though quickening, as for hope, the intensity of her look at him. "Oh he went off without an alarm."

"And he must have gone off also without a hope."

"Ah that, certainly."

"Then it *was* mere base revenge. Hasn't he known her, into the bargain," the young man asked—"didn't he, weeks before, see her, judge her, feel her, as having for such a suit as his not more perhaps than a few months to live?"

Mrs. Stringham at first, for reply, but looked at him in silence; and it gave more force to what she then remarkably added. "He has doubtess been aware of what you speak of, just as you have yourself been aware."

"He has wanted her, you mean, just *because*—?"

"Just because," said Susan Shepherd.

"The hound!" Merton Densher brought out. He moved off, however, with a hot face, as soon as he had spoken, conscious again of an intention in his visitor's reserve. Dusk was now deeper, and after he had once more taken counsel of the dreariness without he turned to his companion. "Shall we have lights—a lamp or the candles?"

"Not for me."

"Nothing?"

"Not for me."

He waited at the window another moment and then faced his friend with a thought. "He *will* have proposed to Miss Croy. That's what has happened."

Her reserve continued. "It's you who must judge."

"Well, I do judge. Mrs. Lowder will have done so too—only *she*, poor lady, wrong. Miss Croy's refusal of him will have struck him" —Densher continued to make it out—"as a phenomenon requiring a reason."

"And you've been clear to him *as* the reason?"

"Not too clear—since I'm sticking here and since that has been a fact to make his descent on Miss Theale relevant. But clear enough. He has believed," said Densher bravely, "that I may have been a reason at Lancaster Gate, and yet at the same time have been up to something in Venice."

Mrs. Stringham took her courage from his own. " 'Up to' something? Up to what?"

"God knows. To some 'game,' as they say. To some deviltry. To some duplicity."

"Which of course," Mrs. Stringham observed, "is a monstrous supposition." Her companion, after a stiff minute—sensibly long for each—fell away from her again, and then added to it another minute, which he spent once more looking out with his hands in his pockets. This was no answer, he perfectly knew, to what she had dropped, and it even seemed to state for his own ears that no answer was possible. She left him to himself, and he was glad she had declined, for their further colloquy, the advantage of lights. These would have been an advantage mainly to herself. Yet she got her benefit too even from the absence of them. It came out in her very tone when at last she addressed him—so differently, for confidence—in words she had already used. "If Sir Luke himself asks it of you as something you can do for *him,* will you deny to Milly herself what she has been made so dreadfully to believe?"

Oh how he knew he hung back! But at last he said: "You're absolutely certain then that she does believe it?"

"Certain?" She appealed to their whole situation. "Judge!"

He took his time again to judge. "Do *you* believe it?"

He was conscious that his own appeal pressed her hard; it eased him a little that her answer must be a pain to her discretion. She answered none the less, and he was truly the harder pressed. "What I believe will inevitably depend more or less on your action. You can perfectly settle it—if you care. I promise to believe you down to the ground if, to save her life, you consent to a denial."

"But a denial, when it comes to that—confound the whole thing, don't you see!—of exactly what?"

It was as if he were hoping she would narrow; but in fact she enlarged. "Of everything."

Everything had never even yet seemed to him so incalculably much. "Oh!" he simply moaned into the gloom.

IV

The near Thursday, coming nearer and bringing Sir Luke Strett, brought also blessedly an abatement of other rigours. The weather changed, the stubborn storm yielded, and the autumn sunshine, baffled for many days, but now hot and almost vindictive, came into its own again and, with an almost audible paean, a suffusion of bright sound that was one with the bright colour, took large possession. Venice glowed and plashed and called and chimed again; the air was like a clap of hands, and the scattered pinks, yellows, blues, sea-greens, were like a hanging-out of vivid stuffs, a laying-down of fine carpets. Densher rejoiced in this on the occasion of his going to the station to meet the great doctor. He went after consideration, which, as he was constantly aware, was at present his imposed, his only, way of doing anything. That was where the event had landed him—where no event in his life had landed him before. He had thought, no doubt, from the day he was born, much more than he had acted; except indeed that he remembered thoughts—a few of them—which at the moment of their coming to him had thrilled him almost like adventures. But anything like his actual state he had not, as to the prohibition of impulse, accident, range—the prohibition in other words of freedom—hitherto known. The great oddity was that if he had felt his arrival, so few weeks back, especially as an adventure, nothing could now less resemble one than the fact of his staying. It would be an adventure to break away, to depart, to go back, above all, to London, and tell Kate Croy he had done so; but there was something of the merely, the almost meanly, obliged and involved sort in his going on as he was. That was the effect in particular of Mrs. Stringham's visit, which had left him as with such a taste in his mouth of what he couldn't do. It had made this quantity clear to him, and yet had deprived him of the sense, the other sense, of what, for a refuge, he possibly *could*.

It was but a small make-believe of freedom, he knew, to go to the station for Sir Luke. Nothing equally free, at all events, had he yet turned over so long. What then was his odious position but that again and again he was afraid? He stiffened himself under this consciousness as if it had been a tax levied by a tyrant. He hadn't at any time proposed to himself to live long enough for fear to preponderate in his life. Such was simply the advantage it had actually got of him. He was afraid for instance that an advance to his distinguished friend might prove for him somehow a pledge or a committal. He was afraid of it as a current that would draw him too far; yet he thought with an equal aversion of being shabby, being poor, through fear. What finally prevailed with him was the reflexion that, whatever might happen, the great man had, after that occasion at the palace, their young woman's brief sacrifice to society—and the hour of Mrs. Stringham's appeal had brought it well to the surface—shown him marked benevolence. Mrs. Stringham's comments on the relation in which Milly had placed them made him—it was unmistakeable—feel things he perhaps hadn't felt. It was in the spirit of seeking a chance to feel again adequately whatever it was he had missed—it was, no doubt, in that spirit, so far as it went a stroke for freedom, that Densher, arriving betimes, paced the platform before the train came in. Only, after it had come and he had presented himself at the door of Sir Luke's compartment with everything that followed—only, as the situation developed, the sense of an anti-climax to so many intensities deprived his apprehensions and hesitations even of the scant dignity they might claim. He could scarce have said if the visitor's manner less showed the remembrance that might have suggested expectation, or made shorter work of surprise in presence of the fact.

Sir Luke had clean forgotten—so Densher read—the rather remarkable young man he had formerly gone about with, though he picked him up again, on the spot, with one large quiet look. The young man felt himself so picked, and the thing immediately affected him as the proof of a splendid economy. Opposed to all the waste with which he was now connected the exhibition was of a nature quite nobly to admonish him. The eminent pilgrim, in the train, all the way, had used the hours as he needed, thinking not a moment in advance of what finally awaited him. An exquisite case awaited him—of which, in this queer way, the remarkable young man was an outlying part; but the single motion of his face, the motion into which Densher, from the platform, lightly stirred its stillness, was his first renewed cognition. If, however, he had suppressed the matter by leaving Victoria he would at once suppress now, in turn, whatever else suited. The perception of this became as a symbol of the whole pitch, so far as one might one's self be concerned, of his visit. One saw, our friend further meditated, everything that, in contact, he appeared to accept—if only, for much, not to trouble to sink it: what one missed was the inward use he made of it. Densher began wondering, at the great water-steps outside, what use he would make of the anomaly of their having there to separate. Eugenio had been on the platform, in the respectful rear, and the gondola from the palace, under his direction, bestirred itself, with its attaching mixture of alacrity and dignity, on their coming out of the station together. Densher didn't at all mind now that, he himself of necessity refusing a seat on the deep black cushions beside the guest of the palace, he had Milly's three emissaries for spectators; and this susceptibility, he also knew, it was something to have left behind. All he did was to smile down vaguely from the steps—they could see him, the donkeys, as shut out as they would. "I don't," he said with a sad headshake, "go there now."

"Oh!" Sir Luke Strett returned, and made no more of it; so that the thing was splendid, Densher fairly thought, as an inscrutability quite inevitable and unconscious. His friend appeared not even to make of it that he supposed it might be for respect to the crisis. He didn't moreover afterwards make much more of anything—after the classic craft, that is, obeying in the main Pasquale's inimitable stroke from the poop, had performed the manœuvre by which it presented, receding, a back, so to speak, rendered positively graceful by the high black hump of its *felze*.[1] Densher watched the gondola out of sight—he heard Pasquale's cry, borne to him across the water, for the sharp firm swerve into a side-canal, a short cut to the palace. He had no gondola of his own; it was his habit never to take one; and he humbly—as in Venice it *is* humble—walked away, though not without having for some time longer stood as if fixed where the guest of the palace had left him. It was strange enough, but he found himself as never yet, and as he couldn't have

1. A gondola's canopied passengers' seat.

reckoned, in presence of the truth that was the truest about Milly. He couldn't have reckoned on the force of the difference instantly made—for it was all in the air as he heard Pasquale's cry and saw the boat disappear—by the mere visibility, on the spot, of the personage summoned to her aid. He hadn't only never been near the facts of her condition—which counted so as a blessing for him; he hadn't only, with all the world, hovered outside an impenetrable ring fence, within which there reigned a kind of expensive vagueness made up of smiles and silences and beautiful fictions and priceless arrangements, all strained to breaking; but he had also, with every one else, as he now felt, actively fostered suppressions which were in the direct interest of every one's good manner, every one's pity, every one's really quite generous ideal. It was a conspiracy of silence, as the *cliché* went, to which no one had made an exception, the great smudge of mortality across the picture, the shadow of pain and horror, finding in no quarter a surface of spirit or of speech that consented to reflect it. "The mere æsthetic instinct of mankind—!" our young man had more than once, in the connexion, said to himself; letting the rest of the proposition drop, but touching again thus sufficiently on the outrage even to taste involved in one's having to *see*. So then it had been—a general conscious fool's paradise, from which the specified had been chased like a dangerous animal. What therefore had at present befallen was that the specified, standing all the while at the gate, had now crossed the threshold as in Sir Luke Strett's person and quite on such a scale as to fill out the whole precinct. Densher's nerves, absolutely his heart-beats too, had measured the change before he on this occasion moved away.

The facts of physical suffering, of incurable pain, of the chance grimly narrowed, had been made, at a stroke, intense, and this was to be the way he was now to feel them. The clearance of the air, in short, making vision not only possible but inevitable, the one thing left to be thankful for was the breadth of Sir Luke's shoulders, which, should one be able to keep in line with them, might in some degree interpose. It was, however, far from plain to Densher for the first day or two that he was again to see his distinguished friend at all. That he couldn't, on any basis actually serving, return to the palace—this was as solid to him, every whit, as the other feature of his case, the fact of the publicity attaching to his proscription through his not having taken himself off. He had been seen often enough in the Leporelli gondola. As, accordingly, he was not on any presumption destined to meet Sir Luke about the town, where the latter would have neither time nor taste to lounge, nothing more would occur between them unless the great man should surprisingly wait upon him. His doing that, Densher further reflected, wouldn't even simply depend on Mrs. Stringham's having decided to—as they might say—turn him on. It would depend as well—for there would be practically some difference to her—on her actually attempting it; and it would depend above all on what Sir Luke would make of such an overture. Densher had for that matter his own view of the amount, to say nothing of the particular sort, of response it might expect from him. He had his own view of the ability of such a personage even to understand such an appeal. To what extent could he be prepared, and what importance in fine could he attach? Densher asked himself these questions, in truth, to put his own position at the worst. He should miss the great man completely unless the great man should come to see him, and the great man could only come to see him for a purpose unsupposable. Therefore he wouldn't come at all, and consequently there was nothing to hope.

It wasn't in the least that Densher invoked this violence to all probability; but it pressed on him that there were few possible diversions he could afford now to miss. Nothing in his predicament was so odd as that, incontestably afraid of himself, he was not afraid of Sir Luke. He had an impression, which he clung to, based on a previous taste of the visitor's company, that *he* would somehow let him off. The truth about Milly perched on his shoulders and sounded in his tread, became by the fact of his presence the name and the form, for the time, of everything in the place; but it didn't, for the difference, sit in his face, the face so squarely and easily turned to Densher at the earlier season. His presence on the first occasion, not as the result of a summons, but as a friendly whim of his own, had had quite another value; and though our young man could scarce regard that value as recoverable he yet reached out in imagination to a renewal of the old contact. He didn't propose, as he privately and forcibly phrased the matter, to be a hog; but there was something he after all did want for himself. It was something—this stuck to him—that Sir Luke would have had for him if it hadn't been impossible. These were his worst days, the two or three; those on which even the sense of the tension at the palace didn't much help him not to feel that his destiny made but light of him. He had never been, as he judged it, so down. In mean conditions, without books, without society, almost without money, he had nothing to do but to wait. His main support really was his original idea, which didn't leave him, of waiting for the deepest depth his predicament could sink him to. Fate would invent, if he but gave it time, some refinement of the horrible. It was just inventing meanwhile this suppression of Sir Luke. When the third day came without a sign he knew what to think. He had given Mrs. Stringham during her call on him no such answer as would have armed her faith, and the ultimatum she had described as ready for him when *he* should be ready was therefore—if on no other ground than her want of this power to answer for him—not to be presented. The presentation, heaven knew, was not what he desired.

That was not, either, we hasten to declare—as Densher then soon enough saw—the idea with which Sir Luke finally stood before him again. For stand before him again he finally did; just when our friend had gloomily embraced the belief that the limit of his power to absent himself from London obligations would have been reached. Four or five days, exclusive of journeys, represented the largest supposable sacrifice—to a head not crowned—on the part of one of the highest medical lights in the world; so that really when the personage in question, following up a tinkle of the bell, solidly rose in the doorway, it was to impose on Densher a vision that for the instant cut like a knife. It spoke, the fact, and in a single dreadful word, of the magnitude—he shrank from calling it anything else—of Milly's case. The great man had not gone then, and an immense surrender to her immense need was so expressed in it that some effect, some help, some hope, were flagrantly part of the expression. It was for Densher, with his reaction from disappointment, as if he were conscious of ten things at once—the foremost being that just conceivably, since Sir Luke *was* still there, she had been saved. Close upon its heels, however, and quite as sharply, came the sense that the crisis—plainly even now to be prolonged for him—was to have none of that sound simplicity. Not only had his visitor not dropped in to gossip about Milly, he hadn't dropped in to mention her at all; he had dropped in fairly to show that during the brief remainder of his stay, the end of which was now in sight, as little as possible of that was to be looked for. The demonstration, such as it was, was in the key of their previous acquaintance, and it was their previous acquaintance that had made him come. He was not to stop longer than the Saturday next at hand, but there were things of interest he should like to see again meanwhile. It was for these things of interest, for Venice and the opportunity of Venice, for a prowl or two, as he called it, and a turn about, that he had looked his young man up—producing on the latter's part, as soon as the case had, with the lapse of a further twenty-four hours, so defined itself, the most incongruous, yet most beneficent revulsion. Nothing could in fact have been more monstrous on the surface—and Densher was well aware of it—than the relief he found during this short period in the tacit drop of all reference to the palace, in neither hearing news nor asking for it. That was what had come out for him, on his visitor's entrance, even in the very seconds of suspense that were connecting the fact also directly and intensely with Milly's state. He had come to say he had saved her—he had come, as from Mrs. Stringham, to say how she might *be* saved—he had come, in spite of Mrs. Stringham, to say she was lost: the distinct throbs of hope, of fear, simultaneous for all their distinctness, merged their identity in a bound of the heart just as immediate and which remained after they had passed. It simply did wonders for him—this was the truth—that Sir Luke was, as he would have said, quiet.

The result of it was the oddest consciousness as of a blest calm after a storm. He had been trying for weeks, as we know, to keep superlatively still, and trying it largely in solitude and silence; but he looked back on it now as on the heat of fever. The real, the right stillness was this particular form of society. They walked together and they talked, looked up pictures again and recovered impressions —Sir Luke knew just what he wanted; haunted a little the dealers in old wares; sat down at Florian's for rest and mild drinks; blessed above all the grand weather, a bath of warm air, a pageant of autumn light. Once or twice while they rested the great man closed his eyes—keeping them so for some minutes while his companion, the more easily watching his face for it, made private reflexions on the subject of lost sleep. He had been up at night with her—he in person, for hours; but this was all he showed of it and was apparently to remain his nearest approach to an allusion. The extraordinary thing was that Densher could take it in perfectly as evidence, could turn cold at the image looking out of it; and yet that he could at the same time not intermit a throb of his response to accepted liberation.The liberation was an experience that held its own, and he continued to know why, in spite of his deserts, in spite of his folly, in spite of everything, he had so fondly hoped for it. He had hoped for it, had sat in his room there waiting for it, because he had thus divined in it, should it come, some power to let him off. He was *being* let off; dealt with in the only way that didn't aggravate his responsibility. The beauty was also that this wasn't on system or on any basis of intimate knowledge; it was just by being a man of the world and by knowing life, by feeling the real, that Sir Luke did him good. There had been in all the case too many women. A man's sense of it, another man's, changed the air; and he wondered what man, had he chosen, would have been more to his purpose than this one. He was large and easy—that was the benediction; he knew what mattered and what didn't; he distinguished between the essence and the shell, the just grounds and the unjust for fussing. One was thus—if one were concerned with him or exposed to him at all—in his hands for whatever he should do, and not much less affected by his mercy than one might have been by his rigour. The grand thing—it did come to that—was the way he carried off, as one might fairly call it, the business of making odd things natural. Nothing, if they hadn't taken it so, could have exceeded the unexplained oddity, between them, of Densher's now complete detachment from the poor ladies at the palace; nothing could have exceeded the no less marked anomaly of the great man's own abstentions of speech. He made, as he had done when they met at the station, nothing whatever of anything; and the effect of it, Densher would have said, was a relation with him quite resembling that of doctor and patient. One took the cue from him as one might have taken a dose—except that the cue was pleasant in the taking.

That was why one could leave it to his tacit discretion, why for the three or four days Densher again and again did so leave it; merely wondering a little, at the most, on the eve of Saturday, the announced term of the episode. Waiting once more on this latter occasion, the Saturday morning, for Sir Luke's reappearance at the station, our friend had to recognise the drop of his own borrowed ease, the result, naturally enough, of the prospect of losing a support. The difficulty was that, on such lines as had served them, the support was Sir Luke's personal presence. Would he go without leaving some substitute for that?—and without breaking, either, his silence in respect to his errand? Densher was in still deeper ignorance than at the hour of his call, and what was truly prodigious at so supreme a moment was that—as had immediately to appear—no gleam of light on what he had been living with for a week found its way out of him. What he had been doing was proof of a huge interest as well as of a huge fee; yet when the Leporelli gondola again, and somewhat tardily, approached, his companion, watching from the water-steps, studied his fine closed face as much as ever in vain. It was like a lesson, from the highest authority, on the subject of the relevant, so that its blankness affected Densher of a sudden almost as a cruelty, feeling it quite awfully compatible, as he did, with Milly's having ceased to exist. And the suspense continued after they had passed together, as time was short, directly into the station, where Eugenio, in the field early, was mounting guard over the compartment he had secured. The strain, though probably lasting, at the carriage-door, but a couple of minutes, prolonged itself so for our poor gentleman's nerves that he involuntarily directed a long look at Eugenio, who met it, however, as only Eugenio could. Sir Luke's attention was given for the time to the right bestowal of his numerous effects, about which he was particular, and Densher fairly found himself, so far as silence could go, questioning the representative of the palace. It didn't humiliate him now; it didn't humiliate him even to feel that that personage exactly knew how little he satisfied him. Eugenio resembled to that extent Sir Luke—

to the extent of the extraordinary things with which his facial habit was compatible. By the time, however, that Densher had taken from it all its possessor intended Sir Luke was free and with a hand out for farewell. He offered the hand at first without speech; only on meeting his eyes could our young man see that they had never yet so completely looked at him. It was never, with Sir Luke, that they looked harder at one time than at another; but they looked longer, and this, even a shade of it, might mean on his part everything. It meant, Densher for ten seconds believed, that Milly Theale was dead; so that the word at last spoken made him start.

"I shall come back."

"Then she's better?"

"I shall come back within the month," Sir Luke repeated without heeding the question. He had dropped Densher's hand, but he held him otherwise still. "I bring you a message from Miss Theale," he said as if they hadn't spoken of her. "I'm commissioned to ask you from her to go and see her."

Densher's rebound from his supposition had a violence that his stare betrayed. "*She* asks me?"

Sir Luke had got into the carriage, the door of which the guard had closed; but he spoke again as he stood at the window, bending a little but not leaning out. "She told me she'd like it, and I promised that, as I expected to find you here, I'd let you know."

Densher, on the platform, took it from him, but what he took brought the blood into his face quite as what he had had to take from Mrs. Stringham. And he was also bewildered. "Then she can receive—?"

"She can receive you."

"And you're coming back—?"

"Oh, because I must. She's not to move. She's to stay. I come to her."

"I see, I see," said Densher, who indeed did see—saw the sense of his friend's words and saw beyond it as well. What Mrs. Stringham had announced, and what he had yet expected not to have to face, *had* then come. Sir Luke had kept it for the last, but there it was, and the colourless compact form it was now taking—the tone of one man of the world to another, who, after what had happened, would understand—was but the characteristic manner of his appeal. Densher was to understand remarkably much; and the great thing certainly was to show that he did. "I'm particularly obliged. I'll go to-day." He brought that out, but in his pause, while they continued to look at each other, the train had slowly creaked into motion. There was time but for one more word, and the young man chose it, out of twenty, with intense concentration. "Then she's better?"

Sir Luke's face was wonderful. "Yes, she's better." And he kept it at the window while the train receded, holding him with it still. It was to be his nearest approach to the utter reference they had hitherto so successfully avoided. If it stood for everything, never had a face had to stand for more. So Densher, held after the train had gone, sharply reflected; so he reflected, asking himself into what abyss it pushed him, even while conscious of retreating under the maintained observation of Eugenio.

Book Tenth

I

"Then it has been—what do you say? a whole fortnight?—without your making a sign?"

Kate put that to him distinctly, in the December dusk of Lancaster Gate and on the matter of the time he had been back; but he saw with it straightway that she was as admirably true as ever to her instinct—which was a system as well—of not admitting the possibility between them of small resentments, of trifles to trip up their general trust. That by itself, the renewed beauty of it, would at this fresh sight of her have stirred him to his depths if something else, something no less vivid but quite separate, hadn't stirred him still more. It was in seeing her that he felt what their interruption had been, and that they met across it even as persons whose adventures, on either side, in time and space, of the nature of perils and exiles, had had a peculiar strangeness. He wondered if he were as different for her as she herself had immediately appeared: which was but his way indeed of taking in, with his thrill, that—even going by the mere first look—she had never been so handsome. That fact bloomed for him, in the firelight and lamplight that glowed their welcome through the London fog, as the flower of her difference; just as her difference itself—part of which was her striking him as older in a degree for which no mere couple of months could account—was the fruit of their intimate relation. If she was different it was because they had chosen together that she should be, and she might now, as a proof of their wisdom, their success, of the reality of what had happened—of what in fact, for the spirit of each, was still happening—been showing it to him for pride. His having returned and yet kept, for numbered days, so still, had been, he was quite aware, the first point he should have to tackle; with which consciousness indeed he had made a clean breast of it in finally addressing Mrs. Lowder a note that had led to his present visit. He had written to Aunt Maud as the finer way; and it would doubtless have been to be noted that he needed no effort not to write to Kate. Venice was three weeks behind him—he had come up slowly;

but it was still as if even in London he must conform to her law. That was exactly how he was able, with his faith in her steadiness, to appeal to her feeling for the situation and explain his stretched delicacy. He had come to tell her everything, so far as occasion would serve them; and if nothing was more distinct than that his slow journey, his waits, his delay to reopen communication had kept pace with this resolve, so the inconsequence was doubtless at bottom but one of the elements of intensity. He was gathering everything up, everything he should tell her. That took time, and the proof was that, as he felt on the spot, he couldn't have brought it all with him before this afternoon. He *had* brought it, to the last syllable, and, out of the quantity it wouldn't be hard—as he in fact found—to produce, for Kate's understanding, his first reason.

"A fortnight, yes—it was a fortnight Friday; but I've only been keeping in, you see, with our wonderful system." He was so easily justified as that this of itself plainly enough prevented her saying she didn't see. Their wonderful system was accordingly still vivid for her; and such a gage of its equal vividness for himself was precisely what she must have asked. He hadn't even to dot his i's beyond the remark that on the very face of it, she would remember, their wonderful system attached no premium to rapidities of transition. "I couldn't quite—don't you know?—take my rebound with a rush; and I suppose I've been instinctively hanging off to minimise, for you as well as for myself, the appearances of rushing. There's a sort of fitness. But I knew you'd understand." It was presently as if she really understood so well that she almost appealed from his insistence—yet looking at him too, he was not unconscious, as if this mastery of fitnesses was a strong sign for her of what she had done to him. He might have struck her as expert for contingencies in the very degree of her having in Venice struck *him* as expert. He smiled over his plea for a renewal with stages and steps, a thing shaded, as they might say, and graduated; though—finely as she must respond—she met the smile but as she had met his entrance five minutes before. Her soft gravity at that moment—which was yet not solemnity, but the look of a consciousness charged with life to the brim and wishing not to overflow—had not qualified her welcome; what had done this being much more the presence in the room, for a couple of minutes, of the footman who had introduced him and who had been interrupted in preparing the tea-table.

Mrs. Lowder's reply to Densher's note had been to appoint the tea-hour, five o'clock on Sunday, for his seeing them. Kate had thereafter wired him, without a signature, "Come on Sunday *before* tea—about a quarter of an hour, which will help us"; and he had arrived therefore scrupulously at twenty minutes to five. Kate was alone in the room and hadn't delayed to tell him that Aunt Maud, as she had happily gathered, was to be, for the interval—not long but precious—engaged with an old servant, retired and pensioned, who had been paying her a visit and who was within the hour to depart again for the suburbs. They were to have the scrap of time, after the withdrawal of the footman, to themselves, and there was a moment when, in spite of their wonderful system, in spite of the proscription of rushes and the propriety of shades, it proclaimed itself indeed precious. And all without prejudice—that was what kept it noble—to Kate's high sobriety and her beautiful self-command. If he had his discretion she had her perfect manner, which was *her* decorum. Mrs. Stringham, he had, to finish with the question of his delay, furthermore observed, Mrs. Stringham would have written to Mrs. Lowder of his having quitted the place; so that it wasn't as if he were hoping to cheat them. They'd know he was no longer there.

"Yes, we've known it."

"And you continue to hear?"

"From Mrs. Stringham? Certainly. By which I mean Aunt Maud does."

"Then you've recent news?"

Her face showed a wonder. "Up to within a day or two I believe. But haven't *you?*"

"No—I've heard nothing." And it was now that he felt how much he had to tell her. "I don't get letters. But I've been sure Mrs. Lowder does." With which he added: "Then of course you know." He waited as if she would show what she knew; but she only showed in silence the dawn of a surprise that she couldn't control. There was nothing but for him to ask what he wanted. "Is Miss Theale alive?"

Kate's look at this was large. "Don't you *know?*"

"How should I, my dear—in the absence of everything?" And he himself stared as for light. "She's dead?" Then as with her eyes on him she slowly shook her head he uttered a strange "Not yet?"

It came out in Kate's face that there were several questions on her lips, but the one she presently put was: "Is it very terrible?"

"The manner of her so consciously and helplessly dying?" He had to think a moment. "Well, yes—since you ask me: very terrible to *me*—so far as, before I came away, I had any sight of it. But I don't think," he went on, "that—though I'll try—I *can* quite tell you what it was, what it is, for me. That's why I probably just sounded to you," he explained, "as if I hoped it might be over."

She gave him her quietest attention, but he by this time saw that, so far as telling her all was concerned, she would be divided between the wish and the reluctance to hear it; between the curiosity that, not unnaturally, would consume her and the opposing scruple of a respect for misfortune. The more she studied him too—and he had never so felt her closely attached to his face—the more the choice of an attitude would become impossible to her. There would simply be a feeling uppermost, and the feeling wouldn't be eagerness. This perception grew in him fast, and he even, with his imagination, had for a moment the quick forecast of her possibly breaking out at him, should he go too far, with a wonderful: "What horrors are you telling me?" It would have the sound—wouldn't it be open to him fairly to bring that out himself?—of a repudiation, for pity and almost for shame, of everything that in Venice had passed between them. Not that she would confess to any return upon herself; not that she would let compunction or horror give her away; but it was in the air for him—yes—that she wouldn't want details, that she positively wouldn't take them, and that, if he would generously understand it from her, she would prefer to keep him down. Nothing, however, was more definite for him than that at the same time he must remain down but so far as it suited him. Something rose strong within him against his not being free with her. She had been free enough about it all, three months before, with *him*. That was what she was at present only in the sense of treating him handsomely. "I can believe," she said with perfect consideration, "how dreadful for you much of it must have been."

He didn't however take this up; there were things about which he wished first to be clear. "There's no other possibility, by what you now know? I mean for her life." And he had just to insist—she would say as little as she could. "She *is* dying?"

"She's dying."

It was strange to him, in the matter of Milly, that Lancaster Gate could make him any surer; yet what in the world, in the matter of Milly, wasn't strange? Nothing was so much so as his own behaviour—his present as well as his past. He could but do as he must. "Has Sir Luke Strett," he asked, "gone back to her?"

"I believe he's there now."

"Then," said Densher, "it's the end."

She took it in silence for whatever he deemed it to be; but she spoke otherwise after a minute. "You won't know, unless you've perhaps seen him yourself, that Aunt Maud has been to him."

"Oh!" Densher exclaimed, with nothing to add to it.

"For real news," Kate herself after an instant added.

"She hasn't thought Mrs. Stringham's real?"

"It's perhaps only I who haven't. It was on Aunt Maud's trying again three days ago to see him that she heard at his house of his having gone. He had started I believe some days before."

"And won't then by this time be back?"

Kate shook her head. "She sent yesterday to know."

"He won't leave her then"—Densher had turned it over—"while she lives. He'll stay to the end. He's magnificent."

"I think *she* is," said Kate.

It had made them again look at each other long; and what it drew from him rather oddly was: "Oh you don't know!"

"Well, she's after all my friend."

It was somehow, with her handsome demur, the answer he had least expected of her; and it fanned with its breath, for a brief instant, his old sense of her variety. "I see. You would have been sure of it. You *were* sure of it."

"Of course I was sure of it."

And a pause again, with this, fell upon them; which Densher, however, presently broke. "If you don't think Mrs. Stringham's news 'real' what do you think of Lord Mark's?"

She didn't think anything. "Lord Mark's?"

"You haven't seen him?"

"Not since he saw her."

"You've known then of his seeing her?"

"Certainly. From Mrs. Stringham."

"And have you known," Densher went on, "the rest?"

Kate wondered. "What rest?"

"Why everything. It was his visit that she couldn't stand—it was what then took place that simply killed her."

"Oh!" Kate seriously breathed. But she had turned pale, and he saw that, whatever her degree of ignorance of these connexions, it wasn't put on. "Mrs. Stringham hasn't said *that*."

He observed none the less that she didn't ask what had then taken place; and he went on with his contribution to her knowledge. "The way it affected her was that it made her give up. She has given up beyond all power to care again, and that's why she's dying."

"Oh!" Kate once more slowly sighed, but with a vagueness that made him pursue.

"One can see now that she was living by will—which was very much what you originally told me of her."

"I remember. That was it."

"Well then her will, at a given moment, broke down, and the collapse was determined by that fellow's dastardly stroke. He told her, the scoundrel, that you and I are secretly engaged."

Kate gave a quick glare. "But he doesn't know it!"

"That doesn't matter. *She* did by the time he had left her. Besides," Densher added, "he does know it. When," he continued, "did you last see him?"

But she was lost now in the picture before her. "*That* was what made her worse?"

He watched her take it in—it so added to her sombre beauty. Then he spoke as Mrs. Stringham had spoken. "She turned her face to the wall."

"Poor Milly!" said Kate.

Slight as it was, her beauty somehow gave it style; so that he continued consistently: "She learned it, you see, too soon—since of course one's idea had been that she might never even learn it at all. And she *had* felt sure—through everything we had done—of there not being between us, so far at least as you were concerned, anything she need regard as a warning."

She took another moment for thought. "It wasn't through anything *you* did—whatever that may have been—that she gained her certainty. It was by the conviction she got from me."

"Oh it's very handsome," Densher said, "for you to take your share!"

"Do you suppose," Kate asked, "that I think of denying it?"

Her look and her tone made him for the instant regret his comment, which indeed had been the first that rose to his lips as an effect absolutely of what they would have called between them her straightness. Her straightness, visibly, was all his own loyalty could ask. Still, that was comparatively beside the mark. "Of course I don't suppose anything but that we're together in our recognitions, our responsibilities—whatever we choose to call them. It isn't a question for us of apportioning shares or distinguishing invidiously among such impressions as it was our idea to give."

"It wasn't *your* idea to give impressions," said Kate.

He met this with a smile that he himself felt, in its strained character, as queer. "Don't go into that!"

It was perhaps not as going into it that she had another idea—an idea born, she showed, of the vision he had just evoked. "Wouldn't it have been possible then to deny the truth of the information? I mean of Lord Mark's."

Densher wondered. "Possible for whom?"

"Why for you."

"To tell her he lied?"

"To tell her he's mistaken."

Densher stared—he was stupefied; the "possible" thus glanced at by Kate being exactly the alternative he had had to face in Venice and to put utterly away from him. Nothing was stranger than such a difference in their view of it. "And to lie myself, you mean, to do it? We *are*, my dear child," he said, "I suppose, still engaged."

"Of course we're still engaged. But to save her life—!"

He took in for a little the way she talked of it. Of course, it was to be remembered, she had always simplified, and it brought back his sense of the degree in which, to her energy as compared with his own, many things were easy; the very sense that so often before had moved him to admiration. "Well, if you must know—and I want you to be clear about it—I didn't even seriously think of a denial to her face. The question of it—*as* possibly saving her—was put to me definitely enough; but to turn it over was only to dismiss it. Besides," he added, "it wouldn't have done any good."

"You mean she would have had no faith in your correction?" She had spoken with a promptitude that affected him of a sudden as almost glib; but he himself paused with the overweight of all he meant, and she meanwhile went on. "Did you try?"

"I hadn't even a chance."

Kate maintained her wonderful manner, the manner of at once having it all before her and yet keeping it all at its distance. "She wouldn't see you?"

"Not after your friend had been with her."

She hesitated. "Couldn't you write?"

It made him also think, but with a difference. "She had turned her face to the wall."

This again for a moment hushed her, and they were both too grave now for parenthetic pity. But her interest came out for at least the minimum of light. "She refused even to let you speak to her?"

"My dear girl," Densher returned, "she was miserably, prohibitively ill."

"Well, that was what she had been before."

"And it didn't prevent? No," Densher admitted, "it didn't; and I don't pretend that she's not magnificent."

"She's prodigious," said Kate Croy.

He looked at her a moment. "So are you, my dear. But that's how it is," he wound up; "and there we are."

His idea had been in advance that she would perhaps sound him much more deeply, asking him above all two or three specific things. He had fairly fancied her even wanting to know and trying to find out how far, as the odious phrase was, he and Milly had gone, and how near, by the same token, they had come. He had asked himself if he were prepared to hear her do that, and had had to take for answer that he was prepared of course for everything. Wasn't he prepared for her ascertaining if her two or three prophecies had found time to be made true? He had fairly believed himself ready to say whether or no the overture on Milly's part promised according to the boldest of them had taken place. But what was in fact blessedly coming to him was that so far as such things were concerned his readiness wouldn't be taxed. Kate's pressure on the question of what had taken place remained so admirably general that even her present enquiry kept itself free of sharpness. "So then that after Lord Mark's interference you never again met?"

It was what he had been all the while coming to. "No; we met once—so far as it could be called a meeting. I had stayed—I didn't come away."

"That," said Kate, "was no more than decent."

"Precisely"—he felt himself wonderful; "and I wanted to be no less. She sent for me, I went to her, and that night I left Venice."

His companion waited. "Wouldn't *that* then have been your chance?"

"To refute Lord Mark's story? No, not even if before her there I had wanted to. What did it signify either? She was dying."

"Well," Kate in a manner persisted, "why not just *because* she was dying?" She had however all her discretion. "But of course I know that seeing her you could judge."

"Of course seeing her I could judge. And I did see her! If I had denied you moreover," Densher said with his eyes on her, "I'd have stuck to it."

"I mean that to convince *you* I'd have insisted or somehow to convince her you'd have insisted or somehow proved—?"

"I mean that to convince *you* I'd have insisted or somehow proved—!"

Kate looked for her moment at a loss. "To convince 'me'?"

"I wouldn't have made my denial, in such conditions, only to take it back afterwards."

With this quickly light came for her, and with it also her colour flamed. "Oh you'd have broken with me to make your denial a truth? You'd have 'chucked' me"—she embraced it perfectly—"to save your conscience?"

"I couldn't have done anything else," said Merton Densher. "So you see how right I was not to commit myself, and how little I could dream of it. If it ever again appears to you that I *might* have done so, remember what I say."

Kate again considered, but not with the effect at once to which he pointed. "You've fallen in love with her."

"Well then say so—with a dying woman. Why need you mind and what does it matter?"

It came from him, the question, straight out of the intensity of relation and the face-to-face necessity into which, from the first, from his entering the room, they had found themselves thrown; but it gave them their most extraordinary moment. "Wait till she *is* dead! Mrs. Stringham," Kate added, "is to telegraph." After which, in a tone still different, "For what then," she asked, "did Milly send for you?"

"It was what I tried to make out before I went. I must tell you moreover that I had no doubt of its really being to give me, as you say, a chance. She believed, I suppose, that I *might* deny; and what, to my own mind, was before me in going to her was the certainty that she'd put me to my test. She wanted from my own lips—so I saw it—the truth. But I was with her for twenty minutes, and she never asked me for it."

"She never wanted the truth"—Kate had a high headshake. "She wanted *you*. She would have taken from you what you could give her and been glad of it, even if she had known it false. You might have lied to her from pity, and she have seen you and felt you lie, and yet—since it was all for tenderness—she would have thanked you and blessed you and clung to you but the more. For that was your strength, my dear man—that she loves you with passion."

"Oh my 'strength'!" Densher coldly murmured.

"Otherwise, since she had sent for you, what was it to ask of you?" And then—quite without irony—as he waited a moment to say: "Was it just once more to look at you?"

"She had nothing to ask of me—nothing, that is, but not to stay any longer. She did to that extent want to see me. She had supposed at first—after he had been with her—that I had seen the propriety of taking myself off. Then since I hadn't—seeing my propriety as I did in another way—she found, days later, that I was still there. This," said Densher, "affected her."

"Of course it affected her."

Again she struck him, for all her dignity, as glib. "If it was somehow for *her* I was still staying, she wished that to end, she wished me to know how little there was need of it. And as a manner of farewell she wished herself to tell me so."

"And she did tell you so?"

"Face-to-face, yes. Personally, as she desired."

"And as *you* of course did."

"No, Kate," he returned with all their mutual consideration; "not as I did. I hadn't desired it in the least."

"You only went to oblige her?"

"To oblige her. And of course also to oblige you."

"Oh for myself certainly I'm glad."

" 'Glad'?"—he echoed vaguely the way it rang out.

"I mean you did quite the right thing. You did it especially in having stayed. But that was all?" Kate went on. "That you mustn't wait?"

"That was really all—and in perfect kindness."

"Ah kindness naturally: from the moment she asked of you such a—well, such an effort. That you mustn't wait—that was the point," Kate added—"to see her die."

"That was the point, my dear," Densher said.

"And it took twenty minutes to make it?"

He thought a little. "I didn't time it to a second. I paid her the visit—just like another."

"Like another person?"

"Like another visit."

"Oh!" said Kate. Which had apparently the effect of slightly arresting his speech—an arrest she took advantage of to continue; making with it indeed her nearest approach to an enquiry of the kind against which he had braced himself. "Did she receive you—in her condition—in her room?"

"Not she," said Merton Densher. "She received me just as usual: in that glorious great *salone*,[1] in the dress she always wears, from her inveterate corner of her sofa." And his face for the moment conveyed the scene, just as hers equally embraced it. "Do you remember what you originally said to me of her?"

"Ah I've said so many things."

"That she wouldn't smell of drugs, that she wouldn't taste of medicine. Well, she didn't."

"So that it was really almost happy?"

It took him a long time to answer, occupied as he partly was in feeling how nobody but Kate could have invested such a question with the tone that was perfectly right. She meanwhile, however, patiently waited. "I don't think I can attempt to say now what it was. Some day—perhaps. For it would be worth it for us."

"Some day—certainly." She seemed to record the promise. Yet she spoke again abruptly. "She'll recover."

"Well," said Densher, "you'll see."

She had the air an instant of trying to. "Did she show anything of her feeling? I mean," Kate explained, "of her feeling of having been misled."

She didn't press hard, surely; but he had just mentioned that he would have rather to glide. "She showed nothing but her beauty and her strength."

"Then," his companion asked, "what's the use of her strength?"

He seemed to look about for a use he could name; but he had soon given it up. "She must die, my dear, in her own extraordinary way."

"Naturally. But I don't see then what proof you have that she was ever alienated."

"I have the proof that she refused for days and days to see me."

"But she was ill."

"That hadn't prevented her—as you yourself a moment ago said —during the previous time. If it had been only illness it would have made no difference with her."

"She would still have received you?"

"She would still have received me."

"Oh well," said Kate, "if you know—!"

"Of course I know. I know moreover as well from Mrs. Stringham."

"And what does Mrs. Stringham know?"

"Everything."

1. Drawing room.

She looked at him longer. "Everything?"

"Everything."

"Because you've told her?"

"Because she has seen for herself. I've told her nothing. She's a person who does see."

Kate thought. "That's by her liking you too. She as well is prodigious. You see what interest in a man does. It does it all round. So you needn't be afraid."

"I'm not afraid," said Densher.

Kate moved from her place then, looking at the clock, which marked five. She gave her attention to the tea-table, where Aunt Maud's huge silver kettle, which had been exposed to its lamp and which she had not soon enough noticed, was hissing too hard. "Well, it's all most wonderful!" she exclaimed as she rather too profusely—a sign her friend noticed—ladled tea into the pot. He watched her a moment at this occupation, coming nearer the table while she put in the steaming water. "You'll have some?"

He hesitated. "Hadn't we better wait—?"

"For Aunt Maud?" She saw what he meant—the deprecation, by their old law, of betrayals of the intimate note. "Oh you needn't mind now. We've done it!"

"Humbugged her?"

"Squared her. You've pleased her."

Densher mechanically accepted his tea. He was thinking of something else, and his thought in a moment came out. "What a brute then I must be!"

"A brute—?"

"To have pleased so many people."

"Ah," said Kate with a gleam of gaiety, "you've done it to please *me*." But she was already, with her gleam, reverting a little. "What I don't understand is—won't you have any sugar?"

"Yes, please."

"What I don't understand," she went on when she had helped him, "is what it was that had occurred to bring her round again. If she gave you up for days and days, what brought her back to you?"

She asked the question with her own cup in her hand, but it found him ready enough in spite of his sense of the ironic oddity of their going into it over the tea-table. "It was Sir Luke Strett who brought her back. His visit, his presence there did it."

"He brought her back then to life."

"Well, to what I saw."

"And by interceding for you?"

"I don't think he interceded. I don't indeed know what he did."

Kate wondered. "Didn't he tell you?"

"I didn't ask him. I met him again, but we practically didn't speak of her."

Kate stared. "Then how do you know?"

"I see. I feel. I was with him again as I had been before—"

"Oh and you pleased him too? That was it?"

"He understood," said Densher.

"But understood what?"

He waited a moment. "That I had meant awfully well."

"Ah, and made *her* understand? I see," she went on as he said nothing. "But how did he convince her?"

Densher put down his cup and turned away. "You must ask Sir Luke."

He stood looking at the fire and there was a time without sound. "The great thing," Kate then resumed, "is that she's satisfied. Which," she continued, looking across at him, "is what I've worked for."

"Satisfied to die in the flower of her youth?"

"Well, at peace with you."

"Oh 'peace'!" he murmured with his eyes on the fire.

"The peace of having loved."

He raised his eyes to her. "Is *that* peace?"

"Of having *been* loved," she went on. "That is. Of having," she wound up, "realised her passion. She wanted nothing more. She has had *all* she wanted."

Lucid and always grave, she gave this out with a beautiful authority that he could for the time meet with no words. He could only again look at her, though with the sense in so doing that he made her more than he intended take his silence for assent. Quite indeed as if she did so take it she quitted the table and came to the fire. "You may think it hideous that I should now, that I should *yet*"—she made a point of the word—"pretend to draw conclusions. But we've not failed."

"Oh!" he only again murmured.

She was once more close to him, close as she had been the day she came to him in Venice, the quickly returning memory of which intensified and enriched the fact. He could practically deny in such conditions nothing that she said, and what she said was, with it, visibly, a fruit of that knowledge. "We've succeeded." She spoke with her eyes deep in his own. "She won't have loved you for nothing." It made him wince, but she insisted. "And you won't have loved *me*."

II

He was to remain for several days under the deep impression of this inclusive passage, so luckily prolonged from moment to moment, but interrupted at its climax, as may be said, by the entrance of Aunt Maud, who found them standing together near the fire. The bearings of the colloquy, however, sharp as they were,

were less sharp to his intelligence, strangely enough, than those of a talk with Mrs. Lowder alone for which she soon gave him—or for which perhaps rather Kate gave him—full occasion. What had happened on her at last joining them was to conduce, he could immediately see, to her desiring to have him to herself. Kate and he, no doubt, at the opening of the door, had fallen apart with a certain suddenness, so that she had turned her hard fine eyes from one to the other; but the effect of this lost itself, to his mind, the next minute, in the effect of his companion's rare alertness. She instantly spoke to her aunt of what had first been uppermost for herself, inviting her thereby intimately to join them, and doing it the more happily also, no doubt, because the fact she resentfully named gave her ample support. "Had you quite understood, my dear, that it's full three weeks—?" And she effaced herself as if to leave Mrs. Lowder to deal from her own point of view with this extravagance. Densher of course straightway noted that his cue for the protection of Kate was to make, no less, all of it he could; and their tracks, as he might have said, were fairly covered by the time their hostess had taken afresh, on his renewed admission, the measure of his scant eagerness. Kate had moved away as if no great showing were needed for her personal situation to be seen as delicate. She had been entertaining their visitor on her aunt's behalf—a visitor she had been at one time suspected of favouring too much and who had now come back to them as the stricken suitor of another person. It wasn't that the fate of the other person, her exquisite friend, didn't, in its tragic turn, also concern herself: it was only that her acceptance of Mr. Densher as a source of information could scarcely help having an awkwardness. She invented the awkwardness under Densher's eyes, and he marvelled on his side at the instant creation. It served her as the fine cloud that hangs about a goddess in an epic, and the young man was but vaguely to know at what point of the rest of his visit she had, for consideration, melted into it and out of sight.

He was taken up promptly with another matter—the truth of the remarkable difference, neither more nor less, that the events of Venice had introduced into his relation with Aunt Maud and that these weeks of their separation had caused quite richly to ripen for him. She had not sat down to her tea-table before he felt himself on terms with her that were absolutely new, nor could she press on him a second cup without her seeming herself, and quite wittingly, so to define and establish them. She regretted, but she quite understood, that what was taking place had obliged him to hang off; they had—after hearing of him from poor Susan as gone—been hoping for an early sight of him; they would have been interested, naturally, in his arriving straight from the scene. Yet she needed no reminder that the scene precisely—by which she meant the tragedy that had so detained and absorbed him, the memory, the shadow, the sorrow of it—was what marked him for unsociability. She thus presented him to himself, as it were, in the guise in which she had now adopted him, and it was the element of truth in the character that he found himself, for his own part, adopting. She treated him as blighted and ravaged, as frustrate and already bereft; and for him to feel that this opened for him a new chapter of frankness with her he scarce had also to perceive how it smoothed his approaches to Kate. It made the latter accessible as she hadn't yet begun to be; it set up for him at Lancaster Gate an association positively hostile to any other legend. It was quickly vivid to him that, were he minded, he could "work" this association: he had but to use the house freely for his prescribed attitude and he need hardly ever be out of it. Stranger than anything moreover was to be the way that by the end of a week he stood convicted to his own sense of a surrender to Mrs. Lowder's view. He had somehow met it at a point that had brought him on—brought him on a distance that he couldn't again retrace. He had private hours of wondering what had become of his sincerity; he had others of simply reflecting that he had it all in use. His only want of candour was Aunt Maud's wealth of sentiment. She was hugely sentimental, and the worst he did was to take it from her. He wasn't so himself—everything was too real; but it was none the less not false that he *had* been through a mill.

It was in particular not false for instance that when she had said to him, on the Sunday, almost cosily, from her sofa behind the tea, "I want you not to doubt, you poor dear, that I'm *with* you to the end!" his meeting her halfway had been the only course open to him. She was with him to the end—or she might be—in a way Kate wasn't; and even if it literally made her society meanwhile more soothing he must just brush away the question of why it shouldn't. Was he professing to her in any degree the possession of an aftersense that wasn't real? How in the world *could* he, when his aftersense, day by day, was his greatest reality? Such only was at bottom what there was between them, and two or three times over it made the hour pass. These were occasions—two and a scrap—on which he had come and gone without mention of Kate. Now that almost as never yet he had licence to ask for her, the queer turn of their affair made it a false note. It was another queer turn that when he talked with Aunt Maud about Milly nothing else seemed to come up. He called upon her almost avowedly for that purpose, and it was the queerest turn of all that the state of his nerves should require it. He liked her better; he was really behaving, he had occasion to say to himself, as if he liked her best. The thing was absolutely that she met *him* halfway. Nothing could have been broader than her vision, than her loquacity, than her sympathy. It appeared to gratify, to satisfy her to see him as he was; that too had its effect. It was all of course the last thing that could have seemed on the cards, a change by which he was completely *free* with this lady; and it wouldn't indeed have come about if—for another monstrosity—he hadn't ceased to be free with Kate. Thus it was that on the third time in especial of being alone with her he found himself uttering to the elder woman what had been impossible of utterance to the younger. Mrs. Lowder gave him in fact, on the ground of what he must keep from her, but one uneasy moment. That was when, on the first Sunday, after Kate had suppressed herself, she referred to her regret that he mightn't have stayed to the end. He found his reason difficult to give her, but she came after all to his help.

"You simply couldn't stand it?"

"I simply couldn't stand it. Besides you see—!" But he paused.

"Besides what?" He had been going to say more—then he saw dangers; luckily however she had again assisted him. "Besides—oh I know!—men haven't, in many relations, the courage of women."

"They haven't the courage of women."

"Kate or I would have stayed," she declared—"if we hadn't come away for the special reason that you so frankly appreciated."

Densher had said nothing about his appreciation: hadn't his behaviour since the hour itself sufficiently shown it? But he presently said—he couldn't help going so far: "I don't doubt, certainly, that Miss Croy would have stayed." And he saw again into the bargain what a marvel was Susan Shepherd. She did nothing but protect him—she had done nothing but keep it up. In copious communication with the friend of her youth she had yet, it was plain, favoured this lady with nothing that compromised him. Milly's act of renouncement she had described but as a change for the worse; she had mentioned Lord Mark's descent, as even without her it might be known, so that she mustn't appear to conceal it; but she had suppressed explanations and connexions, and indeed, for all he knew, blessed Puritan soul, had invented commendable fictions. Thus it was absolutely that he *was* at his ease. Thus it was that, shaking for ever, in the unrest that didn't drop, his crossed leg, he leaned back in deep yellow satin chairs and took such comfort as came. She asked, it was true, Aunt Maud, questions that Kate hadn't; but this was just the difference, that from her he positively liked them. He had taken with himself on leaving Venice the resolution to regard Milly as already dead to him—that being for his spirit the only thinkable way to pass the time of waiting. He had left her because it was what suited her, and it wasn't for him to go, as they said in America, behind this; which imposed on him but the sharper need to arrange himself with his interval. Suspense was the ugliest ache to him, and he would have nothing to do with it; the last thing he wished was to be unconscious of her—what he wished to ignore was her own consciousness, tortured, for all he knew, crucified by its pain. Knowingly to hang about in London while the pain went on—what would that do but make his days impossible? His scheme was accordingly to convince himself—and by some art about which he was vague—that the sense of waiting had passed. "What in fact," he restlessly reflected, "have I any further to do with it? Let me assume the thing actually over—as it at any moment may be—and I become good again for something at least to somebody. I'm good, as it is, for nothing to anybody, least of all to *her*." He consequently tried, so far as shutting his eyes and stalking grimly about was a trial; but his plan was carried out, it may well be guessed, neither with marked success nor with marked consistency. The days, whether lapsing or lingering, were a stiff reality; the suppression of anxiety was a thin idea; the taste of life itself was the taste of suspense. That he *was* waiting was in short at the bottom of everything; and it required no great sifting presently to feel that if he took so much more, as he called it, to Mrs. Lowder this was just for that reason.

She helped him to hold out, all the while that she was subtle enough—and he could see her divine it as what he wanted—not to insist on the actuality of their tension. His nearest approach to success was thus in being good for something to Aunt Maud, in default of any one better; her company eased his nerves even while they pretended together that they had seen their tragedy out. They spoke of the dying girl in the past tense; they said no worse of her than that she had *been* stupendous. On the other hand, however—and this was what wasn't for Densher pure peace—they insisted enough that stupendous was the word. It was the thing, this recognition, that kept him most quiet; he came to it with her repeatedly; talking about it against time and, in particular, we have noted, speaking of his supreme personal impression as he hadn't spoken to Kate. It was almost as if she herself enjoyed the perfection of the pathos; she sat there before the scene, as he couldn't help giving it out to her, very much as a stout citizen's wife might have sat, during a play that made people cry, in the pit or the family-circle. What most deeply stirred her was the way the poor girl must have wanted to live.

"Ah yes indeed—she did, she did: why in pity shouldn't she, with everything to fill her world? The mere *money* of her, the darling, if it isn't too disgusting at such a time to mention that—!"

Aunt Maud mentioned it—and Densher quite understood—but

as fairly giving poetry to the life Milly clung to: a view of the "might have been" before which the good lady was hushed anew to tears. She had had her own vision of these possibilities, and her own social use for them, and since Milly's spirit had been after all so at one with her about them, what was the cruelty of the event but a cruelty, of a sort, to herself? That came out when he named, as *the* horrible thing to know, the fact of their young friend's unapproachable terror of the end, keep it down though she would; coming out therefore often, since in so naming it he found the strangest of reliefs. He allowed it all its vividness, as if on the principle of his not at least spiritually shirking. Milly had held with passion to her dream of a future, and she was separated from it, not shrieking indeed, but grimly, awfully silent, as one might imagine some noble young victim of the scaffold, in the French Revolution, separated at the prison-door from some object clutched for resistance. Densher, in a cold moment, so pictured the case for Mrs. Lowder, but no moment cold enough had yet come to make him so picture it to Kate. And it was the front so presented that had been, in Milly, heroic; presented with the highest heroism, Aunt Maud by this time knew, on the occasion of his taking leave of her. He had let her know, absolutely for the girl's glory, how he had been received on that occasion: with a positive effect—since she was indeed so perfectly the princess that Mrs. Stringham always called her—of princely state.

Before the fire in the great room that was all arabesques and cherubs, all gaiety and gilt, and that was warm at that hour too with a wealth of autumn sun, the state in question had been maintained and the situation—well, Densher said for the convenience of exquisite London gossip, sublime. The gossip—for it came to as much at Lancaster Gate—wasn't the less exquisite for his use of the silver veil, nor on the other hand was the veil, so touched, too much drawn aside. He himself for that matter took in the scene again at moments as from the page of a book. He saw a young man far off and in a relation inconceivable, saw him hushed, passive, staying his breath, but half understanding, yet dimly conscious of something immense and holding himself painfully together not to lose it. The young man at these moments so seen was too distant and too strange for the right identity; and yet, outside, afterwards, it was his own face Densher had known. He had known then at the same time what the young man had been conscious of, and he was to measure after that, day by day, how little he had lost. At present there with Mrs. Lowder he knew he had gathered all—that passed between them mutely as in the intervals of their associated gaze they exchanged looks of intelligence. This was as far as association could go, but it was far enough when she knew the essence. The essence was that something had happened to him too beautiful and too sacred to describe. He had been, to his recovered sense, forgiven, dedicated, blessed; but this he couldn't coherently express. It would have required an explanation—fatal to Mrs. Lowder's faith in him—of the nature of Milly's wrong. So, as to the wonderful scene, they just stood at the door. They had the sense of the presence within—they felt the charged stillness; after which, their association deepened by it, they turned together away.

That itself indeed, for our restless friend, became by the end of a week the very principle of reaction: so that he woke up one morning with such a sense of having played a part as he needed self-respect to gainsay. He hadn't in the least stated at Lancaster Gate that, as a haunted man—a man haunted with a memory—he was harmless; but the degree to which Mrs. Lowder accepted, admired and explained his new aspect laid upon him practically the weight of a declaration. What he hadn't in the least stated her own manner was perpetually stating; it was as haunted and harmless that she was constantly putting him down. There offered itself however to his purpose such an element as plain honesty, and he had embraced, by the time he dressed, his proper corrective. They were on the edge of Christmas, but Christmas this year was, as in the London of so many other years, disconcertingly mild; the still air was soft, the thick light was grey, the great town looked empty, and in the Park, where the grass was green, where the sheep browsed, where the birds multitudinously twittered, the straight walks lent themselves to slowness and the dim vistas to privacy. He held it fast this morning till he had got out, his sacrifice to honour, and then went with it to the nearest post-office and fixed it fast in a telegram; thinking of it moreover as a sacrifice only because he had, for reasons, felt it as an effort. Its character of effort it would owe to Kate's expected resistance, not less probable than on the occasion of past appeals; which was precisely why he—perhaps innocently—made his telegram persuasive. It had, as a recall of tender hours, to be, for the young woman at the counter, a trifle cryptic; but there was a good deal of it in one way and another, representing as it did a rich impulse and costing him a couple of shillings. There was also a moment later on, that day, when, in the Park, as he measured watchfully one of their old alleys, he might have been supposed by a cynical critic to be reckoning his chance of getting his money back. He was waiting—but he had waited of old; Lancaster Gate as a danger was practically at hand—but she had risked that danger before. Besides it was smaller now, with the queer turn of their affair; in spite of which indeed he was graver as he lingered and looked out.

Kate came at last by the way he had thought least likely, came as if she had started from the Marble Arch;[1] but her advent was response—that was the great matter; response marked in her face and agreeable to him, even after Aunt Maud's responses, as nothing had been since his return to London. She had not, it was true, answered his wire, and he had begun to fear, as she was late, that with the instinct of what he might be again intending to press upon her she had decided—though not with ease—to deprive him of his chance. He would have of course, she knew, other chances, but she perhaps saw the present as offering her special danger. This, in fact, Densher could himself feel, was exactly why he had so prepared it, and he had rejoiced, even while he waited, in all that the conditions had to say to him of their simpler and better time. The shortest day of the year though it might be, it was, in the same place, by a whim of the weather, almost as much to their purpose as the days of sunny afternoons when they had taken their first trysts. This and that tree, within sight, on the grass, stretched bare boughs over the couple of chairs in which they had sat of old and in which—for they really could sit down again—they might recover the clearness of their prime. It was to all intents however this very reference that showed itself in Kate's face as, with her swift motion, she came toward him. It helped him, her swift motion, when it finally brought her nearer; helped him, for that matter, at first, if only by showing him afresh how terribly well she looked. It had been all along, he certainly remembered, a phenomenon of no rarity that he had felt her, at particular moments, handsomer than ever before; one of these for instance being still present to him as her entrance, under her aunt's eyes, at Lancaster Gate, the day of his dinner there after his return from America; and another her aspect on the same spot two Sundays ago—the light in which she struck the eyes he had brought back from Venice. In the course of a minute or two now he got, as he had got it the other times, his apprehension of the special stamp of the fortune of the moment.

Whatever it had been determined by as the different hours recurred to him, it took on at present a prompt connexion with an effect produced for him in truth more than once during the past week, only now much intensified. This effect he had already noted and named: it was that of the attitude assumed by his friend in the presence of the degree of response on his part to Mrs. Lowder's welcome which she couldn't possibly have failed to notice. She *had* noticed it, and she had beautifully shown him so; wearing in its honour the finest shade of studied serenity, a shade almost of gaiety over the workings of time. Everything of course was relative, with

1. Designed more or less after the Arch of Constantine in Rome, the Marble Arch, first erected in front of Buckingham Palace, was reconstructed as the entrance to Hyde Park. It is also very close to Tyburn, for centuries England's place of execution.

the shadow they were living under; but her condonation of the way in which he now, for confidence, distinguished Aunt Maud had almost the note of cheer. She had so by her own air consecrated the distinction, invidious in respect to herself though it might be; and nothing, really, more than this demonstration, could have given him had he still wanted it the measure of her superiority. It was doubtless for that matter this superiority alone that on the winter noon gave smooth decision to her step and charming courage to her eyes—a courage that deepened in them when he had presently got to what he did want. He had delayed after she had joined him not much more than long enough for him to say to her, drawing her hand into his arm and turning off where they had turned of old, that he wouldn't pretend he hadn't lately had moments of not quite believing he should ever again be so happy. She answered, passing over the reasons, whatever they had been, of his doubt, that her own belief was in high happiness for them if they would only have patience; though nothing at the same time could be dearer than his idea for their walk. It was only make-believe of course, with what had taken place for them, that they couldn't meet at home; she spoke of their opportunities as suffering at no point. He had at any rate soon let her know that he wished the present one to suffer at none, and in a quiet spot, beneath a great wintry tree, he let his entreaty come sharp.

"We've played our dreadful game and we've lost. We owe it to ourselves, we owe it to our feeling *for* ourselves and for each other, not to wait another day. Our marriage will—fundamentally, somehow, don't you see?—right everything that's wrong, and I can't express to you my impatience. We've only to announce it—and it takes off the weight."

"To 'announce' it?" Kate asked. She spoke as if not understanding, though she had listened to him without confusion.

"To accomplish it then—to-morrow if you will; *do* it and announce it as done. That's the least part of it—after it nothing will matter. We shall be so right," he said, "that we shall be strong; we shall only wonder at our past fear. It will seem an ugly madness. It will seem a bad dream."

She looked at him without flinching—with the look she had brought at his call; but he felt now the strange chill of her brightness. "My dear man, what has happened to you?"

"Well, that I can bear it no longer. *That's* simply what has happened. Something has snapped, has broken in me, and here I am. It's *as* I am that you must have me."

He saw her try for a time to appear to consider it; but he saw her also not consider it. Yet he saw her, felt her, further—he heard her, with her clear voice—try to be intensely kind with him. "I don't see, you know, what has changed." She had a large strange smile. "We've been going on together so well, and you suddenly desert me?"

It made him helplessly gaze. "You call it so 'well'? You've touches, upon my soul—!"

"I call it perfect—from my original point of view. I'm just where I was; and you must give me some better reason than you do, my dear, for *your* not being. It seems to me," she continued, "that we're only right as to what has been between us so long as we do wait. I don't think we wish to have behaved like fools." He took in while she talked her imperturbable consistency; which it was quietly, queerly hopeless to see her stand there and breathe into their mild remembering air. He had brought her there to be moved, and she was only immoveable—which was not moreover, either, because she didn't understand. She understood everything, and things he refused to; and she had reasons, deep down, the sense of which nearly sickened him. She had too again most of all her strange significant smile. "Of course if it's that you really *know* something—?" It was quite conceivable and possible to her, he could see, that he did. But he didn't even know what she meant, and he only looked at her in gloom. His gloom however didn't upset her. "You do, I believe, only you've a delicacy about saying it. Your delicacy to me, my dear, is a scruple too much. I should have no delicacy in hearing it, so that if you can *tell* me you know—"

"Well?" he asked as she still kept what depended on it.

"Why then I'll do what you want. We needn't, I grant you, in that case wait; and I can see what you mean by thinking it nicer of us not to. I don't even ask you," she continued, "for a proof. I'm content with your moral certainty."

By this time it had come over him—it had the force of a rush. The point she made was clear, as clear as that the blood, while he recognised it, mantled in his face. "I know nothing whatever."

"You've not an idea?"

"I've not an idea."

"I'd consent," she said—"I'd announce it to-morrow, to-day, I'd go home this moment and announce it to Aunt Maud, for an idea: I mean an idea straight *from* you, I mean as your own, given me in good faith. There, my dear!"—and she smiled again. "I call that really meeting you."

If it *was* then what she called it, it disposed of his appeal, and he could but stand there with his wasted passion—for it was in high passion that he had from the morning acted—in his face. She made it all out, bent upon her—the idea he didn't have, and the idea he had, and his failure of insistence when it brought up *that* challenge, and his sense of her personal presence, and his horror, almost, of her lucidity. They made in him a mixture that might have been rage, but that was turning quickly to mere cold thought, thought which led to something else and was like a new dim dawn. It affected her then, and she had one of the impulses, in all sincerity, that had before this, between them, saved their position. When she had come nearer to him, when, putting her hand upon him, she made him sink with her, as she leaned to him, into their old pair of chairs, she prevented irresistibly, she forestalled, the waste of his passion. She had an advantage with his passion now.

III

He had said to her in the Park when challenged on it that nothing had "happened" to him as a cause for the demand he there made of her—happened he meant since the account he had given, after his return, of his recent experience. But in the course of a few days—they had brought him to Christmas morning—he was conscious enough, in preparing again to seek her out, of a difference on that score. Something *had* in this case happened to him, and, after his taking the night to think of it he felt that what it most, if not absolutely first, involved was his immediately again putting himself in relation with her. The fact itself had met him there—in his own small quarters—on Christmas Eve, and had not then indeed at once affected him as implying that consequence. So far as he on the spot and for the next hours took its measure—a process that made his night mercilessly wakeful—the consequences possibly implied were numerous to distraction. His spirit dealt with them, in the darkness, as the slow hours passed; his intelligence and his imagination, his soul and his sense, had never on the whole been so intensely engaged. It was his difficulty for the moment that he was face to face with alternatives, and that it was scarce even a question of turning from one to the other. They were not in a perspective in which they might be compared and considered; they were, by a strange effect, as close as a pair of monsters of whom he might have felt on either cheek the hot breath and the huge eyes. He saw them at once and but by looking straight before him; he wouldn't for that matter, in his cold apprehension, have turned his head by an inch. So it was that his agitation was still—was not, for the slow hours, a matter of restless motion. He lay long, after the event, on the sofa where, extinguishing at a touch the white light of convenience that he hated, he had thrown himself without undressing. He stared at the buried day and wore out the time; with the arrival of the Christmas dawn moreover, late and grey, he felt himself somehow determined. The common wisdom had had its say to him—that safety in doubt was *not* action; and perhaps what most helped him was this very commonness. In his case there was nothing of *that*—in no case in his life had there ever been less: which association, from one thing to another, now worked for him as a choice. He acted, after his bath and his breakfast, in the sense of that marked element of the rare which he felt to be the sign of his crisis. And that is why, dressed with more state than usual and quite as if for church, he went out into the soft Christmas day.

Action, for him, on coming to the point, it appeared, carried with it a certain complexity. We should have known, walking by his side, that his final prime decision hadn't been to call at the door of Sir Luke Strett, and yet that this step, though subordinate, was none the less urgent. His prime decision was for another matter, to which impatience, once he was on the way, had now added itself; but he remained sufficiently aware that he must compromise with the perhaps excessive earliness. This, and the ferment set up within him, were together a reason for not driving; to say nothing of the absence of cabs in the dusky festal desert. Sir Luke's great square was not near, but he walked the distance without seeing a hansom. He had his interval thus to turn over his view—the view to which what had happened the night before had not sharply reduced itself; but the complexity just mentioned was to be offered within the next few minutes another item to assimilate. Before Sir Luke's house, when he reached it, a brougham was drawn up—at the sight of which his heart had a lift that brought him for the instant to a stand. This pause wasn't long, but it was long enough to flash upon him a revelation in the light of which he caught his breath. The carriage, so possibly at such an hour and on such a day Sir Luke's own, had struck him as a sign that the great doctor was back. This would prove something else, in turn, still more intensely, and it was in the act of the double apprehension that Densher felt himself turn pale. His mind rebounded for the moment like a projectile that has suddenly been met by another: he stared at the strange truth that what he wanted *more* than to see Kate Croy was to see the witness who had just arrived from Venice. He wanted positively to be in his presence and to hear his voice—which was the spasm of his consciousness that produced the flash. Fortunately for him, on the spot, there supervened something in which the flash went out. He became aware within this minute that the coachman on the box of the brougham had a face known to him, whereas he had never seen before, to his knowledge, the great doctor's carriage. The carriage, as he came nearer, was simply Mrs. Lowder's; the face on the box was just the face that, in coming and going at Lancaster Gate, he would vaguely have noticed, outside, in attendance. With this the rest came: the lady of Lancaster Gate had, on a prompting not wholly remote from his own, presented herself for news; and news, in the house, she was clearly getting, since her brougham had stayed. Sir Luke *was* then back—only Mrs. Lowder was with him.

It was under the influence of this last reflexion that Densher again delayed; and it was while he delayed that something else occurred to him. It was all round, visibly—given his own new contribution—a case of pressure; and in a case of pressure Kate, for quicker knowledge, might have come out with her aunt. The possibility that in this event she might be sitting in the carriage—the thing most likely—had had the effect, before he could check it, of bringing him within range of the window. It wasn't there he had wished to see her; yet if she *was* there he couldn't pretend not to. What he had however the next moment made out was that if some one was there it wasn't Kate Croy. It was, with a sensible shock for him, the person who had last offered him a conscious face from behind the clear plate of a café in Venice. The great glass at Florian's was a medium less obscure, even with the window down, than the air of the London Christmas; yet at present also, none the less, between the two men, an exchange of recognitions could occur. Densher felt his own look a gaping arrest—which, he disgustedly remembered, his back as quickly turned, appeared to repeat itself as his special privilege. He mounted the steps of the house and touched the bell with a keen consciousness of being habitually looked at by Kate's friend from positions of almost insolent vantage. He forgot for the time the moment when, in Venice, at the palace, the encouraged young man had in a manner assisted at the departure of the disconcerted, since Lord Mark was not looking disconcerted now any more than he had looked from his bench at his café. Densher was thinking that *he* seemed to show as vagrant while another was ensconced. He was thinking of the other as—in spite of the difference of situation—more ensconced than ever; he was thinking of him above all as the friend of the person with whom his recognition had, the minute previous, associated him. The man was seated in the very place in which, beside Mrs. Lowder's, he had looked to find Kate, and that was a sufficient identity. Meanwhile at any rate the door of the house had opened and Mrs. Lowder stood before him. It was something at least that *she* wasn't Kate. She was herself, on the spot, in all her affluence; with presence of mind both to decide at once that Lord Mark, in the brougham, didn't matter and to prevent Sir Luke's butler, by a firm word thrown over her shoulder, from standing there to listen to her passage with the gentleman who had rung. "*I'll* tell Mr. Densher; you needn't wait!" And the passage, promptly and richly, took place on the steps.

"He arrives, travelling straight, to-morrow early. I couldn't not come to learn."

"No more," said Densher simply, "could I. On my way," he added, "to Lancaster Gate."

"Sweet of you." She beamed on him dimly, and he saw her face was attuned. It made him, with what she had just before said, know all, and he took the thing in while he met the air of portentous, of almost functional, sympathy that had settled itself as her medium with him and that yet had now a fresh glow. "So you *have* had your message?"

He knew so well what she meant, and so equally with it what he "*had* had" no less than what he hadn't, that, with but the smallest hesitation, he strained the point. "Yes—my message."

"Our dear dove then, as Kate calls her, has folded her wonderful wings."

"Yes—folded them."

It rather racked him, but he tried to receive it as she intended, and she evidently took his formal assent for self-control. "Unless it's more true," she accordingly added, "that she has spread them the wider."

He again but formally assented, though, strangely enough, the words fitted a figure deep in his own imagination. "Rather, yes—spread them the wider."

"For a flight, I trust, to some happiness greater—!"

"Exactly. Greater," Densher broke in; but now with a look, he feared, that did a little warn her off.

"You were certainly," she went on with more reserve, "entitled to direct news. Ours came late last night: I'm not sure otherwise I shouldn't have gone to you. But you're coming," she asked, "to *me?*"

He had had a minute by this time to think further, and the window of the brougham was still within range. Her rich "me," reaching him moreover through the mild damp, had the effect of a thump on his chest. "Squared," Aunt Maud? She was indeed squared, and the extent of it just now perversely enough took away his breath. His look from where they stood embraced the aperture at which the person sitting in the carriage might have shown, and he saw his interlocutress, on her side, understand the question in it, which he moreover then uttered. "Shall you be alone?" It was, as an immediate instinctive parley with the image of his condition that now flourished in her, almost hypocritical. It sounded as if he wished to come and overflow to her, yet this was exactly what he didn't. The need to overflow had suddenly—since the night before—dried up in him, and he had never been aware of a deeper reserve.

But she had meanwhile largely responded. "Completely alone. I should otherwise never have dreamed; feeling, dear friend, but too much!" Failing on her lips what she felt came out for him in the offered hand with which she had the next moment condolingly pressed his own. "Dear friend, dear friend!"—she was deeply "with" him, and she wished to be still more so: which was what made her immediately continue. "Or wouldn't you this evening, for the sad Christmas it makes us, dine with me *tête-à-tête?*"

It put the thing off, the question of a talk with her—making the difference, to his relief, of several hours; but it also rather mystified him. This however didn't diminish his need of caution. "Shall you mind if I don't tell you at once?"

"Not in the least—leave it open: it shall be as you may feel, and you needn't even send me word. I only *will* mention that to-day, of all days, I shall otherwise sit there alone."

Now at least he could ask. "Without Miss Croy?"

"Without Miss Croy. Miss Croy," said Mrs. Lowder, "is spending her Christmas in the bosom of her more immediate family."

He was afraid, even while he spoke, of what his face might show. "You mean she has left you?"

Aunt Maud's own face for that matter met the enquiry with a consciousness in which he saw a reflexion of events. He was made sure by it, even at the moment and as he had never been before, that since he had known these two women no confessed nor commented tension, no crisis of the cruder sort would really have taken form between them: which was precisely a high proof of how Kate had steered her boat. The situation exposed in Mrs. Lowder's present expression lighted up by contrast that superficial smoothness; which afterwards, with his time to think of it, was to put before him again the art, the particular gift, in the girl, now so placed and classed, so intimately familiar for him, as her talent for life. The peace, within a day or two—since his seeing her last—had clearly been broken; differences, deep down, kept there by a diplomacy on Kate's part as deep, had been shaken to the surface by some exceptional jar; with which, in addition, he felt Lord Mark's odd attendance at such an hour and season vaguely associated. The talent for life indeed, it at the same time struck him, would probably have shown equally in the breach, or whatever had occurred; Aunt Maud having suffered, he judged, a strain rather than a stroke. Of these quick thoughts, at all events, that lady was already abreast. "She went yesterday morning—and not with my approval, I don't mind telling you—to her sister: Mrs. Condrip, if you know who I mean, who lives somewhere in Chelsea. My other niece and her affairs—that I should have to say such things to-day!—are a constant worry; so that Kate, in consequence—well, of events!—has simply been called in. My own idea, I'm bound to say, was that with *such* events she need have, in her situation, next to nothing to do."

"But she differed with you?"

"She differed with me. And when Kate differs with you—!"

"Oh I can imagine." He had reached the point in the scale of hyprocrisy at which he could ask himself why a little more or less should signify. Besides, with the intention he had had he *must* know. Kate's move, if he didn't know, might simply disconcert him; and of being disconcerted his horror was by this time fairly superstitious. "I hope you don't allude to events at all calamitous."

"No—only horrid and vulgar."

"Oh!" said Merton Densher.

Mrs. Lowder's soreness, it was still not obscure, had discovered in free speech to him a momentary balm. "They've the misfortune to have, I suppose you know, a dreadful horrible father."

"Oh!" said Densher again.

"He's too bad almost to name, but he has come upon Marian, and Marian has shrieked for help."

Densher wondered at this with intensity; and his curiosity compromised for an instant with his discretion. "Come upon her—for money?"

"Oh for that of course always. But, at *this* blessed season, for refuge, for safety: for God knows what. He's *there*, the brute. And Kate's with them. And that," Mrs. Lowder wound up, going down the steps, "is her Christmas."

She had stopped again at the bottom while he thought of an answer. "Yours then is after all rather better."

"It's at least more decent." And her hand once more came out. "But why do I talk of *our* troubles? Come if you can."

He showed a faint smile. "Thanks. If I can."

"And now—I dare say—you'll go to church?"

She had asked it, with her good intention, rather in the air and by way of sketching for him, in the line of support, something a little more to the purpose than what she had been giving him. He felt it as finishing off their intensities of expression that he found himself to all appearance receiving her hint as happy. "Why yes—I think I will": after which, as the door of the brougham, at her approach, had opened from within, he was free to turn his back. He heard the door, behind him, sharply close again and the vehicle move off in another direction than his own.

He had in fact for the time no direction; in spite of which indeed he was at the end of ten minutes aware of having walked straight to the south. That, he afterwards recognised, was, very sufficiently, because there had formed itself in his mind, even while Aunt Maud finally talked, an instant recognition of his necessary course. Nothing was open to him but to follow Kate, nor was anything more marked than the influence of the step she had taken on the emotion itself that possessed him. Her complications, which had fairly, with everything else, an awful sound—what were they, a thousand times over, but his own? His present business was to see that they didn't escape an hour longer taking their proper place in his life. He accordingly would have held his course hadn't it suddenly come over him that he had just lied to Mrs. Lowder—a term it perversely eased him to keep using—even more than was necessary. To what church was he going, to what church, in such a state of his nerves, *could* he go?—he pulled up short again, as he had pulled up in sight of Mrs. Lowder's carriage, to ask it. And yet the desire queerly stirred in him not to have wasted his word. He was just then however by a happy chance in the Brompton Road, and he bethought himself with a sudden light that the Oratory[1] was at hand. He had but to turn the other way and he should find himself soon before it. At the door then, in a few minutes, his idea was really—as it struck him—consecrated: he was, pushing in, on the edge of a splendid service—the flocking crowd told of it—which glittered and resounded, from distant depths, in the blaze of altar-lights and the swell of organ and choir. It didn't match his own day, but it was much less of a discord than some other things actual and possible. The Oratory in short, to make him right, would do.

IV

The difference was thus that the dusk of afternoon—dusk thick from an early hour—had gathered when he knocked at Mrs. Condrip's door. He had gone from the church to his club, wishing not to present himself in Chelsea at luncheon-time and also remembering that he must attempt independently to make a meal. This, in the event, he but imperfectly achieved: he dropped into a chair in the great dim void of the club library, with nobody, up or down, to be seen, and there after a while, closing his eyes, recovered an hour of the sleep he had lost during the night. Before doing this indeed he had written—it was the first thing he did—a short note, which, in the Christmas desolation of the place, he had managed only with difficulty and doubt to commit to a messenger. He wished it carried by hand, and he was obliged, rather blindly, to trust the hand, as the messenger, for some reason, was unable to return with a gage of delivery. When at four o'clock he was face to face with Kate in Mrs. Condrip's small drawing-room he found to his relief that his notification had reached her. She was expectant and to that extent prepared; which simplified a little—if a little, at the present pass, counted. Her conditions were vaguely vivid to him from the moment of his coming in, and vivid partly by their difference, a difference sharp and suggestive, from those in which he had hitherto

1. The Brompton Oratory, or the Oratory of St. Philip Neri, was served by priests without vows and dedicated to plain preaching and popular services. Patterned after the institute of the Oratory founded in Rome in 1564, the practice was introduced in England by John Henry Newman in 1847. The present structure, in the Italian Renaissance style, was opened in 1884 and completed in 1897.

constantly seen her. He had seen her but in places comparatively great; in her aunt's pompous house, under the high trees of Kensington and the storied ceilings of Venice. He had seen her, in Venice, on a great occasion, as the centre itself of the splendid Piazza: he had seen her there, on a still greater one, in his own poor rooms, which yet had consorted with her, having state and ancientry even in their poorness; but Mrs. Condrip's interior, even by this best view of it and though not flagrantly mean, showed itself as a setting almost grotesquely inapt. Pale, grave and charming, she affected him at once as a distinguished stranger—a stranger to the little Chelsea street—who was making the best of a queer episode and a place of exile. The extraordinary thing was that at the end of three minutes he felt himself less appointedly a stranger in it than she.

A part of the queerness—this was to come to him in glimpses—sprang from the air as of a general large misfit imposed on the narrow room by the scale and mass of its furniture. The objects, the ornaments were, for the sisters, clearly relics and survivals of what would, in the case of Mrs. Condrip at least, have been called better days. The curtains that overdraped the windows, the sofas and tables that stayed circulation, the chimney-ornaments that reached to the ceiling and the florid chandelier that almost dropped to the floor, were so many mementoes of earlier homes and so many links with their unhappy mother. Whatever might have been in itself the quality of these elements Densher could feel the effect proceeding from them, as they lumpishly blocked out the decline of the dim day, to be ugly almost to the point of the sinister. They failed to accommodate or to compromise; they asserted their differences without tact and without taste. It was truly having a sense of Kate's own quality thus promptly to see them in reference to it. But that Densher had this sense was no new thing to him, nor did he in strictness need, for the hour, to be reminded of it. He only knew, by one of the tricks his imagination so constantly played him, that he was, so far as her present tension went, very specially sorry for her—which was not the view that had determined his start in the morning; yet also that he himself would have taken it all, as he might say, less hard. *He* could have lived in such a place; but it wasn't given to those of his complexion, so to speak, to be exiled anywhere. It was by their comparative grossness that they could somehow make shift. His natural, his inevitable, his ultimate home—left, that is, to itself—wasn't at all unlikely to be as queer and impossible as what was just round them, though doubtless in less ample masses. As he took in moreover how Kate wouldn't have been in the least the creature she was if what was just round them hadn't mismatched her, hadn't made for her a medium involving compunction in the spectator, so, by the same stroke, that became the very fact of her relation with her companions there, such a fact as filled him at once, oddly, both with assurance and with suspense. If he himself, on this brief vision, felt her as alien and as ever so unwittingly ironic, how must they not feel her and how above all must she not feel them?

Densher could ask himself that even after she had presently lighted the tall candles on the mantel-shelf. This was all their illumination but the fire, and she had proceeded to it with a quiet dryness that yet left play, visibly, to her implication between them, in their trouble and failing anything better, of the presumably genial Christmas hearth. So far as the genial went this had in strictness, given their conditions, to be all their geniality. He had told her in his note nothing but that he must promptly see her and that he hoped she might be able to make it possible; but he understood from the first look at her that his promptitude was already having for her its principal reference. "I was prevented this morning, in the few minutes," he explained, "asking Mrs. Lowder if she had let you know, though I rather gathered she had; and it's what I've been in fact since then assuming. It was because I was so struck at the moment with your having, as she did tell me, so suddenly come here."

"Yes, it was sudden enough." Very neat and fine in the contracted firelight, with her hands in her lap, Kate considered what he had said. He had spoken immediately of what had happened at Sir Luke Strett's door. "She has let me know nothing. But that doesn't matter—if it's what *you* mean."

"It's part of what I mean," Densher said; but what he went on with, after a pause during which she waited, was apparently not the rest of that. "She had had her telegram from Mrs. Stringham; late last night. But to me the poor lady hasn't wired. The event," he added, "will have taken place yesterday, and Sir Luke, starting immediately, one can see, and travelling straight, will get back to-morrow morning. So that Mrs. Stringham, I judge, is left to face in some solitude the situation bequeathed to her. But of course," he wound up, "Sir Luke couldn't stay."

Her look at him might have had in it a vague betrayal of the sense that he was gaining time. "Was your telegram from Sir Luke?"

"No—I've had no telegram."

She wondered. "But not a letter—?"

"Not from Mrs. Stringham—no." He failed again however to develop this—for which her forbearance from another question gave him occasion. From whom then had he heard? He might at last, confronted with her, really have been gaining time; and as if to show that she respected this impulse she made her enquiry different. "Should you like to go out to her—to Mrs. Stringham?"

About that at least he was clear. "Not at all. She's alone, but she's very capable and very courageous. Besides—!" He had been going on, but he dropped.

"Besides," she said, "there's Eugenio? Yes, of course one remembers Eugenio."

She had uttered the words as definitely to show them for not untender; and he showed equally every reason to assent. "One remembers him indeed, and with every ground for it. He'll be of the highest value to her—he's capable of anything. What I was going to say," he went on, "is that some of their people from America must quickly arrive."

On this, as happened, Kate was able at once to satisfy him. "Mr. Someone-or-other, the person principally in charge of Milly's affairs—her first trustee, I suppose—had just got there at Mrs. Stringham's last writing."

"Ah that then was after your aunt last spoke to me—I mean the last time before this morning. I'm relieved to hear it. So," he said, "they'll do."

"Oh they'll do." And it came from each still as if it wasn't what each was most thinking of. Kate presently got however a step nearer to that. "But if you had been wired to by nobody what then this morning had taken you to Sir Luke?"

"Oh something else—which I'll presently tell you. It's what made me instantly need to see you; it's what I've come to speak to you of. But in a minute. I feel too many things," he went on, "at seeing you in this place." He got up as he spoke; she herself remained perfectly still. His movement had been to the fire, and, leaning a little, with his back to it, to look down on her from where he stood, he confined himself to his point. "Is it anything very bad that has brought you?"

He had now in any case said enough to justify her wish for more; so that, passing this matter by, she pressed her own challenge. "Do you mean, if I may ask, that *she*, dying—?" Her face, wondering, pressed it more than her words.

"Certainly you may ask," he after a moment said. "What has come to me is what, as I say, I came expressly to tell you. I don't mind letting you know," he went on, "that my decision to do this took for me last night and this morning a great deal of thinking of. But here I am." And he indulged in a smile that couldn't, he was well aware, but strike her as mechanical.

She went straighter with him, she seemed to show, than he really went with her. "You didn't want to come?"

It would have been simple, my dear"—and he continued to

smile—"if it had been, one way or the other, only a question of 'wanting.' It took, I admit it, the idea of what I had best do, all sorts of difficult and portentous forms. It came up for me really—well, not at all for my happiness."

This word apparently puzzled her—she studied him in the light of it. "You look upset—you've certainly been tormented. You're not well."

"Oh—well enough!"

But she continued without heeding. "You hate what you're doing."

"My dear girl, you simplify"—and he was now serious enough. "It isn't so simple even as that."

She had the air of thinking what it then might be. "I of course can't, with no clue, know what it is." She remained none the less patient and still. "If at such a moment she could write you one's inevitably quite at sea. One doesn't, with the best will in the world, understand." And then as Densher had a pause which might have stood for all the involved explanation that, to his discouragement, loomed before him: "You *haven't* decided what to do."

She had said it very gently, almost sweetly, and he didn't instantly say otherwise. But he said so after a look at her. "Oh yes—I have. Only with this sight of you here and what I seem to see in it for you—!" And his eyes, as at suggestions that pressed, turned from one part of the room to another.

"Horrible place, isn't it?" said Kate.

It brought him straight back to his enquiry. "Is it for anything awful you've had to come?"

"Oh that will take as long to tell you as anything *you* may have. Don't mind," she continued, "the 'sight of me here,' nor whatever—which is more than I yet know myself—may be 'in it' for me. And kindly consider too that, after all, if you're in trouble I can a little wish to help you. Perhaps I can absolutely even do it."

"My dear child, it's just because of the sense of your wish—! I suppose I'm in trouble—I suppose that's it." He said this with so odd a suddenness of simplicity that she could only stare for it—which he as promptly saw. So he turned off as he could his vagueness. "And yet I oughtn't to be." Which sounded indeed vaguer still.

She waited a moment. "Is it, as you say for my own business, anything very awful?"

"Well," he slowly replied, "you'll tell me if you find it so. I mean if you find my idea—"

He was so slow that she took him up. "Awful?" A sound of impatience—the form of a laugh—at last escaped her. "I can't find it anything at all till I know what you're talking about."

It brought him then more to the point, though it did so at first but by making him, on the hearthrug before her, with his hands in his pockets, turn awhile to and fro. There rose in him even with this movement a recall of another time—the hour in Venice, the hour of gloom and storm, when Susan Shepherd had sat in his quarters there very much as Kate was sitting now, and he had wondered, in pain even as now, what he might say and mightn't. Yet the present occasion after all was somehow the easier. He tried at any rate to attach that feeling to it while he stopped before his companion. "The communication I speak of can't possibly belong—so far as its date is concerned—to these last days. The postmark, which is legible, does; but it isn't thinkable, for anything else, that she wrote—!" He dropped, looking at her as if she'd understand.

It was easy to understand. "On her deathbed?" But Kate took an instant's thought. "Aren't we agreed that there was never any one in the world like her?"

"Yes." And looking over her head he spoke clearly enough. "There was never any one in the world like her."

Kate, from her chair, always without a movement, raised her eyes to the unconscious reach of his own. Then when the latter again dropped to her she added a question. "And won't it further depend a little on what the communication is?"

"A little perhaps—but not much. It's a communication," said Densher.

"Do you mean a letter?"

"Yes, a letter. Addressed to me in her hand—in hers unmistakeably."

Kate thought. "Do you know her hand very well?"

"Oh perfectly."

It was as if his tone for this prompted—with a slight strangeness —her next demand. "Have you had many letters from her?"

"No. Only three notes." He spoke looking straight at her. "And very, very short ones."

"Ah," said Kate, "the number doesn't matter. Three lines would be enough if you're sure you remember."

"I'm sure I remember. Besides," Densher continued, "I've seen her hand in other ways. I seem to recall how you once, before she went to Venice, showed me one of her notes precisely *for* that. And then she once copied me something."

"Oh," said Kate almost with a smile, "I don't ask you for the detail of your reasons. One good one's enough." To which however she added as if precisely not to speak with impatience or with anything like irony: "And the writing has its usual look?"

Densher answered as if even to better that description of it. "It's beautiful."

"Yes—it *was* beautiful. Well," Kate, to defer to him still, further remarked, "it's not news to us now that she was stupendous. Anything's possible."

"Yes, anything's possible"—he appeared oddly to catch at it. "That's what I say to myself. It's what I've been believing you," he a trifle vaguely explained, "still more certain to feel."

She waited for him to say more, but he only, with his hands in his pockets, turned again away, going this time to the single window of the room, where in the absence of lamplight the blind hadn't been drawn. He looked out into the lamplit fog, lost himself in the small sordid London street—for sordid, with his other association, he felt it—as he had lost himself, with Mrs. Stringham's eyes on him, in the vista of the Grand Canal. It was present then to his recording consciousness that when he had last been driven to such an attitude the very depth of his resistance to the opportunity to give Kate away was what had so driven him. His waiting companion had on that occasion waited for him to say he *would;* and what he had meantime glowered forth at was the inanity of such a hope. Kate's attention, on her side, during these minutes, rested on the back and shoulders he thus familiarly presented—rested as with a view of their expression, a reference to things unimparted, links still missing and that she must ever miss, try to make them out as she would. The result of her tension was that she again took him up. "You received—what you spoke of—last night?"

It made him turn round. "Coming in from Fleet Street—earlier by an hour than usual—I found it with some other letters on my table. But my eyes went straight to it, in an extraordinary way, from the door. I recognised it, knew what it was, without touching it."

"One can understand." She listened with respect. His tone however was so singular that she presently added: "You speak as if all this while you *hadn't* touched it."

"Oh yes, I've touched it. I feel as if, ever since, I'd been touching nothing else. I quite firmly," he pursued as if to be plainer, "took hold of it."

"Then where is it?"

"Oh I have it here."

"And you've brought it to show me?"

"I've brought it to show you."

So he said with a distinctness that had, among his other oddities, almost a sound of cheer, yet making no movement that matched his words. She could accordingly but offer again her expectant face, while his own, to her impatience, seemed perversely to fill with another thought. "But now that you've done so you feel you don't want to."

"I want to immensely," he said. "Only you tell me nothing."

She smiled at him, with this, finally, as if he were an unreasonable child. "It seems to me I tell you quite as much as you tell me. You haven't yet even told me how it is that such explanations as you require don't come from your document itself." Then as he answered nothing she had a flash. "You mean you haven't read it?"

"I haven't read it."

She stared. "Then how am I to help you with it?"

Again leaving her while she never budged he paced five strides, and again he was before her. "By telling me *this*. It's something, you know, that you wouldn't tell me the other day."

She was vague. "The other day?"

"The first time after my return—the Sunday I came to you. What's he doing," Densher went on, "at that hour of the morning with her? What does his having been with her there mean?"

"Of whom are you talking?"

"Of that man—Lord Mark of course. What does it represent?"

"Oh with Aunt Maud?"

"Yes, my dear—and with you. It comes more or less to the same thing; and it's what you didn't tell me the other day when I put you the question."

Kate tried to remember the other day. "You asked me nothing about any hour."

"I asked you when it was you last saw him—previous, I mean, to his second descent at Venice. You wouldn't say, and as we were talking of a matter comparatively more important I let it pass. But the fact remains, you know, my dear, that you haven't told me."

Two things in this speech appeared to have reached Kate more distinctly than the others. "I 'wouldn't say'?—and you 'let it pass'?" She looked just coldly blank. "You really speak as if I were keeping something back."

"Well, you see," Densher persisted, "you're not even telling me now. All I want to know," he nevertheless explained, "is whether there was a connexion between that proceeding on his part, which was practically—oh beyond all doubt!—the shock precipitating for her what has now happened, and anything that had occurred with him previously for yourself. How in the world did he know we're engaged?"

V

Kate slowly rose; it was, since she had lighted the candles and sat down, the first movement she had made. "Are you trying to fix it on me that I must have told him?"

She spoke not so much in resentment as in pale dismay—which he showed he immediately took in. "My dear child, I'm not trying to 'fix' anything; but I'm extremely tormented and I seem not to understand. What has the brute to do with us anyway?"

"What has he indeed?" Kate asked.

She shook her head as if in recovery, within the minute, of some mild allowance for his unreason. There was in it—and for his reason really—one of those half-inconsequent sweetnesses by which she had often before made, over some point of difference, her own terms with him. Practically she was making them now, and essentially he was knowing it; yet inevitably, all the same, he was accepting it. She stood there close to him, with something in her patience that suggested her having supposed, when he spoke more appealingly, that he was going to kiss her. He hadn't been, it appeared; but his continued appeal was none the less the quieter. "What's he doing, from ten o'clock on Christmas morning, with Mrs. Lowder?"

Kate looked surprised. "Didn't she tell you he's staying there?"

"At Lancaster Gate?" Densher's surprise met it. " 'Staying'?—since when?"

"Since day before yesterday. He was there before I came away." And then she explained—confessing it in fact anomalous. "It's an accident—like Aunt Maud's having herself remained in town for Christmas, but it isn't after all so monstrous. *We* stayed—and, with my having come here, she's sorry now—because we neither of us, waiting from day to day for the news you brought, seemed to want to be with a lot of people."

"You stayed for thinking of—Venice?"

"Of course we did. For what else? And even a little," Kate wonderfully added—"it's true at least of Aunt Maud—for thinking of you."

He appreciated. "I see. Nice of you every way. But whom," he enquired, "has Lord Mark stayed for thinking of?"

"His being in London, I believe, is a very commonplace matter. He has some rooms which he has had suddenly some rather advantageous chance to let—such as, with his confessed, his decidedly proclaimed want of money, he hasn't had it in him, in spite of everything, not to jump at."

Densher's attention was entire. "In spite of everything? In spite of what?"

"Well, I don't know. In spite, say, of his being scarcely supposed to do that sort of thing."

"To try to get money?"

"To try at any rate in little thrifty ways. Apparently however he has had for some reason to do what he can. He turned at a couple of days' notice out of his place, making it over to his tenant; and Aunt Maud, who's deeply in his confidence about all such matters, said: 'Come then to Lancaster Gate—to sleep at least—till, like all the world, you go to the country.' He was to have gone to the country—I think to Matcham—yesterday afternoon: Aunt Maud, that is, told me he was."

Kate had been somehow, for her companion, through this statement, beautifully, quite soothingly, suggestive. "Told you, you mean, so that you needn't leave the house?"

"Yes—so far as she had taken it into her head that his being there was part of my reason."

"And *was* it part of your reason?"

"A little if you like. Yet there's plenty here—as I knew there would be—without it. So that," she said candidly, "doesn't matter. I'm glad I am here: even if for all the good I do—!" She implied however that that didn't matter either. "He didn't, as you tell me, get off then to Matcham; though he may possibly, if it *is* possible, be going this afternoon. But what strikes me as most probable—and it's really, I'm bound to say, quite amiable of him—is that he has declined to leave Aunt Maud, as I've been so ready to do, to spend her Christmas alone. If moreover he has given up Matcham for her it's a *procédé*[1] that won't please her less. It's small wonder therefore that she insists, on a dull day, in driving him about. I don't pretend to know," she wound up, "what may happen between them; but that's all I see in it."

"You see in everything, and you always did," Densher returned, "something that, while I'm with you at least, I always take from you as the truth itself."

She looked at him as if consciously and even carefully extracting the sting of his reservation; then she spoke with a quiet gravity that seemed to show how fine she found it. "Thank you." It had for him, like everything else, its effect. They were still closely face to face, and, yielding to the impulse to which he hadn't yielded just before, he laid his hands on her shoulders, held her hard a minute and shook her a little, far from untenderly, as if in expression of more mingled things, all difficult, than he could speak. Then bending his head he applied his lips to her cheek. He fell, after this, away for an instant, resuming his unrest, while she kept the position in which, all passive and as a statue, she had taken his demonstration. It didn't prevent her, however, from offering him, as if what she had had was enough for the moment, a further indulgence. She made a quiet lucid connexion and as she made it sat down again. "I've been trying to place exactly, as to its date, something that did happen to me while you were in Venice. I mean a talk with him. He spoke to me—spoke out."

"Ah there you are!" said Densher who had wheeled round.

"Well, if I'm 'there,' as you so gracefully call it, by having refused to meet him as he wanted—as he pressed—I plead guilty to being so. Would you have liked me," she went on, "to give him an answer that would have kept him from going?"

1. Procedure, behavior.

It made him a little awkwardly think. "Did you know he was going?"

"Never for a moment; but I'm afraid that—even if it doesn't fit your strange suppositions—I should have given him just the same answer if I had known. If it's a matter I haven't, since your return, thrust upon you, that's simply because it's not a matter in the memory of which I find a particular joy. I hope that if I've satisfied you about it," she continued, "it's not too much to ask of you to let it rest."

"Certainly," said Densher kindly, "I'll let it rest." But the next moment he pursued: "He saw something. He guessed."

"If you mean," she presently returned, "that he was unfortunately the one person we hadn't deceived, I can't contradict you."

"No—of course not. But *why*," Densher still risked, "was he unfortunately the one person—? He's not really a bit intelligent."

"Intelligent enough apparently to have seen a mystery, a riddle, in anything so unnatural as—all things considered and when it came to the point—my attitude. So he gouged out his conviction, and on his conviction he acted."

Densher seemed for a little to look at Lord Mark's conviction as if it were a blot on the face of nature. "Do you mean because you had appeared to him to have encouraged him?"

"Of course I had been decent to him. Otherwise where *were* we?"

" 'Where'—?"

"You and I. What I appeared to him, however, hadn't mattered. What mattered was how I appeared to Aunt Maud. Besides, you must remember that he has had all along his impression of *you*. You can't help it," she said, "but you're after all—well, yourself."

"As much myself as you please. But when I took myself to Venice and kept myself there—what," Densher asked, "did he make of that?"

"Your being in Venice and liking to be—which is never on any one's part a monstrosity—was explicable for him in other ways. He was quite capable moreover of seeing it as dissimulation."

"In spite of Mrs. Lowder?"

"No," said Kate, "not in spite of Mrs. Lowder now. Aunt Maud, before what you call his second descent, hadn't convinced him—all the more that my refusal of him didn't help. But he came back convinced." And then as her companion still showed a face at a loss: "I mean after he had seen Milly, spoken to her and left her. Milly convinced him."

"Milly?" Densher again but vaguely echoed.

"That you were sincere. That it was *her* you loved." It came to him from her in such a way that he instantly, once more, turned, found himself yet again at his window. "Aunt Maud, on his return here," she meanwhile continued, "had it from him. And that's why you're now so well with Aunt Maud."

He only for a minute looked out in silence—after which he came away. "And why *you* are." It was almost, in its extremely affirmative effect between them, the note of recrimination; or it would have been perhaps rather if it hadn't been so much more the note of truth. It was sharp because it was true, but its truth appeared to impose it as an argument so conclusive as to permit on neither side a sequel. That made, while they faced each other over it without speech, the gravity of everything. It was as if there were almost danger, which the wrong word might start. Densher accordingly at last acted to better purpose: he drew, standing there before her, a pocket-book from the breast of his waistcoat and he drew from the pocket-book a folded letter to which her eyes attached themselves. He restored then the receptacle to its place and, with a movement not the less odd for being visibly instinctive and unconscious, carried the hand containing his letter behind him. What he thus finally spoke of was a different matter. "Did I understand from Mrs. Lowder that your father's in the house?"

If it never had taken her long in such excursions to meet him it was not to take her so now. "In the house, yes. But we needn't fear his interruption"—she spoke as if he had thought of that. "He's in bed."

"Do you mean with illness?"

She sadly shook her head. "Father's never ill. He's a marvel. He's only—endless."

Densher thought. "Can I in any way help you with him?"

"Yes." She perfectly, wearily, almost serenely, had it all. "By our making your visit as little of an affair as possible for him—and for Marian too."

"I see. They hate so your seeing me. Yet I couldn't—could I?—not have come."

"No, you couldn't not have come."

"But I can only, on the other hand, go as soon as possible?"

Quickly it almost upset her. "Ah don't, to-day, put ugly words into my mouth. I've enough of my trouble without it."

"I know—I know!" He spoke in instant pleading. "It's all only that I'm as troubled *for* you. When did he come?"

"Three days ago—after he hadn't been near her for more than a year, after he had apparently, and not regrettably, ceased to remember her existence; and in a state which made it impossible not to take him in."

Densher hesitated. "Do you mean in such want—?"

"No, not of food, of necessary things—not even, so far as his appearance went, of money. He looked as wonderful as ever. But he was—well, in terror."

"In terror of what?"

"I don't know. Of somebody—of something. He wants, he says, to be quiet. But his quietness is awful."

She suffered, but he couldn't not question. "What does he do?"

It made Kate herself hesitate. "He cries."

Again for a moment he hung fire, but he risked it. "What *has* he done?"

It made her slowly rise, and they were once more fully face to face. Her eyes held his own and she was paler than she had been. "If you love me—now—don't ask me about father."

He waited again a moment. "I love you. It's because I love you that I'm here. It's because I love you that I've brought you this." And he drew from behind him the letter that had remained in his hand.

But her eyes only—though he held it out—met the offer. "Why you've not broken the seal!"

"If I had broken the seal—exactly—I should know what's within. It's for *you* to break the seal that I bring it."

She looked—still not touching the thing—inordinately grave. "To break the seal of something to you from *her*?"

"Ah precisely because it's from her. I'll abide by whatever you think of it."

"I don't understand," said Kate. "What do you yourself think?" And then as he didn't answer: "It seems to me *I* think you know. You have your instinct. You don't need to read. It's the proof."

Densher faced her words as if they had been an accusation, an accusation for which he was prepared and which there was but one way to face. "I have indeed my instinct. It came to me, while I worried it out, last night. It came to me as an effect of the hour." He held up his letter and seemed now to insist more than to confess. "This thing had been timed."

"For Christmas Eve?"

"For Christmas Eve."

Kate had suddenly a strange smile. "The season of gifts!" After which, as he said nothing, she went on: "And had been written, you mean, while she could write, and kept to *be* so timed?"

Only meeting her eyes while he thought, he again didn't reply. "What do *you* mean by the proof?"

"Why of the beauty with which you've been loved. But I won't," she said, "break your seal."

"You positively decline?"

"Positively. Never." To which she added oddly: "I know without."

He had another pause. "And what is it you know?"

"That she announces to you she has made you rich."

His pause this time was longer. "Left me her fortune?"

"Not all of it, no doubt, for it's immense. But money to a large amount. I don't care," Kate went on, "to know how much." And her strange smile recurred. "I trust her."

"Did she tell you?" Densher asked.

"Never!" Kate visibly flushed at the thought. "That wouldn't, on my part, have been playing fair with her. And I did," she added, "play fair."

Densher, who had believed her—he couldn't help it—continued, holding his letter, to face her. He was much quieter now, as if his torment had somehow passed. "You played fair with me, Kate; and that's why—since we talk of proofs—I want to give *you* one. I've wanted to let you see—and in preference even to myself—something I feel as sacred."

She frowned a little. "I don't understand."

"I've asked myself for a tribute, for a sacrifice by which I can peculiarly recognise—"

"Peculiarly recognise what?" she demanded as he dropped.

"The admirable nature of your own sacrifice. You were capable in Venice of an act of splendid generosity."

"And the privilege you offer me with that document is my reward?"

He made a movement. "It's all I can do as a symbol of my attitude."

She looked at him long. "Your attitude, my dear, is that you're afraid of yourself. You've had to take yourself in hand. You've had to do yourself violence."

"So it is then you meet me?"

She bent her eyes hard a moment to the letter, from which her hand still stayed itself. "You absolutely *desire* me to take it?"

"I absolutely desire you to take it."

"To do what I like with it?"

"Short of course of making known its terms. It must remain—pardon my making the point—between you and me."

She had a last hesitation, but she presently broke it. "Trust me." Taking from him the sacred script she held it a little while her eyes again rested on those fine characters of Milly's that they had shortly before discussed. "To hold it," she brought out, "is to know."

"Oh I *know!*" said Merton Densher.

"Well then if we both do—!" She had already turned to the fire, nearer to which she had moved, and with a quick gesture had jerked the thing into the flame. He started—but only half—as to undo her action: his arrest was as prompt as the latter had been decisive. He only watched, with her, the paper burn; after which their eyes again met. "You'll have it all," Kate said, "from New York."

VI

It was after he had in fact, two months later, heard from New York that she paid him a visit one morning at his own quarters—coming not as she had come in Venice, under his extreme solicitation, but as a need recognised in the first instance by herself, even though also as the prompt result of a missive delivered to her. This had consisted of a note from Densher accompanying a letter, "just to hand," addressed him by an eminent American legal firm, a firm of whose high character he had become conscious while in New York as of a thing in the air itself, and whose head and front, the principal executor of Milly Theale's copious will, had been duly identified at Lancaster Gate as the gentleman hurrying out, by the straight southern course, before the girl's death, to the support of Mrs. Stringham. Densher's act on receipt of the document in question—an act as to which and to the bearings of which his resolve had had time to mature—constituted in strictness, singularly enough, the first reference to Milly, or to what Milly might or might not have done, that had passed between our pair since they had stood together watching the destruction, in the little vulgar grate at Chelsea, of the undisclosed work of her hand. They had at the time, and in due deference now, on his part, to Kate's mention of her responsibility for his call, immediately separated, and when they met again the subject was made present to them—at all events till some flare of new light—only by the intensity with which it mutely expressed its absence. They were not moreover in these weeks to meet often, in spite of the fact that this had, during January and a part of February, actually become for them a comparatively easy matter. Kate's stay at Mrs. Condrip's prolonged itself under allowances from her aunt which would have been a mystery to Densher had he not been admitted, at Lancaster Gate, really in spite of himself, to the esoteric view of them. "It's her idea," Mrs. Lowder had there said to him as if she really despised ideas—which she didn't; "and I've taken up with my own, which is to give her her head till she has had enough of it. She *has* had enough of it, she had that soon enough; but as she's as proud as the deuce she'll come back when she has found some reason—having nothing in common with her disgust—of which she can make a show. She calls it her holiday, which she's spending in her own way—the holiday to which, once a year or so, as she says, the very maids in the scullery have a right. So we're taking it on that basis. But we shall not soon,

I think, take another of the same sort. Besides, she's quite decent; she comes often—whenever I make her a sign; and she has been good, on the whole, this year or two, so that, to be decent myself, I don't complain. She has really been, poor dear, very much what one hoped; though I needn't, you know," Aunt Maud wound up, "tell *you*, after all, you clever creature, what that was."

It had been partly in truth to keep down the opportunity for this that Densher's appearances under the good lady's roof markedly, after Christmas, interspaced themselves. The phase of his situation that on his return from Venice had made them for a short time almost frequent was at present quite obscured, and with it the impulse that had then acted. Another phase had taken its place, which he would have been painfully at a loss as yet to name or otherwise set on its feet, but of which the steadily rising tide left Mrs. Lowder, for his desire, quite high and dry. There had been a moment when it seemed possible that Mrs. Stringham, returning to America under convoy, would pause in London on her way and be housed with her old friend; in which case he was prepared for some apparent zeal of attendance. But this danger passed—he had felt it a danger, and the person in the world whom he would just now have most valued seeing on his own terms sailed away westward from Genoa. He thereby only wrote to her, having broken, in this respect, after Milly's death, the silence as to the sense of which, before that event, their agreement had been so deep. She had answered him from Venice twice, and had had time to answer him twice again from New York. The last letter of her four had come by the same post as the document he sent on to Kate, but he hadn't gone into the question of also enclosing that. His correspondence with Milly's companion was somehow already presenting itself to him as a feature—as a factor, he would have said in his newspaper—of the time whatever it might be, long or short, in store for him; but one of his acutest current thoughts was apt to be devoted to his not having yet mentioned it to Kate. She had put him no question, no "Don't you ever hear?"—so that he hadn't been brought to the point. This he described to himself as a mercy, for he liked his secret. It was as a secret that, in the same personal privacy, he described his transatlantic commerce, scarce even wincing while he recognised it as the one connexion in which he wasn't straight. He had in fact for this connexion a vivid mental image—he saw it as a small emergent rock in the waste of waters, the bottomless grey expanse of straightness. The fact that he had on several recent occasions taken with Kate an out-of-the-way walk that was each time to define itself as more remarkable for what they didn't say than for what they did—this fact failed somehow to mitigate for him a strange consciousness of exposure. There was something deep within him that he had absolutely shown to no one—to the companion of these walks in particular not a bit more than he could help; but he was none the less haunted, under its shadow, with a dire apprehension of publicity. It was as if he had invoked that ugliness in some stupid good faith; and it was queer enough that on his emergent rock, clinging to it and to Susan Shepherd, he should figure himself as hidden from view. That represented no doubt his belief in her power, or in her delicate disposition to protect him. Only Kate at all events knew—what Kate did know, and she was also the last person interested to tell it; in spite of which it was as if his *act*, so deeply associated with her and never to be recalled nor recovered, was abroad on the winds of the world. His honesty, as he viewed it with Kate, was the very element of that menace: to the degree that he saw at moments, as to their final impulse or their final remedy, the need to bury in the dark blindness of each other's arms the knowledge of each other that they couldn't undo.

Save indeed that the sense in which it was in these days a question of arms was limited, this might have been the intimate expedient to which they were actually resorting. It had its value, in conditions that made everything count, that thrice over, in Battersea Park—where Mrs. Lowder now never drove—he had adopted the usual means, in sequestered alleys, of holding her close to his side. She could make absences, on her present footing, without having too inordinately to account for them at home—which was exactly what gave them for the first time an appreciable margin. He supposed she could always say in Chelsea—though he didn't press it—that she had been across the town, in decency, for a look at her aunt; whereas there had always been reasons at Lancaster Gate for her not being able to plead the look at her other relatives. It was therefore between them a freedom of a purity as yet untasted; which for that matter also they made in various ways no little show of cherishing as such. They made the show indeed in every way but the way of a large use—an inconsequence that they almost equally gave time to helping each other to regard as natural. He put it to his companion that the kind of favour he now enjoyed at Lancaster Gate, the wonderful warmth of his reception there, cut in a manner the ground from under their feet. He was too horribly trusted—they had succeeded too well. He couldn't in short make appointments with her without abusing Aunt Maud, and he couldn't on the other hand haunt that lady without tying his hands. Kate saw what he meant just as he saw what she did when she admitted that she was herself, to a degree scarce less embarrassing, in the enjoyment of Aunt Maud's confidence. It was special at present—she was handsomely used; she confessed accordingly to a scruple about misapplying her licence. Mrs. Lowder then finally had found—and all unconsciously now—the way to baffle them. It wasn't however that they didn't meet a little, none the less, in the southern quarter, to point for their common benefit the moral of their defeat. They crossed the river; they wandered in neighbourhoods sordid and safe; the winter was mild, so that, mounting to the top of trams, they could rumble together to Clapham or to Greenwich. If at the same time their minutes had never been so counted it struck Densher that by a singular law their tone—he scarce knew what to call it—had never been so bland. Not to talk of what they *might* have talked of drove them to other ground; it was as if they used a perverse insistence to make up what they ignored. They concealed their pursuit of the irrelevant by the charm of their manner; they took precautions for the courtesy they had formerly left to come of itself; often, when he had quitted her, he stopped short, walking off, with the aftersense of their change. He would have described their change—had he so far faced it as to describe it—by their being so damned civil. That had even, with the intimate, the familiar at the point to which they had brought them, a touch almost of the droll. What danger had there ever been of their becoming rude—after each had long since made the other so tremendously tender? Such were the things he asked himself when he wondered what in particular he most feared.

Yet all the while too the tension had its charm—such being the interest of a creature who could bring one back to her by such different roads. It was her talent for life again; which found in her a difference for the differing time. She didn't give their tradition up; she but made of it something new. Frankly moreover she had never been more agreeable nor in a way—to put it prosaically—better company: he felt almost as if he were knowing her on that defined basis—which he even hesitated whether to measure as reduced or as extended; as if at all events he were admiring her as she was probably admired by people she met "out." He hadn't in fine reckoned that she would still have something fresh for him; yet this was what she had—that on the top of a tram in the Borough he felt as if he were next her at dinner. What a person she would be if they *had* been rich—with what a genius for the so-called great life, what a presence for the so-called great house, what a grace for the so-called great positions! He might regret at once, while he was about it, that they weren't princes or billionaires. She had treated him on their Christmas to a softness that had struck him at the time as of the quality of fine velvet, meant to fold thick, but stretched a little thin; at present, however, she gave him the impression of a contact multitudinous as only the superficial can be. She had throughout never a word for what went on at home. She came out of that and she returned to it, but her nearest reference was the look with which, each time, she bade him good-bye. The look was her repeated prohibition: "It's what I *have* to see and to know—so don't touch it. That but wakes up the old evil, which I keep still, in my way, by sitting by it. I go now—leave me alone!—to sit by it again. The way to pity me—if that's what you want—is to believe in me. If we could really *do* anything it would be another matter."

He watched her, when she went her way, with the vision of what she thus a little stiffly carried. It was confused and obscure, but how, with her head high, it made her hold herself! He really in his own person might at these moments have been swaying a little aloft as one of the objects in her poised basket. It was doubtless thanks to some such consciousness as this that he felt the lapse of the weeks, before the day of Kate's mounting of his stair, almost swingingly rapid. They contained for him the contradiction that, whereas periods of waiting are supposed in general to keep the time slow, it was the wait, actually, that made the pace trouble him. The secret of that anomaly, to be plain, was that he was aware of how, while the days melted, something rare went with them. This something was only a thought, but a thought precisely of such freshness and such delicacy as made the precious, of whatever sort, most subject to the hunger of time. The thought was all his own, and his intimate companion was the last person he might have shared it with. He kept it back like a favourite pang; left it behind him, so to say, when he went out, but came home again the sooner for the certainty of finding it there. Then he took it out of its sacred corner and its soft wrappings; he undid them one by one, handling them, handling *it*, as a father, baffled and tender, might handle a maimed child. But so it was before him—in his dread of who else might see it. Then he took to himself at such hours, in other words, that he should never, never know what had been in Milly's letter. The intention announced in it he should but too probably know; only that would have been, but for the depths of his spirit, the least part of it. The part of it missed for ever was the turn she would have given her act. This turn had possibilities that, somehow, by wondering about them, his imagination had extraordinarily filled out and refined. It had made of them a revelation the loss of which was like the sight of a priceless pearl cast before his eyes—his pledge given not to save it—into the fathomless sea, or rather even it was like the sacrifice of something sentient and throbbing, something that, for the spiritual ear, might have been audible as a faint far wail. This was the sound he cherished when alone in the stillness of his rooms. He sought and guarded the stillness, so that it might prevail there till the inevitable sounds of life, once more, comparatively coarse and harsh, should smother and deaden it—doúbtless by the same process with which they would officiously heal the ache in his soul that was somehow one with it. It moreover deepened the scarced hush that he couldn't complain. He had given poor Kate her freedom.

The great and obvious thing, as soon as she stood there on the occasion we have already named, was that she was now in high possession of it. This would have marked immediately the difference—had there been nothing else to do it—between their actual terms and their other terms, the character of their last encounter in Venice. That had been *his* idea, whereas her present step was her own; the few marks they had in common were, from the first moment, to his conscious vision, almost pathetically plain. She was as grave now as before; she looked around her, to hide it, as before; she pretended, as before, in an air in which her words at the moment itself fell flat, to an interest in the place and a curiosity about his "things"; there was a recall in the way in which, after she had failed a little to push up her veil symmetrically and he had said she had better take it off altogether, she had acceded to his suggestion before the glass. It was just these things that were vain; and what was real was that his fancy figured her after the first few minutes as literally now providing the element of reassurance which had previously been his care. It was she, supremely, who had the presence of mind. She made indeed for that matter very prompt use of it. "You see I've not hesitated this time to break your seal."

She had laid on the table from the moment of her coming in the long envelope, substantially filled, which he had sent her enclosed in another of still ampler make. He had however not looked at it—his belief being that he wished never again to do so; besides which it had happened to rest with its addressed side up. So he "saw" nothing, and it was only into her eyes that her remark made him look, declining any approach to the object indicated. "It's not 'my' seal, my dear; and my intention—which my note tried to express—was all to treat it to you as not mine."

"Do you mean that it's to that extent mine then?"

"Well, let us call it, if we like, theirs—that of the good people in New York, the authors of our communication. If the seal is broken well and good; but we *might*, you know," he presently added, "have sent it back to them intact and inviolate. Only accompanied," he smiled with his heart in his mouth, "by an absolutely kind letter."

Kate took it with the mere brave blink with which a patient of courage signifies to the exploring medical hand that the tender place is touched. He saw on the spot that she was prepared, and with this signal sign that she was too intelligent not to be, came a flicker of possibilities. She was—merely to put it at that—intelligent enough for anything. "Is it what you're proposing we *should* do?"

"Ah it's too late to do it—well, ideally. Now, with that sign that we *know*—!"

"But you don't know," she said very gently.

"I refer," he went on without noticing it, "to what would have been the handsome way. Its being dispatched again, with no cognisance taken but one's assurance of the highest consideration, and the proof of this in the state of the envelope—*that* would have been really satisfying."

She thought an instant. "The state of the envelope proving refusal, you mean, not to be based on the insufficiency of the sum?"

Densher smiled again as for the play, however whimsical, of her humour. "Well yes—something of that sort."

"So that if cognisance *has* been taken—so far as I'm concerned —it spoils the beauty?"

"It makes the difference that I'm disappointed in the hope—which I confess I entertained—that you'd bring the thing back to me as you had received it."

"You didn't express that hope in your letter."

"I didn't want to. I wanted to leave it to yourself. I wanted—oh yes, if that's what you wish to ask me—to see what you'd do."

"You wanted to measure the possibilities of my departure from delicacy?"

He continued steady now; a kind of ease—from the presence, as in the air, of something he couldn't yet have named—had come to him. "Well, I wanted—in so good a case—to test you."

She was struck—it showed in her face—by his expression. "It *is* a good case. I doubt whether a better," she said with her eyes on him, "has ever been known."

"The better the case then the better the test!"

"How do you know," she asked in reply to this, "what I'm capable of?"

"I don't, my dear! Only with the seal unbroken I should have known sooner."

"I see"—she took it in. "But I myself shouldn't have known at all. And you wouldn't have known, either, what I do know."

"Let me tell you at once," he returned, "that if you've been moved to correct my ignorance I very particularly request you not to."

She just hesitated. "Are you afraid of the effect of the corrections? Can you only do it by doing it blindly?"

He waited a moment. "What is it that you speak of my doing?"

"Why the only thing in the world that I take you as thinking of. Not accepting—what she has done. Isn't there some regular name in such cases? Not taking up the bequest."

"There's something you forget in it," he said after a moment. "My asking you to join with me in doing so."

Her wonder but made her softer, yet at the same time didn't make her less firm. "How can I 'join' in a matter with which I've nothing to do?"

"How? By a single word."

"And what word?"

"Your consent to my giving up."

"My consent has no meaning when I can't prevent you."

"You can perfectly prevent me. Understand that well," he said.

She seemed to face a threat in it. "You mean you won't give up if I *don't* consent?"

"Yes. I do nothing."

"That, as I understand, is accepting."

Densher paused. "I do nothing formal."

"You won't, I suppose you mean, touch the money."

"I won't touch the money."

It had a sound—though he had been coming to it—that made for gravity. "Who then in such an event *will?*"

"Any one who wants or who can."

Again a little she said nothing: she might say too much. But by the time she spoke he had covered ground. "How can I touch it but *through* you?"

"You can't. Any more," he added, "than I can renounce it except through you."

"Oh ever so much less! There's nothing," she explained, "in my power."

"I'm in your power," Merton Densher said.

"In what way?"

"In the way I show—and the way I've always shown. When have I shown," he asked as with a sudden cold impatience, "anything else? You surely must feel—so that you needn't wish to appear to spare me in it—how you 'have' me."

"It's very good of you, my dear," she nervously laughed, "to put me so thoroughly up to it!"

"I put you up to nothing. I didn't even put you up to the chance that, as I said a few moments ago, I saw for you in forwarding that thing. Your liberty is therefore in every way complete."

It had come to the point really that they showed each other pale faces, and that all the unspoken between them looked out of their eyes in a dim terror of their further conflict. Something even rose between them in one of their short silences—something that was like an appeal from each to the other not to be too true. Their necessity was somehow before them, but which of them must meet it first? "Thank you!" Kate said for his word about her freedom, but taking for the minute no further action on it. It was blest at least that all ironies failed them, and during another slow moment their very sense of it cleared the air.

There was an effect of this in the way he soon went on. "You must intensely feel that it's the thing for which we worked together."

She took up the remark, however, no more than if it were commonplace; she was already again occupied with a point of her own. "Is it absolutely true—for if it is, you know, it's tremendously interesting—that you haven't so much as a curiosity about what she has done for you?"

"Would you like," he asked, "my formal oath on it?"

"No—but I don't understand. It seems to me in your place—!"

"Ah," he couldn't help breaking in, "what do you know of my place? Pardon me," he at once added; "my preference is the one I express."

She had in an instant nevertheless a curious thought. "But won't the facts be published?"

" 'Published'?"—he winced.

"I mean won't you see them in the papers?"

"Ah never! I shall know how to escape that."

It seemed to settle the subject, but she had the next minute another insistence. "Your desire is to escape everything?"

"Everything."

"And do you need no more definite sense of what it is you ask me to help you to renounce?"

"My sense is sufficient without being definite. I'm willing to believe that the amount of money's not small."

"Ah there you are!" she exclaimed.

"If she was to leave me a remembrance," he quietly pursued, "it would inevitably not be meagre."

Kate waited as for how to say it. "It's worthy of her. It's what she was herself—if you remember what we once said *that* was."

He hesitated—as if there had been many things. But he remembered one of them. "Stupendous?"

"Stupendous." A faint smile for it—ever so small—had flickered in her face, but had vanished before the omen of tears, a little less uncertain, had shown themselves in his own. His eyes filled—but that made her continue. She continued gently. "I think that what it really is must be that you're afraid. I mean," she explained, "that you're afraid of *all* the truth. If you're in love with her without it, what indeed can you be more? And you're afraid—it's wonderful!—to be in love with her."

"I never was in love with her," said Densher.

She took it, but after a little she met it. "I believe that now—for the time she lived. I believe it at least for the time you were there. But your change came—as it might well—the day you last saw her; she died for you then that you might understand her. From that hour you *did*." With which Kate slowly rose. "And I do now. She did it *for* us." Densher rose to face her, and she went on with her thought. "I used to call her, in my stupidity—for want of anything better—a dove. Well she stretched out her wings, and it was to *that* they reached. They cover us."

"They cover us," Densher said.

"That's what I give you," Kate gravely wound up. "That's what I've done for you."

His look at her had a slow strangeness that had dried, on the moment, his tears. "Do I understand then—?"

"That I do consent?" She gravely shook her head. "No—for I see. You'll marry me without the money; you won't marry me with it. If I don't consent *you* don't."

"You lose me?" He showed, though naming it frankly, a sort of awe of her high grasp. "Well, you lose nothing else. I make over to you every penny."

Prompt was his own clearness, but she had no smile this time to spare. "Precisely—so that I must choose."

"You must choose."

Strange it was for him then that she stood in his own rooms doing it, while, with an intensity now beyond any that had ever made his breath come slow, he waited for her act. "There's but one thing that can save you from my choice."

"From your choice of my surrender to you?"

"Yes"—and she gave a nod at the long envelope on the table—"your surrender of that."

"What is it then?"

"Your word of honour that you're not in love with her memory."

"Oh—her memory!"

"Ah"—she made a high gesture—"don't speak of it as if you couldn't be. *I* could in your place; and you're one for whom it will do. Her memory's your love. You *want* no other."

He heard her out in stillness, watching her face but not moving. Then he only said: "I'll marry you, mind you, in an hour."

"As we were?"

"As we were."

But she turned to the door, and her headshake was now the end. "We shall never be again as we were!"

THE END

Textual Appendix

Notes on the Text

Compared with the history of the composition and revision of some of Henry James's other novels and tales, the history of his writing and rewriting *The Wings of the Dove* seems simple and straightforward. Only three relevant documents are known to have survived: the first American edition of Charles Scribner's Sons, the first English edition of Archibald Constable and Company—both published in late August 1902—and the New York Edition, carefully revised by James and published by Scribner's in 1909 as volumes XIX and XX of the author's "Collective and Definitive Edition."[1] There was for this novel no serialized magazine version, and so there are no complications and curiosities such as the omitted and the inverted chapters of *The Ambassadors*. Nor is there extant James's lengthy synopsis of the story, James himself having destroyed it after concluding that he could not—or would not—treat his subject with an eye toward satisfying the constraints and requirements of conventional twelve-part magazine publication.[2] Whatever early drafts he dictated to his typist no longer survive, nor does the final typescript he sent off to Constable on May 20, 1902. And whereas James's own marked-up copy of the 1881 American edition of *The Portrait of a Lady* has been preserved, the first-edition volumes of *The Wings of the Dove* in which he made all his 1909 revisions are apparently lost.

Those revisions cannot be said to constitute the same radical reshaping of his original work as do, say, the New York Edition versions of *Daisy Miller*, *The American*, and *The Portrait of a Lady*. James's later characterization of Daisy, for instance, is charged with a tragic dimension that the young girl of the 1878 magazine version was incapable of carrying. In revising *The American* over a quarter century after its initial printing, James took the occasion to reexamine his earlier presuppositions about European social values as well as the relationship between the romance and the novel forms. His early and late visions of Isabel Archer comprise two dramatically different portraits of that "heiress of all the ages." But when James was originally finishing *The Wings of the Dove* in 1901 and 1902, he was already at the end of a long and gradual process of revision regarding his portrayal of Milly Theale—a process that stretched back as far as *Daisy Miller* and included his 1884 tale, "Georgina's Reasons," and notebook entries for *The Wings of the Dove* in 1894. By 1902, then, James's conception of his subject and the mature and complex style by which he rendered it already had the essential signature of his "late manner," his "major phase." Consequently, his New York Edition revisions seven years later may

1. *The Letters of Henry James*, ed. Percy Lubbock (London: Macmillan, 1920), II, 70.
2. For a full discussion of the textual complications caused in *The Ambassadors* by its serialization in a monthly format, see the Norton Critical Edition of the novel, edited by S. P. Rosenbaum.

seem narrow by comparison with those he made in his earlier fiction. Nonetheless James made literally hundreds of acute and penetrating changes when he reread *The Wings of the Dove,* and in their cumulative force they enhance the sustained power of his prose idiom. However minor many of these verbal changes appear when considered individually, they have the collective effect, not of a precious polishing, but of a masterful clarification and fulfillment of that late manner. For the attentive reader—and James reminds us in his Preface that this novel "might have a great deal to give, but would probably ask for equal services in return"—these changes have an air of quiet drama that typifies virtually every aspect of James's most mature fiction.

If we know less than we would like about James's total process of revision—during the long years in which the subject germinated for him and in the time in which he actually wrote the story—hitherto unpublished letters show that, contrary to his expectations, composition came slowly. On September 12, 1900, he wrote to his London literary agent James B. Pinker that he agreed to Archibald Constable's proposal of a £300 advance on royalties for a novel of 100,000 words, to be completed by September 1, 1901.[3] Engaged at the time with *The Ambassadors* and confident of finishing that novel quickly, James, true to his creative habit of working simultaneously on more than one project, had already made some progress on *The Wings of the Dove.* Completing *The Ambassadors,* however, proved a struggle, in part no doubt because of his painstaking efforts to conform to the exigencies of serialization.[4] He was not able to send Pinker the last three installments until July 1901. Meanwhile, though Pinker had made arrangements with Scribner's for simultaneous American publication of *The Wings of the Dove,* James had been compelled to put that novel aside. On June 21[?], 1901, he informed Pinker that he had already requested from Constable "a delay to the end of the year—say *Dec.* 31*st*" and asked his agent to write Scribner's about "the inevitable delay." *The Ambassadors,* he said, had been "a long, long job. . . . It is simply that the thing itself has taken the time—taken it with a strong & insistent hand. —This Constable one will, for intrinsic reasons, take less; besides being already well started. (I did *that* more than a year ago.) . . . I hate the delay actually inflicted; & within the time I shall now positively work it."[5] Although James might be referring here only to the synopsis he had prepared in the hope of serialization in an American magazine, his words seem to imply that he had actual chapters already in hand. In any case he was unable to keep this promise. He was, perhaps, distracted by the fact that —as he put it years later in his Preface—"the work had ignominiously failed, in advance, of all power to see itself 'serialised.' " This news hit him at the same time that, pressed for cash, he had to contend with the failure of Harper's to pay him an advance on royalties for *The Ambassadors* as well

3. This letter and all other previously unpublished manuscript letters quoted or paraphrased here are housed in the Collection of American Literature of the Beinecke Rare Book and Manuscript Library, Yale University, hereinafter cited as YCAL.

4. In a letter of July 10, 1901, James told Pinker: "I've kept back (out of this 'to-be-serialized' form,) three or four chapters (3 & ½ strictly speaking,) which I shall desire to include in the volume. I have withheld these only for the shortness of the Parts, & they will be indispensable in the book" (YCAL).

5. YCAL.

as the firm's hesitation to proceed with that serialization. His inability to make headway "into a world of periodicals and editors, of roaring 'successes' " undoubtedly brought home to him the hard news of his flagging popularity. In addition, his domestic tranquillity was disrupted when his housekeepers of some sixteen years became so plagued with alcoholism that James finally had to dismiss them in September.[6]

It was not until November 6 that he could speak again to Pinker of substantial progress: "I am happy to say I am going very steadily and straight with the novel I am finishing for *Constable*. And now, when I've done it, I shall want to engage for another."[7] The final sections of the novel, treating of Milly Theale's death, may have strained James severely. His writing slowed. The end of the year came, and the novel remained unfinished. In January 1902, he sent to Constable the five hundred pages of typescript he had by then dictated to his typist, Miss Mary Weld, and planned apparently to write the final chapters as he was correcting the proof sheets of the earlier parts.[8] Then, as if his life were imitating his art, he was beset throughout late January and February by an incapacitating illness. Another delay became necessary—in part because of his poor health, in part for reasons having to do with the book trade. A letter from Archibald Constable to Pinker on March 19, 1902, implies that James had proposed putting off publication till the following fall. The publisher's insistent counter-proposal suggests James's large anxiety about "conditions of publication" generally and the reason he alludes to them years later in his Preface:

> We have carefully looked into this question, and have come to the conclusion that the best time to publish this book would be early in, or the middle of, July. We are aware that this is not always considered a good season, but we, for our part, have had some of our best successes with books published at this time. The season would not be over, and people, as a matter of fact—more particularly the people to whom Mr James appeals—do read books during their summer holidays in the country after the season is over. Books will often get much more adequate reviews at this time of year, and in addition to this, we hear that several important books will be kept back for the autumn season; and there is in our opinion every prospect of an equal glut of publications during the next autumn to that which occurred during the autumn past. . . . Kindly therefore arrange for publication at the date named.[9]

Two days later James, recovering in Torquay, wrote to Pinker of his plans, his progress, and certain stipulations:

> I am writing Constable & Co. to-day that if they will give me till *May* 15th (not "end of April,") to hand them the remainder of my Ms. for "Wings of the Dove" I assent to their proposal to publish in July. This will be impossible to me without the full time till May 15th, however. But so I am directly writing them. Can you arrange with Scribner—I mean for same date? I shall tell them it depends on that. They (Constable & Co.) have my corrected &, almost all, revised, proof up to page 355. But there will be 100 pages more. I *can* do it—by May 15th—

6. Leon Edel, *Henry James, The Master: 1901–1916* (New York: J. B. Lippincott, 1972), p. 101.
7. YCAL.
8. In a letter of February 20, 1902, James mentioned to Pinker that "proof comes in" (YCAL).
9. YCAL.

> clearly as of those 100 pages I have already a fraction at home prepared for delivery.[1]

James miscalculated—he would need about 220 more pages to bring the novel to its close—but his creative energies allowed him to dictate this much in just two months. He sent off the remainder of his typescript on May 20.[2]

Plans now called for publication on July 1, and James was concerned that the American edition be issued simultaneously with Constable's so that he would be protected against unauthorized printings which would detract from sales and royalties. He had taken precautions to guarantee that the English edition should not be published too soon: on February 20 he had directed Pinker that "The copy for the *Wings of the Dove* to be sent to Scribners had much best be a set of my clean *Revised* from Constables."[3] Constable did not publish the novel on July 1, however, and a week later James made what has the appearance of an impatient complaint to Pinker: "I shall come & ask you when it is that I may look to Constable & Co. to publish my novel. They have not communicated to me on the subject since Meredith adjured me . . . , at the end of March, to finish it by May 20*th* that it might appear July 1*st*. I finished it to the day, but still I wait."[4] Yet on July 31 Pinker received from a Mr. O. Ryllman of Constable's this letter expressing the publisher's own discontent and frustration regarding publication delays:

> I made a point of inquiring as to the date on which proofs were sent to Mr. Henry James, and we cannot find that there was any delay on our part whatever. You probably know that we were kept waiting a long time for copy, even after we had received some copy. I have just looked over the agreement, and I see that the author undertook to deliver the MS. complete on the 1*st* September 1901 and bound us to publish not later than October 1901. Relying on the fact that when once the book was complete no obstacle would be placed in the way of our publishing on the date we thought most advantageous both to Mr. James and to ourselves, we advertised the book in advance, secured advance copies for subscription to the trade and did what we could to promote interest in this novel. . . . I cannot help feeling that the continued delay and uncertainty about the date of publication will most naturally affect the sale. We are particularly sorry that this should be the case, as we hoped to give this book—the first with which Mr. Henry James has entrusted us —every possible chance, and it is a great disappointment to us that our plans are frustrated.[5]

What this suggests is that James, correcting and revising duplicate sets of proof sheets, deliberately delayed sending the last pages to Constable until he was certain the Scribner's set had reached New York. His strategy finally succeeded only too well, for the American edition was ready for publication before the London edition. On August 15 James lamented to Pinker about "the date of my novel on Scribner's part, as to which I am very, very sorry—as much so as helplessly so."[6] It is likely that either he

1. Letter dated March 21, 1902 (YCAL).
2. James to Pinker, letter dated July 8, 1902 (YCAL).
3. YCAL.
4. Letter dated July 8, 1902 (YCAL).
5. YCAL.
6. YCAL.

or Pinker asked Scribner to hold off. Although announced as published on August 21, the Scribner edition of 3,000 copies was "not issued until eight days after formal publication date," just one day before the Constable edition of 4,000 was published.[7]

The textual differences between the Scribner and Constable editions indicate that James sought to revise substantially the proof sheets for the American text while only correcting obvious errors for Constable. In the London edition are several dozen typographical blunders either not caught by James or left uncorrected by the compositors: typical of these are misspelled words such as "sublety" and "hullucination," numerous instances of the omission of quotation marks necessary to set off dialogue, and various ungrammatical or inaccurate constructions—"that's" for "that" and "had been extended" for "had extended." That James did not prepare the Constable text as carefully as he did the Scribner is demonstrated by the error in the first sentence of chapter II, Book Tenth: whereas the English edition reads "the impression of this inconclusive passage," James emphatically corrected the Scribner proof sheets to read "the deep impression of this inclusive passage." Yet the first American edition is finally no freer of obvious errors, James having had no chance to proofread advance sheets of that text prior to publication. Besides misspellings such as "ingenius," "spontaniety," "ideed," and "namble" (for "nameable"), that edition introduces numerous other typesetting errors which seriously affect sense: "more" for "move," "advantage" for "adage," "three" for "there," "if had" for "if it had," "I" for "He," "could not come" for "couldn't not come," and "lightly" for "slightly."

These errors are most likely the work of compositors and copy editors. Beyond them are the conscious verbal changes—single words, phrases, the addition of a few sentences—which James made with a range of purposes. Very few of these alterations appear to be attempts to adjust his diction for an American audience. Early in the novel, when Kate Croy and Merton Densher speak of the terms of their relationship, James substitutes "vulgar" for "*banal*." The word occurs frequently in James's late revisions and marks his response to that "dread of vulgarity" which F. O. Matthiessen has described as "characteristic of his whole phase of American culture."[8] Several of the revisions correct visual or verbal awkwardnesses. In the Constable text, for example, Densher "stood as on one foot." In the American he "stood as one fast." (James, satisfied with neither image, deleted this description when preparing the New York Edition). The Constable phrase "how she

7. Leon Edel and Dan H. Laurence, *A Bibliography of Henry James* (London: Rupert Hart-Davis, 1957), 120–21. In a letter of March 3, 1903, to Pinker (YCAL), James acknowledged receipt of £67.2.9, his royalties on "the sale of the author's 'Wings of the Dove' since publication," a sum equivalent then to about $325. The Constable edition likewise suffered low sales—so low that the publisher dropped plans to publish *The Golden Bowl:* ". . . in view of the fact that the Libraries refuse to take any fiction published at a higher price than 6/–, and as Mr. Henry James's books are of very considerable length, the cost of production and the fact that we cannot expect to sell more than the copies we sold of *The Wings of the Dove*, render it impossible to pay more than £200 in anticipation of royalty. As I think I understand from you that you refuse to accept less than £300 we fear that we shall reluctantly have to forego the pleasure of publishing for Mr. Hrney [sic] James" (Letter dated March 13, 1903, from O. Ryllman to James B. Pinker, YCAL).

8. *Henry James: The Major Phase* (New York: Oxford University Press, 1944), p. 155.

kept in remembrance how" James changed to "how she kept in remembrance that." The need for such changes—as well as others which improve euphony, heighten verbal felicity, and intensify conversational tones—can probably be traced directly to James's method of composing by dictation: it was a method that undoubtedly gave rise to instances of unwanted repetition but one that James insisted worked best for him.[9] What his process of rereading and revising does is to complement that primary "spoken" style with the quality of a "written" style.

Many of the revisions anticipate those that James would later make for the New York Edition. A number of these changes find him attending to those exacting connectives and qualifiers that lie at the very center of his art. In this sentence of the Constable text, for instance, Densher is thinking about Milly's unopened letter: "The intention announced in it he should but too probably know; but that would have been, for the depths of his spirit, the least part of it." James's simple revision in the American edition is telling: "The intention announced in it he should but too probably know; only that would have been, but for the depths of his spirit, the least part of it." James's style is by no means a contemporary American prose style: indeed, part of our interest in him would seem to stem from the vast differences we sense between our language and his. Yet such revisions remind us that his polished syntax says most precisely what it has to say, says it, in fact, if surprisingly, in the fewest words as well as with the most acute emphasis possible.

But that style also has a capacity to offend us, offend us in much the same way it aggravated William James, whose objections have spoken for many readers with a strong preference for the literal-minded:

> You can't skip a word if you are to get the effect, and 19 out of 20 worthy readers grow intolerant. The method seems perverse: 'Say it *out*, for God's sake,' they cry, 'and have done with it.' And so I say now, give us *one* thing in your older directer manner, just to show that, in spite of your paradoxical success in this unheard-of method, you *can* still write according to accepted canons. Give us that interlude; and then continue like the 'curiosity of literature' which you have become. For gleams and innuendoes and felicitous verbal insinuations you are unapproachable, but the *core* of literature is solid. Give it to us once again.[1]

Nowhere is James's late manner more taxing on the reader than in the pervasiveness of his use of abstract, psychological nouns and the complexity of

9. James defended his method vigorously. What he says of his compositional habit regarding *The Golden Bowl* he might very well have said about the writing of *The Wings of the Dove*: "But I can work only in my own way—a deucedly good one, by the same token! —and am producing the best book, I seem to conceive, that I have ever done. I have really done it fast, for what it is, and for the way I do it—*the* way I seem condemned to which is to *overtreat* my subject by developments and amplifications that have, in large part, eventually to be greatly compressed, but to the prior operation of which the thing afterwards owes what is most durable in its quality. I have written, in perfection, *200,000* words . . .—with rarest perfection!—and you can imagine how much of that, which has taken time, has had to come out. It is not, assuredly, an economic way of work in the short run, but it is, for me, in the long . . ." (James to Pinker, letter dated May 20, 1904, YCAL).

1. William James to Henry James, letter dated May 4, 1907, in *The Letters of William James,* ed. Henry James (Boston: Atlantic Monthly Press, 1920), II, 278.

his commonplace pronoun references. Those nouns, signifying various mental processes of cognition and perception, invariably translate what we normally regard as external, physical events and actions into moments and movements of consciousness; they transform those events and actions into intangible ideas as if to insist that such "ideas" constitute the most solid core of both literature and life. James's pronoun references collaborate in this process and are instrumental in registering ideas as objects, events, actions. One of his revisions illustrates well the way in which the largest and solidest meanings in his fictional world swing oftentimes on the smallest hinges. Where this revised sentence in the American edition reads "they" the Constable text prints "she": "Milly clearly felt these things too, but they affected her companion at moments—that was quite the way Mrs. Stringham would have expressed it—as the princess in a conventional tragedy might have affected the confidant if a personal emotion had ever been permitted to the latter." The revision forces the reader to ask: what is it that affects Mrs. Stringham so? Milly herself, the nearest antecedant, whom the rest of the sentence "fits" so well? Or, as James would have it, the content of the entire lengthy preceding paragraph addressing Susan Stringham's youthful past? Both readings make very good sense, but the rejected one—"she"—omits virtually all the real-life grit in those allusive abstractions that James's style asks us to attend to. The superior reading—difficult, to be sure, because of all the facts of consciousness it embraces—not only helps to characterize the essential qualities of Mrs. Stringham's mind but dramatizes as well something of the source of her passionate involvement with Milly as a mysterious extension of her sense of her own past selfhood. The change epitomizes the extent to which James's language is designed, not to treat single and separate phenomena, but to hold in suspension a sweeping multiplicity of references. His style is urgently multidimensional, and his desire to fulfill that ideal is evident even in word changes that appear totally insignificant. Thus, for example, in this passage in which Densher tells Kate Croy of his newspaper assignment in America, James changed the Constable text's "briefly blocked" to the Scribner reading "blocked a little": "The way for that had been blocked a little by his news from Fleet Street." Here James expands and amplifies Densher's consciousness, and does it by replacing a one-dimensional—temporal—modifier with a simple phrase which, however worn, has connotations at once not only of both the temporal and the spatial but of something we might call psychological extent and duration.

If the first dominant note of James's late manner is his insistence on presenting the solid core of reality in the intangible shapes of consciousness, the second is his virtuosity in elaborating those realities of consciousness so as to make them overwhelmingly concrete. James delights, clearly, in endowing his abstractions with weight and palpability, in making thoughts physical. Thus, "Densher regarded this" becomes "Densher took this in"; "much miscellaneous refreshment" becomes "much scattered refreshment"; "the awful ornaments" of Mrs. Lowder's furniture—and personality—descend upon Densher as "the huge, heavy objects"; and a truth which, in the Constable text, had "not quite come to the surface" is one that, in the first American edition, had "not quite cropped out."

Of the few revisions that affect characterization directly, the most interesting concern Milly and Kate. One corrects what are untypically and undesirably harsh ironies in Milly's language. In the first hour of the gathering at Matcham, Milly, assessing the import of Mrs. Lowder's behavior, thinks of her as having "harangue[d] herself into nobler assurances." The American reading casts Milly's judgment in diction more generous if still ironic: Kate's Aunt Maud had "talk[ed] herself into a sublimer serenity." Another revision deletes what might be construed as a hint of selfishness in Milly. In the Constable text, Kate remarks to Densher: "She has so much to lose. And she wants so much more." In the American edition the second "so much" is omitted. If James's changes tend to exalt Milly, several touching on Kate throw doubt on the moral substance of her attitudes and preoccupations. In her efforts to analyze the surprising hospitality with which her aunt welcomes Densher's visits, Kate finds that the explanations were "all amusing—amusing, that is, in the line of the almost extravagant penetration cultivated by Kate." The Scribner text has those explanations "all amusing —amusing, that is, in the line of the sombre and brooding amusement cultivated by Kate." Several sentences later Kate concludes that Mrs. Lowder wishes to know Densher only "to see best where to 'have' him. That was one of the results of our young woman's sweep of the horizon." James's revision for the Scribner text narrows the scope of Kate's vision and makes it far more subjective: "That was one of the reflexions made in our young woman's high retreat." The texture of the metaphoric fabric in which James wraps Kate consistently denies her that expansive breadth of vision possessed by Milly. From the first time we see his condemned heroine, "seated at her ease" at the "dizzy edge" of an Alpine abyss taking "a 'view' pure and simple, a view of great extent and beauty, but thrown forward and vertiginous," she has, like Milton's Eve, all the world before her. Kate's "high retreat," on the other hand, offers her no embracing "sweep of the horizon" but is instead a sign of her unswerving single-mindedness, a condition of consciousness first suggested by the abrasive interior of Lionel Croy's cramped Chirk Street quarters and then developed in Aunt Maud's "tall rich heavy house," which had figured to Kate "through childhood, through girlhood, as the remotest limit of her vague young world." Mrs. Lowder's house seemed to Kate, "by a rigour early marked, to be reached through long, straight, discouraging vistas, perfect telescopes of streets, . . . which kept lengthening and straightening." Whereas Milly surveys depths and distances from her initial perch in the mountains, what Kate sees from her high retreat on a "dark December afternoon" is all the flatness of "the great grey map of Middlesex spread beneath her lookout." The effect of such changes is to make the resonances of James's complex metaphorical development of his characters more integral and more inexorable in their logic.

James was to revise more fully, more intensely seven years later for the New York Edition. Those last changes clearly engaged his passionate attention. That they did so is still another sign of his dedication to the art of fiction, inasmuch as sales of the previous volumes in the Edition had been shockingly small and financial incentive was lacking. He had been enthusiastic when he began the laborious project of rewriting his earlier fictions, and, seeing copies of the first volumes, *Roderick Hudson* and *The American,* on New Year's Eve 1907, he wrote to Pinker: "They are in every way felicitous, they do every one concerned all honour, & our enterprise has now only to march magnificently on. I have but to glance over the books to feel, I rejoice to say, how I have been a thousand times right to revise & retouch them. Lastly in the manner & in the degree in which I proposed to myself to do it. My effort has taken effect & borne excellent fruit—I have, I feel sure, surer than ever, immensely bettered and benefitted them."[2] By late October, 1908, before he had taken up revising *The Wings of the Dove,* he had learned of the Edition's disappointing sales: whereas the first ten volumes had been printed in issues of 1,500 copies, the later ones were reduced to 1,000 copies. There were no royalties nor prospects of royalties. James had revised over a dozen volumes by this time—some of them he can almost be said to have recreated, so sweeping were the changes—and the public was not buying even in modest numbers the work he looked upon as the monument of his life. On October 23 he bared some of his despair to Pinker: "I am afraid my anti-climax *has* come from the fact that since the publication of the Series began no dimmest light or 'lead' as to its actualities or possibilities of profit has reached me." He had allowed himself to hope for a moderate return, he said, "beguiled thereto also by the measure, known only to myself, of the treasures of ingenuity & labours I have lavished on the amelioration of every page of the thing, & as to which I felt they couldn't *not* somehow 'tell.' " The rest of the letter, in part a formal complaint to his purse, is a refreshing reminder that James, too often thought of as a writer who recognized real experience only as etherealized and attenuated, lived himself with a hand-to-mouth awareness of the mundane pressures to pay the daily household bills:

> . . . I have committed, thank God, no anticipatory follies (the worst is having made out my income-tax return at a distinctly higher than at all warranted figure!—whereby I shall have early in 1909 to pay—as I even did last year—on parts of an income I have never received!)—&, above all am aching in every bone to get back to out-&-out 'creative' work, the long interruptions of which has [*sic*] fairly sickened and poisoned me. (That is the real witch!) I am afraid that moreover in my stupidity before those unexplained—though so grim-looking!—figure-lists of Scribner's I even seemed to make out that a certain $211 (a phrase in his letter seeming also to point to that interpretation) *is,* all the same, owing me. But as you say nothing about this I see that I am again probably deluded & that the mystic scrud meant it is still owing *them*! Which is all that is wanted, verily, to my sad rectification. However, I am now, as it were, prepared for the worst, & as soon as I can get my decks absolutely clear (for, like the convolutions of a vast smothering boa-constrictor, such voluminosities of Proof—of the Editions—to be carefully read—still keep rolling in,) that mere fact will by itself considerably relieve me. I have such visions and arrears of inspiration—![3]

Yet despite the pressure of such distractions, James was able to make extensive changes in *The Wings of the Dove.*

He prepared printer's copy for the New York Edition by inserting into

2. YCAL.

3. YCAL.

the margins of copies of the first American edition his corrections and revisions. His rereading of the novel was careful enough that he caught a number of subtle typographical errors, and it was sufficiently sustained that he substantially altered the texture of his prose style. The most abundant changes have to do with slight shifts in word order, the omission of commas and pronouns, and the use of contractions. These so-called "accidentals" of revision, only some of which are included in the list of variants below, have together the substantive effect of making James's style less parenthetical and involuted, more conversational and colloquial. The typical sentence of the New York Edition is at once simpler than that of the 1902 texts and more complex: simpler because the rearrangement of various, largely adverbial, modifiers allows James to catch more fully the rhythms of speech as well as to clarify the pulses of inward consciousness; more complex because these modifiers, relocated, intensify the fluid interpenetration of fleeting points and passing durations of time occuring in both the minds of his characters and in James's "central intelligence." The American text's "He was on his feet, by this time, to take leave, and also because he was at last too restless" becomes "He was by this time on his feet to take leave, and was also at last too restless." "He tried it then for three weeks, and with the sense, after a little, of not having failed" becomes "He tried that for three weeks, with the sense after a little of not having failed." And "The fact that he had, now, on several occasions, taken with Kate an out-of-the-way walk, that had, each time, defined itself . . ." is revised to "The fact that he had on several recent occasions taken with Kate an out-of-the-way walk that was each time to define itself. . . ." As these examples suggest, many of James's changes of syntax and modification affect Densher most directly; they constitute one aspect of James's effort to heighten the drama of Densher's role as "reflector" and to put the processes of his consciousness and what he "darkly pieces together" more decisively at the center of the novel.

A second category of pervasive revisions shows James making his abstractions resound as physical, weighty realities. Kate's interview with her father is no longer one "for which she prepared herself" but a more stressful encounter "to which she braced herself." In the early texts she refused to "judge herself cheap," but James's revision has her refusing to "hold herself cheap." Lionel Croy stands, not "in the presence of offence," but "under the touch of offence." The various processes of intellection are typically rendered as vigorously physical activities and have at times the aura of athletic contest. Susan Stringham, originally only "full of" discriminations, in the New York Edition "bristled with" them. In the 1902 texts Densher "took in" the look of Lord Mark; in the 1909 revision he "seized" it. An announcement that "was made" to Densher is turned in 1909 to one that "met" him. Kate and Densher at first understand themselves to be playing merely "a waiting game," but in the New York Edition they are conscious of the need to play "patience, a prodigious game of patience." In the early texts Densher "reminded her of this," but in the revision he "put the question to her again." On boarding the train, Kate "had found a place," whereas in the 1909 text she "took her place." And whereas Kate "looked at" Milly in the 1902 editions, James intensifies the action in his revision:

"Almost heedless of the danger of overt freedoms, she eyed [the heroine]." States of consciousness which we tend to perceive as relatively passive James takes care to surround with the energy of activity and movement. At that dramatic moment, for example, at which Susan Stringham tells Densher that Milly "has turned her face to the wall," Mrs. Stringham is initially said to be "intensely conscious now of the step she had taken." In the New York Edition James has her "intensely alive now to the step she had taken." When Milly takes her measure of Lord Mark as one of those "people in England who concealed their play of mind so much more than they advertised it," she thinks of his behavior as "a thing he so definitely insisted on." In the revision, however, it becomes "a trick he had apparently so mastered."

When James spends more words, his additions invariably sharpen descriptions. At Matcham, Milly is at first aware of "kind, lingering eyes" upon her; in the New York Edition they are "kind lingering eyes that took somehow pardonable liberties." When Lord Mark originally describes to Milly Mrs. Lowder's London social circle, he asks: "*Was* it a set at all, or wasn't it, and were there not really no such things as sets, in the place, any more?—was there any thing but the senseless shifting tumble, like that of some great greasy sea in mid-Channel, of an overwhelming melted mixture?" In the New York Edition the language following the dash is dramatically concrete: "—was there anything but the groping and pawing, that of the vague billows of some great greasy sea in mid-Channel, of masses of bewildered people trying to 'get' they didn't know what or where?" And at times James's elaborations can be audacious in their comic mixture of concrete and abstract. Milly's desire in going off to London, we are told, is not social acquaintances but "the human, the English picture itself"—originally "the world imagined always in what one had read and dreamed," but in the revision "the concrete world inferred so fondly from what one had read and dreamed." Mrs. Stringham's cautionary response to Milly's view compels her initially to remark that "it might be a comfort to know in advance even an individual." In the 1909 text her response is that "it might be a comfort to know in advance one or two of the human particles of its concretion." Among the guests at a Lancaster Gate gathering is a person Densher originally refers to—with a literal-concrete sarcasm—as the "innocuous young man." James's lively revision in 1909 toys with the sort of abstract-concrete combination we might more quickly assign to the style of Stephen Crane: Densher now perceives the fellow *as* his clothes, perceives him as the "less expansive of the white waistcoats. . . ." When he tells Kate of his youth and education, Densher finds that the experience "perched him there with her for half an hour, like a cicerone and his victim on a tower-top, before as much of the bird's-eye view of his early years abroad. . . ." In the 1902 texts the description is not only less pictorial but less integral with James's characterizing metaphors: Densher had seen it "put him, for half an hour, on as much of the picture of his early years abroad. . . ."

Repeatedly, even in what at first appear to be less notable revisions, James succeeds in rescuing dead or submerged metaphorical content. Relatively amorphous terms are replaced by those having specific coloration:

"attached it" is transformed into "hung out the premium," mere "results" become "fruits," things in the New York Edition tend to "settle" rather than "define" themselves, to "shine out" rather than be made "manifest." Makeup that "was exact" is turned to makeup that "had had the last touch," "an occasion" is converted to "ground," "a perfectly palpable quality" to "an office nobly filled." A "way" is made a "wave," a "line" becomes a "turn," a "light" is revised to a "radiance," a "great thing" to a "benediction," an "it" is called "this adventure." Lifelessly vauge or neutral diction is made active, specific, pointed. A "sense" becomes a "pulse," an "impression" an "apprehension," a "circumstance" is made into an "afterglow," and an unqualified "balloon" James shapes out into a "great seamed silk balloon." At least eight times James finds active variations on "hesitate" and "hesitation"—words such as "debating," "cast about," "waited." Not only his nouns and verbs but his adverbs, adjectives, and connective words participate in these stylistic-textural revisions. Colorless idiom such as "in one way" is dramatized as "to one tune"; bland qualifiers such as "all the same" are sharpened into "despite everything." Densher, denied entrance to the Palazzo Leporelli, finds in the 1902 texts the taste of his ordeal being "of least savour." In the New York Edition, however, negative phenomena of this sort are often presented in ironically positive terms: there the taste is for Densher "most acrid." There, too, Mrs. Lowder sees him no longer as "more harmless" but as "less formidable." Ideas, perceptions, fluid states of cognition, emotion, and attitude become endowed with an almost spectral presence: "let her know" becomes "give her a glimpse of," a "silence that had followed" Kate's "last words" becomes a "silence resting on her last words," a nebulous "sort of respect" is restated as a "strange shade of respect." Kate, cherishing possessively Densher's long glances and conscious of the fact that she and Densher are lovers, no longer "measured it 'every which way' " but "looked it well in the face." Some of the revisions delete unintended ironies and ambiguities: for Lionel Croy, Kate "was in her way a tangible value," not a "sensible" one. Others heighten ambiguity and dispel clichés. Kate's father, who "kindly sighed" in the early editions, "sighed as from the depths of enlightened experience" in James's final revision. Susan Stringham no longer describes Milly as "an angel" but as "a reigning seraph, a sort of vice-queen of an angel."

As James's Preface is a superb introduction to the novel—indeed, it is a masterful replication, in critical language, of the story's dramatic form and action—so too is it in many ways a brilliant gloss on James's revisions. Those revisions and that Preface constitute together the single large process of James's *seeing* his novel again. Most of the changes so far described here are actualizations of what James in the Preface calls "my game . . . of driving portents home," "that play of the portentous which I cherish so much as a 'value' and am accordingly for ever setting in motion." They are in large part likewise reflections of his artistic consciousness of that "blest wisdom that no expense should be incurred or met, in any corner of picture of mine, without some concrete image of the account kept of it, that is of its being organically re-economised." He had, he knew, not only heightened the sense of picture and scene, he had not only filled the corners of his canvas as Veronese filled the corners of his *Marriage Feast at Cana*; in this very long fiction James had also achieved, in part by virtue of the revisions in his metaphor-making argument, "an economy of composition . . . interesting in itself." That economy derives not from block deletions of material but from oftentimes minor adjustments in the warp and woof of his verbal fabric, adjustments and shifts of nuance that knit more integrally together what he calls his "centres" and "circumferences" of meaning. Another thematic thread running through the Preface is what James found "striking, charming and curious, the author's instinct everywhere for the *indirect* presentation of his main image." James would tell all the bearable truth about the dying Milly but would, in the manner of Emily Dickinson, insist on the perceptual imperative to "tell it slant," to have its "success" lie in "circuit," so that it might "dazzle gradually." Although, as he reminds us, his heroine is only "superficially so absent" in Book First—although, that is to say, all of his revisions finally incarnate *her*—those changes that touch her directly are rare. One of the most notable, a change reminiscent of those by which James had transformed Daisy Miller into a tragic figure, has its precise counterpart in the Preface. Nothing, James says there, could more engage him in his development of Milly Theale "than to recognise fifty reasons for her national and social status." In the 1902 texts he had referred to "the great national feminine and juvenile ease" possessed by Milly; in the New York Edition, Milly, carrying the full weight of James's most mature vision of the destiny of the American character, is not mere girl but fabular princess, possessed now of "the great national, the great maidenly ease."

Far from being "perverse," far from making him a "curiosity of literature," James's strategic design—his design in conceiving his heroine as literally absent from Books First and Second and as present only through indirection in so much of her entire story—is identical to the design of many of the poems of Robert Frost, poems widely felt as somehow profoundly American as well as invitingly plain-spoken. To present Milly as James does is to expand to the limits of a prolonged and elaborate poetic texture of full-length fiction what Frost achieves in, say, "The Road Not Taken," where speaker and reader alike are immersed in a fascination of an experience which, as the poem's title proclaims, is *missed*, an experience literally not there in actual reality but is paradoxically, for that very reason, recorded indelibly in the mind as overwhelmingly there and real. In focusing on experience in this way James keeps before us what he termed "the possible other case." If Milly herself is the symbolic equivalent of the road Frost's speaker does not take, Kate Croy and Merton Densher—their circumstances, their consciousnesses—describe the novel's principal equivalents of the path that speaker actually travels. The novel, like the poem, would lead characters and readers alike into a contemplation, not simply of what "has made all the difference," but rather of the mysterious, irreversible fact of all that difference. As the poem ends, so too the novel: " 'We shall never be again as we were!' "

Defining the novel's "main dramatic complication" as Kate and Densher's "predicament," James saw the need to "create the predicament promptly and build it up solidly, so that it should have for us as much as possible its ominous air of awaiting" Milly. Numerous revisions reinforce the urgency of

James's intentions here. In the 1902 texts, for example, Milly perceives Kate early on as "real," but in the New York Edition Kate becomes for her "the amusing resisting ominous fact." Later, Milly finds that Kate "stood for nothing but herself" instead of "was all her own memento." Other changes heighten Kate's self-consciousness of her own manipulative behavior. Comparing her own fortunes to Milly's, she thinks of the heroine ironically as a girl who "so easily might have been, like herself, only vague and cruelly female"—not "fatally" female. Kate is aware of the need to be, not "a creature of precautions," but "a baser creature, a creature of alarms and precautions." Densher's awareness of their joint deceptions becomes blunter, more forceful: he and Kate would have to deal in a "crafty manner," rather than in a "subtle spirit." He speaks of their having flatly "bamboozled" Mrs. Lowder—not, euphemistically, having "beguiled" her. In the Preface James is careful to suggest the crucial importance of his shifting "centres" of consciousness: although Kate and Densher share at points a "practical *fusion*" of collaborative consciousness, each exercises also an independent consciousness in conflict with the other's. Some of the revisions have the purpose of dramatizing more sharply the "interplay" of these "conspiring and conflicting agents." Densher questions what form of "penalty" rather than "payment" Kate will "coerce" from him. He sees Kate as having him "kept and treasured, so still, under her grasping hand," no longer as "so dear and so perfectly proved and attested." Kate complains to Densher that he shows his love not only "too much" but "too much and too crudely." He allows her not simply to "manipulate" his sexual passion but to "apply antidotes and remedies and subtle sedatives." James remarks in his Preface that "I had scarce availed myself of the privilege of seeing with Densher's eyes . . . [but] I had intelligently marked my possible, my occasional need of it." Perhaps the primary import of his revisions in this area is to endow the character with a more vigorous moral passion and thus to strengthen the credibility of his renunciation of Milly's fortune as the wherewithal of his love for Kate. The language with which James surrounds him in the New York Edition is generally more active: instead of "His corner was so turned . . ." we have "He had so rounded his corner . . . ." And it is more open and honest: instead of seeing Susan Stringham's demands on him as involving on his part a "conscious responsibility," he knows it as an "expectation of performance."

One last intriguing change, illustrative perhaps of the subtle density and sweep of James's process of revision as a whole, should be mentioned here. Besides correcting one error of historical fact (in 1902 he had mistakenly identified the famous pair of Venetian columns "of the Saint Theodore and of the Lion" as the columns "of St. Mark and of the Lion"), James made just one change in the names of his characters. A minor one indeed, "Lady Wells"—undescribed other than as "the friend of Mrs. Lowder's"—was originally, in the early editions, "Lady Mills." She is present only once —in Book Eighth, chapter III—at Milly's rented palazzo, and she is known exclusively by her name. That name is mentioned five times there, four of them by—or in relation to—Kate, who is all eagerness to introduce Densher to the lady. It is in this scene that Densher and Kate at last make their ultimate commitments and accommodations to each other, and the scene is charged with their urgent necessity to find the exact words for their actions: " 'If you want things named you must name them,' " Kate insists. And Densher "had quite, within the minute, been turning names over; and there was only one, which at last stared at him there dreadful, that properly fitted. 'Since she's [Milly's] to die I'm to marry her? . . . So that when her death has taken place I shall in the natural course have money?' " Moments later, understanding himself "master in the conflict," he presses home his corresponding demand upon Kate: " 'You'll come?' " he asks. " 'I'll come' " is Kate's reply. Their acts of giving names to their most ardent desires—desires now in subtle, anxious opposition—are punctuated by their seemingly distracted awareness of Lady Wells: their awareness, first, of her awaiting them and, at the end, of her walking inexorably towards them. The flow of their talk is punctuated too by their repeated references to Milly's oncoming death and by no fewer than a dozen occurrences of the adverb "well." As Densher and Kate make their most intimate assignations secretively, James ironically embodies the resonant implications of those decisions for his characters, puts those implications there in the flesh, in this grand public personage insistently approaching them. Neither they nor the reader has ever seen Lady Wells before, and she will neither be seen nor heard of again. Her brief appearance marks that moment at which, on the surface, Kate and Densher seem to enjoy their most intense "*fusion*" of consciousness; but beneath that surface it marks also the point at which their consciousnesses diverge. Lady Wells "inspired" in Densher "no eagerness," but instead "the question, in germ, of whether this was the kind of person he should be involved with when . . . [he and Kate] were married." Their divergence of view would seem to match the shift in nuance which James himself sought in revising the name. Both "Mills" and "Wells" are ancient, classical English surnames, and each is weighted with its opposing cluster of connotations: the connotations in "mill" of a grinding process, and in "well" the connotations—just to begin with—of a virtually bottomless cavity or abyss. The names occur in a novel and in a scene which pivot on darkly primitive questions of health, of "ill" and "well," and on the swirling crosscurrents of ambiguity which reside even in our simplest language. The novel is in one sense—for James and his characters and his readers alike—a strenuous exercise in putting the most sensitive and accurate definitions on words. As the novel continually dramatizes for us those conflicting and interpenetrating forces of "fortune" defined as "destiny" and "fortune" seen as "wealth," so James's revision here arouses all the ironies in our conceptions of "well-being"—well-being as suggestive of a spiritual wholeness, well-being as requiring economic freedom and luxury. As Lady Wells moves toward Kate and Densher, Milly from the far side of the room "sent across toward them . . . all the candour of her smile, the lustre of her pearls, the value of her life, the essence of her wealth."

It was in his "Preface" to *The Wings of the Dove* that James first alluded to himself publicly as "the poet." The evidence is impressive that he was not using the word carelessly.

Textual Variants

This Norton Critical Edition corrects the New York Edition text in twelve instances: six of these emendations can be described as substantive; the others consist of obvious typographical errors and typesetting faults. Each of the Norton corrections is listed or described here, preceded by page/line numbers from this edition and followed by a bracket; the second reading in each entry is the New York Edition variant.

Volume I

3.5 of a] a of
50.34 company: one] company : one
112.7 felicities] [slipped type]
182.13 fact] facts

Volume II

253.20 companion] companions
286.7 to call] it call
300.8 was: one] was : one
332.35 About what] [irregular spacing]
352.41 obliged. I'll] obliged, I'll
353.5 everything,] everything;
355.17 Mrs.] Mrs,
366.13 association: he] association : he

With the exception of the six readings mentioned above at 3.5, 182.13, 253.20, 286.7, 352.41, and 353.5, the following list of Textual Variants records all the substantive variants between the Norton–New York Edition text and the two earlier editions of the novel, identified as follows:

E the first English edition published in London by Archibald Constable and Company in August, 1902

A the first American edition published in New York by Charles Scribner's Sons in August, 1902

The list constitutes a historical comparison which allows the reader to see at just what point a variant reading was introduced into the novel. The word or words in boldface, preceded by page/line numbers from this Norton Critical Edition, give the reading of the Norton–New York Edition text. All variant readings are given in regular type following a boldface entry. Where, as in the majority of entries, the symbols "**E**" and "**A**" do not appear, both earlier editions differ in the same way from the Norton–New York Edition text. In entries in which only one of these symbols appears the other text is understood to be in conformity with the Norton–New York Edition. Ellipses are used in readings of any length only when the omitted words contain no substantive variants. Considerations of space forbid the inclusion here of the hundreds of differences in spelling, capitalization, and internal sentence punctuation.

Volume I

21.24 of personal personal
21.29 to which she had braced for which she had prepared
21.38 words and words, into
21.39 words nor any words, no
22.7 Wasn't it Was it not
22.34 hold judge
22.35 no at least
22.35 for auction for the auction
23.5 her he her that he
23.8 for the perversities he called his reasons for perversities that he called reasons
23.17 nor or
23.21 penetralia *penetralia*
24.2 straightness straitness **E;** strait-/ness **A**
24.7 told the quiet tale told, in a manner, the happy history
24.13 absurd funny
24.16 absurd funny
24.17 this that
24.38 and had and she had
24.39 tangible sensible
25.1 had no such measure was not a sensible value
25.20 if looking, in consequence of her words, for if, in consequence of her words, looking for
25.43 No—I No. I
26.10 uncompanion'd uncompanied
26.14 tangible sensible
26.15 appraised every point of his appraised his
26.16 these points his own
26.17 they it
26.18 its eternal its old, eternal
26.31 me you me that you
26.33 Mr. Mr **A**
26.34 took the place in took in the place
26.35 with in
26.39 gave point put a point
26.41 put to her inquired
27.3 sighed as from depths of enlightened experience kindly sighed
28.1 of feebler intelligence a bigger fool
28.10 I. I am.
28.14 offer to offer you to
28.16 relevance: relevance,
28.32 free funny
28.41 under the touch in the presence
29.9 poor ruin of an old dad poor old dad
29.10 ruin dad
29.32 you quite a you a quite
29.43 lapse drop
31.9 companion had hereupon companion, hereupon, had
31.12 sponge I sponge that I
31.15 indeed well
31.35 these words this
33.3 demand ask
33.8 reprobation disgust,
33.11 went on demanded
33.17 boobies and boobies asses and asses,
34.8 her sister Marian
34.13 she doubtless she, no doubt,
34.29 vistas, perfect telescopes of streets, and which vistas, which
34.43 with wider knowledge with the aid of knowledge
35.4 yet hadn't had yet not
36.22 times circulate more endlessly times move endlessly **E;** times/more endlessly **A**
37.3 compared likened
37.21 on in
37.37 fact as a besieger, we have hinted, that fact, we have hinted, as a besieger that
38.18 have almost nothing direct to have, directly, almost nothing to
39.8 the more you gave yourself the less of you was left the more one gave oneself the less of one was left
39.10 snatch at you snatch at one
39.11 eating you up eating one up
39.29 understood cared for
40.32 in consequence for it
40.45 up out
41.19 at any rate a grave example a grave example, at any rate,
41.41 feel that for the present I've been feel as if, for the present, I have been
41.42 that as if
42.24 mechanical perfunctory
43.3 of the lowest dreadful
43.6 you'll you may
43.34 that resource it
43.40 conveniently nevertheless
44.6 Kate turn for the time Kate, for the time, turn
44.11 elapsing . . . before that . . . elapsed before
44.32 for the pleasure of to oblige
44.45 hung out the premium attached it
45.6 content pleased
45.18 any one anybody
46.7 civil pleasant
46.12 sceptical he was sceptical
46.32 prompt critic than a prompt follower respecter, in general, than a follower
47.38 able to able in any degree to
47.44 in presence in the presence
48.8 ingenious ingenius **A**
48.20 which Kate, by a rare privilege, found which, by a rare privilege, Kate found
48.32 a slightly slightly
48.33 a not not
48.38 this that
48.41 for the value of in respect to

48.42 by midnight the tone was the tone was by midnight
49.2 nothing to look at or handle, but was somehow everything to feel and to know; nothing, but it was somehow everything—
49.5 regarding looking at
49.7 that in itself after all would have been a small affair for two such handsome persons that, after all, would have been a small affair if there hadn't been something else with it **E;** that. after all, would have been a small affair, if there hadn't been something else with it **A**
49.27 took her place had found a place
49.31 seating placing
49.32 stretch of a desert level of the desert
49.37 abstentions silence
49.39 sure the sure that the
49.40 clear he clear that he
50.6 expressed without expressed between them without
50.11 then worked between then between
50.15 nothing—Kate nothing to her—she
50.45 time as surprisingly time surprisingly
50.45 The occasion had been in every way It had been in every way, the occasion, **E;** It had been, in every way, the occasion, **A**
51.8 sombre and brooding amusement almost extravagant penetration
51.20 reflexions made in our young woman's high retreat results of our young woman's sweep of the horizon
51.25 deputy; it deputy. It **E**
51.27 implication implications **A**
51.34 would seem seemed
51.37 in their keeping on on their keeping on
51.45 fruits results
52.4 ambitious, furthermore, ambitious besides, **E**
52.5 decide settle
52.13 recognised produced
52.16 particular phases of apparent earnestness in phases of apparent earnestness, in particular, in
52.19 "A "a **A**
52.39 scattered miscellaneous **E**
52.42 of course always remarkable in London, and of course, in London, remarkable, and
52.45 thing she was clearly incapable thing, clearly, she was incapable
53.38 She looked it well in the face, she took it She measured it 'every which' way, took it **E**
53.41 that, in her way, she was, she took that she essentially was, she took **E**
54.20 all shameless shameless
54.26 quite positive constitutional **E**
54.41 your conscience one's conscience
54.45 nevertheless all the same
54.46 brand on brand in **E**
55.26 had it all again from her had it again all from her
56.2 and was and she was
56.5 quite as if almost as if
56.10 would—in would—or in **E;** would—or, in **A**
56.18 always struck him she had always seemed to him that she had
56.22 annals make annals to make
57.5 accord—this was very accord, very **E;** accord very **A**
57.9 done: done. **E;** done; **A**
57.11 knew it understood it **E;** knew —it **A**
57.11 I recall my saying I recall that I said
57.18 world seem at times world at times seem **E;** world, at times, seem **A**
57.26 returned declared
57.34 known—only known. Only **E**
57.36 about." about London.' **E**
58.3 debating hesitating
58.4 asked inquired
58.10 as is possible as possible **E**
58.11 Densher took this in with marked but generous wonder Densher regarded this with visible, yet generous, wonder **E;** Densher took this in with visible, but generous, wonder **A**
58.14 only but
58.16 this that **E**
58.19 finer rarer **E**
58.26 on. "He on; "he **A**
58.33 showed again how inveterately he felt in her tone something marked in him again his feeling in her tone, inveterately, something **E;** marked in him, again, his feeling in her tone, inveterately, something **A**
58.38 personally. I've seen it make him wonderful. He personally. He
58.41 cried Densher Densher exclaimed
59.15 stuck to that sustained it
59.17 down; I down. I **E**
59.33 by with
60.4 He gave rather a glazed smile He gave a smile a trifle glassy
60.9 quite beautiful beautiful
60.9 vulgar *banal* **E**
60.11 that which
60.13 vulgar banal **E**
60.13 course," she admitted, "I do see my danger course I do see my danger,' she admitted **E;** course, I do see my danger," she admitted **A**
60.16 you. Don't you; don't
60.21 'them'?"—and the "them"?' The **E;** 'them'?" and the **A**
60.21 man extravagantly marked man strongly, extravagantly marked
60.30 her." [¶] He stared. "Make her.' [¶] 'Make **E**
60.32 seen." [¶] He thought. "Seen seen.'[¶] 'Seen **E**
60.40 a great seamed silk balloon a balloon
61.11 a part several **E**

61.19 this day his day **E;** that day **A**
61.27 that "factor" (to use one of his great newspaper-words), and that, and
61.32 it—which was enough—as it—which was enough as
62.10 huge heavy objects awful ornaments **E;** huge, heavy objects **A**
62.13 noted said
62.13 of her to her niece of Mrs. Lowder to her niece
62.18 characterise the poor woman as dull imply that Aunt Maud was dull
62.31 of. [¶]His of. He stood as on one foot.[¶]His **E;** of. He stood as one fast.[¶]His
63.1 he felt sure he flattered himself
63.1 so many things so unanimously ugly anything so gregariously ugly
63.4 an article—an article that an article—that
63.13 certain at all sure
63.16 and abounded and they abounded
63.25 in presence in the presence
64.6 it immediately made discussion frank it made discussion, immediately, frank
64.15 gave one away let one in
64.16 need for need of
64.35 adage advantage **A**
64.35 always infallibly **E**
64.42 you flatter yourself you know it you flatter yourself that you know it
65.22 that's it's
65.29 of his having shown for flippant, perhaps even for low of having affected her as flippant, perhaps even as low
66.2 grand magnificent
66.34 was to speak spoke
66.35 by that time thus **E;** then **A**
67.38 she should miss him too dreadfully she should miss him intensely
67.42 real true
68.4 because he didn't nose about and babble, because he wasn't because he didn't nose about and wasn't
68.5 out. It out; it
68.21 blocked a little briefly blocked **E**
68.25 had spoken with a wisdom indifferent to that, and had just spoken of the future as if they now really possessed it, and
68.28 her question on the score of their being to appearance able to play patience, a prodigious game of patience, with success her question in respect to the appearance of their being able to play a waiting game with success
68.31 of the appearance of that appearance
68.44 this that
69.2 odd funny
69.6 associated with her name named in her programme
69.9 saw how strange a smile was saw that a strange smile was
69.13 think I think that I
69.19 comparisons comparison
69.29 plenty to amuse herself with plenty to consider
69.34 allowed conceded
70.27 This, if it had been so, That, if it were so,
70.28 perched him there with her for half an hour, like a cicerone and his victim on a tower-top, before as much of the bird's-eye view of put him, for half an hour, on as much of the picture of
70.36 blessedly more imagination and blessedly more sympathy so much more imagination
70.38 as much of both as all
70.40 yet what yet of what
71.25 "placing" disposal
71.35 wings—he had wings, had
71.36 indelible ineffaceable
71.39 gravely too much
71.42 was various and complicated, complicated by wit and taste, she was complicated and brilliant she
72.1 more helpless; so that he was driven in the end to accuse her any thing less; so that he was reduced in the end to accusing her
72.3 She was making him out as all abnormal in order She was making out how abnormal he was in order
72.4 since as
73.2 discretion wisdom and patience
73.6 propitiate their star cultivate their destiny
73.12 hour moment
73.14 hour moment
73.17 put it inquired
73.29 secured to us protected
73.38 They were practically united and splendidly strong They were practically united and they were splendidly strong
74.2 make the most of that drop of the tension make the most of it
75.6 named it— said—
76.35 important truth constant fact
76.38 it had extended to it had been extended to **E**
76.44 two-and-twenty summers, in two-and-twenty in
77.11 in particular was in particular, she was
77.13 convinced as she had to be that it was greater convinced as she was that it was much greater
77.19 finest moment deepest moment
77.33 Yet But
78.2 bristled with discriminations was full of discrimination
79.26 and, if not beauty, at least in and, if not beauty, at least, in
80.9 Maeterlinck Maeterlink
81.26 The difficulty, however, by good fortune, cleared away as The difficulty, by the happiest law, came to nothing as **E**
81.32 this qualification, and it was really to assert it that she this qualification,—really to assert which she **E**

82.33 the state it
82.35 a any
83.20 She reduced, them, Mrs. Stringham would have said, to a She reduced them, Mrs. Stringham would have said, reduced them to a
83.25 by on
84.2 pretend she pretend that she
85.13 they she
85.22 an office nobly filled a perfectly palpable quality
85.23 represented been,
85.45 it prevailed even as the it was, all the same, the
87.2 volume the volume that the
87.19 at into
87.33 had partly a had a partly
88.10 after which then
88.11 she had had
88.20 during still another wait even after another interval
89.37 the words he had then uttered what he had then said to her
89.45 presented announced
90.4 this that
90.7 due assurance this assurance
90.27 confidence—he confidence, and he
90.32 this that
91.22 debated hesitated
92.4 with the pulse of her going with the sense of going
92.12 diligence *diligences* **E;** *diligence* **A**
92.24 curtains drawn curtains were drawn,
92.37 a piece of that very "exposition" dear to the dramatist the very beginning of a drama
93.20 as in as if in
93.35 concrete world inferred so fondly from world imagined always in
93.37 this concrete world this world
93.39 one or two of the human particles of its concretion even an individual
94.2 the partner of these hours her interlocutress
94.6 "bright" clever
95.16 and this the end and that this was the end
95.38 now appeared to our friend interesting now struck our friend as interesting
96.1 florid, alien, exotic florid, exotic and alien
96.12 that this
97.24 lady bore herself in truth lady, in truth, bore herself
97.26 had doubtless just been the had just been, doubtless, the
97.28 couldn't had not
97.37 hadn't she had she not
98.13 seemed part seemed a part
98.17 beauty which particularly beauty, and it particularly
99.1 and all to turn pale again, with and turned pale with
99.4 had for her both so sharp a ring and so deep an undertone had for her so positive a taste and so deep an undertone
99.19 whether if
99.39 years days
99.44 She was the amusing resisting ominous fact, none the less, and each other person and thing was just such a fact; She was real, none the less, and everything and everybody were real;
100.11 was there anything but the groping and pawing, that of the vague billows of some great greasy sea in mid-Channel, of masses of bewildered people trying to "get" they didn't know what or where? was there any thing but the senseless shifting tumble, like that of some great greasy sea in mid-Channel, of an overwhelming melted mixture?
100.21 as packed a concretion as as great a reality as
100.29 that mystery it
100.32 advertised showed
100.34 a trick he had apparently so mastered? a thing he so definitely insisted on?
100.36 took all care for vividness off his hands; that was enough insisted for him; but that was all
101.10 element she element that she
102.6 afterwards she afterwards that she
102.8 characteristic note: pertinent note for her:
102.19 without waiting for a return visit, without waiting for without waiting for a return visit, waiting for
102.30 asked without excessive delay presently asked
102.33 I had I've
103.10 Milly cast about Milly hesitated
103.43 she surrendered so to the inevitable in it—being she surrendered to the inevitability of being
103.45 seen enough seen here enough **A**
104.5 nameable namble **A**
104.18 this that
104.25 had seen
106.14 wouldn't think of such a thing for wouldn't for
106.14 suppose think
106.16 suppose think
106.24 all as all—as
106.29 divination that in any case divination, in any case, that
106.45 flagrantly diverted completely as diverted
107.13 why did Milly none the less why, none the less, did Milly
107.23 would perhaps might
108.16 something he did feel something that he felt
108.20 had doubtless been a note of had been a note, doubtless, of
108.39 that is of the failure of her honesty to be proof that is of her honesty not being proof
109.4 feeling she feeling that she
109.16 was really, no doubt, what was indeed doubtless what
109.35 made make
111.26 their two spirits their fancies

112.4 since for
112.25 course; these two rejoicing not less in course, both rejoicing in
113.14 nature and fortune and covered thereby with the freshness of the morning. Kate nature and fortune. Kate
114.9 for in
114.14 these in these
114.27 discrimination reservation
114.35 cruelly fatally
115.25 itself frankly itself as frankly
115.33 a humbug an idiot **E**
115.33 were as yet, so to speak, all were all, as yet, so to speak,
115.38 humbug failure **E**
115.45 bring up the rear come up in the rear
116.14 brute fraud **E**
117.7 it hadn't for a long time for a long time, it hadn't
117.10 had found found
117.18 agreed to this agreed with her
118.1 clearly more dangers roundabout more dangers, clearly, roundabout
119.9 informant mate
119.22 seen how extraordinarily "small," as every one said, was the world. seen that, as every one said, the world was extraordinarily "small."
119.24 also too
119.32 minute moment
119.37 your friend she
120.24 by reason of for
120.35 wave way
120.38 Kate she
121.3 that gentleman's Mr. Densher's
121.13 a labyrinth labyrinthine **E;** labyrinthe **A**
121.19 attached belonging
121.28 truth"! truth!"
121.28 hadn't in fact quite cropped out had not quite come to the surface **E**
121.31 on all this might cover in Aunt Maud that on this rich attitude of Aunt Maud's that
121.32 could might
121.36 by its containing measurably a by reason of its containing a
122.10 toward towards
122.17 hadn't she had she not
123.2 clear Mrs. clear that Mrs.
123.3 wouldn't have would not, in short, have
123.8 if whether
124.19 indescribably specially
124.20 companion exalted companion as exalted
124.28 a delay to answer an hesitation
124.42 replied answered
125.34 masterful clever
126.19 the girl Milly
126.25 "Oh how can I say? "Oh, I don't know
126.27 as for comfort as if for comfort
127.5 'tip' tip
127.12 their relation might have been afloat their relation was as if afloat
127.13 represented made
128.18 as with gaiety as if with gaiety
128.22 fact of his having fact that he
128.24 a little bit at all
128.27 moment and as moment, as
128.39 had actually undertaken had undertaken
129.20 distinctly doesn't does *not*
129.34 something, after all something, that is, after all
130.21 superficially with Mrs. Lowder with Mrs. Lowder, superficially,
131.9 just clearly
131.37 talk herself into a sublimer serenity harangue herself into nobler assurances **E**
132.4 settle define
132.10 through in
132.9 of one's being of being
133.3 sure she sure that she
133.4 to exert exerting
133.12 despite everything all the same
133.22 Didn't it by this time sufficiently shine out Wasn't it by this time sufficiently manifest
133.25 made clear demonstrated
133.31 accessory truths intermixed truths
134.2 tone"? "Since tone? Since
134.33 The young person under her protection Her interlocutress
135.8 comprehensive unmistakeably free **E;** unmistakably free **A**
135.12 a grand natural force a natural force
135.32 clusters groups
135.39 had begun had began **E**
136.4 eyes that took somehow pardonable liberties. eyes.
136.7 flagrant sensible
137.23 splendidly dressed magnificently dressed
138.20 had has
139.8 felt gathering, felt directing felt gathering, directing
139.23 sighing signing
140.16 the perversity being how she kept in remembrance that Kate the perversity being that she kept in remembrance how Kate **E;** the perversity being that she kept in remembrance that Kate **A**
141.21 herself to herself, in short, to
142.25 Kate the latter
142.26 asking her help asking her for help
142.32 still even
142.41 hadn't it had it not
144.25 at a distance from before
144.26 great contiguous square great square
144.43 she stood for nothing but herself she was all her own momento
145.41 asked here and asked there asked here and there
147.2 been thoroughly a secret been, for example, a secret
148.21 his own *being* the highest his *being* the even highest
149.3 his its **A**
149.6 to one tune or another in one way or another
149.10 whatever"—but whatever." But

149.19 he even showed amusement for it. "I he discreetly indulged her; "I
149.43 spontaneity spontaniety **A**
150.24 the minutes or so ten minutes or so
151.35 any rate anyrate **E**
152.2 that effect this effect
152.31 had come came
152.44 after the fashion of as
153.23 the character this character
153.25 this that
153.39 digesting the information, recognising it digesting the information, feeling it altered, assimilated, recognising it
153.39 again as againas E
154.7 an accepted spell a sort of spell
155.10 final and merciful final, merciful
156.18 independent long long independent
156.21 tempting to wonder for an hour tempting, for an hour, to wonder
157.8 were apparently not weren't, apparently,
158.6 it in it, that is, in
159.3 need take
159.6 into their places into places
159.17 well?" well."
159.33 need take
162.32 for as
162.34 therefore in short therefore, therefore in short
162.36 for the moment perhaps, however, perhaps, however, for the moment,
162.41 waited hesitated
163.2 went, in went for her, in
163.4 lie awake for lie awake, at all events, half the night, for
163.31 on my knowing as knowing
164.15 natural Mrs. Lowder natural that her interlocutress
164.16 subtlety sublety **E**
164.17 written her in reply written to her in answer
164.26 But the But ah, the
164.36 didn't likewise likewise didn't
165.7 could affect the girl as quickly and as sharply could, at once, affect the girl as sharply
165.19 friend and breaking friend, breaking
165.31 quest interlocutress
165.41 for in
166.31 long and discurtained long, discurtained
167.15 room—almost room, and almost
170.20 further moreover
170.27 moreover furthermore
170.32 on it all, as well, moreover, on it all,
170.34 feel she feel that she
171.25 remonstrance reproach
174.4 at last now
174.21 view sight
175.39 this that
176.10 as to about **E**
176.13 and also how and how
176.25 spoken, who spoken./who **E**
177.19 this that that that
177.20 it this
178.11 and was and he was
178.15 nor or
178.20 if the opportunity in question hadn't saved her were it not that the opportunity in question had saved her
178.39 accommodation service
178.39 Whatever the Whatever were the
179.12 in Fifth Avenue in the Fifth Avenue
179.29 with luncheon as well as with her return with luncheon, with her return,
180.39 of his recovery of recovery
181.4 bethinking bethought
181.15 the States the "States"
181.22 question complete question as complete
182.16 noticed noted

Volume II

[187].18 crafty manner subtle spirit
[187].30 a baser creature, a creature of alarms and precautions a creature of precautions
188.8 in regard to that subject on that subject
189.1 with things that maddened. with the maddening.
189.3 to treat them to meet it
189.4 convenience, one convenience one **E**
189.14 that, prolonged and exasperated, made that, prolonged, made
189.17 could feel from such a cause; could be with it;
189.19 to apply antidotes and remedies and subtle sedatives. to manipulate it.
189.21 horribly vulgar vulgar
189.30 produce show
190.8 an equal want of invention and of style a want of fancy
190.18 enough to appease him. enough for him.
190.19 enough to render her a like service. enough for herself.
190.20 enough for that purpose—she as good as showed enough for herself—she showed
190.25 have him, all kept and treasured, so still, under her grasping hand, as have him so dear and so perfectly proved and attested as
190.30 indeed ideed **A**
190.34 remained a while remained awhile
190.37 prodigiously amazingly
191.17 answered rejoined
191.20 Little Miss Theale's individual history was not stuff for his newspaper Little Miss Theale's history was not stuff for his paper
191.31 That appearance in fact, if he

dwelt on it, so ministered to apprehension This fact now became for him so sharp an apprehension
191.33 **He shook off the suspicion to some extent . . . by the aid of a** He to some extent shook if off . . . by a
191.40 **a while** awhile
192.20 **explanation** explanations
192.20 **lot, yet could** lot; these could
192.26 **this** his **A**
192.37 **put the question to her again that afternoon** reminded her of this, that afternoon
192.40 **answered; recalled the moment** answered; the moment
193.12 **lack** want
193.14 **it will be the end; just now therefore it's nothing to ask.** it will be the end, just now; therefore it's nothing to ask.
194.21 **for** to
194.38 **think possible** fancy
196.1 **inconvenient and elusive** elusive
196.10 **had** has **A**
196.23 **ever so intimately appreciable** solid
196.26 **real to her.** real.
196.35 **Means** They
197.4 **should** would
197.16 **on this article of** in respect to
197.16 **after** as to whom
197.18 **at** on
197.18 **this, "that** this, that
197.27 **about us to-day** about to-day
197.28 **her room** her own room
197.31 **returned** inquired
197.35 **ask for** ask
197.40 **brought out** said
197.43 **afterglow** circumstances
198.1 **this adventure** it
198.6 **reappeared. "I** reappeared, 'I
198.17 ***this*** this
199.5 **reverted** came back
200.3 **Yes,"** 'Yes,'
200.26 **" 'Denied it'?** ' "Denied it?" **E**; " 'Denied it?' **A**
201.8 **too much and too crudely** too much
201.24 **must** will
202.1 **an instant** for an instant
202.4 **him he** him that he
202.5 **by** in
202.14 **who** that
204.3 **as harmless and blameless.** as a harmless young man.
204.7 **less formidable** more harmless
204.13 **their hostess** her aunt
204.22 **he** our young man
204.31 **her make-up had had the last touch** her make-up was exact
204.33 **the performer's** Kate's
204.37 **performer** actress
205.1 **in any case** at any rate,
206.18 **hadn't she** had she not
206.29 **the remarkable fact** the fact
206.44 **perceived (with . . . others) that** perceived—with . . . others—that
207.6 **The less expansive of the white waistcoats** The innocuous young man
207.10 **appreciate (especially . . . funny) some** appreciate—especially . . . funny—some
207.28 **him. "You** him. [¶]"You
207.40 **said Kate with much gay expression, though what it expressed he** said Kate with a pleasant spirit, though whether for his own or for Mrs. Stringham's benefit he
208.1 **more things in that head than any of them in any other; unless** more things in mind than any of them, unless
208.32 **hadn't he** had he not
208.33 **seemed desirous** seemed to want
208.42 **much** well
209.17 ***since*** since
209.33 **then incontinently vanish** then vanish
210.2 **exhibited** applied
212.11 **What in the world's the matter** What's the matter
212.15 **What in the world's the matter** What's the matter
212.19 **cast about** had an hesitation
212.26 **that poor lady** she
212.43 **be:** be,
213.2 **flights he** flights that he
213.15 **had been** were
213.39 **"The shadow, you consider, of some physical break-up?"** "That of what you allude to as some physical break-up?"
213.41 **wants more** wants so much more **E**
214.17 **Well, she had it ready. "You** "Well, she had it ready. You **A**
214.29 ***You*** You
214.34 ***will*** will
214.43 **curable?"** curable? **E**
215.1 **answer:** answer,
215.30 **eyes** eye
215.31 **wandered, and as** wandered, as
216.3 **that** this
216.14 **as from the** as if under the
216.23 **knives!" Then after an instant: "One** knives! One **E**
216.24 **guess."[¶]Yes** guess." Yes **A**
217.27 **kept his eyes on Densher.** had his eyes on Densher while he inquired further.
217.32 **That young man concluded in** Densher was sure, however, in
217.44 **their observer** our young man
218.13 **Kate seemed for a little to** Kate, for a little, seemed to
219.23 **balanced** looked
220.14 **again giving out all it had in answer, and** again, in answer, giving out all it had, and
220.29 **understand she** understand that she
220.39 **must have involved** consisted in
220.45 **that** which
221.1 **take them** do
221.3 **take them** do
221.12 **returned** exclaimed
221.16 **say I haven't** say that I have not

221.43 man he man whom he
221.43 appraised made out
222.12 gather see
222.19 them it
222.32 Kate's mastery of the subject Kate's intensity
222.33 *become* become
223.3 took for felt as
223.17 smooth smooth, **A**
223.26 "I'm I'm **A**
223.28 Distinct he felt Distinctly, he felt
223.31 as well, while equally, as **E;** as well as **A**
224.42 open to him workable
225.2 such ground as such an occasion as
225.13 wise enough to mark the case intelligent enough to recognise the cases
225.21 he should surely be rather a muff not to manage by one turn he would surely be rather a muff not to manage on one line
225.26 enthusiasm excitement
225.35 had the attraction of Milly were as charming as Milly
225.38 That This
225.43 it was therefore scarce supposable it need therefore scarce be supposed
226.39 nobody else's business the business of nobody else
227.7 give her a glimpse of it let her know it
227.9 read clear, at first with amusement and then with a strange shade of respect, what made sure, at first with amusement and then with a sort of respect, of what
227.17 that degree of tenderness that tenderness
227.41 he should find himself appreciating he would find himself liking
228.1 mightn't soon himself wouldn't himself
228.13 which there were at the same time but too palpably such difficulties about his uttering. which, at the same time, but too palpably, there were such difficulties about one's uttering.
228.14 be virtually as indelicate to be indelicate, in a way, to
228.22 supremely sovereignty
229.16 having overdone it, having made having overdone it, made
229.17 their entertainer his interlocutress
229.33 remembrance of remembering
229.35 now so complicated, whether by what they said or by what they didn't say now, whether from what they said or from what they didn't say, so complicated
230.17 foretold told
230.32 of help rendered him of helping him
231.13 no. We no—we
231.34 'done' spent
231.43 stupid mistakes any mistakes
232.29 it's it is
233.31 how that
233.41 display proportion
234.19 This They **E**
235.21 very like very much like
235.25 associate or cultivate, as associate, as
235.35 the sense of having rounded his corner. He had so rounded it that he felt himself lose the sense again that his corner was turned. It was so turned that he felt himself to have lost
237.17 "In that case, 'Well, then, **E;** "Well then **A**
237.28 Since it's all for that For it's only for that
238.5 "Won't Won't **E**
238.13 shade sort
239.17 He had so rounded his corner His corner was so turned
239.25 to luncheon into luncheon
239.31 front face
239.33 kept in place, against kept standing, as against
240.3 at for
240.30 Susie. Nobody Susie—nobody
241.12 He's He is
241.44 and shall and I shall
242.28 you comfortable you, comfortable **E**
243.14 as to as if to
243.19 place! place.
244.14 should would
244.40 give away give way **E**
245.1 won't own't **E**
246.14 apron lap
246.22 what's what is
246.24 'case'? "case?" **E**
247.11 is—!" is—' **E;** is—" **A**
247.27 'all.' all.
248.16 way! way.
248.30 reached taken
248.37 pass as not a little passing as something
249.11 her, as within her as, within
250.40 you'd you would
251.14 dealt with met
253.20 this that
253.23 That This
253.24 he quite understood he could but reply that it was all right. he quite understood, he could but reply that it was all right.
253.28 thinks of thinks—of
253.39 rather in a way,
253.40 since because
253.43 even should he even if he should
254.9 him: he would enjoy his use of it, and him; he would enjoy his use of it; and
254.21 That This
255.30 she *she*
256.32 I quite recognise I recognise
256.38 entourage *entourage*
256.40 'entourage' *entourage*
257.32 of—?" of—"
258.16 London, it ministered to her London, her
258.37 care ease
259.17 felt she felt that she
260.9 stillness they stillness that they
260.25 of American of the American
261.28 should would

262.5 a shy, an abject a shy, abject
265.1 was had
266.25 as before as if before
267.7 sala *sala*
267.7 sala *sala*
269.19 it they'll it that they'll
270.15 despite this all the same
270.15 confidence I confidence; I
270.35 even with with even
271.1 smiled. "I'm smiled; "I'm
272.33 hadn't he had he not
273.20 her—breaking her, breaking
273.32 returned rejoined
274.22 nevertheless however
274.31 think you're think that you're
274.38 friend one
275.22 point out demonstrate
275.27 *all* all **E**
275.31 *me* me **E**
276.41 that.[¶]"I that. 'I **E**
277.27 wished he would take himself off, so wished that he would get off quickly, so
277.30 sala *sala*
277.33 sashed and starched besashed and bestarched
278.20 during other visits in the other years
278.31 growth sense
278.34 the recognised house, he made out house in question, he made out
279.26 looked a fool looked like a fool
280.45 rage at rage for
281.16 pure direct
281.21 pure direct
282.11 him—it lurked him, lurking
282.17 padrona *padrona*
282.17 radiance light
283.18 been in the prospect from the first a from the first, in the prospect, a
284.13 case after case even after
284.31 before his departure on his withdrawing
284.39 tested sounded
285.13 by night at night
285.32 question of how question how
286.38 had been all there, been was all there, was
286.40 if it had if had **A**
287.1 unmistakeably— unmistakeably, **E**; unmistakably, **A**
287.19 and it's all I've meant and all I have meant
287.31 those, not less, who represent that. those with it who represent it.
287.38 explain *explain*
289.3 Saint Mark's St. Mark
289.13 of course the least the least, of course,
289.24 help it while help having, while
290.24 them the
290.43 silence resting on silence that had followed
291.10 seemed to bethink herself hesitated
291.12 had bethought herself. "We had hesitated. But she decided. "We
291.16 He questioned her in a moment on a different matter, which had been in his mind a week He asked in a moment for something else instead, something that had been in his mind for a week
291.23 else. else?
293.3 me." [¶]She appeared to wonder. "And me." [¶]"And
293.4 what is it I don't—?" what is it?"
293.14 bamboozled beguiled
293.30 this it
293.42 felt his rebellion more tasted his rebellion as more
293.4 her an instant her for an instant
294.15 it was for a minute as if it was quite, for a minute, as if
294.23 you?"[¶]"Come you?" She spoke low. [¶]"Come
295.16 They themselves suggested They suggested
295.28 good for what he wanted. good.
295.44 the wonderment always stirred in him by glimpses the wonderment that was always with him before glimpses
296.6 his own himself
296.8 monstrous and awkward unnatural
296.15 for himself was for himself it was
296.19 In what Where
296.22 Kate—not Kate, and not
296.26 represent his dignity and his honour. represent his honor.
296.27 His dignity and his honour His honor
296.30 oblige her by accepting it. oblige.
296.33 serve do
296.35 and presently and he presently
297.11 appear show as
297.32 from London in London
297.34 something—to let it begin at once. something—just, this evening, to begin.
298.11 he had in his anxiety about them but he had but
298.15 for of
298.21 that weight as of expected performance which these very moments with Mrs. Stringham caused more and more to settle on his heart. that weight, on his heart, which these very moments with Mrs. Stringham caused more and more to settle.
298.24 the expectation of performance conscious responsibility
298.36 asked inquired
298.40 princess—" princess"— **A**
299.4 certainty she certainty that she
299.7 and also that she gave him a and that she gave him moreover a
299.12 thing Kate thing that Kate
299.13 only wanted it only she wanted it
300.1 on the spot feel a brute feel on the spot like a brute
300.6 how that
300.8 a reigning seraph, a sort of vice-queen of an angel an angel
300.28 means he mayn't be shows him as not

301.14 diffuse in wide warm waves the spell of a general, a beatific mildness as diffusing, in wide warm waves, the spell of a general, a kind of beatific mildness
301.16 he in he, at any rate, in
302.3 judging her determined seeing her as determined
302.15 words (all . . . lightness) with words—all . . . lightness—with
302.27 in London and in in London in
302.36 to affect him that he made out
302.38 penalty payment
302.43 as unmistakeable so unmistakeably **E;** so unmistakably **A**
302.45 so she so that she
303.11 conquest victory
303.31 Almost heedless of the danger of overt freedoms, she eyed Milly She looked at Milly
303.33 with the members of her with her
303.35 native humours—things quite in the line of native freedoms that were quite in the note of
304.18 Yet But
304.24 him Densher
304.25 truly, in the case with which in fact, in the case in which
305.8 in great feather gay
305.13 them!" them! **E**
305.39 marked noted
306.13 Lady Wells Lady Mills
306.14 Lady Wells Lady Mills
306.30 the state the true state
306.39 your seeing your way so little how little you see your way
306.43 emotion (to . . . that) was emotion, to . . . that, was
307.11 verily in truth
307.29 love my love
307.45 *have* have **E**
308.13 *do* do **E**
308.40 Lady Wells Lady Mills
309.15 he I **A**
310.33 *justesse* he *justesse* that he
310.34 since for
310.43 It brought them together again with faces . . . plan. Kate It brought them, with faces . . . plan, together again; Kate
311.22 yourselves go go yourselves
311.29 thing a mask, a stopgap and a "dodge." thing was a mask, a "dodge."
311.32 Lady Wells Lady Mills
311.37 go off leave
311.37 go leave
311.40 Lady Wells Lady Mills
312.19 as a cluster of pleasant memories all melted memories and harmonies **E**
313.2 now not **A**
313.13 hallucination hullucination **E**
313.41 slightly lightly **A**
314.9 was not less effectual than imperative was imperative
315.2 stretched on, was possible but was prolonged, was only possible
315.16 trivial common
315.17 for money or clothes, for letters or for orders for money, or for clothes, or for letters, or for orders
315.20 there thus **E;** three **A**
315.25 of his feeling incapable of promptness quite in the same degree in which a gentleman whose pocket has been picked feels in which he found himself incapable of promptness quite as a gentleman whose pocket has been picked finds himself
315.32 put such a question ask
315.37 had been guessing imagined
316.14 uttering bringing out
316.35 should would
316.37 his suffered snub his snub
317.24 bury Kate's so signal snub sink Kate's snub
317.26 under in
317.30 it one **E**
317.35 that this
317.36 this that
318.45 so brief an exchange this exchange
319.2 to become clear clear
319.15 won't go! won't! **E**
319.18 anything I anything that I
319.33 This was the way she just looked him again, and it was of no attenuation that She looked *him* again, for the moment, and it made nothing better for him that
319.43 so far far
320.1 cast about hesitated
320.16 test. [¶] "Then test. "Then
320.21 held said
320.37 that it
320.41 He was by this time on his feet to take leave, and was also at last too restless. He was on his feet, by this time, to take leave, and also because he was at last too restless.
321.2 didn't he didn't
321.14 getting he had got
321.17 When half an hour before, at the palace, he had turned about to Milly on the question of the impossibility so inwardly felt, turned about on the spot and under her eyes, he had acted, by the sudden force of his seeing When he had turned about to Milly, at the palace, half-an-hour before, on the question of the impossibility he had so strongly felt, turned about on the spot and under her eyes, he had acted, as a consequence of seeing
321.25 or shouldn't or he shouldn't
321.26 have close reference to have reference, directly, to
321.30 all motionless motionless
321.36 injunction to keep from that moment injunction, from that moment, to keep
321.37 several different ways for his doing the different ways of doing
322.2 should be were
322.11 as studying to create as creating, studiously,
322.15 Street wouldn't at this juncture Street, at this juncture wouldn't

322.22 he should probably be able, he felt, to stay his breath and his hand. He should be able to be still enough through everything. he could probably, he felt, be still enough.
322.24 that it then
322.24 weeks, with weeks, and with
322.38 relation they found themselves concerned in relation with which they found themselves concerned **E;** relation which they found themselves concerned in **A**
322.40 the great national, the great maidenly ease the national feminine and juvenile ease
322.41 diviningly and responsively diviningly, responsively,
322.43 it—wouldn't have been fine for want of it, for want, in fine, of
323.13 facilitation facility
323.17 liked in order perhaps only liked, if only
323.19 conception notion
323.21 the line they found most completely workable their most completely workable line
323.28 entirely completely
323.28 made up her made her
323.29 granted. granted in her.
322.31 He knew in his nervousness that he was living at best He was living at best, he knew, in his nervousness
323.33 yet but
323.36 but as as but
323.37 still so who was
323.41 met him, in the court, on the lips of one of the gondoliers, met him was made him, in the court, by one of the gondoliers, and made
323.45 the mere receivable the receivable
324.4 *poco bene* not well
324.5 was anything *was* well
324.6 noted observed
324.11 laid within the palace on laid, in the house, on
324.12 The state of her health was never Her health, or her illness, was not
324.13 How much it might deeply be taken for Whether it was inwardly known as
324.15 question inquiry
324.15 This His
324.19 friend; seeing it was so elegantly presumable he friend because it was unmistakeable that he **E;** friend because it was unmistakable that he **A**
324.24 a view of him not less finely formal than essentially vulgar, but which at the same time he couldn't himself raise an eyebrow to prevent. a vulgar view of him, which was at the same time a view he was definitely hindered from preventing.
324.33 all imputations; the imputation in particular that, clever, tanto bello, and not rich, the young man from London was . . . pressing Miss Theale's fortune hard. the vulgar view; the view that, clever and not rich, the young man from London was . . . after Miss Theales' fortune.
324.36 ineffable intimation that a gentleman implication that he
324.39 casual appendage superficial person
324.40 These interpretations were odious to Densher for the simple reason that they might have been so true of the attitude of an inferior man The view was a vulgar one for Densher because it was but the view that might have been taken of another man
325.5 view, the view and the
325.6 an inferior man another man
325.8 inferior men another man
325.10 of him in him
325.13 taken for granted imputed to
325.28 a profundity, a true deviltry of a refinement of
326.2 in presence in the presence
326.18 no (what . . . all) even no—what . . . all—even
326.20 so mattered mattered
326.29 columns of the Saint Theodore and of the Lion were the frame of columns of St. Mark and of the Lion were like the lintels of
326.35 to Densher precisely as precisely, to Densher, as
327.27 seized took in
327.37 might could
327.39 walk, this walk—and this
328.6 should be was
328.22 twice; he found twice, and found
328.25 but left but he left
329.14 shocks he shocks that he
329.16 which he positively, with occasion, which, positively with the occasion, he
329.35 his return should have the better effect his presence there were better
329.38 come back return
330.15 most acrid of least savour
331.19 appeared part appeared a part
331.32 alive now to conscious now of
332.4 he saw plainly
332.19 popped up characteristically characteristically, popped up
332.34 *me?"* *me."*
332.44 it withal it
333.11 a thick association an association
333.31 which Kate was always showing which was Kate showing
333.41 flower flowers **A**
334.7 it all it
334.8 a wan a kind of wan
334.35 felt saw
335.32 an irritation, which he saw grow in her, from the truth itself an impatience, which he saw growing in her, of the truth itself
335.35 feel we feel that we
336.19 if he had for the time if, for the time, he had
336.28 considered hesitated
337.19 that virtue in him that

338.2 perpetually flowering, right and left perpetually, right and left, flowering
338.15 cast on it suffused it with
338.25 if she had in fact if, in fact, she had
338.44 her." her?"
339.19 left with left there with
339.23 appeared. [¶]He appeared. He **E**
339.28 scruple, which she spoke as if not to press. scruple, and she spoke as if not to press it.
339.40 him—there him, and there
340.25 returned replied
340.43 sole only
341.9 possibly right with her, right with her, possibly
341.20 Lowder." Lowder?"
341.28 " 'This'?" ' "This?" ' **E;** " 'This?' " **A**
341.30 Mrs. Lowder she
341.38 Maud that he was seeing Mrs. Lowder, because of seeing
342.2 'guess,' think,
342.16 putting to his visitor a question making an inquiry of his visitor
342.22 with Milly, never for six weeks for six weeks, with Milly, never
342.25 blushed anew blushed, once more,
342.40 Oh! Oh,
343.1 quickening quickened
343.24 moment and then faced moment; then he faced
343.34 on upon
343.43 sensibly long long, sensibly,
345.23 aversion shrinking
345.26 young woman's friend's
345.30 was in was in fact in
345.41 in presence in the presence
346.1 Opposed to In presence of
346.4 he needed he had needed
346.8 from on
346.10 would at once suppress now, in turn, would suppress now, in a minute, instead,
346.12 symbol of the whole pitch, so far as one might one's self be symbol for Densher of the whole pitch, so far as Densher himself might be
346.15 missed didn't see
346.25 All he did was to smile down vaguely He only, vaguely, smiled down
346.32 supposed it supposed that it
347.4 boat disappear boat to disappear **A**
347.6 counted so as had been such
347.24 crossed the threshold come in
347.26 whole precinct whole of the space
347.38 this that
347.41 not on any presumption not, to any appearance,
348.14 consequently therefore
348.15 Densher invoked this violence to all probability; Densher hoped for a visit in that particular light;
348.21 the visitor's his
348.28 whim fancy
348.32 something he after all something, after all, he
348.42 horrible. It horrible. [¶]It **A**
349.16 fact, and in fact, in
350.7 this that
350.22 and was and this was
350.33 was also was, too,
350.40 benediction great thing
350.41 between the essence and the shell, the just between the just
350.45 grand beautiful
351.6 they met they had met
351.13 Densher again and again again and again, Densher
351.24 had was
351.38 our poor gentleman's Densher's
352.8 mean on his part mean, in him,
353.3 utter uttered
353.8 maintained sustained
353.38 a the **E**
354.8 elements accidents
354.21 appearances appearance
354.30 degree of her having in Venice degree in which, in Venice, she had
354.39 tea-table. [¶]Mrs. tea-table. Mrs. **E**
354.43 tea time
354.45 and hadn't and she had not
355.11 observed, Mrs. Stringham would observed, would
356.2 simply be a feeling be a feeling, simply,
356.15 at the same time he he, at the same time,
357.38 by the time when
358.12 that I I
358.25 it that it then that
358.26 born, she born, as she
358.31 her he her that he
359.7 a the
359.25 that's how so
359.43 to. "No; to. [¶]"No; **A**
360.6 signify matter
360.7 "Well," Kate in a manner persisted, "why Well, Kate in a manner persisted. 'Why **E**
360.9 know that seeing know seeing
360.25 *might* might **E**
360.41 suppose supposed **E**
361.8 'strength'!" "strength!" ' **E;** 'strength!' " **A**
361.9 Otherwise, since . . . you, what was What then, at least, since . . . you, was
361.31 " 'Glad'?"—he ' "Glad?" ' He **E;** " 'Glad?' " he **A**
362.19 She seemed to record the promise. She took it as a generous promise.
363.43 did." did. **E**
364.12 that that's
364.40 the deep impression of this inclusive passage the impression of this inconclusive passage **E**
365.10 had first had at first **E**
365.12 fact she fact that she
365.13 that than **A**
366.35 Such only was at bottom what there That was at bottom all that there

366.38 that almost as never yet he had license to that, almost for the first time, he was free to
367.10 on the ground of in respect to
367.17 see—!" see—"
367.24 had said said **E**
369.14 separated at the prison-door separated, in the prison-cell,
369.22 occasion: with occasion with
369.32 took in the scene again at moments at moments, took in the scene again
369.33 man far off and in man, far off, in
369.36 himself painfully together not to lose it. himself, not to lose it, painfully together.
369.40 what the young man had been conscious of of what the young man had been conscious
369.42 all—that all: that
370.7 which, their which, with their
370.11 needed self-respect to needed, for self-respect, to
370.21 in the London of in London, in
370.35 as it did it as did
370.36 costing it cost
371.9 the present this one
371.9 This That
371.19 prime beginnings
371.20 swift motion quick walk
371.21 swift motion quick walk
371.32 apprehension impression
372.3 by her own air consecrated consecrated, by her own air,
372.7 alone simply
372.9 presently got to what he did want. got, after a little, to what he wanted.
372.40 *That's* That's **E**
373.15 everything, and things he refused to; everything—and things he wouldn't
373.18 it's it is
373.20 do *do*
374.6 him, she made him and making
374.8 irresistibly, she forestalled, the irresistibly, the
374.20 at once instantly
374.37 where on which
375.18 not now
375.36 this his **E**
376.12 for from
376.41 couldn't not come could not come **A**
376.43 he added he yet added **E**
377.17 a figure deep in his own imagination an image deep in his own consciousness
377.23 came late last night came, last night, late
377.39 aware conscious
377.43 Failing on her lips what she felt . . . which she had the next moment What she felt, failing on her lips, . . . which, the next moment, she had
378.17 He was made sure by it . . . never been before He perceived from it . . . never done before
378.27 pace, within . . . had clearly been peace, clearly, within . . . had been
378.34 Of With
378.45 scale matter
379.36 indeed he was at the end of ten minutes indeed, at the end of ten minutes, he was
380.2 hadn't it had it not
380.27 sleep he sleep that he
381.38 exiled exiles
382.3 assurance certainty
382.11 failing in default of
382.30 had her telegram from Mrs. Stringham had, from Mrs. Stringham, her telegram
383.4 Besides—!" Besides—"
383.21 wasn't weren't
383.33 in any case however
384.4 for to
384.14 none the less however
384.31 that, after all, if you're in trouble I can that I, after all, if you're in trouble, can
385.12 wrote—!" wrote—"
385.22 is *is*
386.5 believing seeing
386.6 still as still
386.11 for sordid . . . he felt for as sordid . . . he saw
386.41 offer show
386.42 seemed perversely to fill with another seemed to fill, perversely, with still another
386.45 said. "Only said, "but
387.20 remember the other day. remember.
387.31 nevertheless however
387.31 whether if
387.41 showed he showed that he
387.43 anyway any way
389.29 Then bending his head he Then, bending, he
390.16 "He's not really a bit intelligent."[¶]"Intelligent enough "He's not clever." [¶]"He's clever enough
392.7 but he but she **A**
392.29 as if they had been an accusation, an accusation . . . there was like an accusation, but like an accusation . . . had been
393.21 peculiarly specially
393.22 Peculiarly Specially
393.41 that which
394.2 as to as if to
394.12 addressed him addressed to him
394.14 front, the front, to the **A**
394.19 and to the and the
394.24 undisclosed unrevealed
394.37 give her her head till she has had enough of it. give her, till she has had enough of it, her head.
395.41 had on several recent occasions had now, on several occasions,
395.43 was each time to define had, each time, defined
396.26 what gave them for the first time what, for the first time, gave them
397.14 the courtesy they a courtesy that they
397.20 droll funny

397.44 She had throughout never a word for what Moreover, throughout, she had nothing to say of what
398.10 really in truth
398.20 such freshness and such delicacy as that freshness and that delicacy that
398.32 only that would have been, but for but that would have been, for **E**
398.35 This That
398.42 sound he sound that he
399.2 moreover deepened deepened moreover
399.16 recall in recall, in short, in
399.31 declining any without an
400.7 ***that*** that
400.21 from in
400.24 couldn't yet couldn't as yet
400.27 whether if
400.39 corrections correction **E**
401.1 yet at the same time didn't yet didn't, at the same time,
401.20 he she
401.24 explained said
401.26 said returned
402.7 about as to
402.10 place—!" place—"
402.11 help breaking help from breaking
402.12 at once immediately
402.14 instant nevertheless instant, all the same,
402.22 is you is that you
402.25 small." small. **E**
402.39 more? more.
403.22 slow, he slow to him, he

The Author and the Novel

Editors' Commentary

In his Preface to the New York Edition, James indirectly alerts the reader to his germinal source for *The Wings of the Dove* when he speaks right away of the novel's representing "to my memory a very old—if I shouldn't perhaps rather say a very young—motive." The allusion is to his cousin Mary, or Minnie, Temple, whose tragic death in 1870 at twenty-four from tuberculosis had for James's heart deep psychic reverberations and for his mind profound cultural significance. Minnie's engaging naturalness of character and her stricken condition James was to transmute into two of his most memorable heroines, Isabel Archer of *The Portrait of a Lady* (1881) and Milly Theale of *The Wings of the Dove* (1902). It might be said that, whereas Isabel more resembles Minnie Temple in personality, Milly alone reflects fully her tragic circumstances. A third heroine, and the earliest (1878)—Daisy Miller—possessed both a spontaneity of character and, as things turned out, a fate of doom. Yet, despite the high skill and enamel finish of *Daisy Miller*, James's treatment of theme in that accomplished story is comparatively superficial. His psychological penetration, several years later, into Isabel Archer's character and the symbolic amplitude with which, much later still, he overlaid the psychological realism of Milly Theale's story testify to James's evolution of consciousness, his unwillingness to stand pat. Of the three young American heroines in question, it is Milly Theale, not Isabel or Daisy, who bears the same initials as James's young cousin and is to be formally associated with her. If one reflects on the development of James's sensibility and considers also the fact that Minnie Temple had been dead eight years when *Daisy Miller* was published, one begins to see an extraordinary continuity that extends from Minnie Temple through Daisy Miller and Isabel Archer to Milly Theale—and then on to the unforgettable recreation of Minnie Temple herself in James's autobiographical *Notes of a Son and Brother*, published in 1914, just two years before his own death.

As is so often the case with his Prefaces in the New York Edition, James's own phrasing, that his book exhibits "a very old—if I shouldn't perhaps rather say a very young—motive," gives us the most apt perspective from which to view the novel, especially as regards its sources and backgrounds. James's conception is indeed a matrix of things at once "very old" and "very young." There is, of course, his own youth with his Albany cousins, which James saw as a parallel to his country's mid-century innocence and great expectations—an ambience that he dramatized and individualized in the opening scenes of *The Portrait of a Lady*. And there are other pressing old memories and associations from his youthful past: his sense of the beginning of his own career as a writer; the influence of Hawthorne; the development of his "early" literary idiom and method, epitomized in the successful and popular *Daisy Miller*; his youthful decision never to marry.

But all these "very young motives," as he calls them, had evolved into "very old" ones by the time he undertook writing *The Wings of the Dove*. For one thing, his "later manner" and idiom are, as he indicates to his brother William James, now so "inevitable" that the success of *Daisy Miller* has been left behind and he can no longer, as he informs H. G. Wells in another letter, hope to see any more of his books serialized.

In *The Wings of the Dove* are still other transformations of young into old "motives," including his reconception—literally a "re-vision"—of what had once struck him as the fresh, natural American girl, in whom he now saw a potential "heir of all the ages." This late evolution of an early idea provided James both a character and a situation: a young American girl whose special seal and national inheritance of independence release and liberate that character, ironically, into the chilling discovery of mortality. This grim and poignant discovery that James would suffer Milly Theale to make he had already made himself in a succession of such discoveries. It is the discovery Emily Dickinson had rendered in her poem "Success is counted sweetest." And, if Henry Adams's *Education*, Mark Twain's darker fables, and Scott Fitzgerald's vision—along with James's own—are reliable indicators, such discovery marks a drama broadly applicable to American culture.

Still another of James's transformations involves his use in *The Wings of the Dove* of multiple, successive registers or "deputies" of consciousness. This procedure is in its way as innovative as his earlier mastery of the single viewpoint character, the method which culminated in the formal perfection and symmetry of *The Ambassadors*—the novel James finished just before writing *The Wings of the Dove*. Perhaps in James's reconception of narrative lies the reason for, if not a Hawthorne influence, at the very least a new appreciation of and a turning again toward Hawthornean romance: Hawthorne had, in a sense, pioneered a method of successive "registers of consciousness" in *The Scarlet Letter*. One can sense James's reengagement with Hawthorne, in any case, in his 1904 letter composed for the Hawthorne Centenary: he speaks, for example, of romance in Hawthorne's work as being altogether deeper than a "mechanical . . . list of romantic properties." And he goes on to declare his own relationship to Hawthorne's fiction in language startlingly suggestive of the Minnie Temple/ Milly Theale relationship: "But being present by projection of the mind," he observes, referring to his own necessary distance from the celebration, "present afar off and under another sky, *that* has its advantages too—for other distinctions, for lucidity of vision and a sense of the reason of things."[1] These remarks, like *The Wings of the Dove* itself, show James's fine, paradoxical understanding of the value of memory to art, of the multiplied perspectives the artist gains by being "present afar off." In his now classic study, *Hawthorne* (1879), James had clearly revealed that the earlier writer represented for him the native voice and American cultural situation in art; his cousin Minnie Temple represented for him just that voice and situation in life. *The Wings of the Dove*, in its subject matter and in its treatment, points back to these two figures.

In *Notes of a Son and Brother* (1914), written when James was seven-

1. Henry James, *The American Essays of Henry James*, edited by Leon Edel (New York: Vintage Books, 1956), p. 25.

ty-one, he formally enunciated Minnie Temple's death as the end of his youth and that of his brother William. But he also spoke of her death, while concluding his autobiographical volume, as "so of the essence of tragedy that I was in the far-off aftertime to seek to lay the ghost by wrapping it . . . in the beauty and dignity of art." This statement does more than refer to *The Wings of the Dove*. It in effect stretches back in time to that "very young" moment in 1870 when the youth of the two Jameses ended; it then projects forward into a "far-off aftertime," that is, toward the "very old" memory and moment registered in James's Preface to the New York Edition of 1909; and then it projects forward again toward an even "older" moment, that present moment in 1914 when an aged James wrote his *Notes* as the copestone to his autobiographical recreation of his youth, his "very young" memories and motives. James's autobiographical consciousness, like his artistic consciousness, was to rely on the principle of being "present afar off."

The same reversing and fusing of the "very young" and "very old" resonates throughout *The Wings of the Dove* itself. It occurs, for example, in the conjunction of Milly's "old" New York history, her "old" family, and the fact that all the members of that family died prematurely, leaving James's heroine orphaned. (While James unquestionably mourned his cousin Minnie's death with a special passion, there were, he knew, other deaths behind hers: although Minnie lived only twenty-four years, she lived longer than her four brothers and sisters put together—even though one brother served as a captain and was killed in battle during the Civil War.) Milly's deceased family, however, is itself for James part of an earlier "younger," more sweepingly cultural memory. To think of James writing *The Wings of the Dove* is, in this sense, to think of the dying Melville, author of *Moby-Dick* in 1851, trying forty years later to finish *Billy Budd*. Both writers, each in his own way, were confronting an epoch which seemed to become poetic and legendary only when brutally dealt with, betimes, by life and fate. James saw, finally, a brutal poetry in the life of his most loved cousin Minnie, and brutal poetry becomes the shape and pattern of Milly's short life too. In his fiction it is James's genius that he makes his "reversings" his "fusings," and one such instance in *The Wings of the Dove* lies in Milly's remarkable likeness to a young woman in a very old portrait by Bronzino: Milly, on the brink of life, looking at her likeness, sees clearly that the woman in the painting is "dead, dead, dead." As the Bronzino painting is to Milly Theale, so *The Wings of the Dove* itself is to Minnie Temple.

Another instance of reversal and fusion, later in the novel, involves Milly's choice of residence in Venice. Venice is very old, yet its surpassing beauty, its poetic and legendary quality, is defined inevitably by its doomed condition. It is a city whose "poetry of misfortune," as James phrased it in his travel literature, was based upon a deep and mysterious reconciliation of opposites. "Is it the style," he inquires, while pondering Venice's immemorial beauty,

> that has brought about the decrepitude, or the decrepitude that has, as it were, intensified and consecrated the style? There is an ambiguity about it all that constantly haunts and beguiles. . . . The misfortune of Venice

> being, accordingly, at every point what we most touch, feel and see, we end by assuming it to be of the essence of her dignity. . . . What was most beautiful is gone; what was next most beautiful is, thank goodness, going—that, I think, is the monstrous description of the better part of your thought. Is it really your fault if the place makes you want so desperately to read history into everything?

This passage suggests the relationship between Milly's death in Venice and her transfiguration at the end of the novel. But it also suggests in a deep way the metamorphosis of Minnie Temple into Milly Theale; or, more accurately, it exhibits an analogue to that process. The "old" New York background of Milly and then her eventual death in the old city of Venice work together to create once again the contrast, yet fusion, present in the novel and implicit in James's subject and source. On a thematic level, these two cities can perhaps be said to contrast, but *not* fuse with, the city of London, which functions in this novel as the real, unpoetic and in a sense unredeemed center of hypocrisy and human manipulation. And yet, on another deeper level, the level of the novel's own organic expression of its subject, the fusion *is* there, inevitably so. For note that James in the passage above recognizes there is something "monstrous" in the way human nature responds and attaches itself to "the poetry of misfortune"; so too James, the essential novelist, placing literally his beginning, middle, and end in London, insists on making that city the center of his book. His London people, the "English gang," as Howells calls them in his critical essay, do indeed respond and attach themselves "monstrously" to Milly. For James the elements of romance are part of the real, the "poetry" part of the "monstrous."

While James's notebook entries seem to begin at the point where his complex personal motives leave off, with the fictional situation itself and its possibilities for "drama," some of his letters present us with his ex post facto sense of the problem of the book's structure. This criticism he voices both in the Preface to the New York Edition and again, by way of contrast with the ease and symmetry of *The Ambassadors*, in his Preface to that novel. Whatever one's judgment of James's disappointment with the structure of *The Wings of the Dove*, that structure is intimately interconnected with his presentation of Milly. It is especially important to recall that James himself traces any structural awkwardness and asymmetry in the novel to his own "instinct everywhere for the *indirect* presentation of his main image," his need "to approach [Milly] circuitously, deal with her at second hand. . . . All of which proceeds, obviously, from her painter's tenderness of imagination about her, which reduces him to watching her, as it were, through the successive windows of other people's interest in her." Yet in the 1914 letters to Mrs. William James and Mrs. Richard Gilder, James maintained that, despite the pain involved, he *did* succeed in his recreation of Minnie Temple in *Notes of a Son and Brother*. It is hard to escape the conclusion that his satisfaction with this last effort proceeds from his sense of having solved the problem he had faced earlier in *The Wings of the Dove*. We should note that in the 1914 autobiography James chose to "do" Minnie largely and directly through her own letters. These are letters of the sort that "speak" throughout. Minnie's voice is distinctly audible in them and the characteristic elements of her personality are clearly exposed. To read these letters and then to recall James's comments in his New York Edition Preface to *The Wings of the Dove* about an inevitable conflict between the principles of "picture" and "drama" is to have the following conviction: Henry James in his later phase, mind, and heart instinctively and increasingly saw fictional issues as versions of nonfictional ones, historical elements as also poetic ones, and cultural drama as the extension of individual temperament. All such matters were for him even less compartmentalized than for most creative writers. One senses, in fact, that his vision challenges our usual inclination to separate the invented from the historical, technical processes from fundamental meaning or, as so often assumed in psychoanalytic discussion, the author's formal "pretext" from his hidden, passional substratum of motive.

A most important instance of the intersection of the actual with the imaginary in James's Hawthornean novel concerns his use of the Bronzino portrait, a little-known Renaissance painting of a Venetian noblewoman. The painting, reproduced here for the first time in any edition of *The Wings of the Dove*, adds to James's insistently "indirect" treatment of his heroine a fresh perspective, a visual embodiment. In the story itself the Bronzino plays a part by no means incidental but crucial. Milly Theale is not just compared to the lady but literally equated with her in appearance. As a number of scholars, following James, have pointed out, the novelist builds the center of his story around the incident in Book Fifth in which Milly is shown by Lord Mark the portrait—her "painted sister." Indeed, the estate where the portrait hangs is called "Matcham." But what is so crucial to the episode is the extent to which this particular Bronzino painting functions as an "objective correlative" to Milly's situation. In London a scant three weeks or so, Milly has already become a triumphant success in Maud Lowder's circle of friends, a group that includes among others Kate Croy and Lord Mark. Milly recognizes this astonishing success while at Matcham and describes it to herself as "a sort of magnificent maximum, the pink dawn of an apotheosis coming so curiously soon"—an expression that bespeaks her own absence of ego. But upon confronting the portrait that all the guests at Matcham agree resembles her, Milly immediately finds herself looking at it "through tears." She stares at the portrait and recognizes, both in the historical fact of the subject and in the treatment of the figure, that the woman with whom she is identified is dead. And Milly speaks through her tears: "I shall never be better than this."

It is the statement and the moment in the novel when Milly Theale absorbs and enunciates the penetrating truth about her condition, the moment she first responds to the fact of her mortality. The Bronzino functions, then, as a reflexive truth-teller for the central character and for the reader. The fact that the Bronzino is a real painting means that we are allowed to see Milly, as it were, physically; more importantly, the portrait lets us see symbolically her tragic situation. The most dominant imagery surrounding James's heroine throughout the novel is that of an abyss, the figurative vehicle that represents the looming imminence of her death. What struck James about the Bronzino is that all the vibrant color and sensuousness of the lovely woman are countered dramatically by the ominous dark void of the sculpture niche she is seated in front of. Thus, as painting, the Bronzino truly matches the thrust of James's verbal depiction of his heroine's moment and condition. That Milly Theale's intuition, prompted by her sight of the Bronzino, is profoundly pivotal to the entire development of the novel is clearer still when we remember two additional details about the moment. First, it is Lord Mark who brought her, "in nooks and opening vistas," to the Bronzino painting "deep within" the house. And Lord Mark is that character who will eventually break Milly's will to live when he reveals to her, later in the novel, that Kate Croy and Merton Densher are engaged. Second, it is Kate Croy who appears at just the moment Milly regards the portrait: Kate, whom Milly requests to accompany her to the office of Dr. Luke Strett the next morning. Milly's two killers in effect complete the scene.

But the same portrait—and here we have another of James's fusions and reversals—conveys the novel's redemptive theme as well. One can observe the transformed "halo" of the young woman's braided hair and the replacement of the traditional Madonna's child with a book. The first time we see Milly in the novel she has wandered away from a small bench high in the Alps and, having laid aside her book, is gazing out over a precipice: she has in a sense moved out of the painting and into the possibility, and the treachery, of life. Like the two psalms which provided James his title for the book, these two details in the portrait pick up the sacramental tension that James infuses his story with.

To speak of the novel's redemptive theme is to call to mind James's late essay, "Is There a Life After Death?" This long, dense, deeply reflective and poetic meditation was his contribution to a 1910 symposium on immortality. Since his brother William's death occurred the same year, James's argument, at once for him unusually personal and philosophical, may perhaps be in part a memorial statement for William James. In any event, though it is even now virtually unread, it possesses just those dramatic complexities and elaborately extended conceits which characterize *The Wings of the Dove*. In this document James confronts the argument that, since consciousness is necessarily a function of the brain, the life of the physical mechanism must define the limits of consciousness. While his attempt to refute this position may be of interest in relation to contemporary trends in the philosophy of science, its greater import here is its revelation to us of James's views on the extension of human consciousness to include intimations of the supernatural. The essay is itself an extraordinary analogue to the redemptive theme in *The Wings of the Dove* and likewise provides the best way to perceive a bridge between such a theme and James's concurrent work in his stories of the quasi-supernatural—his "ghostly" tales.[2] We have already seen him allude to *The Wings of the*

2. For a fuller discussion of this issue see Richard A. Hocks, *Henry James and Pragmatistic Thought: A Study in the Relationship between the Philosophy of William James and the Literary Art of Henry James* (Chapel Hill: University of North Carolina Press, 1974), pp. 188–229. Although we have included a generous portion of James's long immortality essay, we have still left out almost half of it. Of additional interest may be his view concerning the validity of mediums; the essay likewise contains further comments on the pertinence of immortality to the artist. A complete text of this little-known work can be found in F. O. Matthiessen, *The James Family* (New York: Alfred A. Knopf, 1947), pp. 602–14.

Dove in his autobiography as an effort "to lay the ghost" of his memory of Minnie Temple "in the beauty and dignity of art." It is significant, in such a context, to hear him speak at one early point in the immortality essay about our attempt as human beings to "flutter away from that account of ourselves [as "material organs" without a "soul"], on sublime occasion, only to come back to it with the collapse of our wings." But it is more startling yet to hear him, at the other end of the essay, speak about the exact opposite "account of ourselves" in these words: ". . . who shall say over what fields of experience, past or current, and what immensities of perception and yearning, it shall *not* spread its wings?"

In preparing this Norton Critical Edition we have been struck repeatedly by the fact that, while *The Wings of the Dove* continues to have a fairly small number of readers, it has for some time assumed one of the strongest positions critically in James's entire canon. Given this circumstance, we are presenting in the Criticism section a predominance of affirmative and varied readings. Our notion is a little that of reintroducing the reader, whether student or teacher, to a novel which already possesses its classic interpretations, even though those readings, like the book itself, are not likely to be as familiar as those attending other novels of equal stature —including at least two of James's own, *The Portrait of a Lady* and *The Ambassadors*. Perhaps Oscar Cargill is not too far from the mark when he tells us: "*The Wings of the Dove* is not for every reader of Henry James. . . . Ability to recognize subtle, dramatic tensions, the proliferation of poetic imagery, the iteration of symbols, the rich interweaving of themes, and the control of multiplicity of elements comes only from a long saturation in James. The readers with such a saturation find *The Wings of the Dove* an immensely rewarding book and an immensely personal one."[3] This assessment may not sound too surprising, since it deals in terms and considerations which can apply to any one of several of James's major and more difficult novels. What may be surprising, however, is the discovery that Cargill, in his massive study of James—one in which he reviews and assimilates all the criticism before 1961 on James's novels, major and minor—concludes that *The Wings of the Dove* is first among James's works.[4] The Criticism section of this Norton Critical Edition suggests the extent to which Cargill's judgment finds support among Jamesian scholars and critics.

At the same time, the novelist's own qualification about the book should not be ignored, even though *The Wings of the Dove* appears in both the lists James gives in his letter to Mrs. Prothero. Although the fundamental issue in any assessment of his novel must come round inevitably to the success or failure of James's treatment of his protagonist Milly Theale, the novel clearly exhibits in Kate Croy and Merton Densher especially—but also in Maud Lowder, in Susan Stringham, Lord Mark, and others such as Luke Strett—a wealth of matter for debate and discussion, an opportunity for close critical explication. Both the Criticism section and the Selected Bibliography reflect the novel's multiplicity of perspectives.

3. Oscar Cargill, *The Novels of Henry James* (New York: Macmillan Company, 1961) pp. 374–75.

4. Ibid., p. 429.

HENRY JAMES

From His Notebooks†

34 De Vere Gardens, W., November 3d, 1894.

Isn't perhaps something to be made of the idea that came to me some time ago and that I have not hitherto made any note of—the little idea of the situation of some young creature (it seems to me preferably a woman, but of this I'm not sure), who, at 20, on the threshold of a life that has seemed boundless, is suddenly condemned to death (by consumption, heart-disease, or whatever) by the voice of the physician? She learns that she has but a short time to live, and she rebels, she is terrified, she cries out in her anguish, her tragic young despair. She is in love with life, her dreams of it have been immense, and she clings to it with passion, with supplication. 'I don't want to die—I won't, I won't, oh, let me live; oh, save me!' She is equally pathetic in her doom and in her horror of it. If she only could live just a little; just a little more—just a little longer. She is like a creature dragged shrieking to the guillotine—to the shambles. The idea of a young man who meets her, who, knowing her fate, is terribly touched by her, and who conceives the idea of saving her as far as he can—little as that may be. She has known nothing, has seen nothing, it was all beginning to come to her. Even a respite, with one hour of joy, of what other people, of what happy people, know: even this would come to her as a rescue, as a blessing. The young man, in his pity, wishes he could make her taste of happiness, give her something that it breaks her heart to go without having known. That 'something' can only be—of course—the chance to love and to be loved. He is not in love with her, he only deeply pities her: he has imagination enough to know what she feels. His impulse of kindness, of indulgence to her. She will live at the most but her little hour—so what does it matter? But the young man is entangled with another woman, committed, pledged, 'engaged' to one—and it is in that that a little story seems to reside. I see him as having somehow to risk something, to lose something, to sacrifice something in order to be kind to her, and to do it without a reward, for the poor girl, even if he loved her, has no life to give him in return: no life and no personal, no physical surrender, for it seems to me that one must represent her as too ill for *that*

† From *The Notebooks of Henry James,* edited by F. O. Matthiessen and Kenneth Murdock (New York: Oxford University Press, 1947), pp. 169–74, 187–88.

particular case. It has bothered me in thinking of the little picture —this idea of the physical possession, the brief physical, passional rapture which at first appeared essential to it; bothered me on account of the ugliness, the incongruity, the nastiness, *en somme*,[1] of the man's 'having' a sick girl: also on account of something rather pitifully obvious and vulgar in the presentation of such a remedy for her despair—and such a remedy only. 'Oh, she's dying without having had it? Give it to her and let her die'—that strikes me as sufficiently second-rate. Doesn't a greater prettiness, as well as a better chance for a story, abide in her being already too ill for that, and in his being able merely to show her some delicacy of kindness, let her think that they might have loved each other *ad infinitum* if it hadn't been too late. That, however, is a detail: what some dim vision of a little dramatic situation seems to attach to is the relation that this encounter places him in to the woman to whom he is *otherwise* attached and committed and whom he has never doubted (any more than this person herself has) that he loves. It appears inevitably, or necessarily, preliminary that his encounter with the tragic girl shall be *through* the other woman: I mean that *she* shall know all about her too (they may be relatives —brought together after an absence or for the first time) and shall be a close witness of the story. If I were writing for a French public the whole thing would be simple—the elder, the 'other,' woman would simply be the mistress of the young man, and it would be a question of his taking on the dying girl for a time—having a temporary liaison with her. But one can do so little with English adultery —it is so much less inevitable, and so much more ugly in all its hiding and lying side. It is so undermined by our immemorial tradition of original freedom of choice, and by our practically universal acceptance of divorce. At any rate in this case, the anecdote, which I don't, by the way, at all yet *see*, is probably more dramatic, in truth, on some basis of marriage being in question, marriage with the other woman, or even with both! The little action hovers before me as abiding, somehow, in the particular complication that his attitude (to the girl) engenders for the man, a complication culminating in some sacrifice for him, or some great loss, or disaster. The difficulty is that the beauty of the thing is precisely in his not being in love with the girl—in the disinterestedness of his conduct. She is in love with him—that is it: she has been already so before she is condemned. He *knows* it, he learns it at the same time that he learns—as *she* has learnt—that her illness will carry her off. Say that she swims into his ken as the cousin—newly introduced— of the woman he is engaged to. Say he *is* definitely engaged to this

1. "In short."

elder girl and has been engaged some time, but that there is some serious obstacle to their marrying soon. It is what is called a long engagement. They are obliged to wait, to delay, to have patience. He has no income and she has no fortune, or there is some insurmountable opposition on the part of her father. Her father, her family, have reasons for disliking the young man; the father is infirm, she has to be with him to the end, he will do nothing for them, etc., etc. Or say they have simply no means—which indeed has the drawback of not being very creditable to the hero. From the moment a young man engages himself he ought to have means: if he hasn't he oughtn't to engage himself. The little story *que j'entrev*ois[2] here suddenly seems to remind me of Ed. About's *Germaine,* read long years ago and but dimly remembered. But I don't care for that. If the young couple have at any rate, and for whatever reason, to *wait* (say for her, or for *his,* father's death) I get what is essential. *Ecco.*[3] They are waiting. The young man in these circumstances encounters the dying girl as a friend or relation of his fiancée. *She* has money—*she* is rich. She is in love with him—she is tragic and touching. He takes his betrothed, his fiancée, fully into his confidence about her and says, 'Don't be jealous if I'm kind to her—you see *why* it is.' The fiancée is generous, she also is magnanimous—she is full of pity too. She gives him rope—she says, 'Oh yes, poor thing: be kind to her.' It goes further than she quite likes; but still she holds out—she is so sure of her lover. The poor child *is*—most visibly—dying: what, therefore, does it matter? She can last but a little; and she's so in love! But they are weary of their waiting, the two fiancés—and it is their own prospects that are of prime importance to them. It becomes very clear that the dying girl would marry the young man on the spot if she could.

November 7th, 1894. I dropped the foregoing the other day—I was pressed for time and it was taking me too far. There are difficulties in it—and what I meant was really only to throw out a feeler. I had asked myself if there was anything in the idea of the man's *agreeing with his fiancée that he shall marry the poor girl in order to come into her money and in the certitude that she will die and leave the money to him*—on which basis (his becoming a widower with property) they themselves will at last be able to marry. Then the sequel to that?—I can scarcely imagine any—I doubt if I can—that isn't ugly and vulgar: I mean vulgarly ugly. This would be the case with the girl's not, after all, dying—and that's not what I want, or mean. Moreover if she's as much in love with the young

2. "That I glimpse."

2. "Behold."

man as I conceive her, she would leave him the money without any question of marriage. I seem to get hold of the tail of a pretty idea in making that happiness, that life, that snatched experience the girl longs for, BE, *in fact*, some rapturous act of that sort—some act of generosity, of passionate beneficence, of pure sacrifice, to the man she loves. This would obviate all 'marriage' between *them*, and everything so vulgar as an 'engagement,' and, removing the poor creature's yearning from the class of egotistic pleasures, the dream of being possessed and possessing, etc., make it something fine and strange. I think I see something good in *that* solution—it seems dimly to come to me. I think I see the thing beginning with the 2 girls—*who must not love each other*. This idea would require that the dying girl, whom family or personal circumstances have brought into relation with the other, should not be fond of her, should have some reason to dislike her, to do *her* at least no benefit or service. One may see the story begin with them—the two together; brought a little nearer by the younger girl's illness and trouble—so that the *other* is the FIRST witness of her despair and has the FIRST knowledge of her doom. The poor girl breaks out to her, raves, can't help it. The elder girl is privately, secretly engaged to the young man, and the other hasn't seen him when the doom aforesaid is pronounced. She sees him and she loves him—he becomes witness of her state and, as I have noted, immensely pities her. It is with a vision of what she could do for *him* that she renewedly pleads for life. *Then* she learns, discovers—or rather she doesn't discover at first—that the 2 others—her relative and the young man—are engaged. I seem to see what passes between the young man and his fiancée on the subject. The fiancée has a plan—she suddenly has a vision of what may happen. She forbids her lover to tell the girl they are engaged. Her plan is that he shall give himself to her for the time, be 'nice' to her, respond, express, devote himself to her, let her love him and behave as if he loved her. She foresees that, under these circumstances, the girl will become capable of some act of immense generosity—of generosity by which her own life, her own prospect of marriage will profit—and without her really losing anything in the meanwhile. She therefore *checks* her lover's impulse, and he rather mystifiedly and bewilderedly assents. He 'reads her game' at last—she doesn't formally communicate it to him. She knows the girl dislikes her—say she has jilted the girl's brother, who has afterwards died. At any rate there is a *reason* for the dislike—and she, the elder woman, knows it. So much as this the latter tells her lover—for she has, after all, to *give* him a reason—explain to *him*, too, the dislike. In fact, in giving it, she virtually communicates her idea. 'Play a certain game—and you'll have money from her. But if she knows the money is to help you to marry me, you *won't* have it; never in the world!' My idea is that the poor (that is the rich) girl *shall,* at last, know this—learn this. *How* does she learn it? From the inexorable father? From the jilted brother (if he be *not* dead)? From the man (some other man, that is) whom the inexorable father *does* want her (i.e., want the elder girl) to marry; and who, disgusted with her, turns, in a spirit both vindictive and mercenary, to the rich little invalid? I seem to see, a little, THAT. I seem to see a penniless peer, whom my elder girl refuses. Her father will help her if she does that—if she makes the snobbish alliance. Her merit, her virtue is that she *won't* make it, and it is by this sacrifice that she holds her lover—*en le faisant valoir*[4]—and makes him enter, as it were, into her scheme. Lord X. is a poor creature and has *nothing* but his title. The girl's sacrifice is a sacrifice of that—but of nothing else. If Lord X. goes, then, rebuffed, mercenarily and vindictively to the dying girl and tells her the other woman's 'game' (that is, her presumed, divined, engagement, from which she little by little, piece by piece, or in a vivid flash of divination, *constructs* the engagement), I seem to get almost a little 3-act play—with the main part for a young actress. I get, at any rate, a distinct and rather dramatic *action,* don't I?—*Voyons un peu.*[5] The poor dying girl has an immense shock from her new knowledge—but her passion, after a little, is splendidly proof against it. She rallies to it—to her passion, her yearning just to taste, briefly, of life *that* way—and becomes capable of still clinging to her generosity. She clings, she clings. But the young man learns from her that she *knows*—knows of his existing tie. This enables him to measure her devotion, her beauty of soul—and it produces a tremendous effect upon him. He becomes ashamed of his tacit assent to his fiancée's idea—conceives a horror of it. In that horror he draws close to the dying girl. He tells his prospective bride that she knows—and yet how she seems determined to behave. 'So much the better!' says the prospective bride. My story pure and simple, very crudely and briefly, appears to be that the girl dies, leaving money—a good deal of money—to the man she has so hopelessly and generously loved, and whom it has become her idea of causing to contribute to her one supreme experience *by* thus helping, thus, at any cost, testifying to a pure devotion to. Then the young man is left with the money face to face with his fiancée. It is what now happens between them that constitutes the climax, the denouement of the story. She is eager, ready to marry now, but he has really fallen in love with the dead girl. Something in the other woman's whole attitude in the matter—in the 'game' he consented in a

4. "Setting him off to advantage."

5. "Let's see."

manner to become the instrument of: something in all this revolts him and puts him off. In the light of how exquisite the dead girl was he sees how little exquisite is the living. He's in distress <about> what to do—he hangs fire—he asks himself to what extent he can do himself violence. This change, this regret and revulsion, this deep commotion, his betrothed perceives, and she presently charges him with his infidelity, with failing her now, when they've reached, as it were, their goal. Does he want to keep the money for himself? There is a very painful, almost violent scene between them. (How it all—or am I detached?—seems to map itself out as a little 3-act play!) They *break*, in a word—he says, 'Be it so! —as the woman gives him, in her resentment and jealousy (of the other's memory, now) an *opening* to break—by offering to let him off. But he offers her the money and she *takes* it. Then vindictively, in spite, *with* the money and with her father's restored countenance, she marries Lord X., while he lives poor and single and faithful—faithful to the image of the dead. Of course in the case of a play that one might entertain any hope of having acted, this denouement would have to be altered. The action would be the same up <to> the point of the girl's apparently impending death —and the donation of money would be before the EVENT. The rupture between the two fiancés would take place also before—he would buy her off with the money, the same way—and the hero would go back to the poor girl as her very own. Under this delight she would revive and cleave to him, and the curtain would fall on their embrace, as it were, and the *possibility* of their marriage and of her living. Lord X. and the betrothed's flunkeyizing father would be characters, and there would have to be a confidant of the hero's *evolution*, his emotions. I seem to see a vivid figure, and perhaps, for the hero, THAT figure—i.e., the 'confidant'—in the dying girl's *homme d'affaires*.[6] I seem to see her perhaps as an American and this personage, the *homme d'affaires*, as a good American comedy-type. His wife would be the elderly woman. I seem to see Nice or Mentone—or Cairo—or Corfu—designated as the scene of the action, at least in the 1st act, and the gatherability of the people on some common ground, the salon of an hotel or the garden of the same.

* * *

34 D. V. G., W., February 14th, 1895

* * *

I have been reading over the long note—the 1st in this book[7]—I

6. Business agent.

7. James is referring here to Notebook IV, which extends from November 3, 1894, to October 15, 1895.

made some time since on the subject of the dying girl who wants to live—to live and love, etc.; and am greatly struck with all it contains. It is there, the story; strongly, richly there; a thing, surely, of great potential interest and beauty and of a strong, firm artistic *ossature*.[8] It is *full*—the scheme; and one has only to stir it up *à pleines mains*.[9] I allude to my final sketch of it—the idea of the rupture at last between the 2 fiancés: his giving her the money and her taking it and marrying Lord X. * * * As I ask myself the question, *with* the very asking of it, and the utterance of that word so charged with memories and pains, something seems to open out before me, and at the same time to press upon me with an extraordinary tenderness of embrace. Compensations and solutions seem to stand there with open arms for me—and something of the 'meaning' to come to me of past bitterness, of recent bitterness that otherwise has seemed a mere sickening, unflavoured draught. Has a *part* of all this wasted passion and squandered time (of the last 5 years) been simply the precious lesson, taught me in that roundabout and devious, that cruelly expensive, way, *of the singular value for a narrative plan too* of the (I don't know *what* adequately to call it) divine principle of the Scenario? If that *has* been one side of the moral of the whole unspeakable, the whole tragic experience, I almost bless the pangs and the pains and the miseries of it. IF there has lurked in the central core of it this exquisite truth—I almost hold my breath with suspense as I try to formulate it; so much, so *much*, hangs radiantly there as depending on it—this exquisite truth that what I call the divine principle in question is a key that, working in the same *general* way fits the complicated chambers of *both* the dramatic and the narrative lock: IF, I say, I have crept round through long apparent barrenness, through suffering and sadness intolerable, to that rare perception—why my infinite little loss is converted into an almost infinite little gain. The long figuring out, the patient, passionate little *cahier*,[1] becomes the *mot de l'énigme*,[2] the thing to live by. Let me commemorate here, in this manner, such a portentous little discovery, the discovery, probably, of a truth of real value even if I exaggerate, as I daresay I do, its *partée*,[3] its magicality. <Now?> something of those qualities in it vivifies, backwardly—or appears to, a little—all the horrors that one has been through, all the thankless faith, the unblessed work. But how much of the precious there may be in it I can only tell by trying.

* * *

8. Bone structure.
9. Energetically.
1. Notebook.
2. "Key to the puzzle."
3. Possibly an error for *portée*, meaning "range" or "scope."

HENRY JAMES

From His Letters†

To William Dean Howells

Lamb House, Rye[1]
Sept. 12th, 1902.

* * * Meanwhile, let me add, I have directed to Scribners to send you a thing of my own, too long-winded and minute a thing, but well-meaning, just put forth under the name of *The Wings of the Dove.*

* * *

To Mrs. Cadwalader Jones

Lamb House, Rye.
October 23d, 1902.

* * *

But I am not thanking you, all this time, for the interesting remarks about the book I had last placed in your hands (The Wings of the Dove), which you so heroically flung upon paper even on the heaving deep—a feat to *me* very prodigious. I won't say your criticism was eminent for the time and place—I'll say, frankly, that it was eminent in itself, and all full of suggestion. The fact is, however, that one is so aware one's self, even to satiety, of the rights and wrongs of these matters—especially of the wrongs—that freshness of mind almost fails for discriminations, however benevolent, of others. Such is the price of having written many books and lived many years. The thing in question is, by a complicated accident which it would take too long to describe to you, too inordinately drawn out, and too inordinately rubbed in. The centre, moreover, isn't in the middle, or the middle, rather, isn't in the centre, but ever so much too near the end, so that what was to come after it is truncated. The book, in fine, has too big a head for its body. I am trying, all the while, to write one with the opposite disproportion—the body too big for its head. So I shall perhaps do if I live to 150. Don't therefore undermine me by general remarks. And dictating,

† Except for the last two letters, the selections in this section are from *The Letters of Henry James,* edited by Percy Lubbock (New York: Charles Scribner's Sons, 1920), I, 399, 402–3, 404–6, 407–8; II, 332–33, 362, 402.

1. James's handsome home in the ancient village of Rye, on the Sussex coast south of London—his principal residence after 1898.

please, has moreover nothing to do with it. The value of that process for me is in its help to do over and over, for which it is extremely adapted, and which is the only way I can do at all. It soon enough, accordingly, becomes, *intellectually*, absolutely identical with the act of writing—or has become so, after five years now, with me; so that the difference is only material and illusory—only the difference, that is, that I walk up and down: which is so much to the good.—But I must stop walking now.[2]

* * *

To H. G. Wells

Lamb House, Rye.
November 15th, 1902.

My dear Wells,

It is too horribly long that I have neglected an interesting (for I can't say an interested) inquiry of yours—in your last note; and neglected it precisely *because* the acknowledgment involved had to be an explanation. I have somehow, for the last month, not felt capable of explanations, it being my infirmity that when "finishing a book" (and that seems my chronic condition) my poor enfeebled cerebration becomes incapable of the least extra effort, however slight and simple. My correspondence then shrinks and shrinks—only the least explicit of my letters get themselves approximately written. And somehow it has seemed highly explicit to tell you that (in reply to your suggestive last) those wondrous and copious preliminary statements (of my fictions that are to be) don't really exist in any form in which they can be imparted. I think I know to whom you allude as having seen their semblance—and indeed their very substance; but in two exceptional (as it were) cases. In these cases what was seen was the statement drawn up on the basis of the serialization of the work—drawn up in one case with extreme detail and at extreme length (in 20,000 words!)[3] Pinker saw that: it referred to a long novel, afterwards (this more than a year) written and finished, but not yet, to my great inconvenience, published;[4] but it went more than two years ago to America, to the Harpers, and there remained and has probably been destroyed. Were it here I would with pleasure transmit it to you; for, though I say it who should not, it *was*, the statement, full and vivid, I think, as a statement could be, of a subject as worked out. Then Conrad saw a

2. James means he is likewise dictating this letter.
3. This refers to James's "Project for Novel," his outline for *The Ambassadors* sent to Harper and Brothers.
4. *The Ambassadors* (1903) appeared after *The Wings of the Dove* (1902), although it was written earlier.

shorter one of the *Wings of the D.*—also well enough in its way, but only half as long and proportionately less developed. *That* had been prepared so that the book might be serialized in another American periodical, but this wholly failed (what secrets and shames I reveal to you!) and the thing (the book) was then written, the subject treated, on a more free and independent scale. But *that* synopsis too has been destroyed; it was returned from the U.S., but I had then no occasion to preserve it. And evidently no fiction of mine can or *will* now be serialized; certainly I shall not again draw up detailed and explicit plans for unconvinced and ungracious editors; so that I fear I shall have nothing of that sort to show. A plan for *myself*, as copious and developed as possible, I always do draw up—that is the two documents I speak of were based upon, and extracted from, such a preliminary *private* outpouring. But this latter voluminous effusion is, ever, so extremely familiar, confidential and intimate—in the form of an interminable garrulous letter addressed to my own fond fancy—that, though I always for easy reference, have it carefully typed, it isn't a thing I would willingly expose to any eye but my own. And even *then*, sometimes, I shrink! So there it is. I am greatly touched by your respectful curiosity, but I haven't, you see, anything coherent to produce. Let me promise however that if I ever do, within any calculable time, address a manifesto to the dim editorial mind, you shall certainly have the benefit of a copy. Candour compels me to add that that consummation has now become unlikely. It is too wantonly expensive a treat to them. In the first place they will none of me, and in the second the relief, and greater intellectual dignity, so to speak, of working on one's own scale, one's own line of continuity and in one's own absolutely independent *tone*, is too precious to me to be again forfeited. Pardon my too many words. I only add that I hope the domestic heaven bends blue above you.

Yours, my dear Wells, always,
HENRY JAMES.

To William Dean Howells

Lamb House, Rye.
December 11th, 1902.

My dear Howells,

Nothing more delightful, or that has touched me more closely, even to the spring of tears, has befallen me for years, literally, than to receive your beautiful letter of Nov. 30th, so largely and liberally anent *The W. of the D.* Every word of it goes to my heart and to "thank" you for it seems a mere grimace. The same post brought me a letter from dear John Hay, so that my measure has been full. I haven't known anything about the American "notices," heaven save the mark! any more than about those here (which I am told, however, have been remarkably genial;) so that I have *not* had the sense of confrontation with a public more than usually childish—I mean had it in any special way. I confess, however, that that is my chronic sense—the more than usual childishness of publics: and it is (has been,) in my mind, long since discounted, and my work definitely insists upon being independent of such phantasms and on unfolding itself wholly from its own "innards." Of course, in our conditions, doing anything decent is pure disinterested, unsupported, unrewarded heroism; but that's in the day's work. The *faculty of attention* has utterly vanished from the general anglo-saxon mind, extinguished at its source by the big blatant *Bayadère* of Journalism, of the newspaper and the *picture* (above all) magazine; who keeps screaming "Look at *me, I* am the thing, and I only, the thing that will keep you in relation with me *all the time* without your having to attend *one minute* of the time." If you are moved to write anything anywhere about the W. *of the D.* do say something of that—it so awfully wants saying. But we live in a lovely age for literature or for any art but the mere visual. Illustrations, loud simplifications and *grossissements*,[5] the big building * * * the "mounted" play, the prose that is careful to be in the tone of, and with the distinction of a newspaper or bill-poster advertisement—these, and these only, meseems, "stand a chance."

* * *

To Mrs. G. W. Prothero

Rye.
Sept. 14th, 1913.

This, please, for the delightful young man from Texas,[6] who shews such excellent dispositions. I only want to meet him half way, and I hope very much he won't think I don't when I tell him that the following indications as to five of my productions (splendid number—I glory in the tribute of his appetite!) are all on the basis of the Scribner's (or Macmillan's) collective and revised and prefaced edition of my things, and that if he is not minded somehow to obtain access to *that* form of them, ignoring any others, he forfeits half, or much more than half, my confidence. So I thus amicably beseech him—! I suggest to give him as alternatives these two slightly different lists:

5. Blowups, enlargements.
6. Stark Young, who had asked Mrs. George Prothero, wife of the well-known editor, for guidance in reading James.

1. Roderick Hudson.
2. The Portrait of a Lady.
3. The Princess Casamassima.
4. The Wings of the Dove.
5. The Golden Bowl.

---

1. The American.
2. The Tragic Muse.
3. The Wings of the Dove.
4. The Ambassadors.
5. The Golden Bowl.

The second list is, as it were, the more "advanced." And when it comes to the shorter Tales the question is more difficult (for characteristic selection) and demands separate treatment. Come to me about that, dear young man from Texas, later on—you shall have your little tarts when you have eaten your beef and potatoes. Meanwhile receive this from your admirable friend Mrs. Prothero.

HENRY JAMES.

To Mrs. William James

21 Carlyle Mansions
Cheyne Walk, S. W.
March 29th, 1914.

* * * I hoped of course you would find in the book[7] something of what I difficultly tried to put there—and you have indeed; you have found all, and I rejoice, because it was in talk with you in that terrible winter of 1910–11 that the impulse to the whole attempt came to me. Glad you will be to know that the thing appears to be quite extraordinarily appreciated, absolutely acclaimed, here—scarcely any difficulties being felt as to "parts that are best," unless it be that the early passage and the final chapter about dear Minnie seem the great, the beautiful "success" of the whole. What I have been able to do for *her* after all the long years—judged by this test of expressed admiration—strikes me as a wondrous stroke of fate and beneficence of time: I seem really to have * * * made her emerge and live on, endowed her with a kind dim sweet immortality that places and keeps her—and I couldn't be at all sure that I was doing it; I was ao anxious and worried as to my really getting the effect in the right way—with tact and taste and without overstrain. * * *

7. *Notes of a Son and Brother.*

To Mrs. Richard W. Gilder

Lamb House, Rye
Sept. 2nd, 1914.

* * * Therefore when you express to me so beautifully and touchingly your interest in my "Notes" of—another life and planet, as one now can but feel, I have to make an enormous effort to hitch the allusion to my present consciousness. I knew you would enter deeply into the chapter about Minnie Temple, and had your young, your younger intimacy with her at the back of my consciousness even while I wrote. I had in mind a small, a very small, number of persons who would be peculiarly reached by what I was doing and would really know what I was talking about, as the mass of others couldn't, and you were of course in that distinguished little group. I could but leave you to be as deeply moved as I was sure you would be, and surely I can but be glad to have given you the occasion. I remember your telling me long ago that you were not allowed during that last year to have access to her; but I myself, for most of it, was still further away,[8] and yet the vividness of her while it went on seems none the less to have been preserved for us all alike, only waiting for a right pressure of the spring to bring it out. What is most pathetic in the light of to-day has seemed to me the so tragically little real care she got, the little there was real knowledge enough, or presence of mind enough, to do for her, so that she was probably sacrificed in a degree and a way that would be impossible to-day. * * *

From William James, Fall 1902†

I have read *The Wings of the Dove* (for which all thanks!) but what shall I say of a book constructed on a method which so belies everything that *I* acknowledge as law? You've reversed every traditional canon of story-telling (especially the fundamental one of *telling* the story, which you carefully avoid) and have created a new *genre littéraire* which I can't help thinking perverse, but in which you nevertheless *succeed*, for I read with interest to the end (many pages, and innumerable sentences twice over to see what the dickens they could possibly mean) and all with unflagging curiosity to know what the upshot might become. It's very *distingué* in its way, there are touches unique and inimitable, but it's a 'rum' way; and the worst of it is that I don't know whether it's fatal and inevitable

8. James was in Europe at the time of his young cousin's death in early 1870.

† This letter and Henry James's reply, which follows, are from F. O. Matthiessen, *The James Family* (New York: Alfred A. Knopf, 1947), p. 338.

with you, or deliberate and possible to put off and on. At any rate it is your own, and no one can drive you out or supplant you, so pray send along everything else you do, whether in this line or not, and it will add great solace to our lives.

"In its way" the book is most *beautiful*—the great thing is the way—I went fizzling about concerning it, and expressing my wonder all the while I was reading it.

To William James, Fall 1902

Your reflections on *The Wings of the Dove* greatly interest me. Yet, after all, I don't know that I can very explicitly *meet* them. Or rather, really, there is too much to say. One writes as one *can*—and also as one sees, judges, feels, thinks, and I feel and think so much on the ignoble state to which in this age of every cheapness I see the novel as a form, reduced, that there is doubtless greatly, with me, the element of what I would as well as of what I 'can.' At any rate my stuff, such as it is, is inevitable for me. Of that there is no doubt. But I should think you might well fail of joy in it—for I certainly feel that it is, in its way, more and more positive. Don't despair, however, even yet, for I feel that in its way, as I say, there may be still other variations of way that will more or less *donner le change*.[9]

HENRY JAMES

From His Preface to *The Ambassadors*†

* * * Fortunately thus I am able to estimate this[1] as, frankly, quite the best, "all round," of all my productions; any failure of that justification would have made such an extreme of complacency publicly fatuous.

I recall then in this connexion no moment of subjective intermittence, never one of those alarms as for a suspected hollow beneath one's feet, a felt ingratitude in the scheme adopted, under which confidence fails and opportunity seems but to mock. If the motive of "The Wings of the Dove," as I have noted,[2] was to worry me at moments by a sealing-up of its face—though without prejudice to its again, of a sudden, fairly grimacing with expression

9. Mislead, deceive.

† Henry James, *The Ambassadors* (New York: Charles Scribner's Sons, 1909), XXI, vii.

1. *The Ambassadors.*

2. James is alluding here to his Preface to *The Wings of the Dove*, which introduces volume 19 of the New York Edition.

—so in this other business I had absolute conviction and constant clearness to deal with; it had been a frank proposition, the whole bunch of data, installed on my premises like a monotony of fine weather. (The order of composition, in these things, I may mention, was reversed by the order of publication; the earlier written of the two books having appeared as the later.) * * *

HENRY JAMES

From *Italian Hours*†

[*St. Mark's*]

* * * The condition of this ancient sanctuary is surely a great scandal. The pedlars and commissioners ply their trade—often a very unclean one—at the very door of the temple; they follow you across the threshold, into the sacred dusk, and pull your sleeve, and hiss into your ear, scuffling with each other for customers. There is a great deal of dishonour about St. Mark's altogether, and if Venice, as I say, has become a great bazaar, this exquisite edifice is now the biggest booth.

* * *

[*The Venetian People*]

* * * One grows very fond of these people, and the reason of one's fondness is the frankness and sweetness of their address. That of the Italian family at large has much to recommend it; but in the Venetian manner there is something peculiarly ingratiating. One feels that the race is old, that it has a long and rich civilisation in its blood, and that if it hasn't been blessed by fortune it has at least been polished by time. It hasn't a genius for stiff morality, and indeed makes few pretensions in that direction. It scruples but scantly to represent the false as the true, and has been accused of cultivating the occasion to grasp and to overreach, and of steering a crooked course—not to your and my advantage—amid the sanctities of property. It has been accused further of loving if not too well at least too often, of being in fine as little austere as possible. I am not sure it is very brave, nor struck with its being very industrious. But it has an unfailing sense of the amenities of life; the poorest Vene-

† From "Venice" (1882), "The Grand Canal" (1892), and "Two Old Houses and Three Young Women" (1899); reprinted in Henry James, *Italian Hours* (New York: Horizon Press, 1968), pp. 11, 22–23, 25–26, 43–45, 46–47, 89–91, 100–101.

tian is a natural man of the world. He is better company than persons of his class are apt to be among the nations of industry and virtue—where people are also sometimes perceived to lie and steal and otherwise misconduct themselves. * * *

[*Relation of Art to Life in Venice*]

* * * But you must go to Venice in very fact to see the other masters, who form part of your life while you are there, who illuminate your view of the universe. It is difficult to express one's relation to them; the whole Venetian art-world is so near, so familiar, so much an extension and adjunct of the spreading actual, that it seems almost invidious to say one owes more to one of them than to the other. Nowhere, not even in Holland, where the correspondence between the real aspects and the little polished canvases is so constant and so exquisite, do art and life seem so interfused and, as it were, so consanguineous. All the splendour of light and colour, all the Venetian air and the Venetian history are on the walls and ceilings of the palaces; and all the genius of the masters, all the images and visions they have left upon canvas, seem to tremble in the sunbeams and dance upon the waves. That is the perpetual interest of the place—that you live in a certain sort of knowledge as in a rosy cloud. You don't go into the churches and galleries by way of a change from the streets; you go into them because they offer you an exquisite reproduction of the things that surround you. All Venice was both model and painter, and life was so pictorial that art couldn't help becoming so. With all diminutions life is pictorial still, and this fact gives an extraordinary freshness to one's perception of the great Venetian works. You judge of them not as a connoisseur, but as a man of the world, and you enjoy them because they are so social and so true. * * *

[*The Vast Mausoleum with a Turnstile at the Door*]

* * * "Venetian life" is a mere literary convention, though it be an indispensable figure. The words have played an effective part in the literature of sensibility; they constituted thirty years ago the title of Mr. Howells's delightful volume of impressions; but in using them to-day one owes some frank amends to one's own lucidity. Let me carefully premise therefore that so often as they shall again drop from my pen, so often I beg to be regarded as systematically superficial.

Venetian life, in the large old sense, has long since come to an end, and the essential present character of the most melancholy of cities resides simply in its being the most beautiful of tombs.

Nowhere else has the past been laid to rest with such tenderness, such a sadness of resignation and remembrance. Nowhere else is the present so alien, so discontinuous, so like a crowd in a cemetery without garlands for the graves. It has no flowers in its hands, but, as a compensation perhaps—and the thing is doubtless more to the point—it has money and little red books. The everlasting shuffle of these irresponsible visitors in the Piazza is contemporary Venetian life. Everything else is only a reverberation of that. The vast mausoleum has a turnstile at the door, and a functionary in a shabby uniform lets you in, as per tariff, to see how dead it is. From this *constatation*, this cold curiosity, proceed all the industry, the prosperity, the vitality of the place. The shopkeepers and gondoliers, the beggars and the models, depend upon it for a living; they are the custodians and the ushers of the great museum—they are even themselves to a certain extent the objects of exhibition. It is in the wide vestibule of the square that the polyglot pilgrims gather most densely; Piazza San Marco is the lobby of the opera in the intervals of the performance. The present fortune of Venice, the lamentable difference, is most easily measured there, and that is why, in the effort to resist our pessimism, we must turn away both from the purchasers and from the vendors of *ricordi*.[1] The *ricordi* that we prefer are gathered best where the gondola glides—best of all on the noble waterway that begins in its glory at the Salute and ends in its abasement at the railway station. It is, however, the cockneyfied Piazzetta (forgive me, shade of St. Theodore—has not a brand new café begun to glare there, electrically, this very year?) that introduces us most directly to the great picture by which the Grand Canal works its first spell, and to which a thousand artists, not always with a talent apiece, have paid their tribute. We pass into the Piazzetta to look down the great throat, as it were, of Venice, and the vision must console us for turning our back on St. Mark's.

* * *

[*The Resident Palaces of Venice*]

* * * On the other side of the Canal twinkles and glitters the long row of the happy palaces which are mainly expensive hotels. There is a little of everything everywhere, in the bright Venetian air, but to these houses belongs especially the appearance of sitting, across the water, at the receipt of custom, of watching in their hypocritical loveliness for the stranger and the victim. I call them happy, because even their sordid uses and their vulgar signs melt somehow, with their vague sea-stained pinks and drabs, into that

1. Souvenirs, memories.

strange gaiety of light and colour which is made up of the reflection of superannuated things. The atmosphere plays over them like a laugh, they are of the essence of the sad old joke. They are almost as charming from other places as they are from their own balconies, and share fully in that universal privilege of Venetian objects which consists of being both the picture and the point of view.

[*The Poetry of Misfortune*]

The evening that was to give me the first of them[2] was by no means the first occasion of my asking myself if that inveterate "style" of which we talk so much be absolutely conditioned—in dear old Venice and elsewhere—on decrepitude. Is it the style that has brought about the decrepitude, or the decrepitude that has, as it were, intensified and consecrated the style? There is an ambiguity about it all that constantly haunts and beguiles. Dear old Venice has lost her complexion, her figure, her reputation, her self-respect; and yet, with it all, has so puzzlingly not lost a shred of her distinction. Perhaps indeed the case is simpler than it seems, for the poetry of misfortune is familiar to us all, whereas, in spite of a stroke here and there of some happy justice that charms, we scarce find ourselves anywhere arrested by the poetry of a run of luck. The misfortune of Venice being, accordingly, at every point, what we most touch, feel and see, we end by assuming it to be of the essence of her dignity; a consequence, we become aware, by the way, sufficiently discouraging to the general application or pretension of style, and all the more that, to make the final felicity deep, the original greatness must have been something tremendous. If it be the ruins that are noble we have known plenty that were not, and moreover there are degrees and varieties: certain monuments, solid survivals, hold up their heads and decline to ask for a grain of your pity. Well, one knows of course when to keep one's pity to oneself; yet one clings, even in the face of the colder stare, to one's prized Venetian privilege of making the sense of doom and decay a part of every impression. Cheerful work, it may be said of course; and it is doubtless only in Venice that you gain more by such a trick than you lose. What was most beautiful is gone; what was next most beautiful is, thank goodness, going—that, I think, is the monstrous description of the better part of your thought. Is it really your fault if the place makes you want so desperately to read history into everything?

* * *

2. I.e., the first of three "pictures" that James proposes to "paint" from his memories of Italy.

[*Three Venetian Sisters*][3]

* * * Too much for a rough sketch was to be seen and felt in the home of the three sisters, and in the delightful and slightly pathetic deviation of their doing us so simply and freely the honours of it. What was most immediately marked was their resigned cosmopolite state, the effacement of old conventional lines by foreign contact and example; by the action, too, of causes full of a special interest, but not to be emphasised perhaps—granted indeed they be named at all—without a certain sadness of sympathy. If "style," in Venice, sits among ruins, let us always lighten our tread when we pay her a visit.

Our steps were in fact, I am happy to think, almost soft enough for a death-chamber as we stood in the big, vague *sala*[4] of the three sisters, spectators of their simplified state and their beautiful blighted rooms, the memories, the portraits, the shrunken relics of nine Doges. If I wanted a first chapter it was here made to my hand; the painter of life and manners, as he glanced about, could only sigh—as he so frequently has to—over the vision of so much more truth than he can use. What on earth is the need to "invent," in the midst of tragedy and comedy that never cease? Why, with the subject itself, all round, so inimitable, condemn the picture to the silliness of trying not to be aware of it? The charming lonely girls, carrying so simply their great name and fallen fortunes, the despoiled *decaduta*[5] house, the unfailing Italian grace, the space so out of scale with actual needs, the absence of books, the presence of ennui, the sense of the length of the hours and the shortness of everything else—all this was a matter not only for a second chapter and a third, but for a whole volume, a *dénoûment* and a sequel.

This time, unmistakably, it *was* the last—Wordsworth's stately "shade of that which once was great"; and it was almost as if our distinguished young friends had consented to pass away slowly in order to treat us to the vision. Ends are only ends in truth, for the painter of pictures, when they are more or less conscious and prolonged. One of the sisters had been to London, whence she had brought back the impression of having seen at the British Museum a room exclusively filled with books and documents devoted to the commemoration of her family. She must also then have encountered at the National Gallery the exquisite specimen of an early Venetian master in which one of her ancestors, then head of the State, kneels with so sweet a dignity before the Virgin and Child. She was perhaps old enough, none the less, to have seen this pre-

3. Another of James's "pictures" from memory. James does not identify the young women.

4. Apartment.

5. Decayed.

cious work taken down from the wall of the room in which we sat and—on terms so far too easy—carried away for ever; and not too young, at all events, to have been present, now and then, when her candid elders, enlightened too late as to what their sacrifice might really have done for them, looked at each other with the pale hush of the irreparable. We let ourselves note that these were matters to put a great deal of old, old history into sweet young Venetian faces.

HENRY JAMES

From *Notes of a Son and Brother*†

[*The Character of Minnie Temple*]

* * *

Immediately, at any rate, the Albany cousins, or a particular group of them, began again to be intensely in question for us; coloured in due course with reflections of the War as their lives, not less than our own, were to become—and coloured as well too, for all sorts of notation and appreciation, from irrepressible private founts. Mrs. Edmund Tweedy, bereft of her own young children, had at the time I speak of opened her existence, with the amplest hospitality, to her four orphaned nieces, who were also our father's and among whom the second in age, Mary Temple the younger, about in her seventeenth year when she thus renewed her appearance to our view, shone with vividest lustre, an essence that preserves her still, more than half a century from the date of her death, in a memory or two where many a relic once sacred has comparatively yielded to time. Most of those who knew and loved, I was going to say adored, her have also yielded—which is a reason the more why thus much of her, faint echo from too far off though it prove, should be tenderly saved. If I have spoken of the elements and presences round about us that "counted," Mary Temple was to count, and in more lives than can now be named, to an extraordinary degree; count as a young and shining apparition, a creature who owed to the charm of her every aspect (her aspects were so many!) and the originality, vivacity, audacity, generosity, of her spirit, an indescribable grace and weight—if one might impute weight to a being so imponderable in common scales. Whatever other values on our scene might, as I have hinted, appear to fail, she was one of the first order, in the sense of the immediacy of the impression she produced, and produced altogether as by the play of

† Henry James, *Notes of a Son and Brother* (New York: Charles Scribner's Sons, 1914), pp. 76–79, 457–59, 460–63, 491–94, 514–15.

her own light spontaneity and curiosity—not, that is, as through a sense of such a pressure and such a motive, or through a care for them, in others. "Natural" to an effect of perfect felicity that we were never to see surpassed is what I have already praised all the Albany *cousinage* of those years for being; but in none of the company was the note so clear as in this rarest, though at the same time symptomatically or ominously palest, flower of the stem; who was natural at more points and about more things, with a greater range of freedom and ease and reach of horizon than any of the others dreamed of. They had that way, delightfully, with the small, after all, and the common matters—while she had it with those too, but with the great and rare ones over and above; so that she was to remain for us the very figure and image of a felt interest in life, an interest as magnanimously far-spread, or as familiarly and exquisitely fixed, as her splendid shifting sensibility, moral, personal, nervous, and having at once such noble flights and such touchingly discouraged drops, such graces of indifference and inconsequence, might at any moment determine. She was really to remain, for our appreciation, the supreme case of a taste for life as life, as personal living; of an endlessly active and yet somehow a careless, an illusionless, a sublimely forewarned curiosity about it: something that made her, slim and fair and quick, all straightness and charming tossed head, with long light and yet almost sliding steps and a large light postponing, renouncing laugh, the very muse or amateur priestess of rash speculation. To express her in the mere terms of her restless young mind, one felt from the first, was to place her, by a perversion of the truth, under the shadow of female "earnestness"—for which she was much too unliteral and too ironic; so that, superlatively personal and yet as independent, as "off" into higher spaces, at a touch, as all the breadth of her sympathy and her courage could send her, she made it impossible to say whether she was just the most moving of maidens or a disengaged and dancing flame of thought. No one to come after her could easily seem to show either a quick inward life or a brave, or even a bright, outward, either a consistent contempt for social squalors or a very marked genius for moral reactions. She had in her brief passage the enthusiasm of humanity—more, assuredly, than any charming girl who ever circled, and would fain have continued to circle, round a ballroom. This kept her indeed for a time more interested in the individual, the immediate human, than in the race or the social order at large; but that, on the other hand, made her ever so restlessly, or quite inappeasably, "psychologic." The psychology of others, in her shadow—I mean their general resort to it—could only for a long time seem weak and flat and dim, above all not at all amusing. She burned herself out; she died at twenty-four.

[*Memories of Cultural Innocence*]

* * * Our circle I fondly call it, and doubtless then called it, because in the light of that description I could most rejoice in it, and I think of it now as having formed a little world of easy and happy interchange, of unrestricted and yet all so instinctively sane and secure association and conversation, with all its liberties and delicacies, all its mirth and its earnestness protected and directed so much more from within than from without, that I ask myself, perhaps too fatuously, whether any such right conditions for the play of young intelligence and young friendship, the reading of Matthew Arnold and Browning, the discussion of a hundred human and personal things, the sense of the splendid American summer drawn out to its last generosity, survives to this more complicated age. I doubt if there be circles to-day, and seem rather to distinguish confusedly gangs and crowds and camps, more propitious, I dare say, to material affluence and physical riot than anything we knew, but not nearly so appointed for ingenious and ingenuous talk. I think of our interplay of relation as attuned to that fruitful freedom of what we took for speculation, what we didn't recoil from as boundless curiosity—as the consideration of life, that is, the personal, the moral inquiry and adventure at large, so far as matter for them had up to then met our view—I think of this fine quality in our scene with no small confidence in its having been rare, or to be more exact perhaps, in its having been possible to the general American felicity and immunity as it couldn't otherwise or elsewhere have begun to be. Merely to say, as an assurance, that such relations shone with the light of "innocence" is of itself to breathe on them wrongly or rudely, is uncouthly to "defend" them—as if the very air that consciously conceived and produced them didn't all tenderly and amusedly take care of them. I at any rate figure again, to my customary positive piety, all the aspects now; that in especial of my young orphaned cousins as mainly composing the maiden train and seeming as if they still had but yesterday brushed the morning dew of the dear old Albany naturalness * * *

[*Minnie as Heroine*]

* * * If drama we could indeed feel this as being, I hasten to add, we owed it most of all to our just having such a heroine that everything else inevitably came. Mary Temple was beautifully and indescribably *that*—in the technical or logical as distinguished from the pompous or romantic sense of the word; wholly without effort or desire on her part—for never was a girl less consciously or consentingly or vulgarly dominant—everything that took place around

her took place as if primarily in relation to her and in her interest: that is in the interest of drawing her out and displaying her the more. This too without her in the least caring, as I say—in the deep, the morally nostalgic indifferences that were the most finally characteristic thing about her—whether such an effect took place or not; she liked nothing in the world so much as to see others fairly exhibited; not as they might best please her by being, but as they might most fully reveal themselves, their stuff and their truth: which was the only thing that, after any first flutter for the superficial air or grace in an acquaintance, could in the least fix her attention. She had beyond any equally young creature I have known a sense for verity of character and play of life in others, for their acting out of their force or their weakness, whatever either might be, at no matter what cost to herself; and it was this instinct that made her care so for life in general, just as it was her being thereby so engaged in that tangle that made her, as I have expressed it, ever the heroine of the scene. Life claimed her and used her and beset her—made her range in her groping, her naturally immature and unlighted way from end to end of the scale. No one felt more the charm of the actual—only the actual comprised for her kinds of reality (those to which her letters perhaps most of all testify), that she saw treated round her for the most part either as irrelevant or as unpleasant. She was absolutely afraid of nothing she might come to by living with enough sincerity and enough wonder; and I think it is because one was to see her launched on that adventure in such bedimmed, such almost tragically compromised conditions that one is caught by her title to the heroic and pathetic mark. It is always difficult for us after the fact not to see young things who were soon to be lost to us as already distinguished by their fate; this particular victim of it at all events might well have made the near witness ask within himself how her restlessness of spirit, the finest reckless impatience, was to be assuaged or "met" by the common lot. One somehow saw it nowhere about us as up to her terrible young standard of the interesting—even if to say this suggests an air of tension, a sharpness of importunity, than which nothing could have been less like her. The charming, irresistible fact was that one had never seen a creature with such lightness of forms, a lightness all her own, so inconsequently grave at the core, or an asker of endless questions with such apparent lapses of care. * * *

[*The Death of Minnie Temple*]

* * * This disposition in her, and the way in which, at the least push, the gate of thought opened for her to its widest, which was to the prospect of the soul and the question of interests on *its* part

that wouldn't be ignored, by no means fails to put to me that she might well have found the mystifications of life, had she been appointed to enjoy more of them, much in excess of its contentments. It easily comes up for us over the relics of those we have seen beaten, this sense that it was not for nothing they missed the ampler experience, but in no case that I have known has it come up for me so much. In none other have I so felt the naturalness of our asking ourselves what such spirits would have done with their extension and what would have satisfied them; since dire as their defeat may have been we don't see them, in the ambiguous light of some of their possibilities, at peace with victory. This may be perhaps an illusion of our interest in them, a mere part of its ingenuity; and I allow that if our doubt is excessive it does them a great wrong—which is another way in which they were not to have been righted. We soothe a little with it at any rate our sense of the tragic.

> . . . The irretrievableness of the step (her sister E.'s marriage)[1] comes over my mind from time to time in such an overwhelming way that it's most depressing, and I have to be constantly on my guard not to let Temple and Elly see it, as it would naturally not please them. After all, since they are not appalled at what they've done, and are quite sure of each other, as they evidently are, why should I worry myself? I am well aware that if all other women felt the seriousness of the matter to the extent I do, hardly any would *ever* marry, and the human race would stop short. So I ought perhaps to be glad so many people can find and take that "little ease" that Clough talks about, without consciously giving up the "highest thing." And may not this majority of people be the truly wise and my own notions of the subject simply fanatical and impracticable? I clearly see in how small a minority I am, and that the other side has, with Bishop Blougram, the best of it from one point of view; but I can't help that, can I? We must be true to *ourselves*, mustn't we? though all the rest of humanity be of a contrary opinion, or else throw discredit upon the wisdom of God, who made us as we are and not like the next person. Do you remember my old hobby of the "remote possibility of the best thing" being better than a clear certainty of the second best? Well, I believe it more than ever, every day I live. Indeed I don't believe anything else—but is not that everything? And isn't it exactly what Christianity means? Wasn't Christ the only man who ever lived and died *entirely* for his faith, without a shadow of selfishness? And isn't that reason enough why we should all turn to Him after having tried everything else and found it wanting?—turn to Him as the only pure and *unmixed* manifestation of God in humanity? And if I believe this, which I think I do, how utterly inconsistent and detestable

1. James's parenthetical note. The extracts here are two of several letters by Minnie Temple which James prints in *Notes of a Son and Brother.*

is the life I lead, which, so far from being a loving and cheerful surrender of itself once for all to God's service, is at best but a base compromise—a few moments or acts or thoughts consciously and with difficulty divested of actual selfishness. Must this always be so? Is it owing to the indissoluble mixture of the divine and the diabolical in us all, or is it because I myself am hopelessly frivolous and trifling? Or is it finally that I really don't *believe*, that I have still a doubt in my mind whether religion *is* the one exclusive thing to live for, as Christ taught us, or whether it will prove to be only *one* of the influences, though a great one, which educate the human race and help it along in that culture which Matthew Arnold thinks the most desirable thing in the world? In fine is it the meaning and end of our lives, or only a moral principle bearing a certain part in our development ——?

Since I wrote this I have been having my tea and sitting on the piazza looking at the stars and thinking it most unfaithful and disloyal of me even to speak as I did just now, admitting the possibility of that faith not being everything which yet at moments is so divinely true as to light up the whole of life suddenly and make everything clear. I know the trouble is with *me* when doubt and despondency come, but on the other hand I can't altogether believe it wrong of me to have written as I have, for then what becomes of my principle of saying what one really thinks and leaving it to God to take care of his own glory? The truth will vindicate itself in spite of my voice to the contrary. If you think I am letting myself go this way without sufficient excuse I won't do it again; but I can't help it this time, I have nobody else to speak to about serious things. If by chance I say anything or ask a question that lies at all near my heart my sisters all tell me I am "queer" and that they "wouldn't be me for anything"—which is, no doubt, sensible on their part, but which puts an end to anything but conversation of the most superficial kind on mine. You know one gets lonely after a while on such a plan of living, so in sheer desperation I break out where I perhaps more safely can.

* * *

The next night dear Dr. Metcalfe came, whom I love for the gentlest and kindest soul I have ever seen. To start with he's a gentleman, as well as an excellent physician, and to end with he and my father were fond of each other at West Point, and he takes a sort of paternal interest in me. He told me that my right lung is decidedly weaker than my left, which is quite sound, and that the hemorrhage has been a good thing for it and kept it from actual disease; and also that if I can keep up my general health I may get all right again. He has known a ten times worse case get entirely well. He urged me not to go to Washington, but decidedly to go to Europe; so this last is what I am to do with my cousin Mrs. Post if I am not dead before June. In a fortnight

I'm to go back to New York to be for some time under Metcalfe's care. I feel tired out and hardly able to stir, but my courage is good, and I don't propose to lose it if I can help, for I know it all depends on myself whether I get through or not. That is if I begin to be indifferent to what happens I shall go down the hill fast. I have fortunately, through my mother's father, enough Irish blood in me rather to enjoy a good fight. I feel the greatest longing for summer or spring; I should like it to be always spring for the rest of my life and to have all the people I care for always with me! But who *wouldn't* like it so? Good-bye.

To the gallantry and beauty of which there is little surely to add. But there came a moment, almost immediately after, when all illusion failed; which it is not good to think of or linger on, and yet not pitiful not to note. One may have wondered rather doubtingly —and I have expressed that—what life would have had for her and how her exquisite faculty of challenge could have "worked in" with what she was likely otherwise to have encountered or been confined to. None the less did she in fact cling to consciousness; death, at the last, was dreadful to her; she would have given anything to live —and the image of this, which was long to remain with me, appeared so of the essence of tragedy that I was in the far-off aftertime to seek to lay the ghost by wrapping it, a particular occasion aiding, in the beauty and dignity of art. The figure that was to hover as the ghost has at any rate been of an extreme pertinence, I feel, to my doubtless too loose and confused general picture, vitiated perhaps by the effort to comprehend more than it contains. Much as this cherished companion's presence among us had represented for William and myself—and it is on *his* behalf I especially speak—her death made a mark that must stand here for a too waiting conclusion. We felt it together as the end of our youth.

HENRY JAMES

From Is There a Life After Death?†

Part I

* * * How *can* there be a personal and a differentiated life "after," it will then of course be asked, for those for whom there has been so little of one before?—unless indeed it be pronounced conceivable that the possibility may vary from man to man, from

† Henry James, "Is There a Life After Death?" in *In After Days: Thoughts on the Future Life* (New York and London: Harper & Brothers, 1910), pp. 201, 205–206, 207, 208, 213, 214–16, 217, 219–20, 221–22, 223–24, 229–33.

human case to human case, and that the quantity or the quality of our practice of consciousness may have something to say to it. If I myself am disposed to pronounce this conceivable—as verily I expect to find myself before we have done—I must glance at at a few other relations of the matter first.

* * *

Whatever we may begin with we almost inevitably go on, under the discipline of life, to more or less resigned acceptance of the grim fact that "science" takes no account of the soul, the principle we worry about, and that, as however nobly thinking and feeling creatures, we are abjectly and inveterately shut up in our material organs. We flutter away from that account of ourselves, on sublime occasion, only to come back to it with the collapse of our wings, and during much of our life the grim view, as I have called it, the sense of the rigor of our physical basis, is confirmed to us by overwhelming appearances. The mere spectacle, all about us, of personal decay, and of the decay, as seems, of the whole being, adds itself formidably to that of so much bloom and assurance and energy—the things we catch in the very fact of their material identity. There are times when *all* the elements and qualities that constitute the affirmation of the personal life here affect us as making against any apprehensible other affirmation of it. And that general observation and evidence abide with us and keep us company; they reinforce the verdict of the dismal laboratories and the confident analysts as to the interconvertibility of our genius, as it comparatively is at the worst, and our brain—the poor palpable, ponderable, probeable, laboratory-brain that we ourselves see in certain inevitable conditions—become as naught.

It brings itself home to us thus in all sorts of ways that we are even at our highest flights of personality, our furthest reachings out of the mind, of the very stuff of the abject actual, and that the sublimest idea we can form and the noblest hope and affection we can cherish are but flowers sprouting in that eminently and infinitely diggable soil. * * * It is to the personality that the idea of renewed being attaches itself, and we see nothing so much written over the personalities of the world as that they are finite and precarious and insusceptible. All the ugliness, the grossness, the stupidity, the cruelty, the vast extent to which the score in question is a record of brutality and vulgarity, the so easy nonexistence of consciousness, round about us as to most of the things that make for living desirably at all, or even for living once, let alone on the enlarged chance—these things fairly rub it into us that to *have* a personality need create no presumption beyond what this remarkably mixed world is by itself amply sufficient to meet. * * * The mere fact in short that so much of life as we know it dishonors, or at any rate falls below, the greater part of the beauty and the opportunity even of this world, works upon us for persuasion that none other can be eager to receive it.

* * *

* * * This fact, as after middle life we continue to note it, contributes to the confirmation, within us, of our seeming awareness of extinct things *as* utterly and veritably extinct, with whatever splendid intensity we may have known them to live; an awareness that settles upon us with a formidable weight as time and the world pile up around us all their affirmation of *other* things, and all importunate ones—which little by little acts upon us as so much triumphant negation of the past and the lost; the flicker of some vast sardonic, leering "Don't you see?" on the mask of Nature.

* * * So it is, therefore, that we keep on and that we reflect; we begin by pitying the remembered dead, even for the very danger of our indifference to them, and we end by pitying ourselves for the final demonstration, as it were, of their indifference to us. "They must be dead, indeed," we say; "they must be as dead as 'science' affirms, for this consecration of it on such a scale, and with these tremendous rites of nullification, to take place." We think of the particular cases of those who could have been backed, as we call it, not to fail, on occasion, of somehow reaching us. We recall the forces of passion, of reason, of personality, that lived in them, and what such forces had made them, to our sight, capable of; and then we say, conclusively, "Talk of triumphant identity if *they*, wanting to triumph, haven't done it!"

Those in whom we saw consciousness, to all appearance, the consciousness of *us*, slowly *déménager*,[1] piece by piece, so that they more or less consentingly parted with it—of *them* let us take it, under stress, if we must, that their ground for interest (in us and in other matters) "unmistakably" reached its limit. But what of those lights that went out in a single gust and those life passions that were nipped in their flower and their promise? Are these spirits thinkable as having emptied the measure the services of sense could offer them? Do we feel capable of a brutal rupture with registered promises, started curiosities, waiting initiations? The mere acquired momentum of intelligence, of perception, of vibration, of experience in a word, would have carried them on, we argue, to *something*, the something that never takes place for us, if the laboratory-brain were *not* really all. What it comes to is then that our faith or our hope may to some degree resist the fact, once accom-

1. Fade away.

plished, of watched and deplored death, but that they may well break down before the avidity and consistency with which everything insufferably *continues* to die.

Part II

I have said "we argue" as we take in impressions of the order of those I have glanced at and of which I have pretended to mention only a few. I am not, however, putting them forward for their direct weight in the scale; I speak of them but as the inevitable obsession of those who with the failure of the illusions of youth have had to learn more and more to reckon with reality. * * * I speak as one who has had time to take many notes, to be struck with many differences, and to see, a little typically perhaps, what may eventually happen; and I contribute thus, and thus only, my grain of consideration to the store.

I began, I may accordingly say, with a distinct sense that our question[2] didn't appeal to me—as it appeals, in general, but scantly to the young—and I was content for a long time to let it alone, only asking that it should, in turn, as irrelevant and insoluble, let *me*. This it did, in abundance, for many a day—which is, however, but another way of saying that death remained for me, in a large measure, unexhibited and unaggressive. The exhibition, the aggression of life was quite ready to cover the ground and fill the bill, and to my sense of that balance still inclined even after the opposite pressure had begun to show in the scale. * * *

During which period, none the less, as I was afterward to find, the question subtly took care of itself for me—waking up as I did gradually, in the event (very slowly indeed, with no sudden start of perception, no bound of enthusiasm), to its facing me with a "mild but firm" refusal to regard itself as settled. That circumstance once noted, I began to inquire—mainly, I confess, of myself—why it should be thus obstinate, what reason it could at all clearly give me; and this led me in due course to my getting, or at least framing my reply: a reply not perhaps so multitudinous as those voices of the universe that I have spoken of as discouraging, but which none the less, I find, still holds its ground for me. What had happened, in short, was that all the while I had been practically, though however dimly, trying to take the measure of my consciousness—on this appropriate and prescribed basis of its being so finite—I had learned, as I may say, to live in it more, and with the consequence of thereby not a little undermining the conclusion most unfavorable to it. I had doubtless taken thus to increased living in it by reaction against so grossly finite a world—for it at least *contained* the world,

2. The question, that is, of immortality.

and could handle and criticise it, could play with it and deride it; it had *that* superiority: which meant, all the while, such successful living that the abode itself grew more and more interesting to me, and with this beautiful sign of its character that the more and the more one asked of it the more and the more it appeared to give. I should perhaps rather say that the more one turned it, as an easy reflector, here and there and everywhere over the immensity of things, the more it appeared to take * * *

* * * It is not that I have found in growing older any one marked or momentous line in the life of the mind or in the play and the freedom of the imagination to be stepped over; but that a process takes place which I can only describe as the accumulation of the very treasure itself of consciousness. I won't say that "the world," as we commonly refer to it, grows more attaching, but will say that the universe increasingly does, and that this makes us present at the enormous multiplication of our possible relations with it; relations still vague, no doubt, as undefined as they are uplifting, as they are inspiring, to think of, and on a scale beyond our actual use or application, yet filling us (through the "law" in question, the law that consciousness gives us immensities and imaginabilities wherever we direct it) with the unlimited vision of being. This mere fact that so small a part of one's visionary and speculative and emotional activity has even a traceably indirect bearing on one's doings or purposes or particular desires contributes strangely to the luxury—which is the magnificent waste—of thought, and strongly reminds one that even should one cease to be in love with life it would be difficult, on such terms, not to be in love with living.

* * * And, once more—speaking for myself only and keeping to the facts of my experience—it is above all as an artist that I appreciate this beautiful and enjoyable independence of thought and more especially this assault of the boundlessly multiplied personal relation (my own), which carries me beyond even any "profoundest" observation of this world whatever, and any mortal adventure, and refers me to realizations I am condemned as yet but to dream of. For the artist the sense of our luxurious "waste" of postulation and supposition is of the strongest; of him is it superlatively true that he knows the aggression as of infinite numbers of modes of being. His case, as I see it, is easily such as to make him declare that if he were not constantly, in his commonest processes, carrying the field of consciousness further and further, making it lose itself in the ineffable, he shouldn't in the least feel himself an artist. As more or less of one myself, for instance, I deal with being, I invoke and evoke, I figure and represent, I seize and fix, as many phases and aspects and conceptions of it as my infirm hand allows me strength for; and in so doing I find myself—I can't express it other-

wise—in communication with *sources*; sources to which I owe the apprehension of far more and far other combinations than observation and experience, in their ordinary sense, have given me the pattern of.

* * *

* * * Consciousness has thus arrived at interesting me too much and on too great a scale—that is all my revelation or my secret; on too great a scale, that is, for me not to ask myself what she can mean by such blandishments—to the altogether normally hampered and benighted random individual that I am. Does she mean nothing more than that I shall have found life, by her enrichment, the more amusing here? But I find it, at this well-nigh final pass, mainly amusing in the light of the possibility that the idea of an exclusively present world, with all its appearances wholly dependent on our physical outfit, may represent for us but a chance for experiment in the very interest of our better and freer being and to its very honor and reinforcement; * * * which shall have been not unlike the sustaining frame on little wheels that often encases growing infants, so that, dangling and shaking about in it, they may feel their assurance of walking increase and teach their small toes to know the ground. I like to think that we here, as to soul, dangle from the infinite and shake about in the universe; that this world and this conformation and these senses are our helpful and ingenious frame, amply provided with wheels and replete with the lesson for us of how to plant, spiritually, our feet. That conception of the matter rather comes back, I recognize, to the theory of the spiritual discipline, the purification and preparation on earth for heaven, of the orthodox theology—which is a resemblance I don't object to, all the more that it is a superficial one, as well as a fact mainly showing, at any rate, how neatly extremes may sometimes meet.

My mind, however that may be, doesn't in the least resent its association with all the highly appreciable and perishable matter of which the rest of my personality is composed; nor does it fail to recognize the beautiful assistance—alternating indeed frequently with the extreme inconvenience—received from it; representing, as these latter forms do, much ministration to experience. The ministration may have sometimes affected my consciousness as clumsy, but has at other times affected it as exquisite, and it accepts and appropriates and consumes everything the universe puts in its way; matter in tons, if necessary, so long as such quantities are, in so mysterious and complicated a sphere, one of its conditions of activity. Above all, it takes kindly to that admirable philosophic view which makes of matter the mere encasement or sheath, thicker, thinner, coarser, finer, more transparent or more obstructive, of a spirit it has no more concern in producing than the baby-frame has in producing the intelligence of the baby—much as that intelligence may be so promoted.

I "like" to think, I may be held too artlessly to repeat, that this, that, and the other appearances are favorable to the idea of the independence, behind everything (*its* everything), of my individual soul; I "like" to think even at the risk of lumping myself with those shallow minds who are happily and foolishly able to believe what they would prefer. It isn't really a question of belief—which is a term I have made no use of in these remarks; it is on the other hand a question of desire, but of desire so confirmed, so thoroughly established and nourished, as to leave belief a comparatively irrelevant affair. * * * I can't do less if I desire, but I shouldn't be able to do more if I believed. Just so I shouldn't be able to do more than cultivate belief; and it is exactly to cultivation that I subject my hopeful sense of the auspicious; with such success—or at least with such intensity—as to give me the splendid illusion of doing something myself for my prospect, or at all events for my own possibility, of immortality. There again, I recognize extremes "neatly meet"; one doesn't talk otherwise, doubtless, of one's working out one's salvation. But this coincidence too I am perfectly free to welcome—putting it, that is, that the theological provision happens to coincide with (or, for all I know, to have been, at bottom, insidiously built on) some such sense of appearances as my own. If I am talking, at all events, of what I "like" to think I may, in short, say all: I like to think it open to me to establish speculative and imaginative connections, to take up conceived presumptions and pledges, that have for me all the air of not being decently able to escape redeeming themselves. And when once such a mental relation to the question as that begins to hover and settle, who shall say over what fields of experience, past and current, and what immensities of perception and yearning, it shall *not* spread the protection of its wings? No, no, no—I reach beyond the laboratory-brain.

Criticism

ANONYMOUS

Mr. Henry James's New Book†

Mr. Henry James is to be congratulated. It is a long time since modern English fiction has presented us with a book which is so essentially a book; a thing conceived, and carried on, and finished in one premeditated strain; with unbroken literary purpose and serious, unflagging literary skill. "The Wings of the Dove" is an extraordinarily interesting performance. We know nothing of Mr. James's to compare with it in fulness of intention, and close, rich, elaborate workmanship but the "Tragic Muse" and, possibly, "Roderick Hudson"; and in neither of these works do we find the same element of grave and penetrating tenderness. Mr. James's methods of minute, qualifying, cumulative detail have not altered; but he has added to them. There is a new, a humanizing, note in his long portrait-study of Milly Theale, the stricken little "princess" from New York, "with her frankness, sweetness, sadness, brightness, her disconcerting poetry." "For Milly was indeed a dove . . . with that element of wealth in her which was a power, which was a great power, and which was dove-like only so far as one remembered that doves have wings and wondrous flights, have them as well as tender tints and soft sounds."

This is, we repeat, an extraordinarily interesting performance, but it is not an easy book to read. It will not do for short railway journeys or for drowsy hammocks, or even to amuse sporting men and the active Young Person. The dense, fine quality of its pages—and there are 576—will always presuppose a certain effort of attention on the part of the reader; who must, indeed, be prepared to forgo many of his customary titillations and bribes. Mr. James's novels are often accused of lacking the supreme authority of an overwhelming emotion. But they are not alone in that. And what the average reader misses in them is far more a familiarity, a sense of good-fellowship, and a common attitude towards life. For Mr. James, so to speak, never buttonholes his public; he does not even take it by the arm. There is something of the classic in his sense of aloofness, his detachment from his reader; and the pampered modern reader is apt to call the attitude inhuman. As a matter of fact, it is not the illusion of Life, it is the illusion of Art which Mr. James sets before us. And that is why a book like "The Wings of the Dove" does not make so much for obvious pleasure as for a sort of deep and increasing satisfaction in its admirable workmanship; in its sense of

† *Times* (London) *Literary Supplement*, September 1902, p. 263.

atmosphere, its sense of character, its humour, its ingenuity of epithet, its untiring, discriminating curiosity about life. From first to last every impression, even the facts about the "situations," reach us by a series of reflections and complicated counter-reflections—a set of polished mirrors, as it were, reflecting other mirrors. The *scènes à faire* take place off the stage; and it is by reverberation, by allusion, by inference, that we are gradually drawn into the circle of what is, first and last, an elaborated work of art.

It is idle—it shows stupidity—to resent any artistic method which ultimately reaches its goal; and to enjoy Mr. James the reader must quite simply be ready to meet him halfway; to place himself at the writer's point of view, and frankly to accept his stipulations. As a matter of fact, this is the essential condition which every literary artist exacts. It is only the journalist who yields everything; who makes things easy, and amuses and excites us with one acute eye for ever fixed upon our line of least resistance. And it is precisely the contrast between this friendly familiar aspect of the mass of modern fiction (since the journalistic attitude of mind, after all, does not necessarily imply the newspaper)—it is the sharp contrast between this and Mr. James's habitual air of making no personal claim, of leaving the subject under discussion to the reader's intelligence without disconcerting appeals to his emotion—which makes a novel like "The Wings of the Dove" so significant and so distinct.

Take, for an example—and we select it at random—these few lines from a popular new book (which we notice below):—

> A muddy sea and a dirty grey sky, a cold rain and a moaning wind. Short capped waves breaking to leeward in a little hiss of spray. The water itself sandy and discoloured. Far away to east, where the green-grey and the dirty grey merge into one, a windmill spinning in the breeze: Holland.

That is Mr. Seton Merriman; and no one can deny that the impression is vivid and just; the words effective in their deliberate baldness. Then compare this description of a Venetian palace, where

> The warmth of the southern summer was still in the high, florid rooms, palatial chambers where hard, cool pavements took reflections in their lifelong polish, and where the sun on the stirred sea-water, flickering up through open windows, played over the painted "subjects" in the splendid ceilings—medallions of purple and brown, of brave, old, melancholy colour, medals as of old reddened gold, embossed and beribboned, all toned with time and all flourished and scolloped and gilded about, set in their great moulded and figured concavity (a nest of white cherubs, friendly creatures of the air) . . . which did everything to make of the place an apartment of state.

Each of these descriptions is the description of a realist—and they seem extreme examples of two opposing schools. But the truth is, one represents the realism of impression and the other the realism of association. They stand to each other as a cleverly chosen photograph to the precise and suggestive line-drawing of an old Master—and indeed the multitudinous careful outlines of figures and places in "The Wings of the Dove" often remind us of a collection of such drawings. We imagine a whole series of them, spread out before us, under glass, in the clear tempered light of some Italian gallery. Here is no popular urgency of colour; the work only charms and rewards the trained and loving eye. It is hardly a place for the crowd—who while we are about it may well be imagined as gathered together in the courtyard below shouting to the inspiriting strains of Mr. Hall Caine's vigorous brass band, or listening to Miss Corelli's surprising soprano up-raised in modern oratorio—the place is not perhaps crowded, but surely it is one of the qualities of all finer work that it can afford to be itself and wait.

WILLIAM DEAN HOWELLS

Mr. Henry James's Later Work†

* * *

The feminine enmity to Mr. James is of as old a date as his discovery of the Daisy Miller type of American girl, which gave continental offence among her sisters. It would be hard to say why that type gave such continental offence, unless it was because it was held not honestly to have set down the traits which no one could but most potently and powerfully allow to be true. The strange thing was that these traits were the charming and honorable distinctions of American girlhood as it convinced Europe, in the early eighteen-seventies, of a civilization so spiritual that its innocent daughters could be not only without the knowledge but without the fear of evil. I am not going back, however, to that early feminine grievance, except to note that it seems to have been the first tangible grievance, though it was not the first grievance. * * *

It has been the curious fortune of this novelist, so supremely gifted in divining women and portraying them, that beyond any other great novelist (or little, for that matter) he has imagined few heroines acceptable to women. Even those martyr-women who have stood by him in the long course of his transgressions, and main-

† From William Dean Howells, "Mr. Henry James's Later Work," *North American Review*, 176 (January 1903), 126–31.

tained through thick and thin, that he is by all odds the novelist whom they could best trust with the cause of woman in fiction, have liked his anti-heroines more,—I mean, found them realer,—than his heroines. I am not sure but I have liked them more myself, but that is because I always find larger play for my sympathies in the character which needs the reader's help than in that which is so perfect as to get on without it. If it were urged that women do not care for his heroines because there are none of them to care for, I should not blame them, still less should I blame him for giving them that ground for abhorrence. I find myself diffident of heroines in fiction because I have never known one in life, of the real faultless kind; and heaven forbid I should ever yet know one. In Mr. James's novels I always feel safe from that sort, and it may be for this reason, among others, that I like to read his novels when they are new, and read them over and over again when they are old, or when they are no longer recent.

II

At this point I hear from far within a voice bringing me to book about Milly Theale in *The Wings of a Dove*, asking me, if *there* is not a heroine of the ideal make, and demanding what fault there is in her that renders her lovable. Lovable, I allow she is, dearly, tenderly, reverently lovable, but she has enough to make her so, besides being too good, too pure, too generous, too magnificently unselfish. It is not imaginable that her author should have been conscious of offering in her anything like an atonement to the offended divinity of American womanhood for Daisy Miller. But if it were imaginable the offended divinity ought to be sumptuously appeased, appeased to tears of grateful pardon such as I have not yet seen in its eyes. Milly Theale is as entirely American in the qualities which you can and cannot touch as Daisy Miller herself; and (I find myself urged to the risk of noting it) she is largely American in the same things. There is the same self-regardlessness, the same beauteous insubordination, the same mortal solution of the problem. Of course, it is all in another region, and the social levels are immensely parted. Yet Milly Theale is the superior of Daisy Miller less in her nature than in her conditions.

There is, in both, the same sublime unconsciousness of the material environment, the same sovereign indifference to the fiscal means of their emancipation to a more than masculine independence. The sense of what money can do for an American girl without her knowing it, is a "blind sense" in the character of Daisy, but in the character of Milly it has its eyes wide open. In that wonderful way of Mr. James's by which he imparts a fact without stating it, approaching it again and again, without actually coming in contact with it, we are made aware of the vast background of wealth from which Milly is projected upon our acquaintance. She is shown in a kind of breathless impatience with it, except as it is the stuff of doing wilfully magnificent things, and committing colossal expenses without more anxiety than a prince might feel with the revenues of a kingdom behind him. The ideal American rich girl has never really been done before, and it is safe to say that she will never again be done with such exquisite appreciation. She is not of the new rich; an extinct New York ancestry darkles in the retrospect: something vaguely bourgeois, and yet with presences and with lineaments of aristocratic distinction. They have made her masses of money for her, those intangible fathers, uncles and grandfathers, and then, with her brothers and sisters, have all perished away from her, and left her alone in the world with nothing else. She is as convincingly imagined in her relation to them, as the daughter of an old New York family, as she is in her inherited riches. It is not the old New York family of the unfounded Knickerbocker tradition, but something as fully patrician, with a nimbus of social importance as unquestioned as its money. Milly is not so much the flower of this local root as something finer yet: the perfume of it, the distilled and wandering fragrance. It would be hard to say in what her New Yorkishness lies, and Mr. James himself by no means says; only if you know New York at all, you have the unmistakable sense of it. She is New Yorkish in the very essences that are least associable with the superficial notion of New York: the intellectual refinement that comes of being born and bred in conditions of illimitable ease, of having had everything that one could wish to have, and the cultivation that seems to come of the mere ability to command it. If one will have an illustration of the final effect in Milly Theale, it may be that it can be suggested as a sort of Bostonian quality, with the element of *conscious* worth eliminated, and purified as essentially of pedantry as of commerciality. The wonder is that Mr. James in his prolonged expatriation has been able to seize this lovely impalpability, and to impart the sense of it; and perhaps the true reading of the riddle is that such a nature, such a character is most appreciable in that relief from the background which Europe gives all American character.

III

"But that is just what does not happen in the case of Mr. James's people. They are merged in the background so that you never can get behind them, and fairly feel and see them all round. Europe *doesn't* detach them; *nothing* does. 'There they are,' as he keeps making his people say in all his late books, when they are not calling one another dear lady, and dear man, and prodigious and magnificent, and of a vagueness or a richness, or a sympathy, or an opacity. No, he is of a tremendosity, but he worries me to death; he kills me; he really gives me a headache. He fascinates me, but I have no patience with him."

"But, dear lady," for it was a weary woman who had interrupted the flow of my censure in these unmeasured terms, and whom her interlocutor—another of Mr. James's insistent words—began trying to flatter to her disadvantage, "a person of your insight must see that this is the conditional vice of all painting, its vital fiction. You cannot get behind the figures in any picture. They are always merged in their background. And there you are!"

"Yes, I know I am. But that is just where I don't want to be. I want figures that I *can* get behind."

"Then you must go to some other shop—you must go to the shop of a sculptor."

"Well, why isn't *he* a sculptor?"

"Because he is a painter."

"Oh, that's no reason. He ought to be a sculptor."

"Then he couldn't give you the color, the light and shade, the delicate *nuances*, the joy of the intimated fact, all that you delight in him for. * * *

* * *

"He gives you a sense of a tremendous lot going on, for instance, in *The Wings of a Dove*, of things undeniably, though not unmistakably, happening. It is a great book."

"It is, it is," she sighed again. "It wore me to a thread."

"And the people were as unmistakable as they were undeniable: not Milly, alone, not Mrs. Stringham, as wonderfully of New England as Milly of New York; but all that terribly frank, terribly selfish, terribly shameless, terribly hard English gang."

"Ah, Densher wasn't really hard or really shameless, though he was willing—to please that unspeakable Kate Croy—to make love to Milly and marry her money so that when she died, they could live happy ever after—or at least comfortably. And you cannot say that Kate was frank. And Lord Mark really admired Milly. Or, anyway, he wanted to marry her. Do you think Kate took the money from Densher at last and married Lord Mark?"

"Why should you care?"

"Oh, one oughtn't to care, of course, in reading Mr. James. But with any one else, you would like to know who married who. It is all too wretched. Why should he want to picture such life?"

"Perhaps because it exists."

"Oh, do you think the English are really so bad? I'm glad he made such a beautiful character as Milly, American."

"My notion is that he didn't 'make' any of the characters."

"Of course not. And I suppose some people in England are actually like that. We have not got so far here, yet. To be sure, society is not so all-important here, yet. If it ever is, I suppose we shall pay the price. But *do* you think he ought to picture such life because it exists?"

"Do you find yourself much the worse for *The Wings of a Dove?*" I asked. "Or for *The Sacred Fount?* Or for *The Awkward Age?* Or even for *What Maisie Knew?* They all picture much the same sort of life."

"Why, of course not. But it isn't so much what he says—he never *says* anything—but what he insinuates. I don't believe that is good for young girls."

"But if they don't know what it means? I'll allow that it isn't quite *jeune fille* in its implications, all of them; but maturity has its modest claims. Even its immodest claims are not wholly ungrounded in the interest of a knowledge of our mother-civilization, which is what Mr. James's insinuations impart, as I understand them."

"Well, young people cannot read him aloud together. You can't deny that."

"No, but elderly people can, and they are not to be ignored by the novelist, always. I fancy the reader who brings some knowledge of good and evil, without being the worse for it, to his work is the sort of reader Mr. James writes for. I can imagine him addressing himself to a circle of such readers as this REVIEW's with a satisfaction, and a sense of liberation, which he might not feel in the following of the family magazines, and still not incriminate himself. I have heard a good deal said in reproach of the sort of life he portrays, in his later books; but I have not found his people of darker deeds or murkier motives than the average in fiction. I don't say, life."

"No, certainly, so far as he tells you. It is what he *doesn't* tell that is so frightful. He leaves you to such awful conjectures. For instance, when Kate Croy—"

"When Kate Croy—?"

"No. I *won't* discuss it. But you know what I mean; and I don't believe there ever was such a girl."

"And you believe there was ever such a girl as Milly Theale?"

"Hundreds! She is true to the life. So perfectly American. My husband and I read the story aloud together, and I wanted to weep. We had such a strange experience with that book. We read it half through together; then we got impatient, and tried to finish it alone. But we could not make anything of it apart; and we had to finish it together. We could not bear to lose a word; every word—and there were a good many!—seemed to tell. If you took one away you seemed to miss something important. It almost destroyed me, thinking it all out. I went round days, with my hand to my forehead; and I don't believe I understand it perfectly yet. Do you?"

* * *

F. O. MATTHIESSEN

[James's Masterpiece]†

'The Figure in the Carpet' has struck many readers as an instance where James' curiosity has been anything but idle, where, indeed, it has run into the ground. All the characters in that story are so obsessed with pursuing the hidden meaning of Hugh Vereker's novels that their criticism turns into a nightmarish game as the very issues of life and death are engulfed in their excessive and finally futile ingenuity. But James' intention was much fresher than his effect. His preface tells us that he had designed virtually a fable on behalf of analytic appreciation, a plea for perception, the very secret of which was in danger of being lost altogether by the careless readers of the new mass novel of the day. And in his notebook draft James had his novelist assure the young critic that what could be likened to the complex pattern in a Persian carpet 'isn't the "esoteric meaning," as the newspapers say: it's the *only* meaning, it's the very soul and core of the work.' He spoke of it also as the 'special beauty' that had presided over his books, that had controlled and animated them.

James' fable has yielded a symbol for critics by reminding them that their task is not fulfilled unless they have passed beyond the trees to the wood, and have seen an artist's achievement in its entirety. In a more restricted but very relevant sense one may also look for the essential design, not through the successive stages of an artist's whole development, but in his masterpiece, in that single work where his characteristic emotional vibration seems deepest and where we may have the sense, therefore, that we have come to 'the very soul.'

Such a book in James' canon is *The Wings of the Dove,* the animating beauty of which is its heroine, Milly Theale. James began his preface by saying that this book represented to his memory 'a very old—if I shouldn't perhaps rather say a very young—motive,' since he could scarcely remember the time when its situation had not been vividly present to him. He went into no further explanation there, but in the final chapter of his *Notes of a Son and Brother* (1914), the chapter that completed his account of William's and his own young manhood, he was to uncover the long hidden source of the threads he had tried to weave into the center of his novel. For Milly Theale, to the greatest degree that James

† From F. O. Matthiessen, *Henry James: The Major Phase* (New York: Oxford University Press, 1944), pp. 42–43, 50–52, 55–60, 62–80.

ever based one of his characters on actual life, is his tribute to his cousin Minny Temple, who had died of tuberculosis at twenty-four. His sense of this loss, remaining at the core of his personal life and yet ramifying outward through the long years of his subsequent social experience, empowered him to create in Milly Theale the most resonant symbol for what he had to say about humanity. * * *

* * *

But the pathos of early death, dramatizing the agony of both the intensity and the insecurity of life, was hardly a theme special to James. It has been a peculiarly recurrent American theme. It is startling to realize that the subject of *The Wings of the Dove* is precisely what Poe formulated as the greatest possible subject for poetry, the death of a beautiful woman. For Poe's kind of romanticism, to be sure, James had little taste, announcing, in his unsympathetic essay on Baudelaire, that an enthusiasm for Poe's poetry was 'the mark of a decidedly primitive stage of reflection.' But the theme of deprivation, of loss, of lack of fulfillment was a characteristic product of James' milieu. Henry Adams was to symbolize the end of his youth and his first full awareness of life's brutality in the tragic death of his sister. After the loss—through suicide—of his wife, the Clover Hooper whose intellectual grace James had remarked, Adams was to devote his deepest intellectual energies to understanding the medieval cult of the Virgin; and was to endow his portrait of Her with much the same rare distinction of subtlety and refinement that James bestowed upon his heroines.

Both Adams and James grew increasingly conscious of the waning of old energies. Both looked back to an American world that had been shattered by the Civil War, a world in which the Adams family had had power, and in which the James family had been able to live in a charmed circle of leisure, happily oblivious of the rising giants of business. Neither Adams nor James could be said to have remotely understood the American world of their maturity. Adams could approach its new energies only by a brilliant but dubious analogy between the laws of history and of thermodynamics. James repeatedly confessed that the world an American Balzac would have to master—the world of industrial and finance capitalism—had been a closed book to him from his youth. Inevitably, therefore, the emotional symbols of these writers were feminine. They wrote in an elegiac spirit, and were further exemplars of the lack of male principle in our literature that Emerson had deplored. But if we read James instead of deploring him, we may be impressed that what started as a personal motive became socially, indeed almost nationally representative of a phase in our history when, whether we liked it or not, the American girl, the heiress of all the ages, was the sign by which cultivated Europe knew us.

* * *

James, who tended to discuss his finished works solely in terms of their realized form, was not satisfied with this book. He wrote to Howells that it was 'too long-winded'; to another friend, that it had 'too big a head for its body,' or, speaking more exactly, that its center wasn't 'in the middle.' What he meant by this notion of the misplaced middle he developed in his preface, as he had previously done in that to *The Tragic Muse*. He believed that he had fallen into too great amplitude in his opening treatment of Kate Croy against her family background. This fault, as he wrote to Wells, might have been the result of the fact that, to his disappointment, his plans for serialization had failed ('. . . evidently no fiction of mine can or *will* now be serialized'); and he had gone ahead and developed his scenario 'on a more free and independent scale.' Whatever the cause, he had devoted so much initial space to Kate and Densher that when he had come to his main theme he had had to foreshorten mercilessly, and was afraid that in the last half in particular he had been too crowded, and had produced 'the illusion of mass without the illusion of extent.'

The reader may be inclined to agree, and certainly there is not the symmetrical structure which James achieved in both *The Ambassadors* and *The Golden Bowl*. But the characterizing feature in the method of *The Wings of the Dove*, to which James' preface scarcely does justice, is its deliberately *indirect* presentation of its heroine. The very nature of the theme, involving the fact that Milly is essentially the sufferer rather than the actor, makes it imaginatively right that she should seem surrounded by the others, and that, at the close, because of her illness, she should have been long off stage. That does not mean that her final image is any the less intense, as the ordonnance of the ten books can show.

The first two are given over entirely to Kate and Merton Densher. Milly is not even mentioned, but the London world and the particular situation into which she is to be projected are presented with impressive solidness. The short third book tells us what we need of Milly's background, and brings her to Europe with Susan Shepherd Stringham, a lady writer from Boston who plays the rôle of the Jamesian confidante. The next book introduces them to England, and, through Susan's having formerly known Kate's Aunt Maud Lowder, directly into the circle of their complications. The fifth book, which, without the restrictions of the serial, can become much longer, embraces the whole swift course of Milly's social triumph in London; and though James thought that his foreshortening here had still made his action pivot too rapidly, no passage in all his work gives us more of the felt splendor of life. The sixth book sets in motion Kate's scheme of Densher's being 'kind' to Milly; and the seventh, where the scene changes to Venice, is the last to center around the heroine. In the eighth she makes her final public appearance, at an evening party for her friends, where her frail form is silhouetted against the glamorous setting she is so soon to lose. Thereafter we see her only once more, in a conversation with Densher, in which she voices her last passionate declaration of wanting so much to live, just before Lord Mark turns up with his brutal news that Kate and Densher have been engaged all the time. This news smashes her delicate hold on life, and it was James' instinct that the way to handle such a denouement was entirely without big scenes. The reader of other fiction may feel cheated that he gets at first hand neither her talk with Lord Mark nor her final interview with Densher, in which she forgives him. But James' device of having his heroine not appear during the last fifth of the novel—just as she had not in the opening sections—and of having the final book in London record her death far away in Venice, succeeds extraordinarily in making us feel as though Milly has been wrapped around and isolated by sinister forces, almost as though she has been literally smothered off stage by Kate's terrifying will.

His detailed treatment of Kate at the outset, no matter how much it may have interfered with later proportions, had been absolutely necessary if he was to account for her character and conduct. She is by no means the nakedly brutal villainness that he had projected in his notebook. She is a much more living mixture of good and evil, a far more effective register of James' mature vision of human complexity. She is handsome, she has immense vitality, and she is without resources. Moreover, her selfish family—her sister who frets in the squalor of her lower-middle-class marriage, her father who has been involved in unspecified shady dealings—expect her to do well by them. She is aware that material things speak strongly to her also, and, to help her family's situation and her own, she has gone to live with her wealthy and ambitious aunt. Kate recognizes that Aunt Maud is 'unscrupulous and immoral'; she knows that she has been accepted into the house only as a potential social asset who must make an important marriage—and she has fallen in love with Merton Densher, a young journalist with no more money than she has. The importance of wealth had not been ignored in *The Ambassadors*: as Strether declared, it was 'the root of the evil' in his difficult situation with Mrs. Newsome. But Strether's heart was not set on money, and even without Mrs. Newsome's, he would not be really poor; whereas for Kate, once she is tempted, desire for money becomes the great corrupter.

James makes an incisive contrast between Kate and Densher. He specifies that they have little in common except their affection, that Densher tends to be as passive as Kate is active, that her talent is all for life and his for thought. Indeed, James has created here, somewhat more affectingly than in Strether, the kind of hero which our age has associated with the sensibility of the metaphysical poets, one whose 'remembered thoughts . . . at the moment of their coming to him had thrilled him almost like adventures.' They face together the impossibility of their situation: as Kate says, they are 'hideously intelligent' in the lucidity with which they see that their secret engagement cannot look for sympathy from any quarter. But James does not scant the strength or the beauty of their attachment. To those inattentive critics who keep insisting that James is always flinching from physical passion, the final pages of book two, just before Densher leaves for a special assignment in America, should be ample refutation.

The contrast which James develops between Kate and Milly is one of quantity against quality, of blood against nerves, of robust health against haggard delicacy. It is sustained through every detail of their appearance. Kate's striking handsomeness depends on clearness of eye and skin, on the regularity of her features, on the smooth distinction of her social charm. Milly's pallor makes her hair seem exceptionally red, while her large irregular nose and mouth could allow her to be called beautiful only by those who are attracted by 'American intensity.' It may be an accidental residue of romanticism that, as was the usual practice of Hawthorne and Melville, the innocent heroine is fair, and the dangerous worldly girl is dark.

But the more one scrutinizes the technique of this novel, the more one perceives that, despite James' past-masterly command over the details of realistic presentation, he is evoking essentially the mood of a fairy tale. He wanted to raise his international theme to its ultimate potentiality. He was no longer satisfied to endow an Isabel Archer with a legacy sufficient to allow her to confront Europe independently. He was bent on extending the sources of his splendor to the farthest conceivable degree. Milly was to be a fabulous millionairess. He deliberately wove an atmosphere of enchantment around her by the device of having Susan Stringham regard her as a 'princess.' Susan herself makes the comparsion between them as that between 'the potential heiress of all the ages' and 'a mere typical subscriber . . . to the *Transcript*.' But Susan's imagination has been fed on Pater and Maeterlinck. Hers is explicitly the Puritan imagination 'finally disencumbered' of its background and determined to make up for all its 'starved generations' by discovering in Milly the richest possibilities of romance. Even the girl's utter loss 'of parents, brothers, sisters' can be construed by Susan as 'all on a scale and with a sweep that required the greater stage; it was a New York legend of affecting, of romantic isolation . . .' With such a confidante for interpreter and chorus, James can introduce even fairy-tale imagery without its seeming forced or out of tone. The open sesame by which Susan's earlier friendship with Aunt Maud brings them at once to the heart of the London season is playfully likened by Milly to the wand of a fairy godmother; and in this brilliant new world of dinner parties which, in an echo from *The Tempest*, Milly finds 'rich and strange,' she feels as though she is sustained by 'an Eastern carpet.'

This would seem an appropriate occasion to consider the particular rôle played by imagery in James' writing, since, with his later books, as indicated by such titles as *The Sacred Fount*, *The Wings of the Dove*, *The Golden Bowl*, *The Ivory Tower*, images have become so important that they have passed over into symbols. Moreover, the use of images in *The Wings of the Dove* is so functional that we may keep our discussion of them integrally related to the rest of our discussion of this novel.

* * *

A * * * frequency of images of floating might be noted in *The Wings of the Dove*, where the serene 'high-water mark' of Milly's London success must be contrasted with her view of 'the troubled sea' that looms ahead, with the shipwreck that may lie in store for 'the ark of her deluge.' Since the recurrent pattern of an artist's imagery is the most telling evidence of how he envisages the qualities of life, another odd variant of James' water-images is worth citing. In all three of his great final novels he conceives on occasion his social group as being 'like fishes in a crystal pool,' held together in 'a fathomless medium.' What James seems to want most to suggest through such an image is the denseness of experience, the way in which the Jamesian individual feels that he is held into close contact with his special group, the slowly circulating motion of their existence all open to the observing eye, and, particularly as Densher develops this image, with an oppressive sense of the complexities in which he is immersed, of being plunged into an element 'rather more strangely than agreeably warm.'

If you proceeded to enumerate and categorize all of James' leading images, as has recently been done with Shakespeare's, you would undoubtedly gain a great deal of intimate insight both into the way his imagination worked and into what it worked upon. But the author of a long novel can scarcely depend on iterative imagery to produce atmosphere to the heightened degree that a poet can in the compressed length of a play, and we may learn more about James' art by examining the function of a few of his most elaborated images than by pursuing the sequence of their scattered and often minor echoes.

At the close of the chapter in which he introduced Milly, James wanted to sum up effectively the various and intricate aspects of the impression she had made upon Susan, and was designed to make upon the reader. During their brief sojourn in the Alps, Susan comes upon Milly one afternoon seated on the 'dizzy edge' of a precipice. She stifles a cry at the danger there of 'a single false movement,' at the possible latent betrayal in Milly's caprice of 'a horrible hidden obsession.' But as she watches, she is reassured: 'If the girl was deeply and recklessly meditating there she wasn't meditating a jump . . . She was looking down on the kingdoms of the earth, and though indeed that of itself might well go to the brain, it wouldn't be with a view of renouncing them. Was she choosing among them or did she want them all?' Through such a pictorial image we have borne in upon us one aspect of Milly's situation which James wants us never to forget, that the menace of death is always near her. But as Susan realized, Milly wouldn't try a quick escape 'from the human predicament': 'she knew herself unmistakably reserved for some more complicated passage . . . It would be a question of taking full in the face the whole assault of life.' By that extension James enables us to look ahead to his drama. He centers anticipation through Susan's consciousness of what must lie in store for a girl of Milly's type, of 'her history, her state, her beauty, her mystery.'

One thing notably absent from such a compelling image is any apparent awareness by James of its full religious implications. When Hawthorne had Miriam and Donatello reenact the fall of man, he was thoroughly conscious of the roots of his scene in the Bible, and especially in Milton. But James is concerned only with the beautiful sweep of the possible kingdoms at Milly's feet. At no point in this novel does he want to suggest that she is tempted by the devil in her choice of this world. So, too, with James' casual introduction of an image to suggest the chief source of Densher's attraction for Kate. This lies in the greater range of his intellectual experience, which James expresses by Densher's 'having tasted of the tree and being thereby prepared to assist her to eat.' All that James wants to suggest is the tree of knowledge; he seems to have forgotten that such an image is inescapably one of temptation, since it is certainly not Kate who is led into evil by Densher. Such carelessness or obliviousness on James' part shows how far he had drifted from the firm Christian knowledge that Hawthorne possessed* * *.

The type of image with which James is most successful is that which allows him to draw on the whole reach of his plastic resources. * * * On the very next page after Milly has introduced the image of 'an Eastern carpet,' she is brought to the peak of her enchantment. As she is escorted by Lord Mark to see the wonderful Bronzino in the great house, which picture, as everyone agrees, looks so like her, James has completed his spell and transformed his heroine into a Renaissance princess. By virtue of insisting on this likeness he has caused Milly to feel that she has entered 'the mystic circle': 'things melted together—the beauty and the history and the facility and the splendid midsummer glow: it was a sort of magnificent maximum, the pink dawn of an apotheosis coming so curiously soon.' But at this exalted moment Milly also foresees that none of her happiness will last. Even as she looks, she realizes that the joyless lady on the canvas is 'dead, dead, dead'; and the words reverberate for us as an omen of her own future.

This scene before the Bronzino operates almost like a musical theme: it strikes the first note of the transition to Venice, where Milly plays out her make-believe rôle in the gorgeous rented palace which increases the ironic contrast 'between her fortune and her fear.' There her setting becomes explicitly a Veronese, and Susan, to whom again this comparison occurs, deems all the sumptuous magnificence to be only fitting, since Milly's is 'one of the courts of heaven, the court of a reigning seraph, a sort of a vice-queen of an angel.' Milly herself, in conversation with Lord Mark, feels suddenly her 'excluded disinherited state' in the presence of so much borrowed charm, and murmurs: 'Ah, not to go down—never, never to go down!' Lord Mark, as obtuse to her feelings as he had been when showing her the Bronzino, takes this, not as her anguished dread that she must soon sink from this exalted level, but as a reference to the fact that she no longer goes downstairs.

The continual emphasis on Milly's health faced James with a problem that he solved in his own special way. As his preface affirmed, it is 'the act of living,' not that of dying, by which characters appeal, though that appeal may be heightened 'as the conditions plot against them and prescribe the battle.' One of the leading conditions here was the degree to which Milly was threatened from the start. But the pressure of the danger does not become apparent to others beside Susan until, at the very moment of her rare pleasure before the Bronzino, the girl has a spell of faintness. In this oblique way James hints at a linkage between his themes of love and death. The very next day she goes to consult the great doctor, Sir Luke Strett, and feels, in James' equivalent for a confessional, 'as though she had been on her knees to the priest.' We never know precisely what diagnosis Sir Luke makes of her, since it is James' method to give us such knowledge only through the refracted reports of other characters. He may have felt it necessary to play down the difficult fact of physical infirmity by never saying directly what Milly's illness is, though for many readers this operates as a tedious mystification. Susan might naturally shrink away from knowing the horrible details; but when Kate says to Densher that Milly's trouble is 'not lungs, I think,' either she is lying for purposes of her own, as James' characters often do, or he is dealing in deliberate obfuscation. For as Milly behaves, she can hardly be dying of anything except tuberculosis, as Minny Temple died, at a period when no coherent cure had yet been devised.

One aspect of her situation that he penetrates with psychological depth is the relation between her delicate vitality and the will to live. Sir Luke knows that she needs love to sustain her, to relax the tension of her loneliness, and—though there is the hint in the background that he may have decided at once that there was no lasting hope for her no matter what she did—he urges her to 'take the trouble' to live.

Once again, as in *The Ambassadors*, we have a scene built upon this theme. Milly leaves the doctor's office, knowing that her situation is grave, but buoyed up by his sympathy and his challenge. She has a sense of sharing more than before in the general human lot. She starts to walk through London's streets, a rich girl 'hoping' that she has found the slums. She comes out finally into Regent's Park: 'Here were wanderers anxious and tired like herself; here doubtless were hundreds of others just in the same box. Their box, their great common anxiety, what was it in this grim breathing-space, but the practical question of life? They could live if they would; that is, like herself they had been told so: she saw them all about her, on seats, digesting the information, recognizing it again as something in a slightly different shape familiar enough, the blessed old truth that they would live if they could.'

That reversal seems at first the easy fancy of a sheltered ignorant girl, but James knew what he was doing. As Milly sits meditating upon the odds against her future, upon the rent she will have to pay, she looks around her again, with the kind of comprehension of the favored difference in her lot that makes the reader respond to her with full sympathy, since, no matter how favored, she too is up against death. She saw 'her scattered melancholy comrades—some of them so melancholy as to be down on their stomachs in the grass, turned away, ignoring, burrowing: she saw once more, with them, those two faces of the question between which there was so little to choose for inspiration. It was perhaps superficially more striking that one could live if one would; but it was more appealing, insinuating, irresistible in short, that one would live if one could.'

Shortly after this point James introduces the image that was to become the symbol of his title. A more or less full account of this image, of its morphology, so to speak, may help us to distinguish James from other symbolists. He is so fond of animal-imagery of all sorts that it is hard to say whether, on the occasion when he likens Aunt Maud to an eagle with 'gilded claws,' he is preparing the way for the contrasting image of the dove, or is simply responding to his painter's instinct to make every inch of his canvas as lively as possible. For elsewhere Aunt Maud is a lionness, a glossy embodiment of Britannia herself; just as, again, to Densher's eyes, Milly, worn down by the social crush, becomes 'a Christian maiden, in the arena, mildly, caressingly martyred,' not by the nosing 'of lions and tigers but of domestic animals let loose as for the joke.' But there would seem to be deliberate preparation of his chief characterizing image for Milly in her own contrasting statement that she has used 'the wisdom of the serpent' to find in Sir Luke Strett the special man for her need. For one quality of this 'dove' is that she is not so innocent as she looks. She may be fooled by the new social complexity into which she has been plunged, she may trustingly not suspect that Aunt Maud and Kate both have designs upon her. But in the scene where the dove-image is introduced, she has her own strategy of how to play the part. Aunt Maud has left the two girls together, with the request that Milly find out for her whether Densher has returned yet from America. One look at Kate virtually convinces Milly that he has. Then as Kate paces the room 'like a panther,' Milly is startled as at the foreboding of some sinister charged energy. It is when Kate becomes aware of Milly's strained feelings that she turns to her more gently and pronounces her 'a dove.' This speech serves to bring out again the contrast between the force and the delicacy of the two. But at that moment Aunt Maud reappears, whereupon Milly decides to appear at her 'most dovelike,' and yet to tell her, out of loyalty to Kate's unspoken secret, that she doesn't think Densher is back.

The next use of the image is during the great climactic scene in Venice, where Milly, her dress changed for the only time in the book from mourning robes to white, makes her most radiant appearance—and her last. As Kate and Densher stand watching her across the great room, a heavy 'priceless chain' of pearls around her neck, Kate says once again, 'She's a dove.' Densher agrees that that figure best describes Milly's spirit, but he then realizes how strongly the dove-like color of pearls also enters into Kate's impression. The power of wealth, he reflects, 'was dovelike only so far as one remembered that doves have wings and wondrous flights, have them as well as tender tints and soft sounds. It even came to him dimly that such wings could . . . spread themselves for protection. Hadn't they, for that matter, lately taken an inordinate reach, and weren't Kate and Mrs. Lowder, weren't Susan Shepherd and he, wasn't *he*, in particular, nestling under them to a great increase of immediate ease?' As Kate continues to dwell on the beauty of the pearls, he realizes with a twinge that 'pearls were exactly what Merton Densher would never be able to give her.' It is at this moment that Kate, who up until now has concealed the final range of her intention, comes out with her proposal that since Milly can't live, he is to marry her for her money. Just as Kate has delivered this proposal, Milly sends across the room to them 'all the candour of her smile.'

With this ample instance of how James could extend a metaphor into a symbol, we may see him in relation to the development of modern symbolism. In several of his earliest stories, as in *The Romance of Certain Old Clothes* and *Benvolio*, he had depended on allegory in the manner of Hawthorne; and if we look closely at *Roderick Hudson*, we realize that that novel is still essentially an allegory of the life of the artist. As he went on to master all the skills of realism, he grew dissatisfied with allegory's obvious devices; and yet, particularly towards the end of his career, realistic details had become merely the covering for a content that was far from realistic. He was quite aware of the newer French movement. In fact, he stages one of the later conversations between Kate and Milly in its manner: 'Certain aspects of the connexion of these young women show for us, such is the twilight that gathers about them, in the likeness of some dim scene in a Maeterlinck play; we have positively the image, in the delicate dusk, of the figures so associated and yet so opposed, so mutually watchful: that of the angular pale princess, ostrich-plumed, blackrobed, hung about with amulets, reminders, relics, mainly seated, mainly still, and that of the upright restless slow-circling lady of her court who exchanges with her, across the black water streaked with evening gleams, fitful questions and answers. The upright lady, with thick dark braids down her back, drawing over the grass a more embroidered train, makes the whole circuit, and makes it again, and the broken talk, brief and sparingly allusive, seems more to cover than to free their sense.'

Yet James was no *symboliste*. His interest in Maeterlinck was in the possibilities of a richer, more poetic drama; but he was unlike the symbolist poets in that the suggestiveness of music was not his chief concern. His own analogies for his work were always with painting or with the stage, and he possessed none of the technical knowledge of music that was to be exhibited by both Proust and Mann. His leading symbols are all literary and pictorial. The four that furnished titles for his books are biblical allusions, to which he proceeded to give concrete embodiment with little reference to the Bible. His method of arriving at his symbols and what he hoped to achieve by them may be suggested by the fact that though he left an extensive scenario for the unfinished *Ivory Tower,* this does not mention the symbol itself, any more than do his shorter notebook drafts for the other books. In other words, he did not, like Mallarmé, start with his symbol. He reached it only with the final development of his theme, and then used it essentially in the older tradition of the poetic metaphor, to give concretion, as well as allusive and beautiful extension, to his thought.

The contrast with more recent practice is striking. Unlike Mann, James was not influenced by Wagner; he has nothing like the elaborate and studied recurrence of musical themes. And though he came to work essentially in the genre of the fairy tale, he had not become conscious of the possibilities of dealing explicitly with myth. That consciousness, in its modern form, was the product of a somewhat later period, of the period that had been pervaded by Freud. James may be seen to be moving in the direction of that psychology in his suggestion through 'the sacred fount' of the springs of sexual vitality. But the full influence of Freud was to produce the compulsive symbols of Kafka, whose 'castle,' for instance, is not the last refinement of an already developed theme, but a dense central core of meaning beyond the reach of any articulation that the author's mind could give to it. And, as a final delimitation to James' handling of symbols, there is the fact that, again unlike subsequent writers, he had naturally not felt the impact of more recent anthropology. He sought for his universals in the well-lighted drawing rooms of his time. When he groped his way back to 'the sense of the past,' it was only to the dawn of the nineteenth century, for the sake of a contrast with later social manners. He was not to become aware of the obsessive presence of all times, of the repetition of primitive patterns in civilized life, as Eliot tried to express it through his anthropological symbol of 'the waste land.'

When James did make a thematic use of symbols, it tended to be in the fashion of earlier poetic drama. He had declared in his 'summing up' that the 'dramatic poem' seemed to him 'the most beautiful thing possible,' and in a work like *The Wings of the Dove* he was finally producing his equivalent for it. He even made a Shakespearean use of storm and calm. When Lord Mark, jealous that Milly won't accept him, confronts her with the ugly truth of Densher's engagement, he does it in a Venice where the serene summer is over, where a black sky and a cold lashing rain accentuate how 'all of evil' seems to have broken out. Equally symbolically, when Sir Luke arrives for his final visit, the storm is superseded by 'autumn sunshine,' and the renewed beauty of the city is 'like a hanging-out of vivid stuffs, a laying-down of fine carpets.'

But even in such renewed mellowness—to follow the book now to its conclusion—we no longer see Milly directly. Densher has at last become terribly aware that he has 'never been near the facts of her condition.' As he realizes how the whole 'expensive vagueness, made up of smiles and silences and beautiful fictions and priceless arrangements,' had conspired to charm from the picture any 'shadow of pain and horror,' we probably have James' chief reason for so muffling the question of Milly's illness. He wanted to emphasize how her companions had fled from reality into a 'conscious fool's paradise.' But the facts are all there, as Densher now acutely feels them: 'the facts of physical suffering, of incurable pain, of the chance grimly narrowed.'

Densher is the chief means by which James keeps his romance from becoming dissevered from reality, his tale of enchantment from becoming a tale of escape. If James created the spell of a fairy tale, he did it, as the great fabulists have always done, for the sake of evoking universal truths. Densher is also an important factor in preventing Susan Stringham's intensely 'literary' version of Milly as a princess from becoming merely silly. He is in love with Kate, and Milly, to his eyes, is no princess; she is simply 'little Miss Theale,' the odd-looking American girl who had been so kind to him in New York. This wholly unglamorous view of her is also of the highest significance in the denouement, in the gradual, inescapable transformation of both Densher and Kate.

James' moral drama here is his most thoroughgoing. The issue between Kate and Densher is finely drawn. He is always dominated by her vitality. Even before he discerns where her scheme is tending, he feels himself caught in her 'wondrous silken web.' In the scene of the compact between them, her will operates like that of a Lady Macbeth. When he wants to break off the pretence, Kate says: 'Do you want to kill her? We've told too many lies.' So he weakly agrees to stay in Venice for Milly, but preserves his self-respect by insisting that he will do so only on the condition that Kate will pledge her unchanged love by coming to him in his rooms for complete physical union. He clings also to the scruple that he will himself offer no proposal to Milly, but will simply wait for what she proposes. And though such a distinction may seem tenuously Jamesian, it serves to reveal the gulf that is already opening between him and Kate. For what she foresees as the result of her manipulations is, as she says, 'quite ideal'—a terrifying phrase by its utter obliviousness to any moral implications.

Densher continues to insist that he has no feelings about Milly, that he hasn't 'even the amount of curiosity that he would have had about an ordinary friend.' But as the other English people return to London and he remains behind, he begins to have increasingly a sense of 'her disconcerting poetry.' He feels her as somehow 'divine in her trust, or at any rate inscrutable in her mercy.' When, at the shock of Lord Mark's news, she has 'turned her face to the wall,' the enormity of the situation strikes home to him.

But his change is given to us only gradually and piecemeal. We learn that he has been back in London for two weeks before letting Kate know. On seeing her, he is impressed with 'how terribly well' she looks. But he finds that he can no longer feel free with her, and that oddly he must turn to her aunt in his need to talk about Milly. It is Aunt Maud who says, at the news of Milly's death, 'Our dear dove, then, as Kate calls her, has folded her wonderful wings.' But it would be unthinkable that Densher could share with Aunt Maud the essence of what he now feels about Milly. For, as Aunt Maud pursues her image—'unless it's more true . . . that she has spread them the wider,'—she is thinking of the possible money. And what is uppermost for him is that when Milly had summoned him, through Sir Luke, for their final interview, 'something had happened to him too beautiful and too sacred to describe. He had been, to his recovered sense, forgiven, dedicated, blessed.'

Yet he must seek out Kate, and it is significant of the motivating drive which James attaches to her background that Densher finds her at her sister's, in the ugliness where she seems so little to belong. In the last scenes between them Kate's oppressive sense of her father's sordid evil is always in the air, as is also Densher's sense of her enormous 'talent for life': 'What a person she would be if they *had* been rich—with what a genius for the so-called great life, what a presence for the so-called great house.' But he has come through to the firmness of decision. They are not to be rich. He has grown to have 'horror, almost' of her lucidity and tenacity. As she says, in the final occurrence of the controlling image: 'I used to call her, in my stupidity—for want of anything better—a dove. Well, she stretched out her wings, and it was to *that* they reached. They cover us.'

'They cover us,' Densher said.

'That's what I give you,' Kate gravely wound up. 'That's what I've done for you.'

But even as she speaks, she knows with what liberty of choice he will face her, that she may have either him or the money which Milly, true to her generosity, has left him. The wings have covered them in another sense than Kate had bargained for. Densher may insist that he 'never was in love' with Milly; but Kate replies: 'Her memory's your love. You *want* no other.'

'He heard her out in stillness, watching her face but not moving. Then he only said: "I'll marry you, mind you, in an hour."

"As we were?"

"As we were."

But she turned to the door, and her headshake was now the end. "We shall never be again as we were!" '

Kate is right. Densher has been transformed by the dead girl's hovering presence. Like the hero in any great tragedy he has arrived at the moral perception of the meaning of what has befallen him. As far as Kate is concerned, James has left the reader with the kind of choice which he believed to constitute an essential element in the relation of art to life. He has dropped one idea that was in his outline. There is no remote possibility that Kate will marry Lord Mark. But the other alternative is still in the air. This is not due to careless ambiguity. James held that an artist could convey the real complexity of life only by suggesting, through such a device of multiple choice, a wider circle beyond the restricted one he had selected to illuminate. Milly is dead. Densher has learned the meaning of loss and renunciation. Whether Kate's life has also been irrevocably altered by the brush of Milly's spirit, or whether her hard handsomeness and the desperateness of her situation will still allow her to seek her own kind of shelter beneath the spread of those opulent wings, the reader can determine only by the kind of sustained attention to the whole novel that James was always demanding. And even then James would want his reader's strongest sense to be at the end that the denseness and uncertainty of life are such that we should never pronounce too complacently or too arrogantly upon what lies ahead.

In the preface to *The Portrait of a Lady,* James discussed whether a writer could make his heroine the main support of his theme, and quoted George Eliot's conviction that 'In these frail vessels is borne onward through the ages the treasure of human affection.' But he knew that Maggie Tulliver and Rosamond Vincy, as well as Juliet and Cleopatra, were never allowed to be the 'sole ministers' of appeal. Milly Theale has almost become such. Even though the maturing of Densher may be, in its devious way, as impressive as Romeo's, he is never brought to the center of our concern. The question then presses itself whether a character like Milly's is of sufficient emotional force to carry a great work. The comparison with her original is significant. She does not possess Minny Temple's questing mind; she does not ask about the meaning of faith. The originality and the audacity which so impressed James in his cousin have been keyed down to the gentleness of the dove. But he posited for Milly the same 'excess of joy' in living, and gave to her 'crowded consciousness' the sense that it was her doom to live fast.' It was essential to his theme that his 'anxious fighter of the battle of life' should be arrayed against insuperable odds, that her high-strung American nerves should feel Europe too 'tough' for her.

But the issue is whether such a theme can yield more than exquisite pathos, whether it has enough substance to make tragedy. James believed that it had, that essential evil was revealed in Kate and in Lord Mark through their pursuit of the money, and that essential terror could be conveyed through Milly's own anguished horror of death. He had said in his notebook, 'She is like a creature dragged shrieking to the guillotine—to the shambles.' Densher was to make his own development of that image, as he meditated on Milly's 'unapproachable terror of the end': she 'had held with passion to her dream of a future, and she was separated from it, not shrieking indeed, but grimly, awfully silent, as one might imagine some noble young victim of the scaffold, in the French Revolution, separated at the prison-door from some object clutched for resistance.'

It is revelatory of James that, as was the case with Madame de Vionnet's loss, he again uses an image from the French Revolution, this time an image entirely aristocratic in its associations. That will mark for many readers how far James was from being capable of projecting a real American tragedy of his own time. But the controlling facts of tragedy are neither time nor place, but the urgency with which we are made to feel life and death. James has reduced his ore to the last possible refinement, but what is left is the purest metal. It is not merely the 'vague golden air' of Susan's enchantment; it is rather, as in Donne's image,

like golde to airy thinnesse beate.

There is much more of pity than of terror in Milly's confronting of fate. Her passive suffering is fitting for the deuteragonist rather than for the protagonist of a major tragedy, for a Desdemona, not for an Othello. But if James has shown again that the chords he could strike were minor, were those of renunciation, of resignation, of inner triumph in the face of outer defeat, he was not out of keeping with the spiritual history of his American epoch. Art often expresses society very obliquely, and it is notable that the most sensitive recorders of James' generation gave voice to themes akin to his. In the face of the overwhelming expansion, the local colorists felt compelled, like Sarah Orne Jewett, to commemorate the old landmarks before they should be entirely swept away and obliterated. Emily Dickinson discovered that the only way she could be a poet in such an age was by withdrawal, by depending, virtually like a

Jamesian heroine, upon the richness of her own 'crowded consciousness.' And the least feminine, most robust talent of the age, Mark Twain, who may seem at the farthest pole from James, did not find his themes in the facile myths of manifest destiny or triumphant democracy. His masterpiece was also an elegy. It gave expression to the loss of the older America of his boyhood, which, no less than the milieu of Henry James and Minny Temple, had been destroyed by the onrush of the industrial revolution.

R. P. BLACKMUR

[Dramas of the Soul in Action]†

In his three novels, *The Ambassadors, The Wings of the Dove*, and *The Golden Bowl*, written one a year as he approached the age of sixty, Henry James made a spiritual trilogy which, with each succeeding volume, approached nearer and nearer the condition of poetry. This is one way of stating James' achievement as a novelist and one way of qualifying the stature of his imagination. I mean that the authority and the mystery—the riches and the waste places—of these novels tend increasingly to lie in the poetry of his language, but that the poetry is the poetry of the soul in action. These novels, then, constitute poetic dramas of the inner life of the soul at the height of its struggle, for good and for evil, with the outer world in which it must live and to which it must respond, the world which it must deny, or renounce, or accept. It is by such means that the soul seems, in these novels, to do something to actual life and is itself changed by them through a shifting equilibrium in which a very little soul may by its spiritual intensity balance a great deal of life. Something of this sort is what is meant when we refer to the novel as a way of looking at life, or, better, it is what we might mean if we said that the novel provided us with a theoretic form for life. The novel gives the imaginative parts of our minds a theoretic form for life which will modify or correct the forms which other parts of our minds—all the conceptual and administrative and routine parts—provide; and the novel does this precisely by providing forms in which we can see the soul in action. It is novelists like James who best support this claim.

For it is novelists like James who best show us how in the novel the *craft* of the form—the whole institution of the novel—must intervene between the soul and its actions as the medium absolutely necessary if we are to see anything at all. The more spiritual you are ultimately, the more surely you must be immediately in the senses

† From R. P. Blackmur. Introduction to Henry James, *The Golden Bowl* (New York: Grove Press, 1952), pp. v–x.

and the more certain you must be, for both, that you have the aid of mechanical devices and familiar conventions. It is hard for either spiritual things or sensuous things to reach form in themselves (at least in language), and it would seem they are bound to take lodgings in the conventional forms nearest at hand and of the oldest architecture; if successful, they will emerge, as in these novels of James, as new masters of the house, and the house will be beautiful because once again lived in. Each of these novels is a tale of illicit love, two of them about adultery; the one (*The Ambassadors*) the lovely aspiring adultery, the other (*The Golden Bowl*) the hideous intolerable adultery. In each novel the crash of things comes about through the shock by which the illicit love is recognized. In each the act of illicit love is the tragic fault—the *hamartia* of Aristotle—the act which can be explained but cannot be justified. In each the movements of the plot are carefully calculated to ensure this recognition and this revelation. This is the plot which derives from the impact of the mechanically well-made play—as in Scribe and Dumas and Brieux, and later as in Maugham and Coward and Philip Barry—upon the novel; and taken in that aspect, James made certain of the existence in English of the well-made novel. But this is not the plot which Aristotle called the soul of the action; it is only the mechanical scaffold, proved strong through long experience and wide current practice in popular writing, which would give support, outer convenience, and mechanical form to movements of the soul otherwise (within James' reach) ineluctable. It is like Dostoevsky with his series of great novels based upon the mechanical form of the murder mystery.

Perhaps the more ineluctable in itself the real plot is, the more necessary is the preliminary and final existence of the mechanical plot. The imaginative mind must use many modes of seeing in order to come upon a single view and especially so when, as in our age, there is no existing single view to which the imagination gives universal credit and what is universal seems rather what is made fresh. James, at any rate, in writing about his own work emphasized the mechanical aspects of his technique and even created a whole language for its discussion, at the very moment when he was regarding the freshest and most universal of his creations, such as the three novels we have here in mind * * * . For there is in each of these novels a plot which does truly constitute the soul of the action, which does truly imitate the conditions and aspirations of human life as seen in the actions of men and women of more than usual worth and risk. Between the operations of the two plots we gain the condition prescribed by Coleridge as the ideal condition of poetry, the condition of "a more than usual state of emotion and a more than usual order." How then shall we describe these true plots?

When we try to describe them, we see at once that James had a many-moded mind, and that there is no simple single formula for any of them. Possibly we can say that the mechanical plot is what the action is about as anecdote and that the true plot reveals the being of the people to whom the action happens and *thus* reveals the action of the soul in its poetic drama. In *The Ambassadors* Strether finds in the midst of adultery a virtuous connection which makes, though too late for him, life full and free and worth living. In *The Wings of the Dove*, Milly Theale's life stops, when she discovers her young man has deceived her with her best friend, just at the moment when the nature of freedom and fullness of life have become plain to her. In *The Golden Bowl*, Maggie, the little Princess, seizes fast on the freedom and fullness of life in full assent to its cost in treachery and woe—as illustrated, in her case, by the adulterous relation between her husband and her father's young wife. In each novel, the hero or heroine is an almost inconceivably lonely person—so lonely as to be no more than a shade or the dream of a human being—and yet as quick with life as our own flesh cut with a razor or paper's edge. In each novel, too, the hero or heroine, across the gap of loneliness, works permanent ravage and ruin, the shameless punishment and the shameful penance of passion upon itself, on the couples who have been enduring illicit love however lovely or natural or treacherous to the point of mere lust (Venus without Cupid, as Montaigne says) the love had been. Chad Newsome and Marie de Vionnet separate forever (in *The Ambassadors*), Merton Densher and Kate Croy (in *The Wings of the Dove*) are riven by the woe of their very humanity, and Amerigo, the Prince, and Charlotte Verver create a lie between themselves which will separate them ocean-wide forever. Nor do the heroic agents of these separations fare any better. Strether renounces the chance of getting anything for himself out of his embassy, otherwise so successful, to Europe. Milly Theale denies life at the moment she has grasped it. Maggie Verver accepts life with a conviction so violent that it breaks her to pieces and, at the last moment we see her, is unable to look in her husband's eyes at the cost of the life and loyalty her conviction has created there. They are indeed dread shades into which, with their creations in the lives and loves of their victims, they dissolve, leaving only a vital or a mortal pang, vital as beauty, mortal as incentive, when set upon by the evil that springs in the dusk of life.

When set upon by the evil in life it is the good, in James, that in the instance perishes however it may endure in essence or ideal, in the heaven of man's mind. Here I think is the element in James' novels that gives them their fabulous air; we believe in them only as we believe in hellish or heavenly fables, as we might believe in some fabulous form of the uncreated shades of ourselves. These shades have always been the springs of poetry, of individual insight into collective moral experience and created images of moral beauty alike. They trouble our conscience, and indeed are our conscience, not of particular ill doing or omission, but of life itself; and so likewise these troublings teach us ways of love—of human relatedness—to which even as we see them we are inadequate but to which ever-afterwards we aspire.

So it is with these novels of James. Each of the three persons named—Lambert Strether, Milly Theale, and Maggie Verver—looms on the consciousness of the other persons as an image of moral beauty, strikes them as conscience (the agenbite of inwit), and teaches them a new possible, impossible (James' own phrase) mode of love in which conscience and moral beauty are joined. Through these three persons the others learn what they want, what they are, and what, in the conditions into which they have warped their actual world, they cannot have. The anguish is as great as the beauty, the possible as the impossible. Strether and the two girls suffer as much as the victims of their goodness, their conscience, and their love; they suffer as shades always must in the anguish of the actual world, the certainty either of degradation or extinction, or both. It is of great interest, lastly, that these three suffer in distinctly different ways but in a rising scale of the value grasped at, missed only by the hair's breadth of life itself and so grasped at all the more. They suffer in accord with the plan or division of nature of Dante, that master who first brought love into European literature as a primary subject. Lambert Strether suffers all that is possible to the senses, Milly Theale what is possible as allegory or created meaning, Maggie Verver is in intention rather like Beatrice in the *Divine Comedy*, the Lady of Theology, and suffers the pangs of the highest human love. I will not say that the one mode of love is in the act superior to the others, and I am certain that our sense of any one modifies our sense of the others * * *

ERNEST SANDEEN

The Wings of the Dove and *The Portrait of a Lady*: A Study of Henry James's Later Phase†

I

Whatever Henry James's feelings may have been toward his favorite "Albany cousin," Mary ("Minny") Temple, while she lived, it is clear that at her death in 1870, she left with him an

† From Ernest Sandeen, "*The Wings of the Dove* and *The Portrait of a Lady*: A Study of Henry James's Later Phase," *PMLA* 69 (December 1954), 1060–61, 1064–75.

indelible image that made available to him as a writer large areas of human experience. This image figured more or less obscurely in several of his stories and minor female characters but according to his own testimony was most fully and consciously operative in his creation of Isabel Archer in *The Portrait of a Lady* and of Milly Theale in *The Wings of the Dove.*[1]

Certainly there was the danger in either of these novels that James's view of the human situation which the symbol of Minny Temple revealed might be distorted by his strong personal feelings for Minny herself. He confessed to his "tenderness of imagination" about Milly Theale in the "Preface" to *Wings* which he wrote for the New York Edition of his works. Yet when he came to create this later heroine, James was able to assimilate his private sentiments more completely into his art than he had been when he had created Isabel Archer.

In both *Portrait* and *Wings* the Minny Temple image points toward the same effect, and the sequence of events by which the two protagonists are led to their destiny is basically the same. Isabel and Milly are American girls, they are intelligent and sensitive, and they are equipped with wealth and personal charm. They are introduced into the great world of European society and there they enjoy a brilliant hour of triumph which includes the luxury of declining the "ordinary" form of success, marriage to a member of the English nobility. However, after they form what they believe are attachments of their own free choice, they discover that they have been betrayed by persons interested chiefly in their wealth.

The essential element in this common pattern is the ironic disparity between the great endowments of the heroine and the defeat she suffers, between the high hopes entertained for her and the dismal reality that overtakes her. From the first, James's picture of his cousin Minny had been refracted through his sense of her incongruous relation to the world. At the time when he was trying to adjust himself to the new fact of her death what impressed him most about the living Mary Temple as he remembered her was "that life—poor narrow life—contained no place for her."[2] "Her character may be almost literally said to have been without practical application to life."[3]

In view of the correspondences between the stories of Isabel Archer and Milly Theale it is not surprising that the two casts of characters surrounding the principals should be roughly equivalent

1. For the story of the relationship between Henry James and Mary Temple and an account of its effect upon James's fiction, see Leon Edel, *Henry James: The Untried Years, 1843–1870* (Philadelphia and New York, 1953), pp. 226–238, 323–333.

2 R. C. LeClair, "Henry James and Minny Temple," *AL*, XXI (1949), 40.

3. F. O. Matthiessen, *The James Family, Including Selections from the Writings of Henry James Senior, William, Henry and Alice James* (New York, 1947), p. 260.

to each other. The resemblances are not in their personal qualities, however, but only in the literary functions they serve. For example, Henrietta Stackpole when placed beside her fellow-journalist, Susan Shepherd Stringham of *Wings*, appears more distinctly than ever as a caricature. Yet the two women stand in much the same relation to the heroine. Both betray an admiration for her which rises to a kind of anxious idolatry, and both assume the role of confidante, though Susan is more securely placed in that position than Henrietta.

Again, Mrs. Touchett of *Portrait* could never be confused, as a person, with Maud Manningham Lowder of *Wings*, but James uses both of them for the same purpose. As matrons of European society, they furnish a social entree for the heroine and thus make possible her initial success and her eventual failure. Although Lord Mark is a more cynical portrait of the English aristocracy than Lord Warburton, each is used to develop the irony attaching to the heroine's refusal of his offer of marriage in favor of a more humble and what she believes, mistakenly, is a more genuine petition. Most obviously parallel are the two pairs of "villains," Madame Serena Merle and Gilbert Osmond in *Portrait*, Kate Croy and Merton Densher in *Wings*. Yet the sinister quality in Merle and Osmond, restrained as it is, is converted to a more sympathetic form of frailty in Croy and Densher.

The crucial difference between the two novels, the one which registers most of the other differences, is that in *Wings* there is no character to correspond to Ralph Touchett in *Portrait*. This omission in *Wings* dramatizes James's development of the story which Minny Temple had given him.

* * *

A comparison of *The Portrait of a Lady* with *The Wings of the Dove* brings out the literary weaknesses which the character Ralph Touchett represents in the former novel. He is seen, in this perspective, as an expression of James's great personal tenderness for the woman who lived in his memory and was the archetype for his heroine. It may have been that James's private emotions were as strong when he wrote *Wings*, but here they were not condensed and personified as they had been in *Portrait*; they were, instead, absorbed into the main channels of his protagonist's story. The absence in *Wings* of any character like Ralph Touchett means that James, in effect, has absented himself. A connection is at once suggested between this absence and the greater artistic "toughness" with which James projects the Minny Temple myth in the later novel. The result is the greater depth and the wider range of Milly Theale's tragedy as compared with Isabel Archer's. In brief, the character Ralph Touchett testifies negatively to the truth of the dictum that "the more perfect the artist, the more completely separate in him will be the man who suffers and the mind which creates; the more perfectly will the mind digest and transmute the passions which are its material."[4]

A simple economy of means in *Wings* makes a counterpart to Ralph Touchett superfluous: the functions he might perform do not exist. In the first place, no one is needed to arrange a large inheritance for Milly Theale at an appropriate moment in the story, because Milly is introduced at the outset as a great heiress. There is nothing of the "from-rags-to-riches" theme in *Wings* which, in a greatly refined form, dominates Isabel's early career. In *Portrait* James betrays an idealist's anxiety to justify his heroine's wealth. Isabel must first prove her great qualities and when she has passed the test to the satisfaction of all who observe her, including the reader, she is rewarded as people like her undoubtedly deserve to be but seldom are. James has been careful to motivate the process but an air of contrivance hovers over it, at best. Isabel's inheritance figures, in the last analysis, as the author's management of plot; it never becomes a part of her character.

No apology is offered for Milly Theale's great fortune. She is not required to "earn" it, and yet it is treated frankly as an important source of the power which everyone feels in her presence. Milly manages her wealth with an ease which is at once grand and unselfconscious. She is not at all made uncomfortable by her money; she is not, like Isabel, looking for someone to share the moral responsibility of her good luck. Of course, Milly's greatness is ultimately a matter of character, but no one can think of her personal qualities as altogether detached from her riches. The impression which people have of Milly is that if her fortune is immense, she appears to be equal to it. Even Susan Stringham, Milly's companion, who adores and almost worships Milly, perceives that money is an intrinsic element in her picture of this American "princess." Susan recognizes it as "the truth of truths that the girl couldn't get away from her wealth. . . . it was in the fine folds of [her] helplessly expensive little black frock . . . it was in the curious and splendid coils of [her] hair, 'done' with no eye whatever to the *mode du jour* . . . it lurked between the leaves of [her] uncut but antiquated Tauchnitz volume. . . . She couldn't dress it away, nor walk it away, nor read it away, nor think it away; she could neither smile it away in any dreamy absence nor blow it away in any softened sigh. She couldn't have lost it if she had tried—that was what it was to be really rich. It had to be *the* thing you were."

4. T. S. Eliot, "Tradition and the Individual Talent," in *Selected Essays*, new ed. (New York, 1950), pp. 7–8.

Another instance of James's greater artistic hardness in *Wings* is his willingness to subject his heroine to the same early death which belonged to his memory of Minny Temple. Once again, he has no need for a Ralph Touchett. Milly is not provided with a patron-guardian who is also a sacrificial victim, and this explains in part why she is a more profoundly tragic figure than Isabel Archer. James's hardheaded acceptance of Milly's fortune as a great human power complements his refusal to rescue her from the doom to which Minny Temple had condemned her. It is the combination of her wealth and her disease, of the promise of an illimitable future and the threat of an impending death, that makes Milly peculiarly vulnerable, within and without, to the deception she encounters. The menace of death sharpens her natural desire for a love which she does not want to buy with her money. Yet "wouldn't her value," it dawns upon her, "for the man who should marry her, be precisely in the ravage of her disease? *She* mightn't last, but her money would." If she were an heiress in perfect health, or if she were mortally ill without a fortune, she would not provoke the fate which she eventually suffers.

The harsh realities surrounding Milly Theale are not blurred and softened. Her predicament is more terrible and more pitiable than Isabel Archer's, and it is also more convincing. In order to throw herself into the trap set by Madame Merle and Gilbert Osmond, Isabel has to defy the suspicion and disapproval of all her friends. When she becomes engaged to Osmond, she is warned of her danger by Mrs. Touchett and by Ralph Touchett in very plain language, to say nothing of the less disinterested opposition of Caspar Goodwood, Lord Warburton and Henrietta Stackpole. The forces of deception ranged against Milly Theale are much more formidable. The conspiracy to delude Milly may be engineered by Kate Croy and Merton Densher, but it is one in which everyone in the story, except Lord Mark, eventually takes a part.

Everyone sees in Milly's developing relations with Densher an opportunity either for himself or for someone else. Maud Lowder, who according to her lights has her niece's best interest at heart, finds in the "affair" a chance to end Kate's infatuation with Densher and to promote a better match between Kate and Lord Mark. But Sir Luke Strett, Milly's physician, who takes both a personal and a professional interest in Milly's own welfare, also favors the attachment. Paradoxically, Milly's most loyal friend, Susan Stringham, is willing to carry the deception as far as anyone else, farther in fact than Merton Densher is willing to carry it. Of course, her motives are of the best. She believes that love—even if only a delusion—may help Milly to live or, at the very least, give her the sense of having lived if it cannot repair her health. For these good reasons, then, Susan urges Merton Densher to deny to Milly's face Lord Mark's charge that Densher and Kate are engaged—a charge which Susan plainly believes to be true. But Densher refuses to countenance this depth of deceit.

It cannot be denied that the responsibility for the plot to beguile Milly Theale comes back to Kate Croy and Merton Densher. In their purely functional roles in the action these two greatly resemble Madame Merle and Gilbert Osmond of *Portrait*. In a pattern of precedence in guilt which recalls Genesis the woman in each novel conceives the plan to delude the heroine, and the man at the woman's urging tries to carry it out. But in character the two couples have little in common. The Gothic tinges which distinguish Merle and Osmond from the other characters in *Portrait* have been elaborately subdued in the portraits of Kate and Merton. Much art and space are given over in *Wings* to blending the darker guilt of Kate Croy and her lover into the general gray of human frailty which surrounds the heroine and which here and there dulls even her luminosity.

Merle and Osmond look upon each other with the mild contempt of those who share the memory of a "romantic" experience long ago gone stale. Their common interest is their illegitimate daughter and each parent looks upon her in a way which reveals only a self-centered concern. Kate and Merton, though terribly knowing and sophisticated, still represent "young love"; they see each other in respect to the future, not the past, and much is forgiven them because even their least worthy actions spring from their genuine loyalty to each other.

It is true that Kate perceives in Milly's situation a chance to have her cake and eat it too, to marry the man she loves and at the same time enjoy the fortune she covets. Then she will be free of her Aunt Maud who promises her the wealth she desires but only on condition that she reject Densher and marry Lord Mark. Ideally, of course, Kate should sacrifice to her love all prospects of material well-being. But it is characteristic of James's maturity in *Wings* to emphasize the complexity and the limitations of human behavior. James takes pains, for example, to dramatize Kate's economic responsibilities to others. If she married Densher in opposition to her aunt's will, Kate would, in effect, abandon to final poverty her widowed sister, Mrs. Condrip, with her brood of children, to say nothing of abandoning her father to the disreputable stratagems by which he manages to live on nothing a year. There are further considerations which weaken the case against Kate Croy. There is, first, the indisputable fact of her nature that she finds her proper self only in a setting of opulence. When Densher meets her in the limited context of her sister's house, he recognizes the glaring incongruity which she poses against such a backdrop. Further, her love for Densher being sincere and deep, Kate's willingness to share him with another woman even temporarily exacts from her a genuine sacrifice. Finally, Kate believes as Susan Stringham does, that Densher's paying court to Milly will be of benefit to the dying girl. She is convinced that she can serve Milly's interests at the same time as she serves her own.

James has placed Maud Lowder's large figure in such a position as to shade Kate Croy from the glare of unambiguous, solitary guilt. The real contest, in fact, is between these two evenly matched adversaries, not one between the worldly-wise English girl and the guileless American girl. Actually it is Mrs. Lowder who first sets in motion the scheme to mislead Milly Theale. Kate perceives at once how her aunt intends to make use of Milly in order to promote her own plans, i.e., to fob off on Milly the penniless, unpedigreed Densher so that the way will be clear for Kate to marry Lord Mark. Kate decides not to expose the scheme—though she is tempted to do so—but instead, with Densher's help, to encourage it and so finally beat Mrs. Lowder at her own game. In brief, Kate's primary objective is not to deceive her friend Milly but to outwit her Aunt Maud.

Merton Densher carries out the design upon Milly's innocence, yet he is even less culpable than Kate Croy, his instigator. At first he stumbles unwittingly into her intrigue, believing that she wants him merely to make sure of a convenient meeting place for the two of them in Milly's rooms. At a later stage Kate argues that he should take the trouble to solace Milly because it is the least he can do for a girl who is probably very ill. Whatever Kate's scheme is, he feels that he must back her up in it, though he is puzzled to find that Mrs. Lowder and Mrs. Stringham encourage him in his attentions to Milly quite as much as Kate does. When he begins to understand the part he is expected to play, he discovers that without being exactly false he has nevertheless gone too far.[5] Before he fully realizes it, he has "turned his corner" and retreat seems impossible. Kate gives him a chance to escape but he swears blind obedience to her wishes. He will see the deception to the end: when Mrs. Lowder and Kate return to London, he will remain in Venice and will visit Milly every day. He will even marry her if she will have it so, but only if she takes the initiative.

However, if he is to endure this ordeal alone, Densher feels justified in demanding some proof of equality with Kate in love and

5. Densher never tells Milly a downright lie about his relationship with Kate. Kate herself may be less scrupulous; at least, Milly tells Lord Mark that Kate has sworn she is not engaged. Yet the reader is never allowed to catch Kate telling Milly an unambiguous falsehood. For the most part, Kate and Merton in misleading Milly depend upon the power of suggestion and the untruths provided by others, e.g., by Mrs. Lowder and Mrs. Condrip.

responsibility. He asks her to spend a night with him in his rooms and she complies. In essence what Merton is asking of Kate is whether she wants merely the money which she believes he can get out of Milly or whether she wants him *and* the money. In their final meeting, bringing the novel to a close, the alternatives which he offers are more grimly distinct. Merton will give Kate the fortune that Milly has left to him or he will marry her. He will not do both.

The real guilt of Densher and Kate Croy is not excused, condoned, or diminished, but their motives are made understandable and are shown to be not altogether evil. What is more, all of the other people, even the least selfish, are implicated in the attempt to delude the heroine. Milly herself is implicated in her delusion: she has the innocence of the dove but fails in the wisdom of the serpent. If the plan had succeeded, it seems probable, as all her deceivers hoped, that it would have worked for Milly's benefit. Even as it turned out, it may be true—though Kate who suggests the possibility is trying to rationalize her own position—that despite her cruel disillusionment Milly actually got from her relation with Densher what she so desperately wanted from life—"The peace of having loved. . . . Of having *been* loved. . . . Of having . . . realized her passion."

Lord Mark who exposes the plot and tells Milly the truth about Kate and Merton is far from being an idealist who cannot endure the thought of duplicity. In fact, of all the persons in the story he shows the least moral discrimination and principle. Indifferent to the effect of his revelation upon Milly, he speaks merely in order to be avenged on Densher who is the cause, he suspects, for his proposals to Kate and Milly being refused. It should be added that both of his proposals are dishonest and cynically materialistic in intention.

Such moral ambiguities and complexities reveal James's growing appreciation of the fine shadings in human motives and of the paradoxes and anomalies in human behavior. They do not mean, as has been asserted, that James was inclined in his later years to dissolve ethical values in purely aesthetic enthusiasms. At the same time, however, his greater sensitivity to moral distinctions is indicated by a refinement of his art. *Wings* is a more profound criticism of life than *Portrait* because in the later novel James shows greater artistry and detachment in developing the Minny Temple image. As has been shown, the presence of the character Ralph Touchett in *Portrait* suggests that in this story James was disposed to a romantic softness that blunted his tragic effects and came close to sentimentalizing the moral realities of Isabel Archer's world.

In *Wings* James's perception of the human scene is at once wider in scope and more accurate in detail. Without losing any of Isabel Archer's concreteness, Milly Theale loses much of Isabel's limited particularity. Even as a representative American figure, Milly rises to a higher level of significance than Isabel. Though she remains fragile and flower-like, Milly is consistently displayed as "the heiress of all the ages."

But the "international light" does not shine with great intensity in *Wings*. Milly Theale is much more important as a figure that dramatizes the whole human condition, the story of man's great powers for adventure and achievement enacted under the shadow of mortality. The broadly human implications of Milly's doom are poetically elaborated. When Milly went to the great physician, Sir Luke Strett, for a physical examination, she received what must surely be one of the most subtly expressed diagnoses on record. It was not, however, too subtle for Milly; she realized at once the great danger hovering over her. Emerging from the Doctor's office, she went for a long walk through the poorer sections of London. For this jaunt she wanted no close companion. "She literally felt, in this first flush, that her only company must be the human race at large, present all around her, but inspiringly impersonal, and that her only field must be, then and there, the grey immensity of London." She ended up in the Regent's Park,

> round which on two or three occasions with Kate Croy her public chariot had solemnly rolled. But she went into it further now; this was the real thing; the real thing was to be quite away from the pompous roads, well within the centre and on the stretches of shabby grass. Here were benches and smutty sheep; here were idle lads at games of ball . . . here were wanderers anxious and tired like herself; here doubtless were hundreds of others just in the same box. . . . All she thus shared with them made her wish to sit in their company; which she so far did that she looked for a bench that was empty, eschewing a still emptier chair that she saw hard by and for which she would have paid, with superiority, a fee.

Both *Portrait* and *Wings* exemplify that "idea of treachery, the 'Judas complex,'" which Graham Greene points to as James's "ruling passion"[6] and which was imbedded perhaps in his memory of Minny Temple. But in *Wings* the treason is more firmly rooted in the general fallibilities of human nature. As was noted before, Susan Stringham, the very picture of the faithful friend whose loyalty is fortified with all the rigor of the New England conscience, is at last as entangled in Milly's deception as Kate Croy, the type of the faithless friend. Merton Densher and Lord Mark are also brought together in the same community of human weakness,

6. *The Lost Childhood and Other Essays* (London, 1951), p. 44.

though the moral distance betwen them is scrupulously kept. When he learns that Lord Mark has callously disabused Milly of her illusion for the sake of personal revenge, Merton is outraged. He is filled with the indignation of a superior virtue and moral delicacy, yet in view of the part he has been playing, who is he to throw the first stone? Lord Mark has wished to marry Milly simply in order to inherit her money after her death, an event he believes is very near. Merton in deluding Milly has at least been acting out of a sincere love for Kate Croy, a woman he would marry in a minute whether she had money or not. Yet it is Merton Densher, after all, who deceives Milly and it is Lord Mark who tells her the truth.

The final effect of these ironies is to suggest a total human complicity in error and guilt. Both Isabel Archer and Milly Theale are cruelly deceived, but in Isabel's story there are clearly marked deceivers; in Milly's there is only deception. Isabel is betrayed by two morally specified human beings; Milly is betrayed by human nature.

II

Just as notable as the absence in *Wings* of a counterpart to Ralph Touchett is the absence in *Portrait* of any sustained metaphors of the kind that run through the later novel. Again, the difference is crucial, one that marks the greater depth and reach of Milly Theale's story. The two figures, "princess" and "dove," which are used to reveal the heroine and to emphasize the incongruity which is the essence of her tragedy, give to *Wings* a symbolic range which *Portrait* does not have. These pervasive images do not have the effect of reducing the story to abstract allegory but they do add to it certain common associations of thought and feeling which tend to universalize it. It is immediately apparent that the two figures are ordinary to the point of cliché. All who remember their childhood reading feel at once familiar with a heroine who is also a princess, and the dove is a commonly accepted symbol of innocence. James takes advantage of the wide currency which these simple figures have to ring his own changes upon them and to enrich them with his own ironic effects.

It is Susan Stringham who gives Milly the title of "Princess"; it names what Milly stands for in Susan's view—a gracious, charming embodiment of power. With her beauty, intelligence, youth and immense fortune Milly is about to realize her inheritance, which is nothing less than all the best of all the ages. But it turns out that Milly is a princess who loses everything—love, even at last the illusion of love, even life itself. Susan's title for Milly underscores the irony of Milly's tragedy. But the princess image has another, less austere association. Milly wields her scepter with an unconscious ease that suggests a wand and relates her to the heroines of fairy tales. In fact, Milly *is* a royal figure of fairyland who for a time is overwhelmed by those sinister principalities and powers which also exist in fairyland, as every child knows. At last, however, her influence can be felt in beautiful triumph over the forces that deceive and kill.[7]

The other image under which Milly Theale appears, that of a dove, refers to the opposite pole of the axis around which her tragedy revolves. The figure suggests her innocence, her weakness, her capacity to be beguiled. It is therefore appropriate that this analogy should come from the realistic imagination of Kate Croy. Susan may see Milly in the light of gentle, triumphant power; Kate sees her as a potential victim.

The first time Kate calls Milly a dove, she does so with dramatic suddenness, and yet the metaphor bursts out of the context of their conversation logically enough. After suggesting that her Aunt Maud has plans in mind for Milly as well as for herself, Kate issues an exasperated warning: "We're of no use to you—it's decent to tell you. You'd be of use to us, but that's a different matter. My honest advice to you would be . . . to drop us while you can." Milly does not gather the full import of what Kate has said but she is nevertheless frightened. The next morning it occurs to her "that she had felt herself alone with a creature who paced like a panther." When Kate observes, a moment later, "Oh you may very well loathe me yet!" Milly breaks down. "Why do you say such things to me?" she asks. The abrupt question has an immediate softening effect upon Kate and she replies, "Because you're a dove." And she kisses Milly, "not with familiarity or as a liberty taken, but almost ceremonially and in the manner of an *accolade*; partly as if, though a dove who could perch on a finger, one were also a princess with whom forms were to be observed." To a certain degree Milly was aware that the image was appropriate. It seemed to her "an inspiration. . . . revealed truth; it lighted up the strange dusk in which she lately had walked. *That* was what was the matter with her. She was a dove. Oh, *wasn't* she?" But Milly here is thinking only of Maud's attempt to use her to pry information out of Kate about Densher's whereabouts. She has not yet begun to penetrate the shadows of duplicity that surround her.

The next time Kate has occasion to return to the dove image she is with Densher and the two of them are watching Milly as she entertains her guests in her hired Venetian palace. Here Kate blends the figure of Milly's innocence with an emblem of Milly's power which is more substantial than Susan's transcendent one—a "long, priceless chain" of pearls which Milly is wearing, "wound

7. F. O. Matthiessen, *Henry James: The Major Phase* (New York, 1944), p. 59, says that in *Wings* James "is evoking essentially the mood of a fairy tale."

twice around the neck." "She's a dove," Kate observes, "and one somehow doesn't think of doves as bejewelled. Yet they suit her down to the ground." "Yes—down to the ground is the word," Merton replies and he begins to reflect upon Kate's metaphor.

> Milly was indeed a dove; this was the figure, though it most applied to her spirit. Yet he knew in a moment that Kate was just now . . . exceptionally under the impression of that element of wealth in her which was a power, which was a great power, and which was dove-like only so far as one remembered that doves have wings and wondrous flights, have them as well as tender tints and soft sounds. It even came to him dimly that such wings could in a given case—*had*, truly, in the case with which he was concerned—spread themselves for protection. Hadn't they, for that matter, lately taken an inordinate reach, and weren't Kate and Mrs. Lowder, weren't Susan Shepherd and he, wasn't *he* in particular, nestling under them to a great increase of immediate ease?

The title of the novel indicates that this shift in focus from the dove to the wings of the dove is an important one. The wings image, insofar as it implies "wondrous flights," signifies effortless superiority to earthly forces, and can readily be associated with the picture of a fairy princess. But another meaning is brought out when the dove is seen to spread her wings, not for flight, but for the protection of others. Of course, this new value also merges easily into the image of the storybook heroine.

All these possibilities of the figure are played upon and further extended near the end of the story when Mrs. Lowder refers to Milly's "wings" in a conversation with Densher. She is discussing the news of Milly's death, actually the first report of it he has had, although Mrs. Lowder believes that he has already been informed. It is therefore a solemn moment for Merton Densher.

> "Our dear dove then, as Kate calls her, has folded her wonderful wings."
>
> "Yes—folded them."
>
> . . . .
>
> "Unless it's more true," she . . . added, "that she has spread them the wider."
>
> He again but formally assented, though, strangely enough, the words fitted a figure deep in his own imagination. "Rather, yes—spread them the wider."
>
> "For a flight, I trust, to some happiness greater—!"
>
> "Exactly. Greater," Densher broke in.

Here the dominant idea, that of flight, is one which Densher previously introduced when musing upon Kate's use of the dove image. In Mrs. Lowder's picture of her folding her wonderful wings, Milly is seen coming to rest after her "wondrous flight," and the quickly reversed image which follows suggests a flight still more wondrous, one which blends into the conventional figure of the redeemed soul ascending to heaven or being borne to heaven on the wings of angels.

Mrs. Lowder's reference to Milly's flight contains an allusion which James probably intended her to be ignorant of, for if she knew of the allusion, she would not be likely to use the image at all. It cannot be assumed, however, that James was likewise unaware of it. He must have hoped that the reader would recognize the phrase which he made the title of his story and would be able to restore it to its context. Psalm 55 is typical in that the psalmist asks God to destroy the enemies that surround him. But the enemy in this Psalm is of a peculiarly treacherous kind.

> And I said, Oh that I had wings like a dove! for then would I fly away, and be at rest.
>
> Lo, then would I wander far off, and remain in the wilderness. . . . for I have seen violence and strife in the city. . . .
>
> Wickedness is in the midst thereof: deceit and guile depart not from her streets.
>
> For it was not an enemy that reproached me; then I could have borne it: neither was it he that hated me that did magnify himself against me; then I would have hid myself from him:
>
> But it was thou, a man mine equal, my guide, and mine acquaintance.
>
> We took sweet counsel together. . . .
>
> He hath put forth his hands against such as be at peace with him: he hath broken his covenant.
>
> The words of his mouth were smoother than butter, but war was in his heart: his words were softer than oil, yet were they drawn swords.

James has led Mrs. Lowder to utter what she does not know, and her portrayal of Milly's death as the flight of a dove to a place of greater happiness is therefore steeped in irony. Through the long latter part of the novel when she is suffering most, Milly Theale is never brought before the reader in person—an achievement in literary tact which James points to with some pride in his "Preface." But the Biblical allusion which Mrs. Lowder unknowingly introduces suggests how Milly during her last days might have seen herself in the figure of the soaring dove. After learning how she had been betrayed, after she had, in Susan's phrase, also Biblical, "turned her face to the wall," it is easy to imagine that she might have yearned for "wings like a dove" in order to escape from the city of deceit and guile and to fly from those who pretended to be her friends—Mrs. Lowder herself, Merton Densher and Kate Croy. She had taken "sweet counsel" with those who broke their covenant; their "words were softer than oil, yet were . . . drawn swords."

It is appropriate that Kate Croy who invented it should be the last to recall Milly Theale under the image of the dove. In the final "scene" in the novel as Kate and Merton assess the effect which Milly has had upon their relations to each other, Kate declares that Milly died for them so that they might understand her.

> "I used to call her, in my stupidity—for want of anything better —a dove. Well she stretched out her wings, and it was to *that* they reached. They cover us."
>
> "They cover us," Densher said.
>
> "That's what I give you," Kate gravely wound up. "That's what I've done for you."

Here Kate is revising her original concept of Milly as an innocent victim in favor of an image less condescending. In fact she has adopted the symbol of Milly's royal protective power which occurred to Densher when he first heard Kate describe Milly as a dove. What impresses Kate now is that although Milly discovered the deception practised upon her, she nevertheless willed most of her fortune to the man she knew would marry Kate Croy. This is what Kate means by saying that Milly's wings cover her and Densher. As far as results are concerned, the plot that failed has succeeded and Kate promptly takes credit for her management of the affair: "That's what I give you. . . . That's what I've done for you."

But Kate discovers a moment later that the happy consummation is not to be. Densher will not allow her to have both him and Milly's money. That is to say, in their relation to each other, Kate and Merton are as they were before Milly appeared, except that these two, as Kate lucidly observes, will never again be as they were. It is Milly who has made the profound difference. Returning good for evil she has proved her superiority but she has also had her revenge: without intending it she has heaped coals of fire upon the heads of those who tried to wrong her. It has turned out that Susan Stringham was right and Kate Croy was mistaken; Milly Theale was not a helpless dove but a princess magnificent in power.

CHRISTOF WEGELIN

The Lesson of Spiritual Beauty†

Thematically, *The Wings of the Dove* is a companion piece to *The Ambassadors*. In both novels the international contrast is an integral part of the theme of the lived life. Both show the exposure

† From Christof Wegelin, *The Image of Europe in Henry James* (Dallas: Southern Methodist University Press, 1958), pp. 106–109, 112–15, 117–21.

of American innocence to a knowing Europe, but with a different critical focus. While the Paris of the first represents the beautiful order which results from a continuity of social experience, the second is concerned with the corruption, the perversion of motives attendant upon the process of refinement when social organization becomes subservient to greed. In a sense, therefore, *The Wings of the Dove* is a return to an earlier contrast; yet in spite of certain similarities, it is thematically no mere new version of *The Portrait of a Lady*.

The most obvious difference from that earlier novel is that the expatriate snob has left the picture so that the conflict is now entirely between America and Europe proper. More important and at first sight more puzzling, James's sympathies here are much less clearly placed: at the same time that Milly Theale, the American heroine, is highly idealized, her European antagonists, though brutal in their greed, are not simply condemned. The reason is that while *The Portrait of a Lady* was written primarily from the point of view of Isabel, while it is almost purely a story of the American experience of "Europe," *The Wings of the Dove* is both that and, even more, the story of the European experience of America. It is written from, fundamentally, two points of view—Milly's and Merton Densher's, the Englishman's. Milly's, though, is supplemented by that of her American companion, Susan Stringham, whose function as a "choral" *ficelle* is to supply "an *animated* reflexion of Milly Theale's experience of English society,"[1] to give what Milly herself would give if she were less purely spirit incarnate. *The Wings of the Dove*, then, just as much as *The Ambassadors*, avoids the "platitude of statement" and instead gives two versions of the story which is its physical action.

This is why in spite of so shabbily sordid a plot it is so subtle a book. What matters is not the physical action but the gradual revelations which it brings to Milly and above all to Densher. Hence the stylistic peculiarities: the lyrical and reflective passages in which the physical action is veiled, the fact that there are memories of conversations almost more than actual conversations. Hence also the structural peculiarity which results in an ambiguity easily misunderstood: the fact that we never get inside Kate Croy, the third major character, who is almost totally responsible for the physical action. Kate is tremendously present as a force, a form, a beautiful apparition, "the handsome girl," as Milly keeps thinking of her—a symbol of the English society which is the subject of Milly's fascinated observation and from which Densher finally emancipates himself

1. Preface to the New York Edition; see *The Art of the Novel*, p. 299; James's italics. This chapter owes a large debt to R. P. Blackmur's discussion of *The Wings of the Dove* in an evening seminar which he conducted at Princeton in what must have been the winter of 1950–51. Needless to say, he is not responsible for any errors of mine.

thanks to the light which Milly has thrown on it for him. Kate in fact is all action, while Milly is spiritual sufferance and Densher physical response and finally intellectual rejection. Kate acts, Milly is, Densher judges. The relations between the three make up the substance of the story, and the peculiar "difficulty" of the book is that Kate, whose personal "story" the reader does not get except in so far as he gets it through the "fusion" of her consciousness with Densher's,[2] is the most vivid fact in the stories of the others and through them in the reader's mind.

Kate, then, is the one who creates the physical action. But the germinal idea, as the *Notebooks* show, was in the character and predicament of Milly—in the words of James's preface, "a young person conscious of a great capacity for life" but early stricken by a fatal disease and "passionately desiring" to achieve before her death, "however briefly and brokenly, the sense of having lived."[3] Milly's striking curiosity about London society, about people she does not know and has no specific motive for wishing to know, is a symbolic manifestation of her eagerness for experience, a desire which her involvement with Kate and Densher more than fulfils.

In his preliminary notes James envisaged that, moved by the pathos of her situation, Densher would devote himself to Milly for wholly charitable reasons, that with the sympathetic consent of his lover, Kate, he would "show her some delicacy of kindness," and that a dramatic complication would result from the tension between Kate's magnanimity and her awakening jealousy.[4] As he developed his "action," however, Densher's and Kate's motives changed, and in the final execution Densher is the pliable and for a long time blind instrument of a design of Kate's which is an ambiguous mixture of charity and greed. Since Milly is in love with Densher, thus Kate calculates, she will doubtless leave him her fortune and thus make possible his marriage to Kate, which "poverty" so far prevents. Their engagement, Kate's and Densher's, therefore is to be kept secret. On this plan they proceed with success until Lord Mark, a disappointed suitor for Kate's as well as Milly's favor, guesses their game and informs Milly. This is the essence of the experience which England supplies for Milly, and the shock of the discovered deception breaks her will to live—the will which alone has kept her from succumbing to her fatal illness.

It is, however, not the final consummation of her experience. In outlining his action, James briefly stumbled on the difficulty of imagining a conclusion that would not be "ugly and vulgar." But he saw the difficulty only to find immediately a way out: the saving turn was to make the happiness, the snatched experience Milly

2. Ibid.
3. Ibid., p. 288.
4. *Notebooks*, p. 170.

longs for *be* "some act of generosity, of passionate beneficence, of pure sacrifice, to the man she loves"—be, in fact, "something fine and strange."[5] Thus James planned it in *The Notebooks;* and in the finished novel, though from the moment she is aware of the betrayal Milly, as far as we are allowed to know, feels nothing but the deepest pain, pain at the loss of love and life together, yet the last note is that of her magnanimity, the virtue which shines most blindingly now that it knows of evil. She is indeed a transfiguration of the American girl. It is as if someone had said to James, "It is easy for these American girls to be so pure when they lack experience," and as if he had answered, "Ah, but see how far and straight they will go even when they know. Why, knowing the world will show up their moral beauty only the more splendidly!" As far as *The Wings of the Dove* is Milly's story it is a peculiarly American tragedy, the ravishment of innocence, of moral beauty, by a worldliness so knowing that it has forgotten the knowledge of innocence.

This is, however, less than half the story, for Milly's drama becomes the drama of Kate Croy and above all of Merton Densher too. As they use her for interests of their own, we see them, in the words of James's preface, "inheriting from their connexion with her strange difficulties and still stranger opportunities"; above all we see Densher "confronted with rare questions and called upon for new discriminations," as a result of which the "success" of their scheme is of no use to them;[6] for as Kate puts it at the last, they are not as they were before. Densher is possessed by his memory of Milly and therefore willing to marry Kate only on condition that they give up Milly's millions and only for the sake of his loyalty to Kate—bases, both, which Kate cannot accept, so that the end, in spite of the total success of their common enterprise, finds them ironically separated as nothing has been able to separate them before. In a word, Densher has been "bribed away" from the orbit of his previous life.[7]

* * *

* * * *The Wings of the Dove* is no allegory on a biblical subject. It is a drama not of unambiguous conflict between heaven and hell, but of the contrast between two kinds of human ethics. What the biblical overtones and symbols suggest is the extreme to which the contrast between Milly's unencumbered spirit and Kate's "talent for living" can be reduced philosophically—the contrast between the simplicity of American idealism and the complexity of English empiricism. Here, in contrast with *The Ambassadors,* James focuses on the purity of the first and the dubiety of the second; but it must

5. Ibid., pp. 171–72.
6. *Art of the Novel,* p. 291.
7. Ibid.

always be remembered that the drama, as in *The Ambassadors* almost wholly internal, is a drama of mutual initiation: Milly's into the ambiguous "quantities" of the "accumulated contents" of English social organization, and Densher's into the possibilities of a totally different mode of conduct. For the evaluation, mutual also, takes place entirely in the individual consciousness. In particular, the high idealization of Milly is in large part of Densher's doing, is part of his emotional response to the dramatic circumstances of his involvement in the conflict between the two civilizations.

Densher's story can be summarized as the story of his conversion from the worship of Kate to the worship of Milly, based on a process of gradually deepening vision which is the counterpart of Strether's. But the process is much less simple and clear than the terms to which it finally leads him. In the preface to *The Portrait of a Lady* James speaks of the "dependence of the 'moral' sense of a work of art on the amount of felt life concerned in producing it."[8] The felt life which projects James's moral sense in *The Wings of the Dove* is above all the felt ambiguity of the choices Densher is confronted with. Densher's crisis is the direct result of his involvement with Kate, but it arrives only when he has finally become aware of Kate's scheme—"Since she's to die I'm to marry her?" Densher has asked. "So that when her death has taken place I shall in the natural course have money?" "You'll in the natural course have money," Kate has answered. "We shall in the natural course be free" to marry. But the execution of the scheme is up to Densher alone; Kate refuses to go into the details of that: "from the moment you don't wash your hands of me," she tells him, "you must act as you like and as you can." With this, after Kate has sealed the bargain by spending a night with him, Densher is left alone with Milly in Venice and the book is from here on almost exclusively the story of the education of his conscience.

What he is faced with is not a simple moral choice between good and bad, but a dual dilemma. Loyalty to Kate, which by her surrender to him has become a moral obligation in addition to being an inclination, is in conflict with his sense of decency. Even more problematic, honesty toward Milly is in conflict with kindness toward her, since what has kept her alive has been the will to live for his love. So that for the sake of kindness to Milly as well as of loyalty to Kate, Densher feels himself forced to play the thoroughly equivocal game. Yet he squirms under his sense of the falseness of his relation to Milly. It drives him to strange moral accommodations. He perceives that if he can still feel that his relation to Milly is "innocent," it is Milly herself who has purged it. Something in her national character, "the great national, the great maidenly ease"

8. Ibid., p. 45.

of the American girl is a "boon inappreciable." Something incalculable in that, he feels, works for him and Kate, "something outside, beyond, above themselves, and doubtless ever so much better, than they"—to this he keeps coming back—makes for "daily decency."

Milly herself, "divine in her trust" or "inscrutable in her mercy," as she strikes Densher, is aware of this, though not of the pointed irony her comment has for Densher's ears when she says, "you like us to be as we are because it's a kind of facilitation to you that we don't quite measure: I think one would have to be English to measure it!" With this fragment of remembered conversation Densher remembers also that strangely enough Milly has said it "without prejudice to her good nature." Yet with all this, Densher can still feel that not to profit by Milly's good nature would be to go directly against it, and that "the spirit of generosity" which it engenders in him could feel "no greater pang than by his having to go directly against Milly." Thus he temporizes, and whatever doubts he may still have about the dishonesty of his procedure he muffles with the idea of "tact," the virtue of "the sensitive and the kind." He is not "inhuman," he assures himself, so long as "tact" will serve. And for three weeks he can feel that tact and the simple intention to be kind—with the help, to be sure, of the incalculably purifying air of Milly's disposition—are sufficient guides by which to steer his course.

How long they might have thus served neither Densher nor the reader knows. At the end of the period, at any rate, he finds that Milly will not receive him and his sense of smooth sailing immediately deserts him. Loyalty to Kate and kindness to Milly have indicated the same course, but since loyalty to Kate reminds him inevitably of the lie in his kindness to Milly, his *modus vivendi* has been to keep the two apart, to keep the sense of Kate shut away in his rooms, where the memories of her surrender and quittance linger "as an obsession importunate to all his senses." Now, with Milly withdrawn, Kate reasserts herself with the result of his seeing himself as Kate's agent, a view which makes him immediately sensitive to the light in which Milly's servants have been seeing him—as a simple fortune hunter. It is, Densher feels, a vulgar view because it is the view which "might have been taken of an inferior man." Still, he knows that "the particular attribution of motive" does him after all no wrong. This is the beginning of a series of moral perceptions which are to lead him finally to abandon Kate, but for the time being he still clings to his disbelief in his own wrong.

* * *

* * * It remains to show that Milly and Kate are representative of the civilizations which have formed them. Something of

Densher's and Milly's sense of the matter we have seen already, but there is more. In the preface, for instance, grouping Milly with the Daisy Millers, James explains that Milly's predicament provided a chance to confer upon the type of the American girl "a supremely touching value"[9]—which may serve as a summary of the gradual transformation of Densher's vision of Milly. At first, she is to him simply "little Miss Theale," the typical American girl, one of the "many little Miss Theales" he has seen in New York, one of "the irrepressible, the supereminent young persons" who strike the Englishman as a typical American phenomenon. At the end, she has become "supremely touching," has in Densher's vision indeed acquired what Howells once described as "the charming and honorable distinctions of American girlhood" which demonstrated for Europe "a civilization so spiritual that its innocent daughters could be not only without the knowledge but without the fear of evil."[1] James himself would doubtless have found this manner of putting it too naïve for unqualified assent. But it is not far from what Densher sees in Milly, and both the novel and the preface emphasize her national character.

If Milly is in a sense typical, so is Kate. Both personify the moral bases of their native civilizations. For Kate this means a world in which conduct is governed not by objective principle but by subjective interest. As she explains to Milly at one point, in England "every one who had anything to give—it was true they were the fewest—made the sharpest possible bargain for it, got at least its value in return"; and remembering the statement later, Milly finds it only the stranger that all this can amount to the "happy understanding" of a social system whose wheels are so "wonderfully oiled." Of this world all of Milly's new English friends are part, and each for private reasons of his own contributes to the conspiracy against her—which is the reason why Densher finally measures the odium of his weakness by the fact that he has pleased everybody. It is the reason also why he can make himself understood to Kate's wealthy aunt Maud no more than to Kate herself. Aunt Maud, he feels, responds to the tale of his revelation very much "as a stout citizen's wife" might respond to a tear-jerker, with "why in pity" should she not have lived, "with everything to fill her world? The mere *money* of her, the darling, if it isn't too disgusting at such a time to mention that—!" Across this gulf communication is impossible. For as Milly has put it, with nothing but "the finest outward resonance," these people are "familiar with everything, but con-

9. Ibid., p. 292.

1. "Mr. Henry James's Later Work," reprinted from the *North American Review* of January 1903, in *The Question of Henry James*, ed. F. .W Dupee (New York, 1945), p. 7.

scious, really of nothing"; they lack—and she has used James's own old term—"imagination."

The fundamental contrast between Milly and the England of her abysmal experience is elaborated in a multitude of ways, but dramatized most pointedly through Kate. Kate has representative value because, as James shows with meticulous care, her character and conduct are determined largely by the circumstances of her life—the monstrous caddishness of her flashy father, the sordid squalor of her sister, the vulgar opulence of her aunt Maud, who frees her from poverty only to enslave her by the strong appeal of "material things." The unmitigated materialism of her environment is the ultimate cause of her disfigurement, the reason why her great gift, her splendid "talent for life," turns into the simple "greatness of knowing" what she wants, and finally into something which can be called talent only with the bitterest of ironies or the most cold-blooded of cynicisms. Nothing makes the deep perversion of her sense of values more painfully clear than that she makes a virtue of subordinating her passion for Densher to her passion for wealth: she does not like his courting of Milly but, she tells him, "when you know me better you'll find out how much I can bear." The irony of it becomes clear to the reader only when he too knows her better. She can, indeed, bear too much; for the sake of the "great" future, she can do violence to the integrity of her own feelings. Her deep corruption lies in the *use* she makes of her own love and of her own great endowments, in her *abuse* of one sort of value for ends of quite another sort.

Yet, to the very end one is aware of James's sympathy for the dark brilliance of Kate's presence, a sympathy almost reminiscent of his feelings for some quite different children of his imagination—for Isabel Archer, for example, and *her* mistaken belief in the sufficiency of her own mind and will, or for Strether and his sense that life could not have been different for him. For Kate is not a free agent either. If her "talent" is all her own, she has not chosen the channels into which it has been forced. Even Milly raises the question of free will. One day, as she sits on one of the benches in Regent's Park, she sees herself "in the same box" with the multitudes around her, the box of the "great common anxiety," of "the practical question of life." Like herself, those "hundreds of others" have doubtless been told that "they could live if they would," a piece of information, she comes to feel, which strangely merges into "the blessed old truth that they would live if they could." Finally she feels that there is little to choose between the two faces of the question: it is "perhaps superficially more striking that one could live if one would," but it is "more appealing, insinuating, irresistible, in short, that one would live if one could." Highly unusual, this near-identification of two views of life usually thought of as irreconcilably opposed to one another. And one wonders whether Milly's final magnanimity is perhaps in part a recognition of the fact that Kate and Densher, too, live not to much as they will but —in Strether's phrase—as they can,[2] as England has taught them.

That James lets even Milly thus meditate, that he lets her see her "ultimate state" as that of "a poor girl—with her rent to pay," explains perhaps—as Strether's vision of Marie de Vionnet's abasement does in *The Ambassadors*—the coexistence of judgments grown from the belief in the sovereign power of the spirit and judgments grown from the sense of a necessity in human affairs. But though necessity makes Kate and Milly sisters in suffering, it does not void moral judgment here any more than it does in *The Ambassadors*, and this fact puts a final emphasis on their significance as national symbols. The difference between Kate and Milly is the difference between the civilizations which have molded them. Nothing, finally, strikes Densher more than the moral inadequacy of the civilization which has led him and Kate into the "dreadful game" they have played for Milly's money with Milly's life. He has, James tell us, a "vivid mental image" for this difference: the more he realizes their common abjection, the more urgent is his need of being at least absolutely "straight" with Kate. But "straightness" is the honesty of thieves, the virtue of an order in which no one does anything for nothing, and it turns morally stale on his hands. His one act of disloyalty to Kate, a secret exchange of letters with Susan Stringham about Milly's memory, therefore comes to appear to him "as a small emergent rock in the waste of waters, the bottomless grey expanse of straightness." And the lesson he finally draws is that for "daily decency" the well-oiled social mechanism of which they have been part needs something "beyond and above" itself. Even at best, it is a mere gray watery waste, in which the emergent rock of the spirit alone can give a sense of moral security. With this final image Densher's conversion from the cunning of the serpent to the wisdom of the dove is defined.

Like *The Ambassadors*, then, *The Wings of the Dove* is a story of conversion. But the direction is reversed. Whereas the first dramatizes the values of empirically derived forms of conduct by contrast with the pitfalls of moral absolutism, the second dramatizes the

2. Strether's phrase is the phrase he uses in his speech in Gloriani's garden. But there are other such parallels between the two novels. Milly s sense of communion with the little people in the Regent's Park of London and Strether's in the *Postes et Télégraphes* of Paris both are focal points for important moral statements. And Milly's vision of her "ultimate state" as that of any "poor girl—with her rent to pay" is strikingly close to Strether's view of Marie de Vionnet as "a maidservant crying for her young man."

insufficiency of any moral knowledge purely empirical, *its* liability to corruption, by contrast with an image of supreme spiritual beauty. * * *

J. A. WARD

Social Disintegration in *The Wings of the Dove*†

In his half-century as observer and historian of the western world, Henry James developed from a chronicler of national differences to a prophet of a social disintegration international in scope.[1] James's late novels reflect what his notebooks and letters often state—his vision of the impending collapse of western civilization, of "this overwhelming, self-defeating chaos or cataclysm toward which the whole thing is drifting."[2] That James was unable to continue work on *The Ivory Tower* after the outbreak of World War I testifies not only to the dependence of his fiction on his day-to-day response to history, but also to his apprehension of what was actually taking place—the visible destruction of all that had meaning to the civilized consciousness.

James always remained faithful to the Balzacian concept of the novelist as cultural historian, but his method was increasingly to be through intensity rather than through expansiveness. Jamesian intensity involves metaphor, symbolism, and ambiguity, all realized through the scenic and pictorial methods. Through intensity, James, always the historian of fine consciences, became more and more acute in relating the individual intelligence to its historical context.

One way of defining James's ideal of civilization is to say that not only should society offer the individual a contact with the aesthetic and social values of history—art and manners—but also that these values must be consistent with actual human behavior. In James's works there are four major deviations from this ideal: in America there is no past, and thus none of its values informs the present; in the Europe of *The American, The Portrait of a Lady*, and the other international stories of the seventies and eighties, past and present are inseparable, but inherent in the beauty of age is the evil of age; London, the scene of James's "middle period" fiction, has renounced the past for the glaring vulgarities and immoralities of the

† From *Criticism* 2 (Spring 1960), 190–95, 198–99, 200–201, 202–3.

1. I am indebted here, and elsewhere in this essay, to R. P. Blackmur, "The Loose and Baggy Monsters of Henry James," *The Lion and the Honeycomb* (New York, 1955), 268–288; and R. W. B. Lewis, "The Vision of Grace: James's 'The Wings of the Dove,'" *MFS*, III (Spring, 1957), 33–40.

2. *The Notebooks of Henry James*, ed. F. O. Matthiessen and Kenneth B. Murdock (New York, 1947), p. 207. See also p. 196.

present; finally, in the works of James's "major phase," Americans and Europeans alike undermine and at the same time struggle to maintain the values of the past. In this last stage, forms, surfaces, and manners have become all but incompatible with the human standards they should ideally reflect.

In *The Ambassadors, The Wings of the Dove,* and *The Golden Bowl,* James varies slightly his dominant theme of appearance and reality to dramatize his vision of the American-European world straining to preserve itself from internal destruction. Appearance, the historical heritage of art and manners, is no longer reality: at best it is a thin disguise lending meretricious splendor to a behavior alien to it; at worst it is a thing to be kept in museums, a refuge from reality. The reality of greed, with its mechanics of intrigue and duplicity, seeks the appearance of art and manners. There is a consistent dichotomy between the form and the content of civilization, between past and present, between society and individual. When the form collapses, society becomes anarchy and merely the sum-total of individual grasping egos. The value of the form is ambiguous, for it adds the horror of deceit to the evil of economic and human plunder; but also it is a restraint: it provides a uniformity of standards and a social cohesiveness without which there would be no community at all. Society and civilization collapse together when Strether sees the duplicity of Mme. de Vionnet and Chad, and when Lord Mark reveals Densher's plot to Milly. * * *

* * *

The Wings of the Dove treats a later stage in the collapse of western civilization than *The Ambassadors. The Ambassadors* deals with the last gasping breath of the old order; by the time of *The Wings* the old order is dead, visible only in its decay. Strether is the last Jamesian pilgrim to gain a relationship with what James has termed the "*visitable* past,"[3] as Mme. de Vionnet is the last European whose beauty is not solely a pretense, a false allure.

The scene of *The Wings of the Dove* is the western world: the New York home of Milly Theale[4] and the London and Venice set-

3. *The Art of the Novel: Critical Prefaces by Henry James,* introduction by R. P. Blackmur (New York, 1934), p. 164.

4. America is less an operative force in *The Wings* than in *The Ambassadors* and *The Golden Bowl.* However, what James says in his preface about Milly's nationality deserves comment: he speaks of there being "fifty reasons for her national and social status. She should be the last fine flower . . . of an 'old' New York stem . . ." (*The Art of the Novel,* p. 292). In Milly James is invoking the memory not only of Minny Temple, but also of the New York of his youth, which, as his late fiction (especially "A Round of Visits" and "Crapy Cornelia") makes abundantly clear, has lost its charm and innocence. To James's mind materialism and vulgarity have corrupted America as well as England, so that in the world of *The Wings of the Dove* only an anachronism will serve James as a suitable tragic victim, for the moral attributes which James required of his heroine he could no longer detect in Anglo-American culture.

tings embrace the moral as well as the geographical limits of western culture. The England which has its center in Lancaster Gate (ironically the entrance to the English past leads but to hideous modernity) is given over completely to materialism. Its art has degenerated to the colossal vulgarity of Maud Lowder, the "Britannia of the Market Place," in whom "There was a whole side of Britannia, the side of her florid philistinism, her plumes and her trains, her fantastic furniture and heaving bosom, the false gods of her taste and false notes of her talk. . . ." The England of Maud Lowder has found the aristocratic legacy of manners at odds with the material drive, and has thus drained it of content. Force it finds more effective. Imperial and gross, Maud is a lioness; she is imagined as outfitted with "a helmet, a shield, a trident and a ledger." The emblematic Maud is blind to all but mass and quantity. Like her predecessor Mona Brigstock of *The Spoils of Poynton*, she "is *all* will, without the smallest leak of force into taste or vision, into any sense of shades or relations or proportions."[5] Maud is "the most remarkable woman in England" because she sets the tone for an empire, because she is "unscrupulous and immoral" in an absolute way. The lesser figures about her, Lord Mark and Lionel Croy, are less typical only in that they are less effective. Maud Lowder's London is essentially the London of *What Maisie Knew* and *The Awkward Age*, with the major difference that in *The Wings* James has made it unmistakably clear that the part stands for the whole.

Money is the controlling force in *The Wings of the Dove*; in the London world the economic drive is the normal motivation. Milly recognizes early that her English friends "appeared all . . . to think tremendously of money." Economic values subvert human values throughout, not just in Kate's identification of Milly with her wealth, the easy assumption that leads to the central action of the novel, but in the systematic reduction of all quality to quantity. For example, Kate's father and sister reject Kate's offer of family loyalty in favor of her potential cash value as Aunt Maud's ward. Aunt Maud visualizes Kate as a financial hold: " . . . I've been keeping [Kate's presence] for the comfort of my declining years. I've watched it long; I've been saving it up and letting it, as you say of investments, appreciate, and you may judge whether, now it has begun to pay so, I'm likely to consent to treat for it with any but a high bidder." Milly to Maud also has negotiable value, as a bribe to Densher: "The pieces fell together for him as he felt her thus buying him off, and buying him . . . with Miss Theale's money." The relationship between Kate and Densher gradually becomes corrupted through association with the acquisitive drive; the natural has been made unnatural, so much so that Kate's visit to Densher's

5. *The Art of the Novel*, p. 131.

rooms is thought of by both as a payment for services rendered. Densher fondly thinks of "The force of the engagement, the quantity of the article to be supplied, the special solidity of the compact, the way above all, as a service for which the price named by him had been magnificently paid. . . ." Kate, before she formulates her plan, predicts that "Milly would pay a hundred per cent.—and even to the end, doubtless, through the nose. . . . " Milly, though she is morally detached from her wealth and innocent in spite of her millions, dies a victim of economic competition.

It is particularly significant that Milly's great deed consists of a bestowal of her money. It is an act of love, an expression of forgiveness, and a transcendence of self. Nevertheless, since money is the destructive force in the novel, the nature of the act is tainted although its motive is not. Milly's benevolence cannot purify her money. It is appropriate that the practical result of her gift is to sever Kate and Densher, for it was a want of money that kept them from marrying in the beginning. Milly is not corrupted by her money; yet the possession of it causes her destruction. Money destroys those who are associated with it—those who have it, those who desire it, those who contend for it.

Thus one's moral stature is determined by the degree to which he is free from money. Maud Lowder is surely damned from the beginning; and Kate demonstrates her own damnation at the end, when she rejects spirit for matter, when she burns the unread letter of grace but rips open the envelope containing the check. In giving her the money, Densher gives "poor Kate her freedom": the ambiguity of her being poor spiritually when rich materially and enslaved morally when free economically points the hard lesson of James's novel. Milly grows dependent on money only when social pressures compel her to buy the sanctuary of Palazzo Leporelli and the protection of Eugenio. She uses her wealth as "a counter-move to fate." Yet she gains her lasting salvation only when she renounces money utterly.

* * *

Beginning with Book Sixth the strain of appearances drives Milly to art—to her rented Venetian palace, which is inadequate because its beauty, its inherent traditional values, its silent profundity reflect nothing of the Europe of the early twentieth century. James dramatizes throughout the second volume the meaning of Venice in the modern world: it, like London, has made the sacrifice of art to matter (James invokes the commercial as well as the aesthetic past of the Italian city), so that Palazzo Leporelli has the same relation to the controlling ethos of Venice as does Matcham to that of London. "Palazzo Leporelli held its history still in its great lap, even like a painted idol, a solemn puppet hung about with decorations." The imagery suggests artificiality and sterility, for the essential Venice is better represented by the shady commercialism of Eugenio and Pasquale. Although granted a luster by Susan Stringham's journalistic imagination and by Milly's presence, the old palace along the grand canal is but a relic of a decayed past.

The Venetian past is purposely present not in its beauty, but in its evil—the two components of Europe that formed an inseparable unity to the earlier James. Densher, the man of intellect, sees the Venetians of the present as "members of a race in whom vacancy was but a nest of darkness—not a vain surface, but a place of withdrawal in which something obscure, something always ominous, indistinguishably lived."[6] When Lord Mark awakens Milly to the monstrous plot against her, the Venetian scene reflects the personal catastrophe and gives it extensive dimensions. The great black storm means tumult and cataclysm. "It was a Venice all of evil that had broken out . . . a Venice of cold lashing rain from a low black sky, of wicked wind raging through narrow passes, of general arrest and interruption. . . ." The Piazza San Marco, symbolic of European civilization as a whole, is darkened to blackness and overwhelmed by violence: "the whole place, in its huge elegance, the grace of its conception and the beauty of its detail, was more than ever like a great drawing-room, the drawing-room of Europe, profaned and bewildered by some reverse of fortune." The effort of all to contain evil by appearances fails. Milly Theale's death is the death of a civilization: the gray of a London dominated by materialism and the black of a Venice traditionally malign combine to kill her.

* * *

Through Milly's developing awareness of the irrelevance of the art of the past to modern life, James dramatizes the disintegration of civilization. Throughout the novel he reveals the ever widening breach between individual needs and the social framework. One inevitably finds himself in a position where he must define himself through either his social position or his isolated self. Deprived of access to meaning through art or manners, Maud Lowder derives her motivations and morality from British culture in general. We find her in the beginning as we find her in the end—a loyal apostle to money. But Kate, Densher, and Milly are, in the beginning, un-

6. Seventeen years before *The Wings of the Dove*, James wrote of Venice as having a tradition of immorality, especially in commercial matters, though the jocular tone of the early comments conveys nothing of the atmosphere of evil which pervades Venice in *The Wings*: "[The Venetian race] has not a genius for morality, and indeed makes few pretensions in that direction. It scruples not to represent the false as true, and is liable to confusion in the attribution of property" (*Portraits of Places* [Boston, 1885], p. 21).

defined by status or creed. The novel records their efforts and decisions toward achieving identity. For each the existing situation is inadequate.

Kate's personal qualities are great: she esteems family loyalty over private gain, the need for love over the need for profit, and moral freedom over moral commitment. But her father, her sister, and her aunt comprise for her a world in which selfhood and vulgarity set the tone, in which the material urge is unrefined by sentiment or sensibility. Thus, in her visit to her father's squalid rooms, we find Kate for the most part glancing into the mirror, holding fast to that which is herself.

In Kate's case the standard Jamesian ambiguity towards money has an added twist. The ordinary dilemma is there: to acquire money is ugly, but the possession of it is the *sine qua non* for the good life. In most of James's novels, however, the social scene itself remains aloof from the economic process: fortune hunter and business man alike are anomalies, inconsistent with the placid solemnity of age and beauty. But the London world can be understood only in terms of money. To pursue magnificence Kate has no choice but to accept the code of Aunt Maud. Her effort to reconcile the human value of love and the barbaric value of money must fail. Therefore, when she seeks her own image in Densher's mirror in the novel's final scene, she signalizes her separation from her lover, whose own renunciation of money forces Kate to retreat to the damning security of wealth.

Kate's initial conflict is between acceptance of family poverty for the sake of loyalty and acceptance of Aunt Maud's wealth for the sake of magnificence. When Kate, rebuffed by her father and sister, moves to Lancaster Gate, she hesitates to surrender her will to Maud. In "her actual high retreat" above Maud's "countinghouse," she is precariously detached and uncommitted. The parallel to Milly in her tower is clear enough. Here Kate's relation to Maud forecasts Milly's eventual relation to Kate. But when Kate descends she reconciles the standards of Maud with her love for Densher, and thus becomes converted to society; whereas Milly holds firm to her personal values, her moral integrity.

What we find in Kate is a great will who accepts and then uses society on its own terms. Her object is money and her method is manners. Once she initiates her plot, from the moment she decides not to tell Milly about her engagement to Densher, she remains inflexible. To Densher, Kate is "deep," "a whole library of the unknown, the uncut," but ironically there is nothing beneath the surface but the will: the moral intelligence has surrendered itself to money.

* * *

Densher is a forerunner of a dominant character type of modern literature: he leads to Eliot's Prufrock, Conrad's Heyst, and Greene's Scobie. He is the non-heroic yet perceptive man, driven to self-understanding by his weakness of will and horror of ugliness. Like Kate and Milly, Densher plunges into the abyss, which for him as for the others is both internal and external—the private depths and the social depths. If Milly's descent to the abyss reveals spiritual love and Kate's reveals only will, Densher's reveals, not the will he had sought to find, but a capacity for sanctifying grace. For he remains weak always. His suffering is most acute when he is isolated—after his moral rejection of Kate, but before his acceptance of Milly's love. When Sir Luke leaves the dying Milly to Densher alone, the physician's unspoken plea that he love Milly leads Densher to ask himself "into what abyss it had pushed him. . . ." Densher soars from the abyss, too late to save Milly, but not too late to be saved by her; he embraces spirit over flesh.

In a world whose institutional and aesthetic heritage has been drained of moral meaning, there can be no ultimately valid achievement for the James character without (in M. D. Zabel's phrase) "the final authority of selfhood."[7] Thus the romantic epithets that Susan Stringham applies to Milly Theale lack real significance: the heiress of all the ages has an inheritance of corruption only; the princess reigns in a morally bankrupt empire. But Kate and, for the most part, Densher also miss the point by being too prosaic about Milly. To Kate, Milly is identified primarily with her fortune; to Densher she is the "little American girl." Milly's descent to the abyss precedes the apotheosis of the dove—her transfigured self. Milly can acquire identity only by assaulting life, by risking everything. And not until her great and lonely moral achievement does Milly assume an identity independent of the social, economic, and aesthetic structures which had previously established, for others and for herself, her reality and her being.

DOROTHEA KROOK

[Milly's and Densher's Ordeal of Consciousness]†

* * *

What we perceive at once and with the least difficulty is that it is her American 'innocence' which in the first place lays Milly open to the rapacity and ruthlessness of her English friends. As in her pred-

7. *Craft and Character in Modern Fiction* (New York, 1957), pp. 280–281.

† From Dorothea Krook, *The Ordeal of Consciousness in Henry James* (Cambridge: Cambridge University Press, 1962), pp. 203–15, 221–29. Notes referring to the novel (edited) cite volume, book, and chapter.

ecessors among James's American Girls, this innocence in her springs from a fatal ignorance of the complex pressures operative in the complex world of Lancaster Gate—an ignorance due in the first instance, of course, to her American background. James speaks here of 'the immense profusion, but the few varieties and thin development' of the America of Milly Theale's day, and does not fail to draw again the familiar moral of the international theme, namely, the disabling effects upon the American mind of the simplicities and freedoms of American life, and their effect in particular of placing Americans at a severe disadvantage in their intercourse with the English and the Europeans.

This precisely is what happens to Milly Theale when she is thrown among the English. Her disability is plainly that she has no experience of the pressures, in particular the economic, to which the individual in such a society is perpetually exposed. As in *The Awkward Age,* these economic pressures never show on the surface of the gracious living in the big house at Lancaster Gate; but they are the most powerful subterranean force in the life of a society struggling to maintain a traditionally high standard of life on perpetually dwindling resources. The uneasy relation between an America growing steadily richer and a Britain growing steadily poorer which has become one of the commonplaces of Anglo-American relations since James's day was, it seems, already sufficiently apparent then, at any rate to his discerning eye; and it is this economic fact (with all its moral implications) that lies behind the long sigh of ecstasy and envy that is to be heard in Lancaster Gate every time Milly Theale's English friends touch upon the subject of what they call her good luck. Her 'good luck' is, simply, her money: which they desire, of course, not for its own vulgar sake but for its precious power to secure the freedom they long for—the freedom to enjoy without impediment all that Lancaster Gate would so much like to enjoy, and would know so well how to enjoy.

But Milly knows nothing of these material pressures that lie beneath the gracious surface, and therefore knows nothing of their demoralising effects upon the human spirit, even the most intelligent, most cultivated, most imaginative of human spirits. Indeed particularly (this is James's grand point) upon the intelligent and imaginative—like Milly's dear friend Kate Croy, whose range of enjoyments so greatly exceeds that of the less intelligent and less imaginative, and whose appetite therefore for the power to procure these enjoyments exceeds correspondingly. Lacking such knowledge, Milly Theale is accordingly very slow to see herself, the fabulously rich American, as a proper object of exploitation.

Besides this, however, what makes it so difficult for her to see herself as Lancaster Gate sees her is that the exploitation is not in the least vulgar; nor is it purely mercenary. What is so difficult and puzzling (and profoundly deceptive) is that the exploitation is perfectly compatible, it seems, with the most genuine devotion to Milly herself. Aunt Maud worships the very air she breathes, and is genuinely stricken when she hears of the death of the poor 'moneyed darling'. Kate Croy is genuinely enchanted with Milly: when she says that Milly is as charming as she is queer and as queer as she is charming,[1] she speaks with complete sincerity; and she enjoys their friendship with the most genuine ardour. And Merton Densher, whom Milly so much 'likes', treats her with the most tender deference; and Lord Mark, who makes a point of showing her the Bronzino that everyone says she resembles, intimates in his inexpressive English way that she really ought to 'let a fellow who isn't a fool take care of [her] a little';[2] and all the anonymous guests at the luncheon-parties and dinner-parties can't make enough fuss of her. Everybody in Lancaster Gate, in short, is as charming as possible to her; and here (James wishes us to understand) is another of the characteristic features of the English of that class, another aspect of 'the fathomless depths of English equivocation': that they can feel the most genuine, most sincere, most whole-hearted devotion for those who can serve their interests, and can as genuinely, as sincerely and whole-heartedly cast them off the moment they have ceased to serve their interests—or, alternatively, have begun to make demands that are inconvenient or irksome or just boring.

Of all this Milly Theale has no inkling when she first arrives at Lancaster Gate. She learns most of it, very painfully and slowly, as the story advances, and the most devastating thing of all only at the point of death. She acquires her knowledge in the most incidental, or seemingly incidental, flashes; James's dramatic genius ensures that they shall appear as incidental as in life itself. One of the early flashes occurs when she is talking to Lord Mark at her first dinner-party at Lancaster Gate, and presently discerns that, in spite of his deference and his seeming interest in her, he finds her only diverting, only 'funny'—'a mere little American, a cheap exotic, imported almost wholesale', who has no power to challenge his real interest, and certainly none to engage his stronger feelings.[3] Another, very important, flash occurs when she discovers that Kate Croy cannot endure her friend Susan Stringham. The reason (she discovers on analysis) is, astonishingly, that Kate has in her a streak of brutality —the kind of brutality which enables her to dismiss another human being with the easiest contempt when that human being happens merely to violate her standard of good breeding. Yet this brutality

1. *The Wings of the Dove*, I, iv, 2.
2. Ibid., I, v, 2.
3. Ibid., I, iv, 1.

(Milly also discovers) is characteristically English, in that it has nothing to do with primitive cruelty and everything to do with what in the modern jargon is called a 'defence-mechanism'. It is an instrument of self-preservation, Milly discerns; and pursues her analysis in a passage that is as good an instance as any of the sheer quantity of analytical insight, perfectly dramatised, that can be packed into a few characteristic sentences of James's late style:

> Mrs. Lowder didn't feel it, and Kate Croy felt it with ease; yet in the end . . . she grasped the reason, and the reason enriched her mind. Wasn't it sufficiently the reason that the handsome girl was, with twenty other splendid qualities, the least bit brutal too, and didn't she suggest, as no one yet had ever done to her new friend, that there might be a wild beauty in that, and even a strange grace? Kate wasn't brutally brutal—which Milly had hitherto benightedly supposed the only way; she wasn't even aggressively so, but rather indifferently, defensively and, as might be said, by the habit of anticipation. She simplified in advance, was beforehand with her doubts, and knew with singular quickness what she wasn't, as they said in New York, going to like. In that way at least people were clearly quicker in England than at home; and Milly could quite see, after a little, how such instincts might become usual in a world in which dangers abounded. There were clearly more dangers round about Lancaster Gate than one suspected in New York or could dream of in Boston. At all events, with more sense of them, there were more precautions, and it was a remarkable world altogether in which there could be precautions, on whatever ground, against Susie.[4]

This is the kind of insight into the complex world of Lancaster Gate that Milly is liable to receive from her most casual encounters with her English friends. Her mind, however, is to be still further enriched by her intimacy with Kate Croy. In a great scene at a critical point in the story, Kate 'lets herself go' (as Milly puts it to herself) 'in irony, in confidence, in extravagance' on those qualities of the American Mind, as represented in her friend Milly Theale, that she has come to find peculiarly exasperating—chiefly, its crude naive empiricism, its seemingly inexhaustible capacity for 'exaggerated ecstasy' and 'disproportionate shock', and its consequent propensity to produce upon more developed minds the effects of boredom and irritation. It is an exposure as brilliant as it is bold; and Milly 'follows' it, participates in it, with an intelligence, an appreciation of all Kate's finest shades of veracity, and an irony to match Kate's own, which sets her apart from all her predecessors in the line of James's American Girls and gives her a unique place in the ranks of the late-Jamesian vessels of consciousness:

4. Ibid., I, iv, 2.

> The beauty and the marvel of it was that she [Kate] had never been so frank: being a person of such a calibre, as Milly would have said, that, even while 'dealing' with you and thereby, as it were, picking her steps, she could let herself go, could, in irony, in confidence, in extravagance, tell you things she had never told before. That was the impression—that she was telling things, and quite conceivably for her own relief as well; almost as if the errors of vision, the mistakes of proportion, the residuary innocence of spirit still to be remedied on the part of her auditor had their moments of proving too much for her nerves. She went at them just now, these sources of irritation, with an amused energy that it would have been open to Milly to regard as cynical and that was nevertheless called for—as to this the other was distinct—by the way that in certain connexions the American mind broke down. It seemed at least—the American mind as sitting there thrilled and dazzled in Milly—not to understand English society without a separate confrontation with *all* the cases. It couldn't proceed by—there was some technical term she lacked until Milly suggested both analogy and induction, and then, differently, instinct, none of which were right: it had to be led up to and introduced to each aspect of the monster, enabled to walk all round it, whether for the consequent exaggerated ecstasy or for the still more (as appeared to this critic) disproportionate shock. It might, the monster, Kate conceded, loom large for those born amid forms less developed and therefore no doubt less amusing; it might on some sides be a strange and dreadful monster, calculated to devour the unwary, to abase the proud, to scandalise the good; but if one had to live with it one must, not to be for ever sitting up, learn how: which was virtually in short to-night what the handsome girl showed herself as teaching.[5]

This is Kate Croy's anatomy of the famous American innocence and ignorance; and as such it is uniquely instructive to Milly. But it is intended also to illuminate the complexities of Kate's own nature, in particular her boldness, her audacity, her strange, 'perverse' courage. For Kate by this time is already in the process of conceiving her diabolical design against Milly, and the rest of her 'speech', from the most interesting mixture of motives, is intended also as a warning to Milly—to get out of Lancaster Gate before she is destroyed.[6] Milly, of course, misses the warning, and is consequently doomed; and this submerged tragic irony does much to intensify the powerful dramatic impact of the whole scene.

So Kate Croy, at any rate, is in no doubt that it is Milly Theale's American ignorance and innocence that in the first instance expose her to the destructive power of Lancaster Gate. There are, however, other more subtle reasons that contribute to this condition of exposure. The ignorance and innocence indeed might by themselves

5. Ibid., I, v, 6.

6. Ibid., I, v, 6.

have proved a kind of protection, at any rate against the *conscious* knowledge of her final deception and betrayal. But their potential power to protect is perpetually cancelled out by her very powers of appreciation: by her intelligence, her sensibility, her imagination; and above everything by her passion for 'knowledge'—her fatal curiosity. These together make Lancaster Gate irresistibly fascinating and delightful to her; and by the same token weaken her resistance to its destructive power.

What chiefly weakens her resistance in fact is her supreme Jamesian quality, her self-consciousness. For Milly Theale's passion for knowledge is principally a passion for self-knowledge; and it is for this, more than anything, that she is prepared to suffer pain, confusion and humiliation, and finally total deprivation and loss. That is why (for instance) she participates, in the way we saw, in Kate's analysis of the American mind, entering into Kate's view of herself with an avidity of interest that would be almost masochistic if it were not what it in fact is—the disinterested passion for self-knowledge, characteristic of all the great Jamesian heroes and heroines. The same is true also of her deeply intelligent understanding of the English point of view in other connexions: of the reasons for Kate Croy's streak of brutality; and for Lord Mark's indifference to her; and, most painfully (before she is made to believe he is in love with her), for Merton Densher's indifference. Having received from Kate Croy an unforgettable light on her disabilities as an American Girl, and presently also on her still graver disability, that of being a Dove ('*That* was what was the matter with her. She was a dove'), she has already by the time Densher returns from America begun to see herself through the eyes of Lancaster Gate; and in the quarter of an hour's talk she has with him alone after their first meeting in the National Gallery, she recognises simultaneously both how much she 'likes' him and how much therefore she regrets that he should share 'the view' of her:

> She could have dreamed of his not having *the view*, of his having something or other, if need be quite viewless, of his own. The defect of it [the 'view'] in general—if she might so ungraciously criticise—was that, by its sweet universality, it made relations rather prosaically a matter of course. It anticipated and superseded the—likewise sweet—operation of real affinities. It was this that was doubtless marked in her power to keep him now—this and her glassy lustre of attention to his pleasantness about the scenery in the Rockies.[7]

Again and again in *The Wings of the Dove* we receive such testi-

7. Ibid., I, v, 7.

monies to the range and depth of Milly Theale's self-knowledge.[8] Its tragic implications, however, are not fully disclosed until she has learnt from the great doctor that she is very sick and, on seeking to communicate her secret to Kate Croy, meets with a rebuff that is the more desolating for being so bright and brisk. Then Milly also becomes fully conscious of her own ultimate solitude amidst the buzz of admiration and adulation of the Lancaster Gate circle; and it is this knowledge that adds the last intolerable weight to the burden of her self-consciousness. Her self-consciousness is her glory (James wishes us to understand): Milly is not merely the American Girl 'acting out' her nature unconsciously, like Daisy Miller and the other American girls in James's earlier stories. She is the American Girl grown conscious of herself as acting out the character of the American Girl; and it is this capacity at once for 'being' and 'seeing', for at once suffering intensely and being intensely conscious of the suffering, that defines the kind and quality of her tragedy.

Milly's desperate isolation is created in the first instance, of course, by the combination of her 'good luck', as the English call it, with her 'queerness'—that she should be so rich and yet such a saint, a dove, an exquisite thing. More plainly, what Lancaster Gate finds astonishing beyond comprehension is that Milly Theale should be so little the 'great personage' she ought by virtue of her fabulous good luck to be: that she should, besides being munificently generous, be so mild, so humble, so eager, so 'funny'—in fact, so *good*—when she could so easily afford not to be. They cannot stop marvelling at this; and they do in fact treat her as a great personage, thus consigning her to the lonely eminence symbolised in an early scene in the Swiss Alps.[9] To this even her dear devoted Susan Stringham contributes:

> The girl was conscious of how she [Susan] dropped at times into inscrutable impenetrable deferences—attitudes that, though without at all intending it, made a difference for familiarity, for the ease of intimacy. It was as if she recalled herself to manners, to the law of court-etiquette.[1]

In this aspect, Milly's story may be seen as James's rehandling of another grand melodramatic theme, that of the Poor Little Rich Girl.[2] She is 'rich' in virtue of her money, her exalted position, and

8. In view of the displayed intelligence of Milly Theale, it is astonishing indeed to learn that such a critic as Marius Bewley finds her 'stupid', and another, F. R. Leavis, both stupid and 'embarrassingly sentimental'. One can only guess at the kind of reading of *The Wings of the Dove* that could issue in such judgements; but surely it must have been literal-minded to a degree no serious reading of the later James can afford to be.

9. *The Wings of the Dove*, I, iii, 1.

1. Ibid., I, v, 4.

2. The phrase is virtually used at one point in Milly's meditation in Regent's Park after her second visit to the doctor (I, v, 4).

the expectations of bliss that these spread all around her. She is poor and deprived because through this thick cloud of expectations, this mass of blinding preconceptions about her 'happiness', no human love can penetrate.

What, however, intensifies her solitude to the tragic pitch is her mysterious mortal disease. It is this that finally isolates her from the world she so passionately desires to know and to enjoy. When Lord Mark takes her up to the Bronzino she is supposed to resemble she looks at it with tears in her eyes ('the lady in question . . . was a very great personage—only unaccompanied by a joy. And she was dead, dead, dead'); and Lord Mark, 'though he didn't understand her was as nice as if he had'.[3] Presently in the same scene Kate comes up, and Milly asks her to accompany her on her first visit to Sir Luke Strett, the doctor:

> Kate fixed her with deep eyes. 'What in the world is the matter with you?' It had inevitably a sound of impatience, as if it had been a challenge really to produce something; so that Milly felt her for the moment only as a much older person, standing above her a little, doubting the imagined ailments, suspecting the easy complaints, of ignorant youth. It somewhat checked her.[4]

She is to receive a further and final check after her second visit to the doctor, this time alone. She has spent an afternoon of anguish in Regent's Park pondering with 'her little lonely acuteness' the great man's advice, trying to make out how sick she really is, and deciding that she must, in view of all he had said, be very sick indeed. Back at her hotel Milly awaits Kate's visit. Kate arrives; and her first words of enquiry are, 'Well, what?'

> The inquiry bore of course . . . on the issue of the morning's scene, the great man's latest wisdom, and it doubtless affected Milly a little as the cheerful demand for news is apt to affect troubled spirits when news is not, in one of the neater forms, prepared for delivery. She couldn't have said what it was exactly that, on the instant, determined her; the nearest description of it would perhaps have been as the more vivid impression of all her friend took for granted. The contrast between this free quantity and the maze of possibilities through which, for hours, she had been picking her way, put on, in short, for the moment, a grossness that even friendly forms scarce lightened: it helped forward in fact the revelation to herself that she absolutely had nothing to tell. . . . Almost before she knew it she was answering, and answering beautifully, with no consciousness of fraud, only as with a sudden flare of the famous 'will-power' she had heard about, read about, and which was what her medical adviser had mainly thrown her back on. 'Oh it's all right. He's lovely.'[5]

3. *The Wings of the Dove*, I, v, 2.
4. Ibid., I, v, 2.
5. Ibid., I, v, 4.

After this, there are no further direct references to Milly's sickness; but there is one final comment upon the inaccessibility to death of the living. 'I'm a brute about illness. I hate it', says Kate Croy to Densher, telling him about Milly's case; and adds, 'It's well for you, my dear, that you're as sound as a bell'.

'Thank you!' Densher laughed. 'It's rather good then for yourself too that you're as strong as the sea'.

> She looked at him now a moment as for the selfish gladness of their young immunities. It was all they had together, but they had it at least without a flaw—each had the beauty, the physical felicity, the personal virtue, love and desire of the other. Yet it was as if this very consciousness threw them back the next moment into pity for the poor girl who had everything else in the world, the great genial good they, alas, didn't have, but failed on the other hand of this. 'How we're talking about her!' Kate compunctiously sighed. But there were the facts. 'From illness I keep away.'[6]

This inaccessibility of the living to the experience of death and dying is the immediate cause of Milly's tragic deprivation.[7] The living of Lancaster Gate admire and adore Milly Theale; but they all withhold from her the one thing that would relieve the terrors of her state—their participation, at once intelligent and generous, in 'the ordeal of consciousness' from hour to hour of a young creature with a great capacity for life condemned to die while hating and fearing death. From this terror of Milly Theale's condition they all, like Kate Croy, withdraw. They are all prodigiously intelligent, but not intelligent enough to know what such a condition means; and they are all brave, but not so brave as to risk participation in the twilight life of a soul awaiting death. This, we are meant to see, is the last dreadful infirmity of the brave and beautiful souls that inhabit Lancaster Gate. A final incapacity for love is intimately linked with a final incapacity to confront the fact of death; and, conversely, the incapacity to confront death is the final measure of the coldness, ruthlessness and egotism of the worldly world figured here.

Milly Theale on her side responds to the indifference with her own last infirmity, which is the sin of pride. She refuses to speak of her illness; she is determined to die (as Kate puts it) 'without smelling of drugs or tasting of medicines'. It is of course a sublime virtue, this perfect exercise of fortitude in the face of death: but it is also the last temptation of the devil. For it isolates her more completely than ever from her fellow creatures, cutting her off from her

6. Ibid., II, vi, 4.

7. Readers of Mr. Lionel Trilling's novel *The Middle of the Journey* will remember that the immunity of the strong and healthy to the experience of death and dying is one of its principal themes, and is handled by Mr. Trilling with a penetration and a delicacy that one likes to think James would have admired.

last chance to draw some remnant of loving-kindness out of the cold heart of the world. If Milly Theale (like Maggie Verver in *The Golden Bowl*) had been humble enough, or fearless enough, to renounce her pride, a saving connexion might have been established between herself and the enemy—enough at any rate to render impossible the diabolical design that finally kills her. But she does not renounce it, and thus deprives herself of the last possibility of being saved.

These accordingly are the qualities that together incapacitate Milly Theale against the powers of Lancaster Gate—her American innocence and ignorance, her appreciation, her consciousness, her solitude, her pride. And her mysterious disease is perhaps best seen as at once 'real' and 'symbolic', physical and spiritual. On the one hand, it is a real sickness of the body, which saps her physical resistance; on the other, it is a sickness of the spirit, induced in the first instance by her early intimations, vividly communicated to us by the scene in the Swiss Alps,[8] of the lonely, loveless condition to which she is condemned in spite of (or because of) her fabulous 'luck'. Her spiritual sickness is presently intensified by her experience of the world, and finally confirmed by the ultimate betrayal which causes her to turn her face to the wall and die. She would live if she could be happy, Sir Luke Strett had said;[9] but Milly Theale is so constituted that she cannot wrest happiness out of a world by its nature implacably hostile to her very being. Though she longs to the very last moment to be happy and to live, no mutual accommodation is possible between her and the world she inhabits; and with no physical, 'animal' strength to fall back upon when, for the last time, she struggles to live after the knowledge of her betrayal by her dearest friends Kate Croy and Merton Densher, there is no escape for her from death.

* * *

What is perhaps more masterly than anything else in this master-novel is James's handling of the whole difficult *dénouement* in the last book, which begins with Densher's return to London after the momentous events in Venice and ends with his final parting from Kate Croy. Here Densher is the central figure: it is as if James, having cast him for the part of the male lead to the second leading lady of the drama and kept him strictly subordinate to her up to this point, at last gives him the centre of the stage; and it is wonderful to see how he is 'brought out' in the process—how all that before was implicit or only intimated is now made fully explicit, and how this justifies the special kind and quality of interest that Merton Densher had invited from the start.

8. *The Wings of the Dove,* I, iii, 1.

9. Ibid., II, vii, 1.

Viewed palimpsestically, Densher shows most clearly the lineaments of that long and distinguished line of Jamesian heroes 'who consecrate by their appreciation', which starts with Roland Mallett in *Roderick Hudson,* includes Ralph Touchett, 'little' Hyacinth Robinson (and in some aspects also Nick Dormer), and reaches its apotheosis in Gray Fielder in *The Ivory Tower* and Lambert Strether in *The Ambassadors.* This is James's opening sketch of Densher:

> He was a longish, leanish, fairish young Englishman, not unamenable, on certain sides, to classification—as for instance by being a gentleman, by being rather specifically one of the educated, one of the generally sound and generally civil; yet, though to that degree neither extraordinary nor abnormal, he would have failed to play straight into an observer's hands. He was young for the House of Commons, he was loose for the Army. He was refined, as might have been said, for the City, and, quite apart from the cut of his cloth, he was sceptical, it might have been felt, for the Church. On the other hand he was credulous for diplomacy, or perhaps even for science, while he was perhaps at the same too much in his mere senses for poetry and yet too little in them for art. You would have got fairly near him by making out in his eyes the potential recognition of ideas . . .[1]

What establishes Densher's place in the brotherhood, we soon learn, is 'his weakness for life, his strength merely for thought'. Thus, in respect to Kate Croy,

> Merton Densher had repeatedly said to himself—and from far back—that he should be a fool not to marry a woman whose value would be in her differences. . . . Having so often concluded on the fact of his weakness, as he called it, for life—his strength merely for thought—life, he logically opined, was what he must somehow arrange to annex and possess. This was so much a necessity that thought by itself only went on in the void; it was from the immediate air of life that it must draw its breath. So the young man, ingenious but large, critical but ardent too, made out both his case and Kate Croy's.[2]

But what links him with Lambert Strether in particular is the quality of 'intellect', as distinct from mere intelligence. Like Strether he is a 'writer', a journalist of the superior breed not uncommon, it seems, in James's day; the difference is that in Densher this quality is more integral to the man and more actively important than it ever really is in Strether. It enters intimately, for instance, into his relationship with Kate; she too, on her side, we learn, 'had quickly recognised in the young man a precious unlikeness':

1. *The Wings of the Dove,* I, ii, 1. 2. Ibid., I, ii, 1.

> He represented what her life had never given her and certainly, without some such aid as his, never would give her; all the high dim things she lumped together as of the mind. It was on the side of the mind that Densher was rich for her and mysterious and strong; and he had rendered her in especial the sovereign service of making that element real. She had had all her days to take it terribly on trust, no creature she had ever encountered having been able in any degree to testify for it directly. Vague rumours of its existence had made their precarious way to her; but nothing had, on the whole, struck her as more likely than that she should live and die without the chance to verify them. The chance had come—it was an extraordinary one—on the day she first met Densher; and it was to the girl's lasting honour that she knew on the spot what she was in the presence of.[3]

Densher, however, is also over-written with another 'line' of Jamesian heroes, which includes some members of the previous line but is distinct from it. This, in the works already discussed, is represented principally by Vanderbank in *The Awkward Age*; and it is to culminate in the Prince in *The Golden Bowl*. As we have already learnt from the case of Van, the common characteristic of this fraternity is its combination of the most engaging personal charm and the most sincere goodwill and good faith with a constitutional disposition to evade moral issues—or, rather, moral decisions. The weakness is an inseparable part of the charm, goodwill and good faith; and being for this reason so difficult to isolate as a weakness, it is exceedingly dangerous to its victims. In *The Wings of the Dove* Densher has this sacred terror chiefly, of course, for Milly; for Kate it is reinforced by the 'intellect' (which is absent in Van) and even more by the passion, the distinctively male quality which is absent in all the Jamesian heroes of this line before Densher.[4]

In any case, it is this moral personality of Merton Densher in which intellect, sensibility and passion co-exist with a fatal moral indecisiveness that is chiefly brought out in Book X. We have, of course, seen it repeatedly before this. We remember Densher at his most Van-like when, at a crucial point in his relationship with Milly when he knows that to call on her alone would commit him

3. Ibid., I, ii, 1.

4. It is present only in the rough-diamond heroes, like Basil Ransom in *The Bostonians* and Caspar Goodwood in *The Portrait of a Lady*. That Densher has the 'sacred terror' for Milly is clearly intimated in the scene of the luncheon party at Milly's hotel after her meeting with Densher and Kate in the National Gallery when she grieves secretly over his, too, having 'the view' of her, and recognises that 'whatever he did or he didn't, [she] knew she should still like him—there was no alternative to that.' (I, v, 7). It is powerfully confirmed by Kate at the end when she says to Densher, 'She never wanted the truth. She wanted *you*. She would have taken from you what you could give her, and been glad of it, even if she had known it false. You might have lied to her from pity, and she have seen you and felt you lie, and yet—since it was all for tenderness—she would have thanked you and blessed you and clung to you but the more. For that was your strength. . . —that she loves you with passion.' (II, x, 1).

irrevocably to Kate's plan, he contrives nevertheless to talk himself into the necessity, the desirability, the simple decency of doing so:

> It wasn't so much that he failed of being the kind of man who 'chucked', for he knew himself as the kind of man wise enough to mark the case in which chucking might be the minor evil and the least cruelty. It was that he liked too much everyone concerned willingly to show himself merely impracticable. He liked Kate, goodness knew, and he also clearly enough liked Mrs. Lowder. He liked in particular Milly herself; and hadn't it come up for him the evening before that he quite liked even Susan Shepherd? He had never known himself so generally merciful. It was a footing, at all events, whatever accounted for it, on which he would surely be rather a muff not to manage by one turn or another to escape disobliging.[5]

The moral indecisiveness appears conspicuously at another crucial point in the story when, reflecting on the fearful implications of Kate's design in one of his interior monologues, Densher explicitly recognises that so far as he was concerned, 'Kate's design was something so extraordinarily special to Kate that he felt himself shrink from the complications involved in judging it'.[6] In Book X, however, these characteristics expose themselves most fully because tested in the most challenging situation of Densher's life. There accordingly we have Vanderbank writ large; there James 'goes behind' his hero as he did not in *The Awkward Age*, and as a consequence brings to light new facets of the type, of its graces and virtues equally with its weaknesses, which in the end make Densher one of the principal triumphs of the book. The chief of the new facets disclosed is, we shall see, the sustained self-deception that a man like Densher is capable of when life thrusts upon him an experience that demands a total reorientation of his previous attitudes and beliefs; and this extraordinary power of self-deception, though a function of the moral weakness, is shown to be at the same time a function of his developed moral sensibility (his 'conscience'), his intelligence, his charm and his passion.

The anatomy of Merton Densher actually begins before the opening of Book X when he is left alone in Venice to bring Kate's scheme to its consummation and finds himself, suddenly, portentously, and at first unaccountably, denied access to Milly. As he wanders about in the cold lashing rain, he sees Lord Mark sitting in Florian's, guesses what has happened, and is at first stricken. But presently:

> His business, he had settled . . . was to keep thoroughly still; and he asked himself why it should prevent this that he could feel, in

5. *The Wings of the Dove*, II, vi, 5.
6. Ibid., II, vi, 5.

> connexion with the crisis, so remarkably blameless. He gave the appearances before him all the benefit of being critical, so that if blame were to accrue he shouldn't feel he had dodged it. But it wasn't a bit he who, that day, had touched her [Milly], and if she was upset it wasn't a bit his act. The ability so to think about it amounted for Densher during several hours to a kind of exhilaration. The exhilaration was heightened fairly, besides, by the visible conditions—sharp, striking, ugly to him—of Lord Mark's return. . . . He didn't need, for seeing it as evil, seeing it as, to a certainty, in a high degree 'nasty', to know more about it than he had so easily and so wonderfully picked up. You couldn't drop on the poor girl that way without, by the fact, being brutal. Such a visit was a descent, an invasion, an aggression, constituting precisely one or other of the stupid shocks that he himself had so decently sought to spare her. Densher had indeed drifted by the next morning to the reflection . . . that the only delicate and honourable way of treating a person in such a state was to treat her as *he*, Merton Densher, did. With time, actually—for the impression but deepened—this sense of the contrast, to the advantage of Merton Densher, became a sense of relief, and that in turn a sense of escape.[7]

He cannot, of course, sustain this mood of 'exhilaration,' and accordingly, a few chapters on, when he meets Sir Luke Strett who has just come away from Milly, finds the sweetest consolation in Sir Luke's complete and (as Densher interprets it) gentlemanly abstention from any reference to Milly or Milly's condition or Densher's relation to her:

> He had hoped for it, had sat in his room there waiting for it, because he had thus divined in it, should it come, some power to let him off. He was *being* let off; dealt with in the only way that didn't aggravate his responsibility. The beauty was also that this wasn't on system or any basis of intimate knowledge; it was just by being a man of the world and by knowing life, by feeling the real, that Sir Luke did him good. There had been in all the case too many women. A man's sense of it, another man's, changed the air; and he wondered what man, had he chosen, would have been more to his purpose than this one. He was large and easy—that was the benediction; he knew what mattered and what didn't; he distinguished between the essence and the shell, the just grounds and the unjust for fussing.[8]

Sir Luke, however, just before he boards his train, tells him that Milly has asked to see him, and Book IX ends with Densher arriving at the palace for the last fateful interview.

The first lines of Book X inform us that Densher has been back in London for a fortnight and has only just called to see Kate at

7. Ibid., II, ix, 2.

8. Ibid., II, ix, 4.

Lancaster Gate. The colloquy that follows confirms this first hint of the abyss that has opened between Kate and Densher as a result of his last interview with Milly. Yet throughout the scene (we are told) Kate's beauty, high sobriety and exquisite self-command have lost none of their power for him; on the contrary, with the memory of the consummation of their passion in Venice still unforgettably present to his mind, they inspire in him a joy, pride, tenderness and gratitude greater than ever before; and it is this, we soon perceive, as in all the succeeding scenes between them, that pulls against his growing knowledge of the change in their relationship, perpetually threatening it with extinction.

But the knowledge does come, against all resistance. In the course of their first meeting, Densher tells Kate that it was Lord Mark's visit that had made Milly turn her face to the wall. Kate instantly asks him why he did not deny what Lord Mark had told Milly:

> 'To tell her he lied?' [asks Densher].
>
> 'To tell her he's mistaken' [answers Kate].
>
> Densher stared—he was stupefied: the 'possible' thus glanced at by Kate being exactly the alternative he had had to face in Venice and to put utterly away from him. Nothing was stranger than such a difference in their view of it. . . . Of course, it was to be remembered, she had always simplified, and it brought back his sense of the degree in which, to her energy as compared with his own, many things were easy; the very sense that so often before had moved him to admiration. 'Well, if you must know—and I want you to be clear about it—I didn't even seriously think of a denial to her face. The question of it—*as* possibly saving her—was put to me definitely enough; but to turn it over was only to dismiss it. Besides', he added, 'it wouldn't have done any good'.[9]

What this discloses, among other things, is Densher's special kind of 'stupidity'—the intellectual counterpart, so to speak, of his moral weakness of which we are to have repeated evidence in Book X. Why, if he knows Kate (as by this time he has every reason to know her), should he 'stare' and be 'stupefied' by her suggesting something that is perfectly consistent with the grand scheme in which, up to that point, he had actively participated, and is also, granted the validity of the scheme (which he *had* implicitly granted), perfectly reasonable and 'moral'—at any rate as reasonable and moral as any of the other consequences of Kate's scheme that he had previously assented to? The answer, or one part of it, is that his mind, here as elsewhere, is as confused and self-contradictory as Kate's is clear and rigorously self-consistent; that his right

9. Ibid., II, x, 1.

hand appears not to know what his left is doing; and that he is as 'stupid' in this as Kate is in her tendency to 'simplify'.

But what we are also expected to see is that this stupidity, though present in Densher from the beginning, is now, since the shattering experience of his last meeting with Milly, acutely intensified by the bitter remorse, grief and horror with which the experience has impressed him. He is here so confused and contradictory because, still wanting Kate and still needing therefore to persuade himself that he remains loyal to her and her design, he will not recognise that he has, since he was 'forgiven, dedicated, blessed' by Milly Theale, totally repudiated the dreadful design and with it Kate herself. And that is why in this scene he 'stares' and is 'stupefied' at Kate's suggestion. It is his way of trying, characteristically, to have his cake and eat it: at once to remain loyal to Kate and to repudiate her design—an endeavour in which he is defeated, as we learn in the last line of the book, by Kate's implacable clear-headedness and consistency. This in fact is the *leitmotif* of the whole of Book X: to show Densher, on his side, as incorrigibly confused and inconsistent, and persistently—literally to the last line of the book —refusing to acknowledge with his mind what he has recognised with his moral sensibility, that his last meeting with Milly has made a radical alteration in his relationship with Kate; while Kate, on her side, is shown to be totally deficient in moral sensibility in having to the end no knowledge of what Densher's transforming experience might have been (and probably no great curiosity to know), yet being perfectly clear and self-consistent throughout, and capable both of inferring accurately from the minimal signs she receives what the experience has done to him and of drawing the inescapable conclusions—in particular the most inescapable, that 'we shall never be again as we were'.

If the principal interest of Book X is this gradual, painful disclosure of the differences between Kate Croy and Merton Densher who had seemed such a mutual pair, what makes it especially instructive and poignant is the further disclosure that the differences had been there from the beginning, had previously been obscured by their common participation in the life of the world, but had now been brought to light by the spiritual crisis created for Densher by Milly Theale's extraordinary act of loving kindness. And this (the religious would say) is the characteristic effect of the irruption of the divine order into the natural. It pierces through the appearances, exposing to view the reality that lies beneath—the real identities and differences constituting the natural order; and by the sheer truth of its revelation in the end commands the obedience of those who have received it.

* * *

SALLIE SEARS

[Kate Croy and Merton Densher]†

* * *

In the broadest sense the novel is an anatomy of guilt; of the causes, then the consequences, of deliberate, conscious violation of another human being's existence for the sake of personal gain. Each half the book deals in a general way with one of these two aspects of the subject, so that the major structural break that takes place at the end of Book V corresponds with the shift in thematic focus from the genesis of guilt to its consequences.

James's own image for the novel's subject is a medal hanging free so that "its obverse and its reverse, its face and its back, would beautifully become optional for the spectator." The medal's face is the "stricken state" of Milly Theale, its back "the state of others as affected by her"[1] and, one might add, as affected by themselves in relation to her. As the events of the novel play themselves out, the word "stricken" takes on new meaning, referring finally not so much to the peril to her health as to the blow given to her will to live in spite of it when she discovers the real connection between Kate and Merton. Similarly, the way in which others are "affected by" Milly means one thing at the outset of the story, quite another as she begins in fact to be deceived. In the beginning Kate and Merton are affected by the possibility of using her, in the end by the actuality of having done so and the nightmarish difference that this makes. The emotional complex is shifting and varied, moving for them from greed to remorse, from activity to paralysis and, for Milly, from ignorance to knowledge—which in this context is to say from hope to agony.

The real subject of the book in other words is a dynamic one. It is neither the deceived nor the deceiver who is studied but rather the changing relationship between the two and the phenomenon itself of manipulation; of the circumstances that give rise to it and of the effects it has upon both victim and victimizer. This is what James means, I think, when he speaks, in reference to his narrative method, of scarcely remembering "a case . . . in which the curiosity of 'beginning far back,' as far as possible, and even of going, to the same tune, far 'behind,' that is behind the face of the subject, was to assert itself with less scruple."[2] So he writes that "though my

† From Sallie Sears, *The Negative Imagination: Form and Perspective in the Novels of Henry James* (Ithaca: Cornell University Press, 1968), pp. 63–74, 90–98.

1. Henry James, *The Art of the Novel: Critical Prefaces*, ed. R. P. Blackmur (New York, 1962), p. 294.
2. Ibid., p. 295.

regenerate young New Yorker, and what might depend on her, should form my centre, my circumference was every whit as treatable. . . . One began, in the event, with the outer ring, approaching the centre thus by narrowing circumvallations."[3]

His "outer ring" then is the state of the other characters as affected by Milly and by what she represents at the outset of the novel. It is what he begins with, even though Book I ostensibly deals just with Kate and her family. From the ground laid in that book Milly is only, in James's words, "superficially" absent. Kate is shown under the pressure of various circumstances creating for her a series of dilemmas, all of which, however different in certain respects, have one thing in common: they would not exist if Kate had a fortune like Milly's. These circumstances weave into a web of considerable precision, and if the moth is superficially absent, the spider is waiting; one might say that a general invitation has been issued. Something of the sense of this is what James means when he speaks of having intended Milly's predicament to be created "promptly" and built up "solidly, so that it should have for us as much as possible its ominous air of awaiting her."[4]

The predicament is certainly solid. There is an inexorable and formal irony in the very confluence of events operating on and within Kate that is reminiscent in its way of Hardy. By various vague and nameless deeds Kate's father has brought the family, which includes the four small children of her widowed sister, into dishonor and financial collapse. Her wealthy aunt is willing to rescue Kate on the explicit condition that she renounce all contact with her father and on the unspoken condition that she marry a man of the aunt's choice. Kate herself is beautiful, proud, poor but covetous of wealth, and in love with a penniless man not of her aunt's choice. She is also painfully conscious of the responsibilities and obligations, the silken cords of familial relations, and "the part, not always either uplifting or sweetening, that the bond of blood might play in one's life." She is not free from this bond—as Milly so pre-eminently is—either in fact or, more important, in feeling. "That's all my virtue" she murmurs to Densher, "—a narrow little family feeling. I've a small stupid piety—I don't know what to call it." Finally, she occupies a unique position within the family complex: with her youth, her pride, her presence, and the magnetism that makes her appear "more 'dressed,' often, with fewer accessories, than other women, or less dressed, should occasion require, with more," she is the one piece of solid collateral the disgraced and distressed family possesses, the one tangible asset whose worth to them is the price it will bring at barter. And she knows it. Lionel Croy has few pleasures. Like Gilbert Osmond in *The Portrait of a Lady*,

3. Ibid., p. 294

4. Ibid.

he is concerned with appearances and wears the mask of propriety but feels almost nothing. Yet he does take pleasure, she realizes, in the fact "that she was handsome, that she was in her way a tangible value." And later she repeats to Densher, "My position's a value, a great value, for them both. . . . It's *the* value—the only one they have. . . . It makes me ask myself if I've any right to personal happiness, any right to anything but to be as rich and overflowing, as smart and shining, as I can be made."

So the theme of manipulation, of tampering, of regarding a fellow human being not as a person but as an object for use is present from the beginning of the novel, more horrifying perhaps because of its context within the family setting, where the distortion and reversal of roles are so severe, the primary responsibility of who nurtures whom so askew, that the situation takes on almost cannibalistic overtones: a family party feeding off the younger daughter.

The purpose of these opening chapters according to James was to "account" for Kate: "The image of her so compromised and compromising father was all effectively to have pervaded her life, was in a certain particular way to have tampered with her spring; by which I mean that the shame and the irritation and the depression, the general poisonous influence of him, were to have been *shown*." "They weren't shown," James feels; instead the author's "poor word of honour has *had* to pass muster for the show."[5] And it is true that Lionel Croy's compromising influence does not really seem to have very much to do with Kate's deepest possibilities and energies. But it does not matter; it is not a serious flaw. When we first view Kate gazing into the mirror, the impact of her beauty, vitality, and power speaks for itself. She does not need "accounting for." Her personality with both its resources and its susceptibilities, its passion and its narcissism, is one of the givens of the novel, the concern of which as a study of human guilt is phenomenological rather than psychological. To the extent that the novel is concerned with causes, it is as they exist in the combination of character and circumstance, not as they relate to the origins of character itself. And though James is one of the great scholars of human motives, his interest is in their processes: in the effects, the implications, the reverberations of self-interest and not in its psychodynamics.

Some guilt by association does touch Kate: her sister is abject, her father is full of "folly and cruelty and wickedness," her aunt is "unscrupulous and immoral." It is sufficient for the evil of the day that Kate exists in contiguity with them, that she is the prime object of their various desires, and that she recognizes this and even partially acknowledges its justice. By so doing of course she accepts

5. *The Art of the Novel*, pp. 297, 298.

not only their right to use her but also, by extension, anyone's right to use anyone who might be in a position to be useful. The acceptance of this principle is the primary distortion of human values in the novel, and it operates on a number of levels,[6] reversing the meaning even of ordinary terms of moral discourse. Thus Kate is under pressure from all the members of her family not to be "selfish," that is not to marry a penniless man or, to put it another way, not to marry the man she loves since he not only is penniless but also feels that the "innermost fact . . . of his own consciousness" is his "private inability to believe he should ever be rich."

It is not merely through the eyes of her family, however, that Kate regards herself as an object to be put to use, but through her own eyes as well. Looking at herself in the mirror, she meditates upon the possibility of at least a partial escape from ruin—escape implicit in the fact that she is "agreeable to see." And she is aware of her power: "If she saw more things than her fine face in the dull glass of her father's lodgings she might have seen that after all she was not herself a fact in the collapse. She didn't hold herself cheap, she didn't make for misery." To an extent her vision of herself is one with that of her family: they don't judge her cheap either. The difference is in her intense personal pride, which is reflected in an extension of her self-identification to the "precious" family name, the debasing of which causes her shame and a quality of remorse they themselves do not share. With a certain horror, Kate sees her sister's abjectness, watches her "instinctively neglect nothing that would make for her submission to their aunt," realizes that Marian's lust for profit is "quite oblivious" of dignity, honor, and pride.

One of the most characteristic traits of James's imagination is to see life in terms of mutually exclusive possibilities and negative alternatives. The typical problem faced by his characters is not so much a choice as a dilemma, in which any decision means some major sacrifice, capitulation, or surrender. And for Kate the dilemma rapidly becomes acute; she has accepted her position, even to the extent of questioning her own right to personal happiness, as the family pawn. At the same time it is only she who can or cares to preserve their collective dignity. To preserve it means not to be abject, but not to be abject means in turn "to prefer an ideal of behaviour—than which nothing ever was more selfish—to the possi-

6. Most of the relationships in the book can be looked at from the point of view of who is using whom: Kate's father, sister, and sisters-in-law try to recover their ruined fortune by pressuring her to accept Aunt Maud's offer to "do for" her; Aunt Maud in turn has had Kate "marked from far back" as the means by which she can realize her own social ambitions if Kate under her tutelage marries properly; through Kate's countermanipulations and Densher's passive assistance, Aunt Maud herself becomes the one who is used; and everyone—including Lord Mark, the subtle parasite Eugenio, and even, it could be argued, Susie—uses Milly.

bility of stray crumbs for the four small creatures." So that any way she turns, something, and something important, stands to be lost.

Her one attempt to maintain her spiritual freedom, her integrity, literally her wholeness, of self is her initial offer to her father to stick by him, with or without Densher, and renounce Aunt Maud. This is the first and last unequivocally moral gesture Kate makes in the course of the novel, and part of the inexorability of the patterning of circumstances spoken of earlier lies in its never being allowed to become a genuine option for her. The irony is intensified by the fact that of all the various pressures operating upon and within her, not the least is that of her own "dire accessibility to pleasure" from material things, from "trimmings and lace . . . ribbons and silk and velvet . . . charming quarters."[7] It is an accessibility that makes her feel in danger; in the face of the temptation offered by Aunt Maud, Kate likens herself to "a trembling kid . . . sure sooner or later to be introduced into the cage of the lioness." Yet the source of the danger is internal not external, and Aunt Maud's imagined ferocity is an image for Kate of some possibility within herself that she dreads and that Milly too is soon to dread, recognizing after an interview with Kate that "she had felt herself alone with a creature who paced like a panther."

The intensity of the temptation Kate feels is a measure of the meaning of her gesture to her father. It is no empty offer, but an effort to redeem herself in advance from herself, from what she so clearly senses she might do, and by doing, become. "I did it," she cries to Densher, "to save myself—to escape." To save herself and "the precious name" she is willing at this juncture to give up both love and a possible fortune—a willingness, perhaps understandably, she never demonstrates again.

Given, then, the nature of her own character in the context of circumstances that surround it, there is no set of alternative actions that does not represent a dilemma for Kate. She does not want to give up Densher, yet she does not want to be poor, and she would be poor if she married him. She especially does not want, after the example of the Misses Condrips' who spend their days sniffing out dregs of gossip that might somehow be turned to their financial advantage, to be both poor and unmarried. She does not want to be dishonorable. She does not want to see her family's fortune and honor remain in the mud. She does not want to sacrifice her personal—and familial—dignity to regain that fortune, yet she does not want to have to maintain that dignity at the cost of taking crumbs away from babes. If she maintains her integrity she sacrifices her

7. In respect to material things, of course, her susceptibility is one with her family's; it is only their abjectness in the face of it that she loathes. There is a sense in which their whole relationship with her parodies the forces that in a subtler way most motivate Kate.

family to poverty and, equally to the point, herself as well. So that the choice of any one alternative means the surrender of the other possibilities. And that in turn means the renunciation of her ideal self-image, because that image is precisely a composite of all the possibilities: it is Kate wealthy, dignified, of proud name, charitable in her munificence, and married to Merton Densher.

The one sacrifice on the altar of this vision is her morality. Not the appearance of it, since to seem untouchable and beyond scandal, to have the aura of propriety, is an intrinsic part of her ideal portrait of herself. But certainly the fact of it. So she tells Densher she sees as her one danger the possibility "of doing something base." It is not the danger of "chucking him," as he suggests: "I *shan't* sacrifice you. Don't cry out till you're hurt. I shall sacrifice nobody and nothing, and that's just my situation, that I want and that I shall try for everything."

Kate's cry of yearning is to be echoed in one form or another by all the characters, "good" and "bad" alike, in the late novels. Her situation, that of a person whose longings will recognize no limits and yet who is caught up in circumstances that are unusually limiting, is a microcosm of the fundamental situation James deals with again and again. His imagination so orders reality that the possibilities for happiness that face each character inevitably have an either-or quality about them, and yet the characters are all the kind of people for whom the alternative to the fulfillment of their desires is an empty, pointless existence. And it is in terms of these two extremes that James persistently examines the meaning and significance of "morality." For Kate, the pendulum has swung full swing: if initially she was willing to renounce everything to preserve her spiritual safety, she is now willing to surrender that safety to preserve everything else. In a sense what she does is simply to reject the logical premise of her situation—the premise that she is in a dilemma, that she must choose between one thing and another. But her one peril, that of doing something base, is by definition also a peril to someone else. The shifts in her feeling and attitudes toward herself can be reduced to a series of propositions about the nature of the relationship between self-gratification and morality, and the limits on each imposed by the other. Kate's situation, as she sees it, is such that the price of absolute morality is absolute self-renunciation; the price of partial morality is partial self-renunciation; and finally, the reward of immorality is total self-gratification. It is the novel's concern to disprove this last proposition, but the rigor of her "logic" is nonetheless one of the forces motivating the subsequent events.

This fact, together with the fact that the possession of a fortune is the *sine qua non* of her vision, constitutes the basis of Milly's predicament, and is why it has indeed "its ominous air of awaiting her." Milly has a fortune, Kate needs one; Milly is passive and gentle—a dove; Kate is restless and ruthless—a panther. In addition not only is Milly mortally ill while Kate is vibrantly alive, but also Milly's one English acquaintance happens to be Merton Densher, and she happens to be susceptible to his attractions. Thus every element in Milly's situation has its opposite correspondence in Kate's, and the predicament of the former is a function or extension of the predicament of the latter; it is its logical outgrowth.

One could indeed say that much of the energy of the novel is logistical, rhetorical, dialectical. And clearly both the strengths and the weaknesses of the book are in some important way tied up with this fact. The structuring of the plot, for example, the way the initial dramatic situation is conceived and set up, is characterized by a high degree of formal balance and antithesis, correspondences and oppositions. The way in which what Milly needs and what Milly has to offer so neatly dovetail with what Kate needs, and also has to offer, is almost too good to be true. Or too painful to be bearable, which is the effect James intended. The "soul of drama," he writes, ". . . is the portrayal, as we know, of a catastrophe determined in spite of oppositions. My young woman would *herself* be the opposition—to the catastrophe announced by the associated Fates."[8]

That is, the effect of the remorseless logic of the combined circumstances of the two girls is precisely the feeling of impending catastrophe—and catastrophe that is inevitable, unavoidable, inexorable. Whatever one might argue about the apparent improbabilities, coincidences, even patnesses of the initial situation in the novel, the result is one of ironic contrast, of heightened tension and expectation. There is something ruthless in the manipulation of the events, to be sure, but that very fact contributes to the intensity of the emotional effect, the sense of dread and pity, the feeling of the inevitable mockery and destruction of the deep yearning for life that is so profound a part of Milly's makeup.

The effect is not merely dramatic; it is almost diabolic. There is something reminiscent of a hellish chess game in the book's presentation of the mathematics of narrowing alternatives, in which the loser of the game not only does not know she is losing, she does not even know she is playing. James has an almost Satanic instinct for situation; indeed much of his power as a novelist lies in his remorselessness in this respect.

Remorseless in his delineation of character too, he is one of the great pathologists of human nature we have in modern fiction. His ability to cast a cold eye on a whole spectrum of moral sickness and to present it without flinching is one of the paradoxes of a sensibil-

8. *The Art of the Novel,* p. 290.

ity that in many respects evaded the direct confrontation of powerful emotion. In the midst of the yearning and separation that are characteristic motifs of his imagination is this preoccupation with the darker aspects of the human psyche, a preoccupation characterized by the degree to which the author seems close to and unfearful of its concerns rather than detached or distant from them.

* * *

It must be more clearly recognized that James's vision of human existence is first and last an ironic one, and that it is not he who is deceived by the glitter of the social façade he studies. He was in one sense in search of an ideal society, and the search took place in the two countries of his imagination that in effect constituted a mythological setting: America, the Pale Lady, the boring paradise, and Europe, the Dark Lady, seductive, sensual, totally attractive, totally wicked, the enchanting hell. His novels are all legends of the failure of the quest, because in *his* vision truth and beauty are not one. His Holy Grail is the golden bowl with the imperceptible flaw.

But the success of any ironic presentation depends first of all upon consistency of tone. Reuben Brower defines irony as "meaning . . . narrowed to opposition" and remarks that metaphor and irony "present two levels of meaning which the reader must entertain at once if he is to respond imaginatively to either of these forms of expression. . . . To experience the irony . . . we must entertain both of the clashing possibilities."[9] Even in works (the problem novels, for example) in which James deliberately renders reality from a multiplicity of perspectives, without giving authority to any one of them, each perspective is itself clear, and it is obvious that if either level of meaning (whether or not the clashing viewpoints are resolved ultimately) becomes obscured, or the author's attitude toward it is ambivalent or inconsistent, the ironic effect is lost in confusion. This is finally what happens with the figure of Merton Densher in *The Wings of the Dove*. Up to a point in the delineation of Densher, James's touch is sure and masterly as he keeps a fine and deliberate balance between Densher's increasingly distorted self-image and the more objective image of him held by others. Eugenio, for example, "took a view of him . . . essentially vulgar . . . the imputation in particular that, clever, *tanto bello* and not rich, the young man from London was—by the obvious way—pressing Miss Theale's fortune hard." Densher's passivity, his self-deception and rationalization, his increasing helplessness and loss of

9. *The Fields of Light: An Experiment in Critical Reading* (New York, 1951), pp. 50–51. Brower adds, "So obvious a point needs stressing . . . because some definitions of irony imply that the reader finds the intended or true meaning beneath the apparent, a view that tends to destroy irony both as a literary experience and as a vision of life."

freedom are superbly handled. One of the first consequences of his fall is the diminution in his power of "right reasoning": it is Kate's doing and not his. Or it is Milly's *and* his, freely, not Kate's at all; therefore he is not being manipulated, has not lost his manhood. His ethical position entails obedience to the law, not the spirit; action alone, and not intent or desire, is what is culpable. So long then as he doesn't *do* anything: tell a direct lie, propose marriage himself to Milly, he is blameless. The fact that he knows that both Kate and Aunt Maud have "told the proper lie" for him (that Kate doesn't love him) he passes over. And it will be all right if Milly proposes to him. He has, it is true, moments of clearer awareness, in which he wonders about the validity of his distinction between active and passive participation in the whole affair: "It was Kate's description of him, his defeated state, it was none of his own; his responsibility would begin, as he might say, only with acting it out. The sharp point was, however, in the difference between acting and not acting: this difference in fact it was that made the case of conscience. He saw it with a certain alarm rise before him that everything was acting that was not speaking the particular word" (that is, disabusing Milly of the notion that Kate is indifferent to him).

He decides, however, that it would be "indelicate" to mention the matter to Milly when she would never dream of mentioning it to him, and that further there would be a kind of unnecessary "brutality" in shaking Milly off when she so clearly enjoys his company. At this point, he has not yet given Milly reason to believe that he has any kind of romantic interest in her, though that deception is imminent. The deception itself (what he calls "turning his corner") he perpetrates out of *politeness*: "Clearly what had occurred was her having wished it [that he accompany her on a drive] so that she had made him simply wish, in civil acknowledgement, to oblige *her*." We are to take this extraordinary gesture at face value; he is quite sincere. It is extraordinary because, from here on out, he will not just disoblige but kill her if he does not keep up the pretense. This is the fateful moment, for *now* he would (so far as he knows) merely wound her feelings if he declines her invitation; *later* he would destroy her, as he himself quickly recognizes a few moments later: "If he might have turned tail . . . five minutes before, he couldn't turn tail now."

His politeness is a matter of real concern: he sees she yearns for him, he is touched by her "shy fragrance of heroism." But his displacement of perspective is incredible, particularly in view of his awareness, en route to this very visit, that he was "the kind of man wise enough to mark the case in which chucking [someone] might be the minor evil and the least cruelty." And so the code of chivalry becomes the Law that Merton obeys: "The single thing that was clear in complications was that, whatever happened, one was to behave as a gentleman. . . . The law was not to be a brute—in return for amiabilities."

To be a blue-eyed darling in appearance and a serpent in fact—and not to recognize it. The irony of the portrait is intense, deliberate, and in splendid control until the concluding portions of the book, when something goes askew and the man who has tried so hard not to be a brute becomes what is almost worse, a prig. This was not James's intent of course: Merton was to have gone through a spiritual transformation—literally a conversion—to have conceived a "horror" of the scheme in which he had become involved, as James puts it in his notebooks, and to have emerged morally reborn, "faithful to the [exquisite] image of the dead."[1]

But a conversion implies a degree of self-examination and valuation (rejection of the sinful self) that never takes place in Merton.[2] He dreads public exposure and feels "a dire apprehension of publicity," but this is about the limit of any self-scrutiny that we are shown. Because of this, his conversion is not persuasive, in the sense that we do not feel moved, convinced of some radical spiritual growth. It is one of those cases where instead of being *shown,* as James would put it, we have to take the word of the "poor author" for it. About James's intention, there can be no question: the question is to what degree he realized it. He himself is the first to admit that sometimes an artist's plan is one thing, his result another. One reason we do not feel a sense of Densher's spiritual growth is that his concern is so little with himself, so exclusively and so harshly focused upon Kate. That he should feel a revulsion toward her is not, in itself, surprising, but the way in which he manifests it is very much unlike the "grace" Milly extended to him. He is nearly cruel. He sets little tests and traps for Kate like placing in her hands, to deal with at her option, both the letter from Milly and the envelope from her New York lawyers stating the amount she had left him. When Kate opens it—and who can conceive of her doing anything but—he confesses he is "disappointed": it wasn't the "handsome way" of renunciation he had hoped for; he had hoped she would return it unopened, accompanied by "an absolutely kind letter" of refusal. When she points out that he neglected to express this hope in his letter to her, he explains, "I didn't want to. I wanted to leave it to yourself. I wanted—oh yes, if that's what you wish to ask me—to see what you'd do."

1. *The Notebooks of Henry James,* ed. F. O. Matthiessen and Kenneth B. Murdock (New York, 1955), pp. 173–174.

2. When Saul of Tarsus is on the road to Damascus and hears the voice of Christ saying "Saul, Saul, why persecutest thou me?" it is a private matter of conscience with respect to the implications in the stoning of Stephen. The behavior of the other Jews involved in the persecution is in no way relevant to his experience.

"You wanted to measure the possibilities of my departure from delicacy? . . ."

"Well, I wanted—in so good a case—to test you." And test her he continues to do, up to the bitter end. "He had given poor Kate her freedom," as he puts it: freedom to choose the money without him, or him without the money. So that once again she is in the very dilemma, caught between the same set of negative alternatives, that she was at the outset. There is nothing wrong with this degree of "poetic justice" descending on her shoulders, but there is something wrong with Merton's sanctimonious viciousness, especially when it is coupled with the comparatively gentle, forgiving attitude he has toward himself. He explains to Kate at one point that Sir Luke had understood that he had "meant awfully well"; at another, he senses that Mrs. Lowder gathered the "essence" of his situation: "The essence was that something had happened to him too beautiful and too sacred to describe. He had been, to his recovered sense, forgiven, dedicated, blessed." But he does not extend to Kate the charity he, without tests, has received.

How then are we to understand these events with which the novel closes? Are we intended to make a split judgment, in which Merton is finally exonerated, but Kate not? If this is the intention, it certainly is not realized; in fact the emotional effect is just the opposite. There is a certain beauty in the brave if somewhat harrowing consistency of Kate's character, in her risking everything to gain everything. And this we feel right up through the end, in spite of Merton. Perhaps it is partly due to the principle cited by E. E. Stoll, that readers tend to identify with the active agent rather than the passive, whether that agent is morally acceptable to them or not.[3] At any rate, the bravery of her risk coupled with her refusal to rationalize her behavior, while most of Merton's energy is devoted to rationalization, helps to account for our greater sympathy for Kate. There is something much more unpalatable about immorality when it is in the mask of piety than when it is frank and open.

I suspect that James's *scheme* for the novel, which we have in the notebooks, called for a kind of formal resolution of the plot that was incompatible with the profoundly paradoxical nature of his vision of the source and meaning of human suffering. It was mentioned earlier that much of the energy of the novel is logistical, rhetorical. James's concern with formal balance and opposition, and with fateful logic, is highly effective in the initial portions of the book, where it creates the feeling of impending catastrophe that is not to be eluded by any efforts on Milly's part. But James's preoccupation with the mathematics of situation badly weakens the ending.

3. Elmer Edgar Stoll, "Give the Devil His Due," *Review of English Studies,* XX (April, 1944), 124.

In a way, one could say that the two deepest artistic impulses—concern for shape, form, and aesthetic organization, and concern for truth—obtruded upon each other in this novel at its conclusion. Densher's actions and reactions toward Kate are both harsher and simpler than those of the total work, just as his reactions toward himself are kinder. But because this is the case, the novel can end "neatly," with Densher scarred but beautified and Kate plunged back into the original dilemma upon the altar of which she sacrificed her morality: Kate given and refusing one last option to renounce her lust for money; Kate not spiritually transformed as Densher supposedly is but in fact (that is in *effect*) is not. Kate is thus left formally, though once again this is not the emotional effect, bearing the brunt of the drama of pain that has been enacted. What the book makes so clear and the ending does not is that all three of the principal agents played their role in the events that took place, and that all three are at one and the same time responsible and not responsible. It is this ambivalent sense of things, constantly articulated throughout the book, that the ending does not, or cannot, rise to meet. The ending therefore undermines both the complexity and the emotional intensity of the work as a whole. Densher's sudden access to piety is accomplished with too much ease; he does not suffer enough in the sense that he escapes the self-confrontation that would be the symbolic recognition of and penance for some of the pangs Milly has endured at his hands. This in turn means that the whole moral order of events that centered around his figure has to be questioned: did James after all take him at his own valuation, as a reluctant pawn who is to be exonerated for having tried to be chivalrous in the middle of a compromising situation? And if James did take him that way, what then are we to make of the central ethical problem that is the really interesting and really powerful circumstance of Densher's position: that "case of conscience" which lay in the difference between acting and not acting on his part? If we accept the ending, we must dismiss the case of conscience as a mere rhetorical murmur to himself in the middle of the gentleman's plight. Yet the book, fortunately, will not allow us to do that. In spite of the ending, Densher's passive involvement has implicated him deeply indeed. This at least is the effect, and it is a good thing that it is. If it were not, the whole novel would suffer from a superficiality, even sentimentality, of vision. But James explicitly consigned even to Milly responsibility for the outcome of events, and it is difficult to believe he did not intend at least the same burden of blame for Merton, if not quite a lot more. It does not seem convincing, that is, that James's intention was different from the effect created by the events of the novel up until the end. It is the ending that is unpersuasive, even unreal.

The novel itself survives, but certainly at a cost to its integrity of effect and full realization of its own order of spiritual reality. In that order Merton *is* exonerated, but in a very different sense from that in which he exonerates himself, just as Kate is condemned on quite another level from that on which he condemns her: one considerably less legalistic, literal, and petty. He has of course applied the letter of the law to himself, earlier, so perhaps it is not surprising that he does so to Kate at the end. But the burden of the book rests upon violation not of the word but of the spirit. Is not the whole point that no "word" is spoken to Milly, that the crime and the woe are committed wordlessly but nevertheless absolutely? It is this central human fact of the novel that the ending betrays, and it is in spite of the betrayal that the novel survives.

LAURENCE B. HOLLAND

From *The Expense of Vision*†

[*Language as Fate*]

"It was not till afterwards that, going back to it, I was to read into [Kate's] speech a kind of heroic ring, a note of a character that belittled [Densher's] own incapacity for action. Yet he saw indeed even at the time the greatness of knowing so well what one wanted." The quoted sentences, drawing attention to the heroism of one character (Kate Croy) and comparing it to the passivity of the novel's hero (Kate's fiancé, Merton Densher), occur at the height of the scene which constitutes the drama of *The Wings of the Dove* by bringing the novel's crisis to its culmination and at the same time providing the basis for its resolution. At so crucial a point, James speaks, in the first American edition, for the only time when his voice emerges in the first person to help bring an important matter, Kate's heroism, into definite focus; Densher's ready admiration for her at the time enforces a tribute felt later but openly by James. In the first English edition as in the subsequent New York collection, the "I" is replaced by "he," whether because James detected a typographer's error, corrected his own mistake, or decided on second thought to substitute one form of expression for another. In any case, the "muffled majesty of authorship" and the entire insight into Kate's heroism are delegated in the revisions to Densher—his "bland Hermes," as James was to call him in the

† From Laurence Bedwell Holland, *The Expense of Vision: Essays on the Craft of Henry James* (Princeton: Princeton University Press, 1964), pp. 285–91, 298–301, 306–10.

preface, the god of theft and commerce who gave Apollo his lyre.[1] In all versions the tribute to Kate helps to define the novel's form by straining it, in an effort to encompass both a prospective and a retrospective view, so as to define an act of confession of which the quoted sentences are part.

The act of looking ahead or anticipating the completion of the action and the act of reconsidering it in memory, whether performed ostensibly by James or ostensibly by Densher, are joined in a tribute to Kate's heroism at the moment when she has expressed a willingness to " 'do what I don't like' " in encouraging her own fiancé to marry a dying and wealthy American girl, Milly Theale. James's intervention at this point to pay tribute to Kate, in the unrevised version, would implicate him explicitly in the plot, thus associating him intimately with Kate's and Densher's deed. But the tribute assigned wholly to Densher in the revision is a degree of consciousness and conscience *imputed* to him by James, and it is likewise an effort to confess James's responsibility for the action and to confess as well his form's involvement in the action and his intimate involvement with his medium.

The narrative convention of *The Wings of the Dove* is founded on neither the author's voice alone nor on the center of consciousness alone but on the intimate connection between them, on the shared burden and responsibility which the narrative's gestures confess; it is articulated consistently and frequently, in all versions, when the narrative momentarily reveals James's presence in such carefully unobtrusive phrases as "I say" or "our analysis," "our young lady" and "our subject." Being the very image of the vicarious imagination, the narrative exercises authority by delegating authority and confessing responsibility for it, and the scene which includes the tribute to Kate's heroism twice reveals explicitly, then again veils, James's presence in the phrase "we know."

James's emergence intermittently in the first person is paradoxically both a lapse or flaw in the "guarded objectivity" of his drama and the fulfillment of its logic as a novel which builds, as the preface was to point out, on its own failure. His acknowledgment of the role of narrator, the pretentious "majesty of authorship," is the flaw in his form and a questionable commitment, matching that of Kate and Densher, which must be answered and redeemed. Yet it articulates also James's confession of his commitment. But James's confessed presence is revealed more profoundly, in all versions, in the projected *action* of the scene, for what Kate and Densher do on that occasion—what they do for James—is to "suit the action to the word, the word to the action" of James's novel by agreeing to enact its plot, with Kate forcing Densher to put her plan into words

1. *The Art of the Novel*, p. 298.

and then joining him in the phrasing of it. Moreover James's complicity and the involvement of his form are revealed implicitly also in the rendering of other characters who are James's instruments and who contribute along with Kate and Densher to the plot. Indeed, the very behavior of language itself as an instrument is revealed to be one of the sources of the novel's tragic vision.

If it inheres in the very nature of a language, as Santayana has written, that it gives "perspective" to experience but in that act also "vitiates the experience it expresses," the "kindly infidelities" of language, as Santayana called them, define the verbal action which mediates the tragic vision of *The Wings of the Dove*:[2] the behavior of a medium which at once expresses and betrays its subject or vision and accordingly is inseparable, in *The Wings of the Dove*, from the tragic action it renders. The novel's language is shaped by three principal vocabularies—one commercial, one religious, and one aesthetic—which are defined by characteristic metaphors or phrases: for instance, the phrase "a capital case" which a doctor uses to describe the dying and wealthy heroine; or the description of doves who are "picking up the crumbs of perpetual feasts" in the square before a Christian church in Venice; or the description of the heroine as "embodied poetry." Each of the phrases, and each of the larger vocabularies of which it is part, helps define the novel's relevance to the actual world beyond it—to the institutions, attitudes, formulations of value, and forms that comprise the culture of capitalism, or the Judaeo-Christian tradition, or the fine arts. But the field of relevance they define is a field of behavior in which they act, not a safely remote and independent realm of actualities to which they refer, and the language functions so as to draw the practices and values it suggests *into* the "crucible" of the imagination and into the fictive action, to include them in the world it creates, and, conversely, to bring the "penetrating imagination" into an intimate encounter with its materials, the actualities in the world of which it is part.

The consequence is that the language, as an instrument, is subject not only to all the pressures which have already endowed it with the conventional implications that it brings into the novel but to the pressures it undergoes as the mediating instrument of James's imagination. Its behavior is far from the "merely referential" function which James was to disparage in the preface to *The Ambassadors*, in being at once more anxious or apprehensive and more powerful. It is closer rather to the explorative maneuvers he attributed to himself, as a "wary adventurer," in the preface to *The Wings of the Dove*, "standing off" from the "situation" of the wealthy dying girl, but then "coming back to it," walking "round and round" the

2. George Santayana, *Reason in Art* (New York, 1905), p. 82.

ase" that "invited and mystified" his fascination.[3] The language es not so much stipulate its meanings or describe its action as *susnd* them in a mode which is epitomized by the novel's opening ntences, where Kate Croy's hesitation between departing or naining, between going away or staying to see and help her father, presents the first version of the novel's central action and its basic rhythm. The paleness, the waiting, and the decision to stay, here touched on for the first time, are crucial motives in the novel, and the opening sentences virtually postpone Kate's decision to remain, suspending it in tension with the temptation to go away so as to evade a confrontation with her father, while literally pausing and lingering over her name, the detail of the mirror above the mantel, and her momentarily pale face: "She waited, Kate Croy, for her father to come in, but he kept her unconscionably, and there were moments when she showed herself, in the glass over the mantel, a face positively pale with the irritation that had brought her to the point of going away without sight of him. It was at this point, however, that she remained. . . ."

While the language, in this dramatic suspension, both expresses and betrays its subject, rendering it by approaching it but holding off from it, the prose serves the several functions that are paramount for James's art and govern his characters as well as his language. The prose can be as intimate and compressed in its irony for James as it is for Kate, with her desire when talking of her family's predicament "to work off, for her own relief, her constant perception of the incongruity of things," and to devise, for intimate conversation with her fiancé, a shorthand of "fantastic" phrases and "the happy language of exaggeration," exaggerations which constitute their intimacy and manage to be more true than the less intimate make-believe which they indulge in public. In its analytic probing the prose risks the cruelty of exposure which Kate fears when she learns that she might be written up in a book: " 'Chop me up fine or serve me whole'—it was a way of being got at that Kate professed she dreaded." Yet if it is intimate in its devious exaggerations and painfully close in its exposure of the characters it depicts, the language is, nevertheless, conspicuously restrained even when subservient to James's analytic strategy, as when sheer observation of the ailing heroine becomes a risky adventure for her hired traveling companion, Mrs. Susan Stringham, whose watchful care is dangerous and is inseparable from the reader's and James's own. She knows that she would not (or at least "shouldn't") *lunge* at the girl in her efforts to keep track of her and watch for symptoms of her illness, but she has "almost the sense of tracking her young friend as if at a given moment to pounce" and fears that her aid is

3. *The Art of the Novel,* p. 288.

"secretive," that her "observation" is "scientific." She fears that she is "hovering like a spy, applying tests, laying traps, concealing signs," and while she continues to do this nevertheless, satisfied because "to watch" is "a way of clinging to the girl" and gives access to her "beauty," she does so with the tact of reticence and with restraint. The same probing analysis which risks exposing or chopping up Kate, and spying on or trapping Milly, is, in its restraint, a measure of solicitude and care.

So infused is the language itself with the creative aim it serves and the drama it projects that it becomes at once a rich resource and a virtual fate, endangering and enclosing its subject in the very act of focusing loving attention on it, intimating what lies beyond its vocabularies but failing to free itself from them. The novel distinguishes the heroine's doctor's services from exclusively commercial ones, for instance, but does so in terms which remain distinctly pecuniary: "Sir Luke had appeared indeed to speak of purchase and payment, but in reference to a different sort of cash. Those were amounts not to be named or reckoned, and such moreover as [Milly] wasn't sure of having at her command." Whether because it clings perversely to the terminology of cash when it might try to abandon it, or because it dramatizes by that means art's inescapable dependence on its medium and the "kindly infidelities" which are unavoidable necessities inhering in the nature of language, the prose creates the very possibility of the impending tragedy, prepares the very "fallibility" James was to speak of in the preface as the foundation of artistic mastery, the failure of beguiling intentions which is made part of the very creative process and helps stage the destruction and transformation through wastage—in sum, the tragedy—of Milly Theale.

The "amounts" not "named" or "reckoned" and the failure to name and reckon them are so central to the tragedy that the "kindly infidelities" of words, the verbal drama suspended in the movement of the prose, virtually defines the plot of the novel, when Densher tries to define in his own case the relations among words and action and inaction, telling a lie and "acting it out," telling the truth and keeping it secret. He decides that truth and candor inhere only in naming the names and declaring the reckoning, in openly "speaking the particular word," and that measured by this standard, any behavior short of it—silences, verbal evasions, and inaction as well as overt action—is "acting" in the sense of histrionic illusion or affectation, and that such "acting" in his case makes him responsible for acting out a lie. Accordingly, the very sentences which suspend, postpone, and prolong their import and action, the "kindly infidelities" of the prose which hovers "round and round" its subject in a verbal drama and holds off from naming and reckoning, are, in their style, part of the very drama they help enact. Indeed, the "particular word" that Densher speaks of is a secret that is crucial for the novel's plot—the fact that Kate still is in love with Densher—and Densher goes on to pledge himself to continued silence out of loyalty to Kate and a consequent loyalty to her "design," a design which at that point in the novel has not been fully divulged to Densher, has not been made explicit to the reader, and *may* not even be fully formulated yet by Kate. But that emerging "design" is crucial in James's novel, for it is his own plot which, along with the prose, helps to project the tragic action. It helps to create the design and the movement which James was to call, in the preface to *The Ambassadors,* the full "process of vision," the firm "march" of his novel's "action."[4]

[*Semantics of Social Hierarchy*]

* * *

Unfamiliar in America with the differences in social "position" which prevail in England and the "awfully good manner" which functions to "bridge" the distance between them, Milly arrives in Europe stripped by death even of her immediate family and, with an isolation enforced by her huge fortune, she is " 'independent,' " as Kate declares enviously, of the " 'tiers and tiers' " of groups in an "hierarchical, an aristocratic order." One thing her native society lacks is the vast "interval" between classes, which is associated metaphorically by James with blocks of "skipped" pages in a book or "social atlas." Another thing it lacks is a "manner"—accompanied by a "sinking" or repressing of the "consciousness" (but not the ignoring) of social intervals by both the privileged and unprivileged classes but particularly by the privileged—a manner which bridges the intervals, acknowledging the intervals by the fact of bridging them but repressing the awareness of the differences so as to be able to bridge the intervals at all. In the world of Matcham and Lancaster Gate, social distinctions are still to *some* extent founded on settled arrangements but are also founded on the manipulations, powerful and enterprising, of middle-class Aunt Maud. Not only is she devoting her money, talents, and practiced manner to gaining higher status in the traditional "order" for Kate, and an attractive well-financed wife for the aristocratic Lord Mark; she has brought about by willed effort, virtually created, an otherwise nonexistent social distinction between Kate and her widowed sister Marian—a distinction which to Milly seems forced.

Though the position of the Croys was once "settled" in the successful middle class, static *status* is no longer the apt term for

4. Ibid., p. 308.

Lionel Croy's precarious and shifting position as he moves downward through bankruptcy toward oblivion, and though Marian Croy may have married beneath her station while Kate is being groomed for higher things, James's treatment of the "social atlas" suggests that the "order" is no longer fixed under the impact of Maud's counting-house, that Kate and her sister have not simply fallen or been sorted into different fixed social positions but that a position for Marian has been "established" by Maud's maneuvering, exaggerating whatever interval might otherwise extend between the two sisters, a feat which will be completed if Kate marries the impecunious Lord Mark. The "vast interval" which places Marian on virtually a different "map," in "quite another geography," is defined by skipping, willfully and habitually, "page after page" of the actual social fabric; to locate and acknowledge Marian in the book at all (with a benevolent " 'Here!' " to mark the discovery) is virtually to salvage a community of pages from which she was otherwise willfully excluded. Status and class divisions seem falsely sharp, yet appear more malleable than fixed, in Maud's England as the governing fact of her money produces ferment and the prospect of change. Milly confronts not the old "hierarchical . . . order" of settled divisions but its remnants, in a middle-class world which subjects everything to change in its struggle for power and secure position, and where everyone talks (as Milly notices) of money and threatens to put people and opportunities (as Kate warns Milly) to "use."

James's rendering of Milly's explorative reaction to the world of the Croys and Aunt Maud reveals a characteristic American view in speaking of social divisions as gaps or voids rather than as tangible barriers, as spaces that can be spanned by a manner which responds to the need for it instead of as walled enclosures. The suggestion is not that the intervals are unreal or inconsequential but that they are not impassable. Furthermore, to bridge them (rather than either to obliterate or fortify them) is to define a community which will encompass several geographies without relegating one to another atlas and which will compensate for the "skipped leaves" or pages in the total community—the network of social distinctions and the continuities between them—which the larger contours of class division and Maud's forced exaggerations obscure.

The metaphor of a book—conceived both as an integral whole and as a series of discrete pages—governs James's analysis of Milly's initiation into English society and enables him to define the complex and unresolved relation between that social world and both his heroine's action and his novel's action in it. The glaring, cruel, operative distinctions are there for Milly to discover and confront, the manner which bridges gaps by suppressing consciousness of them is there to emulate. The full sequence of the "atlas" from page to page is there to suggest the density of the existing community behind its more obvious cleavages, but to suggest also the long chain of intervals between pages which must be bridged by a "manner" if the society or book (with its broken sentences and parentheses) is to hold together at elemental levels and attain beyond that the full coherence it seeks. Milly's American manner, like James's, is adopted in the process of coming to understand society and its sharp divisions and, while moderating her consciousness of them, to bridge the intervals which separate her from it or from the groups and individuals in it whom she encounters. In the process, her manner has the effect of enabling Milly to play a role in her world and to share in altering and shaping it. Vulnerable in her illness but powerful with her money, she begins with her manner to take precedence over Aunt Maud and to become the governing center for the schemes and aspirations of the world which begins to form around her under the impact of her power and presence.

* * *

[A *Veronese Canvas: Milly As Sacrament*]

The foreground in which they[5] stand is one of immense scope as is suggested by remarks Susan makes when asking Densher to stay for the party—remarks about one of James's favorite painters, Paolo Cagliari, the expatriate who was known in the Venice where he flourished by the state where he was born, Veronese. To John Addington Symonds, Veronese was "precisely the painter suited to a nation of merchants," who depicted religious martyrs as "composed, serious, courtly, well-fed personages who like people of the world accidently overtaken by some tragic misfortune, do not stoop to distortion or express more than a grave surprise, a decorous sense of pain." For Berenson, writing in the fourth quarter of the last century, Veronese displayed a "happy combination of ceremony and splendour with almost childlike naturalness of feeling," a "frank and joyous worldliness, the qualities . . . we find in his huge pictures of feasts. . . ." Two of Veronese's huge feasts became for James, in one of the boldest appropriations of his expressionism, the instrumental forms for the making of his own composition.[6]

The two are introduced by Susan's reply to Densher's remark about the festive decorations of Milly's palace. She says: " 'bringing out all the glory of the place—makes [Milly] really happy. It's a Veronese picture, as near as can be, with me as the inevitable dwarf, the small blackamoor, put into a corner of the foreground for

5. Kate and Densher. [*Editors.*]

6. Symonds, *The Renaissance in Italy: the Fine Arts* (American Edition, New York, 1888), p. 373; Bernard Berenson, *Venetian Painters of the Renaissance* (New York, 1895), p. 64.

effect.' " She should have a " 'hawk or hound' " or borrow a " 'big red cockatoo' " to " 'perch on [her] thumb for the evening.' " Though Densher feels out of place in so grand a "composition," Susan insists: " 'Besides you're in the picture. . . . You'll be the grand young man who surpasses the others and holds up his head and the wine-cup.' "

One of the paintings is evoked by Susan's echo of Veronese's defense when summoned before the Inquisition (Ruskin had printed a transcript of the proceedings in his guide to the Academy at Venice); it was and is known as *The Supper in the House of Levi*. As recounted in the Bible (Luke v, 27–35), Christ was entertained on that occasion by his wealthy tax-collecting disciple Matthew, along with a company of publicans and sinners. When asked why he associated with such persons, Jesus replied: "They that are whole need not a physician; but they that are sick"; Jesus declared that he came "not to call the righteous, but sinners to repentance," and warned against the day "when the bridegroom shall be taken away."

In Veronese's treatment of the tale, a dwarf stands in the left foreground. (The dwarf aroused the Inquisition's suspicion, but it was placed there, Veronese informed the Inquisitors, "For ornament, as is usually done.") A blackamoor reaches for the bird perched on the dwarf's wrist. Above them on the landing of a staircase in a Venetian palace, in a strikingly mannered pose, stands a figure in green who seems about to descend the stairs and depart; he affords an analogy to Densher. At dinner, far in the background but centered, is the doomed and sacred figure of Christ; he, and his wealthy host, afford analogies to Milly.[7]

The second painting is *The Marriage Feast at Cana*. On that occasion, singled out as Christ's first miracle by the Gospel of John (II, 1–11) and regarded as one of the precedents for the Christian sacrament, Jesus and his mother attended a wedding banquet where the host ran out of wine. Asked to help, Christ first refused, then instructed servants privately to fill the jugs with water and serve that; it proved to be a very fine wine indeed. After tasting it, the banquet's steward made a speech, explaining that most hosts serve their best wine first, then offer cheaper kinds when guests can less easily taste the difference; this host, by contrast, had saved the best wine till the last.

In Veronese's picture (the Louvre version which James knew), a dark-skinned dwarf, with his bird, stands inconspicuously in the left foreground of a sumptuous banquet scene. On the right, holding up a wine cup, stands the steward; he is the figure Susan associates

7. John Ruskin, *Guide to the Principal Pictures in the Academy at Venice* (rev. ed., London, 1891), p. 55.

with Densher. Dominating the composition in the center foreground is a small group of musicians, including a portrait of Titian and a self-portrait of Veronese. They draw the eye in the direction of the figures directly behind, but, in their business as performing artists, they distract attention from the others; behind them at dinner, analogous in their position to Milly, are Mary and Christ.

These are the instrumental forms introduced early in the chapter by Susan's remarks. Later Densher speaks of "the Veronese painting . . . as not quite constituted," but by the end of the chapter the import of Veronese's subjects and the compositional patterns of his canvases have been constituted as part of James's medium, and they inform the composition of James's own canvas and the drama they reveal.

The chapter's central action is enclosed in a frame outside itself (by the proposition which precedes and the assignation which follows) and by one within it. It opens with Susan's urgent request that Densher stay for the party and stay in Venice; it ends with Densher and Kate making urgent requests to each other and consenting. Kate urges Densher to remain in Venice, to pay court to Milly and marry her. Densher agrees to stay. But in return, Densher presses his demand that Kate sleep with him in his rooms, and Kate, reluctantly but without flinching, agrees to do it.

But within this frame of requests and answers, demands and commitments, a proposition and an assignation, lies a vision of Milly which it is the burden of the chapter, and indeed of the entire novel, to make vividly present, a vision which she makes real by enacting it and which sinks so deeply into Densher's consciousness that he can never get away from it, even though at the time he does not fully appreciate it.

It is rendered entirely through Kate's and Densher's perceptions, and while they spend much of the time watching Milly, talking and thinking about her, Milly herself is scarcely even seen. She is far off in the background most of the time, almost obscured in any literal sense by Kate and Densher, the writer, in the foreground. Only once does Milly pass close to the pair and then only to say three words which are not given: it is a "single bright look and the three gay words (all ostensibly of the last lightness) with which her confessed consciousness brushed by him." Densher admires in her the infectious geniality of a civilized hostess and, feeling that she has never before been so much "the American girl," he sees her "as diffusing, in wide warm waves, the spell of a general, a kind of beatific mildness." In the deep waters of that spell, he feels that all of them are swimming around "like fishes in a crystal pool." She is like a " 'new book,' an uncut volume of the highest, the rarest quality," and Densher feels "again and again" the "thrill of turning the page." Later in the chapter, Milly communicates again specifically with Kate and Densher; from across the room she sends a silent message, "all the candour of her smile, the lustre of her pearls, the value of her life, the essence of her wealth."

The closest view of Milly herself, actually, is a look at her costly pearls. Kate points them out to Densher and they both stare at them; the "long, priceless chain, wound twice around the neck, hung, heavy and pure, down the front of the wearer's breast." Looking at these pearls of great price, Kate remarks: " 'She's a dove . . . and one somehow doesn't think of doves as bejewelled. Yet they suit her to the ground.' " Densher agrees, and, as the novel says, a dove "was the figure for her, though it most applied to her spirit."

What lies revealed in the impress of Kate and Densher's experience is that Milly, though sick, has put on the superlative performance of her career so far, as the sumptuous hostess, the spontaneous American, the dove. It is revealed, too, that she has become one with the role she began earlier to play, for the illusion is so amply complete, so intensely and tangibly real, that one of Densher's phrases for her is perfectly apt: he thinks of her as "embodied poetry." And in becoming one with what she seems, she wears a dress whose color Densher notices, for the first time appearing, like Christ at the moment of his transfiguration, in white. The embodied poem, the wealthy dying dove, has become the perfect host. She has spent more lavishly of her money for the party—Densher noticed more candles burning when he entered her " 'temple to taste' "—and she has been spending more lavishly of her energy, her life. Milly has had to miss dinner to save strength for the party, and Densher could even *taste* the question of her health when he entered the palace; toward the end of the chapter, Kate insists that Milly's health is worse. The entire chapter, in its form or composition, focuses attention on Milly while not showing her directly to reveal and shield the torment of her triumph as host, the agony within a radiantly glad and splendid surface. Milly has been inspired by the occasion (chiefly, Densher notices, when Sir Luke arrives), and it is under the nourishing stimulus of this ceremonious affair that she diffuses her "beatific mildness." And while she is finding sustenance in the occasion, Kate and Densher feast their eyes on her. Although Densher at best only half grasps, and Kate now scarcely appreciates at all, what is before their eyes, Milly has become the sacrament, the sacred thing, prefigured in the temples, histories, and legends which the novel evokes but embodied now in its stricken heroine, the treasure, dove, and muse of James's imagination.

* * *

CHARLES THOMAS SAMUELS

[A Flawed Hymn to Renunciation]†

Each of the previous novels[1] is flawed because James's commitment to the protagonist is compromised by admiration for the enemy. *The Wings of the Dove* and *The Spoils of Poynton* are damaged for nearly the obverse reason: in these books evil is persuasive, but virtue—inadvertently—is not. However, since both novels come at the height of James's career and since both are concerned with the central theme of renunciation, neither seems so vulnerable as *The American* or *The Princess Casamassima.* In particular, *The Wings of the Dove* is obviously brilliant, its portrait of corruption supreme. How could a novel fail with Kate Croy?

Kate, the book's chief embodiment of evil, is one of James's major creations. Our first glimpse of her "face positively pale with . . . irritation" in "a vulgar little room" on a "vulgar little street" establishes a reality that never falters. Though powerful in her own right, Kate has been twisted into the shape of evil by other hands. In a world whose only values are material, she belongs to a family that cannot gratify the acquisitive taste it fosters. Moreover, Kate is ashamed of what she is like: "She saw . . . how material things spoke to her. She saw, and she blushed to see, that if in contrast with some of its old aspects life now affected her as a dress successfully 'done up,' this was exactly by reason of the trimmings and lace, was a matter of ribbons and silk and velvet. She had a dire accessibility to pleasure from such sources." Thus, she tries to elude the machinations of her greedy aunt, "Brittania of the Market Place," and at the same time save herself from the greasy poverty of her sister, Mrs. Condrip. With ambition as naively vaunting as classic hybris, she tells her lover, Merton Densher, early in the book: "I shall sacrifice nobody and nothing, and that's just my situation, that I want and that I shall try for everything. That . . . is how I see myself (and how I see you quite as much)." Kate wants more from life than she can get. She thinks she can possess through duplicity and still not lose her soul, but she is wrong; and James traces her error as movingly as the errors of those fastidious moralizers who stand closer to his heart.

With Kate, the author neither blinks at nor misjudges sexual issues that are troublesome in more typically Jamesian characters. Kate's greatest sin is her use of Milly Theale, but to use Milly she

† From Charles Thomas Samuels, *The Ambiguity of Henry James* (Urbana: University of Illinois Press, 1971), pp. 61–65, 66–68, 69–72.

1. *The Sacred Fount, The American, The Princess Casamassima.* [*Editors.*]

must use her own passion for Merton Densher. At our first view of the lovers, Kate is counseling restraint so that they may ultimately possess each other and money. Throughout the book, what is most shocking about her, most indicative of increasing dehumanization, is this way she has of separating herself from her own feeling and of "dol[ing] it out," as Densher says, like a housewife dispensing sugar from her cupboard—or, as one might better say, like a trainer giving inducements to a prize horse. Having misappropriated passion, Kate will suffer its degradation when she is taken by Densher not in healthy lust but in his need to restore the self-direction she had deprived him of. Finally, she will lose his love, not only, as she shallowly thinks, because he has fallen in love with Milly but because she had for too long made his love her instrument. At the end, he is ready to marry her if she will take him for himself. In the end, however, Kate cannot respond to that self, for she has turned it into the means not of passion but of cash.

Kate Croy represents the destructive power of egoism on a selflessness that must exist even in erotic love. Yet she is a tragic and not a melodramatic villainess, because the motive for her villainy is so sympathetic and she acts throughout in the belief that her machinations are expedient, but no worse. In this, she epitomizes a way of life, a kind of polite league of predators that has trained her to be a member of the society in which "it would never occur [to the inner circle] that they were eating you up. They did that without tasting."

Maud, the main lioness in that London zoo, is dreadful at bottom, but her surface is suavely considerate. Like Kate, she is convinced that her exploitation of Milly is acceptable because Milly herself will gain from it. The evil of her set is a banal evil, supported by a ghastly instrumentalism: the greatest good to the greatest number means that a dying girl requires a smaller share. When Milly's attendant, Susan Shepherd Stringham, sits anxiously amidst the inner circle, she looks "very much as some spectator in an old-time circus might have watched the oddity of a Christian maiden, in the arena, mildly, caressingly, martyred. It was the nosing and fumbling not of lions and tigers but of domestic animals let loose as for the joke." The very gentleness of their desecration of Milly is what makes the Lowder set one of James's most profound depictions of "the high brutality of good intentions." When one recalls this polite ruthlessness, the striking biblical imagery which is meant to highlight its significance, and the great scenes in which the animals pace and pounce, it seems obvious that *The Wings of the Dove* deserves a high place in James's *oeuvre*.

Evil in this book is a convincing, because familiar, reality. When we begin to examine its opposite, however, we come to an emptiness whose prototypes we noted in the ghosts, the vampires, the Bellegardes, and the anarchists. The central emptiness in *The Wings of the Dove* is the dove herself. In the novels I have already discussed, James did not adequately face evil because he did not face an evil real enough to vanquish good. For a deeper sentimentality in James's devotion to virtue, Milly Theale is his definitive symbol. Going beyond all reasonable limits of ethical advocacy, his love for her produces expostulations like this: "[Milly] worked—and seemingly quite without design—upon the sympathy, the curiosity, the fancy of her associates, and we shall really ourselves scarce otherwise come closer to her than by feeling their impression and sharing, if need be, their confusion." That James would so compromise his creed of authorial reticence suggests the fervor of his admiration, which attains a volume exceeding even the governess's hosannas: "When Milly smiled it was a public event—when she didn't it was a chapter of history." This claim is made in the impressionable mind of Mrs. Stringham, but James never attempts to qualify its spirit. On the contrary, *his* mind associates Milly with Jesus Christ.

This connection is made when Milly and Susan are journeying through the Alps before they reach Lancaster Gate. Susan gets a glimpse of her companion "looking down on the kingdoms of the earth," and wonders "was she choosing among them or did she want them all?" If one reads *The Wings of the Dove* allegorically, this allusion may seem inspirational, but if we recall that Milly isn't God but rather a fabulously rich girl avid for life, the implication is sinister. James, however, ignores the irony, and later falls into contradiction. He means Milly to be Christ-like in her mercy and selflessness (when she dies, she releases her fortune to the man who had betrayed her), but he also means her to be a brave girl seizing life even at the moment that it is slipping away. Each of these qualities—selfless mercy and appetite for life—is admirable, but in quite incompatible ways. One is directed toward others; the other is self-serving. Though Milly's function in the plot emphasizes the former, her character displays principally the latter.

* * *

Since good characters are notoriously difficult to make convincing in fiction, admirers may safely grant the unfortunate notes of avidity and self-righteousness that Milly sometimes strikes. Her situation and her action, they can say, earn our respect nevertheless. However, should we take this line, we are again faced with a contradiction based on James's desire that Milly win our sympathy in all ways at once. Because she is victimized by something recognizably wicked, we are quite prepared to pity her. Yet James is not satisfied that Milly win the sympathy reserved for victims; he wishes also to make her ordeal heroic because willed. Therefore, Milly connives in her own betrayal in much the same manner as James's major protagonist, Lambert Strether. She is given ample reason to suspect Kate Croy, but, like Strether, she ignores available evidence. However, Strether's ignorance celebrates the putative virtue of Chad and Mme de Vionnet whereas Milly's ignorance is self-interested. Because of her zeal for life, she wants Merton Densher; and if getting Merton Densher means pulling the wool over her own eyes, she is perfectly willing to do so. James tries to have it both ways, to make her a victim who is self-sacrificed, but her sacrifice looks suspiciously like a gambit lost.

When Milly first enters the world of Lancaster Gate, she is certain that Kate is lying about her affairs: "It now came over her as in a clear cold wave that there was a possible account of their relations in which the quantity her new friend told her might have figured as small, as smallest, beside the quantity she hadn't." In subsequent chapters, James clearly shows how the others deceived Milly to quiet her suspicions of Kate, but they do not have to work at it. After her visit to Mrs. Condrip, for example, Susie asks if Milly had been told that Kate is not in love with Densher: " 'You mean she thinks her sister distinctly doesn't care for him?' . . . 'If she did care Mrs. Condrip would have told me.' . . . 'But did you ask her?' 'Ah, no!' 'Oh!' said Susan Shepherd." "Merton Densher was in love," Milly decides, "and Kate couldn't help it—could only be sorry and kind: wouldn't that, without wild flurries, cover everything? Milly at all events tried it as a cover, tried it hard, for the time; pulled it over her, in the front, the larger room, drew it up to her chin with energy. If it didn't, so treated, do everything for her, it did so much that she could herself supply the rest."

I am not suggesting that Milly is any less pathetic for conniving in her own destruction; I am suggesting that she does connive. Since she loves Densher, we can forgive her credulity as a callow sign of her affection; but, in that case, Milly is pathetic, not godlike. However, James wants us to think Milly divinely unselfish, so at the end of Book Four she decides to leave London before Densher's return in order to avoid a confrontation that would reveal their prior friendship and might cause Kate to suspect Densher of infidelity. By leaving London for such a reason, she is affirming to herself a liaison with Densher that never existed. In addition to being callow, the action contains a supersubtle but readily identified sexual interest that is hardly Christ-like.

Densher's willingness to lend himself, however passively, to Kate's design surely makes him responsible for Milly's death. But for reasons we shall presently take up, James wanted to keep Densher's participation from being ostentatious. As a result, the journalist gives the girl little visible reason to believe that he is in love with her, thus placing additional responsibility for Milly's death on her own shoulders. Throughout the book she displays not only a hunger for love but an odd ability to spot it before it occurs. When we recall her desire for Densher, her credulity, and her vanity, we have cause to think her death not a Christ-like renunciation but the sentimental death in Venice of a young girl who couldn't get her man. One doesn't want to make too much of it, but we ought to remind ourselves that Milly's final generosity, whatever else it may produce, wrests Densher from her rival.

* * *

Densher's conversion seems proof of Milly's magnificence, just as Milly's magnificence seems the cause of his conversion. But the relationship between these two main facts in *The Wings of the Dove* is not so smoothly symbiotic. Though Densher's conversion is the surest sign we get of Milly's worth, bringing the two people together necessitates the prior existence of a sexual appetite in Milly that keeps her from being the complete antithesis of Kate Croy—reducing her instead to a rival whose illness is at least partly counterbalanced by her fabulous means. Moreover, Densher's conversion is itself implausible and no less unarguable a sign of Milly's greatness than her own behavior.

Bluntly stated, James wanted Densher to be morally imperceptive, since in proportion as his initial morality is lacking the morality he obtains from Milly is miraculous. But since he is so imperceptive and since James does not dramatize his conversion any more than Milly's martyrdom, the miracle is unconvincing.

"Imperceptive" is hardly the word though. In the early stages of Densher's reaction to Kate's plan, he is almost a moral moron. Thinking that he should refuse Kate's request, he decides to go ahead with it because

> he liked too much every one concerned. . . . He liked Kate, goodness knew, and he also clearly enough liked Mrs. Lowder. He liked in particular Milly herself; and hadn't it come up for him the evening before that he quite liked even Susan Shepherd? He had never known himself so generally merciful. It was a footing, at all events, whatever accounted for it, on which he would surely be rather a muff not to manage by one turn or another to escape disobliging. Should he find he couldn't work it there would still be time enough. The idea of working it crystallised before him in such guise as not only to promise much interest—fairly, in case of success, much enthusiasm; but positively to impart to failure an appearance of barbarity.

(The irony here is coruscating, but that is precisely my point: James will ask us to believe that a man this sophistical can ultimately emerge spotless.) "Wouldn't it be virtually as indelicate to challenge [Milly] as to leave her deluded?" Densher later thinks; "and this quite apart from the exposure, so to speak, of Kate, as to whom it would constitute a kind of betrayal. Kate's design was something so extraordinarily special to Kate that he felt himself shrink from the complications involved in judging it. Not to give away the woman one loved, but to back her up in her mistakes—once they had gone a certain length—that was perhaps the chief among the inevitabilities of the abjection of love." In the thick of the intrigue, separated both from Kate's person and the sophistries which it inspires, Densher is still able to make light of his degradation: "as he hadn't really 'begun' anything," he assures himself, "had only submitted, consented, but too generously indulged and condoned the beginnings of others, he had no call to treat himself with superstitious rigor." On another occasion, he decides he cannot leave Venice because it would be ungenerous to decline Milly's generosity. Sitll later, a few pages before his offstage conversion, he assuages his conscience with the preposterous contention that he had not really understood that Milly was dying.

Densher's stupidities and sophistries constitute a compelling portrayal of decorous evil. Like the characteristics of Kate and Aunt Maud, they comprise one of James's most convincing depictions of a brutality that thrives on ignorance. It is only when James tries to relate this evil to good, tries to prove that good can redeem evil, that the very richness of the depiction becomes an error.

Not only is Milly's goodness meager; being meager, it cannot fill up so cavernous a moral vacuum as Densher. James seems almost to admit as much in his attempt to deny that Densher was evil and thus to make the conversion plausible. Surely this is one reason that James has Lord Mark deliver the deathblow. Densher himself takes this fact as somehow diminishing his own sin, and James never corrects his brutal casuistry. Moreover, James forces the one utterly disinterested member of Milly's entourage, Sir Luke, to nearly exonerate the indirect cause of her effectual murder. In one of his last interviews with Kate, Densher is able to tell her that Luke "understood." "But understood what?" Kate asks. "That I had meant awfully well," Densher replies.

This interview is one of the novel's finest scenes, underlining the suavity of wickedness by transpiring while the lovers serve each other tea, and Kate, recalling an earlier image, doles out Densher's sugar. But it triumphs in depicting evil; as a testimonial to Densher's goodness, it is ingeniously evasive. James apparently wants us to think Densher less depraved because he does not share Kate's willingness to lie to Milly right up to the end: "You might have lied to her from pity, and she have seen you and felt you lie, and yet—

since it was all for tenderness—she would have thanked you and blessed you and clung to you but the more." But his comparative innocence is only impressive if we forget his easy sins of omission. Only his symbolic gesture of entering church and his rather tardy comprehension of Kate declare Densher a new man. We do not see a change but only a long-delayed and undramatized recognition of what he has been.

The novel's plot is as implausible as its heroine, for Milly's virtue and Densher's conversion are equally frail defenses against the solid Lowder world. Yet how can James have written a book so brilliant in conception and so flimsy in detail between a novel that is his masterpiece and one that, however flawed, breaks new ground? Of the last three books, *The Wings of the Dove* is neither a culmination nor a departure but a regression. * * *

Selected Bibliography

Neither the articles reprinted nor the books from which the critical essays in this volume were derived are listed.

CHECKLISTS

Beebe, Maurice, and Stafford, William T. "Criticism of Henry James: A Selected Checklist," *Modern Fiction Studies* XII (Spring 1966), 117–77.

Edel, Leon, and Laurence, Dan H. *A Bibliography of Henry James.* London, 1957; 2nd edition, revised, 1961.

Foley, Richard Nicholas. *Criticism in American Periodicals of the Works of Henry James from 1866–1916.* Washington, D.C., 1944.

Gale, Robert L. "Henry James," in James Woodress, ed. *Eight American Authors: A Review of Research and Criticism.* Revised edition. New York, 1971. Pp. 321–75.

Gard, Roger, ed. *Henry James: The Critical Heritage.* London, 1968.

Stafford, William T. *A Name, Title, and Place Index to the Critical Writings of Henry James.* Englewood, Colorado, 1975.

DISCUSSIONS IN BOOKS

Anderson, Quentin. *The American Henry James.* New Brunswick, N.J., 1957. Pp. 233–80.

Auchincloss, Louis. *Reading Henry James.* Minneapolis, 1975. Pp. 124–32.

Banta, Martha. *Henry James and the Occult: The Great Extension.* Bloomington, 1972. Pp. 183–94.

Bowden, Edwin T. *The Themes of Henry James: A System of Observation Through the Visual Arts.* New Haven, 1956. Pp. 88–96.

Cargill, Oscar. *The Novels of Henry James.* New York, 1961. Pp. 338–82.

Crews, Frederick C. *The Tragedy of Manners: Moral Drama in the Later Novels of Henry James.* New Haven, 1957. Pp. 57–80.

Dupee, F. W. *Henry James.* New York, 1951. Pp. 248–57, 280–81.

Edel, Leon. *Henry James: The Master: 1901–1916.* Philadelphia and New York, 1972. Pp. 108–22.

Egan, Michael. *Henry James: The Ibsen Years.* London, 1972. Pp. 115–46.

Garrett, Peter K. *Scene and Symbol from George Eliot to James Joyce: Studies in Changing Fictional Mode.* New Haven and London, 1969. Pp. 105–7, 123–36.

Geismar, Maxwell. *Henry James and the Jacobites.* Boston, 1963. Pp. 219–55.

Graham, Kenneth. *Henry James: The Drama of Fulfillment.* Oxford, 1975. Pp. 160–232.

Hocks, Richard A. *Henry James and Pragmatistic Thought: A Study in the Relationship Between the Philosophy of William James and the Literary Art of Henry James.* Chapel Hill, 1974. Pp. 191–96.

Jefferson, D. W. *Henry James.* New York, 1960. Pp. 85–90.

Lebowitz, Naomi. *The Imagination of Loving: Henry James's Legacy to the Novel.* Detroit, 1965. Pp. 60–66, 99–107.

Leyburn, Ellen D. *Strange Alloy: The Relation of Comedy to Tragedy in the Fiction of Henry James.* Chapel Hill, 1968. Pp. 148–55, 174–75.

Marks, Robert. *Henry James's Later Novels: An Interpretation.* New York, 1960. Pp. 44–56.

MacKenzie, Manfred. *Communities of Honor and Love in Henry James.* Cambridge, Mass., and London, England, 1976. Pp. 152–65.

Maves, Carl. *Sensuous Pessimism: Italy in the Works of Henry James.* Bloomington, 1973. Pp. 108–17.

Putt, S. Gorley. *Henry James: A Reader's Guide.* Ithaca, 1966. Pp. 309–39.

Sharp, Sister M. Corona. *The Confidante in Henry James.* Notre Dame, 1963. Pp. 181–213.

Ward, J. A. *The Imagination of Disaster: Evil in the Fiction of Henry James.* Lincoln, 1961. Pp. 127–39.
———. *The Search for Form: Studies in the Structure of James's Fiction.* Chapel Hill, 1967. Pp. 164–98.
Wright, Walter F. *The Madness of Art: A Study of Henry James.* Lincoln, 1962. Pp. 219–32.

ARTICLES

Abel, Robert H. "Gide and Henry James: Suffering, Death and Responsibility," *Midwest Quarterly* IX (July 1968), 408, 409–12.
Allott, Miriam. "The Bronzino Portrait in Henry James' *The Wings of the Dove,*" *Modern Language Notes* LXVIII (January 1953), 23–25.
———. "A Ruskin Echo in *The Wings of the Dove,*" *Notes and Queries* 3 (February 1956), 87.
Barzun, Jacques. "James the Melodramatist," *Kenyon Review* V (Autumn 1943), 511–12.
Bell, Millicent. "Jamesian Being," *Virginia Quarterly Review* LII (Winter 1976), 115–32.
Bersani, Leo. "The Narrator as Center in *The Wings of the Dove,*" *Modern Fiction Studies* VI (Summer 1960), 131–44.
Blackmur, R. P. "The Loose and Baggy Monsters of Henry James," *Accent* XI (Summer 1951), 135, 136, 137, 139, 142.
Booth, B. A. "Henry James and the Economic Motif," *Nineteenth-Century Fiction* VIII (September 1953), 145–46.
Cherniak, Judith. "Henry James as Moralist: The Case of the Late Novels," *Centennial Review* XVI (Spring 1972), 105–21.
Clark, H. H. "Henry James and Science: *The Wings of the Dove,*" *Transactions of the Wisconsin Academy of Sciences, Arts and Letters* LII (1963), 1–15.
Conger, Sydney M. "The Admirable Villains in Henry James' *The Wings of the Dove,*" *Arizona Quarterly* XXVII (Summer 1971), 151–60.
Crow, C. R. "The Style of Henry James: *The Wings of the Dove,*" *English Institute Essays* IV (1958), 172–89.
Deaken, M. F. "The Real and the Fictive Quest of Henry James," *Bucknell Review* XIV (May 1966), 82–97.
Dove, John Rowland. "The Tragic Sense in Henry James," *Texas Studies in Literature and Language* II (Autumn 1960), 303–14.
Edgar, Pelham. "Henry James, the Essential Novelist," *Queen's Quarterly* XXXIX (May 1932), 181–92.
Elton, Oliver. "The Novels of Mr. Henry James," *Quarterly Review* CXCVIII (October 1903), 358–79.
Firebaugh, J. J. "The Idealism of Merton Densher," *University of Texas Studies in English* XXXVII (1958), 141–54.
Ford, Ford Maddox. "The Master," *American Mercury* XXXVI (November 1935), 325–27.
Gale, R. L. "Religion Imagery in Henry James' Fiction," *Modern Fiction Studies* III (Spring 1957), 64–72.
Gibson, Priscilla. "The Uses of James' Imagery: Drama Through Metaphor," *PMLA* LXIX (December 1954), 1076–84.
Goode, John. "The Pervasive Mystery of Style: *The Wings of the Dove,*" in *The Air of Reality: New Essays on Henry James.* John Goode, ed. London, 1972. Pp. 244–300.
Habegger, Alfred. "Reciprocity and the Market Place in *The Wings of the Dove* and *What Maisie Knew,*" *Nineteenth-Century Fiction* XXV (March 1971), 455–73.
Hagan, John. "A Note on the Symbolic Pattern in *The Wings of the Dove,*" *College Language Association Journal* X (March 1967), 256–62.
Halverson, John. "Late Manner, Major Phase," *Sewanee Review* LXXIV (Spring 1971), 214–31.
Hamblen, Abigail Ann. "The Inheritance of the Meek: Two Novels by Agatha Christie and Henry James," *Discourse* XII (Summer 1969), 409–13.
Hopkins, Viola. "Visual Art Devices and Parallels in the Fiction of Henry James," *PMLA* LXXVI (December 1961), 561–74.
Itagaki, Konomu. " 'Merciful Indirection' in *The Wings of the Dove,*" *Studies in English Literature* XLI (March 1965), 165–81.
Kimball, Jean. "The Abyss and *The Wings of the Dove,*" *Nineteenth-Century Fiction* X (March 1956), 281–300.
Kornfield, Milton. "Villainy and Responsibility in *The Wings of the Dove,*" *Texas Studies in Literature and Language* XIV (Summer 1972), 337–46.

Lee, Brian. "Henry James' 'Divine Consensus': *The Ambassadors, The Wings of the Dove, The Golden Bowl,*" *Renaissance and Modern Studies* VI (1962), 5–24.

Lewis, R.W.B. "The Vision of Grace: James' *The Wings of the Dove,*" *Modern Fiction Studies* III (Spring 1957), 33–40.

McDowell, B. D. "The Use of 'Everything' in *The Wings of the Dove,*" *Xavier University Studies* II (Spring 1972), 13–20.

McLean, Robert C. " 'Love by the Doctor's Direction': Disease and Death in *The Wings of the Dove,*" *Papers on Language and Literature* VIII, supplement (Fall 1972), 128–48.

Marks, Sita P. "The Sound and the Silence: Nonverbal Patterns in *The Wings of the Dove,*" *Arizona Quarterly* XXVII (Summer 1971), 143–50.

Muecke, D. C. "The Dove's Flight," *Nineteenth-Century Fiction* IX (January 1954), 76–78.

Purdy, Strother B. "Henry James' Abysses: A Semantic Note," *English Studies* LXI (October 1970), 424–33.

Reilly, Robert J. "Henry James and the Morality of Fiction," *American Literature* XXXIX (March 1967), 1–30.

Rowe, John Carlos. "The Symbolization of Milly Theale: Henry James's *The Wings of the Dove,*" *English Literary History* XL (Spring 1973), 131–64.

Thorberg, Raymond. "*Germaine*, James' *Notebooks* and *The Wings of the Dove,*" *Comparative Literature* XXII (Summer 1970), 254–64.

Van Cromphout, Gustaaf. "*The Wings of the Dove:* Intention and Achievement," *Minnesota Review* VI (1966), 149–54.

Vincec, Sister Stephanie. "A Significant Revision in *The Wings of the Dove,*" *Review of English Studies* XXIII (February 1972), 58–61.

Warren, Austin. "Myth and Dialectic in the Later Novels," *Kenyon Review* V (Autumn 1943), 551–68.